BODIE THOENE

Warsaw Requiem

Research and Development By
Brock Thoene

BETHANY HOUSE
MINNEAPOLIS, MINNESOTA

Warsaw Requiem
Copyright © 1991
Bodie Thoene

Cover illustration by Dan Thornberg
Cover design by Sheryl Thornberg

Published by Bethany House Publishers
A Ministry of Bethany Fellowship International
11400 Hampshire Avenue South
Bloomington, Minnesota 55438
www.bethanyhouse.com

Printed in the United States of America by
Bethany Press International, Bloomington, Minnesota 55438

ISBN 1–55661–188–9 (Paperback)
ISBN 0–7642–2432–8 (Mass Market)

In thinking about the dedication of this book,
I have worried about whether it gets old being an editor and
having multiple books dedicated to you.
All the same,
there is no one else who will do for me in this but

Carol Johnson

. . . And so, *Warsaw Requiem* is for my friend.
My dear, one-and-only
Carol-Annie,
who, after Brock, has read
my soul and manuscripts before anybody
and who I love a lot . . .

(Do not edit this, please.)

With more than two dozen novels carrying the byline of BODIE THOENE or BROCK AND BODIE THOENE (pronounced Tay-nee), with more than six million copies in print, and with eight Evangelical Christian Publishers Association Gold Medallion awards, for over a decade this husband-and-wife writing team has captivated the hearts and illuminated the minds of their enthusiastic readers.

The Thoenes have earned Ph.D.'s in creative writing and in history. Bodie's storytelling gifts are supported by Brock's careful research and historical perspective. The resulting novels both inspire and educate, broadening readers' awareness and understanding of important slices of history. Their critically acclaimed collaborations will stand as the benchmark in their category for years to come.

THE ZION COVENANT series comprises six novels covering events in Europe leading up to World War II; the five books in THE ZION CHRONICLES describe the events surrounding Israel's statehood in 1948; the three books of THE SHILOH LEGACY provide an American perspective on the war.

The Thoenes make their home in Glenbrook, Nevada, but travel frequently as they research historical and geographical settings for their novels. They have three grown children and enjoy grandparenting.

For more information on Thoene books and news, please visit their Web site at *www.thoenebooks.com.*

Contents

Prologue

All the reading lamps had gone out, leaving the cabin of the jet muted by the soft twilight of recessed lighting.

Through the small window of the El Al passenger plane, the stars above the Mediterranean seemed hard and cold, unblinking in the thin atmosphere of 35,000 feet.

David Kopecky stared out across the moonlit wing, watching as a red light winked on and off with a steady rhythm. Closing his eyes for an instant, he remembered his own longing as he had watched lights like this pass over the night sky above Russia. Always he had craned his neck to watch, dreaming of the freedom that must surely lie at the end of the journey. He had imagined men and women encased in the sleek silver cocoon of a passenger jet high above his head. *Where are they going?* he had wondered. *And how are they so privileged that they can leave Russia?*

The freedom, the flight, the tiny red beacon on the wingtip had always been for others, not for David Kopecky. Not for his wife Eva, who slept soundly against his shoulder. But on this night, all his dreams and years of longing had at last made him one of those much-envied travelers.

He was sixty-three years old, and this was his first trip on an airplane. But he was unafraid. His son Mikhail had embraced him and begged him to reconsider, to think of the missiles that exploded in Tel Aviv. Was it not possible that one of those missiles might strike the plane before it landed? Could they not delay just a little while after so many years of waiting patiently? Gas masks. SCUD missiles. The cheers and threats of men like Yasser Arafat and Faisal Husseini as explosions rocked the civilian sectors of Israel and sent Israelis running for sealed rooms. *What kind of life is that?* David's son had asked him. Certainly remaining in the Soviet Union was a sensible option now that there was a war going on.

David had patted Mikhail on the cheek and replied quietly, "We are not flying into a new war. We are simply continuing our journey into a very old war."

David did not need to remind his son that Arafat and Faisal Husseini were both blood relations of Haj Amin Husseini, the Muslim leader in Jerusalem who had blocked the immigration of Jewish refugees from Europe before the Holocaust. Mikhail knew well enough that the same family which had terrorized the Jews of Palestine in the time of Hitler was still in the business of terror, still claiming to be the voice of the Palestinian Arabs.

The old war had continued without a break in stride, even after Hitler had perished and the courtroom of Nuremberg had pronounced the last sentence against the mass murderers of the Reich. But the terror of the PLO did not seem so dark as the future David saw for the remaining Jews of Russia and Europe. He felt the evil stir again. Once again he had seen the banners at public rallies declaring: *JEWS TO THE OVENS! FINISH WHAT HITLER BEGAN!*

The banners, the whispered words and the shouted slogans were being accompanied by blows. In Europe men were beating Jews, murdering Jews because they were Jewish. *Again. Once again.*

"You must come soon to Israel, Mikhail. You and Ivana must bring the children and come join us in Israel as soon as your papers are in order."

Mikhail's eyes had betrayed his skepticism. What man would take his wife and children into a land of sealed rooms and gas masks and falling debris?

It was natural that his son would feel that way. After all, David had not spoken to Mikhail of the horrors that had happened in Poland. He had not told his son that he was Jewish until the first breeze of freedom had given him some hope. And then the letter had come from Israel, written in Polish. For the first time in fifty years, David Kopecky learned that he was not the only survivor of the once proud family of Rabbi Aaron Lubetkin!

"My maiden name is Rachel Lubetkin. . . . Grew up in Warsaw . . . My family perished in the occupation. My youngest brother Yacov survived and is here in Jerusalem with me . . . our brother David Lubetkin possibly rescued by a Polish family named Kopecky... Could you help us locate..."

Thus the deception of over fifty years had ended. Only his wife Eva had known, and she had kept silent, guarding his secret, guarding his heart.

He smiled and put his hand on her cheek. She sighed in her sleep and shifted slightly in the cramped seat. She was not Jewish, and yet here she was beside him, leaving her son and grandchildren behind in Moscow to start over again in besieged and troubled Israel.

She, too, felt the hot wind of violence that had sprung up in the Soviet Union. She had left Russia for the sake of her son and his family. "To pave their path," she whispered through her tears. "If we do not leave, then they will not leave. Mikhail will come. He will bring Ivana and the children if we are there."

In that moment David realized that he had married the bravest woman in Russia. Like his own mother, he had married a woman who loved her own child enough to give him up in order to save his life. "Mikhail must come! There are gas masks for the Jews of Israel!"

David looked around the crowded cabin of the plane. Men and women and children of all ages slept leaning on one another in awkward positions. *Are they dreaming sweet dreams,* David wondered, *or the nightmare memories that come to me when I sleep?* He dared not sleep among these strangers for fear of crying out and waking with a start as his mind carried him unwillingly back to Warsaw—to the old war, to the fall. There were no gas masks for the Jewish children of Poland. The flight of refugees was not on bright silver wings, but within a thick, black cloud of fear. The roads were blocked by an endless mass of people—women and children, old men, weak and feeble. The very rich and the very poor mingled together in a groaning tide. That day, Polish Gentile and Polish Jew marched together. They marched *away,* somehow believing that they were fleeing from Death. And yet for anyone who looked closely, it was plain to see that Death was marching along patiently beside them.

Even now, as David Lubetkin Kopecky gazed out over the wing of the passenger plane, he could remember the drone of Stuka engines as they swung over the long columns like vultures. The road had erupted. Villages collapsed. Smoke had drifted across the gentle landscape as if to obscure the retreat of the helpless. David had seen those same images replay in his mind when the first news footage of Kuwaiti refugees had been broadcast. *Not running into a new war. Simply continuing the endless journey. . . .*

David had no fear of coming face-to-face with an Iraqi missile. No, that was not the nightmare which woke him from his sleep. The terrible dream that haunted him was the memory of that first moment when this very old war began for him. That day when he and Samuel had left for school; when the bombs fell, there was no shelter to run to.

Six-thirty in the morning. Hundreds of children laughed and talked as they clattered over the cobbled streets toward the school air-raid shelter. Then there came the high, useless howl of Warsaw sirens as the bombers began their Blitzkrieg on the far end of the Jewish section of town.

In that moment childhood was irrevocably destroyed. Screams were drowned by the whistle of bombs as children ran away from something that could not be outrun, toward a safety that did not exist.

The bigger ones ran faster. Little ones like Samuel were knocked down and trampled. David had thrown himself over his little brother and kicked back the rush of panicked feet. He had stayed with Samuel and so had not died with the others who reached the school just as the first bombs crashed through the roof.

That day, David had lain in the street beside Samuel and wept at the whistle of falling bombs, cringed at the roar of explosions, the grumble of collapsing walls and gutted buildings. *Gottman's Department Store. Menkes' Bakery. An apartment building. The Foundling Home. The school* . . . Blasts shook the foundations of Warsaw. Buildings puffed out and then tumbled down onto the sidewalks all around the two brothers.

And then came the silence—an eerie and profound silence, disturbed only by the sobs of David and Samuel. The shattered bodies of playmates littered the street. There was no more childhood. No more illusions. All dreams vanished forever in that moment.

When it was over, only David and Samuel had survived the bombing of that street. Together they groped their way back through the debris to the frantic embrace and cries of joy waiting at home.

And this was only the first day of the war!

He remembered his family: Mama, named Etta. She was beautiful and good. Papa, Rabbi Aaron, wise and strong. David's sister, Rachel, at thirteen, was a duplicate of Mama. And baby Yacov. Little Yani, they called him. Could that little one be fifty-six years old now, with children and grandchildren? How could he ever bridge the gap of a lifetime of believing they had all died in the bright red ditches of Poland?

Always that first day, the first attack, was the memory that wrenched David from his sleep with a scream of terror. But they had all survived that terrible moment. David lived with indelible images of horror that in the light of day seemed far worse. And yet the hardest memory of all was the one which had blasted away his innocence forever.

And now he was going home once more to see his family. *Little Yacov. Rachel. Beautiful and brave Rachel.* They were alive! The children of Aaron and Etta Lubetkin would once again embrace one another in joy!

Over fifty years had passed, and still the whistle of bombs might mar their reunion. But at least now there were gas masks for Jewish children.

GERMANY POLAND

ENLAND

• Prague

CZECHOSLOVAKIA

HUNGARY

(ONCE AUSTRIA)

NORWAY

SWEDEN

FINLAND

NORTH SEA

GREAT BRITAIN

BALTIC SEA

ESTONIA

LATVIA

LITHUANIA

DENMARK

• Hamburg

POLAND

• Berlin

Warsaw •

London

NETHERLANDS

BELGIUM

GERMANY

SOVIET UNION

• Paris

Prague •

CZECHOSLOVAKIA
(before Munich Agreement)

Munich •

Vienna •

HUNGARY

FRANCE

SWITZERLAND

(ONCE AUSTRIA)

RUMANIA

YUGOSLAVIA

SPAIN

ITALY

ADRIATIC SEA

BULGARIA

CORSICA

• Rome

ALBANIA

MEDITERRANEAN SEA

SARDINIA

GREECE

14

1   When a Sparrow Falls

"MAY 30, 1939"

Karl Ibsen repeated the date three times in order to remind himself that all days were not exactly the same. There was a world beyond the dark confines of his cell where dates meant something more than burned oatmeal for breakfast and thin soup sipped from a dirty tin bowl.

He had counted the days of his imprisonment by scratching rows of tiny notches on the bricks of his cell. Like a calendar, each month was represented by a brick. Six bricks were filled. He carved another notch on the hard red clay of May.

Somewhere it was spring, with flowers blooming in gardens and couples sitting together at sunny tables in sidewalk cafes.

"It is spring," he said aloud.

As if in answer to his words, a small bird fluttered to the bars of his high narrow window and perched on the ledge. It carried a fragment of string in its yellow beak. Only a sparrow, the kind of bird Karl's father had paid him to shoot with a slingshot in the family peach orchard many years ago. Karl had been paid one Pfennig for every ten sparrows he killed in those days. His heart was filled with remorse as he eyed the tiny brown creature and prayed that it would stay to keep him company. The killings were clear in Karl's memory as the bird cocked its head curiously and gazed down upon this man in a cage.

One thousand sparrows fell to my slingshot. I bought Harold Kiesner's old bicycle with my earnings. Forgive my cruelty, little bird . . . and stay.

The sparrow shuddered, dropped its string and hopped three steps before disappearing off the ledge with a momentary flutter.

"Gone," Karl said aloud. And then he groped for the words in the gospel of Matthew. The ones about the sparrows . . . something about God caring even for sparrows, knowing when even *one* sparrow fell to the earth!

Like a knife in his weary heart, he thought about the Thousand and wished he had known then how much more precious they were than the used bicycle! What he would not give to have even one little bird perch on his window ledge now!

But Karl had nothing to give, and so such thoughts were useless. He stared at the barred fragment of blue sky as though his longing might bring the sparrow back. The sky remained as empty as the window ledge.

Karl sank down onto the dirty straw and stared at his calendar. Brick by brick he kept a mental diary of the gray days he had passed in this prison.

Four and one-third bricks had slipped by since the Gestapo agent named Hess had threatened to harm Karl's children if the pastor did not bend his beliefs to the Nazi will. Karl had not yielded in all that time. He was certain now that his children had somehow eluded capture by the Gestapo, or Hess would have made good on his threat to use Jamie or Lori against him. *Perhaps then I would have broken. Ah, Lord, you know how weak I am. I could not remain steadfast and be forced to watch . . . if they hurt my children.*

His gaze skipped back to the notch which marked the day he had heard that his wife had perished in prison. *Helen . . . Helen . . . it must be lovely where you are now. I don't begrudge you that, but I am sorry I can't see it with you.*

Other marks represented days on which news of a less personal nature had been passed along to him. This litany of Nazi victories in nation after nation had been intended to convince Karl that there was no use in one Christian pastor holding out when the whole world capitulated to the Führer's iron will!

Seventeen notches into the January brick, Denmark and the Baltic states of Latvia, Estonia, and Lithuania signed a nonaggression pact with Germany. These tiny nations gave their pledge that they, too, would look the other way no matter what else happened in Europe!

Why do you not see, Prisoner Ibsen, that the Führer has been given a free hand? Do you think it matters to any country that one insignificant man remains stubborn in his beliefs?

On the first mark of February, the government of Czechoslovakia ordered all refugee Jews to leave the country within six months.

The Czechs have at last come to their senses about the Jews.

16

That leaves only you, Prisoner Ibsen!

On the twenty-second notch, the German-American Bund of Fritz Kuhn held a demonstration of 22,000 strong in New York to block additional immigration of refugees to the United States.

And who do you think will speak up for you if you continue to speak up for people no nation will have? Troublemaker! You are despised and forgotten here! Confess your wrong-mindedness and come back to your own people, who will forgive you and welcome you!

With March, the rains had come through Karl's cell window on a strong, cold wind. And with the wind had come news that made him tremble for Jamie and Lori!

On the fifteenth mark of March, the German Army had swept across the line of the Sudetenland, which France and England had offered Hitler in Munich to save the peace. All that remained of the Czech nation had been swallowed up by Germany in one unresisting bite. That night the prison guards were exultant. Hitler himself had ridden into Prague and spent the night at Hradcany Castle! The swastika flag waved proudly over Old Town Prague. German soldiers danced on the Charles Bridge as the Führer's voice rang through the streets announcing that Czechoslovakia was now under the "protection" of the Third Reich. And not one shot was fired. Not one German soldier fell in battle.

Now you will see, Prisoner Ibsen! You will see what will happen to those refugee Jews of yours! Now you will see!

Karl had continued to carve away the days. At night he lay awake and dreamed of Lori and Jamie running from the Gestapo, who smashed the Protestant soup kitchen in Prague. Karl had told his children to flee to Prague. He had sent word ahead to the Refugee Relief Committee to warn them that his children were coming. And now Hitler slept in Hradcany Castle! Those refugee Jews who had been ordered out of Czechoslovakia in February were fleeing for their lives to escape the force that had hounded them throughout central Europe. Karl prayed that Jamie and Lori were not among those masses of desperate humanity.

The notches of March ticked by. Nameless camp was packed to overflowing with human flotsam washed up on the Nazi shore with the sinking of Czechoslovakia. And Karl waited. He waited for his guards to slam into his cell and drag him to a room to

17

watch the torture of his children. He waited, knowing he would say anything they wanted—*anything!*—if only they would not hurt Lori and Jamie!

On the twenty-second notch, the guards came to tell him that Germany had also taken the Baltic seaport of Memel from Lithuania. *Certainly Prisoner Ibsen must see that it is useless to resist the righteous Aryan cause! The Führer has traveled by sea to Memel!*

Karl had smiled with relief because the news was not about Lori and Jamie. The guards had taken his smile as a sign that perhaps he was coming to his senses. They reported his reaction to the warden. Karl was given an extra ration of bread to celebrate the Nazi occupation of the Lithuanian port.

The next day he was interrogated. His smile was questioned. He answered that he had only wondered if the Führer had gotten seasick. For this answer he was beaten, but when he regained consciousness he found that the smile within him had not died. *Somewhere Jamie and Lori were still free!*

In that same month, Spain finally fell to the German-led forces of General Franco. One million had died. Britain and the U.S. recognized the new Spanish government immediately. *Soon the whole world will be Fascist. Everyone but you, Prisoner Ibsen!*

On the first notch of April, the rattle of tin plates in the corridor announced breakfast. Karl heard the guards talking outside his door. England's Prime Minister Chamberlain did not much like the fact that the Führer had taken all of Czechoslovakia without asking. The English and the French were now saying that they would go to war against Germany if the Führer set his sights on the Polish port of Danzig. In reply, the Führer had renounced the British-German naval treaty, telling the English, "Who cares what you do?" Maybe there would be a war after all! Maybe it would come at last . . . over Poland! Even little Holland had mobilized.

The guards sounded pleased. They sounded hopeful. The metal slot in the door clanged open and the plate of burned oatmeal was shoved through.

"Feeding time at the zoo," a voice cried. Amid much laughter, the slot clanged shut again.

Once again Karl smiled. He, too, had been hopeful that day. Perhaps at last the democracies had drawn a line across the pocked face of Europe and said, *"No farther!"* So little Holland had mobilized its army to fight if Germany should, in fact, step over the line! *David against Goliath!*

From that first day of April until today, the thirtieth mark on the brick of May, there had been no further news. No interrogations. No laughter in the outer corridor. Prisoners on either side of Karl's cell had been moved. The silence was complete. His meals were passed to him without comment, his latrine bucket emptied in the dark by a faceless Kapo who entered the cell when Karl slept. The straw in his cell remained unchanged. His confinement became totally solitary. He prayed. He recited scriptures to himself. He let his mind walk through the past again and again until that mental path became worn into a groove that was easy to follow. He called out questions to his captors as they passed him his rations, "Was there a war?" They did not reply. They did not seem to hear him.

Could he be the only man left, as they had warned? Had everyone else gone off to fight in Poland?

Until today, the thirtieth of May, he had found himself slipping into such morbid thoughts. *But today the sparrow had come to his window!* Today he was reminded once again that it was spring! Somewhere there were gardens with flowers blooming. Maybe Jamie and Lori . . . maybe . . . maybe they were out walking—looking at colors, wondering about their father, hoping they would see him again someday soon . . . .

For months in France, important visitors had been picked up at their hotels in Paris and driven through the peaceful countryside of Alsace-Lorraine to tour the great concrete wall of defense, the Maginot Line. Politicians and industrialists, and celebrities such as Charles Lindbergh had all been invited to "take the tour." They had descended into the maze of concrete bunkers and gun emplacements; they had spoken with the French soldiers who manned this fortress; they had emerged again into the bright sunlight of the peaceful French countryside, convinced that there would be no war waged by Germany against France, not with such a massive line of defense to get through.

Today it had been American journalist John Murphy's turn to tour the Maginot Line. He was the logical choice for this week's guest list. As the head of Trump European News Service, he was establishing one of the most successful newspaper and radio news agencies serving America from the Continent.

Added to that, Mr. Murphy was a personal friend of the venerable British statesman, Winston Churchill. The two had crossed the Channel together, stayed at the Ritz in Paris for a day, and now walked through the steel and concrete caverns beside the French captain, Edmone Perpignon. Forty years old, with an erect carriage and snapping brown eyes, Captain Perpignon's entire career in the French Army was tied to the Maginot. He loved its smooth gray walls and bristling gun turrets, which pointed across the Rhine toward similar German fortifications.

"You see," the captain said to Murphy in a soft, thick accent, "General Gamelin said that perhaps you are the sort of person who should *see* the Maginot. Perhaps you will then understand it."

Murphy understood perfectly well how much stock the French put in this cement marvel that stretched from Switzerland all along the border to the lowlands of Belgium. Certainly the German Army would not want to confront such an obstacle. But wasn't it possible that the Germans might simply go around it? The government of Belgium had just announced that it would remain strictly neutral *if* war should break out; Murphy and Churchill had discussed just how much such a declaration would mean to Hitler. A few hours' march across little Belgium, and the German divisions could simply go around this hulking wall like a quarterback doing an end run.

Murphy considered using this analogy with the French captain, but then remembered that the French had no Rose Bowl football games which they might compare to war maneuvers.

The captain was ecstatic. "And if anyone in America doubts for a moment," he said, waving a hand at the long tunnel, "that peace is our only war aim, and defense is our only strategy, tell them this: We have anchored all our millions of dollars worth of great guns in five hundred million dollars worth of concrete!"

Murphy exchanged an uneasy glance with Churchill. Churchill had just been saying that the strength of the German war machine would lie in its mobility. Against armored tank divisions, concrete was indeed a barrier—provided the Germans attempted a frontal attack.

The French captain was in love with the Maginot; he was also in love with the history that had inspired it. "You must promise me you will do an article for the American newspapers about

Lorraine! This place was the gateway used by the barbarians to invade France since the time of Attila the Hun."

Churchill broke his long and thoughtful silence. He paused and relit the stub of his cigar as he eyed the captain. "Yes. I can see the similarities between the barbarians and the Nazis. Herr Hitler would make a commendable Attila." He cleared his throat. "But are you *sure* they will try to come through this way again?"

The captain also paused a moment. He shrugged. "They always have before," he answered.

"Last time they came through Belgium," Churchill remarked dryly.

The captain raised an instructive finger. "We have urged the Belgians to see to their own defenses, and soon we will be extending the Maginot along the Belgian border."

"Why hasn't it been done before now?" Murphy dared to ask. "The crisis is imminent."

No doubt more important men than Murphy and Churchill had asked similar questions. The Frenchman had a ready answer.

"Partly because of cost. Partly because of time. But mostly because if the Belgians see our guns and forts facing them, they might think that we French are as aggressive as the Germans."

"Even though the guns are in concrete?" Churchill asked.

"It will be remedied in time." The captain was undaunted. His faith in this wall was not even scratched by the cannonade of doubts that exploded within Murphy.

They proceeded through enormous air-conditioned galleries linked with rail tracks and separated at various points by fireproof sliding iron doors. Casting all unpleasant thoughts away, Captain Perpignon showed them the floor that could drop inward, hurling any enemy who penetrated so far into pits fifty feet deep. The great guns were on the first floor, the control and chart rooms below them, then the plentiful supply rooms, overflowing with food and medicine and racks of shells, like the honeycomb of a beehive. A maze of oil tanks, machinery, and electrical generators were all duplicated for backup in case one of anything should fall. All of this was indeed impressive. Provided, of course, that Hitler followed the footsteps of Attila the Hun.

Once again Murphy rolled an uneasy thought over in his mind. The Germans were smart. Very smart. What did they know about the Maginot that the French and the Western world could not see? What secret did the strutting German Führer have tucked up the sleeve of his plain brown tunic?

Churchill looked at his watch as if he, too, were considering the same doubts as Murphy. "You are an excellent and convincing guide, *Mon capitaine*," Churchill complimented, still looking at his watch. Hitler was to broadcast from Germany soon, and both Churchill and Murphy wanted to hear what he had to say tonight. Perhaps the success or failure of the French line of defense would be hinted at by some small word or phrase in the Führer's speech.

"*Je fais mon métier*," the captain replied with false modesty. "I am just doing my job."

He was doing more than that, Murphy knew. He was loving this monument to future death and past stupidity. He was waiting and praying for the moment when the guns of the Maginot would boom across the river into Germany. The thought of splintered German tanks and broken bodies filled him with premature pride. "They will come this way," he said. "The Germans are stupid. *Oui!* They will come!"

———

The German occupation of Czechoslovakia on March 15 had put Theo Lindheim back in uniform.

At the orders of Hitler, the German Army had rolled beyond the boundaries of the Sudetenland to smash what was left of Czechoslovakia. In the same hour, the divisions of the Czech Army and Air Force were ordered to abandon their weapons and equipment to their Nazi conquerors.

Instead, the handful of unmarried men who had been a part of Theo's air command had donned their flying gear, fueled their aircraft and headed for England. They hoped they might live long enough to fight for their country one day.

Hitler slept unconcerned in Hradcany Castle while troops marched into Old Town Prague and arrested the men and women who ran the refugee soup kitchen. *Subversives*, the Nazis called them. Hundreds were arrested and executed for resistance.

Hitler toured the great factories of the Skoda Arms Works— quite a prize for Hitler's war machine. Planes considered to be the most modern in Europe were handed over to the German

Luftwaffe. Tanks, rifles, machine guns, and artillery from thirty dismantled Czech divisions were given to the Nazis, and now they pointed at the heart of Poland!

One by one, escaping Czech aircraft flying on fumes made it to a dozen little airfields in England. The pilots collapsed on the ground. They begged for political asylum, just as Theo had done the night England and France had first betrayed Czechoslovakia to Hitler's Munich Agreement.

The night of the Munich Agreement Chamberlain had vowed to fight for Czechoslovakia if Hitler moved any farther than allowed by the treaty. Now, Hitler swallowed the nation in one gulp. Czechoslovakia was no more. Every promise had been broken; men and women dying; the Czech people abandoned.

And Chamberlain did nothing to help.

Members of the exiled Czech government slipped out quietly. Some fled to England, where they were granted asylum like this small group of pilots with Theo tonight.

But England did not fight to save Czechoslovakia. Instead, the British Prime Minister vowed that *this* time he would guarantee assistance to Poland if Poland was attacked.

Days later, the Nazis discovered that the former government of Prague had deposited several tons of gold bullion with the Bank of England for safekeeping. Hitler wanted this gold. He wanted it immediately. After all, Czechoslovakia was part of the Reich now, was it not?

The British government handed the gold over to Hitler, who promptly put it to good use building more tanks.

March had been an amazing month for broken promises and broken lives, Theo thought. The refugee ships had arrived regularly, carrying their loads of brokenhearted children. Many of them were still at the house in London. How sad they were, how quiet. This is what bad politics and stupid politicians had brought them to.

As for the few Czech airmen who had managed to escape, they, too, were grim and bitter. They had saved these precious aircraft for what they saw was soon coming to England. They looked around for former officers who had fled like them.

And they found Theo Lindheim. "They will need us soon enough, Officer Lindheim!" exclaimed a young man whom Theo had trained to fly. "The English gave away our country, but we will stand with them to fight for theirs!"

Would Theo join them? Would he come and train young Czech students to fly?

The time to mourn was past, Theo reasoned. The fight was all that would soon be left for them. He put on his uniform that very day and joined the dozens who had fled in hopes of fighting another day.

The rich, newly plowed fields of France smelled warm and fragrant in the night air as Murphy and Churchill were driven back along the road they had taken that afternoon.

Beyond the dark boundaries of the hedges Murphy could make out the silhouettes of haystacks. In the daylight he had just been able to see the snouts of field guns protruding from the golden heaps. Everywhere for miles and miles of apparently tranquil countryside, machine gun nests hid in half-built cottages. Just beneath the tender shoots of grass, camouflaged pill boxes lay on the hills like snakes waiting to strike. Tank traps bristled with deadly iron spikes. And far away, across the uplands, unbroken coils of barbed wire waited for the return of some reincarnated barbarian to find his path back this way to a quick death in France.

Three hundred yards across the river into German territory, both Murphy and Churchill had seen the figures of German soldiers leisurely digging rifle pits—*in case the French should try to invade?*

Every bridge across the swollen Rhine had been mined. Loyal Frenchmen waited on duty with the button within reach . . . *just in case!* All of this, and yet Europe was at peace! There was no quarrel between Germany and France, or Germany and England! The Führer had said it. *All he wanted now was Danzig!*

Churchill sighed heavily. The moonglow shone on his waxy complexion. "And so it has come to this," he said sadly. "As though babies were born to grow and be hurled into the breach."

Murphy did not reply. He stared silently out the window and thought of Elisa, of their baby. *What kind of world would that little one be born into? Trenches and wire and concrete bunkers. Gas mask drills and . . .* He shook his head as if to force away the images of dead children he had seen in Spain.

"We have been brought to this abyss," Churchill continued with melancholy eloquence. "Germany rearmed in violation of a solemn treaty. Air superiority cast away by us. Just across the river back there they reoccupied the Rhineland. Their Siegfried Line built to match the Maginot. The Rome-Berlin Axis. Austria devoured. Czechoslovakia dismembered by the Munich pact. The mighty arsenal of Skoda now turning out munitions for the German armies. Thirty Czech divisions cast away."

Churchill's match flared, illuminating his round face in eerie light and shadow. "Yes," he finished, "we shall hear it tonight Poland is next. By September, I believe; before the rains can stop the tanks of Germany. By September, there will be war." His slow, certain drawl sent a charge of dread through Murphy as he listened. "The folly of great nations will be paid for by children and mothers. It has come to this at last."

2   Love Like Iron

Thousands of years had passed since Jewish mothers first heard the grinding of Egyptian swords being sharpened for the slaughter of their babies. As the first howls of grief had pierced the morning, a young mother nursed her baby one last time, placed him in a tiny cradle of reeds, and cast him adrift on the waters of the Nile River.

What mother over the centuries did not hear the story and *admire*? To step back from the murky water and watch that fragile ark rocking on the current required love like iron, heated in the fires of anguish and hammered against the anvil of desperation.

In 1939, the grinding wheels of Europe were heard rasping against Nazi swords. Jewish mothers nursed their babies and *knew* . . . They braided the sweet, soft hair of their little girls and they *did not doubt*. . . . They tucked in their little boys and listened to prayers; they tied shoes and doctored scrapes . . . all the while the steady buzz of blade against wheel drifted through the nursery windows. And the little boys grew while mothers waited for the day when they would say goodbye.

Tonight, the docks of Southampton were illuminated in anticipation of the arrival of the ship. But there were no bands, no eagerly waiting husbands or wives, no whistles or shouts or excited waves or confetti. Not for this ship.

Over the weeks, the arrivals of the big passenger liners carrying refugee children from Danzig had been unlike any that Elisa Murphy had ever witnessed—refugees: joyless, homesick children!

Elisa's mother, Anna, and her sister Helen stood shoulder to shoulder on the quay. Their heads slightly tilted toward each other as though they wanted to tell a secret but had forgotten it. Faces were pained, and yet the eyes of both women were eager and hopeful as they scanned the solemn group of refugee children who stared down from the decks of the liner.

Little tugboats nosed the ship toward the dock, much in the way a terrier might nip at the feet of an elephant to make him move.

Little hands clutched the railing. Wide, frightened eyes peered out and wondered what sort of people would take them in. Where would they sleep tonight? Would they be warm and well cared for as their tearful mothers had promised them? Were these English people good and pleasant? Or might they be cross if broken hearts could not remember how to laugh for a while? Would they be sorry when the first tears came, that they had volunteered to take children into their homes?

Elisa looked back at them. She smiled and waved as though they were all old friends. She called out loudly in German, *"Guten Abend, Kinderlach! Willkommen! Willkommen!"*

With that, she turned back to the group of ten musicians who had traveled from London to Southampton for this solemn occasion. And they began to play their instruments. Classical musicians all, they played the brightest snippets of Mozart that they could think of. And finally that drew hesitant smiles from the children.

All the while, the child Elisa carried within her rested quietly, as though sensing the nearness of heartache. These little visits of welcome to Southampton seemed to be the only time the baby was still.

Anna Lindheim and Helen Ibsen had come to assist as interpreters for the homeless children. But they also came with the hope—the prayer—that Helen's children might somehow be found among these who had managed to escape. *Lori Ibsen, age sixteen . . . No, she just had a birthday, didn't she? That is, if . . . if she is still alive. And Jamie Ibsen, ten years old. Last seen being carted off to a Hitler Youth school. That was the last time his mother saw him. Nearly six months ago, it was.*

Aunt Helen showed the photograph of her missing children to several workers who had made the crossing with the few lucky ones. *"No, Mrs. Ibsen. So very sorry. . ."* Aunt Helen looked at the photograph one more time—a longing look, a look that made Elisa put her hand on the baby in her womb and pray that her own life would never come to such a moment.

And each of these little ones who walked down the gangplank represented a mother like Helen who had said goodbye!

All the ships had come quietly into England in exactly the same way. And every arrival caused a lump of gratitude to hang in Elisa's throat. *These few are safe, at least!* But coupled with that gratitude was the uneasiness that comes when grief is very near and real . . . when something in the world is terribly, *terribly* wrong!

Helen Ibsen had never cried before tonight. But she knew there was only one boat left that could bring her children from the Reich to the haven of England. Only one more chance for Jamie and Lori to be on that boat. One more chance.

Elisa looked at the face of her aunt Helen and thought how much she looked like Anna. Sisters. And she remembered how very much Lori Ibsen resembled Elisa when Elisa was that age. Cousins. There were still whole chunks of their hearts that Adolf Hitler held captive. That was true for these little ones, as well. They brought their lives and a future with them tonight. They would start all over again at the age of five or six or ten. But could anyone ever know what great love they left behind?

Only the mothers who let them go could answer such a question. Love had loaded them on this great ship; love had waved goodbye and thrown the final kisses. Love remained behind and watched the ship drift out of sight.

No one on this side of the Channel could replace that.

Elisa had some idea of what it meant. *Love like iron!*

Someone else to tuck him in. Someone else to braid her hair. Someone else to kiss the hurt away. . . .

But these were hurts that could not be kissed away.

The moon was full, bright as a searchlight over the Mediterranean. If he could have done it, Captain Samuel Orde would have shot it out of the sky in order to bring the lads into shore under cover of total darkness. The freighter was supposed to bring them in when there was no moon at all. But engine trouble and endless delays had resulted in the exact opposite result.

Orde and a dozen other members of his Special Night Squad huddled behind the dunes. Just below the lip of moon-drenched sand, a shadow curled over them like a dark wave. There they waited for the signal from the tiny lifeboat that had cast off from the freighter several miles from the coastline of British Palestine.

On the beach, a group of teenaged young people from the kibbutz sat around a roaring bonfire. They sang, they laughed, they roasted bratwurst on long sticks. Their voices seemed a strange counterpoint to the drama of thirty other young men of their own generation who struggled to guide the boat toward the signal fire.

A British military jeep roared up over the sand. Orde thought he recognized the voices of his countrymen as they demanded to know what sort of party was going on here!

A young, unafraid voice replied in concise English, "A birthday party! For Sasha." Then there was laughter and applause as a girl from the kibbutz stood and bowed in acknowledgment.

"You have no chaperon?" demanded the Englishman.

"We left them all in Europe," someone in the group said caustically. This was the sort of remark Orde had warned them against making. He grimaced and glared at the youthful offender from behind the dune.

"But *you* can be our chaperon," called Sasha. She skipped across the firelight and grabbed the arm of the reluctant officer. She pulled him into the group. "Come on! Give me a kiss! It's my sixteenth birthday! No one is serious tonight!"

Good girl! Orde silently cheered her. *Smart girl!* Then he prayed that the lifeboat would not choose that instant to flash its signal as it moved toward the shore!

"No. No. Can't join you tonight. Duty. . ." The Englishman was clearly embarrassed.

"Are you married or something?" asked Sasha, who gave him a kiss amid more shouts of encouragement. "Afraid your general will find out you had a little fun on the beach?"

The other soldier hung back. Orde could see the ramrod-straight back of the Englishman as he decided that he had certainly misjudged the meaning of this gathering. *Just kids, you know. A little party on the beach . . .*

More taunting banter drifted on the wind, half-obscured by the heavy pounding of the waves. The tide had shifted. Not good. High tides and heavy seas would make it impossible to bring in the boat without capsizing it. And could those illegal refugees, a handful of lads from landlocked Poland, swim? He doubted it. That was a terrifying thought added to a long list of unpleasant possibilities tonight.

"Hey! If you come back, bring us some of your English cigarettes, will you?" The request followed the retreating military jeep down the beach to the crude road that led through the dunes.

"They did it," Moshe Sachar hissed and nudged Orde in the ribs.

Orde glared at him in reply. Total silence had been the order. The only voices tonight on the dunes were to be those of young people as they tossed driftwood onto the blazing fire and pretended that they were really just a bunch of kids.

Nearly three hundred young male refugees had been brought in illegally this way over the last four months—escaping Germany, Austria, Czechoslovakia, and now beginning to slip out of Poland as the winds of Hitler's ambitions shifted to blow the inferno ever nearer. But none of those young people had ever landed in this ancient homeland under such threatening circumstances. *The moon. The heightened patrols. And now the tide.*

Orde let his breath out slowly, like steam escaping a pressure cooker. The scheme was to smuggle in young men over the age of sixteen. He had pictured building an army from the ground up, and these young refugees were to be his foundation. Papers could be forged once they arrived; it was much simpler than waiting for the slow wheels of governments to grind these strong, healthy lads to fine dust.

Others were being smuggled in illegally as well, of course. But Orde pretended not to notice them. Old men and women. Little children. They were not the stuff a future fighting force was built from.

The British government knew that simple fact as well. That was why they made it so difficult for young males over the age of sixteen to immigrate.

Well, here was Orde's answer to that—and the answer of the Yishuv! Like the mother of Moses, mothers in Europe darned the socks and underwear of their sons. They kissed them tearfully on their cheeks where the beards of young manhood sprouted, and they sent them off with strangers—with men called Zionists, who spoke of the Promised Land, of the covenant of Zion!

On leaky steamers they came. Under the scornful eyes of bribed captains they vomited over the rails of the ocean's most unseaworthy tubs. And then, nearing this shore, they were once again cast adrift in doubtful little scows, piloted by local fishermen, to run the gauntlet of the English patrol boats!

Their beacon light was a bonfire, a birthday party. Their signal was the voices of other young people who could remember the same long journey.

And when they landed, their shaky legs falling out from under them, they were greeted by men in uniform, led by a British captain named Orde who first terrified them and then astounded them and taught them to be men and Jews returned to their homeland!

It was all a very worthy enterprise. It was also profoundly illegal and dangerous for all involved. Especially for Orde.

Orde did not think of his personal safety now. The voices around the bonfire suddenly grew silent. Orde lifted his head above the crest of the dune and looked out across the water to where a single light flashed. One, two, three short blips and then one long. The signal for *V*. The code for Victory.

One by one, those around the bonfire stood to watch. They brushed sand from their trousers and shorts. They looked at the rows of breaking waves that rolled up on the sand between the fire and the little boat.

The lifeboat was in trouble. Orde and a dozen of the Special Night Squad joined the young men of the kibbutz at the water's edge.

"Who is piloting tonight?" Moshe Sachar asked the tallest of the young men, who had already stripped to his waist and pulled off his shoes.

"Julian," the fellow answered. The roar of waves nearly drowned his voice.

Orde could see the silhouettes of the refugees as the boat slid down the face of a swell and into the silver reflection of the moon.

"Julian knows what he's doing," Orde said, but he pulled off his shirt and shoes and stripped to his shorts as well. Yes. Julian was a good man. A fisherman, he knew the tides and currents of these waters. No doubt Julian knew his boat was in trouble.

A dozen inner tubes from the farm tractors had been threaded through a life rope like donuts on a string. In all the landings of refugees on this beach, the inner tubes had not been needed. Run aground during low tide, the passengers of earlier boats had simply jumped out and waded the hundred yards to shore.

Orde took up the makeshift lifeline and looked around him. Every other man had stripped as well, and now they waited only for Orde's instructions as the lifeboat was thrust up on the boiling foam of a breaker and then spun sideways.

Trouble! Were those cries of terror that echoed above the rumble of the surf?

"Only the best swimmers out! The water will be chest high for fifty yards and then drop away! Hold tight to the tubes and the rope. Don't be afraid, lads! Follow me!"

Like a commander leaping from the safety of a trench into enemy fire, Orde plunged in. He grasped the tube beneath his arm, using it as a shield against the pounding water. He never looked back to see who had come along. They were there. His men were all there. Through hell first and now high water, they would not retreat!

The icy water made his legs and feet and groin ache with pain. But as a boy he had always been first to dive into the frigid waters of the English Channel. Soon enough he would be numb to it.

There were shouts from the men behind him as they jumped into the waves. Lungs and body rebelled against such cold. The mind raged against the folly of stepping into the dark force that pummeled them.

A wave began its slow, crushing curl to Orde's right. He spotted the white flag of its crest and was certain that the wall of water would crash down on him. "Dive under!" he shouted, hoping that the man behind had seen the wave and heard his warning. He plunged into the black wall, dragging the reluctant inner

31

tube after him; then he bobbed up on the other side.

Gasping for air, he could see that two men along the line had been swept back. They struggled to stand and move forward to take their place on the rope again.

Where was Julian's boat? Orde's toes barely brushed the sand. The water was much deeper than he had expected this near to shore! The moon and the tides had formed an alliance against the fragile little boat and the men who fought to reach it!

Orde let the buoyancy of the tube hold him a moment as he searched for the boat. Had it capsized? Were they already too late?

And then he saw it! The bow rose up and slammed down hard as it sledded down the face of an enormous swell. Water pushed it from behind, threatening to swamp and then capsize it. Still fifty yards away and to their left, the screams of terrified young men were clear above the tumult!

Orde kicked hard, aware that he had felt the last of the sand. He dragged the lifeline under yet another bone-crunching wave and swam to where he thought the boat should be.

He had cursed the moonlight before; now he prayed for the moon to light the scene! Julian was in trouble. Thirty young lads were in trouble. Orde was tired, but he fought on, unwilling to admit that he might also be in difficulty.

Ten yards forward! Then the waves pushed him back eight. He caught momentary glimpses of his men, their heads bobbing along the line they grasped as desperately as any drowning man. Behind them rose the eerie orange glow of the watch fire. It spoke of light and warmth and life . . . a distant world from the swirling water!

Yet another wave exploded just in front of Orde. He ducked beneath it but was again pulled back. His inner tube bumped against the man behind him. *Moshe?*

Moshe flailed a moment and then found his buoy again. He shouted, *"Over there! I saw it! She's gone over!"*

Capsized! The refugees would not last in this! Orde could not see where the boat had gone.

"Take the lead!" he called to Moshe who struck out left, directly parallel to the shore line. His stroke was sure and strong, his kick more powerful than Orde's. Orde gratefully took his place as second on the rope.

And then the belly of the capsized boat shone clearly in the moonlight! Julian was sprawled across it. Four others had climbed up beside him and now they reached out to grasp the others in the water who struggled to cling to the boat. Their forms were all light and shadow, like the negative of a photograph, and yet the terror on their faces was clear.

Then came the shout from the rescuers, *"Hold on!"* This was repeated in German, Czech and Polish. Julian turned his head, shouted and waved.

"I told you they would come!"

Those who could swim struck out toward the flotilla of inner tubes. A dozen still clung desperately to the boat while Julian encouraged them.

"You see! Hold on! We're almost home now, boys! Not one will be lost!"

The dossier that linked the political resistance in Austria with connections in Prague and Danzig and Warsaw was several inches thick. Compiled by Major Alexander Hess during his long recovery after being thrown from a train at the Polish border, it was a document that impressed Heinrich Himmler, chief of the S.S. and the Gestapo. For this reason, Himmler requested this private meeting with the Führer only two hours before Hitler's scheduled broadcast regarding the relations between Germany and Poland.

Major Hess, recently promoted from lieutenant, was in attendance this evening to explain the complicated web of connections between the perpetrators of what seemed to be a worldwide plot against the Führer. His facts and theories, listed in the cumbersome document on the coffee table of the Führer's private apartment, needed concise interpretation. Adolf Hitler had no time to read through such dossiers; he had barely enough time to listen. But tonight he was well in tune to talk of plots and possible coups planned against him by the German military and by foreign governments. Hitler did not need evidence to imagine that forces were intent on destroying him and his Thousand-Year Reich. He dreamed such things regularly. He listened to the voices that warned him where to go, where to walk, and whom to trust. Spirits guided him by night, and human voices like that of his Gestapo chief warned him and verified by their research that what the spirits spoke was true! For such a meeting as this, the Führer would delay his broadcast. Tonight the pieces of an unsolved puzzle continued to drop into place, clarifying the picture the Führer claimed to have glimpsed in a foggy dream.

After his ordeal at the border of Poland some months ago, Major Hess walked haltingly, with the help of a cane. The fact that he could walk at all was impressive. The doctors of Berlin had not expected Hess to recover so quickly from the wounds inflicted on him by the guard dogs.

Some wounds would never heal, of course. Major Hess's left eye was gray and clouded across the iris, the result of a fang wound. Loss of vision was total on that side, and yet Hess had spent every spare moment at the pistol range improving his aim and training himself to compensate for the lack of depth perception. His progress was pronounced miraculous.

Tonight the Führer believed that Hess had been spared for the sake of the Reich, for the sake of the Führer and the German people. It was no accident that the man had recovered to be brought to this moment! His research verified the worst fears of Hitler, and the heart of the Führer was touched by the loyalty and persistence of this man.

Himmler adjusted his round wire-rimmed glasses and with a wave of his hand indicated that Hess himself must share the conclusions of the report with the Führer. Hitler's dark blue eyes were rapt with attention as the story unfolded.

Hess removed a front-page photograph of the Führer standing beside two brothers. He smoothed it out before Hitler on the table. Hitler frowned and stared down at their faces.

"Although the caption names the brothers as Peter and Willie Ruger," Hess began, "these two boys are the sons of the Austrian resistance leader, Michael Wallich." Hess then pulled out a picture of the family: *Michael Wallich. Wife, Karin. Son, Peter. Daughter, Marlene. Infant, Wilhelm, a.k.a. Willie.*

Hitler paled visibly. "What does this mean? How did they get so close to me? Where was the failure of security in this matter? This boy—" Hitler pointed to Peter. "He is not that much younger than the young Jew who killed Ernst vom Rath in Paris! It does not take age to make an assassin!"

Hess and Himmler exchanged looks. The Führer was clearly seeing the significance of this matter.

Himmler cleared his throat. "Those around you on the day

the picture was taken at the Berlin terminal have been interrogated. It was the photographer who chose these boys as subjects for this photograph, mein Führer. At first he denied knowing them, but of course with the right persuasion, he confessed everything we expected. He died before we could extract names from him, however."

Hitler's eyes narrowed as he considered the significance of having his picture appear with the sons of the man suspected to have been the head of the Austrian resistance. Did this not prove to all who wished to assassinate the leader of the German people that it was possible—*simple, really*—to get close enough to do it?

And now came the most harrowing point of all. Himmler filled in the blanks. "Agent Hess had been pursuing the children of Karl Ibsen, as you ordered. They were on that same train, it is believed. Agent Hess stumbled upon Peter Wallich in the company of the mistress of Wolfgang von Fritschauer. They were escaping the Reich together." Himmler turned to Hess now to continue.

"When I confronted Lucy Strasburg, informing her that she was under arrest for aiding the escape of Jews, Peter Wallich pulled a gun on me."

"He had a gun?" Hitler stared wildly at the newspaper. "I knew there was something about him! I felt that there was some danger. . . ."

"Who can say why the boy did not use the weapon against you, mein Führer," Himmler responded in quiet agreement.

Hitler sat up very straight. His hands rested on his knees. He did not remove his eyes from the picture of himself holding the baby while the near-assassin grinned wildly at him.

The Führer came to his own conclusion. "It was because I picked up the child. His brother, you say? Yes. That was it. Again I am saved by a force that guided me to make even the smallest move. Peter Wallich did not shoot me because he did not want to hit his brother."

No one could argue with such a possibility. It seemed a reasonable explanation. Himmler nodded. Hess also agreed that was certainly the case.

"You have done well, Major Hess." Hitler was emotional in his gratitude as though the injuries Hess had suffered from Peter Wallich had somehow been in defense of Hitler's own life.

"There is much more, mein Führer," Gestapo Chief Himmler said coolly. He did not enjoy the fact that this little officer received such high praise when it was Himmler who had set the wheels of the Gestapo in motion in this matter. "Of course, there are other factors that the Gestapo has uncovered involving a number of conspirators in various capital cities."

Hitler stretched his neck and drummed his fingers on the arm of his chair. "I am aware that the so-called democracies want nothing more than to see me dead. Where does all this lead? What do you have in there?" He glared down at the dossier.

Himmler nodded for Hess to take the briefing again. "Here is the connection. We know that Michael Wallich was working with a double agent in our own department." A photograph of Otto Wattenbarger was placed on the table. The Führer knew the face well. Wattenbarger was among the best men serving the Reich in Vienna after the Anschluss. Hitler's face darkened at this further evidence of treachery against him in the highest echelons of government.

"Like Michael Wallich, Wattenbarger died before we were able to extract any information from him," Himmler interjected. "Since that time we have been watching the moves of Wolfgang von Fritschauer. Since Wolf's mistress is obviously part of the resistance, we believe that it is only a matter of time before he leads us to her . . . and perhaps to others as well."

"Wolfgang von Fritschauer." The Führer repeated the name of the young aristocrat. "He is suspected? Is it wise to allow him to remain free?"

"Until we trace all the conspirators who have fled the Reich, Wolf must remain at large. He is being closely followed, of course," Hess replied. "His request for transfer to duties in Danzig and Warsaw may well lead us to those who plot against your life, mein Führer."

Himmler pushed his glasses up on the bridge of his nose. "There is a good chance that Wolf is guiltless in this matter." Himmler glared at Hess. Hess had pushed his accusation of Wolf too far. There was no conclusive evidence. "It was Wolf, after all, who arrested Michael Wallich as well as Otto Wattenbarger. I personally am of the opinion that he was simply taken in by Lucy Strasburg, who used him *carte blanche* as a means of getting information and then passing it along."

Hess shrugged with surly reluctance to accept this thesis. He fully believed in the guilt of Wolfgang von Fritschauer. "All the same, Wolf is being trailed. His phone calls are being monitored by an agent who reports to me."

Once again the face of Himmler displayed irritation. "The result of that monitoring at this moment is that Wolf appears to be following orders to track her down. He is also fulfilling his duties in Danzig and Warsaw. Several thousand men are in place within the area of Danzig. Weapons are smuggled across the river nightly. He is performing as you would expect on behalf of the Reich."

Hitler flared. "But is he loyal to *me*? Every traitor claims loyalty to the German Reich. They have forgotten that the Führer is Germany, and Germany is the Führer." He turned to Hess. "Continue your surveillance."

Hitler shifted uneasily in his chair as he considered other factors in the matter of the Austrian resistance. He glared at Hess, who was not getting to the point fast enough to suit the Führer. "It was not your job to deal with the Austrian plotters. You were under orders to break the will of Pastor Karl Ibsen. A simple matter of returning his children to our control." The thought displeased Hitler as he considered that Hess had accomplished none of that. Hitler's mood of growing impatience was a dangerous current to be caught in.

Himmler interceded. "The two issues are inseparable, mein Führer, as you will soon see."

"Then let me see!" Hitler bellowed.

With trembling hands, Hess fumbled through the dossier again. He had not expected such a change of moods. With a sigh of relief he placed the simple diagram of a triangle into the Führer's hands. At the pinnacle of the triangle was the name: ELISA LINDHEIM (MURPHY). From that point, a list of names trailed down the lines on either side. Those who were dead were underlined in red.

"On this side of the line, mein Führer"—Hess ran his finger downward—"you see the players of the Vienna conspiracy."

RUDY DORBRANSKY: Anti-Nazi agent active in smuggling operations on behalf of Jewish children. Performed in Vienna Symphony Orchestra with E. Lindheim. Close association with Michael Wallich.

MICHAEL WALLICH: Leader of Austrian resistance. Owner of

bookstore that served as a front for resistance activities after the Anschluss. Bookstore known to be frequented by E. Lindheim.

OTTO WATTENBARGER: Double agent believed to have passed information to E. Lindheim on various occasions. Lindheim's flat was subsequently leased to Lucy Strasburg after Lindheim fled Austria. Wattenbarger is now known to have had close contact with both Wallich and Dorbransky. Wattenbarger protected the family of Wallich, who were then assisted in escape by:

LUCY STRASBURG.

Hess moved to the other side of the triangle. "There are many less important connections, mein Führer, but here are the most vital."

THOMAS VON KLEISTMANN: Lifetime association with Elisa Lindheim in her years in Berlin. Love affair believed to have been ongoing until his arrest and execution for the murder of Gestapo agent Georg Wand in Paris.

Hess slid his hand past the more obvious names such as Theo Lindheim, Elisa's father. He skipped to the one name that had been his first concern before he had fallen into the center of what he was certain was a vast conspiracy.

PASTOR KARL IBSEN: Uncle of Elisa Lindheim.

There was much more written beside the name of Karl Ibsen, but the Führer saw only that the pastor was a relative of a woman so obviously linked with treachery.

"I have traced the connections, mein Führer," Hess said proudly. "Like a family tree, those who have opposed you all seem to know this one woman. Or they are associated in some way with someone who has been close to her. Vienna on one side, and the Ibsen case on the other."

Hess tapped the dossier. "The Ibsen case is tied to the Lindheim brood. Elisa Lindheim touches Rudy Dorbransky, who leads us to Michael Wallich and, of course, Otto Wattenbarger."

"The links of the chain are tight, mein Führer." Himmler's eyes sparked.

"These are just the underlings, I believe," Hess continued. "They are subordinate to a larger web of deceit that perhaps reaches even here. . . ." Hess swept his hand around the room. "Here to those who surround you. Here, even in the Chancellery."

Hitler's skin grew even paler as he listened and tried to imagine who among his personal entourage might be among this conspiracy. "Then they will be found out!"

"Exactly," Himmler nodded. "It cannot be coincidence that the Ibsen children and the Wallich children escaped to Danzig on the same night. Possibly on the same train. There is some deal that has been struck."

Of course. It all made perfect sense. How could Hitler have missed something so obvious as this? There was a higher force at work to remove him from power. Obviously, disloyal parties were at work against him, and he would have them strung up when they were rooted out!

"So Ibsen may be more than a religious fanatic." Hitler's eyes narrowed. "He does not yield to interrogation."

"He has been tortured. He admits to nothing except that his ruler is not of this world. He has maintained from the first that his children are safe; that they will not be harmed," Himmler said. "Someone has told him this. A bargain has been made with Ibsen—if he does not talk, his children will remain safe."

Hess picked up the folder and hefted it. "He will not talk, will not betray the conspiracy as long as his family is unharmed."

Hitler nodded and snapped his fingers rapidly. "If they are dead and the promises of his confederates prove false—"

"I think Ibsen will crack. He will tell everything he knows. Every day he is of less importance to us as far as his stubborn belief in his God. But, mein Führer." Himmler leaned forward. "He knows more. I am convinced. He is connected to it all. Finding the identity of the traitors within our government may well make the difference of survival for you . . . and for the Reich. For everything you stand for."

"Then find the Ibsen children," Hitler said softly. "And the Strasburg woman. Put agents at the disposal of Agent Hess in London, Danzig, and Warsaw until this matter is laid to rest." His fingers drummed on the chair. "I have felt the nearness of treachery," he mused. "It all makes perfect sense. And I will find the German traitors who would bring me down. They will dance on the end of a wire!"

By now Hess knew that he had completely won the confidence of Adolf Hitler. But he had saved his trump card for last.

"There is one more question that needs to be answered, mein Führer." Hess took the diagram from Hitler and began to write. "If there is a conspiracy against your life, who might be the one political enemy associated with Elisa Lindheim in London who would like to see you dead?"

Hess passed the diagram back to Hitler. At the top of the triangle, written above the name of Elisa Lindheim, was the obvious conclusion. All the indications pointed to one man: *WINSTON CHURCHILL.*

3   Red Lights Over Danzig

The French captain did not speak German, so he drove without comment as Adolf Hitler's speech echoed over the radio of the staff car. He hummed a French tune while Murphy and Churchill listened with rapt attention.

As Murphy listened to the broadcast of the German Führer's speech, he had no doubt that he was hearing a declaration of war against England.

The chirping of crickets through the open window of the car provided a peaceful background to the growling voice of Hitler.

Winston Churchill sat unmoving in the backseat. His brooding eyes reflected the awareness that as Hitler professed peace, he was, in fact, justifying reasons for war.

Today President Roosevelt had sent Hitler an appeal that the issues which fractured Europe should be settled peacefully, without German aggression. Matters could be solved around a world conference table without the use of military force.

Great Britain, Hitler asserted, was the aggressor. England had made a mutual assistance pact with Poland. In the event that Germany—peace-loving Germany—should attempt to take Danzig back, then England would go to war against Germany! This, according to the German leader, was a provocation, an encouragement for the Poles to rise up and invade peaceful Germany!

He then turned his verbal attack on the foreign policies of Great Britain in other lands.

Churchill smirked as the direction of the speech turned. "Here he goes," said Churchill, as though he had been expecting it.

"Now," the voice of Hitler raged with righteous indignation, *"I have just read a speech delivered by Eamon de Valera, the Irish Prime Min-ister. He does not charge Germany with oppressing Ireland, or any other nation, but he reproaches England for subjecting Ireland to continuous British oppression!"*

Churchill shook his head knowingly. "The people of Northern Ireland wish to be severed from England about as badly as the Czechs wanted to be invaded by German divisions."

The voice of Hitler continued. *"In the same way, it has obviously escaped the attention of Mr. Roosevelt that Palestine is not occupied by German troops, but by English."*

At this assertion, Churchill chuckled bitterly. "It is a pity our Captain Orde cannot reply to that, considering the number of German Nazi officers he has found lying dead among the Arab terrorists."

"The Arabs living in that country have not complained of German aggression, but they do voice a continuous appeal to the world, deploring the barbarous methods with which England is attempting to suppress a people who love their freedom and are defending it!"

At this Churchill scoffed. *"Indeed!* I was on the committee that created the Mandate. We penciled in its borders in 1922, giving the vast majority of the Middle East to Arab sheiks who loved their freedom so much they roamed from place to place with herds of camels. Back then the Arabs did not want the little crumb of Palestine. They said it was too desolate to settle in! When we earmarked that tiny fragment for a Jewish homeland, do you know why the Arabs protested? They said that the place was so poor that it could support no one." He lit his cigar and sat back for a moment of reflection. "And after the Zionists made something of the place, these freedom-loving Arabs, who are now so dear to the heart of the Führer, poured across the borders of their lands into the British Mandate at a rate of thirty-five thousand a year!" His eyes narrowed. "Now they fight us with German-made weapons."

Hitler finally reached the point he had been searching for through this long, rambling tirade against British aggression. Had England made a pact with Poland to help if Poland was attacked? Indeed they had.

"In reply to this," Hitler's voice rose as he made a holy pledge to assist the oppressed peoples of Palestine and Northern Ire-

land, *"the German government is prepared to give to these states the same kind of assurance of our help. Indeed, we are already allied with them or at least united by close ties of friendship."*

"That should raise some eyebrows in Parliament," Murphy said in a low voice. "In one breath, Hitler is admitting Nazi assistance to the IRA and the Arab terrorists. The great battle against British aggression."

Churchill reached out switched off the radio as *"Sieg Heil!"* threatened to drown out the song of the crickets. "Herr Hitler fights like a contentious woman," he said. "From point A to point W and back to point S, T, R and G. He is a failure as a logician, I fear." He frowned. "The speech is an ominous vision of what may very well be terrorist warfare in the streets of London as well as Jerusalem. We have heard a man well-schooled in the ways of total evil, Murphy. And I am afraid we are not equipped to deal with it."

The patter of raindrops surrounded the great stone prison of Warsaw with the illusion of peace. Rain this late in the season was unexpected and unwelcome, as unwelcome as the news from Berlin that negotiations must begin immediately on the issue of the Free City of Danzig and its return to Germany.

Uniformed prison guards manned every entrance of the imposing fortress. They smoked and pulled up the hoods of their rain slickers to keep dry, but a strange chill made their hearts tremble as they looked to the south and west and knew that tonight the great army of the Reich surrounded Poland like the claws of a giant crab.

Endless columns of desperate refugees from Czechoslovakia still pressed against the gates, pleading for entry into Poland. They were being turned back at every outpost, returned to satisfy the German appetite for human sacrifice.

Perhaps the Germans will not attack Poland next. . . . Warsaw, of course, did not wish to offend Berlin when it came to the matter of handing over fugitives from Nazi justice. After all, why would people flee the German advance if they were not guilty of something? Even as the Gestapo in Prague cracked down with a violence that rivaled the smashing of the Jews in Vienna, the officials of Poland mimicked the actions of their voracious neighbor. When it came to Jews, Poland agreed with Berlin.

Great friendships between nations had been founded on smaller issues than a mutual hatred of a despised race. In this one matter, Poland and Nazi Germany were inextricably joined. Hatred of Jews was preached on the street corners and in the churches. It was taught to children and babies in the nursery, lectured upon at the universities. And from this night forward, the Jews of Poland would look over their shoulders and sniff the air of Warsaw for danger before they ventured out of their own neighborhoods.

Thus it came as a surprise when the black automobile of the Catholic bishop of Warsaw drove to the gate of the prison compound and stopped.

The window of the vehicle slid down, revealing the face of the bishop himself. Beside him was an ordinary priest, a Jewish rabbi, and a Jewess cloaked in a pale blue shawl.

"We have come to see the warden," said the bishop.

The flustered guard stammered a reply as he looked from the priest to the rabbi, and then to the woman. At last the vehicle was waved through the stone arch of the main prison yard. *No one would believe such a thing!*

Tires crunched over the gravel. Other guards left their posts to stare after the bishop's limousine and whisper among themselves about the meaning of such a visit. *So late at night! And the bishop himself! Not an underling! And with an old Jew in the backseat, and a very striking Jewess as well! What could it mean?*

Two men recognized the diminutive form of Father Kopecky as he stepped from the car and assisted the Jewish woman over the slick flagstones of the courtyard. Behind them came the bishop and the rabbi. *Side by side! What should be the protocol in greeting such a group? Would the warden cross himself? Would he kneel and kiss the hand of His Eminence?*

Only seconds passed before the warden blustered out of the building. His face revealed astonishment, embarrassment, and . . . confusion! Behind him followed two Polish officers, their sword tips clattering over the flagstones as they bowed and stepped back to flank the unexpected celebrities.

The guards lit cigarettes and passed them around from hand to hand. Twenty minutes passed in speculation of what such a visit could mean; then the door of the prison was thrown open. An arch of yellow light spilled out onto the cobblestones. The Polish officers, coatless, hands on the hilts of their swords, emerged first and rushed ahead to open the doors of the limousine. The bishop followed, then the old rabbi, and last the woman, holding tightly to the arm of a prisoner with a blanket around his stooped shoulders. The little priest, Father Kopecky, stood at the elbow of the bowed man. He supported him on his arm and aided him as he shuffled unsteadily to the vehicle. The priest's jaw was set and angry. He glared at one of the officers, who crossed himself after the door was shut and the engine started.

The guards shrugged and speculated. *What was the world coming to when priests and bishops rode in the same car with Jews! And on such a night as this, when Poland walked a very shaky line between Germany and Russia, too!*

———

Mama had decreed it: *"Everything must go on as usual, Rachel—as if Papa is not in Warsaw prison. We must not interrupt the studies of David and Samuel. Your papa would not like that, and so we women will be brave and silent."*

And so it had been for the past months. Since Papa's arrest, the questions of Rachel's younger brothers had been deferred. *Yes. Papa will be home anytime now. But you must study your Torah school lesson, or he will not be pleased.*

Frau Rosen, the housekeeper of the Lubetkin home, was dismissed. Her gloom and unending stream of gossip became too much for Etta Lubetkin and so, for the sake of the children, she had dismissed the old yenta.

Tonight Rachel had been left in charge. Although she was only thirteen years old, she was the eldest and entirely capable of tucking her brothers into bed after supper.

The clock struck nine. The kettle was steaming with water for baby Yacov's bath. *Warm, but not too warm.* Rachel tossed a thick braid over her shoulder and rolled up her sleeves. She tested a drop of water on her wrist as Mama had taught her to do. *Perfect.* Carefully she poured the water into the white enameled pan on the chest beside the baby's cradle. She was an hour and a half later than she should have been in giving Yani his bath, but there had been news on the wireless from Germany. Terrible news! Hitler's threats against Danzig kept Rachel rooted, wide-eyed, in front of the big radio. David and Samuel had fallen asleep on the floor as they listened. It was an easy matter to guide them to their bed and tuck them in when the program was finished. Now there was only baby Yani and the matter of his bath to finish up. Rachel hoped she would be done before Mama came home.

Yani screwed up his face and bleated his displeasure when she removed his diaper and the cool air smacked his little red bottom.

"It is not *so* bad," she laughed.

In reply, Yani let loose with an intermittent stream that soaked her left sleeve and arm.

"Who taught you that!" Rachel gasped. "You Polish peasant!"

Yani cooed happily and kicked his feet in a perverse little dance of freedom. His fists wagged in front of his wide blue eyes as he made ragged attempts to find his toothless mouth.

"I will speak with the Lord and Master and ask that he send me only girl babies," she muttered in disgust as she hefted him into the water.

The bleat turned into a wail of protest as the warm water washed over Yani's plump thighs and belly. "You see," Rachel said soothingly. "I get even with you. You'll think twice next time before you wet on big sister."

Rachel was tender with this little one as she had never been with David and Samuel. Perhaps it was because she was older now. It came to her often that in only a few more years she would, indeed, have babies of her own. Yani was better than the dolls she had played with as a child. He was real. He smiled at her, and laughed sometimes. He held her fingers and moved his eyes toward her at the sound of her voice. Such sweetness eased the stress that each new day seemed to bring to the household since Papa had been taken. When news from the world abroad became too frightening to think about any longer, Rachel fled to the baby's crib.

Here was innocence.

Here was perfection.

Rachel cupped her hand around the velvet soft head and lifted Yani onto the thick towel. She wrapped him up and put her cheek against his cheek to smell his sweet skin. Mama always said it, and it was true—nothing smelled better than a clean baby. And nothing worse than a dirty one. Well, Yani was clean and sweet-smelling. Rachel cradled him in her arms and plunked down in the rocking chair. His warmth seeped through

45

the towel. His thumb popped into his mouth. He sucked on it in drowsy tranquility while she rocked him and hummed and told the Lord and Master that she had not meant what she said about having only girl babies.

The clock struck the quarter hour, and then the half. Yani was asleep, his thumb still crooked at the edge of his mouth. He was diaperless, still wrapped in the towel, when Rachel finally laid him in his crib. The sound of an automobile approached in the square outside the house.

Quickly she diapered him. He awoke with an angry protest and then fell instantly back to sleep as she pulled a gown over his head and wrapped him in an eiderdown quilt.

The front door opened downstairs in the foyer. Mama was home! Rachel rushed to the head of the stairs to call out to her mother, to ask what news about Papa . . .

The light of the foyer lamp cast a golden glow on the black and white tiles of the floor. Except for that, the world seemed colorless.

There was Mama, her face pinched, worried, exhausted beyond anything Rachel had ever seen. And there was the Catholic priest beside old Rabbi Koznon with his yellow skin and yellow beard. Together, Mama and the rabbi held up another old man. Thin and frail and broken . . . beardless and bald.

The stranger's eyes were dark and familiar beneath thick eyebrows. His back was bent as if his head were too heavy to hold up. And yet he managed to look up. Up the stairs. Up into Rachel's questioning eyes, and then his cracked lips smiled. He was missing teeth. The stranger raised a hand.

"Rachel!" The effort of speech was too much. He coughed uncontrollably.

Rachel gasped. She put her hands to her mouth. *"Papa?"* she cried and swayed at the top of the stairs. Had the horror of his appearance been evident in her voice? She tried to control her trembling as she clambered down to the foyer.

"Be careful, Rachel." Etta warned her not to come too close. "Papa is not well. He . . . he is not well," she finished. "Call the doctor."

Rachel stopped two yards away from her father. He smelled terrible—like the public toilets in Warsaw. Like the poorhouse. Could it be? Could this old man be Papa? But yes! Those were his eyes looking back at her, loving her!

46

"Call the doctor," Etta repeated sternly. "Come, Aaron, darling. These clothes! We will bathe you and burn these things." Rachel stood transfixed, staring. There were bugs on Papa. Tiny crawling things. Etta turned and snapped at her. "Rachel! Wake up! Did you hear me! Call the doctor!"

Rachel found her voice. "What doctor? Dr. Letzno is gone. Who shall I call, Mama?" She realized she was crying. What had they done to Papa? What had they done to make him like this? To change him from the rabbi of Muranow into this—

"Dr. Tannenberg, then!" Etta's voice was strained as she and the old rabbi led Papa to the downstairs bath in Frau Rosen's former quarters. Papa in the servant quarters? Yes. Yes. A good idea. He could not be near the baby.

Rachel ran to the study and clenched her fists, trying to make her fingers stop shaking. She could hear Papa coughing, coughing, coughing! He was very sick! If he was so bad from being in Warsaw prison, what would have happened in two more weeks? Or two more days? *He would have died!*

She found the number in Papa's address book, the name and number written in his firm hand.

The phone rang too slowly. One, two, three rings and then a sleepy voice answered.

"Hello, Dr. Tannenberg, please! This is the daughter of Rabbi Aaron Lubetkin of Muranow Square. My father is very ill. *Please!* Come quickly!"

Rachel could distinguish the voice of the Polish priest from that of the doctor. Here in Warsaw, even accent separated Jew from Gentile. It was easy to tell one from the other after the first word was spoken. How strange it was to hear the accent of the Catholic priest emanating through the bedroom door, addressing her mother with such urgency.

"Have you wired your father in Jerusalem about this, Rebbitsin Lubetkin?"

"Not yet. I did not want to worry him. I was hoping that Aaron would be released, you see and . . . my father is old and frail. Things are difficult in Jerusalem just now, as you must know. And so I have not written him about it all."

"You must do more than write him, dear lady," the priest was sympathetic but firm. "Your husband and your family are obvi-

47

ous targets of the political anti-Semites. If things begin to go wrong for Poland, people like your husband will be blamed."

Rachel frowned and stared hard at the toes of her shoes. She thought of what the priest said. This was the same warning she had heard from Eduard Letzno before he left Poland for Palestine.

Papa's furious coughing followed, drowning out Mama's reply to the priest. And then, in a thin, raspy voice, Papa spoke.

"He . . . is right, Etta." He stopped, seized by another fit of coughing. "You must wire your father . . . if not for me . . . then for the children. They . . . must not stay . . . in . . ." His words fell away into more convulsive coughing. Rachel trembled to hear it. Papa sounded as if he could not breathe. The words were so halting; so full of fear. Yet surely he could not think that they would leave Poland for Palestine without him?

"Yes, Aaron. Yes, my dear," Etta soothed. Then she said to the priest, "No more talk of this. Not tonight. This is not the time. Surely you can see—"

"Etta!" Papa's voice was barely recognizable in its strain and desperation. "Listen to—"

"I will carry a wire to the telegraph tonight myself," volunteered the little priest. "Write out what you wish to say, and I will take it now."

A moment of silence passed. Rachel leaned forward and stared at the wood of the door as if she could see through it and read what message Mama wrote out to send to Grandfather. What would such a message say that could make a difference? *Please hurry and get us papers to Palestine? Better to face Arab riots than Polish anti-Semites?*

Rachel imagined the words and knew that if this was, indeed, what Mama wrote out, then things had become very bad for the Jews of Warsaw! Before his arrest, Papa had refused to admit the possibility of any one of them going to Jerusalem. But now, through the croaking voice of a sick old man, he demanded that Grandfather be notified how desperately they needed to leave!

Rachel shuddered. A cold fear crept up and tightened the skin on her neck. In her memory she could hear the shouts and threats of the Saturday people as they had broken down the doors of the synagogue!

Breathing fast, she left her post in front of Papa's sickroom and ran to the window in the front room. The imagined shouts became louder. She stood before the curtained window and pictured throngs of them with hateful eyes and flaming torches and crosses lifted high above their heads! Would they break down this door, she wondered? Would they drag Papa out of bed and carry Mama away on their shoulders to do terrible things? *Terrible things . . .*

Behind her, she heard a door open. The sound of Father Kopecky's feet padded briskly down the hall toward the front door. *"No, no. I will let myself out."*

He passed the archway leading to the front room where Rachel stared at the curtain. He stopped and put on his hat and coat. Then he saw her.

"What is it, child?" he asked, pulling on his gloves and eyeing her pale face with concern.

"Are *they* . . . out there?"

Curses replayed in her mind. The faces of the wicked men who had grabbed Mama swam before her eyes.

"Who?" asked the priest.

"The men . . . who . . . *those* men. You know."

Now he passed under the arch and hurried to the window. Without thinking he pulled back the heavy brocade drape. The rain-slick cobbles glistened by the light of street lamps in the deserted square.

"There is no one out there, child." He glanced back over his shoulder at her with concern.

"I thought I heard them . . . lots of them. I . . . I thought I heard them."

He smiled a sympathetic smile. "There is no one there. Nothing happening." He gestured for her to come to the window, to see for herself. "Just Muranow Square. Everyone is indoors I think, drying their shoes by the fire. Tucked into bed, where you should be now also." He looked at his watch. "You will need to rest so you can help your mother, yes, Rachel?"

He pronounced her name differently than it was spoken among her own people. The sound of it startled her, made her wonder once again why this priest concerned himself with them. She was grateful, and yet uncomfortable at the sound of her name on the lips of a Catholic priest.

"I do not like the goyim," she blurted. "They are a cruel and

49

barbaric people." She raised her chin, daring him to argue on behalf of his own race.

For another moment he looked at the silent square. Then, letting the curtain fall back, he simply nodded his agreement and wished her a good sleep before he hurried out of the house.

It was very late in the night when Werner the cat got up from his sleeping place on Alfie's pillow. The soft fur brushed Alfie's cheek and woke him up when he did not want to be awake. He lay there with his eyes closed and listened to the other boys breathing. Jamie Ibsen wheezed. Mark Kalner, in bed beside Jamie, rattled. Jacob Kalner breathed deep and even. Alfie could always tell just who was where, and which one got up to use the toilet in the dark by the way everyone breathed. He even knew the soft breath of Werner-kitten, who was not really a kitten anymore.

Alfie did not like it when the breathing at night was not like it should be. Sometimes Jamie dreamed unhappy dreams. Jacob tossed on his squeaking cot and fought with dream people who visited here all the way from Berlin. And now, tonight, when everyone was breathing fine and not dreaming at all, Werner was prowling across the bed, jumping on the chest of drawers and . . . sitting on the windowsill.

The cot squeaked when Alfie sat up. He swung his legs over and kicked off the covers. *Maybe Werner needed to go out?* Alfie stepped around the piles of clothes the boys left on the floor. He kicked a shoe that thumped against the frame of Jacob's cot, but Jacob did not wake up. Then Alfie joined Werner on the sill of the tall narrow window that faced north and looked out over Danzig. The city looked very small and dark tonight, compared to the sky!

Alfie pulled back the curtain and asked Werner if he wanted out. But Werner did not want out. He was looking at streaks of color in the sky. Far away, streaks of blue and gold and red moved and faded, then brightened like a curtain of fire across the sky in the north. *Northern lights.* Mama had told Alfie all about them when he was little. Lights like that had called Alfie's papa to go to sea, she said.

Alfie stroked Werner and watched the lights for a long time. They were pretty colors, but they did not make him feel happy inside his heart. The glow reflected in the dark windows of other Danzig houses and looked like fire—like the fire Alfie had seen in Berlin the night he had run away from Sisters of Mercy Hospital. That was never a happy thing for him to remember. It was the sort of thing he usually remembered when everyone was fast asleep and he could not be comforted.

Alfie frowned and bit his lip as the colors in the sky changed to a deep red. The white walls of the house next door, the lace curtains Lori made, Werner-cat's eyes—all were red. Holding up his hand, Alfie could see that his skin was also red like the color of blood.

He did not mean to, but he blurted out Jacob's name. His heart was pounding and he was sweating through his pajamas.

"What!" Jacob sat up straight in bed.

"There . . . there are *lights* in the sky," Alfie said. His voice sounded frightened, but he knew he could not explain why he was afraid.

Jacob moaned. "Stars. Just stars, Alfie." He sounded unhappy to be awake. "Now go to sleep."

"Not . . . not stars," Alfie stammered. The lights made him want to run away. Just like he had run from the ward of the hospital that night when everyone else had been taken. "It is like . . . *fire.*" He tried to swallow, but there was no spit in his mouth.

Jacob came to his side, peering over his shoulder. "Ah." Jacob patted him. "Not a fire; just the northern lights." He was relieved. "Pretty, huh? I thought maybe Marienkirche was burning down or something." Another thump on the back. "Nothing to be afraid of. You and Werner go back to bed." The springs of the cot squeaked and squeaked again as Jacob tried to find his favorite position again. He sighed and soon his breathing was deep and even.

But Alfie did not go back to his cot. He leaned his forehead against the glass pane and watched the lights dancing across the sky. Deep inside a little voice whispered to him, *They are coming here. Coming again. They will bring their fire with them. Run and hide, Alf! Run! They will come here, too.*

Alfie had seen the fire of the Hitler-men in Berlin, and now it played before his imagination like a movie on a screen. "Where should we go now?" he said loudly. Too loudly. The other boys moaned a protest to his voice. He heard Lori's bed creak in the other room and then her soft footsteps.

He knew she was in the doorway, but he did not turn around until she spoke.

"Alf?" She always talked gently to him, like her mama used to. Lori's voice was a lot like her mother Helen's voice. Frau Helen Ibsen had said his name soft like that when Alfie's own mama had died. "*Alf?*"

He turned around and wiped away the tears that had tumbled out of his eyes. "Uh-huh."

"Bad dream?"

"No."

"Are you feeling bad about something?"

Silence. "I heard on the radio. The Hitler-men want this place, too."

"But England will not let them—"

"They are coming here." He gestured toward the sky as though it held the answer. "We should go away soon."

Again there was silence. Alfie knew that Lori was really listening to what he said. Lori did not ever think he was a Dummkopf. He heard her draw a deep breath the way she always did when she had something important to say. "Maybe you are right," she said. "I . . . I will try again to contact my cousin in England. The one who married the American newspaperman."

"Now?"

"Tomorrow. I will write her."

"*Now!*"

Another deep sigh. "All right then. Now. But you must go back to bed, Alf. I will write the letter, and tomorrow we will send it together. How is that?"

Alfie looked at the fire in the sky and then at the shadow of Lori in the doorway. "That is good. It is *smart.*"

The light from Lori's room seeped through the crack under the door of the room where the boys slept. Alfie lay on his cot for a long time until the light went off. Then he closed his eyes and went to sleep because he knew the letter to England was written.

———

Danzig is a jewel imbedded in the backside of the Polish troll. The Führer said so, frequently. He always added his intention to slay the troll and cut out the jewel.

Wolfgang von Fritschauer thought of this as he gazed out the window of the antiquated Danzig local train rattling over the moonlit lowlands of the pygmy state. Only 754 square miles in area, Danzig was a tiny fragment of all the territory that the Reich had claimed as treasure over the last few months. But the leader of Germany planned to use this scrap of land as steel and flint to ignite his final conflagration.

"The decision to attack Poland was arrived at in early spring. Our strength lies in our quickness and our brutality. . . . Poland will be depopulated and settled with the German people. The fate of Russia will be exactly the same. Then will begin the dawn of the German rule of the earth. . . ."

Wolf had been privileged to be in attendance when Hitler had spoken those words. Following that, Wolf had requested transfer to duty in East Prussia, which bordered Danzig and Poland. He had mentioned that he wished to be where the ultimate actions were destined to take place. It would be convenient as well, he suggested, if he could work closer to his Prussian home. His wife and three children were there on the family estate, after all, and neither Vienna nor Prague were places where he felt comfortable.

And so it was Prussia for Wolfgang von Fritschauer. Since March, he had traveled back and forth between the German territory of East Prussia into Danzig with regularity. Through connections with Hitler's foreign minister, Herr von Ribbentrop, Wolf now assumed the role of a businessman—a wine merchant who had constant commerce in the port of Danzig.

Of course he no longer wore his uniform, but he was just as active as he had ever been, supervising the infiltration of agents into the Baltic seaport. When the order came to strike, Danzig would be thick with German soldiers ready to take over the harbor, the Polish Navy, the ship-building facilities, and the gun emplacements facing out to sea. It would be a simple matter of German battleships steaming into port and the Army striking up the Vistula River to Warsaw. A swift blow to the heart and Poland, with its vast resources, would belong to the Reich.

Not once did Wolfgang von Fritschauer mention that there was one additional reason he had requested transfer from Vienna. The matter of Lucy Strasburg and the child she carried would be difficult to explain. Wolf knew that his wife, a possessive and jealous woman at best, would not accept his affair with a woman like Lucy until he was able to put a baby in her arms and say, *"You see, a child for the Fatherland and the Führer! And you must raise him with that in mind. It is your duty. My duty."*

Wolf fully intended that the day would come when he would say those words to his wife. And then he would add, *"The woman who bore this child for you is of no consequence. She is dead, and the child is your own."*

Wolf would make certain that those words were true. Lucy had betrayed him, betrayed her country as well. Death seemed a small punishment considering the depth of rage Wolf carried for her. He thought often of the pleasure he would reap in returning her to German territory and presiding over her execution personally. It would be a small matter to arrange once he located her. And he *would* find her!

Even before Major Hess had mentioned seeing Lucy on the train to Danzig, Wolf had known she had fled to this place. He had found her travel brochures in the apartment. *Poor, stupid Lucy. So provincial. She had chosen the closest thing to Germany without actually choosing Germany.* Wolf did not need the raised eyebrow of Agent Hess and the questioning glare.

"I am certain it was your mistress on the train to Danzig. She was with two suspicious looking boys. Jews, perhaps? I would have spoken with her, but I was attacked by four Jews and thrown from the train a few moments after that."

Wolf did not attempt to explain. He did not tell Hess how she had no doubt warned the family in Otto Wattenbarger's apartment of their imminent arrest, or that she had plotted all along this betrayal of his attentions. He simply shrugged and sipped his glass of wine as though it did not matter. *"The whore. I grew tired of her and threw her out. She'll show up at the side of a general before long, no doubt."*

If Agent Hess knew differently, if he suspected the truth, he at least remained quiet about it. His recovery from the injuries he had experienced that night on the Corridor Express no doubt had occupied his mind more than questions about Wolf's former mistress and her traveling companions. But Wolf knew that his record was no longer untarnished; he could suffer no additional failure.

All of it had simply strengthened Wolf's resolve to find her and finish her once and for all. Danzig was a small place. He had checked the hotels. She had spent four days at the Danziger Hof with two boys she claimed were her nephews. Then she had

checked out and vanished. There was no record of her departure on the steamship lines. She could have easily crossed into
Poland, but Wolf knew her better than that. Lucy must stay
where her own language was spoken fluently, where she could
chat with bellboys and waiters and tell them the story of her life.
No, she would not go to Poland. She would not go to Prague or
Warsaw or France. And she could not go home to Bavaria where
her family lived. Wolf had friends in Munich who double-
checked that possibility. If she became desperate and contacted
her family, he would know within hours.

Wolf was certain that Lucy, with her limited intellect, would
see Danzig as some sort of promised land. It was German in
character, but not Germany. The laws of the Reich could not
touch her here, yet the familiar culture surrounded her.

On this journey, Wolf would stop by the local hospitals. She
was near the time when the child would be born. There was no
running from that fact. Wolf would simply show the doctors a
photograph of his *sister*. He would explain that she was unmarried and ashamed and would no doubt use a false name, and
he would offer a reward for a simple phone call. . . .

The shrill whistle of the train announced that the passage to
Danzig was at an end. Wolfgang von Fritschauer, wine merchant
from Prussia, pulled on his gloves and stared out across the platform of the quaint train station of the free city. His quick eyes
skimmed every face, every form. Passengers hurried toward the
train; men and women kissed in greeting and farewell. Wolf
could feel that Lucy Strasburg was somewhere among the
crowds of Danzig. He sensed her presence as a hunter might
sense the nearness of a stag.

───────

Lucy Strasburg turned her head to the sound of Peter Wallich's weary tread on the steep steps. The stairs to the fourth-
floor one-bedroom flat were steep, but there was something
more labored than usual in the sound of his ascent. *He has
heard the news from Berlin*, she thought. *He has heard the reply
of Poland that they will not give in.*

For some in Danzig, the ominous radio broadcast tonight
made their footsteps light with anticipation. *If there is war, it will
begin here!* For others, like Peter and those thousands who
waited in camps to leave Europe forever, the news put a raging

55

fire at their backs even as they faced the sea.

Lucy rose from her chair and turned up the flame in the sputtering gas lamp on the wall. She had prepared Peter's supper hours ago, expecting him to come home at his usual time. But she knew from the heavy cadence of his step that he had joined with hundreds of others in the streets and listened to the radio broadcast on the loudspeakers. Lucy had opened the window and caught echoed words and phrases from the announcement. *She had heard enough to know!*

Peter's food had grown cold, and so she covered it and put it on the warming shelf until he came home. She tried very hard to cheer Peter up since baby Willie had been sent away—good meals, pleasant conversation. But tonight . . .

It took him longer to reach the landing. Longer to pull out his key. Longer to fight with the stubborn door latch. When the door swung wide, he simply stood in the hall and looked into the room as though he were seeing it for the first time. *Or the last time?*

There was no smile on his face. His curly red hair stood up as though he had been standing in a great wind for a long time. His eyes met hers, and only then did he enter the flat. *Was that fear in his face? What had he seen? Could only words cause him to look so pale?* He closed the door quietly and locked it.

"I kept your supper warm," Lucy said, as though everything were fine.

"Did you hear about it?"

She gestured toward the window. The open window and a good breeze carried the news far. "Bits of it."

"Polish Foreign Minister Beck has told the Führer *no.*"

"Good. Someone should have done that years ago."

"Either way, it means we cannot stay here."

Lucy shrugged and turned to get his plate. "If there is a war over Danzig, then France and England will beat the Nazis, and all our troubles will be over." She smiled and put the plate on the table, pulling out his chair.

He did not move from the center of the shadowy room. "Your baby is due anytime. You cannot stay here in such a place."

"I'm fine. Now sit down and eat. The Nazis are not coming to Danzig without a fight."

Peter's eyes grew dull. He stared at the food. "They are here already, Lucy. Waiting for the word."

"They got the word. From Foreign Minister Beck. I think the word is *NO.*" She tried to go on as if his mood did not put a chill in her heart. "Sit down, Peter. Eat before you hurt my feelings, will you? Never hurt the feelings of a woman who is expecting. She is liable to cry, and then you will be . . ." Her voice trailed away. It was no use trying to pretend. Peter was the one who was crying. A single tear tracked down his cheek. He brushed it away angrily.

"How did it come to this?" His voice sounded much too old for a boy of sixteen. *"How?"*

4 The Specter of Death Guards the Door

The half-moon cast an eerie glow through the clouds as swirling vapors thinned to a glowing film. Dark shadows outlined the muted details of the ancient thatched-roof cottages and rough stone fences of Ireland that traced the road from Dublin to this place.

Inside a cottage half obscured from the road by a stand of trees, three men waited beside a fire. There was no furniture in this one room—only the three men, reaching their hands out for warmth from the flames. An orange glow reflected on their skin as if they, too, were part of the flames. Two of the faces were of middle-age, faces weathered by the harsh Irish winds. Their expressions seemed frozen in an unchanging intensity as they bathed their leathery hands in warmth. Their heavy wool trousers, coats, and thick-soled boots were caked with mud from the ride across the soggy fields.

The third face was younger by a generation. A boyish twenty-five, the eyes of the third man did not stare into the fire as if some message were written there. His eyes flitted from the flames to the faces of his companions and then back to the window which was covered by a flap of dirty canvas. His clothing was American—pleated trousers and city boots too thin for the beating they had just sustained. The hem of his dark blue over-coat was wet, and flecks of mud covered his face and cap.

Outside, their horses stamped impatiently as the wind howled around the corner of the house. The young man looked up sharply as he listened.

"Not yet, Allan," said the stouter of his two companions.

"He'll be here soon enough," said the other, inclining his head slightly with an amused smile as he studied the nervous young American. "He looks like your sister, Colin. Aye. I can see the resemblance." He looked back into the flames and saw a thousand phantoms from his past. "But Maureen was a horse-woman. Indeed. She could sit a horse better'n any lad."

Colin chuckled at the memory and nodded his large head. He ended his chuckle with a sigh. That had been long ago. "What d'ya expect of the lad? Raised in New York City. No horses t' ride. Even the trams are electric."

Allan sniffed, embarrassed by the frantic spectacle he must have made of himself holding on to saddle and mane and lurch-ing about like a drunk man as they rode. He considered telling his uncle that he had ridden a pony once in Central Park, and that there was a mounted police force in New York . . . . Then he thought better of it. The New York mounted police were also Irish, thick of brogue and quick of temper as his mother had been. Allan did not reply. He was fool enough already in the eyes of his Uncle Colin and the IRA captain who had come with them to the meeting.

"You think he'll be able to handle the job?" asked the cap-tain. John Dougherty was his name.

Uncle Colin nudged Allan. The boy must respond to the chal-lenge himself.

"I will not be riding horses in London," Allan said. "And there is not a man among all the IRA who can handle this but me."

Colin raised an eyebrow in approval. Allan had spoken ex-actly true. American born and bred, the boy was nonetheless his mother's child. And she had been as much a fighter as any man in Ireland in those days of the troubles. A toss of her curls and a flash of a smile and she had managed to get more from the Brit-ish soldiers than twenty IRA strong men with clubs could do.

"His mother raised him right. He knows what we're about."

Allan grew bolder. He touched the scar beneath his right eye.

"Raised in Hell's Kitchen in New York," he said. "I learned to fight."

"You're here to watch," said John Dougherty. "Not fight. Not unless we ask you to."

Outside, the horses stamped and whinnied. The sound of hoofbeats rose and fell on the wind. Colin raised his head to listen. "They're here. He's brought them."

The three did not move from their spot, but turned to face the door in case the visitors might be Englishmen instead of their expected guests. They had come here tonight to talk treason against the new King George. It would not do to be surprised.

Allan looked from the face of his uncle to the door and back again. Colin showed no sign of nervousness at this strange rendezvous. A slight smile played on his lips as the tramp of boots and the jangle of bridles and D-rings announced the arrival.

"The boy speaks German?" John Dougherty asked, reconfirming what had been repeated three times.

Colin nodded and drew himself up as the door burst open, and three men came in with a wind that swirled ash from the open hearth around their legs.

The ritual slapping of hands against sleeves and trousers in an effort to knock away the cold was enacted before the three men advanced to crowd around the fire. No one spoke for a moment as the warmth returned to numbed fingers and lips.

Allan stepped back into a shadow at the far right of the fireplace. He looked over the newcomers. He could easily distinguish the one Irishman from the two long-faced Germans who looked around the room with a sort of amused arrogance. Allan recognized the face of Kevin Fahey.

"So, Colin, this is the boy, eh?" Fahey cast a long look at Allan. "Maureen's son?"

Allan nodded, although the question was not addressed to him. Allan had been raised on tales of Fahey, and now the eyes of the IRA hero were turned on him!

"He knows what we're about," Colin replied gruffly. "Maureen raised him right. A fighter."

Now the stern, quiet eyes of Fahey pierced through Allan. The man's expression was different from those of his rough cohorts. Allan knew that here was a leader of men.

"And a scholar, too, I hear?" said Fahey. He extended his

hand past the Germans who stood unmoving between them. Allan took the outstretched hand as if it were offered by a god. He knew Kevin Fahey without introduction. The warm brown eyes were human, humble and real. The red hair was tinged with gray and the face was no longer young as it had been in the mind of Allan when his mother had recited the endless adventures of this man.

"I am Allan Farrell, Maureen's son," he replied with a half smile. His mother's name provided his credentials.

Kevin Fahey frowned into Allan's face and then cried out, "Sweet Mary! I see the resemblance plainly! I would see her in you if no one had told me you were hers!" He embraced Allan as though he were the prodigal son come home. Fahey's own emotion touched Allan. *Family. This felt so much like the family Allan no longer had!* Tears came to his eyes in spite of himself. A pang of shame shot through him; then he saw that the others of his blood had shining eyes as well.

Fahey clapped him hard on the back. "And so she's come back to us too, in a way. She always said she would. Or that she would send her sons home to a free Ireland. We have yet to see that day. We shall have the priest say Mass for her while you're here."

Allan nodded, not certain he could speak. From the moment his mother had died in New York General, he had been surrounded by men who, like her, had fled their native land for America with the British on their heels. Some said that the IRA was as strong in New York as it was in Belfast. When Allan had raised his eyes from her grave, he had been met with faces of men like his uncle who reminded him it was *not finished yet!*

Now, as he stood before his boyhood hero, Allan felt a part of some destiny much greater than his own life. *Maureen's son. Graduate of Johns Hopkins University. B.A. History. Fellow at Georgetown University. On his way to London, where he would complete his doctoral degree.*

All of that had seemed like quite enough until a few weeks ago. And then the call had come. In some small way he was needed for the cause!

"Well now that this is settled" came the thick, dry accent of a German. "We have some business to complete, yes? And then a long way to ride before daylight."

Allan saw that they were looking at him. He returned their

gazes curiously. Kevin stepped back and leaned against the cracking plaster of the wall. The wind howled behind him.

"These are the fellows who will be your contacts in London, Allan." He jerked his head toward the two men who seemed like wax figures compared to the full expressions of the Irishmen in the room.

"My. . . contacts?" Allan frowned.

"Much safer for us. There's not a man among us that won't be hanged by the end of an English rope if we're caught in London. You will report to these men."

Allan's uncle stepped in. "Another case of strange bedfellows wrought by politics and such, Allan."

Allan nodded once. Somehow he had pictured himself within the warm circle of Irish camaraderie. But then, this was a small assignment—a simple matter of nipping at the heels of British John Bull. In London no one would remember or understand the significance of the fact that he was Maureen's son. He would just be another American.

"Well then." Allan stretched his hands out for warmth again. "What is it I am to do?"

Dry clothing. Warm blankets all around. A hot meal for the refugee boys who were not too exhausted from their ordeal to eat. Julian's words had proved true—not one from the little boat had been lost. Three had died in the long overland trek from Czechoslovakia, but twenty-eight had survived to make it here, to the kibbutz in the homeland.

There was one pleasant surprise when the twenty-eight had been herded into the boys' barracks. One of their number, a thin, aquiline-featured fellow, burst into tears and confessed that he was not a boy at all, but a girl named Rebekah!

This confession was perhaps the greatest shock of the evening to the band of refugees: *Frank is really a seventeen-year-old girl from Prague!* She had cut her hair and bound her breasts and joined a group of fugitives in the woods of Bohemia to travel to Eretz Israel. All this way she had come, and no one had ever suspected! Smaller than the others, she had been bullied and threatened and bossed and punched if she did not move fast enough. Only at the moment she stepped into the barracks and saw the communal showers did she begin to weep.

Rebekah, moved to the young women's dormitory, was being pampered and fed as she recited the gruesome tale of fleeing Prague on the very night Hitler arrived to take over Hradcany Castle.

"And all that was small potatoes compared to getting here undetected in the middle of a gang of boys!"

Three remorseful members of the fugitive band took their chocolate cake to the women's dorm and there presented it to Lady Rebekah with their apologies. How relieved they were to find that the one they called *Frank* was not really a feminine-looking boy. "She is quite pretty, you know. How did we not notice?"

Orde instantly forgave the fact that this young female had taken up space of a potential soldier for the Special Night Squad. "A girl so clever and brave," he said, "deserves to be made an honorary member of the Special Night Squad."

Rebekah politely declined the honor and laughed at the pale faces of her comrades. "Enough is enough, thank you!"

Some time after midnight a British military jeep arrived at the gates of the kibbutz and demanded entry. Two British soldiers ordered that any illegal refugees who had come into the kibbutz be brought out to face justice.

Instead, Captain Samuel Orde emerged from his tent to meet with them. Righteous indignation turned into resentment as Orde explained that he had been here all evening. "No one who should not come into the compound has come in—except for you two English intruders."

They left sullenly. Two hours later a message came over the wireless that Orde was summoned to Jerusalem to military headquarters. Perhaps it was coincidence; more likely, suspicion of Orde's protection of the Jewish settlements had finally boiled over.

"No matter," he said returning to his tent. "It can all wait until morning." He instructed the radio operator to transmit the message that the wire had been garbled.

The French village where Murphy and Churchill stopped for the night was still deep within *la zone des armée*, explained the French captain over dinner. "And yet you see how well we French officers dine."

By candlelight in the dining room of the one hotel, Murphy was forced to admit that no other army in the world fed its officers like the French Army. Hors d'oeuvres, salad, salmon, and chicken breast were served with artichokes, and all washed down with *le vin-spécialité: Champagne rosé.*

"Keep the menu for a souvenir," urged the captain. "No matter what happens to France, it will prove to your friends that her officers will always dine like kings."

The food was as fine a meal as Murphy had ever had set before him, but he only picked at it. After listening to the speeches of Hitler and the Polish foreign secretary in Warsaw, the sense of foreboding he felt robbed him completely of appetite.

Bits and pieces of conversation drifted by him. At this moment he could think of nothing but his wife and their child. Their children.

The French captain did not understand either the German language or that of the Poles. He devoured his dinner and drank copious amounts of champagne as he chatted on about the invincibility of the Maginot Line and the strength of one million French soldiers.

Churchill, like Murphy, had simply tuned this jolly babbler out. He, too, sat in solemn contemplation of the dark political shadow that had stepped off the wall to tower above them in three-dimensional terror.

Both Murphy and Churchill declined dessert and coffee. Declaring exhaustion from the long day, they retreated from the too-cheerful company of their French guide.

Churchill's lower lip extended gloomily as they made their way up the stairs. Only when they were out of earshot of the captain did he speak.

"When Poland is attacked," he said, glaring back down the stairs, "the French menu will remain unchanged. They will remain behind their concrete."

"And England?" Murphy ventured.

Churchill raised an eyebrow. "How is Elisa?" He seemed to change the subject. "The baby coming soon?"

"She's fine. At the docks tonight helping with refugee children." Murphy managed a confused smile. "Another two weeks before *the* baby arrives."

Churchill patted him on the back. "When that happens, I

would recommend that you send your family promptly to America. The Maginot Line is not long enough or wide enough. The English Channel is not deep enough or high enough. Take them home, Murphy." He turned as if to go. He had, indeed, answered the question. Two steps farther down the hall he stopped and turned slowly as he reached into his pocket. He pulled out a small revolver and held it out to Murphy. "You do carry a weapon, do you not?" he asked.

"I left it home. For Elisa."

"Here." Churchill chewed his words like a cigar to be savored. "Take this one tonight. I have another." Once again he looked over his shoulder. "In England there are at least twenty thousand organized Nazis. Soon it will be open season on men like you and me. On our beloved families."

Murphy took the revolver and suppressed a shudder. "We have a bodyguard living in the flat downstairs—ever since you recommended it." Murphy hefted the weapon. "Thank you, Winston."

"The best bodyguard may well be the Atlantic Ocean." Churchill remarked as he inserted the key in his door and left Murphy staring after him. The door closed. The latch clicked. Moments later, Murphy could hear the groaning of the chest of drawers being pulled across the floor to rest against the door.

Never before had Murphy so strongly desired to take Elisa home to Pennsylvania as at that moment. Tonight he followed the example of the British statesman known as the Prophet of Doom. He slept with the revolver beside him and the chest of drawers on guard before the door.

Rachel slept in her clothes on the settee in the parlor. She knew that it was morning before she opened her eyes.

Soft light penetrated her eyelids and the voice of Dr. Tannenberg penetrated her consciousness.

"Not typhoid," he said firmly. "No, Rebbitsin Lubetkin, your husband does *not* have typhoid."

She recognized her mother's sigh of relief and then Rachel opened her eyes to see them framed beneath the archway of the foyer. "But what do we do?"

"Still very serious . . . rheumatic fever can be just as deadly, only it is not in itself contagious. No. You need not worry about the children. It is, you see, from the strep infection your husband had six weeks ago. But some symptoms are much like typhoid—it is no wonder the young prison doctor confused the two. The fever. The jerking. The rash. Nodules and lesions. Perhaps the young fellow even thought he was about to have an epidemic of plague." The doctor clucked his tongue in sympathy for the prison doctor. "It is definitely rheumatic fever. It attacks the heart valves. Quite deadly, but not contagious."

"Please," Etta exclaimed in exasperation. "What can we do for him?"

"Just give him the medicine as I told you."

"But there must be something else."

"No. Just the sulfa drug. It is hard on the kidneys, but it will arrest the heart damage." He pulled on his coat. "I will be back this afternoon."

Rachel watched her mother grasp the doctor's sleeve. "I . . . I do not want *them* to know it is not typhoid." She bit her lip and stared up at him. "If they know it is not contagious, maybe they will take him again and then he will die in prison."

Dr. Tannenberg agreed with a single jerk of his head. "Reb-bitsin, I will deceive them in this small matter. But I tell you this, the rabbi may die anyway. There may be other complications. Arthritis. Perhaps an increase in the uncontrolled jerking. But the heart damage is the most severe danger. It may make no difference for your husband if he has *only* rheumatic fever instead of typhoid or plague—"

"But it makes a difference to *them*. They let him come home!"

"No doubt they are hoping he will infect the entire Jewish quarter of the city," he remarked cynically. Then he shrugged. "I will tell no one the nature of the illness. But I cannot make any promises about his recovery, either. You understand? And if it is his time . . ." Another shrug. Rachel stared angrily at Dr. Tannenberg from where she lay. She did not like this doctor. She missed the kind gruffness of Dr. Letzno. He would not have shrugged when talking of death, especially not the possible death of Rabbi Aaron Lubetkin. He would have stayed at Papa's side. He would have administered the medicine himself and made certain that Papa recovered. No, Rachel did not like this doctor.

Etta accepted the doctor's words with dignity. "We will pray that my husband may have full recovery. We thank you for your help. For the medicine. And I implore you to say nothing that might dissuade the people and the authorities from thinking the worst. I cannot help but think . . . the symptoms are so close to typhoid . . . perhaps the Lord and Master has sent this other sickness to my Aaron so he could come home."

"I cannot pretend to know the mind of God, Rebbitsin. However, if I had a choice between coming down with typhoid or rheumatic fever, I do not know which I would personally rather die from. You see?" He smiled a patronizing smile and placed his drooping hat on his curly gray hair. "And so . . . I will return this afternoon, yes?"

On that gloomy thought, the doctor slipped out. Etta stared after him and then closed the door and shuddered from his words.

Rachel coughed, letting Mama know she was awake. Etta looked at Rachel and spoke to her for the first time since she had ordered her to call the doctor last night.

"You heard it all?" Etta asked, remaining in the foyer.

"All of it." Rachel sat up and smoothed back her hair that tumbled from a disheveled braid. "What about baby Yani? And David and Samuel? Can we all be together?"

Etta shook her head. She looked back at the door and frowned thoughtfully. "Our friends will care for the boys. No one must know." She tossed her head as if she had a plan. "This doctor says he might die anyway, but I tell you, Rachel, we will make him well and pray him well and let the specters of infection and plague stand guard at our door. The goyim will not come here. Not to collect a bill. Not to ask a question. Not to take your father from his bed! Nu! And you and I will nurse him without fear of becoming ill. The doctor says rheumatic fever is not so easy to catch." Mama was almost smiling. *Almost!* "Let them think there is typhoid in the Lubetkin house! And let them tremble at the thought of having to interrogate a man so ill." She looked Rachel straight in the eye. "It will all be for the best." Etta smiled in earnest now. "You will help me, Rachel. We will make him well together."

The black bread in the tin bowl was flecked with spots of mold. Karl Ibsen held a chunk of it up to the light and studied the green spores.

The sight of them made him smile. He remembered that Jamie had collected two dozen different mold specimens for a science project in school. Was the mold from black bread different from the mold of rye bread? For weeks the boy had cultivated tiny fuzzy jungles in petri dishes beneath his bed. With these microscopic worlds he had terrorized his sister regularly.

Penicillium blossomed into a wonderfully hairy green bouquet that Jamie placed upon Lori's pillow just before bedtime. Her screams had no doubt awakened the slumbering dead in the churchyard of New Church. And then there was the fascinating experiment in which several dishes of mold were placed in the icebox among the Christmas puddings and mince meat pies. This was done, Jamie explained to his angry mother, to see if coldness inhibited the growth of certain specimens. Helen sternly instructed Jamie to take his entire collection out of the house and into the cold winter night of Berlin. On the back stoop of the parsonage Jamie's beloved miniature mold gardens met their end. Yes, coldness did indeed inhibit the growth of mold.

Karl sighed and shook his head in distant amusement. Here it was hot and humid. Maybe that was why all the bread served at Nameless prison was covered with a soft green coat of penicillium. Karl listlessly brushed at it, but it clung tenaciously to the crust. It would not be gotten rid of so easily in the warm, moist climate of a Nameless prison cell.

"I am not hungry, Lord, and yet I know I must eat. To eat is to hope. I will not give up hoping." He frowned down at the green stuff that sucked nourishment from Karl's bread. Every day he pretended that perhaps there was some vitamin in this spore which somehow was of benefit to his body. He forced himself to close his eyes and take a bite. "For that which I am about to receive, may the Lord make me truly thankful . . . " he murmured.

Chewing on teeth that were sore from malnutrition, he was able to feel warmed by the memory of Jamie and his petri dishes. Wouldn't the boy have delighted in the giant mold specimen that his father now consumed?

———

The storm clouds over Jerusalem had parted. A bank of thunderheads piled against the distant mountains of Moab, but bright sunlight gleamed down on the clean pink stone of the Old City Wall.

The air was fresh and cool; the slight breeze carried the light scent of orange blossoms that bloomed in orchards throughout the British Mandate. In spite of the Arab strike, in spite of the violence that had led to the destruction of tens of thousands of the Zionists' orange trees, the Mufti had failed to uproot them all. And he had failed to uproot the men and women who planted and tended the trees.

His failure, in large part, was due to the efforts of the British captain, Samuel Orde. In six months Orde had turned the meager defenses of the Jewish settlers into a force to be reckoned with.

Orde stood at the open window in the office of Colonel Hallum and looked out toward the Temple Mount where the worst of the riots had begun with the death of Eli Sachar. The ancient pavement was rain-washed, unstained now by the blood of the hundreds who had fallen throughout the winter. The violence had finally receded like the clouds, but there were many dead and broken in its wake. Gazing out over Jerusalem from British headquarters, it seemed impossible to imagine the horrors that had swept across the Holy Land these past few months.

As though he could read Orde's thoughts, Colonel Hallum said quietly, "There is nothing holy about this land. Always has been a bloody, violent hole. Always will be."

Orde pretended not to hear. He drew a deep breath, savoring the scent of the orange blossoms. "Smell that, will you? There will be marmalade in the tearooms of London, after all."

Silence. Hallum knew well that the survival of the settlements was due to Orde. Everyone knew it. From this office all the way to London, no one in the government had missed the newspaper accounts of Captain Samuel Orde and his Jewish Special Night Squads. Several thousand young Jewish settlers had been trained in combat according to British standards. They had protected the water pipelines in the north regions of Galilee. They had saved the skins of a British patrol ambushed near Hanita, and captured the criminals who had kidnapped and tortured to death three British civil servants. And that was only a partial list of accomplishments. General Wavell spoke openly about the benefit of the Night Squads. He supported Orde when others did not.

The scent of orchards in bloom, however, spoke the loudest praise. But that was not enough, it seemed. Not in a world where politics was seldom played by the rules of common sense.

Hallum began again. "The Mufti has been in Berlin. Quite welcome at the table with Herr Hitler, they say."

A slight smile crossed Orde's face. "Have they noticed in the home office that the Japanese ambassador is also at the German Chancellery quite a lot lately? Has anyone in London made the connection that whenever Hitler invites a scoundrel to dine there is inevitably indigestion in the British Empire someplace?" Orde clasped his hands behind his back. He continued to stare at the Dome of the Rock, but he was no longer really seeing it. "And who is der Führer and Haj Amin Husseini serving as main course, I wonder?" Orde knew. He had known for some time. But still he wanted Hallum to have to say it.

"Haj Amin Husseini is exiled from the British Mandate." Hallum's voice was clipped. He resented the game. "The Arab Higher Committee that rules in his place in turn is demanding that officials in our government be brought to some sort of justice."

"Justice." Orde whispered the word, but it rang like a thunder clap of accusation. The very concept of justice had been carved up and devoured by Hitler and his dinner companions.

"To save face, you see. A compromise. Distribute the blame for the violence of the last few months." He paused. Waited for the meaning to penetrate.

Orde understood perfectly. "A scapegoat. Roasted in proper English fashion and served with Yorkshire pudding. Traditional in all negotiations for peace."

"If you will." The colonel raised his chin slightly. "A responsible individual. Someone of high profile but low rank." He cleared his throat as if to give Orde an opportunity to challenge him.

Orde simply bowed slightly in acknowledgment. What did he expect, after all? He had written his own press releases—all under a pseudonym, of course. He had not guessed that he was setting himself up for this moment.

"And?"

"And, they have decided—"

"They?"

"London."

"And Berlin?"

Hallum ignored the jibe. "London. They have found that you were somehow involved in every battle. Every aspect of this fiasco. From the first day on the Temple Mount when Eli Sachar was butchered until now. And so the final blame . . . the only possible—"

Orde shook his head. Not the Victoria Cross for service above the call of duty. Not even a promotion. Not even a "thank you, now please pass the orange marmalade."

"So what is it to be?" Orde asked.

"Posted back to England. Some desk duty for a while until this blows over."

"This will not blow over." Orde finally turned to face the uneasy colonel. "We will need those trained Jewish soldiers to hang on to this hunk of rock once the real storm breaks."

"That may be. But it is not the case now. The Grand Mufti of Jerusalem is in exile!"

"And what is one little British captain? Is that it?"

"Posted to England! That is all! Jews and Arabs are dead. British boys are being shipped home in boxes. And when the beginnings are traced, there *you* are! *Captain Samuel Orde.* On duty, right in the bloody thick of the fray! The Arab Council will be placated no other way."

"Unless I am killed?"

"You and I both know you are lucky to be alive. Every headhunter in the territory is out for you. You are a stubborn idiot, Orde, to believe that you can go on like you have and not end up a martyr!" Hallum's eyes narrowed slightly as he scrutinized Orde's stony face. "Maybe that is what you had in mind—to die like some prophet in the Holy Land?" Hallum rubbed his hand across his cheek. Had he stumbled onto something, perhaps? "Well, you will be offered up on the altar of political expediency, Orde. But I, for one, will not stand by your grave in Jerusalem! Go back to England! Give yourself a rest from this *obsession* of yours! This is not supposed to be a war! We . . . *Britain* . . . are here to keep the peace! You have forgotten that goal."

Orde turned back to face toward the city, toward the golden onion-shaped domes of the Russian convent at the foot of Gethsemane. Victoria Sachar was still there, safe within those walls, mourning for her husband. There had been days when Orde had wished that he himself could have died that day on the

Temple Mount instead of Eli Sachar. Orde knew what it was to lose someone you love and then be forced to go on living life alone. Did Victoria Sachar look back over her days without Eli and trace the beginning of her sorrows to Orde? Ah, well. Perhaps this was to be his punishment. It seemed much worse than dying—to be shuffled off to England and a desk job, there to wither away in obscurity while other men made the *difference* in the world. It was much easier to fall in battle; Hallum was right about that. *A martyr in the Holy Land!*

Hallum broke the silence of Orde's unwelcome reverie. "Look, old fellow..." His tone was that of a friend. "How long has it been since you have been home?"

"Home?" Orde could not quite grasp the question. Did Hallum mean quarters, or...

"England."

Orde nodded. He knew exactly how long it had been. He had left England one month to the day after Katie died. "Four years in June," he said. He did not add that it was also four years since he had buried his wife.

Hallum frowned slightly. "Four years. It is four years since you lost Katie, isn't it?"

Orde resented the fact that Hallum remembered something so personal. So very painful. "You have a keen memory."

"I attended the services, Orde, the day after my fortieth birthday. You bore up well. Everyone said so at the time."

"Why bring this up?" Orde snapped.

"Because it has occurred to me more than once that perhaps you did not bear up as well as we all thought. I have watched you here and—"

Orde raised his hand to interrupt. "Thank you, Colonel. But . . . this is a personal matter. That is not why you called me here. Are we quite finished?" He paused and shook his head resolutely. "In one month my commission is up. I wish to apply for early discharge, if you please."

Hallum regretted mentioning Katie Orde now. It was the final straw. He had pushed too hard. "Think about it."

Orde blinked in the bright light. "I *have* thought about it! Right here I have thought about it!"

"You will not be permitted to remain here in Palestine." Hallum was suddenly stern. "This will do you no good."

"I am requesting early discharge." Orde's face flushed with

emotion. What right had Hallum to link Katie to his performance here as a British officer?

"As you wish, then." Hallum took his seat and opened the file. "Your discharge will be effective the day you set foot in England again." He sniffed, businesslike and unmoving. "Any questions?"

"No. No . . . *sir*." Orde snapped to attention and saluted.

"All right, then. *Dismissed.*"

Orde strode from the building and stood in the sunlight as the British Union Jack snapped on the flag pole above him. He looked toward the Muslim Quarter of the Old City with the certainty that even in exile himself, the Mufti would be very pleased at the news of Orde's disgrace.

He let his breath out slowly. He had not imagined that the betrayal could be so complete. Walking slowly down the steps of the building, he forced himself to acknowledge the salutes of men of lesser rank. Now his rank meant nothing at all. He was of less significance in Jerusalem than the lowliest private in the motor pool.

5 Music for the World

Three times each day, Etta Lubetkin washed and changed her clothes and hurried across the square to nurse baby Yani. Always when she returned, the strain in her face was lessened. It seemed that the baby had somehow nourished her, Rachel thought.

Rachel's chores included going to the teeming marketplace. She looked forward to the excursions, to the noise and the bustle after hours of counting the labored breaths of Papa. She bargained cautiously, as her mother had taught her. And when she returned with cabbages or potatoes or bread or a chicken and recited the price to Etta, she was rewarded with a smile and a nod of approval.

Daily, gifts of meals were also brought to the back doorstep by members of the congregation. Dolek, the milk peddler, brought butter and cheese with his tall gray horse. At least one hot cooked meal a day came from the community soup kitchen. But from his sickbed, the Rabbi Lubetkin had forbidden his flock to enter the house.

Each Sabbath, a regular visitor came. His face at the door had surprised Rachel so much the first time that she had stood speechless before him and had not moved to let him enter.

"Who is there, Rachel?" Etta had called from the kitchen.

The little Catholic priest had bowed his head in greeting. Rachel could not remember his name, only his kindness.

"Father Kopecky, child," he smiled and prompted.

Flustered, she called her reply and stepped aside. "Father Kopecky, Mama. The priest. The Catholic priest!" *Did he want to come in?* she wondered in amazement.

He brushed his boots on the mat. *Yes. He wanted in.*

"Good Shabbat," he had said that first day, almost as if he knew something about a Jewish household.

After that first visit, Father Kopecky came often. On Shabbat, he laughed and called himself the *Lubetkin Shabbes goy!* He built the fires and chopped kindling. He stacked wood and lit the lamps. He cooked—or at least he lifted the kettle onto the stove and made hot tea for everyone. All the duties Jews were forbidden to perform on the Sabbath, this strange, whistling little priest did. On other days he bathed Papa from head to foot. Papa even managed to talk sometimes when the priest came, although at first he had thought he was dreaming.

When Father Kopecky came, Mama had rest. Rachel had time to retreat to her chair and read. And on this particular day, the Catholic priest read to Papa from the Torah; offered him precious words of discussion that mere women were unable to do. "A Shabbes goy?" Mama exclaimed in wonder. "The man talks like a son of the covenant, not some Gentile servant come to build our fire! Did he go to Torah school, I wonder?"

In spite of herself, Rachel looked forward to his coming. She still felt herself stiffen at the sight of his priest's frock. Was he not from the *other side,* from the world of the Saturday people where plaster gods were prayed to and candles were burned to the dead Christ above their altar?

Rachel had never seen these things because she had not ever dared to set foot in one of those places, but she had heard about the great cathedrals. She had seen the drooping dead

Christ leading parades and funeral processions through the streets. She knew what it was to be accused of putting that Christ to death. *Christ-killing Jew!*

These things made the presence of Father Kopecky suspect at times. Rachel wondered why he came and then came back, why he read to Papa in Hebrew. *Why?* And then she remembered the way he had helped Mama in the street the day the Saturday people had attacked them. She remembered, and she really liked him. When he was late, she worried that he might not come. When he had to leave early, she hoped she had not offended him by a puzzled glance or a frank, curious stare.

It should not have surprised her that Papa also looked forward to the company of this man. After all, Papa was known and sometimes disapproved of for his friendships with those outside the faith. Dr. Letzno was one such character, but at least the good doctor had been born a Jew and circumcised on the eighth day. Priests were not circumcised, Rachel knew. They were *goyim,* Gentiles, and so there was no ceremony for them when they were babies.

Still, through his croaking fevered voice, Papa called the priest *"Righteous! A righteous Gentile!"*

Rachel was convinced that Father Kopecky must be the only righteous goy in Warsaw. Maybe in the whole world. She hated every other Gentile. The Saturday people had done this terrible thing to Papa. They had broken down the doors and taken him and made him sick. He was in bed because of what the Saturday people had done.

Maybe Father Kopecky was repenting for all of them, she thought today as she watched him stoke the fire. She held her book so that she could watch him secretly and then turn her eyes back to the pages quickly if he glanced her way.

He was whistling again, sweeping up ashes from the hearth as he always did. Suddenly he turned his head to look at her sitting in the plump over-stuffed chair. She looked quickly down at the pages. She felt her face flush because he had nearly caught her staring. She could not focus her eyes and she raised the book a bit higher to hide her cheeks.

He stopped whistling and said, "Hmmmm. That is very strange."

Rachel's eyes widened as she heard his footsteps move across the flowered rug toward her. He stood in front of her

74

chair, an arm's length away. "Indeed," he said again. "Very peculiar. Rachel?"

At the sound of her name, Rachel felt the color deepen. She pretended not to notice he was speaking to her.

"Rachel? Child?" he asked again, as if requesting politely that she look at him.

It was not very far to look up. He was a short man, shorter than Rachel herself. She raised her eyes. He was smiling at her. Amused. She quickly looked down again. "Yes, Your Honor?" she stammered.

He reached out and took the book from her hands. He held it up and turned it sideways as if to study the words at a strange angle. Then he turned the book over. "You were holding it upside down, child." He gave it back to her. "Is this some new way of holding a book on the Shabbat? Nothing I have heard of. Seems like *work* to me."

Her mouth opened and closed in speechless humiliation. She was caught in the act! *Spying!* And now he was laughing at her.

"Pardon . . . I . . . I was . . ."

"Watching your *Shabbes goy* clean the ashes?" He laughed loudly. "Perfectly all right, child. Understandable. Who would want a Shabbes goy who did not do good work on the Sabbath?"

"I was . . . just . . . I did not mean . . ." Tears stung her eyes. She did not blink for fear that tears might actually fall.

He saw her embarrassment and became instantly contrite for having noticed and commented that she was spying. "Think nothing of it." His voice was fatherly. Priestly. Kind.

"I was not." She stared unblinking at her hands and tried to explain. "It's just that you are so kind. And I was just . . . I do not know why you are so kind. And I was just . . . I do not know why you are so kind when the others are . . ."

"Not?" he finished for her.

But there was no time for him to answer her. Maybe there was no answer anyway.

Mama came into the room. "Your Honor," she gestured toward the big clock on the opposite wall. "Aaron is hoping you might stay this evening."

The priest frowned at the clock face. Had he forgotten that it was time for the BBC broadcast of the symphony from London? "Ah, Rachel, we'll miss it if we don't hurry." He scurried out of the room, leaving a wake of unanswered questions behind. The growl of the radio emanated from Papa's room.

Rachel put down the book but did not move from the chair.

"We'll miss the beginning of the concert," Etta said, searching Rachel's eyes for a moment. "What is it?"

Rachel bit her lip and tried to define just what it was that troubled her about the little priest and his weekly excursions to Muranow Square. "Are there others like him, do you think?"

Etta nodded in reply, and then brushed the conversation away like ashes from the hearth. "Come along now. You know how Papa loves the concerts."

The whine of the BBC in faraway London slid into focus. So she had not made them late for the concert by her silly curiosity. She entered the bedroom where Father Kopecky was chatting pleasantly with Papa.

"I heard this performed by the Vienna Symphony Orchestra at the Czech National Theater in Prague two years ago," the priest explained. "It was a different world then, was it not?"

———

In honor of tonight's BBC broadcast of Mozart's Prague Symphony, Murphy donned his black dinner jacket and had his dress shoes polished. He endured the starched shirt with a smile as he sat in the close atmosphere of the audience in the radio studio.

The gathering was small, just enough people on hand to give the live broadcast the added dimension of applause at appropriate moments.

At five minutes to air time, Elisa took her place as second chair violinist for what would be her last performance until after the baby was born. She had given up playing for the large concerts at Covent Gardens some months before. BBC radio concerts were plenty. Now she could barely lean forward far enough to turn the pages of the music on her stand. She could not place the precious Guarnerius violin on her lap because she had no lap—only baby Murphy thumping around in there, threatening to kick over the music stand or punch a hole in the priceless fiddle.

Elisa had managed to sneak a wink at Murphy, flanked by Charles and Louis. The six-year-old boys were also dressed in matching white dinner jackets. *A very impressive sight,* Elisa thought. Being here with the boys was a loving gesture on the part of Murphy, who in his heart would have much preferred a jazz performance in Soho by *D'Fat Lady Trio*, who were soon to leave for America.

Murphy responded to her wink with the sort of look that let her know he would like to be paid back in kisses from his favorite fat lady as soon as she was once again a performing musician. How far she had come since she had last played this concert with the Vienna Symphony Orchestra on tour across Europe!

Elisa didn't need to turn the pages of the music—this was one score she knew backward and forward! It was this very symphony the old gang from Vienna had performed in Prague on the night she carried Rudy Dorbransky's Guarnerius violin home to Berlin. *Rudy's fiddle.* She raised it to her chin and silently dedicated her last concert to Rudy, who had tried so hard to stop all that had now come upon Europe!

Today it was his birthday, she suddenly remembered. How could she forget such a date? He had gotten drunk and gambled all night, losing everything, including this violin. And then he had come to her in tears to beg for a loan with which he might redeem his fiddle. She had counted out the bills and sent him on his way, never knowing what Rudy was really up to on the back streets of Vienna!

Now she knew. She knew everything. She knew too much. She was going to bring a child into this world, and tonight she longed for the carefree ignorance of those days. *Shimon. Leah. Rudy. All the much-loved members of the orchestra—everyone scattered, or dead, or playing the tune of the Nazis in Vienna.* Ah well, Hitler had chased her out of the arms of Thomas von Kleistmann and into the heart of the lanky American jazz-lover who now sweltered in a dinner jacket in this summer heat because he adored her! *Be thankful for such lovely things!*

The concert master raised his violin. The orchestra tuned up as the seconds ticked by and the red light blinked a warning that air time was approaching. *Time to get serious here.* Elisa raised her bow in salute to Murphy, in salute of all the others who were not performing with her tonight. The introduction made, Sir Thomas Beecham strode out to a smattering of applause. He raised his arms above his big head, and once again Elisa played. *Mozart's Prague Symphony. With Leah. Shimon. Rudy. Happy*

Birthday, Rudy. Did you know the Nazis have taken Prague? Hitler slept in Hradcany Castle. But I'm playing the Prague Symphony all the same. Because I remember what used to be. I remember it's your birthday, Rudy, and I still have your fiddle.

The radio was one thing the Danzig Gang had decided immediately they must have! How else could they know the current events? Or keep up with the latest music from America?

Their apartment may have been sparsely furnished, but the big radio against the wall gave it a touch of refinement. They had traded a small gold pendant from Alfie's treasures in order to purchase it. Lori often said it was worth an entire gold mine to know what was going on.

They had heard the regular broadcasts of *D'Fat Lady Trio* throughout the group's European tour. Now that the American jazz trio was bound for home, Jacob spent the evenings slowly twirling the dials in search of a replacement.

Tonight the low whine of the tuner howled and then suddenly dropped London into the sitting room of the flat. "*SIR THOMAS BEECHAM OF THE LONDON PHILHARMONIC ORCHESTRA . . .*"

Jamie and Mark groaned as Lori gasped and shouted for Jacob not to move the dial.

He turned and scowled at her. "Somewhere there is jazz playing. Or maybe Charlie McCarthy! Please, not this—"

"This is London!" She grabbed Alfie by the sleeve. "Alfie, listen!"

He raised his head as distant applause sounded very near. "What?"

Werner-kitten pounced on Alfie's big feet, batting at the toe that protruded from his sock. Alfie was too absorbed in this battle to take Lori's side in the radio argument.

"Come on, Lori! Enough culture, already," Jamie sneered.

"You have been out of school too long," Lori snapped. Then, as Jacob's fingers twitched, eager to tune out Mozart's Prague Symphony, Lori whirled to face off with him. "You touch that, and I will never speak to you again! That is *London,* you idiots! London! Where our very own Cousin Elisa is now a musician! Maybe playing right now with that very orchestra."

Jacob melted back with respect at such a thought that Lori

and Jamie had a cousin on the radio. Even if it was only classical stuff. "Well, then . . ."

So Lori won. Jamie and Mark still looked disgusted. Edgar Bergen and Charlie McCarthy were more entertaining than this. But . . . well, it was London, after all. And soon a letter from them in Danzig would arrive there—maybe opened by one of the musicians in the very orchestra that was playing now.

That much, at least, was something to think about while the music played.

————

There was only one radio in the entire apartment building where Lucy and Peter shared a tiny one-room studio tucked beneath the eaves of a once-magnificent house.

Bent and crippled from arthritis, the aged concierge of the building had but one pleasure in his life. Last year at Christmas his daughter had sent him a Philco radio from faraway America. The radio would have cost half a year's wages for the old man, and yet he would not have sold the radio for twice that amount. On nights like this, when the reception was especially good, he would turn up the volume and let all the tenants enjoy his great luxury.

Tonight the clear strains of the London Philharmonic Orchestra wound up the steep stairs to the garret where Lucy and Peter lived. The concise British accent of the announcer left no doubt that the broadcast did indeed come all the way from London. In this way the old concierge wordlessly declared the value of the gift his daughter had sent. Somehow his own worth was enhanced by this treasure.

"Tomorrow he will ask me if I heard it," Lucy said softly as she and Peter sat together beside the open window. The view was only the tiles of the adjoining rooftop and beyond that the stars. *These stars are also shining in London,* she thought wistfully.

"How could we not hear it?" Peter was amused. "A very good radio. Four flights of very steep stairs. Not to mention walls and floors, and here it is right in our own flat, as though the radio was ours."

"He is proud of it."

"He has nothing else to be proud of," Peter said with an edge of bitterness.

"Don't be unkind, Peter," Lucy chided as the music soared. Such gentle music. "Just listen. He is giving us a gift."

"Not a gift. He is only being proud."

"Stop." Lucy leaned against the windowsill and closed her eyes to inhale the sweet summer air. "Don't ruin it for me. I am dreaming of faraway places."

"This is the Prague Symphony." Peter's voice was still tinged with disdain. "I hope you are not dreaming of Prague. Hitler is there."

"Not Prague." Lucy still did not open her eyes. "Of London. Where this music is coming from." She opened her eyes. "And it is a gift, Peter. It makes me feel . . . hopeful."

He laughed and turned his back on the stars. "Hopeful? You know what this is? It is a requiem for poor Prague, that is all. It is the melody of what used to be and what has now gone away forever. A requiem for the dead."

"Go to bed if you don't care to listen." He was goading her again, pushing her to talk about things she did not wish to talk about. Every night since the last Hitler broadcast it had been like this.

"You are the one who is not listening," Peter said, taking her arm. "And the next sound you hear may be the tramp of jack-boots on the pavement."

"Stop," she answered in quiet despair. "Please."

"And after that, Wolf will be on the stair and at the door."

"Don't!"

"You must come with me, Lucy! Soon the requiem will be for Danzig."

"I will not . . . cannot go with you to Warsaw." Why did he push her so? Why could she not have one night without this, one moment of pleasure listening to music? Just a symphony from London, and now Peter was at her again to go with him to Warsaw.

"If you do not leave this place, then the requiem may be for you, Lucy. And for the baby. There is no more time. No hope for us here. Do you understand?"

Lucy did not answer. She brushed past him and opened the door of the flat so that the radio of the concierge was even louder. With a backward glance over her shoulder, she stepped out onto the landing and sat down alone on the top step. She hoped he would not follow her. She wished only that he would leave her alone and go to Warsaw if he was so terrified of the future. But she would not go with him into Poland.

The mellow sound of cellos and violins wound up the stairs like green ivy covering a shabby facade with a living cloak. The facade of peace and security for Danzig was ready to crack and fall to pieces, but just for tonight, for this one hour, Lucy did not want to think about it.

She felt the presence of Peter at her back, yet pretended not to know he was there. She prayed he would go back inside and leave her to her dreams.

After a moment, he left, leaving the door open just a crack. Lucy closed her eyes again and thanked God for the thoughtful daughter of the concierge. The symphony of Prague soared above her and around her, finally covering her with its beauty.

For just that hour, Lucy did not think at all. She simply rested in the music and dreamed she was somewhere very far from this place.

———

Orde lay back on his cot as the dulcet tones of the symphony echoed in the stone chamber of his permanent Old City quarters. The BBC Home Service broadcast was delayed by several hours from the original performance. Still, Orde listened to the music and imagined the musicians at their stands as though they were on the stage at Covent Gardens.

Katie had loved the concerts of London. He had merely endured them for her sake. Wearing a stiff collar and cuffs, being stuffed into a dinner jacket, had never been his idea of a pleasant evening. While Katie had shimmered in the glory of such music as this, he had nodded off or put his mind to work on some problem or other.

Now those delayed broadcasts of London concerts had become his one tenuous link with her. In those brief hours Orde allowed himself to think of her as she had been on those evenings. So beautiful, lost in an enjoyment that he had not shared with her while she was alive. Yet now he relived those precious moments at her side as though he, too, had cherished this music. It seemed odd to him now that he had not heard the beauty when she was beside him. And tonight, when he was so very alone, he longed to tell her just exactly what it was about the melody that moved him.

The second movement of the symphony began. Orde stared up into the shadows of the vaulted ceiling of the ancient barracks. Surely other soldiers had lain awake in this very room throughout the centuries. Officers of a dozen armies had stared up at these same stones and dreamed of lost loved ones as some musician played a sad song in the courtyard. The tunes, like those men, had vanished in the dusty air of Jerusalem. *And I, too, am dust.* Orde covered his face with his hands. "Oh, Katie, what is left for me? I did not see you when you were with me. I did not hear the melody of your heart! *A selfish, preoccupied man!* And now what is left?"

He sat up slowly and unlaced his boots, the boots of an officer. "What I would give if I could trade these in for that starched shirt and one evening at a concert in London with you, Katie. But I have nothing to replace this uniform, do I? Nothing at all to come home to." His own voice mingled with the sweet strains of the strings like a prayer. "But now I hear what you heard, Katie. It is beautiful. Yes, love. If only I had heard it before . . ."

6 The Hunter and the Hunted

It was a hot night. "Suffocating," Elisa said, as she tossed uncomfortably on the bed. "Humid as only a London summer night can be."

Murphy moved the mattress through the French doors and out onto the roof garden while Elisa sifted through his jazz recordings, finally settling on the mellow tunes of Glenn Miller.

As the soft tones of a muted trombone drifted out from the house, they lay together beneath the stars and silently gazed over the London rooftops toward the lighted dome of St. Paul's Cathedral. Crickets in the planter boxes chirped in counterpoint to the music. The scent of gardenias and sweet peas filled the air. Far away a siren howled into the night as Murphy sat up to rub Elisa's feet.

"Nice," she said.

"Better?"

"We should move the bed out here. Sleep under the stars."

"The air is not so clean as Pennsylvania." Murphy stroked her ankles. "But the crickets remind me of home."

Elisa did not answer. He thought perhaps she had drifted off to sleep—or maybe she was thinking of the chirping of crickets in some distant memory. "This reminds me," she murmured, her voice soft and loving, "of the night we made love beneath the oak tree in New Forest." Reaching for his hand, she pulled him down beside her. She placed his hand against the steady thumping of the baby within her. "And look what you did that night," she laughed. "Ruined my figure."

Murphy's voice filled with wonder. "He has the hiccups. *Huh!* The little guy is in there tapping away! What do you know!"

Elisa fixed her eyes on the great bright dome of St. Paul's. "Murph?"

"Uh-huh?" He was still preoccupied with the steady tapping inside her belly.

"I know you want us to leave London when it comes—the war, I mean."

He did not take his hand from her, and yet the sense of carefree wonder left him instantly. For a long time he did not respond. "There's more than the two of us at stake here. Charles and Louis. And this little one."

"I won't leave without you."

Were the crickets still singing?

"Maybe we won't have a choice."

"There is always a choice, Murphy. I . . . I don't want to live even a day without you."

"I wish I could go home, Elisa; you know how I feel. But there is something here I have to do." He touched her face and lay close to her. "England may well end up fighting alone. The American isolationists need to hear what's going on over here."

"They won't listen to you."

"Somebody will. There is a story that will have to be told. And what kind of man would I be if I leave when it gets too hot for comfort?"

"But I can't . . . don't want to raise this baby without you. Murphy, haven't we given enough? Done enough?"

"Your parents are still working with the refugee kids in spite of threats from the government that they are far too involved in politics. Can I do less?"

Elisa rolled over on her side to face him. Her eyes were bright in the soft light. Her look said all the things she had no words to say aloud. "I won't leave you, then. No matter what happens." She looked up at the sky. "If the stars fall right through this roof, I'll be here with you."

The image of falling bombs was too vivid for Murphy. *Madrid. Barcelona. Rows of children with blank eyes staring up into the sky. Incendiary bombs falling on the cities like stars . . .*

"Don't." Murphy put a finger on her lips. Warm and soft, those lips smiled at his touch. "We'll talk about it another time."

She was eager to think of other things. *Crickets beneath the oak trees of New Forest.* "Did you like the way I played my fiddle tonight?" she whispered.

"Kiss me," he murmured, pressing his mouth against hers. Here she was in his arms, two weeks away from having a baby, and yet he wanted her.

She chuckled, amused by his desire. "Your tastes have changed," she teased. "I never knew you were attracted to omnibuses."

"Depends on where they take me."

"It's a short ride to New Forest," she smiled. "And you've already ruined my figure. What have I got to lose?"

Major Alexander Hess looked out at the thick pine forests of Poland as the Corridor Express train sped toward Danzig. Providence was smiling on him after his ordeal. He had been given the order to pursue the children of Karl Ibsen as far as he must in order to bring that case to a successful conclusion, but it seemed that his pursuit might have unexpected dividends.

The Führer had taken Hess's mutilated hand in his own hand and had given him this mandate: "If you cannot bring Karl Ibsen's children back alive to face him, then bring back their heads in a sack." He had smiled, but Hess knew well that the Führer was not joking. "In the diplomatic pouch if all else fails, ja? To which you may add the heads of resistance leaders and traitors," he concluded significantly.

Of course the Gestapo had agents in place in London to report if any word came to Elisa Murphy about the Ibsen children. Those agents, in turn, would report to Hess, and when the capture of Lori and Jamie Ibsen was accomplished, Helen Ibsen would also be eliminated. All of this would be done in a way that left no doubt as to the accidental death of the woman, of course. Although she had made no public statements about the imprisonment of her husband, the very fact that she was alive and capable of speech was still a matter of concern to the Ministry of Propaganda. Heads had rolled when it was reported she had escaped. That aspect of the case, of course, was of little concern to Hess. He demanded only that the woman be left alive as a possible source of information regarding her children. If Hess did not find them in Danzig, then he would follow them to France, or England, or Poland. He had promised the Führer that unlike Wallich and Wattenbarger, Pastor Karl Ibsen would not be allowed the luxury of death until he had made a full confession of conspiracy against the Fatherland. And if he would not bend, then he would witness the breaking of his children as a penalty for his obstinacy.

Danzig also held promise of the conclusion of a personal matter that had plagued Hess. Wolfgang von Fritschauer had been assigned to the area, and Hess was quite certain that in some way the man was still connected to Lucy Strasburg. If they were both involved in a smuggling ring on behalf of Jews and political dissidents, then Hess was resolved that he would bring both of them to justice as well.

Hess could never let anyone know the truth that it was Lucy's young companion who had held him at gunpoint and forced him from the train. To have admitted that would have destroyed his career. It was enough for Hess to greet Wolfgang von Fritschauer at the officer's briefing last month and tell him that Lucy had been on board the Corridor Express on the same night he was attacked.

Wolf had paled. Was it anger, or guilt? Perhaps Lucy Strasburg had betrayed Wolf as well as Hess for the sake of those two Jewish children. If that was the case, Wolf did not speak of it. He spoke of his weariness of her; his relief that she was gone. Why, then, was the man so pale at the mention of her name?

Hess felt a kind of disdain for von Fritschauer, whatever the truth might be. He had been involved with a woman more vile and dangerous than the Jews she protected. There was, indeed, room for more heads in the diplomatic pouch. Hess had decided long ago that he must question Lucy and then kill her, rather than attempt to take her back to trial. That was the safest way to keep himself from disgrace. She must not be allowed to give her account of the true circumstances of his leap from the train. With the first twist of Gestapo thumb-screws, the woman would be screaming that she had traveled with an officer named Hess who was knocked out and held with his own gun by a Jewish refugee boy.

A junior agent had been assigned to Hess in Danzig. Between them, Hess was certain that the Ibsen matter and the issue of Lucy Strasburg and Wolfgang von Fritschauer could be settled permanently.

He let the shade fall back and opened the basket of food that had been prepared and packed by the Führer's own chef.

A thermos of tea. Sandwiches. Fruit and cheeses. Hess had brought along his own bottle of schnapps, which he nursed discreetly. Everyone knew that the Führer did not approve of the vice of alcohol—and drinking was, indeed, one of the many vices of Major Alexander Hess. He shrugged the thought away as the whistle shrieked the approach to Danzig. He was, after all, conducting his own private celebration in compartment 17.

It was a miracle, thought Karl Ibsen joyfully when the tiny sparrow returned to the window ledge of his cell. Just a small miracle, but a miracle nonetheless.

Karl dared not move from where he stood in the center of the cell. The bird cocked its head in puzzlement at the sight of this human canary in a cage. A grizzled creature, this human. Did no one ever clean this cage or give water for the human to wash his boney, featherless wings? A pitiful sight, this prisoner. No real bird trapped in a cage was ever treated so badly as this.

Karl knew that he was only imagining the pity he saw in the tiny, unblinking eyes of the sparrow, and yet, even imagined pity made him feel . . . Feel what? What was this emotion that pushed inside his hollow chest? Had loneliness so deep and profound caused him to forget the feeling that now gripped him?

He looked toward the edge of his straw mattress. His ration of bread was wrapped carefully in the remaining rags of his shirt. "Stay," he whispered to the sparrow. "Stay and I will give you the best crumbs of my bread."

Karl decided the bird was a female. Drab brown color. Plain, unpretentious feathers. The tender, sympathetic look. Yes. A female. Had the bird been a male, it would have looked at Karl with terrible scorn. It would have hopped a slalom course around the bars to taunt Karl in a display of its freedom. "See?" it would have chirped. "Nothing to it. One hop and I am in the cell. One hop and I'm out. Spread my wings and I'm back in the forest. Not like you, old man!"

The lady sparrow lifted her head and looked beyond her beak at Karl as if to ask, "Whatever is to become of you?"

Karl replied aloud, "I don't know. Not in this life anyway. If I could fly... if I could fly away like you, then I would. Through the bars... Away. I would not mind leaving this life, and that's the truth. Only Jamie and Lori . . . my children . . ."

His voice became suddenly too unnerving for the little sparrow. There was too much passion here in this man-cage. Too much grief to be contained inside the brick walls. Like a terrible wind, the pent-up emotion of the prisoner broke loose and blew the lady sparrow from the window ledge. One flutter and she was gone. It was just too difficult—even for the tiny heart of a sparrow.

———

"Her name is Lucy." Wolf extended the photograph showing Lucy on the steps of St. Stephan's in Vienna. "Lucy Strasburg."

The stoop-shouldered doctor of the Marienbad Women's Hospital studied the slim and beautiful image for a moment and then shook his head slowly.

"I would remember such a patient. Your sister is very beautiful, Herr von Fritschauer. But—"

"Of course she won't look like this now, Herr Doktor. She is . . . her time must be very near."

"I would remember such a face." The doctor gazed a while longer. "Such innocence in her eyes. It is always the ones like your sister who end up being hurt by some fellow, yes? Pregnant, you say?"

Wolf bit his lip and stared at the picture of Lucy. He had never noticed the childlike expression on her face until now. *Innocent?* He had always imagined it was stupidity and country naivete. The doctor's words sent a fresh surge of anger through him. Lucy Strasburg was neither innocent nor stupid. She was clever and devious. She had made a fool out of Wolf, had she not?

Wolf was pale with emotion. The doctor touched his arm. "Are you unwell, Herr von Fritschauer?"

"This is an ordeal," Wolf mumbled, still staring into those wide eyes. "I have looked at every clinic. Every private doctor. No one has seen her. And you are right; she is not a woman one forgets easily."

"You were certain she was expecting when she disappeared?"

"Yes. Nearly four months."

"The father?"

"A lieutenant in the Army."

"He would not marry her?"

"He is married . . . an affair, you see. He has offered to care for the child, support my sister. She was ashamed. We know she came to Danzig. I have checked steamship lines, offered rewards. This picture . . . you may keep it. I have more. My name and telephone are on the back. If you see her . . . please . . . just call me. Do not attempt to detain her; she will only run again. Our mother is grief-stricken, of course. We only wish to help Lucy."

The doctor nodded slowly as he listened as though he were making a thoughtful diagnosis. "Yes. I will alert my nurses to the situation as well. If she is nearly full term, she will show up. It is certain. No woman would remain alone at such a time."

"That is what we have been praying for." Wolf returned the photograph to the doctor.

He glanced at it. "Where was this . . . taken?"

"St. Stephan's Cathedral in Vienna."

"She is maybe religious, your sister?"

It took a moment for the significance of the question to penetrate Wolf's consciousness. "Yes. *Yes!* Extremely. One of her little quirks."

The doctor laughed a short, knowing laugh. "Take it from a man who works with women. When a lover deserts a female, you will find her grieving one of two places—either to her physician or to her priest. If she has not been to one, then . . ."

Wolf stared at the anatomy chart on the wall of the office. The doctor was right. Lucy the dreamer! Lucy the one who crossed herself before a meal or when passing a shrine on the street, or whenever she heard good news and bad alike! Why had Wolf not gone to the churches of Danzig before this? He had been a fool! He had been looking in places where she might find physical comfort, when he knew she was always looking wistfully at the spires and bell towers of churches they passed! He had teased her once that he was thankful she had not chosen the life of a nun because it would have ruined his pleasure. That remark had made her weep and admit that she had dreamed of such a life when she was a little girl.

He had laughed at her then. And he was laughing as he left the medical clinic and stared out over the spires of Danzig's great churches!

He was close now. Very close indeed! His city map had a directory of the port's many churches, listed by denomination. He ran his finger down the list as he whispered her name, "Lucy, Lucy, Lucy. . ."

Catholic churches. French. German. Polish.

The choices narrowed down to six German parishes scattered throughout Danzig. It was so simple! It was so certain! Wolf could not imagine that he had not thought of it himself. It had taken a healer of the body to remind him of Lucy's overworked concern for her soul! And now the scent was strong.

The train station of the Free City of Danzig was built to match the medieval architecture of the entire town. It looked like some ancient printer's woodcutting; a fifteenth-century engraving come to life.

Lucy Strasburg held Peter Wallich's hand as they walked in the shadows of the tall narrow houses of the old town. Sea birds played on the Baltic winds above the steep gables of the tall tight-packed buildings. A lone cloud scudded across the sky and threatened to impale itself on the spires of the enormous brick church known as Marienkirche.

There were flowers everywhere. Geraniums tumbled from the window boxes on every windowsill. In a small park opposite the train station, hundreds of tulips were planted to create the coat of arms of the last of the city-states; two yellow eagles flanking a red tulip shield.

This was not really the last of the city-states, Lucy thought as she looked at the flowers nodding in the breeze. Danzig and the Vatican City were the only two remaining historical oddities. Peter had told her all about the history of the place where they had fled four months before for refuge. Danzig flew its own flag over a tiny territory consisting of slightly more than 400,000 residents. The multitude of refugees who camped in shanty towns to the south were not counted in the population. The Baltic seaport issued its own currency, had an elected parliament, and was under the protection of the League of Nations. Danzig had a customs union with Poland and provided that great nation with its only access to the Baltic. The times when Danzig was not an independent state, it had been batted back and forth between Germany and Poland like a tennis ball. The Treaty of Versailles after the Great War in 1919 had wrenched Danzig from defeated Germany and brought it to its present precarious condition—claimed by Poland, coveted by Germany.

Lucy looked up to where a dozen Nazi flags spilled out from windows where flower boxes should have been. Even though the mailboxes were Polish and the uniforms of the customs officers were Polish, there was a nasty stirring among the German youth of Danzig. The Horst Wessel song was becoming quite popular. Even Sprinter's ice cream parlor with its glass-topped tables and immaculate wrought-iron chairs was becoming a gathering place for imitators of the Hitler Youth. On Thursdays there were Nazi rallies in the main square, and there was talk among the German population of returning to the Fatherland.

Peter warned Lucy that it was more than talk. Last week, he had placed his baby brother Willie in the arms of a stranger on a children's refugee ship. Then tearfully he had turned to Lucy and said, *"There. I have sent my heart away to England. Willie will be safe now. But there is no reason for me to stay here in this place. My mother and sister are never coming. I do not know what happened to them, but there is no use waiting here in Danzig for them to show up. They might have gone to Warsaw. We have old friends in Warsaw. Come with me, Lucy. Soon it will be as bad here in Danzig as it was in Vienna. Come with me to Warsaw to look for my mother and Marlene."*

Lucy had smiled and shrugged. How serious and concerned this boy sounded! Ah well, he was not really a boy any longer, was he? Peter Wallich had grown up since they had crossed the border of the Reich through the Polish corridor and gone on to Danzig. He was taller, still lean, but his face was fuller and tanned from his work on the wharf. He had done his part. He had taken care of his baby brother. When Lucy was too far along in her pregnancy to continue work as a shop clerk, Peter had managed to provide food for them both. But she could not go with him to Warsaw.

"I want you to come with me, Lucy," he said again. The sun glinted on his copper-colored hair. He looked toward the train station, then back to search her eyes.

"If you were ten years older I would say yes, Peter." She tried to keep her voice light.

"It is not safe here for you—or for me. And your baby is due. Come with me. We will find help in Warsaw, even if I do not find Mother and Marlene."

"You will find them. I am certain of it." Again the half smile of regret. "But, dear Peter, do you know what the Polish name for Danzig is? *Gdansk.* I can barely say it. I could never find work in Poland. The language is so—"

"You are German to the end."

"Ja. And so I'll take my chances here. We run from the same darkness, but for different reasons. My world cannot fit into your world. I have no friends in Poland . . ."

He pressed a slip of paper into her hand. "You do now, Lucy. You have me." He blushed a little at his own boldness.

Lucy knew he was in love with her, this tall, sensitive teenaged Jewish boy. It was flattering and touching, considering that she was unmarried and nearly nine months pregnant with the child of a Nazi S.S. officer. She opened the paper, half expecting some written declaration of his love. But Peter was more sensible than that. He had neatly printed the name and address of his Warsaw destination.

"Thank you." She kissed him lightly on the cheek. "You are a good friend to me, and I will not forget."

He looked away as the train whistle shrilled. "It seems to me they are playing our song again, eh?" He smiled to hide his emotion. "We said hello to that. And now goodbye." He took her hand and shook it as though she were a soccer teammate. "Well . . ."

"Auf Wiedersehen. And . . . *Grüssgott,*" she said in her best Viennese accent. Then she held up the note. "I will write you. When the baby comes, ja?"

Again the whistle. If he didn't hurry, he would miss the train. Maybe he wanted to miss the train. His hand raised. His eyes lingered on her face as he stumbled up the steps. And then, he was gone. Peter Wallich was gone to Warsaw.

And Lucy Strasburg was alone—alone with the unborn child of Wolfgang von Fritschauer.

She almost wept, but then she squared her shoulders and turned away. "There are some things much worse than being alone," she whispered to herself.

———————

The posters were everywhere it seemed—pasted on the news kiosks of London, on the walls of Victoria Station, in the subways, on the markets and stores of Oxford Street.

GAS ATTACK

Big white block letters splashed across a green background—there it was, right here in London: *HOW TO PUT ON YOUR GAS MASK: Always keep your gas mask with you, day and night. Learn to put it on quickly. Practice wearing it.*

It had become a regular drill in the house on Red Lion Square. On Monday, Wednesday and Friday evenings Murphy would unexpectedly call out, *GAS ATTACK!* This sent Charles, Louis, Elisa, and whoever happened to be around scrambling like mad to pull their masks out of the canvas pouches and put them on securely before Murphy shouted ALKA-SELTZER!

"If the mask is not in place by the time I call 'Alka-Seltzer,' " Murphy explained, "you lose."

To lose meant that everyone else got a piece of hard candy, while the loser had to practice putting on his or her gas mask five times in front of everyone else. Charles and Louis and Elisa never lost anymore. But sometimes company did. Charles enjoyed having company. Tonight, Dr. Patrick Grogan, speech therapist and English teacher to Charles and Louis, stayed for dinner, as he often did. He had never stayed for dinner on Monday, Wednesday or Friday, however, and so he was not prepared, even though Elisa warned him that there was likely to be a gas attack after dessert.

The alarm was given, and the mad rush for masks began . . . .

Everyone else sat happily around the table like a family of locusts while Dr. Grogan fumbled and blushed, his face matching his red hair.

"Sorry, Doc," Murphy said from behind the mask. His voice was muffled, as if he were talking into a tin can. "The word is ALKA-SELTZER! You lose!"

Charles and Louis clapped their hands with delight. They ripped off their nasty-bug masks and pointed at Dr. Grogan. Now they could get even for all the times he had made them do it again! *Practice! Practice! Practice! Come now, Charles, once again!*

Grogan was embarrassed. His round face flushed as he accused Murphy, "You planned this! You and these two little heathens! To get even with me. Come on now, admit it!"

Both boys nodded eagerly. Yes, they had planned it. That is why Charles had asked Elisa if Doc might eat with them tonight.

"Yes," Louis laughed.

"Yesssss," Charles agreed, giving the speech therapist a few extra *s's*, since they were a difficult sound for him to make. "Show us . . . how . . . to put it on, Doc!"

Dr. Grogan laughed. His big head rocked on his narrow shoulders and he laughed until his chubby belly ached. Wispy red hair, thinning on top, stood straight up from his first attempt in the Alka-Seltzer drill. He looked like a pudgy little leprechaun in from a windstorm.

Charles liked him, even if he did make him drill hour after hour. Elisa liked him because he was good with the boys. Murphy liked him for a lot of reasons, one of which was that he was American like Murphy.

Murphy passed out the cherry candy while Doc struggled to put on the mask.

"Say it, Doc Grogan!" Louis demanded. "Say the steps!"

"Okay! Okay! Little *heathen*! *Mary and Martha!*" This was Doc's way of saying *good grief,* Charles knew.

"Put it on!" Charles plopped his candy into his mouth and sat back to watch the show.

Doc nodded his big head. "One. *Hold your breath!*" He held his breath and fumbled with the mask. His face got redder. He let out his breath and exclaimed, "How can I hold my breath and recite the blasted steps of this torture?"

"Okay. We'll *say* it," Murphy instructed. "You *do* it." Then Elisa held up her hands like a conductor and they all recited the process together:

"One. *Hold your breath.* Two. *Hold mask in front of face with thumbs inside. . . . INSIDE,* yes. Like that . . . straps. Three . . ." Three was always Charles's favorite part to watch because people who did not practice always made such awkward faces.

"Thrust chin well forward into mask." Out went the chin that was hardly a chin at all. Doc Grogan was mostly shoulders from the ears down, like a bulldog. *Like one of Winston Churchill's bulldogs,* Charles thought. He stuck out his lower jaw and bit his upper lip as he struggled to fit his face into the mask. This was the best-ever after-dinner entertainment! The absolute best!

Elisa laughed and held her big pregnant belly. She begged Doc not to be so funny because it hurt to laugh now that she was so far along. Murphy raised his eyebrows and made his best donkey laugh. A sort of *Hoo-haw-haw-hoo.* Charles and Louis hung on to each other lest they fall out of their chairs at the sight of their taskmaster being taken to task!

At last the bright red face was secure behind the googly eyes of the locust mask. Orange hair protruded from the straps like antenna. Doc Grogan tugged the straps secure to complete the instruction of number three. Then, because everyone else was unable to speak, he completed the process.

"Number four!" he shouted through the mask. *"Run finger around face-piece, taking care head-straps are not twisted."* He crossed his arms in satisfaction and turned to address Charles and Louis. "Wait until your next lesson, me boy-o's."

They were not intimidated. Still, they hooted on as the eyes of the gas mask fogged up.

"Can I take it off and have some candy too?" Off came the torture device, leaving a flaming red crease around Doc's face. Murphy tossed him a candy as he smoothed his hair and glared at the thing. "Don't make me do it again. I beg you. *Mary and Martha!* What a torment! They would be laughing at us in Berlin if they could see what we do in London for entertainment!"

Tears of glee were wiped away. *Would the grown-ups talk politics again tonight? Of course.*

"Not that we will ever need these things," Elisa said as she stacked the dishes. "But at least the British government is finally taking Hitler seriously."

Ever since the Nazis had taken over Czechoslovakia in March, the sandbags around the government buildings in London had been sprouting, multiplying and finally towering like great lumpy heaps of laundry.

They were there around the Houses of Parliament, at the steps of Whitehall, and the foreign office. They protected the trenches dug in Kensington Park and Hyde Park and Grosvener Square, to name just a few.

It was not as if most people really expected war, or actually believed that Germany would press the issue of taking Danzig and the Polish corridor from Poland. Herr Hitler would not go that far, would he? "You bet he would," Murphy said. That was why he took the gas masks seriously. But for most of England, all of this was just precaution, a way to soothe the nerves of the more jittery types in government. And when the sandbags split after the spring rains and weeds began to sprout, there was a big row in Parliament about the matter. After all, there was supposed to be *sand* in the sandbags, not just ordinary garden soil! Then a member of Prime Minister Chamberlain's party suggested that the sandbags serve double duty. Why not plant a few carrots and turnips in the things?

This idea got the biggest laugh the House had heard for weeks.

That same week it was decided that something must be done to demonstrate that England was serious about defense. Murphy was among a troop of fifty journalists who set sail on board the aircraft carrier *Ark Royal* with the earl of Stanhope, first lord of the admiralty, and Colonel Beck, Poland's foreign minister.

As the ship plowed across the Channel, tours were given of the bridge and the galleys, the officers' quarters and the engine room. The day was crowned with an exclusive showing of *Snow White and the Seven Dwarfs*. Midway through the film, two dozen officers hustled out. The movie was stopped in the middle of vital action. The first lord then stood before the image of Dopey the dwarf and announced that the order had been given to put the entire British fleet on alert. "That explains these empty seats," he said calmly as Dopey looked down from the screen.

Murphy felt certain that Walt Disney would be relieved that no one had walked out on his epic by choice. . . .

Photographs of the first lord of the admiralty being upstaged by an animated dwarf made the front pages of a number of publications. *Life Magazine* dedicated a whole page to it, and the British government could almost hear the great guffaws of the German Reich.

Maybe Britain and France were finally taking Germany seriously, but it was a sure bet that Hitler no longer felt that either great nation was much more threat than a band of Disney dwarfs on the rampage.

"You think there will be war then?" Dr. Grogan asked with a hint of disbelief in his voice.

Elisa hustled Charles and Louis up the stairs and out of earshot from Murphy's answer.

He sipped his coffee and waited until their bedroom door was closed. "Unless you want to be in the thick of it," Murphy replied quietly, "I'd start looking into fares back to the States." He raised his eyes toward the room of Charles and Louis. "When it starts—"

"When?"

"When it starts, I'm sending them home. To my folks' place in Pennsylvania. London is a two-hour bomb run from Berlin. I saw what the German Air Force did in Spain, and they were not even officially there." He made the slow whistling sound of a bomb dropping and then the thud of an explosion as he gestured out the window.

Grogan inclined his massive head thoughtfully. "You can't think it will come to that. Chamberlain has given the Führer *carte blanche*, hasn't he? As long as jolly old England is not involved?"

Murphy shrugged. Nobody ever said that a thirty-year-old speech therapist was supposed to understand what was going on. "You'd better make all the notes you can about the structure and use of the English language. Unless something happens, Hitler figures that the whole world will be speaking German. You get me?"

Doc opened his mouth as if to argue the point, but a heavy knocking at the door interrupted what was proving to be an interesting discussion.

With a raised finger, Murphy warned Grogan to hold his thought while he answered the knock.

Harvey Terrill, the overworked night desk editor of TENS burst through the door. Waving an envelope, he pushed past Murphy.

"This came by special courier, Boss! Look! Look at this! Addressed to Elisa *Murry*, care of TENS London!" He slapped the envelope into Murphy's hand. He stammered on, pointing to the return address. "Lori Ibsen! Ain't that the kid who got Timmons into trouble in Berlin? The kid you been lookin' for all these months?"

Murphy turned to call for Elisa, but she was already rushing down the stairs.

"Yes!" Elisa was laughing. *"Lori!* Murphy! Call Mama! Call Aunt Helen! Oh, *Murphy!"*

7   Never Too Much for God

Charles and Louis banged on the steam radiator with a wooden spoon. This was the signal to Freddie and Hildy Frutschy in their apartment below that they were needed.

Freddie was sent in the automobile to fetch Anna and Theo and Aunt Helen while Murphy telephoned Winston Churchill with the news that the children of Pastor Ibsen were alive and well in Danzig. From there calls were made to the British home office and the decision was made that the children should be contacted through the British Consulate in Danzig.

While Hildy Frutschy made pots of coffee and tea, Harvey Terrill hurried down to the cafe to purchase a chocolate cake. Then an unplanned celebration began.

Pastor Williams arrived, and people from the church came to embrace Aunt Helen and see the letter with their own eyes. It was a miracle, it seemed, after so long! *And was there any word of Pastor Ibsen as well?*

No. The miracle was only partly complete. Lori and Jamie Ibsen had escaped Germany along with three other children, Jacob and Mark Kalner and Alfie Halder. They were all quite safe, but the letter asked if Elisa had heard from Pastor Karl and Helen Ibsen or the Kalners.

We thought to travel to Prague as Father instructed us, but now that the Nazis are there as well, we do not know where to go. There is no office for TENS news here in Danzig or we might have gone. The people here in Danzig are German, and many among them now favor Hitler. We have heard the threats of

the Nazis against Poland, and although we are well and not
threatened personally, we fear what may be coming here to
Danzig. I pray that you will receive this letter if you are still in
London, as you were when Mother spoke of you. I am not
certain of the spelling of your last name but pray this will fall
into the right hands and be directed to you. We miss our par-
ents very much. Have you any word. . . ?

Helen Ibsen sat in the rocking chair by the window and read
the letter from her daughter in English to whoever wanted to
hear it. Always at this place in the writing she cried as she had
the first time.

"My children are alive," she said. "You see? The Lord is still
in the business of miracles!" Pressing the letter to her heart she
added softly. "And if Jamie and Lori are safe, then perhaps also
my Karl, ja? It is not too much to hope for. Not too much for
God!"

―――――

Lodgings had been arranged for Allan Farrell in the Bloomsbury district of London. Mills University Hotel at 107 Gower
Street was located not far from the British museum. The charge
of fifty shillings a week for students still would have been steep
for Allan had it not been for the supplement of his meager in-
come by a modest bank account from the IRA.

The money was transferred weekly from New York as though
he had some caring benefactor in the States. *"A small stipend,"*
Colin had told him. *"Call it a reward for your assistance, if you*
like."

In truth, Allan's assignment was so insignificant that he felt
almost ashamed. He was nothing more than an errand boy, a
messenger of sorts. It was not what he had expected. It seemed
almost beneath the dignity of a son of Maureen Farrell. The stories of her exploits were still fresh in the long memories of the
Irish. She had made orphans of many Englishmen's sons in her
day and had rocked the corridors of Parliament at the mention
of her name!

Sheepishly, Allan argued with the proprietor of the Mills
Hotel over an extra weekly charge for boot cleaning and the
washing of bed linen. For the princely sum of fifty shillings a
week, such amenities should be provided as part of the service.

The proprietor cocked an eye at him and mumbled something about rich Yanks wanting everything for nothing. Allan explained that this service was listed in his guidebook and that anything less would be a breach of the printed promise. And so his still-muddy boots were placed outside the door to his small corner room. Clean sheets were promised every Monday provided the fifty shillings was paid one week in advance. One bathroom was shared by five other tenants of the boardinghouse, although Allan did have his own washbasin. Rules and regulations of the establishment were printed and posted on the door of each room. Breakfast and dinner were included in the charge. Luncheon and tea were a matter of the lodger's choice of various plain restaurants about the neighborhood.

Allan felt as though he had landed in high society after a lifetime of wondering where his next meal was coming from. All of this, and his only task was to meet with a couple of fellows who needed to exchange notes!

Allan frowned, certain that this job had been manufactured just for him because he was the son of Maureen Farrell. Like an orphan's pension, the egg-head scholar-boy was being taken care of because his mother had been a great woman.

It was a disgusting thought, one which brought a flush of shame to Allan's cheeks. *How could it be anything else?*

"I am a postman, Mother," he mumbled as he gazed out over the foot traffic of Gower Street. "Well paid for it, too. Room and board, with my boots shined each week like a gentleman."

He touched the scar beneath his eye, the scar he had gotten in Hell's Kitchen as a boy. He had worn that scar like a badge of manhood, never hinting that it had been a girl who hit him with a brick to cause that scar. Asthma had kept him small and weak as a child. Books had kept him company, filling his mind with dreams of adventure.

So here he was, the son of Maureen Farrell—an errand boy.

He shook his head slowly, certain of how this had all come to pass. *"You wrote Uncle Colin, didn't you, Mother?"* he whispered against the glass. *"Told him to look out for me?"*

It was the truth. There could be no other explanation. She was like that, Maureen was—a strong woman who got her way, even from the grave. He could almost hear the letter she must have written: *Young Allan is going to London to study. I've saved a bit . . . not a well boy, even now . . . For the sake of his pride, Colin, as a favor to me. . . .*

They had all commented on how much he favored her, had they not? She was small and delicate-looking herself. *Ah well,* Allan thought as he looked around the room, *I will do what they asked and pretend it matters to the cause all the same.* He had spent his life pretending, wishing . . . remembering he was the son of Maureen.

"I sense the imagination of the lovely Mrs. Murphy behind this request," commented Winston Churchill. "You, Murphy, are only the messenger. Isn't that so?"

"Right as always, Winston. Elisa doesn't travel far these days. As much as she enjoys coming here to Chartwell for visits, she would rather not have the baby here."

"I cannot understand why not," rumbled Churchill. "Most of my brilliant ideas are hatched right here. Why not a little Murphy? In any case, tell her that I will be very pleased to speak at a rally in support of the plight of Pastors Ibsen and Niemöller and the others. Even in their imprisonment, they continue to shine as beacons of righteousness amid the Nazi dark, and we must let them—and more importantly, Herr Hitler—know that they are not forgotten. Have you selected a location?"

"We hope that there will be an enormous turnout, so we plan to use one of the great churches. Perhaps even St. Paul's."

"And the date?"

"Elisa would like to participate in the orchestra, so she wants to allow some time after the baby's arrival—around the end of August, say."

Churchill thrust his hands deep into the pockets of his dressing gown and thrust out his jaw as he nodded. "We must trust that the Nazi terror has not given birth to the child of war before then," he said.

These were the days of arrivals and departures in Warsaw. Across the rooftops of apartments and houses, the train whistle would scream beneath the tin roof of the *Umschlagplatz*. Only a short time later the first groups of newcomers would straggle up Niska Street or Pokorna Steet to arrive with their bundles in Muranow Square.

Some came in search of relatives or old friends. Some came

100

to Warsaw because they could lose themselves among the hundreds of thousands of Poland's Jewish community. All the same, they had a different look about them than Polish Jews. Ragged bundles and cheap suitcases were carried by the lucky ones. Those less fortunate arrived wearing all their possessions. Even in the heat of summer, they bore coats slung over their shoulders or tied onto the top of a valise. The more experienced among the refugees knew that it might be hot now, but that surely a cold winter was coming for every Jew in Europe.

Rachel was sweeping the front steps when the shrill cry of the train whistle announced that shortly new people would come to Muranow Square. Over the rooftops she could see the thick gray haze from the locomotives, as though this dark cloud had come with the wanderers, following them into Warsaw to pollute the blue sky with gloom.

She was watering the rhododendrons when the first family groups reached the square from different routes. Father, mother and two little boys arrived from Niska Street. From the cut of their clothes, Rachel could tell that they were from Czechoslovakia. Only secular Jews from Prague wore caps such as the man had on his head. The woman carried a coat with a silver fox collar. *They must have been wealthy before the Germans came,* Rachel thought.

An overweight man and woman and two teenaged girls limped around the corner of Porkorna Street. *German.* It was as plain as anything. The man was red-faced and had the look of an overworked owner of a beer cellar. The faces of his wife and daughters were flushed from exertion, their mouths twisted downward with disdain and bitterness. They looked around the square at trams and trees and benches. Everything was quite different from Germany and so could not be quite as good. The girls watched as a black-coated Hassid walked by twirling his earlock thoughtfully on his finger. They stared. Such sights were not common in Germany. *Perhaps some grandfather has fled the tyranny of Orthodox life in Poland, bringing his family to live in civilized Germany,* Rachel mused as she leaned against her broom and considered them. *And now look what German civilization offers them in return! Papa says they all would eventually come back to Poland, a thousand times worse off than when they had left!*

Behind this portly German family came a tall, lean red-headed young man, his frame tilted sideways as if the weight of his battered suitcase was going to pull him over. He wore no cap. By this, Rachel knew that he was a secular Jew. Those among her people who were religious always covered their heads with some sort of hat. But this drawn-looking young man had a bare head. His red hair stuck up wildly as if to emphasize his rebellion in this small tradition. He wore a heavy camel-hair overcoat, which added some size to an otherwise thin frame.

Rachel followed him with her eyes. He was the most interesting of the new refugees. He was not much older than she was, yet he was alone. No family. No companion. So youthful, and yet alone. Such a visage spoke of tragedy and ill fortune.

In his free hand, he held a crumpled piece of paper—probably with an address or a name written on it. Had his family sent him out of Germany to the safety of relatives in Warsaw? Was his father in prison perhaps, or his mother too sick to flee the Nazi regime with him?

He looked from the paper to the street sign on the corner and then back again at the paper. His face puckered in thought. His eyes narrowed as he mopped his brow with the sleeve of his elegant coat. A fine coat, a man's coat, not originally cut for him. Rachel wondered who had owned the coat before this red-headed young man. Perhaps his father? Or his uncle? Maybe someone dragged off in the terrible pogrom of November?

Beyond them, the trains of the Umschlagplatz whistled their farewell to Warsaw. On the departing trains were Jews of Polish origin who knew Warsaw too well to consider it safe to remain. Rachel knew that they would soon be playing out this same scene on the other end of the rail line. Straggling into a city square, checking their scribbled addresses against unfamiliar street signs, shifting luggage from one weary arm to the other. . . .

By the time they realized that every place in Europe was the same for a Jew, the homes and flats they had vacated in Warsaw would be filled by these.

Rachel looked up at the slate roofs of the buildings of Muranow Square. Like the set on a theater stage, everything looked the same. The parts were simply to be played by different actors.

She turned away and looked at the facade of her home. Big and yellow, it was a bright flower among lesser blooms in the garden. She had been born here; it was the only home she had ever known. Happy times and sad times had been played out within the safety of those walls. She had looked out her window and seen the first snowfall, the first bud on the great elm trees in the square. And yet now, her mother and father dreamed of leaving this place forever—boarding a train that would carry them far away from Muranow, far away from Warsaw and Poland! But were not all places the same when the tracks finally ended and the last whistle blew?

Such thoughts filled Rachel's young heart with despair. In his fevered dreams Papa moaned about sending them away to Palestine. *"Leave me, Etta!"* he cried to Mama. *"Take the little ones before it is too late!"*

Then Mama soaked a cool cloth and dabbed his forehead, assuring him that there was still lots of time for him to get well.

Rachel traced the path of the red-haired young man, the solitary stranger with no one to walk with on the crowded street. The sight of him made her shudder, as though his visage carried some portent of her own future. *Oh, Eternal!* Her heart cried out with pity for him and pity for herself. *I do not ever want to be like him! Please! Never alone! Alone in a strange land!*

It was better to stay, she decided that afternoon. Better to sit at Papa's bedside, to know the fate of every member of her beloved family! If she were ever given the choice to flee for her life or stay in Muranow Square with her mama and papa and little brothers, Rachel knew what she would do!

She watched the young wanderer until he dodged behind a clanging train and disappeared up Niska Street past the young couple with the two small sons. Only then did she retreat to the safety of the big yellow house on Muranow.

———

There were only thirty-six men in the meeting room of Albert Forster, Danzig's top Nazi official. Wolf stood before them with Gautleiter Forster at his side. He considered the expression on the face of each man. Age and features were all different, and yet the hardness of the eyes, the nodding of heads, the sense that each man was a coiled spring gave the group an almost identical look.

"You are the core of all that will come to Danzig," Forster cried as though he were speaking to thousands. "Only thirty-six men, and yet you are chosen to represent a thousand! You thirty-six will change the history of Danzig and so the history of the world as we know it forever!"

Forster paused, just as Wolf had heard the Führer pause for his audience to fire themselves further with applause and cheers. *Albert Forster is good,* Wolf thought. Berlin had made the right choice in this man. He had mastery over his officers. He lit a fire in their hearts with the promises he echoed from faraway Berlin! *They would make a difference! They would rid their world of Untermenschen. Danzig—and indeed all the East—must be scraped clean and purified by fire for the New World!*

The cheering died reluctantly, and Forster introduced Wolf as the personal emissary of the leaders of the Reich. More cheering erupted. The thirty-six hooted as if they were thirty-six thousand strong! Wolf let them yell, let them break into the Horst Wessel song and scrape back their chairs to stand at proud attention. He sang with them. He raised his arm to the swastika flag on the standard at the front of the room. Among these men he was not the quiet wine merchant on business in Danzig. He was the personal representative of the Führer. Wolf enjoyed the heady feeling of his own power.

The song ended. The thirty-six Brownshirts took their seats and waited in utter silence to hear what the spirit of Hitler would say through the mouth of Major Wolfgang von Fritschauer. Wolf let them wait. . . .

"In the name of Adolf Hitler, I greet you. *You,* who have been waiting here in Danzig for this final release! *You,* who have watched from afar the slow progression of the Reich across the land. I tell you now that *you* now are given the key of all power to unlock the door for the German race and their leader!"

The silence was profound, as though a holy rite were taking place.

Wolf began again. His Prussian accent was closer to the dialect of these men than to that of the party leaders in Berlin. Wolf recognized the profound effect this had on the thirty-six.

"The Führer has declared that Danzig must be united with Germany. Poland and England and France now say that such an event will result in war." Again he paused, letting the word *war* take effect. Stronger than love, stronger than hate, war stirred the passion and imagination of young men like nothing else, just as the idea of motherhood for the state had captured the hearts of the young men as their rite of passage. Bad music and bad reasons all sounded good and righteous and able beneath the banner of race and blood-brotherhood! To savor the bread broken with comrades made the values of war not only acceptable, but desirable. The Führer knew the hearts of his people well.

"For the sake of the German folk and German culture, the Führer sends you this promise: There will be war! War against the enemies of the Aryan people! It is inevitable, comrades. And it will begin here. With *you*! *In Danzig!*"

And so it was said. The Port of Danzig was not negotiable. Poland and England and France had thrown down the gauntlet. They had finally drawn a line, faint and uncertain though it was. The Führer had determined to step over it, and soon. These thirty-six, and thousands behind them, would provide the front line division when the moment arrived.

The certainty of it was a relief. All the youth of Germany had been impregnated by the great god of war. And now, here in Danzig, the bloody child of Death was about to be born.

It was a moment of deep reflection for the few gathered in the little room. Like apostles, they had been chosen to stir the hearts of their young soldiers to follow the crusade! There was no man in attendance who did not feel blessed by some vast force at that moment, filled by some unexplained power, lifted by the dark glory of blood and death!

"You have heard the words of the Führer. If there is to be a war, then let it begin on this issue . . . *Danzig!* Even as he meets the challenge of our enemies, he looks to *you*, depends on *your* loyalty and dedication!"

The rest of the meeting drifted into the practical mechanics of beginning a war. Demonstrations must increase within the Free City of Danzig. The summer must be marred by wave after wave of boycotts and strikes by dock workers and transit employees. Those who did not cooperate must be dealt with severely. German deaths must be attributed to the Polish government and, above all, violence must be pushed to such a degree that Poland would be required to act with force against these leaders and their men.

Yes, they would face death. They themselves might be martyrs to the cause of *One Reich, One Volk, One Führer!* In that they would find a kind of eternal life; eternal memory.

Planned demonstrations must appear spontaneous and widely separated throughout the territory. When Poland stepped in, the German battleships would be standing ready in the gulf of Danzig.

———

Once again the wine merchant, Wolf slipped out the back door of Albert Forster's offices. The long, low bellow of a fog-horn sounded in the dark harbor. The port was quiet, but Wolf knew that even now an entire fleet of U-boats prowled beneath the Baltic Sea just outside of Danzig.

The streets of the city seemed deserted as well, and yet Wolf felt the presence of something . . . *someone* . . . watching him from the shadows. *British agents? French? Polish?* It did not matter. Let them watch and speculate on the late-night meeting of the German wine merchant with Albert Forster. Let them put whatever meaning they desired on it. If it stirred them to action against the ever-growing Nazi party in Danzig, then that act would only speed the beginning of the war. So much the better. Wolf was impatient. All of Germany was impatient. The baying of hounds had gone on too long for the liking of any hunter. It was time for blood to color the landscape. Let it come quickly.

———

All that was left was the title page. Orde stared at the blank sheet of paper for a moment and then printed in block letters the title of his *magnum opus*:

MILITARY TRAINING MANUAL
JEWISH DEFENSE FORCES
OF THE NATION OF ISRAEL
Compiled by
CAPT. SAMUEL ORDE, *In service to his King*

Never mind that there was no nation of Israel. Never mind that British Parliament had gone back on every promise it had ever made to the Jewish people since 1917. Parliament was not the last word, and the King whom Orde served was not the king of England.

No training manual for any army had ever been written quite like this one. Not only was it filled with practical firsthand knowledge about the art of desert warfare, it was reinforced with passages of Scripture, reminders of ancient battles in this same land and the covenant an unchanging God had made with His chosen people.

Now it was finished. Orde laid down his pen and wrapped the two hundred hand-written pages in butcher paper from the Hanita kibbutz kitchen. He tied up the precious package with twine and scrawled across the front: *For my brothers and sisters, my adopted family by the great blessing of our one Lord and King.* He signed his Hebrew name, *Hayedid. The Friend.*

Orde took one last look around the tent he had made his headquarters. He had known what was coming. His heart had warned him, although his mind had resisted. Every additional day he had spent with his men had been a gift. But now the gift of time had run out. Orde felt somehow that all his life had been spent in preparing him for these few months with what he believed was the foundation of an army for a nation yet to be reborn. This was the beginning for them. But what was it for him? What purpose would his life hold now?

He tucked the manuscript under his arm as though it contained orders from the highest general. Perhaps it did, he thought, tugging his beret into its proper angle.

At any rate, the manual was his legacy—his gift of every minute scrap of knowledge he had gleaned from his career as a fighting man. He closed his eyes a moment and prayed that it would be enough to sustain these men he loved, as well as those who followed after them and fought for the survival of the Jewish people. In his prayer, Sam Orde offered back to God what had been given to him. He asked no further blessing on his own life. He felt that he had been set aside by his King; now his life had no further purpose except to float and spin away the time he had left to live.

The skies above Galilee were bright, but Orde felt only darkness above him as he passed down the long line of his troops. They stood proudly at attention as he had taught them the first day he was with them. Now, instead of ragged work clothes, they wore clean pressed khakis for the occasion of their farewell. On their heads were the jaunty Australian bush hats that Orde had demanded from British ordnance and gotten after months of badgering.

Zach Zabinski called for the troops to salute Hayedid a final time. Orde returned the honor and then passed the manuscript into Zabinski's hands as one dying soldier might pass a standard to another.

"It is all there, Zach," he said in a low voice. "God willing, I will come back someday and review the troops of a proper nation." He managed a smile. *"Baruch Hashem."*

Zach saluted again, then tucked the manual beneath his arm as Orde had carried it. How everything had changed because of this one man! They had survived the most terrible of all winters and then a bloody spring because of Samuel Orde.

"Baruch Hashem, dear Hayedid. Shalom to you."

Charles carried Elisa's violin case into the TENS office. Murphy had told her not to carry anything but the baby, and so the boys had enthusiastically taken their chief at his word. They fetched glasses of water, cleared the supper table of dishes, swept the steps and, today, took turns cradling the cherished violin on their way to meet Murphy for lunch.

Murphy's face looked *growly,* as Elisa described it. Charles could clearly see him through the glass partition of his office as they moved through the bustling desks of the journalists.

"Lousy news from Palestine, Mrs. Murphy," one of the younger men called.

"What's with you, Jack?" chided another. "You always have to be the first with the bad news? That's sick!"

"That's why he's a journalist!"

"Ah, you're all sick!"

Smiling through the barrage of American banter, Elisa guided the boys past hands that reached out to muss their hair and sticks of gum tossed their way.

She knocked timidly on the glass door. Murphy was talking angrily to Harvey Terrill and waving a slip of paper in the air.

"So get hold of Mike Tracy in Cairo, that's all!" Murphy said, and then he motioned Elisa and the boys to enter as Harvey slipped out past them with a pained look on his face.

"What's all this about?" Elisa asked, giving him a kiss as he hefted the boys onto his desk.

"Nothing. Well, *something*, but we'll manage."

"Palestine? Jerusalem?" Elisa asked anxiously as Charles looked at Murphy's face for a clue. Leah and Shimon Feldstein were in Palestine. There was a war in Palestine. Just this morning

Elisa had read them some parts of a letter from Leah. She had skipped others, in spite of the fact that Charles and Louis had begged for every word to be read. And now the men in the newsroom had mentioned Palestine.

"First the good news. There's a truce. Temporary to be sure, but the fighting has stopped. The bad news is strictly business. We've just lost our best correspondent in Palestine."

"You only have one."

"Right. Samuel Orde."

"Dead?" Elisa gasped.

"Not killed. Just reprimanded and posted out of Palestine by the British Army. He'll be on his way back to England at the strong insistence of the Arab Higher Committee."

"Oh. I'm sorry." Elisa did not sound very sorry, Charles thought. She sounded more relieved than anything. She was smiling again, talking about a BBC concert rehearsal and ordinary things like how she and Anna and Helen found perfect wallpaper for the baby's room. But Charles and Louis knew the big secret!

Murphy took his coat and hat from the rack and herded them out to the maze of desks where Freddie waited beneath the awning while a steady rain pelted the slick cobbles.

"Will y' be long, sar?" Freddie shook drops of rain from the shoulders of his slicker. "The missus has a few things for me to pick up."

Murphy gladly released their toothless giant to the task of running errands. Freddie's wife, Hildy, had taken up the additional duties as cook for them for the last few weeks, while Freddie had provided an imposing wall of protection for Elisa, Anna, and the boys. This arrangement seemed ideal.

"Take the rest of the afternoon if you like. I'll see Elisa home."

Freddie was granted use of the automobile, and the hungry foursome hugged the facades of the buildings on Threadneedle Street as they hurried through the pouring rain. It was a short walk to the one pub in London where nearly every patron spoke American and thought American and was, in fact, American. Murphy liked the place because of its familiarity to his homeland. Elisa and the boys liked it because it was quite different from any other atmosphere in London.

The publican was an Irishman who had multiple cousins in America, and so was forever up-to-date on the latest stateside news. He had letters from nearly every major U.S. metropolis and could pull them from under the counter at will to recite the home-front news to homesick Americans.

As the foursome entered the close-packed room, the publican was reading the latest news about the IRA bombing. He looked up and spotted Murphy, then hailed him as one Irishman to another.

"The British hate us, y' know, brother Murphy!"

"Can you blame them?" Murphy called back cheerfully.

At that, a dozen greetings were shouted out from various booths which lined the dark paneled wall, separated by wood partitions inset with beveled glass. Brass gas lamps had been converted to electricity and illuminated each table with poor light and shadows that concealed the faces of the diners. The whole place buzzed like a Waterloo railway station, and the smells of smoke mingled with the aroma of fish and chips and warm ale.

Everyone towered over Charles and Louis. People whom they had never met before greeted them as if they were related. Elisa explained that this was not bad manners, but simply an American eccentricity. It was okay with Charles. He had decided long before that he liked Americans a lot. He just smiled a gap-toothed smile and shouted "Hi'ya" right back at them. Helen, Theo, and Anna sat in the back corner booth. Their faces in shadow, it was hard to see them until Theo shifted in his seat and the light brushed over his amused features.

Murphy raised his hand and inched toward them as a stranger brushed by and remarked, "Hey, we got Krauts back there now. Whole place is being taken over by the Nazis, wouldn't you know?"

Murphy ignored him and pushed on. Now he could see that Anna was smiling broadly. It was an expression Murphy had not seen on her face for a long time.

"What's up?" he asked as they slid into the booth.

"Good news!" Theo proclaimed. "Or . . . maybe you have already heard?"

"I'm the last to hear anything. You know that." It was clear from the smug expression on Elisa's face that she also knew the news but had waited until now to share.

"*I* know," Charles giggled.

Murphy feigned unhappiness. "Everybody knows but me,

110

then. Not a good recommendation for the chief of a news bureau, is it?" He had already guessed that the news concerned Helen Ibsen's attempt to contact her children. Smiles all around could mean only one thing.

"Tell him, Helen," Anna urged her sister.

Helen opened her mouth as if to speak, but tears of joy and gratitude choked off the words. "Anna?" she asked.

"All right then." Murphy put on his best newsman scowl. "We've got a deadline, you know. An hour for lunch. Somebody tell me."

Charles raised his hand as Doc Grogan had taught him when he had the answer. Louis' hand went up higher.

"Okay, Charles."

The news exploded from him. "The kids!"

Louis followed. "In Danzig!"

"They was on the telephone!"

"All the way from Danzig."

Suddenly everyone was talking at once. They were all fine. Not hungry or ragged. They lived in a two-room apartment in the older district of the city. Terribly homesick for Helen, they wanted only to get to England as quickly as possible. Theo had already wired funds through American Express to take care of steamer tickets the minute their papers were in order.

"I know Karl has been praying for them," Helen finished the story softly. Her hands trembled as she fingered her soup spoon. "He has prayed, and soon our children will be home."

8 By Dying I Conquer

Before today, Sam Orde had not realized how many prized possessions he had accumulated in three years of service in Jerusalem. Now, each precious item he had purchased in the souks or unearthed on Mount Zion posed a problem for him. How could he take them all with him to England?

Two packing crates were allotted to him. Two were not enough. They sat open and empty on the stone floor of his quarters in the Old City barracks. His cot was cluttered with an assortment of notebooks and rare volumes, ancient maps and parchments gleaned from the antique shops. The smaller things were of no concern. Arrow tips from the archers of Rome. Half a dozen coins from the time of Christ. A stone inkwell discovered near the ruins of an ancient synagogue. Orde stuffed these items into his empty boots.

But how to carry the two rare Persian prayer rugs? And the shofar in the inlaid mahogany box? And the silver menorah candlestick cast in the shape of an oak tree by a long-forgotten Jewish silversmith? His carved desk?

He sat down heavily and sighed. His gaze lingered on a square hand-hewn block of Jerusalem stone against his wall. Long ago marking the resting place of some fallen Crusader, the stone was carved with a cross and bore the chiseled Latin inscription *BY DYING I CONQUER LIFE.* Orde had found it face down among the boulder-strewn rubble at the foot of the Mount of Olives. With the permission of Mother Superior at the Russian convent, he had carried the stone away, cleaned it, and spent many long hours wondering about the man who had lain beneath it. This odd reminder of his own mortality had become his most cherished possession. At one hundred pounds, its weight alone exceeded the limits imposed on personal shipping for the military. His Majesty's government could not be expected, after all, to make room for personal goods on military shipping. Otherwise, every retiring staff sergeant and major would be returning home with enough goods to open an antique store in Bloomsbury.

Somehow, Orde had not imagined that the stone would ever be a problem. He remained in Jerusalem with the feeling that he would be buried here one day, that the ancient Crusader stone would mark his grave as well.

"By dying I conquer life," he whispered, feeling the sting of being singled out as the example of British military folly for the Arab Council. Indeed, at this moment, he considered how much easier it might have been to have died with honor, to conquer unjust life by falling in this undeclared war. He ran his fingers through his close-cropped brown hair and looked around the small room that had been his home for three years. Nobody ever said that life was fair. Better a captain than a colonel, after all. And banishment back to England and the end of a military career was not the absolute end of everything.

Orde glanced over his things and considered his alternatives. The Army might rob him of his occupation, but he would not be forced to leave his belongings behind. He would travel by private freighter rather than military transport. Tomorrow he would buy a steamer trunk and purchase his own passage. By the time he reached England, his commission would be up. He would step onto the soil of his homeland as an ordinary citizen. No use spending another two weeks saluting and *yes-sirring*!

The decision made, Orde relaxed a bit. He fixed himself a cup of tea on a small camp stove, then set to work packing his books.

An hour passed, and a timid knocking sounded at his door.

"Cap'n, sar," called the melancholy voice of the Irish Corporal Hobbs. "Thar's an ol' rabbi here t' see y', sar!"

Since hearing the news about Orde's misfortune, Corporal Hobbs had gone about his duties with a catch in his voice and a tear in his baleful eye. This overdone sympathy irritated Orde, and so he fixed a broad smile on his face before throwing open the door. Hobbs towered over the diminutive form of Rabbi Shlomo Lebowitz. The old rabbi looked past Orde at the cluttered mess and the packing crates behind him. Hobbs shrugged, half saluted and left the rabbi and Orde alone.

"Come in, Rebbe Lebowitz. I cannot offer you a place to sit, but perhaps a cup of tea?" At the sight of the old man, Orde was filled again with a sense of regret. How he had grown to love these peculiar people of the covenant!

The rabbi's face registered dismay. "You are going someplace, Captain Orde?" He stepped into the small cubicle and swept his eyes over the disarray.

"Home to England," Orde managed to say lightly.

The rabbi was silent for a long, awkward moment. "We heard. Hermann Sachar was notified by the British high commissioner's office that the investigation proves you are at fault in some way for the death of his son Eli. A good boy. But noodles for brains to go to the Temple Mount on such a day, God rest his soul." The rabbi extended a crooked hand in sympathy. "The boy was meshugge. Herbert does not blame you. We in the Old City do not blame you. A letter has been sent to the high commissioner telling him so. You have been a good man here, Samuel Orde."

113

All pretense melted away. Orde stood grim but grateful before the old man. "You sent a *letter*?" he said quietly.

"And such a letter! You should unpack! They would not send you away after such a letter!"

Orde did not answer for a moment. "Yes, Rebbe Lebowitz. I fear they have made up their minds. It's England for the likes of me."

"But how can they—" the old rabbi sputtered indignantly.

"It is not for the sake of the Jewish community that I am blamed. The Arab Council, you see. They cannot carry all the fault for the riots. It is not politically wise."

Rebbe Lebowitz let his breath out in a slow, indignant sigh. He tugged his beard. "I thought the Englishmen were above such things."

Now Orde smiled. "Why ever did you think that?"

The rabbi tapped his temple. "I am crazy also, nu?"

"Well, I appreciate your craziness. And your support. I shall ask for a copy of your letter. Perhaps it will help me feel better, at any rate." Orde lit the camp stove and placed the kettle on to boil. Then he cleared a place on his cot for the old man he had come to consider a friend.

Rebbe Lebowitz sat stiffly on the edge of the cot and frowned at the packing crate. "What will you do? More soldiering? Somewhere else?"

"I'm afraid that option is not open to me."

The old man's eyes flashed with indignation. British injustice was full-blown, indeed. "Well then. The Lord and Master must have something else in mind for you." He pressed his lips tightly together. "Yesterday I was coming here to ask you for help when I heard what they had done to you. Such a man should not be treated so badly, I said. But what is right is often forgotten by what is convenient."

"Well spoken, Rabbi." Orde poured the tea and set a bowl of sugar on the crate before his guest.

"So the English are not in the mood for mercy or justice, eh?"

Orde noticed that the rabbi's hands trembled as he spoke. No doubt the old man had also heard of the decision of the Woodhead Commission to limit Jewish immigration to a mere handful each year until 1945, when immigration was scheduled to stop entirely. Had the judgment affected the old man's hope of bringing his family to Palestine?

"Any word about your daughter in Warsaw?" Orde asked gently.

The old man nodded once. He placed his cup back on the crate and pulled a long white envelope from his coat pocket.

"The quotas are filled. Imagine." He shook his head slowly. Orde's situation was momentarily forgotten. There were other matters of justice to discuss. The rabbi's face was pained. "My son-in-law was accused of plotting. He was in prison in Warsaw. He is just a rabbi, but they call him a threat to the community. He was released because of illness. England will not have him here in the Mandate. It seems . . ." His voice fell. "There is no appeal. Like for you, nu? Somebody always has to be accused. Otherwise the guilty will be discovered."

The old man absently opened the envelope and removed the useless passport photos of his daughter and her family. He held them reverently in his hand for a moment and then placed them one by one on the crate beside his teacup. He sighed as he looked at them, and Orde sensed that he was witnessing a private moment of longing in the old rabbi's eyes.

"My Etta." He tapped the photograph of his daughter. "Of course you cannot see how blue her eyes are in a picture, but I tell you . . . such blue."

Orde smiled in agreement. "She is lovely." There was no exaggeration in the statement. Orde did not need to agree out of mere politeness. Even with the austerity of a black-and-white photo, Orde could see how beautiful Etta was. Her slender neck and finely sculpted face were framed with raven black hair. Her skin was pale and smooth.

The depth within the clear gaze of her eyes made him think that in a moment her lips would form a word and she would nod her head and smile at him. He touched the corner of the photograph with his finger. "She is a real person," he muttered, amazed at the thought that this same woman was indeed flesh.

The rabbi smiled. The Jewishness of Orde's statement amused him. "Yes," he agreed, "Etta is a person. A *mensch*, my Etta is." He tapped the other faces in turn, "And these are also little persons. Here is Rachel, the oldest. Samuel. David. And our youngest, little Yacov. Yani, they call him. Here is the papa, Aaron. Before his arrest. Even a rabbi they make to shave his beard in Polish prisons, I am told." He shook his head. "Ah, well. The Poles may tear out our beards, but they cannot steal what is

115

in here!" He thumped his chest defiantly. "There must have been many Jews in prison who need a rabbi, nu? Even one without a beard." He was not speaking to Orde but to himself and to Etta and her children. He fell silent. His eyes were moist. "I would like to hold the little one while he is still a baby," he finished. "But maybe these days they are safer in Poland than in Palestine." He managed a *who-knows* shrug and reached to gather up his little family.

Orde put a hand on the old man's arm to stop him. It was an impulse, probably foolish, but Orde did not want to see the matter fade away in the dusty archives of British immigration files. "I know some people in England." He paused, checking the impulse for a moment, not wanting to raise the hopes of the old man unless there was a possibility. "Perhaps I could put in a word for your daughter's case. After all, she was born here. Your son-in-law was educated in British Palestine. They have some claim, some right, it seems to me."

Rebbe Lubetkin raised his chin as if in thought. He nodded slowly and smiled from behind his beard. "This was the very matter I was coming to discuss with you yesterday. We should not let this matter die, I said to the Eternal! Maybe Captain Samuel Orde could help to find a way! After all, he is an Englishman and can navigate the hidden tracks of the English mind! So! I was hoping for this. Praying for your help." He reinserted the photographs into the envelope and then pulled out a thicker envelope from his pocket. "All the papers are here, you see. I brought them . . . *just in case.*"

The day was warm in Warsaw. Etta Lubetkin opened the windows wide and let the scents and sounds of summer into the house on Muranow Square.

Rachel looked out at the green leaves on the trees that lined the square. She had not noticed when the trees had bloomed or when the leaves covered the branches. It was as though Mama had opened the window and suddenly it was summer. Had spring ever come this year?

Sunlight filtered through the trees, dappling the cobbles like light dancing on the waters of the Vistula River. Trams and autos moved like ships. People skipped along like little sailboats scudding through the traffic. Suddenly Rachel wished she was out among the bustle.

Did Mama hear her thoughts?

"Rachel, your papa has said he would like a sugared roll from Menkes' Bakery. Nothing else will do for him at all, he says."

This was a good sign. Papa's favorite treat had always been the sugared sweet rolls from Menkes'. He had not even asked for one since his release from prison. When Mama had put one on his tray, he had not touched it or commented on it. And now, it was as though his appetite had blossomed like the trees, without any explanation. Just like that! A sweet roll from Menkes'!

Rachel sailed out into the sun, watching her own cheerful shadow with pleasure. Up ahead two Hassidim chatted as they strolled together, their black coats flapping like the wings of birds. When Rachel looked at their shadows she could imagine that the coats were a dozen bright colors, like the cloaks of patriarchs. Like Joseph's coat of many colors.

And what color should she paint her shadow? Maybe her skirt was bright red instead of dull and somber blue. Or maybe yellow with orange flowers on it? Such thoughts were not fitting, perhaps, but they seemed to match the brightness of the day.

Here and there mothers pushed their babies in prams, while other children clung to their mother's skirts and sucked their thumbs. Two bent old men shuffled past a group of young boys on their way home from Torah school who stopped to pet the milk-cart horse.

David and Samuel would be returning from school to Frau Groshenki's house soon. Rachel fingered the coins in her pocket. Mama had instructed her to purchase enough sweet rolls for the boys, to drop them off, in honor of the return of Papa's appetite.

Every few paces someone called her name, asking how her papa was and if anything was needed.

"I'm going for sweet rolls at Menkes'!"

"The rabbi is feeling better, then!" Everyone knew what Papa's favorite treat was.

Rachel pushed through the door of the warm, yeasty-smelling bakery. His hands full of a flat tray filled with warm bread, the baker looked up, surprised to see her.

"Sholem aleichem, Rachel." He slid the tray onto a rack,

then wiped his flour-coated hands on his likewise floured apron.

"Aleichem sholem," Rachel said. She felt like laughing. Baker Menkes had flour even on his bald head. His big ears stuck out like wings. Had she ever noticed that he looked more like a prize fighter than a baker? She decided that she had never noticed anything at all before today. She had been asleep her entire life, but now it was almost summer after a terrible winter. . . .

"Did you forget something?"

She had been here only yesterday afternoon. Had she noticed how good it smelled then? "No," she answered, looking at the buns stacked in neat rows along the top rack. Their tops were thick with a crust of glistening sugar and cinnamon. "Papa is better," she said and his eyes followed her gaze to the rabbi's favorite treat.

Baker Menkes clapped his powdered hands together. He had sent home a sugared roll free with every purchase each time Rachel had come for bread. It had always been untouched by Papa, and so Rachel and Mama had shared it. *But today!*

"The Eternal be praised!" the Baker exclaimed. "A dozen for the good Rebbe Lubetkin! *No, no!* Put away your money! This is for your papa with my blessings!"

Mama would not like it if Rachel did not also buy something from Baker Menkes after such a generous gift. She studied the rows of cookies. The eclairs. The strudels. She would buy something wonderful to take to David and Samuel.

Baker Menkes' eyes flitted up and out the window. His pleasant gaze clouded slightly; the smile faltered, vanished, and when he looked back at Rachel, a preoccupied expression remained on his face. "Anything else?"

She looked over her shoulder as a freight wagon loaded with expensive furniture rumbled past. Muranow Square was filled with such wagons these days. People moving away. People moving in from all over. Why had Baker Menkes made such a face?

The wagon passed like a curtain. On the other side stood the young man in his heavy camel-hair coat. In this weather? His red hair stuck up wildly. His face was thin; too thin for the broad shoulders of the coat he wore. In his hand he carried a scuffed valise. He was staring hard through the window of the bakery. That was why Baker Menkes had frowned. *Hunger* was standing on the sidewalk across from this house of plenty. It was common, but disquieting all the same. The young man was not dressed in the fashion of Poland. He certainly did not fit the pattern of a Warsaw Jew. Maybe German? There were plenty of them streaming into Warsaw these days.

"German," Rachel muttered, suddenly noticing that her own feeling of lightness had vanished, just as Baker Menkes' smile had done a moment before.

"He was out there three days ago," said Menkes. "And then day *before* yesterday. *And* yesterday. His face keeps getting thinner until now there is not much there but hair and eyes. I gave him bread yesterday." He shrugged. "Told him to go to the Community Center at the synagogue. He said he was not religious and did not believe in a Supreme Being. Therefore, how could he take charity from the synagogue, he asked?" Menkes shrugged. "I told him if he was hungry one piece of bread was as holy as another. So here he is again. I won't feed him. He can go to the Community Soup Kitchen. Either that, or I will end up with a stray on my step forever more."

Rachel did not look at the stray again. She sighed and pulled her attention back to the display of strudel. Something for the entire Groshenki household would be suitable. After all, the Groshenki family had put up baby Yani, David, and Samuel ever since Papa had come home.

"There." She tapped the glass. "That big one."

Baker Menkes pulled out the largest of the strudels, wrapped it happily and said he had been saving it just for her today. For this, he let her pay. But he would not take one penny for the sweet rolls.

The transaction complete, Rachel left the shop. The scarecrow redhead who had been across the street was gone now, as though he had sensed Baker Menkes' comments to Rachel. She scanned the crowded square in search of him. He would have been easy to pick out, but he had melted away and suddenly Rachel noticed that there were many more just like him all around. Some sat on curbsides. Others leaned against lamp posts or shaded themselves beneath the awnings of shops. Certainly all had the same lean and hungry look as the red-haired young man. Why did they torture themselves by loitering so near the mouth-watering smells emanating from the bakery? The baker was right not to feed just one. He would have soon taken over the job of the charity soup kitchen.

The package of rolls and strudel felt heavy in her hand.

There was so much in her package, and so many hungry eyes looking at it!

She quickened her pace and looked at her dancing shadow again. It was just a shadow after all. Like the new green leaves on the trees, the homeless beggars seemed to have suddenly bloomed in Warsaw.

Tutoring sessions had taken on an interesting dimension since the children's ships had begun to come to England. On Thursday afternoon, Dr. Grogan gathered not only Charles and Louis under his wing, but a dozen other sad-faced young boys and girls as well, herding them off to the weekly scheduled London field trips.

Charles and Louis, who had been almost everywhere in London at least once, were at the head of the double line. Following Doc Grogan like newly hatched ducklings, the silent group entered the enormous courtyard of the British Museum. Of the dozen new hatchlings, not one spoke a word of English. Their eyes reflected the heartbreaking wonder of children who had spent a lifetime being shut out of public places in Germany.

Grogan walked backward, waving his hands like a conductor over their heads as he explained everything first in their own language and then in English. Charles and Louis enjoyed the introduction of the German language to their tour. Doc had always spoken to them only in English. It was much easier to understand everything when it was explained twice. Charles decided that this would be his best visit to the museum ever.

The broad steps and high double row of columns of the entrance were reminiscent of the great museum in Berlin. A dozen heads turned in fearful unison to gape at the blue uniforms of the bobbies on duty at the top of the steps. Were they there to keep Jewish children out? Were the wonders beyond the doors for English school children only?

"It is free to get in," Louis called in German over his shoulder, as though he were the guide and giver of this great gift.

"Now tell them in English, Charles," Doc instructed as he tipped his hat to the guard and smiled.

"It . . . don't cost—"

"*Doesn't* cost . . ."

"Uh-huh . . . It's free and everybody can go in." He felt as if

120

he owned a piece of the museum when he said that. It was a good feeling.

Still, the ducklings looked worried as they entered the vast portals of the British Museum.

"It is the greatest in the world," Doc said with dignity. So much for Hitler's claims about Aryan culture being the greatest! The museums in all of Germany put together did not have even one-tenth the Egyptian mummies that were right here!

"Let's take them . . ." Charles pronounced his words very carefully, even though their companions could not tell if he was speaking exactly right nor not.

"Take them where?" Doc knew where, but he insisted that it be said.

"To see the mummies."

"To see Ginger!" Louis cried.

So much for the ancient Greek urns, Roman busts and Etruscan bronzes. Pottery, seals, and hieroglyphic characters of the Hittites held little fascination to a tribe of homesick six-year-olds.

It was enough to troop through the endless rooms of ancient artifacts. The sheer enormity of carved pillars from the walls of Assyria were impressive without having to be understood.

Charles and Louis were correct in their assessment of what was guaranteed to make a smash hit for the day. Proceeding straight on to the main staircase and the Northern Gallery, passing through the second Egyptian room and turning left, they entered *Ginger's room*. . . .

All eyes suddenly brightened with fascination. In case A lay *Ginger*, a favorite mummy of Charles and Louis. As withered as a piece of old shoe leather, the little man had a shock of ginger-colored hair and was billed as "the oldest dead man on earth."

Impressive! Now this was a museum worth visiting! Certainly the greatest on earth—who could argue?

Dr. Grogan explained that the fellow had been found buried in the sand; quite possibly he was one of the Hebrew slaves in Egypt. Or perhaps the fellow Moses had killed and buried?

This filled the air with a series of *oooh's* and *ahhhh's*. It gave the exhibit a familiar feeling, because everyone knew about Moses killing the Egyptian. That was back when Egyptians were like Nazis.

Jews were in trouble then, too.

So this was the fellow? Mummies, mummy cases and coffins

were all on display in cases around the walls. Not exactly what the ancient Egyptians had in mind when they sketched the blueprints for the pyramids, to be sure. *A nice Thursday afternoon outing for the young descendants of the slaves who built the great monuments of Egypt. . . .*

Doc Grogan was Moses for the afternoon, guiding them in two hours through a museum where a person could wander forty years if he made a wrong turn.

The most important lesson of the day was the introduction of the lavatories at the end of the tour. *G-LAV for gentlemen. L-LAV for ladies.*

All of *this,* and no officer ever once questioned their right to be there! Afterward, there was ice cream for everyone and a short ride on the London tube.

It was here all along, just across the English Channel. Right here, a few hours from the German Chancellery and the offices of the Gestapo!

There were reminders of Germany all around London, of course, from the sandbags against the sides of the museum to the civil defense posters on the monument to Lord Nelson in Trafalgar Square. But it felt quite different here!

In Germany, the beggars and poor people had been rounded up and shipped off to camps. Today, everyone noticed the blind beggar at the entrance to the tube. He stood with his cup in his hand and a sign around his neck, *I AM BLIND.* In Germany it would have been an offense to place money in his cup. And so it was an amazing thing to see Doc Grogan press a bill into the beggar's hand and wish him good luck. The group of ducklings watched the blind man tap his way down the sidewalk, right under the nose of a policeman! *And the blind man was not arrested!* This was as interesting as Ginger, the mummy Moses killed! Indeed, England seemed to be the promised land to every child that afternoon.

"Maybe next week," Charles said to Doc, "we will go show them the zoo."

From his vantage point in the reporter's gallery, Murphy looked over the heads of the members of Parliament and suppressed a yawn. Prime Minister Chamberlain had been droning on at great length, defending his government's inability to put together a defense agreement with Soviet Russia.

Murphy wondered how Chamberlain could speak so much about *not* doing something. The thrust of the speech seemed to be that complete inactivity was preferable to false starts. The Russians, Chamberlain suggested, wanted a broader mutual defense agreement than Great Britain should entertain.

His attention wandering away from the bland speech, Murphy's gaze traveled the seventy-five-foot length of the hall and up to the clock on the south wall. Around the clock face were grouped nineteen coats of arms—an odd number, to be sure.

Murphy had once asked Winston Churchill what the decorations meant. Churchill had explained that the crests honored the memories of the nineteen members of Parliament who had given their lives in the Great War. Churchill had added, with a loud clearing of his throat, that he hoped that the brave men who had paid the highest sacrifice for their country's stand against German aggression would not be "revolving in their sepulchers" as their banners overheard the present government's shilly-shallying.

Thinking about Churchill's comments made Murphy scan the chamber for him. The statesman was drumming his fingers on the bench beside him as he waited for Chamberlain to finish.

When the Prime Minister at last concluded his prepared remarks, Murphy expected Churchill to jump to the attack. Instead, Churchill deferred to his old mentor and colleague, David Lloyd George.

Lloyd George began by saying that Chamberlain's foot-dragging did not come from reasonable caution, but from a continued reluctance to antagonize Germany by being friendly toward Russia. The older statesman drew both chuckles and hisses when he hinted that Chamberlain's policy owed more to snobbery than to practical considerations.

So far, it was pretty mild criticism in Murphy's opinion, but Chamberlain's critics were just warming up. Lloyd George added that Russia had been willing to sign an agreement for months and was only waiting for a signal that Great Britain was ready to be serious. Anthony Eden firmly pointed out that any alliance intended to prevent aggression which did not include Russia would not be strong enough to prevent a war. Others continued attacking the lack of progress.

Finally Churchill rose to speak. In measured phrases he intoned, "Should war come to Europe, the success of a western front cannot be guaranteed without an eastern front, in which Russia must take part. No eastern front means no western front, and perhaps . . ." He paused ominously. "No west."

Hisses and cries of "Shame, shame" erupted from the benches of Chamberlain's supporters. When the hubbub died down, a voice behind Chamberlain demanded, "How can we trust Moscow?"

Churchill's reply was delivered over the top of his reading glasses, with the air of a master correcting an erring pupil. "In Moscow," he said, "the question is, 'How can we trust Chamberlain?' "

9 The Gifted Ones

Elisa sat beside Helen Ibsen in the small, cramped office of Harold Weyland, case officer in charge of the immigration of Lori and Jamie Ibsen.

Weyland was a bulky, bespectacled man with gray strands of hair combed over the top of his bald head. He wore a blue bow tie and a brown suit that looked as though it belonged to someone of a much smaller size. His white shirt strained at each buttonhole as if one more bite of the half-eaten sandwich on his desk would explode a volley of buttons around the cluttered cubicle. His eyes blinked like a telegraph as he studied the sheaf of information regarding the case. Except for the distant clack of typewriters penetrating the frosted glass of the office door, his wheezing breath was the only sound in the room.

Elisa sat very straight, as though she were in concert. Baby Murphy was doing his usual tap dance along the bottom of her rib cage. She folded her hands on what remained of her lap and silently wished the interview were over.

At last Weyland scanned Lori's letter from Danzig. He raised his eyes, looked at Elisa's stomach suspiciously and frowned, as though he feared she would have the baby right here in his cramped office.

"Mrs. Murphy. . ."

The silence was at last broken! "Yes?"

"You are married to an American." The tone was clipped, impatient.

"That's right. Bureau chief of London TENS. American news—"

He held up a hand to cut her off. "And this is your aunt?" He nodded toward Helen. "And these are your cousins?" He waved the letter and let it float to the top of the stack.

"That is correct," Elisa answered, suddenly self-conscious of the slight tinge of an accent in her voice. Weyland obviously had no patience with foreign accents. For this reason Elisa had come along to help Helen with the interview. Elisa's English was nearly flawless; Helen spoke English with the thick heavy sounds of one who had lived her entire life in Germany.

"Since you are an American by *marriage*—" Weyland cleared his throat to let her know that he knew where she really came from. "Then perhaps this matter of your family. . . these children, Lori and Jamie Ibsen, would be better handled by the American Embassy." He closed the file folder and stared with watery blue eyes.

Was this a dismissal? Helen clutched Elisa's hand and looked at her for explanation. Elisa shook her head in disagreement. "Our entire family is . . . we are in London, you see. My mother and father came with President Beneš from Czechoslovakia, invited by your government. They are here by special arrangement, and . . . the Prime Minister himself . . ."

Weyland drew back and opened the file again. *Why had no one told him this before? The Prime Minister?* "Ah. Well . . ."

More silence passed as he reconsidered the documents with this new information in mind.

"My dear Mrs. Ibsen." He faced Elisa, even though it was Aunt Helen he wanted answers from. Helen's mastery of the English language was acceptable in most circles, but Weyland demanded an interpreter be present in case there was difficulty. "I understand about your own children. And about those other two, the Kalner boys—although Jacob Kalner is over-age. Seventeen, is he not?" He paused to let this fact sink in. "But now there is this other matter . . . Alfie Halder. Tell me again . . . slowly. . . who he is and where he comes from."

Helen understood everything. Elisa did not need to translate.

She and Helen exchanged resigned looks, and Helen began again. "He is a child who . . ."

The thought gave her a chill of fear. "He grew up in our congregation, you see. A sweet child . . ." How could she explain?

Weyland pursed his lips in thought. "There are so many thousands of requests these days. The cut-off age is sixteen. And for those who are younger, we have strict standards of health and intelligence that we check for. Children are being rejected, for instance, if they have decayed teeth or physical ailments, you see."

Helen blanched. Lori and Jamie had good teeth, healthy minds and bodies. But what about Jacob and Mark Kalner? And how could she ever explain about Alfie Halder? She looked to Elisa for help.

"Both parents of Alfie Halder are deceased; he has no family. No one to care for him. My husband and I will sign an affidavit of financial support, of course."

Weyland sniffed and looked down his nose at Elisa and Helen. "My own parents died when I was fifteen," he declared proudly. "And as you can see, I survived on my own quite well. Educated myself, and—" He swept his hand around the tiny cubicle as if to display his achievement. "You can see. You shall have to give a good reason for bringing a fifteen-year-old boy in the place of a younger refugee child who is truly in need."

"But Alfie is . . . *special.*" Helen leaned forward. How could she explain how special he was when children with cavities were rejected?

"Special." He chewed the word. "Ah. I see. Gifted, do you mean?"

"Yes. Gifted. A *gift,* Alfie is, to all who know him."

A new interest sparked in Weyland's dull eyes. "On occasion we do make exceptions for young people who might benefit from our educational system."

Elisa jumped in, grateful for even this impossible hope. "Good! Alfie Halder is special. My husband hopes to employ him."

Weyland frowned and stuck out his lower lip. "*Employ?* Dear me, no. He cannot be employed. Take the place of a British subject in London?"

"As an interpreter." Elisa gulped. "He speaks several . . .

uh . . . unusual languages. Exceptional." She could not look at Helen's pale face.

"And Jacob Kalner?" Helen was flushed. It was warm in the office. Too warm. She felt light-headed. "Perhaps a student visa?"

"Kalner." Weyland frowned and chewed his upper lip. "Seventeen. A man by all guidelines. But perhaps . . . is he also exceptional in intellect?"

Both women spoke at once. "*Yes!*"

"Such visas are dependent on school records from the country of origin."

"Those remain in the Reich. In such a case one cannot call up Berlin and simply ask for them."

"Quite." Weyland was softening some. "Then you must understand that retaining the visa depends on how well a student performs here. And you will guarantee financial support for him as well?" Weyland shuffled through a stack of papers for the correct forms. He looked at them doubtfully. "The final decisions are always made at the consulate of origin. Danzig. All I can do is pass along the information from this side of the Channel. Due to the circumstances of your family situation, there is hope for your daughter, even though she too is seventeen. But the others . . ."

A student-visa application was pulled from the file. Weyland looked as though he was relieved to be done with this matter. Time to move on. Time to finish his sandwich. He clapped his hands together. "Fill out these. Four copies each, as you can see. And for the other children as well. I can make no promises. There are hundreds of thousands of these applications being submitted at every British Consulate on the Continent." He frowned and gestured toward the metal file drawers that lined every wall. "As you can see."

Both women left the office and stood stunned, in the center of the drab corridor. The sound of typewriters and voices echoed around them, but they heard nothing but the replay of Harold Weyland's unpromising words.

————

The telephone call from Holland came in to the London TENS office just as Murphy was rolling down his sleeves and searching for his hat. It had been a long day, with news breaking like a line of dominos clacking down one after another. Murphy was ready to turn the operation over to Harvey Terrill, ready to go home to Red Lion Square, to look at Elisa and the boys and *think on whatever was true, whatever was noble, whatever was right, whatever was pure. . . .*

Murphy, at the suggestion of his father-in-law, had been putting that scripture to a lot of use lately as the news leaking out of Europe grew increasingly grim. For a while, Murphy had begun to believe that there just weren't any good things left in the world to think about. Lately he had come to see that as the darkness had gotten darker, the little pinpoints of light had gotten stronger. There were fewer of those lights, to be sure, but the harder the blackness squeezed, the more vibrant the light became.

With that in mind, Murphy had given Timmons, the Berlin correspondent, the assignment of reporting on those bright spots in the Third Reich. *Who was left in Germany? What were they doing?*

Mindful of the impossibility of getting such a story past the Nazi censors, Timmons had carried it in his mind to Holland, where he placed the trunk call to the TENS bureau chief.

Night desk editor Harvey Terrill looked annoyed as he poked his head into Murphy's office. "Sorry. It's Timmons on the line from Amsterdam. Says he has to talk to you. Just you. Nobody else but you," he said with a shrug. "Doesn't trust me to get it right." It was only the first few minutes of Terrill's shift, but already he was edgy, Murphy thought as he picked up the receiver.

On the far side of the English Channel, the boyish voice of Timmons sounded frantic, as usual. The kid was learning journalism the hard way, after all. He had been picked up and interrogated by the Gestapo in Germany twice already. He did not want to take a chance on another stay in Himmler's resort.

"Must be some story," Murphy said, dispensing with the usual greeting.

"Probably the last we're going to see any of those little lights shining in Germany, Boss," Timmons said. His voice sounded as if he were shouting through a garden hose. "This morning two thousand Christians gathered outside the rubble of New Church. Nine pastors read the names of their colleagues who are now in prison, including Pastor Karl Ibsen and Martin Niemöller. Hitler is saying publicly, *It is them or me. . . .* You know what that means around here. It will be them!"

"Let me get a copy editor. You've got the whole story?"

"I watched from across the street. Not close enough to get arrested. Professor Bauchin spoke for fifteen minutes before the goons moved in and rounded everyone up. There were trucks waiting on the side streets. Nobody tried to make a run for it. Everyone was arrested. An announcement was made by the Gestapo that the German Confessional Church will transfer the use of the cathedrals to the Hitler elite guard for that body's neo-pagan ceremonies. This is the penalty of the church's *Jewish influence* and *the political degeneration of Christianity.*" He paused. "Those are exact quotes, Boss."

"They aren't trying to hide their true purpose anymore, are they, Timmons?"

"Don't have to. The visible church in Germany is dead. No Bibles in the bookstores. I think we've just seen the last two thousand *open* Christians trucked off. Those lights you were looking for have all gone underground, Boss. A certain official from the German press told me that Ibsen is being held because he refuses to accept the *Aryan paragraph* that excludes all Jews and Jewish influence from the German church. Unless he accepts the Nazi version of Hitler's church, they say he's going to rot in there until he's forgotten."

"*Forgotten.*" Murphy repeated the word as though it were the biggest threat to Karl Ibsen and the others who suffered in the same cause. *Whatever is true, whatever is noble, whatever is right, whatever is pure, whatever is admirable, excellent, or praiseworthy . . . think about such things!*

The men within the walls of Hitler's prison camps were all of the above, Murphy reasoned, and then he added *courageous* to the list of things to think on as Timmons dictated the full story of the last Christian Alamo in Berlin.

Murphy was two hours late getting home to Red Lion Square. In that time, he had revised his interpretation of what Scripture meant when it said to *think on these things.* The apostle Paul had written those words while he was in prison, had he not?

Men like Karl Ibsen embodied all the qualities of what was noble and right and true and just. These were the qualities the Führer wanted the world to forget; these were the principles he wanted to rot away in prison so he could continue his plan unopposed. He had promised Ibsen full restoration if only Karl would remain silent! But because he would not compromise, Karl was locked away in the darkest of Nazi holes.

But Ibsen was not silent, Murphy realized. Behind those thick and terrible walls, his heart was still true to his God. His example rang out like a shout from the rooftop of St. Paul's!

Think on these things. . . .

With that in mind, Murphy called Anna and Theo Lindheim, Helen Ibsen, and Winston Churchill. They walked together on the roof garden and looked over nighttime London to where the great dome of St. Paul's Cathedral glistened in the spotlights like a moon rising over a mountain range.

Where the voice of a few brave men had been silenced, the bells of ten thousand churches should toll, reminding the world to *think on these things.* . . .

Allan Farrell read his morning edition of *The Times* as he sunned himself on a bench in Parliament Square. The headlines were all about Hitler. Troop buildups on the borders. Poland. Danzig. Editorials screamed about despots who gobbled up other peoples' land like a hyena tearing the flesh of a wounded animal.

Noble sentiments, considering their source, Allan thought. *Noble and full of hypocrisy.* Like English political philosophy for four hundred years, these words about the German Führer were colored by what was best only for England.

Allan raised his eyes to the weathered stones of Westminster Abbey where Protestant Queen Elizabeth lay buried in the same crypt with her half sister, the Catholic queen known as Bloody Mary. Catholics and Protestants had been slaughtering one another since before the reign of those two sisters. There had been a continuous and brutal war going on a long time before the strutting German Führer appeared on the scene.

James had succeeded Queen Elizabeth as Monarch. He had commanded the publication of his Bible at the same time he ordered English and Scottish Protestants to settle the ancient land of Ireland. In the name of religion, the executions and murders had begun in the early years of the 1600s. The troubles were that old. Seasoned in the keg of bitterness, three and a half centuries had not mellowed the hatred of Irish Catholics for the Protestant usurpers in Ulster. Allan could recite his family tree from the list of those hanging by nooses on its branches. There were no monuments to those men in their own land. Ah, but here in England there were monuments everywhere to the rulers who had hanged them!

Just across St. Margaret's Street, Allan could make out the bronze statue of Oliver Cromwell standing on the green outside of Parliament. Now *there* was a blood-soaked tyrant for the ages! He had plunged England into a civil war for the sake of his religion. He was responsible for the execution of King Charles I just a few miles from this spot! Cromwell had taken the government into his own hands, and melted down the crown jewels to pay his armies. He had smashed the Irish revolt with an iron fist and titled himself *Lord Protector of the Realm*. And now, Cromwell, who had cried out against the graven images of the Catholic church, was himself a graven image on the green of Parliament.

Despots had only to be victorious, Allan thought, *and all their brutality acquired the status of a holy crusade!*

Allan studied the statue of Cromwell for a moment, then looked back at the front-page photograph of Hitler and Mussolini. All these two modern-day dictators had to do was *win*; then they would also be cast in bronze to stand as Europe's most recent graven images. They were no better or worse than all those of any nation who had gone before them. Weapons were more advanced, to be sure. Evil could be refined to an art. But evil had always existed within the lofty world of politicians and kings.

Allan looked at his hands. They were too much like his mother's to be called strong and masculine. He had always been ashamed of his hands, tucked them into his pockets or stood with clenched fists. But her hands had been strong. She had used them to wage war against the oppression three centuries of her kin had suffered. Why, then, were Allan's own hands not strong? Why had Colin and the others marked him as a messenger for the cause, but not a fighter?

He looked at Cromwell. "They have made you a saint, you bloody butcher. You're worse off now than the men you killed, and there's nothing to be done about it, is there?"

Glancing away, Allan sighed. "There is one Irishman sitting across from your shrine, Lord Cromwell. They think I am too weak to do anything but shuttle messages to and fro, do they?" He raised his eyes to Big Ben as the hour hand slid into place

131

and the great bells began to chime noon. He let his gaze glide over the piles of sandbags that were stacked thick and deep along the facade of every public building. The Houses of Parliament, Westminster Abbey, St. Margaret's Church, all looked as if they had been prepared for a flood . . . or at least a heavy German-sent storm.

Sandbags, ditches—all in preparation for what might come from the belly of a German bomber. But what about the damage one lone fighter might do behind those barricades?

Allan's eyes narrowed as he spotted his German contact snapping photographs like a tourist across the square. For now their common enemy, England, had made them allies. On this one point they could agree—it would be a lovely sight if the walls of Parliament came tumbling down. Did it matter if the weapon fell from the sky or came from within?

Allan pulled a small envelope from his coat pocket and folded it into his newspaper. Leaving *The Times* on the bench, he strolled away from the approaching contact. He paused for a moment as if to study the statue of the Earl of Derby. The German took his place on the bench and opened the copy of *The Times*. It was that simple. That antiseptic. Allan did not even know what message the note contained. The secret business of his unlikely allies.

There was nothing in the process that had given him one moment of excitement or nervousness. *Room and board. Clean sheets and polished boots. Good payment. And for what?*

Allan walked slowly along the sidewalk; past the sandbags and the statue of Cromwell. He thought that perhaps the old Lord Protector was worthy of a more active opponent.

Tucking his hands in his pockets, he quickened his pace to catch the red omnibus at the corner.

A fluttering poster nailed to a tree caught Allan Farrell's attention:

REMEMBER THESE MEN!

A list of names followed, as well as the explanation that these men were currently in prison in Nazi Germany. A great rally, a Remembrance Service, was to be held on their behalf on September 1. The bells of all the churches in England and America would ring out a message to the Nazis that those unjustly imprisoned were not forgotten.

Allan pulled the paper from its nail and studied it carefully. At the top of the list of those scheduled to speak was Winston Churchill. Allan frowned. Like Cromwell, Winston Churchill was also an opponent of everything Allan believed in. A hypocrite of the first order, Churchill had opposed the turning over of naval bases to Ireland. He argued on behalf of keeping Ulster chained to the leg of the British Empire!

And yet, Winston Churchill was going to speak on behalf of martyrs imprisoned in Germany! The irony of it was almost too much for Allan. He folded the paper and angrily shoved it into his pocket.

Extra sugar. Extra butter. Extra coffee. The cupboards of the Lubetkin house were overflowing with little bits of this and that brought from the members of the congregation to the rabbi's family. All those little bits had accumulated into so much that there was room for nothing else.

Mama stood in the pantry with her hands on her hips. "You would think we are having a Bar Mitzvah, Rachel!" she called over her shoulder. "So much! Go get David's wagon. Bring it to the kitchen door. We should take most of this to the soup kitchen. Your father says. So go."

Rachel hated pulling David's wagon anywhere. The left front wheel wobbled drunkenly after an unexpected collision with an elm tree in the square. Pulling the wagon was like taking a rabbit for a walk on a long leash. The wagon went its own way no matter which way Rachel tried to guide it. Why had Papa ordered that she should show up at the shul with this thing in tow? Everyone would be there. The members of the congregation who manned the staff often fed their own children there as well. They would all see Rachel in the undignified task of fighting a little red wagon up the street.

"Can't I go later?" She looked at the kitchen clock. Later would be after dark, and after suppertime as well. The kitchen would be empty, or nearly so. No friends or schoolmates to see her—nearly a grown woman—tugging a child's wagon!

Mama looked irritated at the suggestion. "So look at the clock. If you can't tell time, then look at the sky. Later will be dark. You can't go out these days after dark. You know that. Get your brother's wagon and quit kvetching. Your father said *now* take the stuff to the shul!"

Reluctantly, Rachel retrieved the offending vehicle from beneath the shade tree in the back. It was covered with pigeon droppings! *Humiliation heaped upon humiliation!*

It squeaked and resisted all the way to the door. Mama heard it coming. Everyone would hear it coming. Mama was waiting behind the screen with her arms full. She gasped at the sight of the wagon. "You cannot go with it covered in bird droppings," she scolded.

Rachel smiled slightly in spite of the tone of Mama's voice. Here was an unexpected reprieve. She blessed the birds who roosted in the tree! "It is a mess," Rachel said cheerfully.

"Soap. A little water, maybe! So wash it! And hurry, if you please!" *Bang!* The door slammed shut.

Rachel grumbled and scrubbed the wagon. Red paint chipped off in big flakes beneath the brush, giving David's wagon the appearance of something that had been pulled by refugees coming to Warsaw and other refugees going back to Cracow and still others back to Warsaw again.

"They will think I am a refugee," she moaned when the task was completed. She thought of the rag pickers and beggars roaming about Warsaw even now. None of them would stoop to pulling such a pitiful cart.

"Mama, it is not dignified," Rachel said as the last of the food was crammed between the slats, and then bundles of old clothes were placed on top.

"Dignified!" Mama scowled at her. "Five hundred homeless arrived only yesterday in our neighborhood, and you speak of your own dignity! Your father sick on his bed is not thinking of himself! He is thinking about those down at the shul. What would he say about your dignity? I should tell him you don't want to take our contribution to the shul because your pride would be wounded maybe?"

After Mama's speech about dignity, the loud squeaking of the wagon wheels was a pleasant relief. At least until Rachel reached the main street to the shul.

The rhythm was a steady *grooooan, clunk, shriek!* Rachel pulled right and the wagon rolled left. When she went around the streetlamp, the wagon stopped like a dog looking for a place to lift its leg. The thing was alive! An evil spirit seemed to have possessed it.

"Hello, Rachel!" called Frau Potemski from her stoop. "The rabbi, your father, he is better?"

Rachel felt her face color. "He is sending charity to the soup kitchen."

"They won't want the wagon," she laughed.

Rachel forced her lips to smile politely. "Good-day, Frau Potemski." The wagon lurched toward the stoop as though it wished to greet the good Frau.

"If you're going to have a pet, you should teach it to heel." The moon-faced housewife gave the wagon a nudge with her toe.

"Yes, Frau Potemski." Rachel's cheeks were bright red.

She did not look to the right or the left as she struggled up the next block. Friends hailed her and asked after her father. Strangers stared at her with the same curiosity with which she had stared at the red-haired young man in Muranow Square. She looked like one of them! Old clothes bundled on top of a cart. *Why* had Mama not been content to only send food?

"Well, good evening, Rachel!" It was Herr Menkes, the baker. "Running away from home?"

Clunk . . . shriek . . . grooooan . . . clunk . . .

"I am sorry, Herr Menkes, I cannot hear you! This assassin of a cart is making too much noise." She raised her nose slightly and struggled on. "And I cannot stop to talk because I am running away from home."

"You won't get far with that beast you are pulling!" he called after her. "Are you pulling it, or is it pulling you?"

She chose to ignore the jibe of the baker. He was more filled with sarcasm than a jelly donut was full of jelly! She would think especially hard before she went into his shop next time so she could have something clever prepared to say in reply when he teased her.

She approached the corner of the street, its curb looming up like the brink of a steep ravine. Rachel paused. The beast rolled up on her heels, then veered to the left, toward the curb. She tugged back on the handle, jerking the rusty axle around. With a loud moan, the wagon reared up on its hind wheels and then threw itself upside down!

Old dresses! Undergarments! Stockings and worn-out shoes!

Papa's old trousers. Mama's old dresses. Rachel's old blouses and three nightgowns flew out across the sidewalk.

This motley collection of faded finery was followed by the real treasure: butter wrapped in waxed paper. Sugar in a paper bag. Salt. Pepper. Extra loaves of bread. Extra sugared rolls. Extra this and extra that. A little of everything that amounted to quite a lot of mess there on the busy street corner.

"Oh! You terrible monster!" Rachel wailed as the crooked wheel spun around happily in the air. "Now *look* what you've done?"

She stooped and jerked the wagon into a lopsided upright position. It had emptied all of its burden, and before she could stop it, it rolled away, off the curb.

Rachel sat back on her heels as the wagon splintered to a noisy death under the wheels of a taxi. The cab squealed to a stop, and a great commotion arose as men and women appeared to see what had happened.

Rachel covered her face with her hands. Arms lifted her to her feet. Hands brushed her off, and familiar ones mingled with unfamiliar voices in a hundred different explanations of how the daughter of the good Rabbi Lubetkin—God forbid—almost was killed by the taxi that roared around the corner like a wild bull looking for someone innocent to mow down. And of course she was running away from her unhappy home because she could not stand the strain any longer of caring for . . .

No! No! No! She was on a mission of mercy, poor child! Taking items of charity to the soup kitchen when—God forbid—she was almost crushed beneath the wheels of this . . . But, the Eternal be praised! Jumping back just in time, she was snatched from the jaws of a horrible death!

The crowd looked ready to lynch the poor taxi driver.

Rachel was crying by this time. Her tears made matters much worse. Someone suggested that she be taken to a hospital to be checked in case anything was damaged.

"Please," Rachel said quietly, "the wagon just broke loose. It is nothing. I was taking this to the soup kitchen at the shul and the wagon broke away. Nothing. Just . . . I am fine."

The babble of excited voices drowned out her feeble voice. Rachel looked up in search of a reasonable face. Among the crowd of friends and strangers who now blocked traffic, Rachel saw the wry smile of the red-haired young man in the camel-hair coat. He was behind a three-deep line of neighbor women. His head and shoulders towered above their excitedly bobbing heads. He rolled his eyes, and shook his head, as if to say, *Who would believe this?*

He inched his way forward. "I saw it," he said to Rachel through the ruckus. "I'm afraid the wagon is done for, but we may yet save the cargo." He passed her a still-folded nightgown.

"They never listen!" Rachel said, looking down to where someone stood squarely in the middle of the butter. Yellow ooze was squishing out over the toes of scuffed shoes.

The red-haired boy fought his way down to rescue sacks of bread and buns and mismatched shoes. These he passed up to Rachel, who accepted them with a newfound composure as her crisis continued to be discussed by everyone at the same time.

An unbroken bag of sugar was retrieved. Matching shoes were found, rolled socks, shirts and dresses retrieved. Rachel's arms were full. She could carry nothing more. And then the young man rose to his feet. His arms were full as well.

"I was taking it to the soup kitchen," Rachel explained.

"Old shoes make good soup, I am told, if properly seasoned." The young man nudged past her and then began his escape through the press.

Rachel followed. No one noticed that the victim was leaving. Like the broken wagon, the butter and a few additional items were abandoned, left as evidence to the near tragedy.

On the other side of the square, Rachel and this young man with the rebellious red hair could see that the mob had grown to two hundred. The two walked quickly toward the soup kitchen at the end of the block.

"Rachel!" cried Herr Bilenki as he hurried past in the opposite direction. "What! What has happened over there, child, do you know?"

"Somebody—God forbid—is dead," Rachel replied as she kept on walking.

10   On the Beach

The crates were packed and ready for transport to the freighter in Tel Aviv. Orde was expecting the porters; instead, the door opened and a junior officer passed him a cable from London.

A reprieve from his disgrace, perhaps? Or word that he had been posted back to England to help sort out the problems of Palestine?

He tore open the envelope and scanned the brief paragraph. His hopes fell as quickly as they had risen. It was a telegram from John Murphy and the TENS office in London.

CAPTAIN ORDE
    REGRET TO HEAR OF YOUR POSTING BACK TO EN-
GLAND AND SUBSEQUENT DECISION TO RETIRE STOP
TENS CURRENTLY IN NEED CORRESPONDENT IN POLAND
STOP
    BOTH WRITING AND RADIO BROADCASTS REQUIRED
STOP HOPEFUL YOU WILL APPLY FOR POSITION STOP
    SINCERELY JOHN MURPHY
    BUREAU CHIEF TENS LONDON
    REPLY REQUESTED

The offer was kind, but Orde read it with a growing sense of despair. It was not at all the way he had envisioned spending the rest of his life. A journalist? No. Samuel Orde was a soldier from the ground up. The TENS proposal was one that he might think about on the trip back to England, but it was at the bottom of his list.

He folded the cable and stuck it in the pocket of his coat. Another knock sounded on the door.

"Yes?"

Hobbs poked his head in. "The messenger is still here, sar. Will y' be sendin' a reply?"

Orde answered with a curt nod and then scrawled out his message to Murphy on a torn sheet of note paper. It would be several weeks before he reached London, and Orde hoped the position would be filled by then so he would not have to even consider it. *THANKS FOR CONSIDERATION. WILL CONTACT YOU IN LONDON* . . .

There was much he needed to think about, to pray about. He had deceived himself into thinking that the Almighty had chosen him to help the cause of a Jewish homeland. And Orde had rather liked picturing himself in the role of a new Moses.

The thought of his arrogance made him wince. "That's the truth of it, old boy," he muttered to his reflection in the mirror. So here he was; not a Moses at all, but an Englishman punished by his own people because of that desire.

The knife of that reality cut deep into his heart. To work as a journalist meant reporting the history that other men made. Always before, Orde had considered himself a man who could make history happen.

That much of his life had come to an end, and now he had no personal life, no life at all to fill the void.

"Journalist," he muttered, clearly remembering something he had said before about members of the press. *Those who can, do. Those who can do nothing else, write what others have done.*

He wondered what sort of bloke this American John Murphy would be to work for. Probably insufferably arrogant and crude like most Yanks.

There was time enough to consider the proposal. Orde determined that he would discuss it with Winston Churchill when he got back to England. It was Winston, after all, whose infernal meddling had gotten him the assignment of Middle East correspondent.

Somehow Orde connected his own stories with this dismissal. Had he not been so vigorous in his reporting, he would not have drawn attention to himself and . . . *No use thinking of that now.* It was too late. There was no reprieve, it seemed. He was going back to London no matter what.

———

The din of spoons against tin bowls was deafening.

Peter Wallich smoothed out the torn scrap of paper on the long trestle table in the community soup kitchen.

"Here it is, you see." He tapped it with his finger and ignored his bowl even though Rachel knew he must be very hungry. It seemed as though the fragment of yellow paper held all the hope for nourishment that Peter desired. The blue ink was water-stained, leaving only a small portion of the address legible. *"Niska Street,"* Peter said unhappily. "You see. That is all I have to go on."

"Niska is a very long street. It would be difficult these days to wander up and down knocking on the door of every flat to ask if someone had a relative in Vienna," Rachel frowned.

Peter moved his face closer to the paper as he attempted to decipher the water-smeared ink. "This could be an *A* or an *O*. And this maybe an *M* or an *N*. The last three letters are *SKI*. That is one certain thing."

Rachel looked up at him doubtfully. Poor boy. Did he not know that practically everyone in Warsaw had a relative with a last name ending in *SKI*? This was of little use, if any, in helping Peter Wallich locate the family he was searching for in Warsaw. Niska Street ran for miles. Thousands of mail slots were labeled with names ending with the only three legible letters in the name on the paper. "All the way from Vienna you have come for this," she murmured, her words lost beneath the clamor of the crowded dining room. She looked around at the gaunt faces of the diners. So far these tragic people had come, only to end up here!

"It was so absurd." Peter slammed his hand down on the paper.

"You should eat," Rachel urged.

"I was on my way here from Danzig, you see." He seemed to have lost his appetite. "On the train to Warsaw! Just walking through the corridor, and—you know how trains rock!"

Rachel shrugged. She had never been on a train. But in 1939, could she admit that she had never been on a train? *Too childish and provincial.* "I see," she said, using her imagination. *Like a tram, only worse.*

"So there I was, walking toward the third-class dining car," Peter continued. "I met this fellow carrying two cups of coffee. Just then the train hit a bad bump. The man fell into me!" He raised his hands and brought them down across the paper to show how the coffee had soaked him and the precious address to his destination. "And here, you see, is the result! The address in my pocket—all my hopes washed away in that moment."

Rachel sat silently, contemplating the terrible misfortune of Peter Wallich. She looked up to see Frau Sobrinski staring curiously at her from the door of the kitchen. The woman's eyebrows raised in disapproval. *So there was the rabbi's daughter talking to a total stranger of a boy in the soup kitchen! Oy!*

Rachel knew the yentas would talk. She did not care. She would go right home and tell her mother and father what had happened to this poor boy who had helped her carry the items for charity to the shul. Maybe Papa would have an idea what to do.

Frau Sobrinski still stared. Rachel smiled and waved, let the smile cool, and then turned away. The look plainly told Frau Sobrinski that she was being a yenta and she should tend her own soup! *Very good,* Rachel thought. When she looked up again, the woman had scurried away.

"My father is the rabbi here," Rachel said to Peter as if that fact explained everything.

Peter looked alarmed. "I am not religious," he said sternly.

"Yes. I know. Baker Menkes told me you would not eat a meal here for that reason. Is that why you have not touched your soup?"

His expression grew more stern. "Soup is soup when one is hungry." He met her challenge by taking a bite.

"And a rabbi *IS* a rabbi when one needs help finding lost friends," she replied smugly. "So do not be so proud. My father knows everybody. And if he doesn't know *everybody,* he knows enough people who do." She folded her hands primly before her on the table. "So. Do you want help? Of course you do. Then you must tell me everything about your father in Vienna and the man who gave him this address, nu?"

———

It took nearly an hour of explanation about the smashed wagon and spilled cargo before Rachel's parents allowed her to get on to the really important matters. By that time Papa's eyes looked very weary, and Mama was irritable. Mama was often irritable these days from the strain of Papa's illness and the terrible state of politics.

"But, Mama," Rachel protested when her mother told her the story could wait until later, "this is what I wanted to tell you! I just had to start with the wagon because that is where I met him."

"Etta," Papa wheezed, "we'll listen."

141

"Everyone in Warsaw has a story," Etta said. "And you need to rest, Aaron."

Papa raised his hand in a gesture that ordered no argument. Rachel had not meant to cause trouble. Now she wished she had waited until morning to tell the whole story.

"It is all right," Rachel replied. "Really. It can wait."

"Nonsense." Papa's brown eyes flashed. "I like a good story."

"Mama?" Rachel begged her mother's pardon.

"Your father is bored lying here," Mama sighed and shook her head. "One of the joys of being a rabbi is listening to everyone's troubles. As if we do not have enough of our own, Aaron." She managed a smile as she gently patted his arm. "So tell us the troubles of this red-haired boy who replaced the red wagon."

Rachel tried to strain out the unimportant parts, like the fact that Peter Wallich was not Orthodox. Not Conservative. Not religious at all. Starting with the spilled coffee, she traced back to the horrible Night of Broken Glass in Vienna and then Peter's escape to Danzig. By then, Rachel could plainly see that her mother was indeed fascinated and sympathetic as well. *Such* a story!

"His mother and sister were supposed to meet him at the Danziger Hof Hotel in Danzig. They never came! He waited there for some time, hoping for a letter. Each week he went to the hotel and asked if maybe there was a message there for Peter Ruger, which is the name on his false passport. But they never wrote."

Mama clucked her tongue. So sad. Terrible. A son separated from his mother and sister. "And now he is in Warsaw?"

"With only this clue." Rachel passed Etta the yellow coffee-stained paper.

"There is nothing anyone can do with this." Mama passed it to Papa, who held it up to the light.

He shook his head. "Rachel." He sounded disapproving. "When there is no help, it is more harm than good to give someone hope. We can do nothing with this."

"But there is more," Rachel leaned forward. "He remembers things about the man in Vienna who gave his father this address!" She looked very pleased as she paused long enough for the suspense to build.

"Yes?"

"Well? So tell us."

Rachel nodded. "The man was from Warsaw, but very active against the Nazis in Austria. Like Peter's father, he tried to stop the Anschluss. He was killed just before Hitler took over Austria."

Once again Etta and Aaron exchanged looks. Many people were killed during that time. This was not news. "Is there more?" Papa asked, looking very tired indeed.

"Peter remembers something about him—though not his name. If he could remember his name, then Peter would not have such a problem." She paused. "He came to the Walliches' flat always very late at night. Peter says he carried a violin case and wore elegant clothes. Black dinner jacket and a fine overcoat. A musician. Not like the fellows who stand on the street corners and play their fiddles, but a *real* musician, like the men at the concert hall. And he was Jewish. Dark eyes and black hair. Handsome."

This description certainly matched no one in the congregation of Aaron Lubetkin. But maybe it *was* something. How many Jewish violinists had left Warsaw for Vienna and actually made a success in an orchestra there? It was the sort of thing a Jewish mother and father would talk about. *My son the concert violinist. . . .* And then there was the matter of the son being killed. That would have made waves in the community somewhere.

"Good. This is good," Papa urged Rachel on. "There is more, maybe?"

Rachel nodded her head curtly. This was the really good part. "Peter saw this man's photograph in the newspaper. The headlines said he had murdered his mistress—"

At this, Mama looked suddenly disgusted. Rachel was not supposed to know about things like mistresses. That was the sort of terrible thing that happened on the *outside*.

"Finish," Papa said grimly.

"So Peter brought this newspaper to his father. His father got very white and said to Peter, 'This is no one I know. Do not speak of it again.'" Rachel shrugged to indicate that this was the last clue. "When the Nazis came, Peter's father was arrested and killed. His mother kept the address of the musician from Warsaw hidden. She gave it to him before they fled Vienna. And then . . . you know. . . the coffee spilled on it."

Well, this was certainly a story for the yentas of the block to talk about. But maybe not the sort of thing Mama was pleased had entered the ears of her daughter.

"It is enough." Aaron ran his hand across the stubble of his new beard. "It is something."

Hidden in the center of Karl Ibsen's ration of daily bread was a soft core. Not yet stale. Not yet shrouded with mold. This heart of the bread was the one taste of pleasure that Karl enjoyed each morning.

As always, he bowed his head and offered thanks for the bit of nourishment that kept him tied to this world. Then he glanced up toward the window and muttered something about the value of even one sparrow. And then in a voice his warders would have attributed to the madness of solitary confinement, the prisoner cried, "Whatever you do for the least of these, you have done for me."

With that, he rose from his knees and divided the precious heart of his bread into three fragments. Three one-inch squares of bread. Turning his water bucket upside down beneath the window, he stepped up on it. Straining every muscle, he reached up to boost the three small crumbs into the window ledge between the bars.

The bucket tipped and he fell with a clatter onto the filthy floor of his cell. He lay panting on his back for a while, never taking his eyes from the altar where he had laid his offering.

"You said you were hungry and we did not feed you," he said aloud when he found his breath again. "There is no man close enough for me to feed, Lord. And so I cannot share my bread with a person. But also . . . you said you know even when a sparrow falls. Even . . . a sparrow. So I will feed the sparrow in your name. Will a sparrow do? Will the bread crumbs work? I have nothing else to give. My prayers you have already. But while I am still here in this prison called earth, I will feed the sparrow because you said . . . if I feed the smallest, then I have fed you."

The sparrow had not returned for many days. Karl Ibsen sat on the floor of his cell and waited with perfect faith that it would come again.

There were certain places a woman like Lucy Strasburg would most likely patronize. Regardless of her low beginnings,

144

Agent Hess had no doubt that her long association with Wolfgang von Fritschauer had honed her appreciation of the finer things in life. If Wolf had spoken truthfully and had indeed thrown her out, then no doubt she would still be frequenting the more elite of the Danzig clubs and restaurants in search of another male companion of Wolf's financial status. Such a woman could not survive long alone.

This afternoon Hess had chosen Cafe Passage as the location of his meeting with Gustav Ahlman, his assistant investigator in the matter of the Ibsen case. Situated along Dominiks Wall, in an old but elegant district of Danzig, the cafe served excellent wine and had tables on a patio overlooking a busy shopping area.

The sky was clear and blue above the red and white striped umbrellas of the cafe. Every table was crowded with women shoppers. Hess recognized the accents of nearly every country in the League of Nations. These were the wives of those diplomats who even now counseled together and worried helplessly about the future of the free port governed by their organization. Their women seemed oblivious to it all, unconcerned about anything but the rise in shoe prices since the fall of Czechoslovakia.

Hess did not look at the flowers of the Danzig parks. He did not gaze at the charming facades of the medieval buildings along Dominiks Wall. He sipped his schnapps, and from behind dark glasses, he scrutinized the elegant ladies of Danzig. There was only one among them all whom he wanted to see. *Tall. Shapely. Creamy smooth skin. Golden hair and the bearing of a princess with the heart of a back-street whore. This was Lucy Strasburg.* Even amid the elegance of Dominiks Wall shopping arcade, few could come close to such a description. Hess would find her. He was certain of that. After that he would devote his full attention to the matter of the Ibsen case.

Gustav Ahlman stepped from the tram across the square. Dodging traffic, he did not wait for the crossing signal, but headed straight to where Hess had been waiting for a quarter of an hour. The young man's thin face was pinched and harried. He was late. Hess did not like his junior officers to keep him waiting. Better to be hit by a bus while crossing against the signal than to be late.

He was panting as he took a seat. His fine brown hair fell across his high forehead. His eyes blinked rapidly as he looked nervously at his own reflection in Hess's dark glasses. He smoothed back his hair, cleared his throat, and looked nervously over his shoulder.

"Sorry I am late," he said.

Hess inclined his head to acknowledge the apology. He did not forgive the transgression, but he wanted Gustav to know that he had noticed.

"Well?" Hess sipped his schnapps and resumed his visual search of the ladies beyond the patio of Cafe Passage.

Gustav cleared his throat again. He was smiling as he wiped away sweat from his neck. "I have followed him as you instructed." The young voice was too excited. Hess squelched the enthusiasm with a withering look.

"And?"

Gustav Ahlman pulled out a small loose-leaf notebook and flipped it open. "I have it all here."

The waiter came, interrupting the report before it had begun. Gustav ordered tea and pastries. "Identical to those on the opposite table," he instructed like a schoolboy.

Hess eyed him briefly with disdain. Was this the best the Gestapo could come up with for his leg-man? Hess thought he could have hired an errand boy and accomplished the same thing. Ah well, everyone had to start somewhere. Gustav Ahlman had won the assignment of trailing Wolfgang von Fritschauer. He did not know why he was following Wolf, but he had dutifully recorded every move in this little book.

"What have you got for us?" Hess sounded bored already.

Again the intense brown eyes of the young man scanned the page. "Well, he has been to the doctor."

Not exactly earth-shattering news, Hess thought. "Is that all?"

"Actually, he has been to see a dozen different doctors around the city. As far away as the maternity clinic in Sopot."

Maternity? Hess turned his gaze on the eager young fellow. "You said—"

"Maternity." Gustav was triumphant. "I followed him into the waiting room of the last. Heard him talking to the doctor, and then the doctor talking to his receptionist. This Wolfgang von Fritschauer is also on the trail of someone. A woman. And she is . . . she is expecting a child, I heard him say."

This was unexpected news. Hess shook his head as he watched a shapely blond emerge from Neider's clothing store.

146

Displays of the latest fashions and silk stockings mocked him from the showcase windows.

"So she is pregnant," he muttered. "The little slut is carrying a child for the Fatherland. And Wolf is the father, no doubt."

Suddenly it all made sense. The woman had not been thrown out by Wolf; she had left him. She had, like hundreds of willing unmarried S.S. mothers, suddenly become unwilling to give up her child.

"Good news, Agent Hess?" The young man was extremely proud of himself.

"Incomplete." Hess would not reward him with his favor. Not yet. "Find this woman for me. And then we will discuss good news. Stay with von Fritschauer. Report back to me any further developments."

Gustav leaned in close. "Is it a spy ring?" he asked in a whisper.

The tea and pastries came. Hess replied with a laconic shrug. He stared at the heaps of small cakes and eclairs and tried to imagine Lucy Strasburg slow and pregnant. An interesting thought, one which had completely evaded him over the long months of his recovery. Of course that did not alter his plans in any way. The woman would be silenced permanently regardless of her condition. Hopefully this would be accomplished before Wolf managed to find her and she had opportunity to talk about her escape.

––––––––

In his pursuit of Lucy Strasburg, Agent Hess had not neglected his first duty to the Führer. He carried photographs of Jamie and Lori Ibsen in his briefcase. Sections of the city of Danzig had been marked out on the large detailed map on the wall of his hotel room. The search for Lucy had been combined with the hunt for the children until block by block he had checked all the cheap hotels and rooming houses and then crossed them off the list.

Like the loop of a snare, the broad circle of search was being drawn tighter. The outlying districts had been ruled out as possible places of refuge. Now, only the central market districts remained. Each remaining rooming house and block of cheap flats was identified with a red pin.

Hess was not only patient, he was thorough and exacting in

the tedious work of tracking fugitives. One by one the red pins were plucked out and replaced by black pins, which now filled the map of Danzig like an ever-darkening shadow.

Lori insisted that it was not warm enough yet to lie on the beach at Sopot, but Jacob disagreed.

"It is now or never." He bowed with a flourish as Mark and Jamie and Alfie clustered around him to shout their agreement.

"This is a democracy," Jamie instructed his sister.

"Majority rules!" Mark added.

"Ja," Alfie said, a slow smile brightening his broad face. He held up the paw of Werner the cat to vote. "See? Werner also wants to go to the beach, Lori."

She shrugged in mock resignation. "You would think that once in a while Werner would vote with me on something. But we will take coats as well as swimming clothes."

Now the all-male majority of the Danzig Gang cheered little-mother Lori and danced an Indian dance around her as they had seen done in an American movie starring Rex the Wonder Horse last week.

"You're a good sport." Jacob thumped her on the arm as the others tumbled into the boys' quarters to gather their newly purchased swim gear and their heavy coats in case the Baltic breeze was cold at the beach.

"Another week and we will all be in foggy London," Lori said lightly. "And then when we tell people we spent almost five months on the Baltic, they will ask if we ever looked into the casino at Sopot or if the weather was as wonderful at the resort as everybody said. Terrible to admit we had not gone once to the beach." She blushed under Jacob's amused gaze, wondering if he would like the way she looked in her swimsuit. He had not seen her in a bathing suit since last summer, and she had grown up a lot since then. She pretended to busy herself gathering her own things, but he did not leave her room. "Well?" she asked at last. "Are you going? You'd better get your things."

In their excitement, the boys sounded like a growling, yelping pack of weaned puppies. Their squeals and protests penetrated Jacob's silence. He looked away from Lori. "They are killing each other in there," he said and left the room.

She closed the door and leaned against it, grateful for a moment to be alone, a moment without feeling the thoughtful gaze of Jacob Kalner warming her blood like a kettle on a slow fire. Maybe next week they would be in London! She and Jamie would be with Mama. *And where would Jacob and Mark and Alfie stay? Maybe one of the children's camps?* Lori frowned at the thought. She did not like the idea of such a separation. Maybe she could ask Uncle Theo . . . maybe there was some way, someplace where they could still live together in London! The Danzig Gang had been through too much together to be separated. Surely someone would see that. All the way from Berlin to here. They had lived by selling off the jewels Alfie had carried out in his pocket. Jacob had worked at the wharf. Lori took a job at the drugstore and Alfie had even found work as a janitor at Sprinter's ice cream parlor until the Hitler boys had roughed him up. Except for that reminder, life here had not been an ordeal at all, even though the adults in London had all sounded sympathetic and shocked that five children had been forced to survive on their own for six months. Lori had told her mother over the telephone that it was not *all* bad. What she should have said was that except for missing her parents, it was *not bad at all!*

She was the mama and Jacob was the papa. They had kept it all perfectly proper, however. He shared the big room with the boys. Lori slept in the tiny corner room alone, although there were times when she could almost feel his nearness through the door. On those nights she never slept well. On those nights she lay awake and stared into the darkness, grateful that she had *never* felt this way when they had shared sleeping quarters in the bellows room at New Church!

There were other moments when he brushed her hand by accident or looked at her when she had not expected it, and in those moments Lori felt as if she could hardly breathe. She had to make herself exhale and act as though everything were *not* spinning inside her.

Beyond the threats of Berlin, in the clean air of Danzig, something had happened to Lori. She wanted to talk to Mama about it. She would talk to her about it for hours—maybe next week.

"And we were standing in church together sharing the hymnbook, and his hand touched mine, and I thought I would faint. I did not hear the sermon. But he did not notice. He does not seem to be aware. We just . . . you know . . . take care of the boys like you and Papa would have. A regular little family, except . . ."

She slipped on her swimsuit and remembered how last year she had wished she filled out the top a little better. Now she filled it out nicely. The boys on the banks of the Spree back home would have looked at her. And looked again. *Indeed,* Lori thought, *something very nice has happened between last summer and now.* She had become a woman. She wondered if Jacob had noticed the change.

And she was also in love. At least she was practically certain that she was. She thought that probably Jacob would not notice that. And if he did, he would not care because she had been such a complete pain the entire time they had been locked up in New Church together.

He had teased her about being older and more mature when they celebrated their seventeenth birthdays in April. She was three days older than he was, and he said that he figured that was why she was always trying to tell him what to do. He had meant the comment as a joke, but still it stung. That meant he had not forgotten the Lori-of-New Church! Lori who cried often. Lori who complained. Lori who argued about everything! She did so want him to forget about all that!

She wanted him to see Lori-of-the-Danzig-Gang. Good sport. Capable. Happy. Willing to lose in a democratic vote! And now, she wanted him to see Lori-in-the-swimsuit. All grown up. Pretty. She wanted him to feel the same warmth that she felt when he looked at her. There was only one week left here if all went well! They could stand the agony of mutual attraction for one more week. After all, she had stood the agony of unspoken love for months!

She brushed her shoulder-length blond hair and tried it down, and then piled up on her head. She looked older with it up and so she pinned it up, leaving her shoulders bare. A touch of lipstick added to the effect. Satisfied, she pulled on her blouse and skirt, finishing just as the thumping of impatient fists on her door demanded her to hurry or be left behind!

"Come on! Hurry up! We'll miss the tram, Lori!"

And then the chuckle of Alfie and his thick, happy voice, "Meow! Werner says hurry up!"

———

It was only seven and a half miles from Kohlen Market in Danzig to the crisp white beaches of Sopot. Twenty-six minutes by tramway, including stops in the suburbs of Langfahr and Olivia.

The tram, powered by electricity, could have run very well on the excess energy being generated by the boys of the Danzig Gang. Lori sat at the far end of the bright yellow and green tram and tried to pretend she did not know who these noisy, rowdy, gawking travelers were.

All to no avail, of course. They whooped and pointed out the window and yelled down to her over the heads of other prim and disapproving passengers. *"Hey Lori! Lori! Lori! Look at that! Do you see that?"*

When the crescent curve of Danzig Bay appeared there was a sudden roar, the tumult of explorers seeing a new land for the first time and claiming that they really did *see it first*! Lori casually looked at the bright waters of the Baltic as though she had seen the bay a thousand times. She glanced away at the wooded hill sloping up from Sopot as if the new green of leaves were far more interesting. Jamie, Mark, Alfie, and Jacob pressed their faces against the tram windows like a group of caged orangutans reaching for a banana.

"There it is! Look at it! I won because I saw it first!"

"No! I saw it first!"

Just when it seemed there might be violence over who actually laid eyes on Danzig Bay first, Lori stood regally and pronounced, "I saw it first."

Silence descended, and then Alfie shook his head slowly. "No, you don't count . . . because you was not in on it." He seemed indignant over her intrusion in so great a matter. The other passengers looked at her curiously, wondering what she could say to satisfy this big fellow who was obviously not quite all there in the head.

She clutched at the leather strap and swayed for a moment as the tram rattled over the tracks. And then she spotted Werner-cat on Alfie's broad shoulder.

"Werner saw it first," she said. "Werner wins the ice cream, then."

Alfie liked the answer and congratulated his cat for seeing the bay first. The other boys groaned all together and told her to sit down and stay out of it. Then a new bet was born and the old one disregarded.

"First one into the water, then!"

"Not just touching it, but in!"

"Over the head! First one in over the head!"

Werner-cat would not be in this competition, they told Alfie. Cats did not like to swim even when the water was warm, so Werner would have to sit this one out.

"And you too, Lori," Jamie Ibsen warned his sister.

"Ah, you know girls," Mark added. "She won't get her hair wet anyway."

So went the conversation on the Danzig tram to Sopot. The line scooted along the seashore—iridescent blue sea on the right and the famous hotel and casino named Kurhaus right across from the pier. There was Northpark and Southpark where less brave bathers could play under the yew trees or ride a donkey cart. For those who preferred warm water to the real feel of the Baltic, there was the *Warmbad,* a heated pool complete with cabana and a brass oompah band on weekends.

Lori would have been quite happy with that luxury, but as the tram slipped by the wide awning of the building, the orangutans began to chant their cry about *the old lady pool, the pool for infants and convalescing arthritis patients.*

At that instant Lori spotted a jabbering tribe of flabby-thighed mothers being pulled into the entrance by their young children. Ah well, perhaps warm water was not everything.

Directly between Northpark and Southpark, where the courtyard of the Kurhaus Casino faced the Seesteg Pier, the tram grumbled and clanged and stopped.

Lori peered into the glittering entrance of the Kurhaus Casino and then back toward the Baltic. At this moment she remembered her father. This was the place Karl Ibsen had spoken of! Here it was! Why had she not remembered before this moment? *The Tram Ride to Temptation! The casino on one side and the ocean on the other! And there you are, caught between the devil and the deep blue sea!*

Papa had been here as a young man. To this *exact* place! He had told the story often of how he walked through the casino with its baccarat tables and roulette wheels. He had been the only one of his university friends who had not bet and had not gambled away all his funds for vacation.

"So this was the place," Lori whispered as the boys crammed through the tram doors all at the same moment and ran full bore toward the sparkling waters!

Lori simply savored the moment. She felt the nearness of the old story and wished that Papa were here to tell her all over again. She had not been heartsick for him for a long time, but the memory of his laughter and his warning about this very spot made her miss him fiercely!

She stepped off the tram and stood transfixed before the very door where Papa had entered as a young man. *Before he had even met Mama, he said!* She walked toward it, wishing very much to see this wilderness of sin where Papa had been tempted.

Suddenly Jacob spoke her name. "Are you coming, Lori?" He smiled at her. "Or do you want to see the casino?"

Her eyes widened. Did they dare go in? "Do you think. . . ?"

Jacob took her arm, propelling her past the red-coated doorman. "You know our fathers were here together." He hurried through the revolving door. "When they were at University."

"You mean *your* father?" The reek of stale tobacco greeted her. The clear voice of the croupier called out that bets must be placed. Then the whirl and the tick . . . tick . . . tick of the spinning roulette wheel.

"Yes. Our fathers." Jacob was grinning as he took in all the opulent splendor of this enormous gaming hall. "My father said a woman could walk through one of these casinos stark naked and probably nobody would look up . . . too busy losing their own shirts. Father lost all his money, he and the other fellows with him. Only Pastor Ibsen—except your father was not a pastor then, but quite a man about town—well, he was the only one who would not gamble. So everyone else lost their money and would have starved if Pastor Ibsen had not . . ."

Tears came to Lori's eyes. It was foolish of her. Embarrassing. But here she was hearing the other side of a story that was an Ibsen legend! And now . . . where were those two young men who had strolled through the Kurhaus? Where were the fathers of Jacob and Lori now?

A heavy foreboding for her own future came over Lori with that thought. And what was to become of *them* . . . the *Danzig Gang*? If there was a war? If their British visas did not come through? They were having such a lovely day, but all those worries came crashing down on her in the middle of it.

Jacob put his arm around her. "I . . . I'm sorry. I did not mean to. I thought you would think it was funny."

She nodded. "It is . . . or it *was* . . . but . . ." Her words trailed off. The thought that their fathers were both in a Nazi prison or worse . . . after so many wonderful years of friendship, somehow stole the laughter even from old memories. "I am, *really*, all right. I just . . . don't want to ever look back and wish for . . . all the good times *we* have had. All of us together, I mean. To be apart or . . ."

They inched their way through a crowd gathered around the roulette wheel. There was no need to say more. There were ghosts even here, in the laughter of the young men of Kurhaus. Jacob heard them, too. *The laughter of their fathers at age twenty, when they could not have known what the future held for them. Their wives. Their children . . .*

"Stupid of me," Jacob said as they emerged again into the bright clean air. "This is our day," he said gently. "We should make our own memories today, yes? And maybe one day tell our children?" He wiped away her only tear with his calloused thumb. Yet another tram arrived behind him and disgorged its passengers; some to the devil and some toward the deep blue sea.

Jacob sat beside Lori on the beach, but he never looked at her, never noticed the new swimsuit or the new Lori. His eyes were everywhere but on her—on the three boys splashing in the surf; on the little girl building sand castles; on the old couple walking their dog just out of reach of the waves. He studied the clouds that drifted across the sun, cutting off its warmth and then letting it loose again. But he did not notice the goose bumps on Lori's bare arms when the wind came up. He did not know why she did not at least wear her blouse over the swimsuit when bursts of cold breeze blew in from the Baltic.

Lori sighed. Could he really think she was enjoying this ordeal? Why did he not look at her once and *notice* that she was quite grown now? *A woman!* A half-frozen woman forcing a pleasant look on her face as she waited for him to glance her way just once! After that, she reasoned, she would ask to borrow his sweater like Garbo had done in . . . *what was the name of that film?*

Never mind. Jacob looked at the pier when she talked to

him. When she asked him to rub suntan oil on her back, he said, "No thank you. I'm fine."

"Well *I'm* not. I could burn!"

He looked over her head at the heated swimming pool. "Then put your shirt on. Or go inside."

Instead, she turned over and let the sun beat down on her beet-red face. Even a sunburn could not outdo the flush of her embarrassment at his rebuff. She closed her eyes so he would not see how near to tears she was. A cool breeze swept across her skin, but suddenly she was very warm. She wished he would go swim with Alfie and the boys. She was sorry she ever bought this swimsuit, ashamed that she had thought of *Jacob* when she looked at her own reflection in the mirror.

Minutes passed. The dull crash of waves mingled with happy shrieks and dozens of voices. Lori could hear Alfie's deep, pleasant chuckle as he stammered some challenge to Mark and Jamie.

"Bet I . . . I . . . can hold my . . . breath longest . . ."

Jacob heard Alfie too, and now he spoke. "You were right, you know," Jacob said softly. "We could not have left Alfie in Berlin, and—"

She opened her eyes, certain of what he would say next. "We are *all* going together," she said almost angrily.

"But if they don't let him—"

"We have to believe! Papa would say . . . and I say now, God is in charge of even little sparrows. Why would He forsake Alfie?" She sat up and watched as big Alfie, fifteen-year-old Alfie, played contentedly with the little boys.

"But *if* . . . you know, Lori, I would have to stay with him. Find some way to get him out of here. He said it. They are here, the Nazis are. It's a matter of time. And—"

It was instinct. She rammed him hard in the ribs with her elbow and then drew back, as horrified by the blow as he was.

His breath came out with an *oof!*

"What?" He finally looked at her. "Why did you—?"

"Because. *Shut up!* Our *one* day at the beach, and you find *gloom* to talk about! And here I have been all day, wearing *this*. . . ."

At last! At last his eyes swept over her! She wanted to cheer! He looked at her for a moment, at least! Then he looked away quickly, back toward the boys.

"You didn't even notice," she finished quietly.

Jacob drew a deep breath, like a man inhaling the healthy sea air. He drew another breath and exhaled loudly. His eyes seemed glazed. His jaw muscle flexed.

"Are you . . . *all right?*" Now Lori thought perhaps she had hurt him with the jab to his ribs.

He sighed slowly, then put his head in his hands. "Oh," he moaned, "this is not doing any good at all!"

Now she knew she had hurt him! "Oh, Jacob! I'm so sorry!"

He stood, scattering sand on the blanket and on her. Stretching his neck, he squinted at the pier, the sea, the sky, the dog, the bath house. Then, as if he struggled against some powerful force, his face jerked around and he locked his gaze on her. Helpless resignation filled his eyes as he drank her in. Her eyes. Her throat. Shoulder. Arm. *Please, please, not the breasts. . .*Too late. Even as he battled himself, he took in every inch of her beautiful, incredible, too-perfect body.

"There!" He ran a hand through his hair. "All day I have been trying *not* to look—not to notice. And now look!"

It was the wrong thing to do, but Lori smiled up at him in his misery. "You have been the perfect gentleman," she said softly. "But I have not been a lady." She reached for her blouse.

Jacob knelt down beside her and put his hand on her arm. He shook his head slowly and moved nearer, his eyes never leaving hers. *Too late, Lori. Too late. You are beautiful; I knew that anyway, and now you are going to get kissed. . . .*

Waves still crashed against the sand. Children still laughed and shouted at the water's edge. Their voices carried far above Lori and Jacob like the hollow voices in a dream. The breeze was cool, but Lori did not notice anything but his lips against hers.

11 The Prodigal Sister

Wolf had left nothing to chance when he prepared for his first meeting with the priest at Marienkirche. He had called ahead and made an appointment, giving a brief summary of the situation. Posing as the worried and grief-stricken brother of Lucy, he had spoken of her as any brother might speak of a sister who had been deceived and abandoned by her lover.

Naturally, the priest had been most sympathetic and eager to help in any way.

Wolf had additional photos of Lucy copied. Along with the photograph of her on the steps of St. Stephan's, he included one with her in a red low-cut gown. In her raised hand was a glass of champagne. In this one, her face reflected the seductive look that was much more familiar to Wolf than what the doctor had described as Lucy's "innocence." In the mental script Wolf prepared for this interview, he labeled the two photos *before-he-seduced-her* and *after-he-took-her-from-her-family*. Wolf had dealt with these ecclesiastical types before; he was certain that he had only to say these words with the right touch of bitterness and sorrow, and the priest would move heaven and earth to help him locate his "prodigal sister." Even if he had not personally seen Lucy in his great cathedral, this priest would know who Wolf should contact within other Danzig parishes. Coupled with his own personal performance of sorrow, Wolf would offer a reward to the Catholic diocese in Danzig. A charitable contribution from his wealthy Prussian family in exchange for the return of his sister and her illegitimate child to the fold.

Well armed with this story, Wolf took a taxi to the massive Gothic cathedral that dominated the skyline of Danzig. Wolf considered the building not as one might look on a holy site, but as an example of pure German culture. Founded in the fourteenth century by Teutonic knights, Marienkirche was the mightiest example of German architecture in the Baltic. The massive west bell tower consisted of ancient brick rising to a summit 248 feet above the cobblestone street. Ten slender turrets reached heavenward from the gables. Inside, the beautiful grained vaulting was supported by twenty-eight pillars. The aisles and transepts were flanked with private chapels dedicated to German merchant burgomasters and their families. In the walls and floors between the buttresses, the proud and the rich descendants of those first Teutonic knights waited for eternity.

For Wolfgang von Fritschauer, the glory of Marienkirche had nothing to do with the Lord it claimed to glorify. In the gilded high altar, the woodcarvings, and stained-glass images of the apostles and Christ, Wolf did not see the Spirit of the living God—he saw the spirit of Aryan culture. He deified the stone carvers and the ancient painters, the builders of this place. They were his ancestors; those workers of this wonder—German, one and all. If the painted scene were not the image of Christ—if, instead, it were the face of Thor hurling thunderbolts to earth, it would have had equal meaning to Wolf. The great altarpiece depicting *The Last Judgment,* with its swirling smoke and rising flame and the angry face of a vengeful God, could just as easily have been made in the image of the Führer. The judgment of the German people was soon coming on the earth. The victory of German culture would be celebrated with new significance in this place. A new inferno was planned for those unworthy to enter the paradise of national socialism. And worthiness was, of course, determined by German law.

All these things flashed though Wolf's mind as he genuflected before the crucifix and extended his hand to the priest. He felt no awareness of blasphemy in his thoughts. His beliefs were as natural to him as breathing. The fact that he himself was worthy to be called pure of blood was owed to the wisdom of his ancestors. They had known the value of untainted race, and had practiced it long before the bricks of Marienkirche had risen as their monument.

The priest was short and swarthy—obviously of some mixed Slavic blood. He invited Wolf to follow him through a labyrinth of hallways to his office where they might speak privately about the man's sister. The priest could not guess the revulsion and disdain Wolf felt as he stared at the back of his too-round head and sloping shoulders.

"Won't you be seated, Herr von Fritschauer?" The priest kindly indicated a large tooled-leather chair beside his desk.

"Thank you, Father." Wolf opened his briefcase, displaying a stack of Lucy's photographs among his business papers. The priest sat opposite him and listened sympathetically to the story of Lucy Strasburg *before* and Lucy *after*. Not an unusual story these days in Germany. Young women in the *Bund Deutscher Mädel*, the "League of German Girls," were encouraged to have illegitimate children for the Reich.

Wolf brushed over the priest's obvious disapproval of the Nazi policies of rewarding immorality. He held fast to his story: "I am prepared to offer a reward to benefit the charity of your choice if you might help bring Lucy home." He fanned a dozen pictures out on the scarred desk. "Perhaps if you could make some phone calls on behalf of my family, put her picture into the hands of any who might have seen her here in Danzig."

And so it was as simple as that. A model of charity and kindness, the good Father promised to do all he could to return this wayward girl to her family.

The great bells of Marienkirche tolled high noon as Wolf strode confidently from the building.

————

With its bright yellow sides and lime-green roof, the Danzig tram No. 5 glided to a stop like a giant banana on rails. Danzig trams and taxis were the only things that seemed out of character in the medieval city.

Lucy considered the queue of passengers for only one moment of temptation. She fingered the few coins she carried in the deep pocket of her sweater. She had brought along these precious savings today for a special purpose. Although her ankles were swollen and her back ached terribly, she would not squander what little she had left on a tram ride out to shop.

Raising her chin slightly, she pretended that she simply preferred to walk. After all, walking was the best exercise for pregnant women. Women in this condition had been walking to market in Danzig long before these miracles of transportation were even imagined!

Peter had given up riding on the tram as well, but for a different reason. One day near the synagogue on Hunde Strasse the sign above the tram stop had been painted: *HUNDE STRASSE – HOUND STREET: DOGS ALLOWED – NO JEWS.*

Lucy had told him that she would not ride the public tram, either, if such signs were allowed to remain. It was a matter of honor.

159

But Peter was gone to Warsaw now, and if Lucy had only had money enough, she knew that today she would have gladly traded a bit of her newfound principle for even a few moments of luxury.

Never mind that, she told herself. *Hadn't Mama always gone out to milk the cows when she was expecting, even on the days the babies came? It was good for her, Mama said. Good for me, too.*

Lucy found herself thinking a lot about her mother these days—missing her, longing to ask her a thousand questions. But there was no use trying to contact her parents. No doubt Wolf would have them watched. He wanted the child Lucy carried, and she did not doubt that her mother and father had already been questioned and warned. Probably once they learned of Lucy's condition they had gone to the priest and had the Mass read for her. They had mentally buried her in the plot reserved for sinners. She would not have been welcome in her father's house even if there had been some way to get home without being discovered by Wolf.

So there is no use thinking of Mama, except to remember what she did before each baby came.

She struck out along the waterfront known as Speicher-Insel. Here the ancient stucco and half-timbered grain elevators unloaded their freight onto cargo ships as they had done for centuries. Peter had found work here. Now that he was gone, there were a hundred men in line to take his job. The place was teeming with dock workers who would have stopped in their tracks to take a look at her only a few months before. Now not one head turned, Lucy noted in amusement. For the first time since she turned thirteen, men were not gawking at her, raising their eyebrows or winking.

She was just another pregnant Frau on her way to the green gate that led to Langer Market. Pregnancy had blessed her with a cloak of anonymity. She bore little resemblance to the stylish woman who had attended the opera in Vienna with the Nazi party officials. Nothing about her suggested that she had once sat beside the Führer and been admired by the most powerful men in the German Reich. All that was gone. With swollen ankles, swollen belly, and a puffy, weary-looking face, Lucy Strasburg was far from radiant. Perhaps that was the reason the Aryan mothers at the S.S. maternity homes were kept in strict confinement. No doubt the Nazi hierarchy did not wish to disillusion those potential mothers for the Reich who believed that carrying a child for the Führer gave young mothers the status and looks of a goddess.

Some goddess, Lucy thought as she caught her reflection in a shop window. She wondered what Wolf would say if he could see her now. Then she wondered what he would do to her if he ever found her here in Danzig.

Still, even with that remote possibility, she did not regret her decision not to go to Warsaw with Peter.

Lucy Strasburg saw the future of Danzig quite as clearly as Peter saw it. The howling threats of the Führer of Germany against Danzig and Poland were unmistakable. But the certainty of what was about to come made her adamant that she would never go to Warsaw. She had heard the German generals with her own ears as they spoke of the devastation their Air Force and tanks could bring to that place. All of Poland could not stand for a week against the divisions of the Reich. Cavalry units and flashing sabres and suicide charges across the open fields would mean nothing against airplanes and panzer units. And now the giant Skoda armament factories of Czechoslovakia were in German control. Coal and steel mills and great deposits of iron had come into the orbit of *Mein Kampf.*

Lucy knew it. Maybe everyone knew it by now. Peter Wallich had run off to Warsaw, but it was only a matter of time.

And in spite of their promises, England would remain on its side of the Channel. They might declare war, but they would not come to help Poland until the Requiem Mass was read over all the dead of Warsaw. France would sit behind the great concrete wall known as the Maginot Line, and they, too, would wait.

It was not really a matter of language, Lucy thought as she walked through the bustling streets of Danzig. It was simply that one place on the Continent of Europe was no more safe than another. Just because there were no swastika flags replacing flower boxes in Warsaw did not mean that it would not soon be the case.

Not Warsaw for Lucy. Given any choice in the matter, she preferred to be somewhere else when the final bells of the Requiem tolled.

As if to reinforce her thoughts, the bells of Marienkirche boomed out over the city of Danzig. Lucy looked up toward the

161

bell tower, remembering how she and Peter had climbed the steep stairs to watch the bell ringer on his wooden treadmill turning the green-tarnished gears that moved the bells. One strong man in that little squirrel cage caused all this commotion. Pigeons swirled skyward, people checked their watches and shuttered their shops for lunchtime. Danzig ordered its existence by the bells of Marienkirche.

Lucy knew that those bells would soon be ringing a life-shattering event for the Danzigers. *"One day,"* Hitler had shouted, *"the bells of Marienkirche will announce the reunification of German Danzig with the Reich!"*

When that day came, Lucy Strasburg hoped to be somewhere else. Not Warsaw. Not Paris. Not Brussels . . .

Lucy carried two books in the deep pockets of her smock. One book was an English-German dictionary. The other was a thin green volume she had found on the table of a used-book seller in the open market. This book she studied as though it contained the secrets of eternal life. *Her life. The life of her unborn baby. . . .*

WAITING AT TABLE
A Practical Guide
Including
PARLOURMAID'S WORK IN GENERAL
By
MRS. C.S. PEEL, O.B.E.

The bookseller did not know what the *O.B.E.* stood for after Mrs. Peel's name. However, he guaranteed that the former owner of this precious green volume had studied its contents and obtained a British visa, traveling to London, England, as a domestic servant. Lucy had heard of other such miracles. England did not want doctors or lawyers or skilled workers, but they were still in need of domestics—parlormaids who knew how to carve a leg of lamb properly!

Lucy had shelled out her few pennies and had purchased first the book, then the dictionary to help her decipher its secrets.

When the first drone of Luftwaffe engines was heard over Danzig and Warsaw, Lucy hoped to be practicing the fine art of carving loin of lamb, neck of veal, knuckle of veal, breast of veal, ham, hare, or rabbit. This was as far as she had gotten in

162

her studies, and it was all difficult to remember since she had none of these things to actually practice carving. It had been a long time since she had eaten anything but the cheapest sausage and cheese. Reading about real food often made her mouth water. Dishing up such delicacies had filled her dreams. At night she closed her eyes and recited the catechism of carving: *chops should be cut off, beginning with the outer chop, unless these are too large, when slices should be cut the whole length of the joint. . . .*

As the baby kicked and thumped within her, she would drift off to mouth-watering dreams of steaming heaps of lamb on a plate before her. Nightmares about Wolf had long since faded, and the practical issues of food had filled his place nicely.

But in the clear light of day, when temptations beckoned her through the window of Haueisen Confectioners, she turned her face away from the eclair or heaping sandwich. Her fingers tightened around her coin purse. There were more important things to purchase than food. *Diapers. A basket for the baby to sleep in. Two glass baby bottles and spare nipples.*

Not that Lucy expected to need bottles. She would nurse her baby, as her own mother had nursed Lucy and her brothers and sisters.

Still, just in case, she bought canned milk. And it would be wonderful to find a christening robe with lace and little booties and a bonnet! The baby must be christened! Lucy had determined that this little one would be blessed by a priest, in spite of how it had come into being. Lucy was condemned, but she would not let that heartache touch this baby. She loved it, even unborn, and she yearned for it to have all the sweet little things a baby should have.

Lucy looked through the display window of the children's shop. Tiny shirts and gowns and little caps were draped over stuffed bears and a soft pink rabbit. Ruffled blankets and matching sheets adorned a hand-carved rosewood cradle.

She pulled out her list and studied it. *Diapers. Bottles. Alcohol for umbilical cord. Aspirin. Sanitary pads. Disinfectant.*

Lucy had attended two of her mother's deliveries. She had watched the milk cows give birth; seen kittens born. There was no money for a doctor. But the baby of Lucy Strasburg would have a christening gown. Silk and white lace. And matching booties. A bonnet over the velvety head.

This much, Lucy determined, she would do for her baby.

————————

The prow of the White Star Line freighter rose and fell in a steady rhythm against the six-foot swells beyond the Tel Aviv sea wall.

Sam Orde did not look back toward the receding shoreline of Palestine. He stood braced in the windy bow of the ship and fixed his gaze on the gun-metal gray wall of clouds on the horizon. There was a squall up ahead, unusual for this time of year on the Mediterranean.

The cargo hold was filled with enormous flats of citrus fruit. Crates of oranges, lemons, limes, and grapefruits had been loaded by cranes. Fruit was placed in porcelain bowls in the otherwise sparsely provisioned passenger cabins. Fresh orange juice was promised for every breakfast. Lemonade was on hand at any hour. Limes were sliced and readily available for those passengers who preferred gin and tonic in the ship's salon. Orde was grateful the cargo was not onions or garlic.

Eleven other passengers traveled on board the *Lady of Avon*. Orde had boarded before any of them and had slept through their boarding and initial introductions. He dreaded polite conversation and inane questions that inevitably accompanied a small passenger list and a long voyage. The weight of the past few weeks was heavy on him. He hoped only to pass the voyage to England by long hours of sleep and as little human interaction as possible.

A number of the other passengers gathered on the stern of the ship. They strained their eyes for the last glimpse of the Holy Land. When Orde heard them pass by the porthole of his cabin, he emerged to stroll to the opposite end of the freighter. He braced himself in the bow and closed his eyes as he inhaled the cold, salty mist. A sea gull circled above his head, crying, and then wheeled away, back toward the land.

"Captain Orde, is it?" The voice of a young Englishman startled Orde.

No ship was large enough for anonymity, it seemed. He barely glanced at the smiling face of a man he had never met before. How did the fellow know his name?

"Yes. I don't believe I have had the pleasure . . ."

The fellow laughed. "Oh dear me, no. You don't know me.

But I saw your picture in the newspaper. Right after that dreadful incident on the Temple Mount. An interview about the chap who was killed. Dreadful. Hard to forget such a thing. And I never forget a face."

"I see." Orde turned back to face the wind. He was being rude, but then so was this fellow, intruding on Orde's privacy.

"We heard you had resigned. Good heavens. A pity. A chap puts his whole life into the Army and then something like this happens." Perhaps the words were meant to be sympathetic, but an alarm bell sounded in Orde's brain.

Whitecaps topped the swells. The wind was cold, penetrating Orde's heavy cable-knit sweater and corduroy trousers. But he had claimed this spot in the bow and felt strangely unwilling to give up its solitude to anyone. Perhaps if he waited, the young man would grow bored and wander back with the other passengers.

The intruder buttoned his heavy coat and remained in place. He seemed unaware of Orde's melancholy reverie. Or if he knew, he was still determined to stand at the rail.

"Going back home to your wife and family, then are you?" He was oblivious to his own bad manners.

"No. Just going home to Mother England," Orde replied, unwilling to admit that a raw nerve had been struck.

"Well, what will you do with yourself?" He gripped the rail beside Orde. Uninvited. Unwelcome. "I mean, do you have some kind of job?"

Orde turned to face him with the same withering stare he might give a recruit whose gun was not properly cleaned. He raised his chin, exuding his military authority. He did not speak until the young man's exuberant curiosity wilted beneath the glare of rank. "You are just the sort of chap I enjoy getting under my command. A bit of cleaning up and discipline, and you might polish out half decent." Orde rose slightly on his toes with satisfaction at the horrified expression on the stunned face. "However, since I will not have opportunity to teach you manners, and I detest rudeness, I will retreat and leave you the forward position."

With a cold smile, Orde nodded his head and left the fellow staring after him.

Perhaps it was best not to mingle at all with the other passengers, Orde reasoned as he closed the door of his cabin. He could pay a bit more and take his meals in his room. *Wife and family. . . Mother England . . .* His wife was dead, and Mother England was angry with him. What did that leave him? What was he to do now?

Questions and self-doubt led to a wave of self-pity that threatened to drown him. He told himself that his faith in God had not wavered, only his faith that God had any use for him. This was the most devastating doubt of all. Orde had suffered losses before in his life. Katie had died in an auto accident near their home in Surrey. With her had perished their unborn child and all of Orde's hopes to live the normal life of a husband and father. He had raised his head and asked himself, *What now?* In that moment he found total dedication to the military was the only way to fill the empty hours. He embraced Mother England and believed that in fulfilling his duty to the English government in Palestine, he was also serving God. For years he had lived only for that purpose, that fulfillment.

Tonight, the chasm of uselessness opened before him. For the first time since she had gone, Orde allowed himself the luxury of longing for Katie once again. Yes, he had often thought of her; wondered what she would say about this event or that. He had imagined her tenderly in a thousand different ways. But tonight, he longed for her, ached for her, desired her once again.

He closed his eyes against the starlight that glistened through the porthole. Breathing in, he remembered the sweet fragrance of her skin. He reached his hand up into the emptiness above him as if to touch her face, to brush a finger across her lips and pull her down to kiss him.

He swallowed hard and opened his eyes again when the longing became unbearable. *So this was loneliness.* His eyes were moist, and now he questioned not himself, not England, but the God who had taken Katie from him and had cast him adrift.

He sat up and held his head in his hands in despair. Then he switched on the light and rummaged through his duffle bag for the well-worn Bible Katie had given him on their fourth anniversary. Almost desperate for comfort, he flipped open the cover to her delicate handwriting.

My Dearest Husband,
   Four years of joy with you on earth makes me long for an

eternity of joy with you. We will stand together before the Lord, and may He say to each of us, "Well done." Until then, it is your duty to serve Him in faraway and dangerous lands. It is mine to stay behind and bravely watch you go. To pray and believe that He goes with you always, even as He always stays by me in lonely times. Even when we do not see the answers we must pray and believe that our Lord knows all. This faith is all that He asks of us. It is the only real battle we fight. In the end this is why He will say, "Well done."

Your loving wife,
Katie.

Orde read her words as if seeing them for the first time. He wiped away tears with the back of his hand and whispered thanks to her. He had not dreamed that she would one day leave him behind. Nor had he imagined that he would ever face a moment so bleak in his life that he would be forced to say, *"I do not understand, and yet I trust in You, Lord!"*

Tonight, Orde said those words aloud. And for the first time he understood that the biggest battle was not fought against Muslim terrorists on the slopes of Zion, but against the doubt and despair that threatened to destroy true faith in God's love.

In the small dark hours as the ship steadily moved away from Palestine, Orde won that battle. As Jesus prayed in Gethsemane, Orde bowed his head and said, "Not my will, but yours be done."

———

The purple glow of dawn shone through the window of Karl Ibsen's cell. A single morning star was framed between the center bars to wink in at the sleeping prisoner. If he had opened his eyes, he would have felt the nearness of heaven by the light of that star. He would have smiled and imagined that the star was really an angel watching over him. But Karl did not awaken until the sky had ripened into morning and a beam of light penetrated his consciousness.

Far away he heard the song of birds in the forest that ringed Nameless camp, and then he heard the flutter of feathered wings above him. An angel? He did not open his eyes to see. Again the gentle rustle sounded, followed by a small, unmelodious chirp.

The lady sparrow had returned to the window ledge. Karl

opened his eyes but did not move as he watched her peck curiously at the bread he had placed in the center of the bars.

Peck . . . peck . . . peck . . . and then a resounding "cheep!" With this exultant cry, she called another to join her at the feast. A darker-feathered sparrow whirred to her side. She deferred to him, hopping back a step and waiting politely until he plunged his orange beak first into one piece of bread and then into the next. Lady Sparrow cocked an eye toward Karl as if to remark that she knew where the bread had come from and how much she appreciated such an exorbitant gift in a place where starvation was so common. Karl nodded almost imperceptibly.

The big male sparrow hefted a morsel in his beak and then flew out of sight. Lady Sparrow waited a moment longer before she turned her attention away from Karl and likewise wrestled with a piece of bread, grasping it in her beak and hopping off the ledge.

One small square of Karl's offering remained. He knew the sparrows would come back for it. And if they came back once, they would come back a thousand times. They would return for as long as Karl continued to feed them. "Company," Karl whispered. "Thank you. Thank you, Jesus, for caring about sparrows. About me. About Lori and Jamie. . . ."

Father Kopecky arrived at the door of the Lubetkin home with a paper sack of plums and a package of fresh trout from the fish market. Unlike other friends and neighbors of the Lubetkin family, the priest did not bring food prepared in his own unkosher kitchen. For this sensitivity to the ways of a Jewish household, Etta was quietly grateful.

She led him down the hallway to Papa's room. "You see how well he looks!" Papa sat up in bed, waiting impatiently for Rachel to set up the chess board for their game, which was fast becoming a thrice weekly event.

"He looks like a scarecrow," Father Kopecky said with a grin on his impish face. "Today he will not beat me at chess like he did two days ago."

"Man looks at the outside," Papa declared, "while the Eternal knows what is in the mind of an accomplished chess player."

The priest took his seat beside Rachel. "Then God should tell me a few of your chess moves just to be fair about it." He winked at Rachel, which made her blush.

Sometimes she liked the priest. Other times he made her uncomfortable.

"Give it up, my friend," Papa said, rubbing his hands together in anticipation. "You do battle against a son of the covenant." He held up the black king in a threatening way. "Have you forgotten the words of the prophet Balaam? *He has blessed, and I cannot change it. . . . The shout of their King is among them. . . . Their king will be greater than Agag.*" He coughed as his own joke made him laugh. "Besides, you are a lousy chess player." He set his king back in place.

"Etta," cried the priest, "have I come here to be insulted?"

Mama smiled and shrugged. "Don't insult him, Aaron," she chided Papa. "He has brought us fresh plums and trout from the market. Let him win for once."

Then Mama jerked her head for Rachel to come out with her and leave the two friends to their game.

"He is good for your father," Mama said to Rachel as she unwrapped the fish.

"I like him," Rachel agreed. "But I do not trust him always." The headlines of the newspaper caught her attention. It was a Polish newspaper. A publication for the Saturday people who did not like Jews. In the house of Aaron Lubetkin, only Yiddish papers were read and studied. This newspaper was something quite different. It contained advertisements directed at Polish women for fashions from Paris. It held theater and cabaret listings. And today, it displayed a banner headline announcing that German Culture Week had been declared in Danzig! Smaller articles explained that for the occasion, a German battleship was scheduled to come into the port, and that Poland had forbidden such a thing. One thousand Gestapo and two thousand members of the S.A. were reported to be in Danzig. Jewish harassment there was being stepped up. Polish reservists had been called up, and German troops were playing war games across the border where Czechoslovakia used to be.

Etta noticed that even though she was talking to Rachel, her daughter had not heard a word for the last several minutes. She stood at Rachel's shoulder and read the news as seen through the eyes of an outraged Polish government. She looked from the newspaper to the fish and wondered out loud if the priest had wrapped his gift in this edition for any particular reason. Then she gathered it up just as Rachel was getting to the most frightening part of the story: *Poland has three hundred tanks, Germany has two thousand. . . .*

"Just the sort of thing suitable for wrapping fish," Mama said lightly as if the old black print did not send a shiver through her as it did through Rachel.

"It will be all right," Rachel agreed, turning to wash the plums. "Nothing will happen here, Mama. That is why people like Peter Wallich have come to Warsaw from Danzig, isn't it? The German Gestapo would not dare to come here. And as for the tanks, Papa says German tanks cannot outmaneuver the Polish cavalry. We are safe in Warsaw."

Mama heard her. She nodded, but did not reply other than that. German Culture Week in Danzig! Battleships in the harbor—over the Poles' dead bodies! Maybe it would come to that. Over their dead bodies. Maybe Hitler would also come to Warsaw and sleep in Pototzki Palace as he had slept in the castle in Prague.

All these fears were evident in Mama's eyes, although she did not say them to Rachel. And Rachel suddenly felt angry at the priest for wrapping the fish in such an ominous herald of the current events! Had he done such a thing on purpose, to frighten Mama into sending Rachel and David and Samuel and baby Yacov away? But where would they go? Was not one place the same as any other? At least here they had a roof over their heads. Why had the priest been so cruel?

Rachel could see that her mother was very pale. She looked ill. She looked afraid, just as she had the night Papa had been arrested.

"Go tell Frau Groshenki we are bringing the boys home now, tonight," she said, and Rachel saw that her hands were shaking.

"But what about our charade? No one will believe Papa has typhoid if we bring the boys home."

Mama looked at her sadly, as if the illusion did not matter anymore. "We should all be together," Mama said. "Here. Home. Under the same roof."

Rachel stared silently at her mother as the implication sunk in. *In times of trouble, in desperate hours, the family must stay together for as long . . . as long as it remained possible.* Did Mama believe the Germans were coming to Warsaw, too?

Mama looked out the kitchen window as a bee buzzed and

bumped against the glass pane. In that small hum, could she imagine the drone of airplanes overhead?

"Go on, Rachel," Mama said, wadding up the paper and throwing it angrily into the rubbish can. "Bring the boys home now. We have fine fish for supper. A feast."

Rachel left the house reluctantly, feeling as though the sky might tumble down before she got home with her brothers! Was the feast, in reality, about to end?

———

"It is not typhoid fever," Rachel told Frau Groshenki. "Rheumatic fever. Not catching, and so Mama wants us all to be home together."

With this simple statement of truth, Rachel felt a sudden relief. Perhaps the Poles were too busy now worrying about what the German hornet's nest was up to for one little rabbi to matter anymore. And why would they come again to arrest a man as sick as Papa? He would die if they took him. The doctor had said he must not be moved farther than from his bed to the bathroom. No physical exertion. Certainly the Polish police would know that they could not move the rabbi, because then the state would end up having to pay the cost of a burial and no purpose would be served by it.

And so the charade had ended. Frau Groshenki praised the mercy of the Eternal that the beloved Rabbi Lubetkin only had rheumatic fever instead of typhoid! "A miracle!" she exclaimed as she helped Rachel pack the boys' things.

This was the first time Rachel had heard of anyone praising the Eternal that someone had rheumatic fever! Ah well, it was the Jewish way of life, nu? *Things could always be worse....* And when things could not possibly get any worse, it was time to think of possibilities so terrible that one could still declare, "Things *could* always be worse." From there it was a short step to long recitations of how things were *much* worse for this cousin or that uncle. Such conversation made people feel better.

"You hear that, David?" Frau Groshenki said to David as he gratefully hefted his valise. "Your father the rabbi only has rheumatic fever. God be praised. Not typhoid. Or *worse,* like my cousin Mordechai, paralyzed from the neck down and living like the living dead! Oy! Now *that* is the worst."

Rachel gathered Little Yani in her arms. The baby nuzzled

her face in slobbery kisses of infant gratitude, as if to tell her that nothing could be worse than being cooped up in Frau Groshenki's house!

David and Samuel thanked the Frau properly for her hospitality and then, when they were out of earshot, they railed on her for everything from her endless gossip to her piggish table manners.

"She talks with her mouth full of gefilte fish, Rachel!" David declared.

"She dips her pound cake in her teacup," Samuel added with five-year-old disgust. "And then she slurps up the soggy crumbs."

"Sometimes she brushes her teeth . . . but not usually." David wanted to be fair in his reporting.

"And she says the Nazis are going to come here to Warsaw and kill all who are Jews," said Samuel. "Even the *baby*!"

Rachel could tolerate the fact that Frau Groshenki ate like a pig and did not brush her teeth! *After all, things could be worse.* But this repetition of the worst fears in her own heart made her angry.

"She is a *nebech*!" Rachel declared angrily. "She is nothing!"

"What is rape?" David tugged his earlock thoughtfully.

Rachel stopped in the street and whirled to face the Groshenki house. She was furious. Did her brother see how that word angered her?

Little Samuel said in a serious voice, "Frau Groshenki says that when the Nazis come, they will rape the women."

David added, "She says she will die rather than be raped."

Rachel's eyes narrowed as she pictured the fat, wrinkled face of Frau Groshenki looking up at German soldiers and begging them to kill her rather than rape her. "She won't have to die," Rachel said in a haughty tone. "The Germans are not coming, and even if they did, I can promise that they would not be interested in Frau Groshenki!"

"But what if they come here?" Samuel asked as they walked slowly across the square.

Rachel looked up into the linden trees. She pointed to a nest of twigs where a family of sparrows lived. "The little birds would know if Nazis were coming. They fly everywhere, you see. And if they heard that the Nazis were coming to Muranow Square, would they build a nest and raise their children here?"

Samuel gazed somberly at the nest. He looked at the birds

172

and listened to the persistent peep of the babies. "I suppose not."

Rachel gestured toward the big yellow house on the corner. "There is the nest our father built. Would he keep us here if he thought the Nazis would come?"

At this logical explanation, David and Samuel both seemed greatly relieved.

"So the worst will not come."

"Frau Groshenki is nothing but a yenta who sees a cloud around every silver lining, nu?" Rachel had heard this saying on the BBC radio. The priest had explained it to her, and now she explained it to her brothers. By the time they reached the front steps, everyone was quite relieved. By the time they reached the embrace of their father, they had almost forgotten the terrible things Frau Groshenki had said.

12   The Warsaw Link

Allan regretted that he had insisted on having his bed linens changed once a week. The thought of a maid entering his room even for that was now a matter of concern and annoyance. What if she opened the bottom drawer of his bureau? And if she stumbled across his material, would she know what she was looking at?

That thought motivated Allan to travel to the luggage shop in Chelsea. Stacks of luggage took up nearly every square foot of floor space in the little shop. Steamer trunks formed the foundation on which skyscrapers of smaller cases and valises rose to the crown molding of the high ceiling. Allan wondered how those pieces on the bottom could ever be taken out without the whole pile coming down in an avalanche.

"And what size would you prefer, sir?" asked the pretty young shopkeeper.

"Personal size. For a cruise. Waterproof." Allan eyed a pyramid of hard-sided cases in the back of the store. "Like that. Fourth one from the top." A poster of a passenger ship was taped to the display.

It was perfect. Of medium size, the case was light aluminum covered with plain tan leather. The corners were protected by metal to match the lock. The sign on the stack read: *THE LATEST FOR YOUR CRUISE. WATERPROOF.*

"Ideal for ocean travels, sir. And for rainy weather, too." She moved the ladder and climbed up fearlessly. "No need to worry with the Deluxe World Traveler grip. If your ship goes down, you could simply paddle back to Southampton with all your things quite dry inside."

Allan did not bargain with her about the price. He would keep the receipt, and when everything was accomplished, he would present the bill to Colin for reimbursement.

In the meantime he would keep his things locked inside. With both keys around his neck, the hotel maid would not be able to get into it even if she were the curious sort.

The shopkeeper deftly removed the case from the stack like a magician pulling a tablecloth from beneath a set of dishes. A cloud of dust filtered down, causing Allan to cough convulsively. The young woman eyed him remorsefully. She should have dusted, she told him. By way of apology she lowered the price of the purchase by two shillings.

"Voyaging for your health, are you then?" she asked sympathetically. "With this model we will stamp your initials on the handle free of charge."

"Thank you. No time, I—"

"It will only take a few minutes."

"I may wish to sell it later," he replied, feeling pleased that he thought of an excuse so quickly.

"Well then," she whispered conspiratorially, "if you do, send the buyer back here. I'll stamp it for him all the same. Sometimes we have customers come in for initials, and they buy another piece of luggage from us." She winked and passed her card to Allan. "My name is on the back. Carol, you see?" She extended her hand. "You're American?"

"Allan Farrell," he answered, instantly sorry he had said his name. Could she guess what he really intended to do with the purchase? No, of course not. Still, he had a sense of intrigue he never would have had had he remained merely a sideline errand boy.

"Well, Mr. Farrell," she said, looking at his forehead and his mouth and his eyes, "if you change your mind and decide to keep the case, you know where I am. The offer will still be good."

She was speaking of things other than initials, Allan knew. Some other day he might have been flattered, might have made plans to drop in another time. Not now. Maybe never again.

———————

Peter Wallich was early. Rachel watched him walk down the street with his shambling gait. He looked like a scarecrow that had jumped off a post and was now hurrying to escape over a furrowed field.

This morning Peter did not wear the heavy coat. The warm sun gleamed against his red hair, which was still partly wet from a shower. The hair which, already dry, had pulled up into a wild briar-bush curl to tower over the stuff that was too wet to stand up. The trousers Peter wore were too short at the cuffs, revealing brown socks that drooped around the tops of his worn shoes. The belt was pulled tight around his waist, gathering up both trousers and baggy shirt like a sack cinched in the middle. His long skinny arms protruded from short sleeves. He was very pale, and the freckles on his arms were a shade lighter than his hair. His mouth turned down slightly at the corners. His head and eyes were never still. He looked to the right and the left and back over his shoulder, like a little puppy turned loose in a garden.

All this taken together made Rachel think that Peter Wallich would have made a remarkably fine clown in the Imperial Warsaw Circus. Add a little makeup (very little), extend the length of the already big feet, give him a big stick with which he could swat rival clowns, and Peter would be quite at home in the center ring beneath a canvas tent. Only one thing did not fit into this comic appearance: his eyes seemed to contain all the sorrow in the world. Beyond the pale skin and the red hair and the long thin neck were those eyes—the reflection of a tragic life, a soul that had aged and hardened far beyond the gangly body in which it dwelt. Flashing at the perimeters of all that sorrow was the steel edge of bitterness and the glow of smoldering anger.

Those emotions could not be crammed into the resume of Peter's clownish appearance. There was no joy in him, no youth; nothing left behind those eyes that could enjoy laughter or a good prank.

Rachel had instinctively known all these things from their first conversation in the soup kitchen. This young man, not much older than Rachel herself, had seen firsthand in Vienna what the Saturday people could do to Jews once Hitler had declared Jews to be fair game. He had survived the first days of hunting season, but he bore the smell of death away with him. This frightened her, and yet she pitied him with her whole heart. Along with that pity, however, she carried the fear that he might hold up a mirror and show Rachel her own future. *What would I do without Mama and the boys? What if Papa had died in Warsaw prison instead of simply getting sick? What if I were left alone and lost like Peter Wallich? And what if the Nazis came here to Warsaw?*

Just seeing Peter brought all those terrible questions to the front of Rachel's consciousness.

She drew back from her place at the window, as if she did not want him to turn his sorrowing gaze upon her and pass the infection of tragedy to her life.

Peter, seeming to sense the fact that he was much too early for his appointment, stopped and leaned against the streetlamp on the corner of Muranow. He had no watch, but he stared a long time at the clock tower set at the far end of the square. He crossed his arms and waited for the minute hand to slide into place. It did not move fast enough to suit him, and so he turned impatiently and stared up at the big yellow house where the rabbi lived and where Rachel watched him from behind the screen of lace curtains.

She stepped back farther, half wishing she had not offered her father as counselor and adviser to this lost sheep. And then a rush of shame followed quickly as she considered that if she were in Peter Wallich's place, she would long for someone to advise her, to help her find a way back home.

With a shudder, she left the window of her bedroom and scurried downstairs, shouting her superstitious dread away.

"Papa! Peter Wallich is standing outside on the sidewalk! Mama! Should I let him in?"

"He is early." Mama poked her head out of the kitchen as Rachel reached the bottom of the stairs.

"He has nowhere else to go, I suppose," Rachel said.

"I suppose not." Etta looked toward the front door as though she also sensed something. Wiping her hands on her apron she said, "It is hot. I imagine the boy would like some apple juice. Your father is awake. So let your friend in, already."

———

Agent Hess poured himself yet another glass of schnapps as he decoded the dispatch from Berlin. He did not need to complete the work; he knew the message before he was halfway through the jumble of words.

LONDON AGENT REPORTS IBSEN CHILDREN IN CONTACT FROM DANZIG STOP ALL STEPS BEING TAKEN BY FAMILY IN LONDON TO OBTAIN VISAS FOR LORI AND JAMES IBSEN TO IMMIGRATE TO ENGLAND STOP NO DANZIG ADDRESS GIVEN THUS FAR STOP SUGGEST YOU PLACE AN AGENT AT BRITISH EMBASSY AND CHECK STEAMSHIP SCHEDULES STOP

Hess had already hired a man to watch the British Embassy. The fellow was a Jew, a former bank clerk from Bremmen who had managed to slip out of the Reich shortly after *Kristallnacht*. Hess had spent two days milling around outside the British compound as though he, too, were desperate to escape. He had struck up a conversation with the Bremen Jew, explained that his injuries had come as the result of a confrontation with the Gestapo, and won the fellow's confidence. It was only a short step from there to enlisting the Jew in his hunt for the Ibsen children. He presented himself as a member of the German resistance who was concerned for the welfare of a fallen comrade's family. That lie, combined with a promise of a room and regular food, was enough to win the Bremen banker's services as watchdog at the gates of the British Embassy. The fellow had only to keep his eyes open. When and if the lost children arrived, he was to observe them and then follow them back to their living quarters and report to Hess immediately at the Deutscher Hof.

Hess had learned early in his career that it was easy to enlist even the most ardent anti-Nazis on the payrolls of the Gestapo as long as they believed they were working for a righteous cause. Germany and the Western democracies were crowded with such unknowing betrayers. There were almost as many anti-Nazis on the payroll of the Reich Ministry of Information as there were Nazis. Hess had no doubt that if the children should arrive at the embassy, the banker from Bremen would follow his orders to the dot of the Nazi *i*.

———————

Peter Wallich held his glass of apple juice in both hands as he sat in the straight-backed chair across from the bed of Rabbi Aaron Lubetkin.

Rachel thought how much her father looked the part of a great rabbi, in spite of the fact that his hair and beard had been shaved and now bristled at the same length on head and face. He was propped up among the pillows on his bed. The black skullcap was exactly in place, giving him an air of dignity that the unruly red locks on Peter's head did not have.

Here was wisdom advising the sad fool. Here was age and experience assisting the young and inexperienced. And yet . . . there was something in Papa's eyes that matched the sorrow behind the eyes of young Peter Wallich. In the comprehension of tragedy, both were equal. But Papa's expression held none of the bitterness the boy's displayed.

"And so your mother and sister simply vanished?" Papa asked gently.

"They never came to the Danziger Hof. Never sent word."

Papa considered what that meant and searched for some hope that might penetrate the bitterness in Peter's voice. "Your father was a prominent political prisoner. Your mother was also a suspect?"

"Yes. That is why we remained in hiding."

"Ah, well then." Papa's brown eyes flashed with confidence. "You know the Nazis announce the arrest of everyone they consider to be a prominent criminal. Did you ever see the name of your mother in the newspaper in Danzig?"

Something flickered in Peter's eyes. For a moment the black shadow of despair lifted. Here was some beam of hope! He slowly considered the question. "No. I did not. And I read the papers. I even read the Nazi edition of *Der Angriff* so I could have some idea of what they were up to."

Papa's voice was gentle. "They certainly would have made a great announcement about the apprehension of your mother. Don't you think so, Freund Wallich?"

Peter nodded. He looked at his hands for a moment and

frowned as if he was afraid to look into the hopeful face of the rabbi. "I think so."

"Well then . . . *nu*?" By this, Papa meant that Peter had reason to be hopeful. Why should his eyes hold such despair when there was no evidence that the worst had indeed fallen upon his mother and sister?

"But . . . where?"

"They are somewhere," Papa said with a shrug. "We will try and find these people . . . the address on your paper. Just because the letters are washed away, this does not mean that the people are washed away. They, too, are somewhere, nu? Here in Warsaw, even. And since the fellow who fought beside your father against the Nazis in Vienna is a son of Warsaw, then we will find this fellow's family here. But it will take time." Papa raised his chin to instruct the young man. "And it will take *hope* on legs to find them. Do you understand?"

Peter shrugged; he tried to pretend that the rabbi had not glimpsed the depth of his sadness.

Rachel watched her father's eyes fill with compassion as he studied the boy's stony expression. She could see Peter resisting the tenderness, lest it once again allow him to feel hope.

"Maybe they are there. Maybe they are somewhere . . . maybe they are not." He was leaning toward the latter. It was easier to live with despair than with disappointed hopes.

"The Eternal knows such answers," Papa replied.

"I do not believe in the Eternal," Peter snapped. "This is not a religious call."

Papa smiled, unmoved by this new display of bitterness. "It does not matter if you believe, Peter. The Eternal does not need your belief in order to exist. That is why He is Eternal. And if your mother and sister are alive, they do not need your belief in order to remain alive. They eat and sleep and speak to each other. They certainly miss you." Papa paused as emotion filled Peter's hard eyes.

"It is better to expect the worst," Peter reasoned. "Then I will not be disappointed."

Papa shook his head from side to side. "No. Then you live in disappointment all the time. Then you are a slave to bitterness. Then, when good things happen you are only surprised by them. Much better to live on the other side of that mirror, nu? Hope in the survival of your mother and sister. Think of them laughing and talking; looking for you."

"But what if that is not true?"

"Then you can be surprised when you find out. There will be plenty of time then to grieve."

Ah, Rachel thought, *such a rabbi Papa is! So full of life, even thin and frail and weak from his own encounter with misery!* How proud she was of her father as he did battle on his sickbed with the very demon Rachel had seen in Peter's eyes and run from!

"Yes, I see," Peter said, and then he stiffened. "But I will not hope . . . believe in this Jewish God of yours."

"Much better in the end to find out you were wrong for believing, I always say. If I am wrong . . ." Papa shrugged. "Well then?" He lowered his chin. "But if you are wrong, Peter?"

"I did not come here to be made a religious Jew." Peter was stubborn. He would not be moved. "I came for advice. For help to find . . . if they are alive . . . my mother and sister."

"So." Papa rummaged through his papers on the bedside table. "Here is my letter of introduction. Everyone newly come to Warsaw needs something. This may move your case to the front of the queue. Here is also a list of people to speak with."

He passed the two letters to Peter, who took them in trembling hands and skimmed the contents as if he had at last found something to nourish his famished soul.

Rachel smiled a tight-lipped smile. There it was in the eyes of the mirthless clown . . . *hope* . . . alive in him again!

———

The Cliffs of Dover gleamed like a clean white wall off the starboard side of the freighter. Orde felt no joy at this view of England. While others among the small group of passengers chatted excitedly about home, Orde turned from the rail and retreated to his cabin.

Once there, he opened his scuffed leather letter case and pulled out the telegram from the London office of TENS. *Correspondent for Poland.* Beside that on his bunk, he placed the photographs of the Lubetkin family that old Rabbi Lebowitz had entrusted to his care.

Etta Lubetkin's clear blue eyes held a serene beauty even in the starkness of a black and white photo. Her eldest child, Rachel, was also lovely. She appeared much older to Orde than the birthdate on her certificate would indicate.

Orde sighed as he placed the photograph of Aaron Lubetkin beside that of his wife. He pitied the young, stern-looking rabbi; pitied him and envied him as well. How much easier it was for Orde to face the coming cataclysm than it must be for a man with a beautiful wife and such handsome children as these. Photographs of three little boys followed. Orde knew them by name. *David. Samuel. Baby Yacov, whom the family called Little Yani.* Lovingly the old rabbi had repeated the names of his grandchildren. How hopeful he had been when he placed the envelope with their rejected immigration papers in Orde's hands.

Orde touched each face with the same tenderness he had seen in the old man. Then, Orde once again picked up the telegram from John Murphy which expressed the hope that Samuel Orde would consider a position in Warsaw. *Warsaw! Could such a thing be a coincidence?* Orde wondered. *Or is there a link between the job offer and something not yet understood about this family in Warsaw?*

"What is it you want of me?" Orde whispered. "What is it that you see, Lord, which I do not see?"

Such questions, of course, held no tangible answers for Orde. And yet, he felt some link between this telegram and this family. *Something . . . something . . . which he would know in time.*

The shoreline of his homeland loomed outside the porthole, yet Orde could not take his eyes from the faces of the Jewish family. *"It is Poland, isn't it?"* he questioned aloud. *"Warsaw for me?"*

Before the ship bumped against the docks of Southampton, Orde was confident of the answer.

13 Prelude to New Life

It was *enormous,* this unborn baby Murphy!

Lying back in the bathtub, Elisa looked at the bulging mound where a once-slender abdomen used to be. There was no hope of submersing everything in the warm water at once. Dipping a washcloth, she spread the soapy water on top of her belly. *Like a snowcap on Mont Blanc,* she thought.

Suddenly, without permission, the mound shifted to the right. Baby elbows and baby knees and baby rump bopped and gyrated to some unknown baby jazz tune.

This one would never grow up to be a classical musician! *He-she* took after Daddy Murphy! Ha! No doubt this baby would be born snapping its little baby fingers and whistling a tune from *D'Fat Lady Trio!* And Murphy would break into song in his irritating off-key voice, *Yessir, dat's my ba-by!*

And it *was* his baby, too. He ought to try carrying it for one night before he teased her so unmercifully! *"Gee, Elisa, I don't think this bed is big enough for the three of us anymore!"*

This comment came last night because of soda crackers. She did not crunch the crackers, but sucked on them very quietly while *Murphy's child* stoked up the fires of indigestion and warmed its little hands with glee.

"Then go sleep on the sofa!" Elisa ordered through her tears.

Murphy had rolled over and switched on the light, peering at her in astonished horror. *"You're crying!"*

"Insensitive! I . . . said . . . go . . ."

Tousled and hurt, he had taken pillow and blanket and shuffled out to the sofa. It really was for the best. Elisa had cried a little more, crunched her crackers loudly, then sprawled out for her first real night's sleep in a month.

She awakened in the morning with the worried face of Murphy hovering over her. "Anytime now, hon." There was sympathy in his voice. "Didn't the doc say so? Anytime." Then he kissed her and she forgave him for a minute until he patted her bulge and added, "Gotta go now. Let me rub your belly for luck . . ."

This rubbing-her-belly-for-luck was the final indignity. Just the memory of it made her eyes narrow and her lower lip extend in an injured pout. How could he be so calloused? How could he, who had put her in this condition in the first place, not see how much it hurt her when he made sophomoric jokes about the fact that she was no longer slender . . . no longer desirable. *Definitely resistible. Oversensitive. Edgy.* He certainly had not attempted to stay in bed with her last night when she ordered him out!

Not big enough for the three of us . . .

Tears of self-pity stung her eyelids once again. She was nearly two weeks past her due date. Two extra weeks in this purgatory of pregnancy, while the whole world flew by!

This afternoon she had yet another appointment with Dr. Howarth. No doubt he would thump her like a melon, declare her still unripe, and send her back to incubate and expand a few months more. *"So sorry, Mrs. Murphy. Sometimes in rare cases like yours, these things take several years to mature. Shall I call a freight truck to haul you home?"*

Elisa found herself unable to concentrate on anything but what was literally right in front of her. Like a hood ornament on a foggy day, baby Murphy was the clearest thing in sight.

Even though the flat of Anna and Theo Lindheim was packed wall to wall with refugee children in transit to foster homes, Anna had asked to take Charles and Louis for a few days so Elisa could relax. Frankly, the boys had seemed happy to go.

On top of that, Aunt Helen had gotten word from her children that they were safe in Danzig. But a battle was raging with immigration to have Lori and Jamie Ibsen and the others included on the last refugee transport ship scheduled to leave next week.

Elisa thought of Lori and Jamie every day, yet, she prayed for them with a strange sort of detachment. Every emotion, it seemed, was being expended on thinking about *the day*. Every prayer somehow started one place and made a big loop back to *this* baby; *her* child; its safe and healthy arrival.

She had gratefully taken her leave from the orchestra. It was undignified to waddle across the stage to her music stand. Her hours had been filled with packaging clothes for the children arriving on the refugee transport ships, acting as interpreter and counselor to the volunteer families taking children.

She casually mentioned her participation to Dr. Howarth, who had promptly hit the ceiling. He lectured her severely about exposing herself and her unborn child to possible communicable diseases brought to England by these children.

That had been the worst visit. She was also ten pounds overweight and had been warned about that, too. *Ah yes. The tears had flowed that day in Dr. Howarth's little office!*

Elisa had busied herself with painting and papering the nursery. The church and the women of the orchestra had teas for her and provided enough baby things for several babies. It was very nice, but all the same, Elisa longed for the day when she would no longer feel as though she were wearing a kettle drum around her middle!

Elisa hefted herself out of the tub and vowed to think about other things and people today. She braced herself against the sink and attempted to dry her legs as she whispered a guilty prayer for Aunt Helen and the arrival of Jamie and Lori and the others. And then, triggered by the thought of arriving children, she added a little something about baby Murphy once again. *How long, oh, Lord?*

Involuntarily, she imagined that Charles and Louis would probably be grown up before this stubborn baby arrived! If things happened on schedule, pregnancy would be endurable! *But two weeks late and big as a barn?*

Elisa had nightmares that she would be out crossing a busy intersection on Oxford Street or in church or shopping when her water broke. She had spent the day yesterday hiking up and down the apartment stairs in hopes of forcing the issue. *No use.* She would go to Dr. Howarth and he would say, *"So sorry!"* And one of these weeks her water would break and wash away the shoppers at Liberty.

She bent awkwardly to dry her right knee. It was down there somewhere. Maybe if she sat on the edge of the tub?

As she bent down, Elisa's water broke. *Yes! There in the bathroom!* Not shopping at Liberty as she had feared. Not out to tea with her mother. Not hiking up the stairs. But right here in her own bathroom.

There was none of the anticipated pain. Just a warm rush and a lovely release of pressure in her lower abdomen. She laughed and clapped her hands. There was time to clean up and dress. Time to make the bed and do the dishes.

And then those much-waited and longed-for contractions began with the syncopated rhythm of early labor. So much for vows of unselfish thoughts. It was a sure bet that today Elisa would be thinking of only one little person. . . .

––––––––––

This time Alfie had to leave Werner the cat at home. Each of the boys was dressed in his best Sunday suit and shoes. Jacob and Alfie wore trousers because they were older. Mark and Jamie wore knickers and long wool socks. Lori wore her prettiest dress, the one with pink and blue flowers that she had worn on Easter.

"But Werner stays home," Jacob warned. "The British Consulate would not take kindly to having Werner prowling over the desks of secretaries."

Once, Alfie had managed to sneak Werner into church in his pocket when Jacob told him not to. That morning during prayer time, Werner had skipped down the pew, then rushed past the legs of several old ladies and young ladies who screamed loudly one after the other. It had been very bad.

Werner had jumped onto the altar where the Communion plates were, and the whole service had been ruined. It did not matter that Alfie was very sorry and scolded his cat. Everyone was still angry at Alfie for bringing Werner. *Except maybe Jesus,* Alfie thought. He did not think that the Lord was angry. After all, it woke everyone up in what was a very dull church service.

The pastor had whispered too loudly to the choir director that he wished the *Dummkopf* would be left home with the cat. Everyone heard what he said. Alfie heard it and felt very sad. Jacob and Lori heard it and were angry.

After the service Jacob waited in the line to greet the pastor and his wife and Jacob told them both that if the cat and Alfie were not welcome, then none of them would be back because it was the deadest church he had ever been to. But he said it in a nice way, and then he shook the pastor's hand.

All the way back to the flat that day Lori had talked about her own papa, Pastor Ibsen. *"Remember what a sense of humor he had about such little disasters? Remember when Frau Meyer's baby threw up all over that mean old Herr Speer who had just fired his chauffeur in front of the church because he hadn't cleaned the pigeon droppings off the car?"*

Everyone remembered that great day, of course. Pastor Ibsen had tucked his notes away and preached about true humbleness. This memory led to the next. *"And remember when old Herr Speer died and the little dog fell into his grave sometime in the night and then started howling during the service?"*

These stories had made them all laugh again and forget how angry they felt about the preacher and his *Dummkopf* remark. Alfie had not been around when the dog started howling from Herr Speer's grave, but he liked the story a lot and laughed right along with everyone else. By the time they had gotten home, Alfie did not feel like a dummkopf anymore and no one was angry that Werner had frightened the old ladies in the church.

But today, going to the British Consulate was an entirely different matter. Jacob explained it again to Alfie. "They are the fellows who have our papers so we can go to England."

"Will they also have papers for Werner-cat to go to England?"

"No, Alfie, and we must not mention Werner to them."

"But if Werner can't go, I can't go."

"I know that. We will smuggle him on board with us. You must not worry about it." Jacob held up his finger. "But don't say anything at all. Lori and I will do all the talking. If anyone asks you a question you just say *yes* or *no*. And if they ask your name, well, then tell them. But don't say any more. Understand?"

Alfie ran it all through his mind. In a very serious tone he answered the way Jacob told him to. One word. "Yes."

"Good. All right then." Jacob looked very nervous. He straightened Alfie's blue bow tie. He double-checked Alfie's suspenders and tugged at the crease in his trousers. Then he placed a brand new fedora on Alfie's head. He pulled the brim down, stepped back and looked him over from top to toe.

Lori came in and laughed when she saw Alfie all dressed up in his new suit. "Why, Alfie! You look so handsome and adult!"

Alfie tried not to smile too big, tried to act as if it were really nothing at all. He turned to look at his reflection in the mirror. It was very nice. He remembered his own papa wearing a hat like this one and a blue serge suit with suspenders. "I . . . look . . . like Father. Uh-huh."

"Yes! You look *wonderful*! The Englishmen will think you look like a bank officer! The hat is perfect."

Alfie scratched his ear and ducked his head with embarrassment.

"Uh-huh. Englishmen don't like Dummkopfs. They will think I look smart, won't they?"

Lori and Jacob looked at each other in a way that made Alfie wish he had not said *the word*. Lori always said that the word *Dummkopf* made her heart hurt. Alfie had not meant to make her feel bad; he was only asking a question about how the Englishmen at the British Consulate might feel about people the Nazis said were Dummkopfs.

"Alfie," Lori said quietly. She put her hand on his arm. "You *are* smart. It is because of you that we are all alive now, because of you that I wrote Elisa in London. You have the smartest heart of anyone I know."

Alfie smiled down at her. She was very pretty and always so nice. He loved her very much. "Jacob is right," he said. "It would not be good to take Werner with us today to the English. He is just a cat and might say something he should not." Alfie meant that the cat might run against the legs of English women and make them scream like he had in church. Werner-cat could not *say* anything wrong . . . any Dummkopf knew cats do not speak. "You know what I mean?" Alfie asked Lori.

"Yes." Lori patted him and straightened his tie again. "It is smart to leave him home today."

The British Consulate was located in the most convenient section of Danzig. At 14 Stadtgraben, it was near the main train depot and the post office. The consulate occupied three stately baroque mansions that stood side by side on the main thoroughfare. The common walls had been opened up to join the buildings. Secretarial offices were housed in the smallest wing. In the center mansion, all the woodwork had been refurbished and the ballroom had been enlarged for official receptions. The portrait of the king smiled down regally from the wall where a wide mahogany staircase wound up to the offices of the British officials. The third wing had been made into the living quarters for the British staff. Paneled walls and thick wool carpets, paintings depicting idyllic English countryside and great British naval victories, all gave this wing of the consulate the air of an exclusive London club.

Each day at four o'clock precisely, work in the first two wings came to an abrupt halt while tea with sandwiches and pastries was served, just like at the Savoy in London. It was always a comfort to those members of the British Foreign Service that English culture could be satisfied with an assortment of teas and jams.

And so at 3:50 every afternoon, the gates of the consulate swung shut on the faces of the hundreds of refugees who made pilgrimage to this building as though it were a holy place where they might be healed of some terrible disease. They waited quietly in the street as the holy communion of high tea progressed within. They turned their gaunt faces up to the bright spotless windows, hoping that someone might look down and have pity.

But there was little pity at teatime. If diners chanced to look out at the silent masses, they saw people who did not comprehend the afternoon ritual. They saw hungry refugees who desired entry into England when they had not the slightest concept of British culture. This lack of understanding on the part of the hopeless thousands who filed past this building was indeed a sort of fatal disease. They could not share the holy rites of orange pekoe or Ceylon tea with scones and clotted cream. What did they care for orange marmalade?

Often the great decisions of life and death, escape or imprisonment in hostile Europe, boiled down to who would fit in at Piccadilly. Did the British want a steady diet of foreigners with foreign ways mucking up the tearooms of London's hotels?

Lori Ibsen had some idea of this principle, although she could not put it into words—not in German words, or English. But she looked at Alfie Halder with his blissful smile and clumsy gait and she trembled for him as they held their appointment notice through the iron bars of the consulate building. Even all dressed up and scrubbed until his skin was pink, Alfie did not fit. He carried his big head at a slight tilt to the side and down at the chin, his smile too broad, his eyes too wide and childlike.

He looked as though he could comprehend nothing, although Lori knew that Alfie Halder somehow understood everything all too well. Information ran through his mind like tea through a silver strainer, and in the end, it was all perfectly distilled within the cup of his great innocence.

Alfie's faith was what Lori's father had described as "that perfect faith which the Lord spoke of, the faith of a child. . . ." Even this great faith looked up at the windows of the British Consulate and asked, "Do they let . . . boys like me . . . inside, Lori?" He did not use *the word,* but indeed, he understood the issue.

Children like Alfie had been systematically euthanized by the Nazi government. If he were rejected by England because he was "not quite all right in the head," that rejection would be equal to a death sentence. And so many millions stood condemned for less cause than that!

"Lori?" Alfie asked quietly as the guard examined the official notice that these five young people were to come to the consulate at 3:45 exactly.

Lori held a finger to her lips to silence Alfie. The guard looked at his wristwatch and scowled. "You're late. Two minutes. We close at 3:50 for teatime, don't you know?"

Lori was the spokeswoman for the group. "Yes. We know all about four o'clock tea." Her English was quite good. The guard appraised her with a forgiving look, and yet . . .

"Well, you're late."

"These trams, you know," she replied as though public transportation in a foreign country was so very unreliable. "Anyway, shall I tell the official that we were kept waiting at the gate?"

Very good—in attitude as well as accent. "I see you are expected." His tone was apologetic. He glared back at the mob that pressed against the backs of the five visitors as though everyone might come in at once. Raising a hand he shouted, "Everyone back except these five! Back in your line! Only these five admitted!"

It was among the poorest of all the parishes in Danzig. The streets were so narrow beneath the overhang of the gables that a taxi could not drive there.

Wolf paid the cab driver and promised him extra if he would wait here at the end of *Heiliger Geist Strasse*, Holy Ghost Street. This narrow lane was named after the Catholic church where a young priest reported that he may have seen a woman matching the description of Lucy Strasburg. He could not remember if the woman had been expecting. *She was kneeling,* he said; *her face was childlike and glowed with an innocence rarely seen except among the very pious. Could this be the same fallen woman described by her brother? The same woman in the red dress holding the champagne glass?*

The priest was uncertain. He had called the office of the bishop and explained that the woman had left the church before he could retrieve the photograph from his study. Now the young priest carried the picture in the pocket of his cassock, but the woman had never returned. The office of the bishop contacted Wolf with this information. *Perhaps your sister lives in this district?*

There was a strong stench of sewage and rotting fish in the air as Wolf walked down the sloping lane. His eyes flitted from window to window of the dingy medieval rooming houses and cheap hotels. Beer cellars and secondhand shops lined the lower stories. Passing the dark entrance to a bar, Wolf could hear the shrill laughter of women mingled with the coarse voices of foreign sailors.

Yes. This is suitable for Lucy, he thought. *A sow gone to wallow with her own kind. A prostitute in search of a job. Up to the hotel room, and then to church in the morning to ask forgiveness.* This was just the sort of place he would expect to find her.

He felt his anger rising at the thought of how she would raise a baby in such a place. He would find her, take the baby to his own estate, and take Lucy back to the Reich for trial.

Staring up at the drawn shades of the windows, he imagined what she was doing; how she made her living selling herself for bargain prices to the ragged men of Heiliger Geist Strasse.

The ancient, soot-tarnished facade of the church loomed at the end of the curving lane. There was a workhouse across the small square where a line of destitute men and women waited for entry into a public soup kitchen. Their gray, hopeless faces reminded him of the disembodied souls in the painting of *The Last Judgment*. When Danzig was annexed to Germany again, such nests as this would be cleaned out.

At the core of his rage lay the realization that Lucy had chosen this life over him, over all he had offered her! Was that not proof of what she was? Proof enough for anyone with eyes to see.

Wolf entered the dark church building through a heavy wooden side door. This had been the instruction of the priest, lest Lucy see her brother if she was nearby, and not return to the church.

Wolf's jaw was set with anger as he descended the steep stone steps into the basement offices of Holy Ghost Church. One passageway led to the underground crypt and the other led to the library and robing room of the structure.

As arranged, the tall, worried young priest was in the library, hunched over a large volume of commentary. He jerked his head up and blinked at Wolf, as though he had forgotten the reason for his meeting here. Just as quickly, the confusion passed. He stood and nodded and extended his hand. When he spoke, his voice was a ridiculous whisper, as though Lucy might somehow hear him.

"You are the brother of the woman?"

Wolf had conducted secret meetings with agents in Danzig who bore less air of mystery than this priest.

"You have seen my sister?"

"Yes . . . that is, I think it was her. Blond. Pretty. . ." He said the word *pretty* as though it were a forbidden word. Wolf had wondered what thoughts had passed through the priest's hypocritical mind when he saw her.

"She was pregnant?"

He shrugged helplessly. "Kneeling at the altar. I could not tell. And when I turned away and looked back, she had gone."

"I suppose it is possible she has had the child."

The priest nodded. "She prayed before the Madonna and Child, as many women who are expecting do. And mothers come to pray for their children. I suppose—"

Wolf raised his hand to cut him off. "Why did you not try to speak with her? Detain her in some way?"

His voice accused the priest of neglecting his duty. "I was uncertain. And she was praying." He pulled her photograph from his pocket. It was the picture of Lucy on the steps of St. Stephan's. *Wide innocent eyes. Hopeful, slightly confused expression.*

"Is this the woman you saw then?"

"I am almost certain. But much older. Infinitely more . . . sad." His voice trailed off as he studied the picture again. "I carry the picture with me. She will not get away again. We thought you should know. In case she is the one. This neighborhood is quite—"

"I saw it . . . smelled it . . . myself. If my sister is here in such a place—and the baby—we must take her home. To think of her here is—"

"Yes. Heartbreaking. I know. I will do what I can. The bishop felt it wise that we meet. I will keep watch, Herr von Fritschauer. Such a lady as your sister has no place in the squalor of Heiliger Geist Strasse."

And so the chain of unwitting agents had found its final link

191

on Wolf's behalf. Once again Wolf stressed that Lucy should be taken to some counseling office and detained without being made aware that her brother was searching for her. She must not be frightened away. A clever woman, she might slip the snare again, and time was running short.

Lucy's one-room flat was located in a tall narrow building in the Heiliger Giest district of Danzig not far from the ancient city wall. At one time it had been the spacious mansion of a wealthy coal merchant. Of course, that had been three hundred years earlier, before anyone had ever dreamed of indoor plumbing and electric lights.

In 1790, the place had been divided into a dozen flats on each of the first three stories. Much, much, later in its history, a sewer pipe had been installed on each floor, to be shared as communal toilet by the tenants. About that same time, gas lighting was added. A single cold water faucet in each room completed the latest in nineteenth-century conveniences to each flat.

Since that time there had been no improvements made. And so it remained as it had been for sixty years. Dock workers, poverty-stricken students, sailors without ships, and prostitutes in search of business lived here. Twelve flats to a floor, sometimes twelve tenants to a flat, they shared the toilet and accepted the fact that they were only a little better off than the rodents that used the groaning water pipes as thoroughfares from room to room.

But Lucy was on the fourth floor. Nestled in among hand-hewn rafters that might have served as the masts of an ancient galleon in a former life, she somehow felt above the squalor that packed the tenement. Her room had been the poorest room of all when this had been the house of a rich man. It had been his attic, the place he stored old furniture, the place his children played hide-and-seek. Tucked under the eaves at the back of the house, there was only one window, which faced another slate rooftop. Lucy could see the sky if she leaned out and craned her neck. She had pried open the sash and propped the window open with a stick. She did not need curtains; nor did it matter that the aged glass was caked with two hundred years of soot. There was no one to look in, and unless she cared to climb out on the roof to find a view, the window was only for ventilation.

This room was smaller than the others, she was told. It had a faucet and a basin, but she had to walk down one flight to empty her chamber pot. Peter had done that task when he was with her. Now the dreaded chore of entering the filthy closet that passed for a bathroom sickened her. She was grateful that her room was a floor above the stinking, teeming warren of the rest of the building.

She had to climb four steep flights of stairs, and her place was tiny, at best. But it was also cheaper than the rest. And isolated. She and Peter had scrubbed and scraped and scoured every inch until now it was the cleanest flat in Altstadt. At night the rats chattered along the rafters and the pipes. She placed little piles of rat poison at every opening and Peter had nailed tin cans over the broadest rat tunnels to block their highways. Now only a few of the braver rodents skittered past and out again as quickly as possible. Peter had kept an axe handle by his bed. Lucy inherited it when he left. Usually a hard bang on the floor would frighten the midnight invaders away.

This afternoon, in honor of the imminent arrival of the baby, Lucy had once again scrubbed every inch of the room. From the rusty iron frame of her curtained bed, across every splintered plank of the bare wood floor, up the walls and along the rafters, the room was immaculate.

She moved the rickety table next to her bed and laid out everything she knew she would need. String to tie the cord. A sharp knife to cut it. A basin for water to wash. Another basin in which she would put bloodied sheets and towels. Antiseptic. Alcohol. Cotton gauze.

She sat on the edge of the sagging bed and studied her meager array of necessities. She stroked the child within her and looked up toward the shining silver crucifix that hung on the water-stained wall above the foot of her bed. She would be able to look up and see *Him* there. Of course she knew that Holy Christ would have no part of one like her, but the baby... *Would not Christ have mercy for the sake of this child?*

Just beneath the crucifix, Lucy laid out the soft satin christening gown, the matching cap and booties. Along with the silver filigree of the cross, they were the only bright and beautiful objects in the room. They were there, waiting to be filled by someone beautiful; someone tiny and perfect and innocent.

She fingered the soft hem of the christening gown. *White. Clean. Lacy. Like a wedding dress . . .*

Ah well, no use thinking of what will never be. Lucy fixed her imploring gaze on the silver Christ. "I . . . I know. . . you cannot hear me. I am too dark inside for you to hear." She mastered her tears, lest they stain the satin of the christening gown. "And so I will not ask you for myself. Nothing for me. But for this—" She touched the baby, who moved beneath her hand. "Sweet Christ? Please? Do you remember what it was to be . . . born in a stable? Your mother. Was she afraid? Were there rats there, too?" She searched the silver face, so full of agony, the hands, the fingers claw-like around the spikes. Had the mother of Jesus begged mercy for her child?

Lucy swallowed hard and did not look away. "For my baby, I ask—not for me, but for this little one. *I need help!* And I will give the baby to you if you help me. Not to Wolf. Or the Führer or Germany. This will be *your* child! I am past your mercy, not worthy. But—*Oh, God! I am afraid!* Alone. *Please . . . "*

Tears came, though her battle remained strong. What was the use? Why should she expect help? She stood and went to the window, breathing deeply the scent of the sea. She wanted to live. She wanted the baby to live and grow up to be someone better than she ever was. And she did not know how to do that alone.

The churchyard at Winchester had been the last place Orde had stopped before he left England for duty in Palestine. Today it was his first stop on his way back to London as well.

The churchyard gate groaned as Orde swung it open and entered. *Cemetery gates always groan,* Orde mused, swinging it back and forth again before pulling it closed. It was as though the rusty iron had captured the pain in Orde's heart and expressed it audibly for him.

He picked his way through the overgrown headstones to the far corner of the grounds. There, in shiny black granite lay the marker for his Katie:

KATHERINE JENNIFER ORDE
BELOVED WIFE OF. . .

Orde had wanted the stone to bear Katie's name, followed by

the words *AND CHILD*. He was advised that since the baby had not been born, the sentiment would not be appropriate. But to Orde the child had been alive; it had been his, and he regretted that he had let them talk him out of it.

"Hullo, Love," he said quietly, laying the flowers at the base of the stone. "I must be the only one who remembers there are two of you here." He could see his own reflection in the stone. He looked much older. His image of Katie was still young; bright and beautiful as she had been the morning she left the house. "I remember," he said, "even though it's been a while. I remember clear as yesterday how it was. Our plans and such—baby things all put away in the nursery." He frowned and wrung his cap in his hands. "I gave it all away before I left. The house is the same, though. I'll be walking into the same house you walked out of when you went away." He looked up as a group of boys on bicycles rattled by outside the fence. "I'm not looking forward to going back there, I'll tell you. I feel more comfortable here, somehow. This is where I buried my heart. Where I think of myself." He frowned. "I won't be here long, Katie. I'm leaving for Poland, soon, if there's still a job for me." He ran his hand along the lapel of his jacket. "See, the whole world is going to war but me. I'm not a soldier anymore."

Orde sat down on the cool, moist soil beside the grave. He told Katie everything that had happened since he had last been here. And after that he wondered aloud what would happen between this hour and the next time he entered the groaning gate of Winchester where his heart was most at home.

———

Allan Farrell surveyed the materials spread out before him on the floor of his room. *One cutting board. Razors. Boxes of ordinary wooden kitchen matches. A hunk of steel pipe sealed at one end.* The simplicity of his design was ingenious. The fuse had been the most difficult problem, and now Allan had the solution to it quite clear in his mind.

This was the sort of weapon that sandbags and bomb shelters could not keep out. The pipe was small enough that it would fit easily up the sleeve of Allan's jacket. He could enter any public building, any hotel lobby or train station, and no one would know what he had up his sleeve. No one would even think to ask.

Carefully he razored the heads off the matches, dropping each round blue bead into the pipe. It was important that he not accidentally strike a match, he knew, or half of Mills University Hotel would go up in flames!

His hands were steady as he worked. He was not afraid even of the possibility that such a minor mistake could kill him before he had a chance to test his pipe bomb somewhere besides his own room. He had written a note to Uncle Colin, telling him to keep his ears open for unusual news about the IRA in London. If Allan died in his effort, he felt certain that his uncle would figure out what he had been up to. *He really was the son of Maureen Farrell, was he not?*

Allan hoped to live long enough to hear that glorious comment in person. Here was his own small proof that he was made of the same stuff as Colin and Kevin Fahey! More than just a messenger boy, Allan intended to deliver a message to the English that they would long remember!

He touched the scar beneath his eye. After tomorrow it would not matter how he acquired that scar. He would someday claim to have gotten it from the butt of an English soldier's gun, and his comrades would not question him! They would look at him with respect and ask his opinion of this action or that demonstration. The son of Maureen would at last have a name of his own.

14   Even Twigs Can Be Strong

Consulate Officer Brace was scowling down at his appointment book when the five members of the Danzig Gang entered his office. He looked up at them through his round wire-rimmed spectacles as though he wanted them to go away. It was, after all, five minutes until teatime. How could he settle all this in just five minutes?

"You're late," he said, cleaning his glasses.

"The trams, you know," Lori began. "And then all the people outside the consulate. Hard to get through to the gate."

Replacing his glasses on his hawkish nose, he blinked at the group as she made introductions. Bored and impatient, he thumbed through the applications that had been relayed through from London. So these were the children at the center of all the fuss. *Ibsen, Lori. Ibsen, James.* And these other three? Along for the ride. Holding to the coattails of these two Ibsen children. It was political favoritism, undoubtedly, to let these in when there were so many begging at the gates.

He checked his watch. Four minutes until teatime.

"So. You are Lori Ibsen." Out came the young woman's papers. "You look older than seventeen." She looked frightened by that, but she did not reply. "Student visa." He raised his visa stamp and thumped it down hard on her newly issued identity papers. She smiled broadly and exhaled with a burst of relief as she shoved her brother and the littlest Kalner boy forward.

The eyes of Officer Brace narrowed as he looked up at the two boys. "You look your ages." Out came the papers of James and Mark. "James Ibsen?" Jamie stepped forward. Down thumped the stamp. "Mark Kalner?" Mark squeezed in beside his friend. The third thump resounded joyfully, matching the beat of Lori's heart. The papers were shoved across the desk, snatched up and hugged tight to the hearts of the young ones.

Two and a half minutes until tea. "Right." Brace frowned slightly. "And now for the genius. Alfred Halder." Alfie stepped forward as had the others. He wrung his new fedora in his big hands. He blinked hopefully at the officer. *Did they take boys like Alfie?*

Brace stared at the papers and then at the young man in front of him. *Genius?* Ah well, had anyone taken a look at Einstein lately? Hair that looked like the scientist had been hit by lightning. A definite over-bite. Brace shook his head slightly. These genius types were all a bit on the imbecilic-looking side, weren't they?"

"So you are our genius?" Brace asked.

Alfie shrugged and smiled in a gesture that betrayed modesty. "Yes." He answered as Jacob had told him, even though he did not know what the officer had said.

"A linguist, eh?"

Alfie looked at Lori. Was he doing all right? She nodded and smiled, although she was very pale. "Yes," Alfie answered.

"Well, God knows we can use you in the Foreign Service."

197

Brace thumped his rubber visa stamp across the proper square on Alfred Halder's papers. "No one seems to be able to understand a word anyone else is saying these days. Much easier if everyone spoke English."

"Yes," Alfie replied seriously. He took the document and bowed slightly.

"That's another thing. You Germans are much more polite than the French. Now, that is all."

Smiles vanished. Everyone looked at Jacob, who had been standing in the doorway of the tiny office. He had not been called forward. There had been no satisfying crash of the rubber stamp across his papers.

"Wait!" Lori's face grew pale.

Brace looked at his watch. He had been efficient. He deserved first selection on the pastry cart. His hand banged against his desk blotter. "What? What, what, what?"

Jacob broke through his companions. He smiled nervously and nodded. "Myself. I . . . am here the Bruder of Mark Kalner." Another timid smile from this very large young man. He was not a child at all—twenty years old if he was a day!

"Jacob Kalner," Jacob said.

Resentment filled the officer's eyes. "And what is it?"

"My Papiere, bitte. Papers?"

This one spoke rotten English. Besides, he did not look like the intellectual type. More like a rugby player who would take the job of some loyal Englishman as a dock worker.

"Ah, yes." Brace held up Jacob's documents and mumbled through them. "You claim to be seventeen?"

Lori moved to stand beside Jacob. She was frightened. "Yes," she blurted out. "He is. Seventeen."

"Young woman, you are not to interrupt." Brace was cold, official. The wheels of the pastry cart were no doubt in the tearoom by now. He studied the document a moment longer. "It says here you are of an exceptional intellect. How many years of school did you have, Mr. Kalner?" A muscle in his cheek twitched irritably.

"I . . . have . . . you know, the Nazis. They do not let . . . uh . . . non-Aryans stay in . . . the school."

"So? Yes? Well? How many years of schooling?"

Jacob could not remember the English pronunciation for the

number ten. He held up his fingers. "This . . . and then I am made to . . . how do you say it?"

"Expelled." Brace helped him. "Rejected."

"Yes." Jacob did not look at the terrified face of Lori. It was going badly. He knew it. He wished he spoke English better!

"Well then. So this application is specious."

How was he to answer? He did not know that word. "I wish to England to go. With mein . . . Mark, ja?"

Consulate Officer Brace's expression turned to steel. He had enough of this nonsense. By now Phillip Smith had eaten the eclairs and all because of this . . . *imposter*! "I will tell you something, Mr. Kalner. This is obviously falsified." He tapped his finger on the application. "It is my duty to weed out the goats from the sheep in matters such as these and I think your performance is shameful. In the first place, you have no higher education, that is clear. Your mastery of the English language is rudimentary at best. You cannot be seventeen, certainly. And if you were seventeen that would still be above the cut-off date for the emergency child refugee provision." He raised his pointed chin as if to challenge Jacob. "Do you understand my meaning?"

Now Jacob looked painfully at Lori. Her hands were trembling. Tears hung in her eyes. "Please," she begged. "I know Jacob. He is *very* bright! The Nazis forced him from school. If he goes to England he can go to school again!"

"As what? Janitor?" Brace dug in his drawer for the other stamp. "This man is perfectly capable of taking care of himself here on the Continent. I could not live with myself if I let him take the place of . . . one of the children out there." He gestured angrily at the window. The shade was drawn, but he could sense the presence of so many others pressing against the gates.

Down came the rubber stamp with a loud bang. *REJECTED*.

"Please," Lori said again as she rushed forward to grasp the officer's hand.

The gesture was too much for him. He flung her hand away angrily and stood, calling for his secretary to escort these five people from the building.

By then it was three minutes after tea had begun. His day was quite ruined.

———

A furtive knock sounded on Agent Hess's door, betraying the

identity of the visitor even before Hess turned the knob.

The Jewish banker from Bremen, perspiring heavily, leaned against the doorjamb. His labored breathing indicated he had run all the way from his post at the British Embassy gates.

Short, slope-shouldered and balding, the man was a stereotypical Jew. The face was pinched, the nose enormous, and on that nose perched spectacles so thick that the wearer's eyes looked unnaturally large and frightened.

This evening the eyes were even larger than usual. Hess stepped aside, allowing his exhausted accomplice to stumble past him into the room.

"I saw them!" he cried. But there was no victory in the declaration. Something had prevented the banker from fulfilling his entire duty.

"Well? Where are they?"

The Jew shrugged and shrank down onto the edge of the bed in defeat. "They entered just before four o'clock. Teatime at the British Embassy. Everything closes down, but they let these five children in all the same."

"Five children?"

"Yes. The two whom you are seeking were with three other boys. Well, maybe not children. Of late adolescence, I would judge."

Hess was not surprised that the Ibsen children had formed a company with others in their own predicament. That would simply mean that Hess would no doubt have more young charges to transport back to the Reich after their capture. "What about the two?"

The unwitting spy grimaced, giving his face a strangely rodent-like appearance. *Like a rat twitching his whiskers*, Hess thought. The fellow revolted him, yet he maintained his pleasant attitude in spite of it.

"Like I said, they all went in, escorted past the rest of us who had been waiting. Taken right into the building as if they had been invited for tea. Everyone was quite disgusted by such favoritism. We could tell they are not Jews like the rest of us. The British make no secret of their dislike of—"

Hess resisted the urge to slap the little weasel across the face. He let him grumble on about British favoritism and the injustice of Gentiles jumping line. "How long were they in there?"

"Half an hour. No more."

"And where did they go when they came out?"

The fellow looked almost angry. "The Englishmen took them to the side gate. I suppose it was so they would not be required to walk through such a large crowd of truly desperate people."

"You followed them?"

The huge eyes narrowed behind the lenses. "I attempted to follow them, comrade. They were a block ahead of me before I spotted them. Two blocks before I managed to make my way through the crowd. I tried not to look as though I was chasing them . . . as you instructed me. But then they turned onto a side street—"

"What street?" Although Hess knew the outcome of this tale of incompetence, perhaps something could be salvaged from it.

Once again the rat-like face screwed up in thought. The banker shoved his glasses up the thin bridge of his long nose. Hess had witnessed specimens of subhumans much less Jewish in appearance than this Jew being used as examples of all that was loathsome to the German people. It disgusted him that the Jew was sitting on his bed. Hess felt the muscle in his cheek twitch with suppressed fury as he stared hard at the Jew.

"Yes. Let me think. Hmmmm. I think. . . Tischler Strasse. Yes. Yes. It *was* Tischler Strasse. And then . . . the crowds. I did not see them. Could not find them."

Hess whirled to study his map. He traced his finger along the route the Ibsen children must have taken from the embassy. There were only red pins in the entire area. It amused him to think that the last district to be searched would indeed hide the fugitives.

Behind him, Hess could hear the Jew droning on in a high nasal voice about the difficulty of finding anyone with Danzig so full of refugees and everyone wanting to go anywhere else in the world but here. He congratulated himself that he had seen the children at all and that he had managed to follow them as far as he had. The worm would be expecting some sort of reward even though he had done only a fraction of what he had been hired to do. This recitation of difficulties was a prelude to asking for money. Hess could stand no more.

But the fellow was still of some possible use, and so Hess mastered the desire to shoot him between his close-set eyes. Instead, he dug into his pocket and pulled out a gulden, which he thrust into the fellow's hand. Then he grabbed him up by the collar of his jacket and whispered urgently, "We must find them before the Gestapo does, you understand? Stay at your post. No doubt they will be back. This time don't lose them!" With that, Hess jerked open the door and shoved the man out into the corridor.

Slamming the door, he returned to the map. Counting the pins within the last twenty-block area of Altstadt, he felt pleased that the resolution of this matter seemed so near.

It seemed almost providential to Hess that the last area of the hunt was likely to reveal that Lucy Strasburg and the children of Karl Ibsen had been living within a few blocks of one another.

He tapped his finger against the central landmark of the area. "Heiliger Geist Church," he muttered pleasantly.

———

The City of London Maternity Hospital at the corner of Old Street and City Road was the oldest institution of its kind in the kingdom. A green bronze plaque implanted in the cornerstone gave the date of establishment as 1750.

Antiquity was admirable in places like cathedrals and palaces, Murphy said, but a maternity hospital was a different matter—especially the hospital where his baby was about to be born.

The floor creaked as he paced the smoke-filled room where a dozen other expectant fathers waited. The more experienced hands played gin rummy or read the paper. Two fellows slept soundly on a cracked leather sofa—probably an original piece of furniture from bygone days of the hospital's glory.

Murphy felt sick. *Sick!* He wished they had checked out this listing old barn of a medical center before this. Elisa should be someplace with a decent waiting room and clean windows and nurses who had not been born in this very place in the last century.

The wheelchair they had taken Elisa away in was *wicker*, for goodness' sake! Probably willed to the institution by good old Queen Victoria! The electrical wires were all on the outside of the walls and had been painted over a half dozen times! Murphy had not seen round dial light switches of that vintage since he had visited the ancestral farm of the Murphy family as a five-year-old kid! Not exactly the kind of place he wanted to trust with the lives of his wife and child!

Did the terror show on his face? Why did they not let the fathers be with their wives? Anna could be in there. What was happening that they would not let him be with Elisa? And why was this taking so long?

A big man with a weather-beaten face and the clothes of a taxi driver whacked him on the back. "First time, eh?"

Murphy managed a miserable smile and a nod.

"Who's the Doc, then?"

"Howarth," Murphy replied.

"He's a good'n," said the big man. "A fine bloke, that Howarth."

Three other gin-rummy players agreed. *"Right. Good chap. He's taking care of my Maggie as well."*

Heads raised from newspapers. Two more bored-looking men nodded.

"My old lady as well."

In all, he figured that Dr. Howarth was delivering four babies besides Murphy's. That fresh and terrible revelation made him feel faint. He groped for a chair. His head was throbbing. This had been a moderately awful day to begin with, even before Elisa had called him and told him to meet her here. Now it definitely ranked right up there with the most horrible. How could one doctor deliver five babies all in the same day? *Impossible! Elisa would be left alone in some hallway somewhere! They would forget her there on the gurney and she would be calling his name, and . . .*

It was too terrible to contemplate. He hung his head and moaned. "We should have done this in the States."

"Ah, nothin' to it, mate!" growled someone. "Me wife's 'ad all of 'em 'ere!"

"How can he deliver five babies at once?" Murphy moaned.

"One at a time."

"Nothin' to it!"

" 'At's wha' we pay 'im for!"

Pay him. Whatever they paid him it was too much. This did not feel like a maternity hospital for women. It was a veterinary clinic!

Murphy had not paid attention when Elisa had told him that she had found a reasonable doctor. She should not have an unreasonable doctor at a time like this, he had quipped. Then she had said he was a doctor they could afford and hardly noticed the expense. *A specialist,* she said!

He wished he had walked through this place just one time and looked at the wiring. One of these days it was going to burn down. Probably tonight. He wished he had insisted that she have the baby back in America, where everyone spoke the same language and hospitals had not even been built in 1750. Benjamin Franklin had not even invented electricity when this place went up!

"America was still a colony when this place was built," he whispered hoarsely.

Someone laughed proudly. "Aye. We've been doin' this sort of thing a long time in England!"

"Somethin' new for you Yanks, then?"

Murphy stared at his hands. New for him, anyway. New for Elisa. Frightening and terrible and wonderful all at once. He wished he had thought all this through before. Last night she had called him insensitive and she was right. Any sensitive man would have made certain that the hospital his wife was in was at least newer than the Declaration of Independence!

He looked at his wrist and shook his head. His watch was broken, smashed when he tried to go through the door at the TENS office the wrong way. He hoped the man he knocked down was all right. He had not been moving when Murphy left. Maybe he was in a hospital, too. Not this one, though. Accident victims were probably treated better than women in labor.

Murphy did not want to ask what time it was. Daily life in London was tough enough trying to figure out the accent. Tonight he simply could not bear any more. He shook his broken watch. The crystal tinkled out on the floor.

"Break your watch?"

Murphy nodded at the voice. By now they all sounded alike, and he didn't care who said what anymore.

"Almost midnight." Someone answered, though no one had really asked.

Why did this take so long? Did these things always take so long?

"They'll be poppin' out soon enough!"

"Always in the wee hours."

As if on cue, a withered nurse poked her head through the door; she also looked to be of a pre-revolutionary war vintage. The gin-rummy game paused mid-gin. All eyes fixed on the face.

"Mr. Finsbury, please?"

One of the sleeping men shook himself awake. "Yes. Finsbury here."

"Good news! A baby boy."

The man stood and straightened his tie without a word, as if she had told him his car was in a tow zone.

"Jolly good," he commented, leaving his comrades without a second glance.

The card game resumed and then ended with the declaration of *gin*. It promptly began again. The men lit up fresh cigarettes and pipes, crossed their legs at a different angle. The slap of playing cards on the table was the only sound for half an hour more.

Murphy's mind played back every insensitive thing he had ever done or said. He then progressed into borderline insensitivity and onward into realms of guilt and self-recrimination he had never experienced before. He prayed and promised God that if everything came out okay—no pun intended—he would do better by Elisa and the kids. The world might be going nuts; Europe might be about to go up in flames; but Murphy would be a better father and husband!

"Twelve-twenty-six," muttered someone, breaking the silence.

Again the door opened and the prune face of a different nurse poked into the gray swirl of smoke.

"*Mr. Mur-pheeee?*"

"Yes! *Yes!* I *am* Murphy! That's *me!*" He was making a fool of himself, grabbing the arm of the old lady like that.

"*Yanks!*" someone grumbled from the gin table.

———

It was either very late at night or very early in the morning when the taxi pulled up beneath the window.

"He's home!" Charles cried, pouncing on the bed of his still-sleeping brother.

The announcement was something like saying Santa Claus had landed on the roof and was squeezing down the chimney. Louis sat bolt upright and the two scrambled to the window seat to peer down at the rattling black cab pulled to the curb of the little park opposite the house.

No sign of Murphy yet. The glow of gas lamps reflected against the hood of the vehicle. Beyond, the dark and deserted square seemed to be waiting for the arrival of a new baby in its perambulator. Murphy and Elisa had promised the boys they could give the baby rides around Red Lion Square. *Could we begin this morning?* Charles wondered.

The passenger door opened.

"There he is," Louis whispered, pressing his face against the glass.

"Where's Elisa?" Charles frowned when Murphy closed the door without sign of either Elisa or the new baby.

"Where's . . . the kid?" Louis echoed.

Charles thought for a moment. Murphy had said this was a very late kid. He had been saying that for weeks and had been growly more often these days. Elisa had been weepy. A normal thing, Murphy had told the boys man-to-man as they pretended to shave with him yesterday morning.

"Maybe the kid is still . . . late," Charles said.

This was a very disappointing homecoming. Charles and Louis had been forced to spend the evening with Hildy and Freddie. Trying to figure out what Hildy was talking about was a difficult proposition most of the time, but all evening her false teeth had clicked and clacked more than usual as she babbled on. She vacuumed twice and scolded Louis for getting cracker crumbs on the floor in front of the radio. It had been an unpleasant night, and now there was not even a baby to show for it. Would they have to do this *again*?

Murphy looked awful. His fedora was way back on his head. He needed a shave worse than usual. His tie was off; tucked into his coat pocket and hanging out nearly to his knees. He looked tired, *tired*. Worse than the nights when he came home from spending too many hours reporting on something terrible in the news. He walked slowly toward the house. The cab drove away.

Louis grimaced. "No kid."

"Rats."

Hildy was sound asleep on the sofa. Charles could hear her snoring. He wondered if she would someday suck in her false teeth and choke from such snoring. Not even Freddie snored like Hildy. He decided that next time they thought the baby was coming, he would ask if they could stay with Doc Grogan. He would have preferred Anna and Theo, of course, but they also would be at the hospital with Elisa because Elisa was their daughter. So, maybe they could stay with Doc Grogan who spoke real English instead of fractured, garbled stuff like Hildy. He said things like *rats, okay,* and other real American stuff like Murphy.

The boys turned away from the window and waited in the dark as the hollow sounds of Murphy's footsteps climbed the stairs.

Hildy heard him coming in her sleep. She snorted, and the snoring stopped. "Who ist dere, pleeze?"

Murphy replied in a muffled voice that it was he.

"Ach! Mein *Gott!* Mizter Murpheee! Und d' ba-bee ist. . . ?" The door banged back. Murphy's voice was low and quiet. Hildy's voice was loud and unintelligible. The pitch increased. Murphy, still tired, was talking all the same. Talking too quiet!

Something was up. The boys exchanged glances and padded quickly out to the landing where they could see Hildy's plump, wide body blocking Murphy from coming all the way in. If she caught them there she would shake her finger at them and scold them, so they stayed quiet and hoped she would go downstairs to her own place soon.

"Fine . . . fine, Hildy." Murphy managed to get in a word.

"Ach! Gott praise to be! Und danks to Gott, Mizter Mur-phee!"

Murphy's hands took the old woman by her shoulders. "The boys were good for you?" *Uh-oh. The question . . .*

"Like d'an-gels, dey ist! *Per*-fect! An-gels!"

Charles understood her. *Angels?* This was amazing. Murphy managed to switch places with Hildy so she was mostly outside. He was still speaking very low. She was very excited and loud. Crying. Were they happy tears or unhappy?

"You go . . . get some sleep now, Hildy. You must be tired. Thanks a lot . . . tell you all about it tomorrow."

She let out a big laugh and she slapped her hand against her legs like a German folk dancer. "Tomorrow ist already *here!*"

"So it is." Murphy looked at his wrist to check the time but he did not have his watch on. "Late. Early. G'night, Hildy." He shut the door. *Relief!* Murphy was better than anyone at getting Hildy out the door.

He sighed and looked up toward the landing. The tired look went away when he saw the boys waiting there in their pajamas. Something wonderful had happened. Charles could tell by the look on Murphy's face.

"It's okay, fellas," he called. "She's gone. You can come out now."

They clambered down the stairs to embrace him. He smelled like the ashtrays at the newsroom, but he was happy.

"Where's Elisa?"

"Where's the kid?" Louis asked. "Still late?"

Murphy laughed and hoisted them both up to touch the heavy rafters. "You've got a baby sister, boys," he cried. "As beautiful as her mother, too!"

———————

Where the walls of his cell came together at the corner, Karl noticed a shadow just beneath the ceiling where one brick was missing. The sparrows saw it as a place to build their nest.

Karl's human logic could not understand why the sparrows would forsake the fragrant green boughs of a pine-tree home for the rank gloom of this prison cell. But such a miracle was beyond human logic. When Karl reasoned with his heart, he came to the conclusion that these tiny feathered creatures were sent to him as a gift. The sparrows did not belong to him. No. They were free to come and go as they pleased. They belonged to the Lord who cared for all creatures big and small, and God had loaned them to Karl to keep him company. How kind, how thoughtful, God was, Karl concluded. God had known about the missing brick. He had provided the bread. He had sent the sparrows and planted the desire in their hearts to build their home in the very walls that imprisoned Karl.

Twig by string by stem, the sparrows labored over their nest. As they twittered to each other, Karl's heart entered into their conversation. He understood the concerns of parenthood and marriage. Of building a safe place in which to bring up youngsters. All these concerns were acted out in miniature drama in the nitch above Karl's head. Lady Sparrow scolded and the male pouted. He tossed his head and she obeyed . . . but not without protest. Together they lined the nest with downy feathers, creating a soft place for their little ones through their own sacrifice.

Day by day Karl offered them the best morsels of his bread. In return, they sometimes brought him gifts. One day the leaf of an elm tree. The next a faintly fragrant pine needle, which he pressed between his fingers to inhale the scent. Twice, Lady Sparrow dropped the petals of a wild flower. By holding the fragile yellow fragment in his hand, Karl could imagine a whole field of yellow flowers sloping down toward the banks of a broad river.

They brought him pieces of the world. Little bits of beauty from which he could rebuild the memories of the things he had most enjoyed with his own family: Picnics by the River Spree. A hike through the fragrant forests of Bavaria. Late-night talks with Helen about their children. Their future. Their lives. Family...

The memories of long-ago things did not make Karl melancholy. Instead, he found comfort in replaying his life with Helen and Jamie and Lori. He had no regrets. Life had been good. Every day had been brushed with the colors of loving. Even the most ordinary routines now seemed somehow sacred and blessed, a holy sacrament.

Karl looked up at the nest. It was barely visible even though he knew where to look. If his jailors ever came into the cell, they would not see the little family high in the wall. He was grateful for this. The male had gone foraging this morning. Lady Sparrow was nestled in the downy feathers. A miracle was happening today, Karl knew. There would be eggs in the nest by the time her mate returned. This fact gave the cell the aura of a holy place. Karl bowed his head and worshiped the Lord of men and sparrows.

――――――

Only one thing did Rachel enjoy more than the weekly BBC concerts on the radio—the weekly live concerts performed at the Community Hall for free.

Tonight, Father Kopecky came to visit Papa. He had looked surprised that Rachel and Etta were not going to the concert.

"Why should the women stay home," he asked, "when a priest and a rabbi have so much to talk about?"

"And a game of chess to finish," Papa had added.

The boys were put to bed early. Etta French-braided Rachel's hair, giving her the appearance of a nearly adult young lady. Then they had changed into Shabbat clothes and joined the parade traipsing through Muranow Square toward the hall.

There were more strangers here than people who knew the Lubetkins. Fewer and fewer of the old friends and neighbors remained in Warsaw each day. The dress and dialects of the crowd verified that they had come here from everywhere.

Many looked just like the Poles whom Rachel had seen beyond the neighborhood. They would have fit in just as well at the Saxon Garden or on the sidewalks outside the Royal Palace where merchants with little carts cooked Polish sausages. Some wore clothing that once must have been as grand as anything that passed through the lobbies of the Bristol or the Europejski hotels. Others would have fit right in among the fish sellers on the docks of the Vistula.

One thing was certain; the newcomers did not look like Jews. They did not talk like Jews or act like Jews—at least not like the Jews of Muranow Square! Rachel thought that maybe the Catholic priest would have fit into this assembly very well. The thought made her feel indignant and more than a bit uncomfortable. Across the aisle, in an entire row of wooden folding chairs, boys and girls sat all in a line, talking together, *holding hands*! The sight of such familiarity made her flush with embarrassment.

Rachel had heard Papa laughing about such things with the priest. His laughter had shocked her. His comment had sobered her, especially in the face of the terrible news from Germany these days.

"It seems impossible to me that Herr Hitler simply lumps all of us who are Jewish together," Papa had said. "I will give you the straight of it. You may preach a sermon on it, because it has not changed since Jesus walked in Jerusalem."

"Instruct me." The priest had moved his knight across the chess board and grinned at Papa's sour expression.

"Then be instructed." Papa swept a hand over the chessmen. "Our trouble in facing the Nazis is that we do not have one great army with one belief as they do. We are not even right or left. We are not even right, left, center. We are a spectrum." At that he began bumping his chess men from the table. "We are Orthodox, Karaites, Ashkenazim, General Zionists, Poale-Zion Right, Hasid, Mizrochi, Hashomer Hatsoir, Poale-Zion Left, and Communist."

All the little chess pieces lay in a pile, and Papa's king and queen were quite exposed to all the forces on the opposite side.

"I see," said Father Kopecky. "Check and checkmate." Then he said, "And you know why the Christians have been so utterly smashed in Germany as well? We are Catholic, Lutheran, Episcopal, Methodist, Baptist, Mennonite . . ." All his chessmen came crashing down as well. "Everyone with a different idea. All forgetting who God is as we cram Him into doctrinal boxes and squabble over this and that. Not so very different, after all, are we, Aaron?"

"Except that every Jew will die regardless of what he believes if the Nazis come here. If you Christians . . . renounce your faith, or simply alter it to conform . . . you will live."

"Not live, Aaron." He laid the two kings side by side as if they shared a mutual tomb. "Only survive. Breathe and walk in bodies that have lost their souls. And in the end, those who have betrayed their faith will be scraped off the shoe of God right along with the Nazis, I think."

Rachel had been called away from the rest of the discussion, but looking around her at all the different types gathered together under one roof, she recalled every word.

Just then she spotted the ragged form of Peter Wallich as he leaned forward at the foot of the stage and talked in serious tones to the violinist. She knew what Peter was asking about. And from the expression on his face, she knew that he had not found what he was looking for. He still was lost, still without the precious name he needed to find his way home to his mother and sister. That is, if they were really here in Warsaw.

She shuddered as she stared at his increasingly ragged clothes, his bushy, unkempt hair, and his face so thin that his bitter eyes were his most prominent feature.

And then a terrible thought came to her, a thought that made her want to leave the concert. *Peter Wallich is every Jew that was and will be. Lost and looking for home. This is what the enemy wishes to throw in the fire! Not an oak branch, but a bundle of twigs, an army to be defeated one lonely life at a time!*

She put her hand to her head and closed her eyes. Etta leaned close. "Are you all right? Do you have a headache?"

Rachel nodded. "A big one." She opened her eyes and Peter was gone, vanished from the place where she had seen him. She looked around but could not find him. He had simply blended into the crowd. Rich and poor, wise and foolish alike had simply absorbed Peter Wallich into themselves.

Where is home? Rachel wondered as she looked at each twig in the vast bundle and pitied them and herself. *Where is the home we are searching for?*

The spotlight flicked on behind the chairs. The audience applauded as the lights were turned off. The musicians began to play the Mozart Quintet K. 174, and for that moment all hearts listened as one heart, longing for the same home together. Once again Rachel closed her eyes and let her mind sing the words of the prophet Balaam:

> *How can I curse those whom God has not cursed?*
> *How can I denounce*
>   *those whom the Lord has not denounced?*
> *From the rocky peaks I see them,*
>   *from the heights I view them.*
> *I see a people who live apart*
>   *and do not consider themselves*
>   *one of the nations.*
> *Who can count the dust of Jacob*
>   *or number the fourth part of Israel?*
> *Let me die the death of the righteous,*
>   *and may my end be like theirs!*

The melody of those words filled her heart like the music. For a moment, at least, she felt peace. There was much she would have to ask Papa about that passage. Could it be that from heights God did not see a bundle of twigs in Israel, but a solid oak staff that would not bend beneath the weight of persecution, or break under the force of the stones that even now were hurled against this people called Israel?

God has made His walking stick out of brittle twigs, Rachel mused. *But in the hand of God, even twigs can be strong.*

15   The News Never Waits

"Where to, mate?" The taxi driver leaned his head far out the window and called to Samuel Orde. He seemed to be the only remaining taxi at London's Victoria Station tonight.

Orde touched his fingers to the brim of his Panama hat and then climbed into the back of the vehicle without answering the question.

"I say," tried the driver again, "where to?"

It had been a long time since Orde had given anyone the address of his London home. The last time, he had been with Katie. They had ordered a new sofa for delivery to the house. Now the sofa was covered with a sheet, as was all the rest of the furniture. Dusty sheets and lonely rooms. Orde was not anxious to enter that place again.

"I say—" The cabbie looked concerned. "Do you *parley* English?"

"Yes. Sorry. It's been some time since I've been here. For a moment the address—" He waved his hand as if he had forgotten. "Three Kings Yard—" *Katie had loved the name of their street.* "Between Claridge's and Grosvenor Square. Do you know it?"

The taxi had already lurched into motion. "Number?"

"Twelve." Orde looked out the window. All of London seemed asleep. There was hardly any traffic. He could see the reflection of the cab as it passed the showcase windows of the shops and hotels. Yes, London was asleep and Orde was dreaming. He had been dreaming since the day Katie died. Between that moment and this, it seemed that no time at all had passed. He would go home to their house—to the wallpaper she had hung, the furniture she had picked out. The paintings. The carpets. The china and crystal wine glasses they had gotten on their wedding day. And surely Katie would be there, too, waiting for him to wake up. *"Fresh strawberries and cream for breakfast, Sam. You've overslept. The sofa is coming today."* And then she would lean over to kiss him awake. She would tell him to shave and shower quickly *because . . . because . . .*

Orde shook his head. He tapped on the glass partition separating him from the driver. It had been a long time since he had seen the city, Orde explained, and perhaps it would be better to have a look at it while there was no traffic.

The cabbie shrugged in good-natured acquiescence. What did it matter to him if this passenger wanted to rack up unnecessary miles on the meter as long as he could pay for it? It did not occur to him to ask why a man who had been away so long would not be eager to arrive home. The real reason for Orde's sudden urge for this late-night tour of the city was nothing Orde could have articulated even if someone had asked him.

Hyde Park. Marble Arch. Selfridge's Department Store where

Katie had loved to shop. Regent Street to Piccadilly Circus. Once around Trafalgar Square and then back toward Buckingham Palace.

Everywhere Orde looked, sandbags piled like lumpy pillows against the dark hulks of buildings. On the base of every monument, posted signs proclaimed Britain's preparedness for whatever might come. These ominous reminders of the daily headlines finally drew Orde out of the melancholy memories of Katie and set him down squarely in the present. When Katie had died, Spain had not yet erupted. Germany had no army to speak of. Austria was still Austria and there was the solid little democracy of Czechoslovakia in the heart of Europe.

There had been no sandbags in London when Katie left. . . .

Again Orde tapped on the window partition. "What is the date?" he asked the cabbie. "The *year,* I mean?"

With a quick, concerned glance in the rearview mirror, the cabbie answered, "1939."

Orde nodded. "Right. You may drive me home now, if you please. Number 12. *Three Kings Yard.*"

———

London seemed quite awake now. The din of traffic along Fleet Street was deafening. Fumes of omnibuses and taxis threatened to choke the two horses pulling hansom cabs to St. Paul's Cathedral.

Sam Orde double-checked his reflection in the window of a shop next to the London office of Trump European News. He frowned and smoothed the lapels of his ill-fitting tweed jacket. The shoulders were cut too narrow. It had been a year since he last wore it, and he had forgotten about the shoulders needing to be altered. The material of his suit was definitely out of season for the warm month of May. But he had nothing else suitable to wear with the possible exception of his Royal Army uniform. And, of course, as of midnight last night, Orde was a private citizen again.

Ah well, perhaps Mr. Murphy would not notice the cut of Orde's clothes. And if he did, maybe it would not matter.

Orde drew a deep breath of exhaust-filled air. He pulled himself erect and walked—not marched—to the entrance of TENS. Hand on the door, he peered through the glass at the commotion within. Everyone seemed to be up and milling about. The young woman at the switchboard stood leaning against the counter and laughing. Orde could distinctly hear the shouts and laughter of men and women. Some sort of party—at eight-thirty in the morning? Orde wondered if he should have called Mr. Murphy. Of course, Orde had no telephone at the house. It had been disconnected for years. And if he was really going to accept this position as a member of the TENS staff, there was no reason to have it connected again, was there?

Taking another deep breath, Orde wondered if the Warsaw position had been filled. He pulled the door open. A buzzer rang, announcing his entrance, but no one even looked his way. The air inside was more rank than the exhaust fumes outside. *Cigar smoke!* Every man in the place was puffing away on enormous Cuban stogies. The women among them did not seem to mind. At least not much.

Someone shouted to the receptionist. "Hey, Marjorie! Open the door! Prop open the blasted door! We're all going to asphyxiate in here!"

Laughing, the receptionist brushed past Orde, who stood in the lobby. She did not notice him, did not speak to him as she propped the entry door open. Her face seemed perpetually frozen in a gleeful smile. Once the door was open, the noise of Fleet Street combined with the din of the group. The receptionist charged back past Orde as if he were a pillar rooted in the floor.

The swinging half door to her little cubicle slammed shut. She once again leaned against the counter to observe the celebration in the crowded newsroom beyond.

"I hope it doesn't look like you, Murph!" shouted a man who sat on a cluttered desk.

"Nope, looks just like Elisa!" remarked a fellow whose pockets seemed to be jammed with the offending cigars. "Beautiful."

"Ah come on, Murphy! I got three kids myself. Never saw one fresh out of the oven that didn't look like it needed to bake a while longer!" There was a great roar of approval at this truth.

"Nah!" said the cigar man again. "I'm telling you . . . really now. . ." His hands rose up in innocence. "Beautiful. All the rest of them in the nursery look squashed in the face, but not our girl! Just like her mother!"

Wolf whistles rang out in reply.

"Watchit! Watchit!" warned the cigar man. "I'm a father now. A little respect from you mugs, if you don't mind!"

Orde knew that he had walked into something wonderful. The rumpled-looking fellow thumped everyone on the back as he laughed, handed out cigars, and shouted back in joyful banter about his baby. His wife. Indeed, Orde had crashed a celebration; one which made his heart more than a little envious. *That might have been me.* He did not interrupt until someone spotted him hanging back.

"Hey, Murph! There's another one without a cee-gar!"

Three fellows charged through the swinging gate, and then Orde noticed that among the crowd was a policeman, a taxi driver, a chauffeur, and a man wearing a chef's hat.

"Come on! Come on!" They grabbed Orde by his tweed suit and propelled him into the newsroom until he stood face-to-face with the new father.

With a cigar clutched between his teeth, the father pulled another cigar from his jacket pocket. "Congratulate me, pardner. I am the proud father of a seven-pound, eight-ounce baby girl. Mother is doing swell." He handed Orde the cigar. "In honor of Katherine Anna Murphy!" He flicked the match with his thumb, sparking the flame to life and touching it to the top of the stogie.

So this is the boss, Orde thought, accepting the ritual offering. Not bad tobacco. Orde sized up the chap who might well be his employer. He liked him immediately. "Congratulations," he saluted lightly. "And may I ask if the father of Katherine Anna—"

"Katie! Katie, we decided. She's too little for all that Katherine. We just named her after my mother and Elisa's mother, but she looks like a Katie to me."

A slight twinge shot through Orde. A well-loved name: *Katie.* "Very well, then. Katie's father wouldn't happen to be John Murphy?"

"The same." Murphy raised his hands like a soccer player who had just made a goal. Great cheering rose up from the impromptu guests and regulars in attendance. "I'm not asking anyone's name," Murphy said through his cigar, "because I won't remember it."

"All the same, I am Samuel Orde." Orde presented the crumpled telegram to Murphy. "I believe you wished me to see you about a position?"

Like smoke after a Fourth of July fireworks display, a blue cigar haze still hung over the newsroom of London TENS. Heads were bowed over Olivetti keyboards. Crumpled paper overflowed metal trash cans beside each desk. The news could not wait just because John Murphy had become a father last night. And with the one exception of a baby girl named Katie, none of the news was good this morning.

Murphy's face still held a lopsided grin. For him the good news was too good to be tarnished by the latest horror story from Nazi-occupied Prague. Even as he explained to Sam Orde the gravity of the situation in Warsaw, the half smile did not vanish. The distant clatter of typewriters penetrated the glass-enclosed office like the faraway popping of rifle fire.

Murphy passed the latest wire dispatch across the desk. One thousand Czech citizens had been arrested and thrown into prison in retaliation for the killing of a Nazi policeman last night. German troops were reported on the move across Czech territory toward the border of Poland.

"I am convinced Warsaw is the next target," Murphy said. "And that you are the right man to have in place when it finally breaks." He paused, still smiling. "What I can't figure is which way Russia is going to jump in this." The grin finally wavered and faded. "There are a number of men in Parliament who have been trying to form an alliance with Stalin. Warsaw won't have any of it, of course."

"Certainly not. Warsaw dare not make an alliance with Russia for fear that an invasion by Germany would be an invitation for Russia to flood across Poland to fight the Germans. And maybe Stalin might take a liking to Warsaw and never leave."

Murphy seemed pleased by Orde's reply. He had grasped the essence of all Polish foreign policy: straddle a very high fence, and hope the Russians or the Germans did not climb over it. The fear that Murphy had shared with Winston Churchill was that Stalin and Hitler might simply advance to that center line through the heart of Poland, and divide the nation between them.

"Do you think Germany will attempt an alliance with Moscow?"

"In order to divide up Poland," Orde said flatly. Then he nodded. "Here in England the politicians say it cannot happen. And I am certain that the German people would be appalled by such a prospect. Hitler has built his support on a platform of fear about Communist Russia." He frowned and picked at the lint on his trouser leg. "But I cannot see any other way for Hitler to make good his threat about invading Poland. From a military point of view—"

Murphy leaned forward, urging Orde to continue. This was just the sort of insight he had hoped for from this man. "Go on. And once it happens, I'll print it."

"Hitler will not risk invading Poland if it means he must fight the West *and* Soviet Russia at once. Certainly Stalin will not sit back and allow the German divisions to sweep right up to his borders."

"And?"

"And so, Hitler must have some sort of . . . agreement . . . with Stalin. Perhaps a nonaggression pact of the sort he has with Italy. If that happens, then war is a certainty."

"What do you see standing in the way?"

"Hardly anything at all." He shrugged. "Prime Minister Chamberlain resists any alliance with the Russians. The Poles remain on their high wire, hoping that the breeze will not blow. And Hitler is looking eastward, considering how the devil may best make a pact with the bear."

"You have been paying attention while you were in Palestine, Captain Orde," Murphy said, genuinely impressed.

"What is happening in Palestine is very much linked to what is happening in Europe. Only a political moron would not see that." He paused. "Just call me Orde, if you please. Or Samuel."

"All right then. If you will call me Murphy." He reached across the desk to shake hands with a man he considered to be the finest TENS political reporter in all of Europe. Orde had recited the same political scenario that Murphy had heard from Winston Churchill over prime rib and Yorkshire pudding last month. Churchill was seldom wrong in his foresight of coming events.

"When do I begin?" Orde asked, looking around as though a steamer ticket had already been purchased.

"I thought, if you accepted the post, that you might want a bit of time in London to relax."

"I find after one night at home that I am more relaxed elsewhere. I will be ready to leave as soon as arrangements—"

At that moment, Harvey Terrill banged once on the glass door and then poked his head in the office. "Sorry, Boss. It's a trunk call all the way from Danzig. Some little girl . . . your cousin? Elisa's cousin? She speaks pretty good English. Says she tried to get through on the home lines and nobody answers. Collect call. I accepted."

Murphy nodded. The smile reappeared. It had to be Lori, reporting in on the news about their visas. "Sweet kid," Murphy said aloud and then, "Hullo?"

Today the sweet kid was anything but sweet. Anything but calm. Lori related to Murphy the sad tale of Jacob Kalner's rejection by the embassy official. She barely noticed when Murphy told her that the reason no one was home was because Elisa had just delivered a baby. She did not ask if the baby was a boy or girl.

"If Jacob does not come to England, then you must explain to my mother that I am not going either!"

"Wait a minute!"

"I mean what I am saying! He cannot be left in this place alone. Danzig is not a place where anyone should be alone. I will stay here with him until we can figure out another plan. But the boys will come ahead. Tell my mother these things."

She rambled on, her voice betraying her emotional distress. She was not thinking clearly; not weighing the consequence of her turning down a visa. Likely there would be no more offered to her.

Murphy covered the mouthpiece as she talked. "Orde. We've got a situation here . . ." Lori's voice rose to a soprano of near-hysteria, and he simply spoke over her. "I'd like to give you an assistant. Put him on the payroll. He's seventeen. Jewish. In Danzig now. I can have him meet you. Messenger boy, valet, if you like. He speaks German almost exclusively, so the language might be a problem, but—"

Orde could hear every word of Lori Ibsen's long recitation. Within a moment he had a clear grasp of the desperate situation. "I have had seventeen-year-old recruits beside me in trenches before. Often they fight as well as men with ten years on them." He waved a hand. "Tell the girl . . . her chap will be well managed until we can get him to England." Orde smiled. He was still the captain of a very small troop.

———

Within thirty minutes Victoria Station would be packed with

London commuters. It was still only half full when Allan Farrell passed through the main entrance.

Today he looked more like Maureen than himself, he thought as he caught his own reflection in the glass of the doors. He had shaved twice, put on the clothes and shoes of a woman and then a touch of lip rouge and powder to complete the effect. He covered his hair with a wide-brimmed hat and veil. His slim, small-boned structure lent itself well to such a disguise. He carried a large shopping basket and a handbag containing cigarettes and matches along with a handful of change.

His destination was neither ticket kiosk nor train. He moved rapidly across the echoing terminal to the ladies' lavatory. Without hesitation, he entered, walking quickly past a handful of women at the sinks. Two primped before the mirror, fixing their hair and makeup. Allan did not let himself think of their fate if they lingered too long in the ladies' room.

The stalls were mostly empty. He chose the one at the end of the row and locked the door behind him. Within moments the pipe bomb was placed on the water tank of the toilet. Allan fumbled in the handbag, taking out cigarette and matches and a spool of thread. He placed the matches against the cigarette, binding them to it with the thread. Once lit, the tobacco would burn down toward the match heads slowly enough for him to get away. Three minutes later, when the flame reached the matches, they would flare and ignite the contents of the pipe bomb. The result would be devastation.

One minute had passed since he entered the stall. He lit the cigarette fuse, blew on it until it glowed hot, and then placed it in position against the end of the pipe bomb.

With that, he dropped a towel into the toilet bowl and flushed. Instantly, the water filled and overflowed onto the floor, soaking his shoes and spreading rapidly as the ladies in the room squealed and grumbled and clamored to get out of the path of the flood.

"A toilet has broken! Everyone out! Hurry!" He had done his best. He could not think about those women who did not move fast enough to escape what followed. *Those who did not care about wet shoes would soon never have a care again.*

Five women went out the door with him. Two remained inside. They would die, Allan knew. He did not look back. He resisted the urge to run back and pull them from harm's way. Fixing his eyes on the telephone booth, he hurried toward it. One minute remained until the device exploded. He looked over his shoulder as one more disgusted-looking woman emerged.

With trembling hands he picked up the telephone and dialed the number he had memorized. He wanted to be certain the world knew. . .

"Hullo, Trump European News Service. How may I direct your—" Fifteen seconds.

"Shut up and listen. I am at Victoria Station. The explosion you are about to hear is courtesy of the IRA. Got it? IRA . . ."

He let the receiver fall. It was dangling there when the explosion rocked Victoria Station. When the shrieks and shouts of terror filled the chasm of the terminal, TENS was on the line. By the time the first wails of ambulances filled the streets, Allan Farrell was long gone. But they heard it all over the telephone at TENS. They heard everything from the name *IRA* until the moment the first reporters crowded through the police barriers.

Allan read about the incident in his morning issue of *The Times* as he sunned himself in Parliament Square and waited for his contact.

Visiting hours at the City of London Maternity Hospital were not long enough to suit Murphy. He stood for an hour in front of the glass partition of the nursery, tapping on the glass, talking to the little bundle named Katie who slept peacefully in her bassinet between two stout, bawling baby boys.

"An angel," Theo said of his granddaughter. He leaned his forehead against the glass, smiled and waved a tiny wave with the same adoration on his face as Murphy expressed.

"She looks like Elisa." Anna was anxious to hold her granddaughter, but it would be days before that was allowed. "Don't you think so, Helen?"

Helen Ibsen could only nod. The baby also looked like her own baby Lori had looked. She could not see anything behind the glass but the image of tiny Lori as she had been in her crib.

It was already seven o'clock according to the clock inside the nursery. Only one hour left to visit Elisa and then sneak back here for a final peek at Katie.

"Gotta git." Murphy kissed Anna lightly on the cheek. "Thanks," he said as he pumped Theo's hand. He wanted to thank them both for Elisa; their lives had resulted in his life being full to overflowing. But there were no words—just emotion enough to power the lights like a generator. And the sweeping second hand of that clock kept moving.

"Give her a kiss for me," Anna said.

"Kiss my baby girl and tell her I'm proud, ja?" Theo added.

Elisa was sitting up reading her Bible when Murphy walked in. A radio at the end of the ward played a Glenn Miller tune, but something in Elisa's eyes told him clearly that she had also heard the news about the bombing at Victoria Station.

He kissed her three times. "Once for your Mom. Once for Theo. And once for me." He grinned down at her, ignoring the worry in her eyes. "That's just for starters. We have an hour."

"She is so beautiful, isn't she, Murph?" Elisa said. There was more than pride in her voice; there was an edge of worry that they had brought something so perfect into an imperfect world. How could they shield this little one from the same terrible heartache they were seeing again and again among the children from the Reich?

Murphy felt it, too, but he did not speak of it. Instead, he took her hands. "You done good, kid," he said. "Real good. I called my mom. Good connection, too. I told her about the name, and she cried. Imagine! Calling all the way to Pennsylvania and then to have her bawl like that. Pop was pretty happy, too. He says we need to bring you all home soon, to teach Katie to ride a horse and milk cows." He was babbling, trying to pretend that he did not see what was in Elisa's eyes. He had heard the old saying before: *Any man with a baby in the cradle longs for peace in the world.* He had never understood it with his heart as he did now. "Anna and Theo say she looks just like you."

Elisa's brow furrowed with emotion. "And Aunt Helen? What does she say? I held Katie and thought how much she looks like little Lori looked. And then I remembered Lori and Jamie. Murphy, I haven't even asked you about them. Are they coming to London, Murphy? Did they make it through the paper mine field?"

Murphy patted her hand and nodded. She lay her head back on the pillows and sighed with relief. So much to think about . . . so many others to think about when this should be the happiest day of their lives. Murphy did not tell Elisa about Jacob Kalner except to explain that Jacob would be staying behind to work as the assistant of Samuel Orde in the new Warsaw branch of TENS. Putting the news in that light made it seem not at all terrible or threatening for the young man.

The second hand swept too swiftly around the clock face. Murphy did not say much about the Victoria Station bombing except that one toilet had blown up and an unfortunate woman was killed. He avoided mentioning that the woman had been only twenty-seven years old, or that she left behind two toddlers and a husband. Tonight the world should have been a perfect place, a safe place in which to raise someone as precious as little Katie. Mothers should not have to worry about pipe bombs exploding in train stations or Nazis sweeping over half the world.

16 Kyrie

Along with the ordinary mail, two special letters whisked through the mail slot of the Lubetkin home in Warsaw, Poland. Rachel picked them up and scrutinized the postmarks and handwriting to see who had written, when the letters were mailed, and from where.

Mama had told Rachel a thousand times that she must not be so nosey. The mail was almost always addressed to Papa, and so it was not supposed to be any of Rachel's business who was writing.

But Rachel had gotten into the habit when Papa was in prison. No matter who had written, she and Mama had opened the letters and gone over them together. The experience made it difficult to wait patiently for Papa to scan his correspondence and decide which letter was for sharing with the family and which was for his eyes alone.

Rachel knew at a glance that one of the letters was for reading. Addressed to Papa in the spidery handwriting of Grandfather Lebowitz, the letter had been mailed from Jerusalem four weeks ago. This meant that it had arrived two weeks sooner than the usual time of six weeks. And so the news would be two weeks newer, provided Papa did not take his time about reading it!

The Jerusalem letters were always wonderfully long and entertaining. Grandfather wrote them on paper so thin that a person could see through it. He did this to save money on postage, Mama explained. And on this thin, practically transparent paper, he painted long and wonderful pictures of the Holy Land. He started with the weather, which was always six weeks out-of-date. He progressed to funny stories about the Old City neighborhood—what this yenta had said about that yenta and who was squabbling with whom. Or getting married. Or graduating from Yeshiva. Sometimes who had died.

With all of this, Mama's eyes were bright and her face happy or sad, as the occasion dictated. The best part was her running commentary about everything Grandfather wrote. She had grown up in the neighborhood, after all. So, shouldn't she know all the little extra details that made the story more interesting? Of course she should. And she did.

Over the last two years the weather reports and personal news also included a lot about the Muslim uprisings. Mama also commented on this, since she had lived in the Old City before the British had taken over the place and all of the Arabs had moved in from the neighboring countries. Always when Grandfather mentioned the Mufti of Jerusalem, she became indignant. *"So why did the British make the lunatic a Mufti, already? Haj Amin was born in Syria, and they make him Mufti in Jerusalem!"*

Things had been different when she was growing up, she said. Arab and Jew got along wonderfully well. Lately Papa had been saying that he was sure the British would work it all out, and wouldn't it be good to go back there?

Rachel was certain that Grandfather's letter would end on the same note. He would tell them that everything was wonderful and that they should come home as soon as the little details about their papers got sorted out. Grandfather said they could all live with him. Mama said he would have to rent a bigger flat, and then she always looked around wistfully at the pale yellow walls and the fine walnut furniture and the beveled-glass transom windows that made the sunlight into rainbows on the polished wood floor. Before this year, they had all thought it would be impossible to leave the wonderful house on Muranow Square. Rachel still considered the idea unthinkable. But something had changed in the way Mama and Papa talked about Jerusalem. Now there was something wistful in Mama's voice when she mentioned the shops on Julian's Way and the merchants in their stalls along David Street and the covered souks and ancient sites.

Rachel held the envelope up to a rainbow from the window. It was full of colors, sights, sounds, and even smells that Mama would describe for her. But Rachel did not want to go to Jerusalem to see it in person. A letter on onionskin paper to be recited lovingly in the house on Muranow Square was good enough for her. She did not want to end up like the vagabonds who stood in long lines for free soup. She did not want to leave her bedroom furniture for some other girl. Better to lie on her bed and dream about exotic places than to leave her bed behind and go there.

Mama called to her from the kitchen, "Rachel? Are you snooping through the mail again?"

"No, Mama." Rachel furtively examined the postmark on the second faraway correspondence. She gasped at what she saw. "Mama!" she cried. "A letter from Czechoslovakia! From *Turnau*!" She had given herself away. She had been snooping, but at this news about a letter from Uncle Maurice in what was now Nazi-controlled territory was something that drew Mama out from the kitchen in an instant. She did not even scold Rachel as she hurried the letter in to Papa.

"Aaron! Darling!" Mama never called him that if she thought anyone was listening. This was indeed an occasion. "Look, Aaron! A letter from Turnau! Maybe news about your brother!"

Rachel helped her father to sit. She plumped the pillows behind his back as he waited patiently for Mama to open the envelope. A letter from Czechoslovakia! They had been hoping for news from Uncle Maurice ever since the Germans had marched in and taken over. They had been waiting as stories had poured across the border like the desperate refugees. Papa had said a prayer each night for his older brother. He had hoped that Maurice and his sons would show up on the doorstep of the Muranow house unharmed.

"Well?" Papa asked as Mama looked at the signature.

"It is not from Maurice. It is from a friend," she answered, and Rachel could hear her voice tremble when she said the words. "Be patient," she said to Papa. Then she read on. Her face grew pale. Her eyes filled up with terrible visions that she would not read aloud. Then she looked at Rachel and said softly, "Leave the room, Rachel. . . ."

"But—"

Not harsh, but firm. "Leave us."

By this and the weary look on the face of her father, Rachel knew that something terrible indeed had happened in the little town of Turnau, Czechoslovakia. Uncle Maurice was prominent there. He was a Jew. The Nazi invaders no doubt found both of those factors to be distasteful.

The facts concerning the deaths of Maurice Lubetkin and his three sons had been written out in meticulous detail by a friend who had witnessed it all. The friend had taken his own life in his hands by recording their executions and sending the account to Aaron Lubetkin.

Distilled down to simple details, Aaron's brother and his teenaged boys had been chosen at random, lined up against a wall and shot in retaliation for the killing of a German policeman. In this way, according to German reasoning, the innocent learned an important lesson. Everyone paid for the rash act of one person. That same lesson had been taught during *Kristallnacht*.

Aaron Lubetkin was too ill to be allowed traditional mourning and fasting for the dead members of his family. So Etta and Rachel donned their black clothes. They tore the hems of their dresses. They fasted and mourned in silence except for prayers and the few words necessary for daily existence.

The priest came and expressed his dismay to Aaron. Rachel heard them speaking in low tones about the possibility of Nazis coming here to Warsaw. And if they came, the priest told Aaron, all his children should be dispersed among Catholic families of his parish.

Aaron did not argue with this unthinkable proposition. Rachel shuddered at the idea of actually living with the Saturday people who beat Jews on the head with their crucifixes and called them Christ-killers!

She decided that she would never go among them! Rachel would let them put her against a wall and shoot her full of holes, but she would not leave with Father Kopecky and go live with the Saturday people!

Why did her father not tell the priest that he would never consent to such a thing? How could he sit silently on his bed, knowing that the goyim had just murdered his brother and his nephews in Turnau!

Rachel waited in the hallway until the priest was finished talking to Papa. She leaned against the wall with her arms crossed defiantly and her eyes staring at the floor.

She looked up as Father Kopecky emerged. He was surprised to see her there. He knew she had heard.

"Rachel?" he questioned gently.

"I will never go with your kind," she said fiercely in a quiet voice. "Better to die than be with them."

He put out a hand to soothe her. "We were speaking only of the worst case." He shrugged. "It will not come to that."

"Papa would rather see us dead than live with the goyim."

The priest shook his head in disagreement. "You are wrong, I think. Not because your father would ever want you to forsake your people. But he knows, as you do not, that we are not all heartless and brutal. There are a few who see clearly what is good and what is evil. In case of the worst, Rachel, your father would say as a rabbi, *Baruch Hashem*. . . . For the sake of the Name of the Eternal, you must continue to live. It is easier sometimes to stand against the wall and let them shoot. But for the sake of the Name, we are called sometimes to suffer and go on living."

Rachel pushed past him and ran up the stairs to her room. She did not want to hear what he had to say! She did not want to think about suffering!

She stood at her window and looked out over the homeless who had pitched their shanty tents in the square. Had they left behind nice furniture? Fine clothes? Family meals around a big table in the dining room? For what? Were they really alive down there, or were they ghosts who had drifted in before her eyes to show her some grim vision of her future?

Rachel was afraid. Cold, sick fear climbed down her spine and settled in her stomach. She did not fear dying against a wall with her family falling with her. No. She feared the words of the priest much more . . . *Baruch Hashem!* Was God so cruel that He would require her to turn her back on everything just to go on suffering and living?

"Go away," she said to the homeless specters in the square.

But they did not go away. And there, on the fringes, she saw the sunlight glint on the red hair of Peter Wallich. Still lost. Still homeless. He was the most frightening ghost of all! *"Go away!"* she said again, and then she pulled the window shade and turned away.

———

Bracing herself against the wall, Lucy descended the steep stairs from her apartment very slowly. At the bottom, she turned to look up, wondering how many more days it would be before she carried the baby in its christening gown down those same steps.

The time was very near. She sensed it in the same way the heavy-bellied animals on her farm at home had *known*. Feeling the thrill of that reality had frightened her this morning as she looked at the satin gown and wondered. The mix of excitement and dread had driven her from the little nest she had prepared. Never had she felt a more urgent need to walk the three winding blocks to Heilige Geist Church. She needed to close her eyes and listen to all the sounds that were so dear and familiar to her. She needed to pretend that she was home and her mother was close at hand, and that the priest would offer a prayer for her and for the child.

Maybe this was the last time she would carry the baby inside her to the Mass. Maybe next week his little head would turn to the sound of the great pipe organ and the voice of the choir. *Not heaven, little bird, but as close as we can get on earth. . . .*

The morning sun beamed down through the canyon of crooked gables overhead. Lucy inhaled deeply. It was early enough that the stink of rotting fish from the fish market did not yet pollute the clean Baltic air. The street was still quiet. Drunks and prostitutes slept off their hangovers behind drawn shades. Secondhand shops and beer cellars were not yet open. It was a good time to get out. The usual squalor of the neighborhood had not yet flooded out over the street.

Lucy knew that she would be one of only a handful at the early morning Mass, but it did not matter. She usually preferred the anonymity of crowds, but this morning she half hoped that a priest might notice her, speak to her kindly. How good it would be if someone would offer her a kind word today!

No one ever seemed to look her way anymore, except to

wince at the sight of her ponderous waddle. Peter had teased her about it; said she had acquired the rolling gait of a drunken sailor and that now she fit in nicely on Heiliger Geist Strasse. She was secretly glad that he had identified her with a drunken sailor instead of with the painted women who lounged in open doorways and waited. The memory of his laugh gave her a twinge of loneliness. *If only he could have stayed in Danzig a few weeks more! No use thinking about that now. He was right. He could not stay here. Not the way things are going.*

She was out of breath by the time she reached the steps of Heilige Geist Church. Her ankles and feet were more swollen than usual and the heaviness of the baby seemed almost painful.

Entering the high arched portal, she touched her fingers in the holy water and crossed herself as she stole a look at the bulletin board on the back wall of a sanctuary. Sometimes there were offers of employment posted there. *Would it not be a miracle if some good Catholic family in England wanted a skilled parlormaid who knew all about carving?* Not likely in a parish like Heiliger Geist.

There were new summer hours for the soup kitchen. An announcement about the departure of the refugee children's steamship to England. Boxes of used children's clothing were needed for them.

Lucy scrutinized the mimeographed sheet enviously. Some said it was the last children's transport. Departure time was seven o'clock Wednesday morning. How she wished she were a child again! *To go to England!*

Her hand went instinctively to the baby. The pipes of the organ bellowed the first notes, announcing that Mass was about to begin. She took her seat in the last row of chairs in the small side chapel where morning Mass was usually read.

Lucy stared at her clasped hands, then at the back of the empty seat in front of her. There were not more than a dozen worshipers scattered throughout the little chapel. She scanned her companions briefly. Nine old women and three old men. Their faces showed varying degrees of weathering, but all of them could have easily come from the same litter. The clothes were all ragged. The men all needed a shave; the women all carried the same ancient sorrow in their eyes. Lucy had seen these same people everywhere she had ever been, it seemed.

Old. Tired. Waiting and preparing for death. They knelt on stiff knees. They prayed, silently beseeching, with lips that moved almost imperceptibly. Making the sign of the cross, they pulled themselves back into their seats and sat waiting as though the effort had exhausted them.

Lucy looked back at her hands and then toward the little altar where unlit candles waited for a flame. She wondered if she was the only one who had come here this morning in search of life? Had the faces around her ever been young? Ever known joy? Ever looked forward to anything other than that which was beyond the grave?

Her eyes darted to the crucifix again. To the dead Christ. *Are you Lord of the living, as well? Or only of the walking dead?*

The thought came involuntarily, and she blushed at her blasphemy. Who was she to ask such a question? After all, perhaps she was as near to death as these old ones around her. She let her eyes linger on her hands again. Her nails were clipped and unpolished, her fingers so swollen that she could no longer wear the cheap wedding band she had purchased for the illusion of propriety. This was the first time she had ventured into church without that ring. She had fooled shopkeeper and priest alike with it, but today she did not bring her disguise with her. Somehow, the absence of that ring made it seem as though she were seeing her own hands for the first time. *This is me. Just as I am. Today I do not want to hide from you. If you are the God of the living, then I want to know you. I want to live. I want my baby to live. If you can hear me—*

Her thoughts were interrupted as the priest and choir entered. Those in choir robes outnumbered the ragged worshipers.

The congregation all stood slowly as the priest prayed at the foot of the altar and the hymn was sung. Lucy studied the profile of the young priest. He could not have been much older than she was. She had seen hundreds of faces like his standing rank on rank before crowds of cheering Germans. She had toyed and flirted with men much older than this priest. It was a disquieting thought. Did she dare make confession to one so young?

She closed her eyes again as those around her read the Introit: *"When the just cry out, the Lord hears them, and from all their distress He rescues them."*

Could she trust even a priest, considering all she had fallen into? Would he urge her to give away the baby she had come to love? Or would he see her heart, and help her?

Her eyes opened, and she saw the priest looking intently at her, his gaze locked on her face. His eyes were agitated; anxious—as though he knew everything already.

He paused, too long, before beginning the Kyrie. There was no mistaking the fact that her presence at the service signified something to him . . . *something*. He spoke to a young man in the choir who also glanced at Lucy and then left the chapel.

"Lord have mercy," he began. His voice trembled.

"Lord have mercy," the congregation repeated in their cracked voices.

He looked away from her, then back again. "Christ have mercy."

Lucy could not make her lips move with the others. *"Christ have mercy. . . . "* What had the priest said to the young man?

Like an electric shock, a charge of fear coursed through Lucy. *He knows something. Something, but not the truth. Not all the truth. Not my truth . . . Wolf?*

She looked over her shoulder, feeling as though Wolf might stride through the door any moment. She could not think.

"Glory to God in the highest." It was obvious now that the priest held her captive in the corner of his vision.

"And on earth peace to men of good will."

The voices began a chanting echo in her brain.

"Lamb of God, You take away the sins of the world . . . receive our prayer. . . ."

Help me, Lucy breathed, unmoving. *Lord! Mercy! He knows!*

The priest turned to face the altar, breaking the spell that held her motionless. She gathered her little handbag and stood, bumping a chair noisily as she inched toward the aisle. The head of the priest moved at the sound. Was he listening for her escape as well as watching?

Her clumsy feet moved as if they belonged to someone besides Lucy. They slapped too loudly on the bare stone floor as she fled. Red and green votive candles became a blur of color as she ran through the main sanctuary. Then she heard footsteps behind her. *"Wait!"* a voice cried. "We will help you!"

She turned at the door to see the priest with his hand raised at the entrance of the chapel.

"Fraulein Strasburg!" he called.

Lucy gasped and threw herself hard against the massive

wooden door of the Heilige Geist Church. Sunlight exploded into her eyes as she ran blindly into the street.

"Wait! Wait, Fraulein Strasburg . . ."

The door boomed shut behind her, closing off the cries of the priest.

The street was awake—mercifully stinking, noisy, teeming with people. Lucy ran into the shelter of the crowds as she silently begged that they would hide her from anyone who might have followed.

———

Werner was a very handsome kitten. Everyone who saw him with Alfie in the fish market each morning stopped to scratch Werner's chin and tell him what a pretty kitten he was. Fishmongers in oilskin aprons and tall rubber boots offered Werner fish heads and fresh guts on newspapers. Alfie took Werner to a different stall each day so that he would not wear out their hospitality. Mama had told him, *"Fish and company stink in three days."*

Alfie knew that the saying meant that he should not stay too long in the same place, and since fish really started to stink in one day, he figured that he should not visit a fishmonger more than one day each week.

He explained this all very patiently to Werner, who blinked at him with wise kitten eyes. It did not matter to Werner where he got his daily fish head as long as he got it. One fishmonger was as good as another, and everyone along the wharf thought he was a superior cat anyway. Every day someone commented on how much Werner was growing. They congratulated Alfie in raising such a smart and polite cat. Werner was careful to clean his paws after every meal, and Alfie did not tell the men that Werner thought of it all by himself.

"Did you teach him such manners, Alfie?"

"Well . . . Werner . . . he is a smart kitten. He don't need . . . much teaching."

Alfie secretly thought that Werner was probably just licking the last of the fish flavor from his little toes. After all, Alfie always licked the jam from his fingers, so maybe that was how Werner learned it. All the same, it made Alfie feel good to put Werner on his shoulder and walk through the market. Werner was becoming handsomer every day. His black head and back were smooth and shiny. His white legs were always bright like Alfie's socks when Lori did the washing. He carried his tail proud and high like a main mast, and he rode on Alfie's shoulder like the captain on a bridge of a big ship. Alfie hoped very much that there would be a fish market like this in England.

England! For days Alfie had been happy when he thought about England, but today he was not happy. He was going. Lori and Jamie and Mark were going, but England did not want Jacob. Jacob was going to Warsaw to work on a newspaper, *unless . . .* Alfie was not worried about smuggling Werner onto the ship. Werner was small and would fit in a box. But Jacob was too big for a box. Too big even for a steamer trunk. How could they smuggle someone as big as Jacob onto the boat? And then off the boat in England? Couldn't Jacob work for the same newspaper in London instead of going all the way to Warsaw?

This was a problem they had talked about all night. Lori had cried and said she would not go unless Jacob went with her. Jacob had sounded angry and told her she must not talk so foolishly, that he could take care of himself well enough. Then she had run into her room and slammed the door. Lori was not happy about leaving Jacob even though he had a job. The boys had all sat very quietly staring at the floor for a long time.

"*Well?*" Jamie had said while his sister made muffled sobbing noises in her room.

"*Well,*" Jacob said, "*we will call London tomorrow and tell them what's up. Maybe they will have some ideas.*"

Last night had been a very sad night. But now it was tomorrow and Jacob and Lori were calling London to talk to Lori's family. Alfie did not want to go because he never got to talk on the telephone anyway, so here he was at *Herr Frankenmuth's Fresh Fish Daily* watching Werner finish off a herring on top of a newspaper with Hitler's greasy picture on it. Herr Frankenmuth enjoyed putting fish heads on top of the Führer. He told Alfie so. Herr Frankenmuth was a thin, frail-looking man with stooped shoulders and a sour face. He always had a black pipe hanging from his mouth. Alfie supposed it was because tobacco smelled better than fresh-fish-daily. Anyway, Herr Frankenmuth was a nice man who probably did not smile because his pipe might fall out if he did.

Today he noticed that Alfie was not cheerful. He wiped his hands on his fishy apron and looked at Werner. "What's the trouble today, Alfie?" he asked, sucking on his unlit pipe. "You have not smiled, even though today's front page shows Hitler with herring eyeballs and a fin for a mustache, eh? I arranged Werner's plate special today."

Alfie felt badly that he had not laughed at Herr Frankenmuth's cleverness. The fishmonger had gone to a lot of effort, after all. "Hitler looks better like that," Alfie said, but still he could not smile. "We are all going to England, except . . . except for Jacob. He cannot go. Lori cried a lot last night because I think she loves Jacob. Jacob is going to Warsaw to work for Lori's . . . well, I can't remember all of it. But Jacob is not going with us. He does not seem too sad because he likes newspapers and radios. But the rest of us are sad all the same." It was a long story.

Herr Frankenmuth stared angrily at Hitler's fish eyes. He frowned at the news and shifted his pipe from one side of his mouth to the other. He stared at the trays of ice where the fish were laid out side by side; then he looked off beyond the gray canvas awning to where the smokestacks of the big freighters poked up over the warehouses.

"Every day somebody gets left behind," he mumbled. Then he asked, "This friend of yours, Jacob. A big boy, is he?"

"Big."

"Big as you?" His eyes measured Alfie's 5'9" frame as if he were measuring a fish.

"Bigger. Maybe. Yes. I think bigger."

Herr Frankenmuth frowned and squinted his eyes. "When are you all leaving?"

Alfie could not think of the day, but it was soon. "On the children's ship."

Herr Frankenmuth nodded his head. He knew when that was. He leaned down to scratch Werner's chin. "Are you taking Werner?"

Alfie nodded and glanced over his shoulder to make sure no one could overhear him. "In a box . . . Jacob made it. With a . . . a . . ." He could not remember the word.

"False bottom?" Herr Frankenmuth finished for him.

Yes. That was the word Alfie forgot. "False."

"Ah, good. A nice fellow, this friend of yours. Tell him, will you, if he needs anything, I could use a big strong lad around here to help out. Will you tell him that, Alfie?"

"Yes. I will." Alfie pointed to the newspaper. "Maybe you will cheer . . . cheer him up. If he is not too sad."

Herr Frankenmuth did not have time to say anything else because two women came under the awning to buy their supper. Alfie hoped he could come back to say goodbye before the children's ship left. He liked Herr Frankenmuth and wanted to show Lori what Hitler looked like with fish eyeballs on his face.

He picked up Werner and put him on his shoulder. Herr Frankenmuth nodded his head goodbye and Alfie turned back into the crowded alleyway of the market.

Faraway he heard the loud hooting of a ship horn. It sounded like saying goodbye. It reminded Alfie that his own papa had left on a ship and never came home again. When they left Danzig, would they ever see Jacob again? The thought troubled him and he did not smile at his waterfront friends when they called to him.

He was not watching where he was going. Mama always told him to pay attention to where he was going so he would not get lost. But today he was not doing that. He looked at the stacks and booms of the freight boats as he walked along, and then he smashed head-on into a lady who was running down the street.

Werner was knocked off balance and dug his claws through Alfie's shirt. The woman stumbled and managed to brace herself on the side of a market stall. She was young and had a pretty face and looked like the cat Joseph just before Joseph had kittens. Alfie could tell she was going to have a baby. He tried to say how sorry he was for smashing into her, but she never even looked at him. She looked back the way she had come and then pushed past Alfie as if she was running from something.

"Sorry," he called after her. She did not hear him. He stood and watched her because she did not act like everyone else in the fish market. She did not walk slowly through the stalls or stare at the trays of fish. She pushed and tumbled and bumped into a lot of other people besides Alfie.

Alfie looked all around to see who would be mean enough to chase after a woman so big from a baby? He could not see anyone running after her, and so he readjusted Werner on his shoulder and walked back through the market the way he had come.

———

Lucy's lungs felt seared by the time she stumbled up the stairs to her flat. She slammed the door and locked it, then leaned, panting, against it. Gazing wildly around the room she tried to think what she must do. Where could she go?

Warsaw! Peter! "You have a friend. . . . "

Expecting to hear the crash of boots ascending the steps, Lucy pulled her tattered valise from beneath the bed and began jamming her clothing into it. Forgetting how she had placed all the baby things neatly in a row and rearranged them hour after hour, she crammed them into the large basket she had purchased for the little one to sleep in and be carried in.

Bottles. Milk. Diapers. Pins. Talcum powder. Alcohol . . . She folded the satin gown with the cap and booties, then wrapped the bundle in thin paper and tucked the package beneath the blanket on the bottom of the basket.

At that moment, when panic and dread ruled every thought, the first contraction wrapped iron fingers around her.

"Not now!" she cried. *"Oh please, God! Not . . ."* A warm, liquid release of pressure told her that her water had broken. Looking at the crucifix over her bed, she groaned at this, the ultimate betrayal.

No use. No use. Where could she run to now? How could she hide?

The contraction slowly eased. She straightened and stood staring at her bed. Mechanically, she once again removed what she would need from the baby's basket. Without joy, without anticipation, she laid those things out in a neat row as they had been.

There was time enough to prepare the bed and undress before the next contraction came. And then there was time enough to brew a cup of tea and sit waiting by the window.

Minutes of hopelessness ticked into hours, and still no one came to pound against the thin door. Once again Lucy dared to hope. Perhaps no one had seen her. Perhaps she had eluded the priest. Perhaps he had not even attempted to follow her.

The pains came closer and stronger, driving every other thought from her mind at last. She lay down and curled into a ball facing the last light of day that seeped through the window. She was alone. Glad she was alone, and yet, wishing for her mother. Now it seemed there was no relief from the strength of the pain. She did not cry out, but felt certain that if anyone came for her in the morning they would find her dead.

Lord, have mercy! Christ . . . have mercy!

17 To Do What One Can Do

In spite of Doc Grogan's vow that he would never take more than one dozen children on the Thursday educational walk, this morning there were twenty standing in the ranks on the sidewalk outside Red Lion House.

Elisa and the new baby were coming home today, which meant that Anna and Aunt Helen would be busy at the house while Murphy brought wife and baby home from the hospital. Someone had to help out with the new refugee children who had not yet made the transfer to their new families. For most of them, this would be their only opportunity to see London.

Doc squared his shoulders and counted heads. "Eighteen, nineteen, twenty and *twenty-one?*" He scowled down at a fair-haired eight-year-old girl who scowled back at him. "Where did you come from?" he asked in German.

"You counted me twice," she replied, not much liking the attention.

"Then you must get in line only once," Doc chided, then turned to Murphy with a grin. "How about it if we trade places, eh? I will pick up Elisa and the baby, and you take the troops to the Houses of Parliament."

Hildy Frutschy broke her own rule about never speaking German. For the first time ever, Charles could clearly understand the plump little housekeeper as she shouted to the group, "Do you all have your lunch sacks?" Heads nodded in affirmative reply. *"Gut! Sehr gut, Kinder!"* But bobbing heads were not enough for Hildy. Again in German: "Raise your hand if you have your lunch." It appeared that all hands were up. *"Gut! Sehr gut!"* And then, one more check. "And if you do *not* have a lunch, *bitte,* now also raise your hand." No hands went up. *"Gut. Sehr gut!"* Her job was done. She wiped her hands on her apron and retreated to the house to finish her work before the great arrival.

The adults had dwindled down to Murphy and Doc. Murphy was looking impatiently at his empty wrist. His watch was still broken, but he was sure the red double-decker bus was late—or at least it was not early as Murphy had hoped. He was staying on until the bus came. Doc needed the moral support until then. After that he would be on his own.

"We appreciate the help, Doc." He patted the weary-looking academician on the shoulder.

"I am leaving with twenty," Doc replied. "I hope I will return with the same number." As if to emphasize his worry, he shouted to the standing group, "Stay together now! Remember! Everybody *stay together*!"

"Keep away from the subways. No tube stations," Murphy warned. "There was another bomb scare yesterday. Nothing came of it. Probably nothing more afoot here in London after the Victoria bombing, but . . ." He looked over the heads of the children. "They have just come from that sort of thing. No use frightening them here in England."

"Parliament Square should be a safe enough place," Doc sighed. "I'm not so worried about IRA bombs as I am about having one of them wander off." He rubbed his chin thoughtfully. "More people were killed crossing the street last week than in the bombing."

"Only one out of millions in London," Murphy nodded. "Still, it's the idea of the thing. Not knowing where. Makes life a little shaky when you can't even go to the bathroom without wondering if the toilet is going to blow up."

Doc nodded. "Senseless."

"Not if you're a terrorist," Murphy disagreed. "Terror is a powerful weapon." He lowered his voice and looked at the haunted eyes of these mirthless children. "Take a look, Doc. This is the result of six years' worth of terror in Germany. Robbed the kids of their ability to laugh."

Doc nodded. He had indeed noticed and commented on the fact that every week these excursions with the refugee children were silent and somber. Unlike the babble of English school children that echoed in the great halls and museums, these children *marched*! Their little feet against the pavement echoed the tramp of the Nazi jackboots that had pursued them from their homes and smashed their families, scattering them throughout Europe.

"No laughter," Doc agreed. Then he reached out and mussed

the hair of Charles. "Except for this one and his brother!" He chucked Louis under his chin. "Talk, talk, *talk*! And I enjoy hearing every word, too!"

The comment made Charles beam, showing the gap where his front teeth should have been. "I been . . . to Par-li-ment," he said proudly.

"We been every place," Louis added, bobbing up and down.

At first the boys had been disappointed that they would not be on hand when Elisa and their baby sister came home, but Doc and Murphy had explained that Doc needed them to "*ride herd.*" Just like cowboys, keeping the group all together, Charles and Louis were assigned to bring up the rear, looking out for some children who were a lot older than they. The responsibility felt good.

"There is a triple duty police force on patrol, I'm told," Murphy said as the big red bus rounded the corner in a cloud of diesel smoke. "And Scotland Yard has plainclothesmen everywhere as well. Might be a help to the kids if you let them meet a bobby or two. Let them see the difference between here and the Reich. They still aren't going to get it for a while, I guess," Murphy added with a shrug. Then in a low voice he whispered, "You know, Charles is still having nightmares. After the Victoria bombing he slept in my bed. Poor kid."

Doc frowned at that news as though it made his heart hurt. He shook his head and patted his chest. But there was only a moment for reflection about what life in Germany could do to a child's dreams. The bus pulled up with a mighty belch. Doc counted heads as solemn faces piled into the bus. He realized that riding on a public bus was something many of these children had been forbidden to do in their homeland. All of them, without exception, headed straight to the fume-filled back of the vehicle and looked confused and nervous as they took their places.

"I'll bring them back a bit changed, I hope," Doc said to Murphy as he counted out the fares.

"Just bring them *back*, Doc," Murphy teased.

Doc did not seem to hear him. He shouted for everyone to move. "Top of the bus! Everyone up! Front seats, if you please!" It was good for a start.

Hildy opened the window and shouted down that there was a trunk call for Murphy, all the way from Danzig, no less!

Murphy looked impatiently at his wrist and then, muttering to himself about the fact that phone calls were more expensive than steamer fare, he ran up the stairs to face yet another bout with the pleading of Lori Ibsen.

"Can't you also give *me* a job in Warsaw?" she begged. "I do not want to leave Danzig unless we all leave together. *Please*. I am smart. I can work as a secretary! Please let me go to Warsaw with Jacob."

Murphy told her sternly that all positions were filled and that it would be good for Jacob Kalner to have experience as a news journalist's assistant through the rest of the summer. And certainly by autumn when it was time for him to be in school, the mix-up about his papers would be all straightened out. Murphy tried to assure the young woman, although he did not believe most of it. By autumn, Europe would be at war, and everyone who was getting out would be out. Or else.

It did not take a genius to figure out that Elisa's cousin was deeply in love with Jacob Kalner. Even Murphy caught on to that one two sentences into Lori's last long-distance try.

"His boss is a fellow named Sam Orde, just out of the British military. He'll run the Warsaw bureau like an army boot camp, Lori. It's no place for a young lady. But he'll take care of Jacob, that's for sure. He's arriving in Danzig the morning your ship leaves. Said he'd hang around the docks and meet up with Jacob. Okay?"

At last Murphy heard the resignation in her voice. No use trying. Staying was really impossible. She would be more trouble than anyone wanted to deal with if she tried to go to Warsaw.

"All right then," she replied quietly. "I suppose. If you promise he will be in school in the autumn."

Murphy looked at his wrist again. He would be late picking up Elisa and Katie. He hoped Lori would forgive him if, indeed, Jacob ended up being one of the unlucky ones left behind come September. "I will do all I can to make that happen," Murphy promised. What more could he do?

Allan Farrell stepped off the tube at the Westminster Station and bounded up the stairs into the bright sunlight of Parliament Square.

On the east, the square was bordered by the towers of Parliament. On the south was St. Margaret's Church, dwarfed in the shadow of Westminster Abbey. The square was ringed by statues of British statesmen whose heroic deeds were nearly forgotten now. Allan made his way across the area to the fountain that commemorated the abolition of slavery in the British dominions. Since Northern Ireland was still enslaved, Allan considered the symbolism of the fountain a sham; however, the water was cool. The spray dotted his forehead and eased the unrelenting heat. He dipped his handkerchief in the water and mopped his brow, then sat on a bench to wait for the arrival of his contact.

His first scanning of the heat-weary crowds of tourists and school children revealed that there was a disproportionately high number of policemen wandering about the square and standing in the shade of the towers and turrets of the surrounding buildings. Such vigilance on the part of Scotland Yard and the British authorities would be hard to penetrate during his next attack. He imagined that there was a plainclothes officer from Scotland Yard standing on duty at every urinal in the city of London.

The thought pleased him. The news accounts had called the Victoria Station bombing cowardly and depraved. Allan considered that it was just the opposite, and a tremendous success, judging from the visible evidence of so many blue-coated bobbies prowling around the place.

It was astounding how much damage one little pipe and a few match heads would do to the morale of the mighty British Empire. And words like *coward* held no meaning to Allan any longer. He had tasted blood, and like the newly tried hound of a hunt, he was eager for more.

Only this morning he had considered what his next job might be. A bomb right here? He looked at the spurting fountain, this monument to hypocrisy. Well, perhaps not this, he mused. He enjoyed it as his only refuge from the summer heat in his forays to pass information to the contact.

Maybe St. Margaret's Church? Or the abbey itself? That would certainly set all of England on its ear! A pipe bomb exploding in the organ of Westminster Abbey?

A matched pair of bobbies strolled past. They were greeted by yet another pair at the junction of the walkways in the square. Too much risk. It would be foolish to allow himself to be caught when he had only just begun his crusade.

St. Margaret's Street ran into the Old Palace Yard at the edge of the Houses of Parliament. The place was the scene of execution for a number of Catholic conspirators, led by one Guy Fawkes, who had attempted to blow up Parliament and King James I with all his lords as well. Bright fellows, those unfortunate men had been. They had rented a coal cellar that extended beneath the House of Lords and had crammed it full of gunpowder. They would have succeeded too, had it not been for an informer. The cellars were searched and the conspirators captured with a lantern ready to ignite the deadly fuse.

The course of history might have gone differently, Allan knew, if those Catholic dissenters had pulled it off. But half were executed in the Old Palace Yard and the others were killed near the entrance of London's great St. Paul's Cathedral. Protestant England still celebrated the failure of the Gunpowder Plot each year, and now it remained for someone else to carry the lantern and light the fuse beneath the city of London!

Allan had been raised on stories such as these. It was the dream of every brother in the IRA to pick up the tale where King James buried it. Those ideological forebears who had dreamed up the Gunpowder Plot in 1605 were perched on the pedestals of Allan Farrell's mind today as he gazed around the square. He was not so insane as to think that he could succeed where they had failed, but he longed to speak to England through the fire and smoke of terror as they had tried to do.

His sense of justice strengthened as he looked up into the cloudless sky. Pigeons fluttered past to roost in the shadowed cornices of the great facades. Perhaps, in this case, German bombers would one day finish the work of Guy Fawkes and his band of brave men. Allan imagined fire leaping through the roofs of Commons, devouring the great clock tower and turning Big Ben into molten metal.

The image reinforced his belief that all the evil the English had dished out would explode on their heads one day. But such dreams did little to satisfy his own sense of what he must do to hasten that certain day.

He must think; scout London for some unguarded relic, some fortress of well-being where the enemy would never imagine destruction could come upon them. A public lavatory at a train station was just a beginning, and a small beginning at that. But Allan fully intended to keep sleep from the eyes of Scotland

Yard's best men. A small device, a small, tiny flash of destruction, would simply be his foretaste of something big yet to come. He would need help. He would need the proper materials.

When the German agents stepped from the red omnibus and walked slowly toward Allan, he remained where he was. Today he did not merely leave the information tucked into the pages of the London *Times*. Today Allan left a personal note stating that he wanted to extend his role beyond that of mere messenger boy.

Allan Farrell wanted to prove to the world and to himself that he was much more than just the son of Maureen; that he could outdo anything his mother had ever dreamed of! For Allan Farrell, all his life had come down to this moment.

"Well, Murphy, did you get mother and child home safely?"

"Both doing great, Winston."

"And what," inquired Winston Churchill, "was your impression of today's debate over the Prevention of Violence Act?"

"It must be gratifying to you, Winston, to finally see Parliament come to grips with an issue in such complete agreement," responded Murphy. "The government admits that terrorists are real and that special measures and deportations are in order."

Churchill shook his ponderous head slowly. "Don't give them too much credit, Murphy," he warned. "If I have seen a vicious dog bite four of my neighbors *already*, then my wisdom cannot receive a great deal of credit if I let the mongrel come into my yard and bite *me* before I decide that I need to do something about it!"

The great man paused to reflect before continuing. "What this government still does not see is the identity of the *master* of the dog named terrorism. Herr Hitler has done it with Arabs in Palestine, racial Germans in Austria and the Sudetenland and Danzig, and now with Irish extremists in London."

Murphy frowned thoughtfully. "I would have thought you'd be pleased with the home secretary's statement." The newsman paused and referred to a notebook. "Here it is: The terrorists are being actively stimulated by foreign organization."

"Bah," Churchill grumbled. "You'll note that he still does not accuse Nazis by name! I'm not entirely certain that he himself knows. He may be referring to the Irish Republican brotherhood

243

in America! That group, the Clan da Gael, may buy some dog food, but it is still Herr Hitler who commands the dog to jump!

"No, Murphy," Churchill concluded sadly. "For all the rhetoric about expulsions, exclusions, and deportations, Chamberlain and his cronies still do not grasp the gravity of the situation."

Hitler listened as his interpreter, Dr. Schmidt, translated the text of the commons debate about IRA terrorism. The Führer nodded contentedly as Chamberlain's remarks were read. He seemed distracted, as if he were not really paying attention.

Then Schmidt began to translate the responses offered by Lloyd George and Anthony Eden. The Führer's face clouded over, and with each reference to Germany's instigation of the bombings, Hitler's countenance grew darker and darker.

Schmidt glanced up nervously, then back at the transcript, nearly losing his place. He could tell that the storm of Hitler's wrath was about to break.

When Schmidt reached Churchill's remarks, the interpreter was already braced for the explosion. "This English bulldog dares to snarl at us?" Hitler shouted. "This jowled species of British mongrel making watchdog noises!" Flecks of spittle flew from the lips of the leader of the Nazi Reich in his rage.

"Who is Churchill that anyone gives him room to speak?" Hitler demanded of the air. "He is discredited, a failure, a castoff wretch! The British want peace, peace, peace! Why do their papers still report the ravings of this warmongering cur?

"Schmidt!" Hitler snapped his fingers. "Enough! Stop reading! Tell Himmler I need to see him at once!"

Every piece of furniture in Orde's London home was shrouded in dusty sheets. Orde carefully removed the covering from a straight-backed petitpoint chair that he had never sat on before now. He left his favorite overstuffed chair out of sight as if one glimpse of the fabric would bring back too many memories. Better to view the room from this uncomfortable and unfamiliar angle. Katie had purchased the chair because she liked the needlework on the cushion. Now Orde sat firmly on it and thought what a frivolous purchase that had been. To buy a chair no one ever sat in simply because it was pretty.

That sort of impracticality had been out of character for Katie, and so Orde assumed she must have seen something extraordinary in the chair, some faraway purpose she imagined it would serve. *A mourning seat for Orde, so he would not have to take the covers from the really comfortable chairs. So he would not have to sit and remember and doze off to dream that the years without her were just a terrible dream!*

He resisted the insane urge to call for her to make him a cup of tea. He looked at the long dead ashes in the fireplace. He had not cleaned them out after she died. He had let the coals glow and watched the light pass from the embers, leaving his heart there in the ashes on the hearth.

He chided himself for not simply cleaning the place and renting it to some junior diplomat or a university professor on sabbatical. He had been foolish to simply let it sit and gather a coat of dust, while beneath the shroud the colors and pain of memories were as vivid as ever.

Sunlight leaked in through the slats of the shutters. Particles of dust stirred by his presence swirled in the shafts of light. Orde considered opening the windows to let the breeze in, but then he was seized by the thought that somewhere within this atmosphere was the breath of Katie.

He moaned and rested his head in his hands. What was he doing? And why was he making himself suffer like this? Why had he not mourned like a normal man instead of waiting until years later to walk in and be surprised by his own grief?

At that moment something else startled him. There was a soft rapping on the door and then the strident buzz of the doorbell.

A mistake, Orde thought. *Wrong address. Or perhaps a salesman. Who knows I am here? Worse yet, who cares that I am here?*

In spite of that, the bell continued to harass him. He resented this small interruption to his self-pity. Jerking open the door he glared down on the interloper who did not remove his finger from the button.

The handsome, sun-tanned face of Moshe Sachar grinned up at him. "Captain Orde!" Moshe exclaimed. "Glad to see you're really here! I was afraid I may have arrived too late!"

Orde had known that Moshe was about to take up his studies at Oxford, but he had not expected to see him here in London. Maybe he had not expected to ever see the bright young Zionist again. He had not thought of him being anywhere at all besides

Hanita, marching along with the other members of the Special Night Squad. Now he sat on the newly uncovered sofa.

Over tea, which Orde brewed after turning on the water and washing the kettle and the cups, the two men shared mutual stories about their trips. Orde was grateful for the distraction. They talked together like old friends, on a very different plane than that of commander and ordinary soldier.

Only after half an hour of small talk did Moshe finally come to the point of the visit.

"We heard you have accepted the position with TENS as Warsaw correspondent."

We? We heard? Orde knew who WE was, but he could not fathom that anyone of authority had sent a lad like Moshe to discuss anything important.

"How did you hear that?"

"Come on now, Captain—such a question, when you have so helped us to enlarge our understanding of the way the world operates." Moshe shrugged. "It doesn't matter anyway."

"Yes. I'm going to Poland. Hardly significant."

"That's where you're wrong." Moshe grinned, flashing the whiteness of his teeth in the gloomy room. "So. The British think with this last shipment of kids to England that we will give up?" He sipped his tea thoughtfully. "You know what I am about to say. You know what is coming to Poland—to the world. You have trained our young men after they arrive in Palestine. Can you not train them before they get there? Work with them at the Zionist youth camps near Warsaw. Pick the most able, and then . . ." His hand glided through the air like a bird. "Out the back door. Through Hungary to the seacoast of Yugoslavia."

Orde raised his eyebrows and inhaled deeply. "I have accepted a job. A time-consuming—"

"It need not interfere. In fact, it will be an excellent cover for you." Moshe shrugged. "Just train them. Pick a few at a time and send them on their way. The only difference is that they will know your military manual by heart before they ever set foot in Palestine, nu? Economy of resources, I call it. They get off the boat and they are ready to go to work. You've done the same job on the front end that you were doing on the back, and where are the Arabs to stop you? Who is going to call the English government and complain? It seems perfectly logical to us. We are not fools, Captain Orde. A Jew knows a good thing when he sees it. Everyone who has read your manual has commented—"

Orde nodded. He was flattered, but still strangely unmoved by the idea. It was like raising seedlings in a nursery instead of harvesting the crops. Still, it was something. "Yes. It is an excellent book." There was no false modesty about Samuel Orde. "But the Polish government might have something to say—"

"Nonsense! Warsaw is shaking in its boots. You think they will mind if an English Army officer trains a group of schoolboys in survival techniques?"

"If there is time for training even one group before the world explodes, I will be surprised," Orde added. "But how many can we take out?"

"There is talk of hiring a freighter in Ragusa. As many as a thousand children will be taken out if that comes through. Otherwise, we still have a number of fishing trawlers. Less risky, of course, but that cuts the number to three hundred."

Orde bit his lip as he considered the fate of the young man who had just been assigned to work with him in Warsaw. *Jacob Kalner.* Here was a way, if all else failed. And there was the Lubetkin family. "You are thinking only of young males with military potential?"

Moshe nodded. His face clouded slightly as he considered what that meant. *Making choices . . .* "Possibly a few able girls might be included. But they will be expected to march as far and fight as hard as the boys. That will have to be your ultimate selection."

No families. No small children. Few girls. Orde frowned. He nodded. He could hold classes in the Warsaw community centers. Bill it as *Instruction in Desert Survival.*

Moshe left the names and numbers of Zionist activists in Poland with Orde. He made only the promise that he would do what he could do in what he believed was an extremely short time. That satisfied Moshe Sachar, who pumped his hand and called him *Hayedid,* the Friend. Then he saluted and called Orde "Captain" one more time.

Anna straightened the tie of Theo's uniform, and kissed him lightly on the cheek. "You do not look like a grandfather," she smiled.

"Let's keep it at that." He rubbed the ache in his leg. "Don't ask me if I feel like one today, eh?"

Her eyes became solemn with understanding. Today a letter from Wilhelm and Dieter had arrived with the mail from America. Like their father, they had thrown themselves back into training as aviators . . . *"just in case the worst should come."*

An ominous reminder that Theo had served in a war on Germany's behalf only twenty years before, the boys had this news for him:

> *We located the American who saved your life at Belleau. He was at the address you gave us. But the most amazing thing, Father, is that his son, who is just nineteen, is also training as an aviator! If war breaks out and America remains neutral, then he plans to enlist in the Royal Canadian air force. He is a splendid fellow. A fine pilot. Perhaps we, the sons of former enemies, will soon fight together on the same side.*

Such enthusiasm and eagerness in those words made Theo wince. "It takes twenty years to raise a son," he said, "and a moment of war to kill him." He embraced Anna. "The world has a way of coming around again, doesn't it, Anna. Was I spared twenty years ago so my sons could be born to fight? That wasn't the dream. No. When I lay in that ditch and saw the faces of the Americans, they were men like me. I knew they wanted the same for their sons as I wished for mine. *Peace*."

Anna silently tucked the letter from Wilhelm and Dieter into the pocket of his tunic. "You should write your American friend. Perhaps it is important that two old enemies speak to one another about their sons. Yes. That is a good idea, Theo. Perhaps he feels as you do."

"It makes no difference how we feel now, Anna. It seems that we have come around to Belleau Wood once again."

18   In the Fullness of Time

Rachel pushed the black pram slowly beneath the shade trees of the square. The small, perfect hands of little Yacov, her *Yani*, reached up as blackbirds flew overhead. It was so good to have the boys all home again. Mama had been right—their happy laughter put a spark back in Papa's eyes.

Papa gathered them every day around his bed for lessons in the Torah. He instructed them and helped them with their Torah school studies. He piloted the minds and hearts of the household from his pillowed helm. Everything seemed almost normal. Very much better than it had before.

Baby Yani squealed with happiness at the birds that sat on the leafy branches of the linden trees. Like the birds, the baby had no awareness of anything unpleasant beyond the confines of the square.

Three blocks up Niska Street, the steady throbbing of diesel engines hummed as a convoy of Polish Legion vehicles moved equipment into place around the Umschlagplatz. There were anti-aircraft guns and machine guns already mounted on the roof of the train shed, Rachel knew. This was just one more reminder that all was not perfect in the world.

The second reminder approached Rachel from across the street. Peter Wallich was grinning like a mannequin in a shop window. His clothes flapped on his body. The sole of his right shoe flapped as he shambled toward her.

She tried to wheel the carriage around and go the other way. *Too late!*

"Rachel!" he called. "Rachel Lubetkin! Wait!"

Heads turned. They looked at her and then at the apparition that bumped to her side. Peter gaped down into the pram. He grinned at the baby and made baby noises in greeting.

"My brother Yani. Yacov. But I call him Yani," Rachel said coolly. She did not want Peter to pick up the baby, but he leaned down to scoop Yacov into his bony long arms anyway. The contrast between the healthy plumpness of Yacov and the lean, hungry-looking form of Peter was too much like seeing a skeleton caress her beloved brother. "Are you eating anything at all?" she blurted out.

His smile dimmed a bit. "I try. Sometimes it is difficult."

"The food at the kitchen is good," she reprimanded.

His sad eyes looked into hers. "Not like my mother's cooking, though."

She was ashamed of herself for dodging this lonely young man. He was telling her that he could not eat because he missed his mother. Understandable. Terrible. Tragic. "You will find her," she said more gently.

"Yes." He bounced Yacov, who laughed out loud. Then Peter laughed. "This is such a good age for babies, don't you think? I remember when my brother Willie was this age. I bounced him around so much that soon he wanted nothing but to be bounced." Again the sadness flicked through his eyes. "He is in America now. I was lucky enough to get him on one of the children's ships. He was placed with a family in America, last I heard. The British social worker wrote to tell me. . . ." A deeper sadness shadowed his face. "They thought he would get along better if all the ties were broken. He is young, they said. He will forget about me. It is better for him if he forgets, I suppose." Peter bounced Yacov one more time and then put him back into the carriage as if he were breakable, fragile porcelain, as if there were a sign on the pram that said: *OFF LIMITS TO PETER WALLICH!*

"Oh, Peter," Rachel said, feeling even more ashamed. "You can hold Yacov anytime you wish."

He shrugged. This was just a baby, after all. It was not his brother Willie who had so loved being bounced. "Well. Never mind." He drew a breath and exhaled loneliness. "I wanted to tell you that I came up with a brilliant idea!"

Now Rachel tried extra hard to make up for her coolness. "Papa said you are bright."

"Yes, well, not too bright or I would have thought of it before now," he grinned. "I have a friend in Danzig, you know."

Yes. Peter *had* told her about the pregnant former S.S. woman. A shocking story. It had made Rachel blush, even though she admired the woman for helping Peter get away. "Well?"

"I left the address with her."

"You mean *the* address?" This *was* news!

"Yes. Of course. So I wrote her a letter in Danzig, asking her to forward a copy to me at the soup kitchen box number." He snapped his fingers. "I only have to hang on a while. And then I will have it!"

She was genuinely happy for Peter. This tiny fragment of good fortune did a lot to wash away the feeling that Peter Wallich was the most unlucky person in the world. "Imagine! Solved so easily!"

"Yes." He drew himself up straight and smiled a crooked happy smile. Not bitter. Not a clenched-teeth smile like Rachel had seen before on his face. Here was hope.

"Mazel tov," she said.

"Thank you. Tell your father, will you?" With that he waved to another ragged-looking young man across the square and simply left.

Rachel was glad that he had told her his news. He was now telling the other fellow. He would doubtless tell everyone who would listen that his problem was about to be solved.

She watched him a moment. The sun gleamed dully on his hair. She wished that he would eat better and take another bath soon. In spite of that, she was happy for him as she returned to tell Papa his news.

Werner crouched and crept along the edge of the bed, keeping a hunter's eye on his shadow on the floor. Alfie watched the kitten pounce from bed to shadow and wrestle with the air for a moment. Usually Werner made Alfie smile when he played this way, but tonight Alfie could not smile. He wished that Werner would quit trying to make him feel happy. No one was happy tonight.

One suitcase was laid out for each of them—everyone but Jacob. He would travel on to Warsaw like Lori's relative Mr. Murphy told him. Once in Warsaw, Jacob would have a job with the Trump European News Service until some way could be found to get him to England, too.

Jacob was too cheerful. Just like Werner. He opened Alfie's valise to show him once again the false bottom where Werner would fit. Jacob had designed it and made it special himself. Somehow even that made Alfie feel badly. After all, if they were going to sneak Werner-kitten onto the ship, why could they not find some way to get Jacob on board as well?

Lori was not talking. She had hardly said anything since that terrible day in the British Consulate. Every day her eyes looked sadder. Alfie saw the way she looked at Jacob when Jacob was not looking. Alfie knew this was what it meant to love someone so much that it hurt. Alfie knew about such things, even though no one thought he knew.

"Bring Werner here," Jacob ordered brightly. "Let's test it out. See if it works."

Alfie reached for Werner, who reared up on his hind legs and batted Alfie's fingers playfully.

"Not now," Alfie said in an unhappy voice. "I don't want to play no more, Werner." The cat went limp and docile in his big hand, as though Werner finally understood that nobody felt like playing.

He meowed and Alfie put him in the bottom of the valise. Jacob fit the false bottom over the space. Werner meowed more unhappily. Now he was feeling badly too.

"He'll have to be quiet." Jacob frowned as the bag meowed on.

"Shhhh." Alfie patted the valise. "Don't talk, Werner."

But Werner did talk. His faint meow became a distinct howl, an alley-cat dirge, shrieking from the otherwise ordinary-looking piece of luggage.

"You think they'll notice?" Mark scoffed, looking up from the silent game of cards he had played all evening with Jamie.

"They'll notice," Lori said, no mirth in her voice.

Jacob straightened his back but continued to stare down at the racket. "We'll have to do something before you take him to the boat. They'll notice, and then Werner will end up here in Danzig with me!"

That was not a good thing to say. Everyone looked up at Jacob and stared at him. No one said anything until he nudged the suitcase with his toe.

"Hush up, Werner," Jacob instructed, but still the kitten did not hush. It was plain Werner did not take to this terrible imprisonment. He wanted out, and he would tell everyone in Danzig that he wanted out!

"I know," said Lori quietly. "I know what we can do!" For just a moment, she looked almost happy again. She glanced at

252

Jamie who was studying his cards. "Remember the Wieden-beck's cat?"

"Uh-huh."

"The way it wailed all night beneath Papa and Mama's window?"

Jamie smiled, but he did not look away from his cards. "Good idea," he said.

"What about it?" Jacob asked, grateful for this minor diversion from the heaviness in the apartment.

"Papa started feeding him beer every night in a saucer on the back step."

"And?"

"He got drunk. The cat, I mean. Every night he drank as much beer as his belly could hold and then he would stagger away home. Frau Wiedenbeck talked about her drunken cat to Mama. She could not understand who would be so terrible to give a cat beer. She was sure it was beer, because the cat smelled like a brewery and—"

"But did it get quiet?" Jacob asked, eyeing the moaning luggage.

"The perfect drunk, that cat was. Went home and curled up fast asleep every night. For a while it came to our house to wait for its pint, but then it quit coming. Mama said that Frau Wiedenbeck was feeding it beer to keep it home. A very good solution."

"Brilliant," Jacob said to her. "A great idea, Lori."

As soon as Jacob said her name, Lori's smile went away. Alfie could see that her eyes were bright and shining with tears even though she went out of the room to hide them. She cried whenever Jacob said her name. Alfie felt bad. He wished they could have thought about making Werner drunk without having to say Lori's name.

"Um . . . good. Good idea." Alfie did not say *Lori*. "Jacob can feed Werner beer like your papa."

From her room, a small sob leaked out. Then a bigger one. Werner yowled in the case and Lori cried in her room. It was a terrible night—the worst night they ever had since they came to Danzig.

Alfie supposed it was more fitting for Werner to be unhappy like everyone else. For a long time he did not take him out of his little secret case. He let Werner cry so no one would hear Lori as much.

Music from the cabaret drifted through the ghostly streets of Heiliger Geist District. Drunken sailors had gathered the prostitutes under their arms and staggered off to flea-bitten hotel rooms. Only a stubborn few remained in the cabaret now. Those women who were too old or homely to be chosen huddled at tables with men too broke or drunk to care. The barkeeper polished the last of the chipped glasses while the accordion player leaned against his groaning instrument and sipped cheap wine. The janitor up-ended chairs and mopped sour-smelling beer from beneath empty tables. It was like this every night. The Geist Cabaret would not lock its doors as long as there was even one customer buying drinks. It was the last outpost of the hopeless, a purgatory of desperation for men and women with nowhere else to go.

Tonight, Alexander Hess sat alone at a table, half a bottle of schnapps before him on the table. He had paid for the right to drink it all in this place, he told the accordion player, and therefore the music must continue!

He stood, bracing himself on the table as he gathered his cane in one hand and his bottle in the other. He swayed for a moment, then made his way cautiously to the open door of the cabaret. The music slowed, as if in hopes that Hess was leaving.

"*Play!* I *paid* for it! Play until *I say* you can stop!"

The barkeeper and the musician exchanged dubious looks. With a slight shrug, the barkeeper instructed the accordion to begin anew.

"That's more like it!" Hess shouted. He leaned against the doorframe and inhaled. His head cleared a bit as he looked up to scan the facades of the ragged buildings.

Hess imagined the notes of his vulgar song drifting through the ravines of Heiliger Geist's streets. He could almost see the tune and the words creeping up the bricks and through the rickety iron balconies into the rooms of those he sought. "*I am singing to you,*" he slurred. "*Listen! Whores and babies* . . . hear me? Through your windows and your locked doors my shadow comes . . . to pull you down . . . down into darkness."

The distant sound of accordion music seemed a strange

counterpoint to the stillness of the room.

The pile of unwashed sheets lay on the floor where Lucy had thrown them. There was no strength left for her to make the bed, and so she lay down beside the baby on the bare mattress.

The light was dim in the room, and yet she could see that the still form beside her was beautiful. The gray, blood-streaked skin had turned a rosy pink. Ten perfect little toes. Ten perfect little fingers. The mouth was like her mother's; the eyes blue, hair blond and wispy. *Yes. Beautiful.* Just the sort of child a man like Wolf had desired.

She pulled back the fleecy towel. The spindly newborn's legs were drawn close to the rounded abdomen as though the little one still lay within her womb.

How she had prayed that the baby would be a girl! Wolf would have had less interest in taking a baby girl! But Lucy had a son, fine and healthy. . . beautiful. *Perfect!*

Lucy tucked her arm around him and pulled him close. He turned his face to her breast instinctively and she marveled at the miracle that one so new could claim her so immediately. As a girl on the farm she had witnessed the wonders of new life a hundred times. Puppies, calves, and kittens . . . mothers and babies, forgetting the trauma of birth as they settled into the sleepy tranquility of nursing.

Now that miracle was hers. She guided the tiny searching mouth to her breast, wincing slightly at the first hard tug. Stroking the velvet crown, she laid her fingers on the soft spot of his head and felt the steady rhythm of his heartbeat.

"And here you are," she whispered. "Hello." She kissed him lightly and smoothed his fine hair, curling it around her index finger. *Soft. So very soft.* Everything about him astonished her, filled her with joy beyond measure!

Everything her mother had told her was true. She did not remember the pain of giving birth; it seemed like nothing more than a vague dream now. The nightmare reality that Wolf was probably close on her trail, however, lurked like a dark shadow in her consciousness. She closed her eyes, then opened them slowly as though her eyelids were weighted.

"Are you tired, little one?" Her eyes moved to the silver crucifix above her bed. *"For unto me a son is born. . . ."* She could not keep her eyes open any longer. "Thank you," she whispered. "Thank you that Wolf did not find me. Thank you . . . for help-

255

ing . . . us." The child at her breast, Lucy drifted off to a dreamless sleep.

———————

They were playing music at the cabaret especially late tonight, Lori thought. She wondered if people were dancing together even now.

The door to her bedroom was open enough for the light and sounds from beyond the kitchen window to filter softly in. She could just distinguish the white outline of her blouse on the back of her chair and her sneakers on the dark floor beside her bed.

In odd harmony with the distant accordion music, she could hear the assorted wheezes and snorts of the four boys as they slept. She knew which boy belonged to each sound. Alfie snored soundly, like Papa used to after an especially long day. Mark wheezed in and rattled out. *Jamie?* That was easy. She had grown up listening to his asthmatic breathing. From the age of three she had gotten up in the middle of the night and padded down the hall behind her mother to stand quietly beside his bed and listen, to make certain he was properly tucked in.

Old habits were hard to break. Jamie was big enough that she did not need to check him while he slept. Still, from the beginning of their ordeal, Lori had gotten up each night, tiptoed to his bedside and straightened his blankets like Mama would have done. Big sister to little brother. Maybe she would never get over the urge to make certain Jamie's toes were not peeking out, or that his sheets were not kicked onto the floor.

She felt strangely like the character of Wendy in the novel *Peter Pan*—Mother of the Lost Boys. Lori had read the first German translation of the book when she was twelve. She had developed a terrible crush on the imaginary Peter Pan, and even in the cold months of Berlin autumn, she had left her window open in hopes the fairy tale might come true.

And so it had in a way. She and the boys were sailing off to London, while Jacob was doomed to remain in the terrible Never-Never Land of Europe. The weight of their imminent separation made her realize that what she felt for Jacob Kalner was much more than a childhood crush.

How she wished now that she had not let herself love him! This was no fairy tale; there was no promise of *happily-ever-after* in their future. And there was no calling back the love she felt for him. Every minute that passed was a reminder that there was one less moment she could see him; hear his voice; delight even in the simple pleasure of listening to him breathe as he slept.

Lori was awake—more awake than she had ever been; awake in ways she had never dreamed of. Her heart beat faster as she thought of Jacob's kiss, of kisses that had followed to stir up this hunger in her for more.

Her mind warned her that tonight she must not go into the other room to check her lost boys, or she, too, might be lost! She could feel his presence even at a distance. There was no use lying to herself about it, was there? She had left the door open tonight not so she could hear the sleeping boy, but in the hopes that Jacob would come to her. She looked at the vague light and wished that his shadow would block it out.

She prayed that she would fall asleep, that she would not dream of him again. But she did not wait for an answer to her prayer.

Slipping from her bed, she pulled on her robe like every other night. *Time to check the boys.* That was her excuse as she willed him to wake up. It was not Jamie or Mark or Alfie whom she slipped in to check. They could go on breathing without her! *But Jacob!* Would his breath stop once she left him? Would his heart cease to beat because she was not with him?

Lori wondered about the breaking of her own heart as well. How could she leave him? Was that not like leaving a part of herself for the vultures who swung low over Danzig? And if she had to leave her heart with him, could she not give him more than words to remember her by?

She blinked at the shadowed shapes in the room, hardly daring to believe the thoughts that filled her mind now. *Go back! You will hurt him more by this!*

But she did not want to return to her room. Every step away from her own bed was an act of defiance. She did not care! She would not go back to bed alone.

Alfie slept on a mattress on the floor, with Werner-kitten curled up on his chest. The two younger boys were tangled lumps among the sheets on the double bed beneath the window. She pretended she had come to tuck them in. She straightened the blankets and ran her hand across Jamie's tousled hair like always.

Jacob did not stir. He slept on a mattress at the foot of the bed. She wanted him to wake up and find her here, doing her duty as Mother to the Lost Boys. She brushed past him, resisting the desire to kneel and press her lips against his mouth; to stroke his cheek and wrap her arms around him in surrender before they had to say goodbye.

The strength of her emotion frightened her, warning the rational side of her that it was not safe to be so near him tonight.

As if he sensed her presence, Jacob drew a deep breath and shifted slightly on his mattress. She turned to stand over Jamie. *The Little Mother.* She told herself that she had come into the room to tuck Jamie in. *You are lying, Lori. You know why you came.*

The whole truth made her hands tremble as emotion swept through her with a power she had never felt before this moment. She tried to picture the face of her father. And then Mama. What would they say if they knew, *really* knew, what she was feeling?

God help me! She did not dare turn around to look at the shadowed place where Jacob slept. It would be too easy to join him there and be lost forever in another kind of darkness.

Gripping the cold iron headboard of the bed, she tried to pray, tried to steady herself and master her desire so she could walk calmly back to her own room and close the door behind her. *Escape!* Yet how she longed for him to open his eyes and see her there! How she ached to have him take her hand and pull her down to spend a night in his arms!

Only one touch. What would it hurt? She turned from pretense and stooped over him as if to brush his forehead with her fingertips.

From the darkness, his big hand reached up to grasp her painfully by the wrist. He held her there above him a moment and then pushed her back from him, sending her sprawling on the floor. The rough gesture made her gasp; startled her back to her senses.

She started to speak, to explain that she had only come in to—

He stopped her with a whisper. "No, Lori. Not like this. Not now. Go back to bed."

How had he known what she wanted? How had he read her intentions before she even touched his face the first time?

She drew her outstretched hand back and covered her eyes

as desire for him was replaced by the hot flush of shame.

"I was just—" she tried to explain in a hoarse whisper. She knew whatever explanation she gave him would be a lie.

"Don't!" His voice was almost angry.

"I didn't mean . . . to wake you."

"Yes, you did," he challenged.

The steady breathing of the others changed to snorts and whistles of disturbed sleep.

"Tucking Jamie—" Tears of shame stung her eyes. The metal of the bedframe dug into her back.

"Go back to your room," he warned. "Lock the door! You hear me? *Lock it!*"

From Mark's side of the bed came a confused mumbling. "What? Is the door . . . huh?"

Jacob spoke in a loud voice, as though he wanted everyone in the room to wake up. *"Go to sleep, will you!"*

Lori stumbled back into her room. She slammed the door and locked it, although now there seemed to be no need for such precautions. Jacob had shamed her. He had good reason, too.

"Oh, God," Lori whispered miserably, "what have I . . . what was I *doing*?"

The morning light was another miracle for Lucy. She and the baby were still alone. The priest who had called out her name had not followed her, had not found her. Wolf had not come for the child. For all this, she raised her eyes to the sorrowing Christ and thanked Him. She could not let herself think any further than each moment of safety. The future was too uncertain, too frightening; and so she thought about the past, and she thought about now.

Lucy had seen the mother cows up and about the morning after giving birth. She had witnessed her own mother get up from the birthing bed after a few hours to respond to the cry of another child in the house. Why, then, should Lucy not sit up slowly and swing her legs over the edge of the bed?

The baby slept as Lucy washed herself and gathered the sheets to slip the bundle outside the window on the roof of the adjoining building. She shuffled to the stove and fixed herself a cup of tea and two pieces of toast.

At the soft cry of the baby, she felt milk fill her breasts. She bathed him, changed his diaper and doctored the stub of the umbilical cord before she made up the bed and lay down exhausted to feed him.

Like her mother, like the animals on the farm, Lucy was doing what she must do. She found there was at least strength enough for simple tasks.

Unbuttoning her cotton gown, she let him nuzzle her breast and settle into contented nursing once again. She stroked his head and whispered sweet things to him. She told him how lucky she was that he was her own, that she had not ever imagined such love or perfection. They grew drowsy together as the morning sun rose to heat the tiles of the roof just beyond the window, warming the room as well.

Lucy thought of small tasks she would perform when they awakened. To the gentle rhythm of the baby's breath, she sang the lullaby her mother had sung to her:

> *"I am small,*
> *my heart is pure,*
> *no one lives in it*
> *but Jesus alone . . ."*

And then, as if someone had sung the song to her, Lucy fell fast asleep.

"I am certain it was your sister." The young priest looked past Wolf as though he could still see the face of Lucy.

"Pregnant." Wolf clenched and unclenched his fist. He was furious at the ineptness of the priest, but he dared not show his anger. "Still pregnant?"

The priest nodded. "She could not have run far in such a condition."

"But the boy lost her."

"At the far end of the fish market. Philip was simply dwarfed in the crowd. He could not see over the heads of the people, you see. And so your sister escaped him." He frowned and spread his hands in a gesture of apology. "There are only two streets she could have taken. You see here." He passed the small square of the parish map across the desk. "The lad says he last saw her here." He pointed to a street corner and then slid his finger toward the two remaining streets where she might have turned. "That leaves you with three square blocks where you might inquire of her. Certainly someone will recognize her. Some shopkeeper or green grocer." He smiled a weak smile. "It is not so very hopeless any longer, Herr von Fritschauer. And I will pray for her that she might be restored to those who love her and the child."

Wolf's hands trembled with barely controlled rage, which the priest mistook as the emotion of a brother for his wayward sister. "I will not forget what you have done," Wolf said in a low voice. Indeed, he would never forget this show of incompetence—Lucy had been warned now! By now she could have packed up and moved out of the district! She could be halfway across Europe by this time! No, Wolf would not forget. He half-suspected that the priest had warned her himself! Perhaps the story of the chase through the fish market was all a deception as well.

He stepped out of the cool church into the hot sun high above Danzig. Replacing his white Panama hat, he stood for a moment on the steps of Heiliger Geist Church and scanned the square.

Setting his eyes toward the arched portal of the fish market, he retraced the steps she had taken as she fled. There was a small chance—very small—that she had not left the area. It was very near the time she was due to deliver, he knew. There was always that one chance that she had not made it out of the city.

19   The Most Precious Gift

The flowers that Father Kopecky brought to the home of Rabbi Lubetkin were picked, he explained, in the gardens of the great Warsaw cathedral. He presented them to Etta Lubetkin in thanks for the pound cake she had baked for him last week.

"Catholic flowers," Rachel said, eyeing them skeptically.

"They are as kosher as matzo balls," Mama scolded as she trimmed the stems and arranged them in a vase of water.

"Probably grown at the base of a graven idol," Rachel whispered.

Etta sniffed them. "All the same, they smell wonderful." She began to gather the leaves and stem pieces into the newspaper that the priest had wrapped around the bouquet. Etta stopped and peered at the headline. Then she looked at the date. She dropped the leaves into the rubbish container and, completely forgetting the vase of flowers, read the newspaper.

PEACE HOPES WANE
OUTLOOK BLACKEST SINCE 1914
DANZIG NAZI DECLARES "OUR HOUR IS COMING"

Black and white headlines had suddenly made the scent of the flowers unimportant.

"He brings us gifts wrapped in a prophecy of our death," Rachel said gloomily. "Why does he bring us fresh fish wrapped in such terrible news? Why not fish that is three days old? And why flowers that are pretty? More appropriate to pick dead flowers and give them to us. Is he trying to scare us into leaving, Mama?"

Etta shook her head. She did not know anything for sure anymore. Twice, the newspapers the priest had passed along in this unobtrusive manner had been German papers, Nazi publications with full stories of Jews fomenting rebellion in Czechoslovakia. According to the paper, Jews in Warsaw plotted to join Poland with Communist Russia and attack Germany!

And always he asked how progress was coming with the passports. *Would they soon have visas to leave Poland? What plans did they have if the visas did not come through? Would they travel under false documents? Had they prepared the children to talk the ordinary jargon of Polish Catholics in the countryside? Such things were important—as important as a warm coat in winter and a good pair of shoes and socks when one had to walk a long distance!*

Rachel crossed her arms and glared hard at the flowers. Mama did not look up from the heart-stopping news that stared up at her. "He ties up his gifts with a poisonous snake," Rachel said. "I would rather not think of any of it, since there is nothing to be done now. And Papa is sick anyway. How could we leave unless Papa is well?"

Etta raised her eyes slowly from the headlines. "Your father..." She frowned and looked at the flowers as if looking at something beautiful would help her say what was ugly and terrible. "Your father will not be leaving Warsaw, Rachel."

"Then none of us are leaving," Rachel replied with an uncharacteristic defiance. Her brilliant blue eyes flashed anger.

"Your father and I . . . are doing . . . everything we can to find a way out for you and your brothers."

"Mother!"

Etta held up a warning finger. "If what happened in Prague comes to Warsaw, then you are going!"

"Where?"

"Jerusalem. Grandfather Lebowitz."

"Not without you!"

"You have a responsibility, Rachel. You are the oldest! If your father and I cannot . . . will not . . . leave the congregation here in Warsaw, then you must take your brothers and . . ."

Rachel was furious at the priest for bringing the paper into their lives. It was better not to know what the Saturday people were doing! Better not to think about it! She turned away, hearing her mother's faraway voice, but letting none of the meaning penetrate her mind. She closed her eyes and buried her face in the bouquet of flowers. She inhaled the sweet fragrance as Etta talked and talked. *These flowers are only flowers. They grew in a garden and came wrapped in plain paper. There is no news. Warsaw is still Warsaw, a flower garden of Poles and Jews who grow side by side. No Nazis. No Danzig. No Hitler. No news today at all.*

Such mental games were like rearranging the flowers in the vase. Tug a little on the stems of the red blossoms, and they show up better than the yellow ones. In the same way Rachel decided which news she would consider important. *Papa is home. Very important. The boys are home. We are all under the roof of this house together. If one is taken, all will be taken.* No matter what Mama said, she would not abandon her and Papa!

––––––––

Each evening Karl scratched the passing day on his brick calendar. The marks were no longer simply a method of keeping track of lost freedom. Now Karl was counting the cycle until the eggs in the sparrows' nest would hatch. When he prayed for his own children, he prayed for the coming of the sparrow chicks as well.

As he placed the shared morsels of his bread on the window ledge, he whispered this reminder to himself: "What you have said in the dark will be heard in the daylight. What you have whispered in the ear in the inner rooms will be proclaimed from the rooftops." Karl paused and smiled up toward the concealed nest. "You must remember to tell them that," Karl said to Lady Sparrow. "Remember to tell them that Jesus cares for them. Will you tell them that?"

He stepped down from the bucket as the male sparrow fluttered past his ear and up to retrieve the bread crumbs. "When I am gone, little friends, you must preach this sermon to whoever comes into this place after me." He raised his hand. "Don't be afraid of those who kill the body and after that can do no more. . . . Will you tell them that, little sparrow? You see, Jesus spoke those words to fellows who had every right to be afraid. And right after that He mentioned you. . . . Are not five sparrows sold for two pennies? Yet not one of them is forgotten by God. . . ."

Karl stood in the center of the cell and closed his eyes. For a moment he stood beneath the spreading elm trees that surrounded New Church. Above his head the birds hatched their young. He was not afraid of what men could do to him. God cared even for the sparrows, did He not? And these sparrows raised their young in the branches of this tree of brick and bars. Karl looked forward to the moment when he would face his accusers for the last time. He was unafraid of what they would do to him. He was confident that the sparrows would preach his sermon after he was gone.

———

The inside of the Indian restaurant was a cool relief after the wave of heat that beat down on London. The atmosphere was heavy with spices, the decor straight from Bombay, India.

Sam Orde had not forgotten the promise he had made to old Rabbi Lebowitz in Jerusalem. And so Orde hand-carried the passport photographs and rejected immigration applications of the Lubetkin family to his lunch with Harry Norman at Veeraswamy's India Restaurant not far from Piccadilly.

Harry was a former Eton classmate of Orde's. They had entered the military on the same day and had served together in India. Harry had lost his right arm and his army career in a motorcycle accident and now was well-entrenched in government affairs at Whitehall.

The empty sleeve of his pin-striped suit was tucked under

and sewn up. "Like the clipped wing of a pet duck," he said to Orde with a grin. "And as for you, old chap—" Harry tugged on a loose thread hanging from Orde's tweed jacket. "You are as slovenly as ever." Harry's brown eyes were bright with amusement as he appraised his old friend. "Now don't tell me you've rung me up just to come down to Veeraswamy's and reminisce. I know you better than that, Orde. I could tell from your voice you want a favor." He sipped gingerly on his gin and tonic. "A government position, right? Well, if you're going to work for the government, you'll have to do something about your clothes."

Behind their table the discordant twanging of a sitar played a perfect background to the babble of Harry Norman. Orde savored the familiar atmosphere of the place. Dark tapestry and the scent of curry brought back a myriad of memories. Orde considered his old chum's receding hairline and spreading paunch. One thing he had forgotten until now was how much Harry talked. Years ago it had been one of the things Orde enjoyed about him. It had been restful to sit back, enjoy his meal, and let Harry Norman carry on all the conversation. Today, however, the endless chatter was far from restful. First came a monologue about the troubles in India. Then, of course, the current topic of the IRA bombing bubbled up like a broken sewer line. Then on to trouble in the Middle East. Never mind that Orde had been there; Harry Norman had his own immutable opinion. Toward the end of an hour, he rounded a conversational bend and pounced on the subject of the refugees who were attempting to flood the free world in their drive to escape Hitler.

The envelope containing the papers of the Lubetkin family seemed useless baggage now as Harry railed against the admission of ten thousand refugee children into the United Kingdom.

Orde looked at Harry's empty plate. Not one kernel of rice remained, although Orde's plate was still half full. When had Harry taken the time to swallow?

Harry gulped his gin and tonic and looked at his watch. "Five minutes," he announced, "and I'll have to get back to the office. Now what was it you wanted to talk to me about?"

Orde pushed his plate back, and with a sense of futility, pulled the Lubetkin family papers out onto the table.

"Friends of mine." Orde placed each photograph in a line.

"Friends," Harry said flatly. "Jews. I heard you had gotten awfully chummy with the Jews. That's why you're back here Orde, old chap. Too chummy."

Orde pressed on. "The woman," he pointed to Etta, "was born in Jerusalem. Moved to Warsaw with her husband and would like reentry into the Mandate."

"With the rest of her family? Sorry. Not a chance. The quotas, you know."

"I was hoping you could pull some strings."

Harry wiped his mouth and tossed the napkin across his empty plate. "No strings left to pull. The White Paper has clipped them all, I'm afraid," he frowned. "Where are these people now?"

"Warsaw."

"Warsaw? How do you know them? *Warsaw?* A bit far from your last assignment."

"Etta's father is a rabbi in Jerusalem. He asked me to see what I could do here in London. I told him I would."

Harry smiled grimly. "He asked *you?* Good grief, Orde! That's like asking a leper to carry sheets into the hospital, isn't it? Does the rabbi know you're not the most popular fellow in government circles these days? Just having lunch with you is a bit risky, you know. I mean . . . but obviously there is nothing you can do to help anyone these days. Not even yourself."

A drop of tonic water spilled on the corner of Etta Lubetkin's application. Orde blotted it carefully lest the ink run. He shrugged and slipped the precious papers back into the envelope. He had forgotten what an unpleasant person Harry Norman could be. The curry formed a seething lump in his stomach. He regretted having brought up the matter with Harry. It was a mistake. Harry would carry the story back with him to the government offices and retell it with such a vengeance that everyone in London would know that Samuel Orde was prowling about, trying to get around the immigration quotas!

"Forget it. It's not important." Orde feigned indifference. "It's nothing at all. This old man simply asked me to see if there was anything to be done. I knew it was hopeless, but I wanted to keep my word to him." He checked the tab in the dim light. "Thanks, Harry. Marvelous to see you again."

There was nothing remotely marvelous about seeing Harry Norman. It was simply one more reminder to Orde that every-

266

thing he held dear in England was buried in a small plot of earth in Winchester.

———

Allan Farrell was irritated that the London *Times* editorial called his pipe bomb attack "cowardly and amateurish." He read over the words for the hundredth time even as he set up the water glass and the double row of small aspirin bottles.

He forced himself to pay attention to his business when he removed the ground glass stopper from the acid container. The burned, yellow-stained tips of four fingers showed what happened when he did not pay enough attention.

He carefully stirred the mixture with a glass swizzle stick stolen from a bar near Piccadilly Circus. When the smelly concoction was adequately swirled together, he used the glass rod to guide the oily, amber liquid into each tiny bottle.

Allan delicately screwed the lid down on each vial. It would not do to have the acid mixture splash on the metal cap and start eating its way to a premature explosion. Two walnut pipe racks with rows of indentations for briars and protruding pegs for supporting meerschaums served very well to keep his little messages of terror upright and secure.

The Irish American rubbed his hands with satisfaction and inspected the surface of the tiled counter to be certain that no drop of the acid mixture remained. Convinced that it was clean, he proceeded to the next step: he retrieved the cotton garden gloves that had been drying on his windowsill and snipped off each of the fingers with a pair of scissors.

The common household substance that gave each glove finger a crystalline coating felt gritty in his hands. Allan doubted that anyone would notice through the envelopes.

But after he carried out this self-appointed mission, *he* would be noticed. He would not need to give another thought to the fact that the Germans had never bothered to respond to his note. After this, they would be coming to *him*. "Please, Mr. Farrell," they would say, "take charge of this operation for us. Won't you give us your assistance?"

He counted the aspirin bottles and the slipcovers of cotton fingers. Twenty of each, a perfect match. Allan gathered up the dismembered gloves and laid them aside.

Moving to his table, he took up the box of manila envelopes

and the directory of Greater London. He had considered using only fictitious addresses, but he was not sure whether the stamps were canceled before or after being sorted. It would not do to have his pets collecting in some dead-letter office. Allan daydreamed for a moment about the vials being crushed and the acid bursting into flame on contact with the crystals.

He pondered the selection of names and addresses. It did not matter, not really, but he wanted at least the first address to have significance.

At last his eye lit on the perfect choice. In careful strokes of his fountain pen he inscribed, "O. Cromwell. 15 Sunset Lane."

The housekeeper at Winston Churchill's Chartwell estate came to the edge of the garden path with Murphy and Orde. Looking down toward the duck pond, she waved a dishtowel in the early morning sun to signal Churchill's bodyguard that these visitors were expected and approved.

The bodyguard's hand came off the revolver inside his jacket and acknowledged her signal. Behind the bodyguard, a portly mason in coveralls tapped a brick into place with his trowel handle and wiped his balding head with a handkerchief.

Murphy and Orde went directly up to the bricklayer. "Hullo, Winston," Orde acknowledged. "When I was here last you were working on that wall over there." Orde pointed toward a winding brick barricade on the other side of the pond.

"Hello, Orde, Murphy. No, you are wrong. The wall you saw me building was two before that one, on the other side of that clump of elms."

"What is this, Winston?" Murphy teased, "the Churchill Maginot Line? Tank traps to defend Chartwell from the Hun?"

"Bah," Churchill snorted. "This useful work is how I keep my sanity after listening to the drivel of useless and largely insane speeches. Besides," he continued, "my soul is not at ease unless I can claim an honorable profession to offset the corruption of politics and journalism." His voice leaned heavily on the last word. "Sit down," he offered, indicating a completed stretch of wall.

"I'm sorry to say that politics and journalism are both on the agenda for this visit," apologized Murphy. "You have heard that Orde is on his way to Warsaw, and . . ." A deep nod of Churchill's head indicated that he knew what the subject of their discussion was to be.

He wiped his brow again, then tucked the handkerchief away and laced his stubby fingers together. "What I share with you cannot be quoted," he warned. "There is one man in the foreign press department of Goebbels' Ministry of Propaganda. He likes newspapermen—though I can't for the life of me imagine why—and scotch whiskey. The combination seems to loosen his tongue."

"Are you certain he's not a plant?" asked Orde.

"We have tested his information against other sources, and so far, we have uncovered no inaccuracies. He admits that his department has been instructed to spread the message that the West will not go to war over Danzig."

Churchill picked up the trowel and waved it like a baton to silence the objections coming from Murphy and Orde. "We recognize the propaganda machine at work, but there is more. Recently this man was privy to the report of a conversation in which Hitler asked his generals for their predictions regarding the outcome of a general European war."

Murphy and Orde leaned forward attentively. "The consensus is that Germany would win if Russia does not join the conflict. Should Soviet Russia fight against the Nazis, General Keitel says that he is not optimistic, and Field Marshal Brauchitsch reportedly remarked that Germany would lose."

All three men were silent for a moment, letting the implications sink in. At last Orde spoke. "Then Danzig is not really the big question, nor is Poland even the key."

"Precisely," agreed Churchill. "The Führer does not want to fight a war on two fronts, but Poland is not the eastern front to him. He means Russia's three hundred divisions. So long as the Anglo-Soviet defense agreement is stalled, Hitler will do what he likes with tiny Danzig and indefensible Poland, and have no fears about the outcome."

Orde and Murphy exchanged looks. "Winston," Murphy wondered, "is Orde wasting his time going to Warsaw?"

Churchill shook his head emphatically. "The British government must be poked, prodded, and propelled into moving on an agreement with Russia. That instrument alone may save the peace when nothing else will. Captain Orde must report frankly and convincingly of how incapable the Poles are of defending themselves against the Nazis, while I do my humble best to nag Prime Minister Chamberlain from this end."

"Back before Hitler fortified the Rhine—" Churchill pointed to the brick wall across the small lake. "Before Czechoslovakia was betrayed and dismembered—" He gestured at the pond. "Europe had many places on which to stand and proclaim peace. Russia's assistance was not necessary. But now—" He patted the wall on which they sat. "Now I tell you frankly, we need the Russians on our side."

Something was up with Lori. Alfie knew something was up because she was not looking at anyone today. Especially not Jacob. She acted like Werner-kitten had acted when Alfie had let him out of his little cage in the satchel. Werner had shaken himself and gone off to lick his paws. He would not come to Alfie even when Alfie offered him a treat of sardines. It had taken a long time before Werner would let Alfie tickle his chin again. All the while, Alfie had fretted and wrung his hands and said he was very sorry for locking Werner in the cage. Werner did not forgive him until he had licked every paw twice.

Anyway, Alfie thought as he looked at Jacob looking at Lori, something like that was happening here. Lori fixed eggs. She did not sit down with everyone to eat. She fussed in the kitchen, scrubbing the burners on the stove.

"Come eat," Jacob worried.

She did not look at him, did not answer him. When the meal was over she cleared the table herself. Usually she made the boys do it and also wash the dishes. But not today.

Jacob was too cheerful, as he always was when something bothered him. When he was not cheerful, he looked very worried and unhappy. He sneaked looks at Lori. Worry. Worry. Then he whistled and said something bright about the weather or about what a fun time they had at the beach and wouldn't it be nice to go back to Sopot?

Lori never said anything at all. Soon everyone was casting worried looks at her. This was going on a lot longer than Werner licking his paws and feeling put upon!

So Alfie asked her as she washed the dishes herself, "How come you are . . . uh . . . are washing those?"

Lori looked at Alfie. He was the first person she had looked at all day, and it made him feel better. She almost smiled at him too. "Oh, Alf," she said. And then she washed some more.

"How uh . . . come you act like Werner did?"

Lori looked puzzled. "Werner?"

"When I let him out . . . uh . . . the cage. He thought I hurt him, locked him in on . . . uh, purpose." He drew a deep breath. "I would not hurt Werner, but he was mad all the same because I locked him in, because he got to get used to . . . so he don't get hurt. And you are acting like Werner when he licked his paws and don't talk to me because *he* thought . . ." Alfie's voice trailed off. It was a lot of talking, and he lost his place. He grimaced, hoping she knew he was not talking about Werner-kitten, but about her and the way she was acting about Jacob. "You understand, Lori?"

She shook her head. *No.* She had also lost her place. She kept washing the dishes. Not looking when Jacob whistled as he walked by one way and hummed back the other way.

"Can I dry those for you?" Jacob asked.

Lori acted as if she hadn't heard him. Jacob acted as if something was breaking inside him. Alfie watched them both. He did not know he was smiling until Jacob got angry at him.

"What are you looking at?" Jacob said in a loud voice to Alfie.

"Leave him alone!" Lori shouted.

"He's looking . . . smiling . . . this is not something to smile at!"

"He's not doing anything at all! He asked me if he could help! Leave him alone!" She was slinging the dishes into the water, pushing Jacob out of the way while she scrubbed the counter top harder than she had ever scrubbed it before.

"Alfie—" Jacob shook his head and Alfie could tell he was sorry for yelling at him.

"It's . . . all right." Alfie made sure he did not smile now. This was not *about* him. He patted Jacob on the shoulder, man-to-man, and then he went into the other room.

Mark and Jamie had gone out. Alfie picked up Werner and thought that he would also go out for a while. Something was up.

"I didn't mean to hurt you. . . ."

No answer as Alfie put his hand on the doorknob.

"Please, Lori. Please understand. Last night I . . . I could

have . . . *if I had not sent you away. . ."*

Alfie smiled. He slipped out the door. So this really was something like Werner being put in his cage. Lori was nice. Lori was smart. Alfie felt certain that she would see how much Jacob loved her, and then she would quit licking her paws.

He reached up and scratched Werner under the chin. The kitten sat on his shoulder as they swung out into the morning light. He leaned hard against Alfie's big head and purred. Lori would be all right, just like Werner-kitten.

Jacob ran his hand through his hair nervously. "It's a good thing I'm not going with you, that's all."

Lori whirled to face him. "How can you say that? *How?* If you don't feel the way I feel, then why did you tell me you loved me?"

"I do." Jacob stared down at the sink full of suds. Bubbles made little rainbows in the sunlight. He groped for words. It had to be right, what he was about to tell her. What words could he use? "I love you . . . *permanently.* Last night, I was so afraid of hurting you. Hurting us." He finished lamely with a shrug. "You see?"

Lori also stared at the bubbles. Her face reflected the long and sleepless night. "I threw myself at you," she said miserably. "And you threw me out. I . . . I'm so . . . *ashamed.*" She covered her face with her hands and leaned back against the counter.

Jacob looked at her. She was not a girl anymore. She was a woman. The transformation had happened right before his eyes. Sunlight glinted on her golden hair. He reached out and touched it. "You think I don't know the value of the gift you offered me?" he said gently, pulling her against his chest. She did not resist. "You're beautiful. Oh, *Lori!* Like the best package under the Christmas tree. And I look at you and wonder what it would be like to unwrap you. . . ." She let her arms encircle his waist and she laid her cheek against his chest. He thought for a moment he could not breathe. "But, Lori," he said. "It isn't Christmas yet. You can't unwrap the gift until Christmas, or the whole day is ruined. You *know?*"

She nodded. Her face moved up and down against him and her arms tightened around him. Her soft hands stroked his back. "Marry me," she whispered.

"Yes. Yes. When all this is over and we're—"

"No. Marry me today. Now. I want to spend Christmas with you."

He lifted her chin. "You think I could let you leave me if we. . . ?"

"I'm hoping you won't."

He shook his head, trying to make some sense of all this. "Then I won't . . . can't marry you now. Because, Lori, you've got to get out of here. I'll make it out someway. I'll find you again. But you have papers in order and a ticket to leave. You go to England, and—I promise—I'll find you by Christmas."

She was silent. Listening. Thinking. "Marry me before I leave. They'll let you join me if we're married!"

That made sense, but . . . "You know what our folks would say?"

"They would be glad we did things right. Glad we knew enough . . . glad and proud that you sent me away from you last night so we could talk it over by the light of day!" Her eyes were fierce as she looked up into his face. "And it *will* help you get to England if you have a wife there. It doesn't matter that we're young, does it? I'm sure. Sure that . . ." She leaned against him.

"You can't stay with me here," he warned, "even if we marry! You must promise not to ask that of me."

"I promise," she said in a small voice. "Oh, *please*. Let's not waste another minute. There are so few, Jacob. And time with you is my most precious gift. . . ."

Jacob closed his eyes, arguing silently with everything she said. In the end, he lost the argument.

———

"Does that mean you aren't coming to England, Lori?" Jamie looked worried as they all sat together around the table.

"*No!*" Jacob and Lori said at the same time. Then Jacob took over. "She is going. Just like we planned. I will come later."

Lori nodded and nodded as he explained. "You see, when there is a relative—like a mother or a wife already in England—it makes it easier for the person left behind to immigrate."

Mark scowled. "Well, I'm his brother! Aren't I enough?"

Alfie was smiling because Lori looked as if she were purring. Jacob held her hand and their fingers were woven together like a basket. "First you, Mark," Alfie said. "Then Lori will be the wife.

273

And Jamie will be . . . something too. Related."

Jacob shifted in his chair and clapped Alfie on the back. Alfie got it. Why were Mark and Jamie so reluctant to see the benefits of having a wedding today?

Jamie scowled. "What will Mama say? She would want to be there. And . . . and *Papa*! What about that? Walking down the aisle and all that?" As the son of a pastor, Jamie had seen enough weddings that he knew how real weddings were supposed to be conducted. This was missing every possible ingredient for a successful occasion. Who would play the organ? Where were their formal clothes? A wedding dress? "What about the *ring*?" Jamie exploded. "You can't have a wedding without a ring!"

Alfie stood majestically and plopped Werner into Jamie's lap. He hurried back into their room and pulled out a bureau drawer containing his tin soldiers and his treasure sock. Dumping the sock out unceremoniously onto a line of cavalrymen, he found the answer to Jamie's objection. It was a pretty ring, with green stones all around a large diamond. He had been saving it for something special. This seemed special enough.

"I got it!" Alfie cried, not bothering to put his other treasures back into the sock. "The best one!"

He placed it in Jacob's hand and crossed his arms proudly. Mark and Jamie looked at each other and shrugged. Well, they knew *absolutely* that their parents would not approve. They had done their best. No one would blame them for this! Jamie gazed solemnly at the ring. "Emeralds and diamonds," he said in a low, astonished tone. "Alfie, you're a genius."

"A really smart fellow," Mark rephrased the comment. "I suppose that we should forever hold our peace, then. There's no stopping them if they have a ring."

"Papa won't think much of this." Jamie was still reluctant. "At least you better do it in a church."

Lucy's legs trembled when she stood. Her hands shook as she fixed her noonday meal of broth and crackers with a small slice of cheese and apple. Her mother had taught her well that from the cows in the barn to the hens in the coop, offspring fared better if the mothers were well fed. Lucy had no appetite, but she ate for the sake of her baby. She ate because she must be strong in order to leave Danzig soon.

But leave for where? Lucy pulled the chair close to the bed and sat on a pillow to watch the baby sleep. How she wished she could go home again! How she ached to see her mother, to hear words of advice on caring for this precious little one. But there was no going back, even if her parents had been willing to take her in. Wolf would find her there, and the end would be the same as if she had saved herself the trouble and stayed in Vienna!

Behind her through the open window, Lucy could clearly hear the persistent bellow of a ship's whistle. It would be wonderful, she thought as she looked at her little green book. *Waiting at Table . . . England!*

Before the priest had called out to her in the church, Lucy had imagined she had all the time in the world. Now she knew that the world had run out of time. Now, in this desperate moment, she must gather her wits and her strength for the sake of the baby. But she knew she did not have the strength to walk from here down the stairs. How, then, could she walk to the train station? Where would she find the stamina for that now?

Never had Lucy been so tired. Such weariness convinced her once again that if Wolf had not found her by now, perhaps he could not track her down at all.

She pulled back the sheet, revealing the baby's perfectly formed head. *So beautiful.* Lucy's mother would have commented on such a thing. She would have gathered her grandson into her arms and danced around the kitchen. She would have told everyone in the village that there never was a baby born with such a perfect head!

That thought somehow comforted Lucy as she looked down tenderly on the child whom she alone had admired. No doctor. No proud grandparents. No joyful neighbors bringing food. No priest . . .

But the lack of all that did not change the fact that her son was born; beautiful and sweet. He cried only when he was hungry, or when he needed changing. Did he somehow sense the sorrowing heart of his mother? Did an angel whisper in his little ear and tell him they were alone and without help, that he should be a quiet baby, a baby gentle and kind even in these first few hours of life?

It was the child who comforted Lucy, not she who comforted

him. He was sleeping quietly, but she took him into her arms anyway. She pressed her cheek against his forehead as his eyes fluttered open and he considered her. She smiled down at him, and for that moment it did not matter that Lucy was alone. She felt no lack of mother or father or priest or doctor to gather in around her to admire this miracle.

Their absence did not change the fact that the miracle had happened. *"For unto me a son is born,"* Lucy whispered again. "And . . . his name shall be *wonderful*!"

She considered the little face as the baby's fist wobbled up to his toothless mouth. *Those eyes, so serious!* Yes. There was the matter of a name. Even the most wonderful baby could not be called *Wonderful*!

"I will sleep on it," Lucy said quietly as she tucked him close to nurse him back to sleep. "Something worthy of a little boy as good and thoughtful as you."

They lay together on the bed, and he comforted her as the ship's whistle sounded again and yet another ship slipped out of Danzig without Lucy and her son on board.

20 What God Has Joined Together

Concierge was an exalted word for the old man who lived at the foot of the stairs and collected the rent from the tenants of this building.

Hess presented his photographs to the dottering old fool. Crooked fingers clutched the edges awkwardly as dim eyes strained to see the images on the paper.

"Bitte. One moment." He looked up at a light socket where a bulb had been some years past. "The light is bad in here." He squinted and moved his arm back and forth like a trombone player as he attempted to find the proper focus for his eyes.

"A brother and a sister," Hess urged, tapping on the faces of Lori and Jamie Ibsen so the old man would not mistake Karl

Ibsen and his wife as the ones Hess was looking for.

"A nice looking family," the concierge mumbled. "We do not have many of these sort let rooms here." The weathered face wrinkled in distaste as the shrill laughter of a woman drifted down from the upper floors. "In the old days this was a fine boardinghouse. Before the Great War, it was a reputable establishment," he said bitterly. "Now no one cares. No families like this come here anymore."

"I am not looking for the entire family," Hess repeated impatiently. "Just this boy and his sister. They would be with three other children. Not hard to spot. One among them is a Dummkopf, I am told. A big dimwitted boy."

At this the man's eyes sparked with recognition. He looked again at the photograph. "Yes. Not here in my block, but I think . . . the girl would be much older, you say?"

"Yes." Hess resisted the urge to shake the information out of the old man. "Two years older than the photograph, at least."

"Two small boys. Two older? One among them is the dimwit. A friendly fellow. Carries a little cat on his shoulder and has stopped to talk to me several times as I swept the steps." He smiled at the thought. "They are in the neighborhood. Yes. I cannot tell you exactly where, but one does not forget such a group on a street like this."

The old man could tell Hess nothing more. He did not know which direction they lived. Could not recall the names of the other children.

The gnarled hand stretched out, palm up, for a gratuity. Hess tossed a coin to him. It clattered on the chipped tile of the foyer, and he left the concierge groveling on the floor for his tip.

———

Orde had spent the better part of the week shuttling between the BBC and the TENS office on Fleet Street. He was getting acquainted with the mechanics of broadcasting live from the European Continent to the London studio, which would then relay the program to the United States.

Arrangements had already been made for Orde to have a small storefront office in the same block as the building housing Polski Radio. It would serve as his Warsaw broadcasting base.

On the surface, it appeared simple, like sending a message by radio back to GHQ from a forward position. The problem was making the timing of each live broadcast coincide with the tiny window of broadcast time allowed during radio programming.

"Suppose I am covering an important conference in Warsaw and I have nothing to report by airtime?" he asked Murphy and Harvey Terrill.

"Can you sing?" Harvey replied in a resentful tone.

"You'll just have to wing it," Murphy said with a grimace. Such things happened regularly in the new world of radio journalism. "Ask questions—plenty of questions. Get people wondering what's coming. Then they'll tune in when you have the answers." Murphy leveled a look at Orde. "Just remember, talk slow! Americans love the sound of an English accent, but—"

"Right, old chap," Orde replied. "I have heard it a million times from your Doc Grogan . . . *talk slowly and distinctly, please.*"

Murphy had put Dr. Patrick Grogan to work improving the rapid machine-gun dialect of Samuel Orde. The pleasant, round-faced elocution specialist had drilled Orde the way Professor Higgins had taught Eliza in *Pygmalion*, preparing him for every eventuality. With marbles in place in Orde's mouth, Grogan had dared to challenge Orde to heated political discussions. Grogan always took the opposite side of the argument and hammered away until Orde was red in the face with outrage and quite prepared to spit the marbles into the eye of his grinning teacher.

As if on cue, Doc Grogan entered the TENS office with Charles and Louis in tow. Grogan had kept the boys at his side during the day to help out with the arrival of the newest Murphy child. He waved broadly and puffed out his cheeks as a way of greeting Orde.

He did not knock, but entered the office with all the freedom of a TENS employee. "Well, well, it is Samuel Orde! I see you've lost your marbles at last. Here you are with Harv Terrill, and Terrill would kill to get the Warsaw assignment!" Grogan was smiling.

At this comment, Orde noticed the face of Harvey Terrill puckered with ill-suppressed dislike for Patrick Grogan.

Charles tugged Orde's sleeve and smiled at him with a toothless grin. "We will lith-en to the radio."

"Listen!" Louis corrected.

"Yeth. Er . . . *yes-s-s-s*. But talk slow."

Could I do otherwise with so many coaches? Orde wondered.

278

"Even if bombs are exploding under me." He raised his hand in solemn promise.

Orde had never seen the harried night desk editor look anything but tired. Now, as the playful repartee was exchanged between Orde and Grogan, Terrill acted downright irritated. He flashed venomous looks in Grogan's direction. *What is that about?* Orde wondered. *Perhaps two junior officers competing for the approval of the boss?*

As the two boys boisterously clambered into Murphy's desk, Orde observed Terrill purposely bump a stack of papers beside them.

"Enough of this, Boss," Terrill said, as though the boys had knocked the papers over. "This is not some playground," he mumbled and stooped to retrieve and reorganize the documents.

Murphy shrugged apologetically. "I've been working you too hard, Harvey. Or you'd know this *is* a playground." Grogan and Orde laughed. Terrill grunted his disapproval of the interruption.

In deference to the sour mood of his second-in-command, Murphy escorted Grogan and the boys into the outer office. More laughs as Murphy swung Charles upside down until his face hung in front of the busy telephone receptionist. No one seemed surprised or concerned with Terrill's ill-humor. Only Terrill, Orde noted, did not give it up. He stared after Grogan and snapped. "He's in here with those kids at all hours snooping around. Doesn't even knock."

Then it was back to business. Orde had only an hour left to pick up his renewed passport, which now showed him as a civilian entering Poland on a six-month-renewable work permit. Murphy and Terrill went through the sheaf of documents required by the Polish government for broadcasting from Warsaw and Danzig. Frequencies and the names of contacts were rehearsed one final time, and then Murphy invited Orde to stop in at the Red Lion House before he left.

As Orde left the building, he caught a glimpse of Harvey Terrill's sullen face as the night desk editor sifted through the stacks of reports on his own desk. Was he simply overworked, as Murphy said, or did the man really resent the fact that Orde had taken the Warsaw assignment?

———

Even though the London traffic was thick and particularly fumey today, Orde refused to take the underground train to the passport office. He preferred to ride behind the grumbling cab driver and see the city from above ground. Tube stations made marvelous air-raid shelters, Orde thought, but he had never enjoyed traveling like a mole tied to a Roman candle.

The passport office was located at 1 Queen Anne's Gate Building on Dartmouth Street. There were two doorways into the office. One had a long queue of people waiting to pass beneath the hooded arch of the entrance marked: *FOREIGN NATIONALS*. The line of weary-faced hopefuls stretched for an entire block. The question on every face was, *Will they renew my work permit? Or will I be instructed that my stay in England is at an end?*

Orde could hear the distinct, guttural conversation of those from Germany mingled with the language of the Poles. New among the lines today were the soft, fluid accents of the Irish who had been ordered to report for questioning at various government offices since the bombing. Orde easily spotted the Irish among the others—beautiful, ruddy-cheeked people with clear, worried eyes. Orde was quite certain that whoever had been planting the bombs would not be among those who answered the government summons to report here for questioning and registration.

Orde entered the office through the second door, labeled simply, *PASSPORTS—NEW AND RENEWAL*. There was no line to wait in. Perhaps no one in Great Britain was interested in traveling to the Continent of Europe these days. It was too much like hiking through a mine field.

One couple stood at the counter in front of him. They chatted amiably about traveling to New York to attend the World's Fair. The clerk listened patiently to their entire itinerary before bidding them farewell and wishing them a pleasant journey as if he were a travel agent.

He greeted Orde with the same enthusiasm. It was obvious that the clerk was relieved to be on this side of the office, rather than in the midst of all the unpleasantness on the other side.

He found the file containing Orde's new passport. "We could have sent it to you through the post if you were not in such a hurry," the man said apologetically. "This is not the best of times to have to come in to the office, is it?" As Orde grimaced at his dreadful passport picture, the clerk glanced down at the folder once again. "Why, Mr. Orde, is your wife not traveling with you?" He peered closely at a yellowed document.

Orde was mildly surprised at the question. So no one in the passport office had gotten word that Katie Orde had passed away over four years ago. "No," Orde said without explaining.

"All the same," said the clerk hopefully, "her passport is also due to expire. Let me see . . . just three months. You might wish to take care of it now so that if she should change her mind and join you in Warsaw, it would be in order." Without waiting for reply, he passed two renewal applications across the counter to Orde. "In case you make a mistake. Always good to have a practice sheet, I say. You would be surprised the number of people who mail these things in all scratched out, marked up. It goes much easier if you type it." He tapped the blank sheets. "Just like yours. And if you're not in such a hurry, mail it. Usually eight weeks is time enough for renewals. The ladies love having the new photographs made."

Orde smiled and listened to him babble. He accepted the applications without attempting to explain that Katie would definitely not be coming to Warsaw. No use getting into personal conversation with a chap who loved to hear himself talk.

"Enjoy your trip to Warsaw," he called after Orde.

Orde winced at the words. Maybe this fellow did not know what was happening in Warsaw these days, he mused.

Among all the little boys around Muranow Square and in the Torah school, the name of the great and magnificent *Hayedid*, Captain Samuel Orde, was already legend.

Who in the Jewish District did not know somebody—or at least know somebody who knew somebody—who had gone to Palestine? And if everyone knew of a somebody even twice removed in Jerusalem, then of course the daring and stupendous deeds of Captain Orde against the Arab gangs of the Mufti had been reported back to Warsaw. Thus the letter from Rabbi Lebowitz in Jerusalem caused a stir in the community when his aquaintance with the Hayedid was reported.

On the strength of one mention of Orde's name in a letter, David and Samuel Lubetkin announced that the very same courageous Englishman in all the news dispatches was coming to their very house! He was coming to hand deliver a note from their grandfather, they proclaimed. He was coming to discuss the situation with their father! And he was coming for a cup of tea as well, probably.

Such incredible news made both the Lubetkin brothers suspect among their classmates at Torah school. What they had said was something akin to claiming that Moses was coming for dinner. Not just somebody *named* Moses, but the very Moses who parted the Red Sea and brought other miracles to pass on behalf of the slaves in Egypt.

Some boys believed that it was the *real* Hayedid who was coming, but most others looked at one another and said, "There must be someone else with the name Captain Samuel Orde. Possibly it is a common name among the English, just as Moses is a common name among us."

Such logic insulted and angered David Lubetkin. It simply confused his younger brother Samuel. "There is only *one* brave and victorious Captain Orde," David announced outside the school. "It is the same captain who has conquered those who would curse Israel and drive the Jews into the sea!"

"And he is coming to have tea." Samuel's earlocks trembled with earnest excitement.

The doubters pushed their way to the front of the circle. A boy named Mordechai, two grades older than David, crossed his arms and glared down at him in accusation. "Why should the great Hayedid, of whom my uncle has written, come to visit you?"

"Because," ventured a smaller child who bristled with indignation at the doubt of something so tremendous, "the Hayedid is going to see Rabbi Lubetkin. Do not great warriors always hold conversations with holy men?"

Younger heads bobbed. Older heads, more experienced with huge rumors that never came true, raised their chins and lowered their eyelids as an expression of violent skepticism. And after a moment, the boy named Mordechai said *the word*. "Liars. David and Samuel are nothing but liars. Why should Captain Orde come to Warsaw for a conference when Jerusalem is jam-packed full of rabbis? I ask you—why?"

There was little doubt as to who threw the first punch. Actually, David threw more than a punch at Mordechai.

With a growl, David plowed into the belly of the startled boy, hurtling him backward into a wall of onlookers who stepped back with one astonished exclamation. *"A-H-H-H-H!"* they said in mutual approval and enjoyment of the spectacle. Such sights were rare among Torah school pupils, much more common among the other Jews who sent their children to nonreligious school. But here? Oy! Such a fight it was. Shouting and pounding and kicking and more shouting! It felt terrific! Books fell everywhere. A ring of short pants and knobby knees encircled the combatants, moving with them as they pummeled and kicked and rolled down the street!

The real reason of the argument was all but forgotten. The fists of every Torah-school boy were doubled up to punch and jab in vicarious battle!

It was all too wonderful for words until the cries of David's sister were heard. She fought her way through the crowd, elbows flying; she pushed back the startled spectators. For a girl, and a pretty girl at that, Rachel Lubetkin could hit pretty hard!

The presence of a member of the opposite sex put a different slant on the entire contest. Some of the older boys simply picked up their books and skull caps and hurried away. The younger crowd, those who believed in the coming of Captain Orde, were left to shout, all at the same time, that it was all the fault of the great bully Mordechai!

Rachel crossed her arms and stared down at Mordechai who lay on his back on the cobblestones. His nose was bleeding. His right eye was already swollen. David was rumpled and his school clothes were torn, but he seemed in better shape than his opponent.

Rachel was red-faced, furious that anyone had laid a hand on David. She waited until Mordechai sat up slowly and held his kerchief to his nose before she launched in.

"Well, Mordechai! Every time there is a fight, you are always in the middle of it!"

The last fight had been two years ago, and Mordechai had been hit with a rock. It was not his fault, but Rachel brought it up anyway.

"Ha!" said Mordechai behind his kerchief.

"And now you have taken to attacking small children," she continued. "You are twelve! David is ten! And yet here you are brawling in the street like any filthy Polish peasant!!" It was not a nice thing to say, but not dangerous right here in front of the synagogue. There were no Poles around.

"Who is bleeding? Nu!" He shook his kerchief at Rachel and clamped it back on his nose quickly.

"Whose clothes are torn?" Rachel put a protective arm around David's shoulders. David shrugged her arm away. He was doing just fine before she came; who needed an interfering sister, anyway?

Samuel stepped up and tugged her skirt. "Rachel, Mordechai says that Grandfather is a liar."

Her mouth and eyes widened at the same instant. She breathed in until some boys thought her lungs might pop. "*My* grandfather? The great Rabbi Lebowitz who prays each day beside the Western Wall? You say he is what?"

"I never said it," spat Mordechai, slowly climbing to his feet. "David and Samuel are liars and you, Rachel Lubetkin, are a contentious woman that we have just studied about in Proverbs."

Everyone stepped back at those words. Would Rachel follow the example of her brother David and hurl herself against Mordechai?

"I am a peacemaker!" she exclaimed haughtily. "Just because I am a woman I still can see injustice being done and put a stop to it! You think I would abandon my brother to a great bully in the street?"

The argument had veered off the subject. The audience exchanged looks. They did not want to hear who was right and who was wrong or who was winning and who got the worst of it! There was only one great issue today—was the real and authentic British hero for the Zionist cause actually coming to tea?

A deeper male voice called in from the back of the group. "Rachel Lubetkin!" It was Peter Wallich, the ragged lost gypsy of Muranow Square. "Are you all right, Rachel?"

"Fine. Here is a bully for you." She gestured toward Mordechai, whose nose bled on. "He attacked David in the street, called my grandfather a liar, and called me a contentious woman! May his mother hang him by his earlocks!"

"I said I did not believe it!" Mordechai defended. "I said the great and incredible hero of Zionism . . . the British Hayedid, Captain Samuel Orde . . . was not coming to their house for tea! And *then* . . . David Lubetkin attacked me!"

"So? Why shouldn't he hit you?" Peter seemed unimpressed by Mordechai's defense. "If you said I was lying, I might also hit you. Because they are not lying. I don't know about coming for tea, but I just heard from the leader of Zionist Youth that Captain Orde is coming to Warsaw. Muranow Square. He will teach the pioneers survival in the wilderness. A lecture class, he said."

The cheers rose up in a mighty roar. The Torah-school boys rushed in to thump David Lubetkin on his dirt-covered back. They shook his hand and fetched his yarmulke and his books. It was true! It was true! The great military leader was coming right here to take tea at the house of Rebbe Lubetkin! Oy! Such a moment! Moses comes marching into Egypt with his staff in hand!

"And he will teach us!" the little boys cried.

"Not *you*," Peter corrected. "Only boys who have had their Bar Mitzvah. Thirteen and older. *That* is who he will instruct."

Smiles faded almost as suddenly as they had come, and silence fell over the group. Mordechai brushed himself off. He was almost thirteen, he told Peter. Next week was his birthday. He would very much like to attend these lectures of the great and ferocious Hayedid, Captain Samuel Orde.

———

Orde arrived home in Three Kings Yard to find that all the personal belongings he had shipped from Jerusalem had finally arrived. Crates and boxes blocked the entrance to the house. With a shake of his head, Orde climbed over the heap and then began to wrestle it indoors. *Just in time to say goodbye,* he mused as he looked at the new mound of possessions in the center of the shrouded furniture. It would remain there until he returned from Warsaw.

Hands on hips, he gazed at it for a moment until he spotted the wooden box containing the old headstone from Gethsemane. Had it survived the trip? This one thing Orde set to work uncrating.

With a sigh of relief, he cleared away the packing paper and patted the old granite stone.

BY DYING I CONQUER LIFE.

Orde read the inscription again with bitter amusement. "Ah, Katie," he whispered, "if only it was just that easy. The trouble is, you see, in the meantime I have to keep *living* and conquering life."

He straightened slowly and pulled back the slipcover from Katie's writing desk. Opening the drawer, he found Katie's passport. Her birth certificate. Her certificate of death. He opened the passport and wished that she were here to travel with him; wished that she were one of the ladies so delighted to have a new passport picture taken. He smiled down at the gray, colorless picture. Katie had always been so full of life and color—her skin, her eyes, the sun highlighting bits of red and gold in her soft brown hair. *By dying I conquer life.*

Orde thought the ancient headstone had spoken aloud. Still holding the open passport, he turned and stared at the gray lifeless granite, the symbol of someone else's existence. There was something he was meant to understand from the inscription . . . *something!*

"What is it, Lord?" he prayed aloud.

At that moment his briefcase toppled off a crate. The plain manila envelope containing the Lubetkin family immigration material spilled out on the floor.

Without passports they are trapped in Poland. If the Nazis come, that family will be among the first singled out. Then Orde said aloud, "They are alive and cannot get passports. Katie has been dead for four years, and I can renew her papers by post!"

Orde knelt down and fanned out the photographs of the Lubetkin family on the floor—the boys with their earlocks; the rabbi with his beard; Etta in her severe dress—each of these bore the appearance of East European Jews. But the girl . . . *Rachel!* Her pretty young face would do well inside the stiff new cover of a British passport! It was a simple matter of matching her with some long-dead child in an English churchyard and writing in for a birth certificate.

"Can it be that simple?" he wondered aloud.

For a moment he considered sending in the photograph of Etta Lubetkin with Katie's passport renewal form. But Katie would have been much too young. The age discrepancy might be noticed. But there were other women in England who *would* have been the age of Etta had they lived! Perhaps there was a way for the dead to conquer life—at least to help conquer the obstacles of immigration for others to remain living for a while!

He stumbled to the telephone and dialed the number of the passport office. A clipped, officious voice answered.

"Hullo." Orde hoped she could not hear the excitement in his voice. He should sound irritated and unhappy, should he not? "I have lost my passport. All my identification, and I have a rather urgent trip abroad."

"A matter of obtaining your birth certificate and a new photo and bringing it to our office."

"Like a renewal then?"

"Yes. You will need to fill out the application. Nothing to it."

"I'm going north tonight."

"We can handle the matter by post if it is easier."

It was easy enough, Orde thought as he hung up and began to stuff his clothes into his baggage! Why had he not seen it before? A last glance at the headstone gave him courage as he left the house. Perhaps the next time he returned, he would open the shutters and take the dusty sheets off the furniture to see the colors once again!

————

Who would have guessed it would be so difficult to get married in Danzig? The tiny blue flowers woven into Lori's french-braided hair had wilted. Jacob's tie was loose and cocked off to the side. His collar was unbuttoned and he carried his jacket as the party trooped into the park around the corner from city hall in search of a shady bench on which to rest for a while.

Three churches of different Protestant denominations—three pastors, and none of them seemed to believe in holy matrimony, especially without *parental permission in addition to a marriage license!* When Jacob had explained that they could not obtain a license without parental permission, these men of the cloth had simply nodded and showed them the exit.

"Maybe we should give up," Mark said, wiping sweat from his brow.

Lori's eyes narrowed. "*You* give up! It's not your wedding anyhow."

Mark made a face. "Seems to me that a brother in England is as good a relative as a wife. I think you want to get married for some other reason."

"You're right," Jacob mumbled. "Now shut up."

Jamie lifted his chin in an arrogant fashion. "If Papa were here, he'd say that *God* is telling you not to get married."

Jacob scowled. "If your papa were here, we'd have parental permission and then God would be saying *yes!*"

Lori added, "If Papa were here, he'd perform the ceremony himself." She cocked a superior eyebrow at Jamie.

Alfie leaned against a tree behind the bench. Werner jumped

off his shoulder and perched on a branch. There was a sign warning that pets should be on a leash and that it was VERBO-TEN to step on the grass, but Alfie was too hot to care. He decided not to read the sign even though it had words he knew, because then he could stand on the grass without knowing he broke the rules. It made sense in a roundabout way, Lori reasoned when she asked him to read the rules about standing on the grass.

Alfie sighed. "Does this mean I don't get to be the . . . best . . . best . . . uh . . ."

"Man," Jacob snapped. "Not yet. There is a church on nearly every corner in Danzig; we will find one *somewhere* willing to do a proper job of this."

"I think we should go back to Sopot and go swimming," Mark said sullenly.

"Yeah. It's too hot for us to get married today," Jamie agreed.

"I want to be . . . uh . . . best man." Alfie wiped his brow on the sleeve of his once-ironed shirt. "And Lori . . . can sleep in our room if her and Jacob is uh . . ."

At this, looks were exchanged all around. There would be no explaining this to Alfie.

Jamie tried. "Married people sleep in the same room."

"Uh-huh. I said that," Alfie nodded.

"Alone," Mark added.

"Why?" Alfie asked.

It was very warm. Jacob stood and tugged his collar open a bit more. "Maybe we should try the English Mariner's Church on the waterfront," he suggested.

"You don't speak English," Jamie chided. "That's what got you into this mess."

All heads swiveled to pierce him through with black looks. Jamie shrugged and looked at the tram. Now he really wanted to go back to the beach!

"The English church then," Lori said. "I will translate."

"Just tell me when we're really married, will you?" Jacob tossed his jacket over his shoulder and struck out across the park. He did not care that Alfie had to climb the tree to fetch Werner and so almost got lost. Alfie told him it would have been an unlucky thing if the best cat was left in a tree somewhere.

The pastor of the English Mariner's Church was a burly Scot from Edinburgh. He had spent most of his life in the Merchant Marines, denting the walls of bars and assorted unholy places until his ship was torpedoed by Germans in the Great War in 1918. Four days drifting on scraps of lumber had been enough for Seaman Cecil Douglass to see the error of his ways. After several years in seminary he had taken up what he called a front-line position between the wharf and the brothels of the waterfront district.

The church building itself stood in the shadow of the half-timbered warehouses along the waterfront. It looked like any other little church from the English countryside. This fact pleased Pastor Douglass, who felt it stood as a beacon of hope, a reminder of home and family. These were matters of great importance to the pastor, and he preached often on the folly of unfaithful seafaring husbands who took no thought of the commandment against adultery.

All these things Jacob had heard from the fellows who worked with him on the docks. Pastor Douglass had taken his four days on a raft in the Mediterranean quite seriously, it seemed.

From this small bit of personal insight, Jacob and Lori formulated a strategy by which licenses and parental permission might be circumvented.

It was cool inside the little church, and everyone began feeling much better about the wedding. Lori and Jacob sat in the choir loft and spoke in low tones to the enormous pastor while the others stared gratefully at the cool white walls and stained-glass windows.

"Miss Ibsen," remarked the pastor, "I have heard of your father. Indeed I have. A giant of the faith. Suffering for the cause of the kingdom and Christ." He knit his bushy black brows together in consternation. "But without the permission of your father—" He spoke excellent German. There was no need for anyone to translate for Jacob.

"Since Lori's father is in prison, how can anyone expect us to get permission?"

Pastor Douglass smiled sympathetically. "But you are both underage."

"We are both Christians." Lori looked indignant. "We love each other."

The pastor wagged a thick finger at her. "And since Jacob is to be left behind, what sort of a marriage—"

"He will join us in England." Lori took Jacob's hand.

"Ah. Yes. And to do that, I suppose it would be convenient to have a marriage certificate." The frown deepened. "I will not make a mockery of God's holy ordinance of marriage."

Lori drew herself up. "Then when my father gets out of prison, I will tell him that the reason Jacob and I were forced to live in sin is because no Christian pastor would perform the ceremony." She tossed her braid, and wilted flowers tumbled out.

The pastor stared at the flowers and considered that no female puts such things in her hair if the wedding is only for a certificate of marriage to show the immigration officials. Perhaps this was indeed a matter of two hearts before the Lord. Here was this young man in a jacket and tie on such a hot day. Was it reasonable to think he would do that for any other reason than true love?

Pastor Douglass stuck out his lower lip. He scratched his cheek thoughtfully. Peering over the rail of the choir loft, he called, "Who's the best man?"

The big dimwitted chap with the kitten stood up and waved the cat in the air. "Me and Werner."

"And who will give the bride away?"

Jamie stood up and smiled weakly. He was taking Papa's place and was certain he could not do a good job. *"Me."*

"And is there a ring-bearer?"

"Me!" Mark jumped to his feet and dug deep into his pocket for the ring.

Pastor Douglass shrugged and stood. "Well, then. All we need is a bride and a groom."

21 Night Closes In

This was not at all what Alfie had meant when he suggested that Lori could share their bedroom.

While Jacob took his new bride for an ice cream soda at Sprinter's ice cream parlor, Mark, Jamie, and Alfie had hurried back to the flat to move mattresses from the big bedroom into Lori's tiny corner room. Jamie and Mark changed the sheets on the double bed and placed two bouquets of fresh flowers in quart canning jars on the night table and the chest of drawers.

It all looked very pretty, but Alfie had not meant that he and Jamie and Mark would have to move to the little room while Jacob and Lori got the big one. It did not take a smart person to see that three bodies crammed into Lori's small space did not fit as well as all five of them in the big room.

"What do you think?" Mark asked, stepping back and crossing his arms as they surveyed the honeymoon suite.

Jamie was not pleased. "I still say Papa will not like this when he finds out I helped." He stared sourly at the flowers. The yellow petals of the daisies had already begun to wilt and drop onto the night table.

"Jacob owes us for this." Mark nudged Jamie. "He said if we would make the place nice . . . romantic-like . . . that he would treat us three to lemon ice at Sprinter's when they got back."

Alfie licked his lips at the thought of lemon ice. His favorite. He looked at the flowers and imagined the bright colors of the umbrellas over the round tables at Sprinter's. He did not know why all five of them could not have gone there together, however. Instead, it was Jacob and Lori first and then the boys. Alfie thought it was sad that they could not all spend every minute together until the boat left for England.

"Well, I am going to have a double-double ice cream soda after this," Jamie scowled. "He owes us, all right! Some trade. I give my sister away today, and all I get is ice cream in return."

Mark seemed amused. "Like Esau giving Jacob his birthright for a mess of porridge."

Alfie winced in confusion. "Huh?"

"In the Bible," Mark answered.

Jamie sniffed. "A sister is worth more than a mess of porridge. More than a double-double soda." He scowled. "I was supposed to be the man of the family while Papa was gone. Now look what's happened." He gestured toward the perfectly made bed. Clean sheets and pillow cases. Not even a wrinkle.

Alfie was lost. "Your papa won't mind that you made the bed," he soothed.

Mark and Jamie exchanged *the look*. Alfie decided they knew more than they were telling. He scooped up Werner and went into Lori's old room to look at the pile of mattresses on the floor beside her iron cot. Not even a place to walk.

"I say we take the money and catch the train to Sopot," Jamie said. "Let's get out of here before they get back."

"I doubt Jacob would mind if we stayed out as late as ten." Mark sounded enthusiastic about the idea. "I'll write the note."

"Good thinking. Lori wouldn't like it at all if she knew I thought of it. With your handwriting . . . And Jacob will back us up, even if we slept all night on the beach."

"Worse and worse," Alfie mumbled to Werner. Sleep on the beach? Wasn't this tiny room bad enough? Now they had to sleep on the beach?

"Hurry up," Jamie hissed. "Tell him . . . them . . . in honor of their wedding night, we've decided to stay away for a while. How is that?"

No time to reply. A heavy knock sounded against the door. Jacob and Lori were back already. Alfie thought they must have swallowed their sodas in one gulp.

Mark and Jamie moaned. Too late. Jacob and Lori would never agree to let them stay on the beach in Sopot, no matter how hot the flat got tonight. No cool ocean breezes . . . no gentle drumming of the waves . . .

Again the knock sounded. "Open it, Alfie," Mark commanded.

Alfie put Werner on his shoulder and fixed a smile on his face even though he was not happy about the way everything was so confused. He pulled open the door.

"Hullo . . . uh . . ." The smile went away. This was not Lori and Jacob after all.

A thin, frightened little man stood sweating in the corridor. His hatless head was drawn forward toward an enormous nose.

Thick spectacles perched on his beak, making him look very much like a vulture. His wide eyes seemed to whirl behind the lenses. Alfie thought to himself that the stranger's eyes looked like bulging boiled eggs. He did not say that to the man, however, because that would have been rude.

"Hullo," Alfie said again. He shook the fellow's clammy hand. "I am Alfie."

The man looked over his shoulder, then at the number on the door. Alfie also looked at the number, then back at the man who seemed very nervous.

"Who is it?" Mark shouted from the bedroom.

"A man with egg-eyes who is sweating a lot," Alfie answered. Then he frowned because he had not meant to talk about the man's eyes, only his sweat. "He looks nice," he added.

"Please," the man said in a quiet voice. "I need to talk to someone . . . who is in charge. There is a young woman who lives here with you?"

"Lori is having a wedding . . . soda . . ." The man seemed very frightened. Alfie called Jamie. "Jamie, this man wants Lori."

His face set in a scowl, Jamie emerged. He looked past Alfie at the little man. The scowl melted into curiosity and then concern.

"Who do you want to see?" Jamie sounded adult as he challenged the stranger.

"Lori." The nervous glance over the stooped shoulder. "Her name is Lori? It is . . . about you. My business concerns you as well."

Jamie did not walk forward to the door. He hung back as though he was afraid the man might reach out and take him.

"Mark!" he called. Mark was already at his side. The two boys stared silently back at the man.

"Who are you?" Mark demanded.

The man wiped his brow with a yellowed handkerchief. "It does not matter who I am . . . I . . . have reason to believe . . ." He faltered, peering past Alfie who towered above him, blocking his entrance into the flat. "Please. I need to have a word with whoever is in charge."

"*We are*," Mark and Jamie said together.

"What do you want?" Mark drew himself up as he had seen Jacob do before a fight.

"I do not know who you are. Why you are here. But there is

a man in Danzig who wants very much to find you." The stranger's voice was an urgent whisper. "I met him outside the British Embassy. He told me a story. He hired me to watch for you—" He pointed at Jamie. "And your sister. I followed you here, and went to report. He lives at the Deutscher Hof. In his room there was a map. Black pins and red pins. He has searched every district, and now he knows you are here." He waved his hand back toward the stairs. "I did not tell him the name of the rooming house because I thought perhaps . . . when I saw the map . . . He seems not to be what he told me he was." The big eyes darted around the room. "Get out of here. I wanted to tell you. Get out of Danzig. Out of Heiliger Geist District. Stay clear of the Deutscher Hof."

Jamie, Mark, and Alfie stared silently at this prophet of doom. The silence drew out, long and heavy as the heat. Finally Werner moved, and the man looked at the kitten as though he was grateful for some response.

"Well," he shrugged and stepped back from the door. "I can do no more than warn you." And then he was gone. The clatter of his street shoes sounded on the long staircase to the lobby. Alfie stood in the doorway and listened until the footsteps disappeared.

———

"*What did he say?*" Jacob shouted as he pulled Mark up by his arms.

"We *told* you!" Jamie defended. "There was a map with pins in it in the man's room at the Deutscher Hof. Black pins where he had looked for us. Red pins where we might be!"

Alfie pointed at the floor. "Here is a red pin still."

"We can't stay here, Jacob!" Mark cried, responding to his brother's anger with equal feeling. "While we're standing here talking about this . . . Don't you see? We have to get out of Danzig *now!*"

Lori bit her lip and looked toward the window as if she were afraid to get near it. *Could the unnamed pursuer be out there now? Looking toward this flat?* She remembered what Alfie had told her. *They are coming to Danzig. . . .* He had known all along.

The boys gathered up all the packed luggage. It stood ready beside the door.

Jacob's face was ashen. He looked at the luggage and then

at Lori. Had any wedding night ever been shadowed by such portent of disaster?

"They are right," Lori said with resignation. "We shouldn't waste any more time."

Jacob frowned and stared hard at the window. *He felt it, too!*

"The man said stay away from this district, away from the hotels." Jamie's brow furrowed with concern, an expression that made him look much older.

Lori turned away to look at the perfectly made double bed, the flowers in the quart jar vases. *Beautiful and sweet.* The gesture made her want to cry, but there was no time for that now. "Where should we go?" she asked Jacob.

Alfie looked up brightly. "It's hot here," he said. "Let's go . . . uh . . . Sopot is a good place to go!"

Six months ago Jacob might have scoffed at any suggestion Alfie made, but this evening he remembered that God seemed to whisper in Alfie's ear.

The light returned to the eyes of Jamie and Mark. *Sopot! The beach! The Kurhaus! The casino and hotel!*

Jacob raised his head as though he heard the same voice Alfie heard. "Sopot. Perfect. A resort. They would not think of looking for a gang of fugitives at Sopot!" He thumped Alfie on the back. "A very smart idea, Alfie."

"Uh-huh. Do . . . can kittens go in the casino?"

In reply, Jacob opened the false-bottomed valise and dropped Werner in. The racket of unhappy yowling began immediately. Alfie pressed his lips together with concern.

"They will not notice the noise," Lori reassured him. "Papa used to say someone could walk through naked and no one would look up."

That comment made Alfie blush. He could not think that Pastor Ibsen would ever say such a thing as that!

Allan Farrell rode from post office to post office by alternating cab and underground. At each location he nonchalantly removed one manila envelope from a scuffed leather briefcase. He deposited each in a mail slot and strolled unhurriedly back out to the street.

Sometimes he would make his drop at post offices that were close together. Other times he would deliberately ride past several or double back on his path so as to confuse his actual route.

The first of the envelopes blew up at 4:00 P.M. at the branch of the Royal Post Office not far from the British museum. The eyesight of the postal worker who was operating the canceling machine was spared only because he wore glasses; the eruption of flames when the aspirin bottle was crushed burned the outline of his spectacles onto his face.

From there a string of nineteen more explosions rocked the London summer afternoon. At another post office in the city, no one was injured seriously, but two thousand business letters—banking and commerce, shipping and industry—were destroyed. How do you fight a fire of blazing paper except with water? But what does more damage; a flaming pile of envelopes or a two-inch stream of muddy Thames river water?

The most common injury among postal clerks was burns to their hands as they attempted to drag letters away from the bonfires. The more enterprising tried to smother the flames with canvas mail sacks, but unless they thought to soak the bags in water first, they only added fuel to the fires.

One envelope caused a particularly spectacular display. One of the bombs was addressed to an outlying district and so was loaded onto a mail car attached to the 6:15 train from Charing Cross Station. It had not even come near a canceling machine, but the length of time had been enough for the acid to eat through the thin metal cap on the bottle. The clerk later reported smelling a biting, acrid odor just before an entire sack of mail burst into flames!

Throwing open the sliding door and grabbing the canvas bag without regard to the vicious heat searing his hands and arms, the clerk pitched the blazing sack from the moving train. It arced through the air like a meteor streaking to earth, leaving a trail of gray smoke and flaming letters.

Its flight took it directly into the path of another train going the opposite direction. When the fireball was struck, it showered both sides of the railway carriages with burning debris.

Both engines ground to a halt and the tracks were soon swarming with passengers, crew, and curiosity seekers. Some were clutching smoldering fragments of envelopes as souvenirs. The injured mail clerk with blistered hands futilely tried to retrieve the letters from the ditches and the crowd.

By the time this happened, Allan Farrell had long since deposited the last of his weapons of terror and returned home to await results. The scream of sirens that began suddenly and increased rapidly gave him great satisfaction.

———————

The distant sound of a siren pierced the evening air as Orde stepped onto the sidewalk. He raised his head to listen, then hurried inside.

Orde's bags were packed and loaded in the taxi that waited downstairs in front of the house on Red Lion Square. A broad-faced woman poked her head out to watch Orde suspiciously as he climbed the stairs to Murphy's residence. His step was light in anticipation of the plan he was about to present. *Precious British passports!*

"D'Mizzus Murphy, she has just home from the hospital got from the having of the baby!" The woman called after him to indicate he should not visit at such a time.

"I am invited," Orde said softly over his shoulder.

"Okay den, but you don't too long stay because all dis is wearing her out!" Then the door slammed shut. A moment later it opened again. "An' don't too loud on the door knock!" the indignant voice instructed him in a shouted whisper.

As per instructions, Orde rapped softly, doffed his cap, and ran his hand through his hair. Murphy's voice was a tiptoe beyond the door. "That you, Orde?"

He opened the door and stepped back, inviting Orde to enter with a finger placed over his lips. "She's sleeping," Murphy explained. Then Mrs. Murphy . . . Elisa . . . slipped into the room with two women following after. It was plain to see that they were all related. The physical resemblance was strong and impressive to Orde. Fine-looking women, all three of them. Elisa, her mother Anna, and Anna's sister Helen Ibsen.

Elisa Murphy did not look as though anything was wearing her out, Orde thought as he considered the warning of the woman in the stairwell. Dressed in a pale pink cotton skirt topped by a shirt that probably belonged to her husband, she looked as if she had just come in from a stroll on the beach at Brighton. Her short blond hair was swept back. She wore no makeup. Her skin looked fresh and scrubbed. Orde did not let himself look into the blueness of her eyes as he shook her hand. He envied Murphy in that moment. A new baby and a woman who would be a pleasure to wake up next to.

Anna and Helen were different, older versions of the same uncluttered attractiveness. Helen was younger and slightly taller than Anna and Elisa. And when he looked into Helen's eyes, he saw the sadness plainly.

Did she see something behind his face as well? Introductions were made all around; then it was Helen Ibsen who took charge of the meeting. She led Orde to the sofa, sat down, and indicated that he should sit beside her. Elisa and Anna slipped out to make coffee. Helen then told Orde the story of the young man with whom he was about to make contact. *Jacob Kalner, so in need of a passport!*

The story of Jacob Kalner was anything but happy. Reports were confirmed that Jacob's father had been executed in prison. His mother had died of typhus six weeks ago. They had not yet broken the news to Jacob. They had waited, hoping that he would be here in England among friends when he was told. "But he will ask," Helen said quietly. "It would be better if someone was there with him to tell him face-to-face."

Coffee was served, and Helen shared everything she could about him—much more than Orde cared to know. She finished by saying, "My daughter Lori is in love with him. She thinks I don't know, but . . . she is my daughter." Helen frowned. "There was a time when I promised Jacob's mother that we would care for him if something happened. Well, everything has happened. And Jacob is out of reach." She put a hand on Orde's arm. "I want to ask you to take good care of Jacob. He is like my own child. My children are coming home to me and Jacob is staying behind. Until we can find some way. . ." She paused, "He is a good boy, Captain Orde. And he will have no one but you for a while."

At first Helen Ibsen talked over and around the insistent wail of sirens that had begun moments after Orde entered. Then the increasing racket caused everyone to look at one another in concern.

Murphy stood up and went to the window as two more police cars screamed past and rounded the corner. "Excuse me," he mumbled, retreating to the office. "Ambulance chasing gets in the blood."

Murphy's voice could be heard as he telephoned the TENS office to see what news was coming over the police radio frequency. Before he emerged, the rapid stumbling of footsteps sounded on the stairs.

Charles and Louis burst into the room, their eyes wide and horrified. They were shouting a jumble of English and German words. Behind them, at a much slower pace, came Doc Grogan. He, too, looked pale and worried.

He did not say hello, did not seem to notice Orde, or Anna and Helen. "Where's Murphy?" he asked Elisa curtly.

"Here." Murphy stood framed in the doorway.

"Are the Nazis coming?" Charles clung, weeping to Elisa. There was no mistaking the terror in his eyes.

"Bombs." Doc began to talk in a rapid-fire voice that he had repeatedly warned Orde against using on the radio. "We took a taxi. I was afraid to take the underground with the boys." He shook his head. "Bombs all over London. Every district post office has been hit. I mean *every* post office we passed."

The hammering wail of sirens filled the air. Tomorrow the children of Helen Ibsen were leaving Danzig for the imagined safety of London. But apparently there was no safety. Not anywhere.

Orde looked toward his briefcase, which held the photographs of the Lubetkin family. He had not had a chance to explain his idea to Murphy. In an hour, Orde had to be on his ship, yet Murphy and Grogan were saying goodbye and rushing out the door. There was no use trying to pull Murphy into the office and explain his idea with all this going on.

Rocking on his heels, Orde stood at the window for a few minutes and watched fire trucks and ambulances speeding past. How best to approach these women with the plan for obtaining passports for Jacob Kalner and the others among the Lubetkin family?

The boys were crying. Baby Katie awoke unhappily as the noise grew louder. Over this confusion, Orde sat down and took a sip of tepid tea. What if they did not appreciate the logic of his plan? What if they. . . ? *Oh well,* he thought, *spill it.*

In the midst of this chaos, Orde displayed each photograph on the coffee table beside Katie's passport. No one noticed the sirens anymore as Orde explained his plan.

"I think the photograph of Rachel Lubetkin is good enough to pass easily for British. The pictures of the rest of her family will have to be retaken."

"What about Jacob?" asked Helen.

"It is only a matter of getting the passport pictures to you here in England. In the meantime, you should immediately begin looking in cemeteries."

The woman exchanged nervous glances. "We have been warned by certain British officials," Anna explained. "We are fairly certain they are watching us closely."

Orde had a ready reply. "Brass rubbing," he said. "A piece of paper, a crayon. Put it over the stone and rub. It is quite popular among the British. People studying genealogies. A pleasant summer pastime which no one will question."

"It looks as though we are back in business," Elisa said cheerfully as she took down the violin case from the cupboard. "Mother? How many do you think we can reasonably manage?"

Anna looked skyward. "It depends on how much time the politicians give us." Then to Orde, "This means you will have to make difficult choices. Appearance and mannerisms will be important. Language. It would not do to send someone on a steamer to Southampton who could not address the steward in English."

Orde was accustomed to difficult discussions. "Have the birth certificates ready to go. I am hoping to have the photographs in your hands within a fortnight of the time I arrive in Poland. I will send them by air courier among the regular news photographs. From there it will be a matter of submitting the passport applications and waiting a few weeks."

"And then smuggling the documents to you in Warsaw," Anna said.

Elisa looked at the battered violin case and remembered. "It cannot be half as hard in Poland as it was in the Reich."

"As long as Poland is not also the Reich," Orde added with a grimness that gave fulfillment of the plan a new desperation.

Hess knew from the first reply that he had at last found the right apartment building.

"So who wants to know about them?" asked the overweight middle-aged woman who owned the building and managed it herself.

"There is a reward," Hess remarked, sliding the photograph back into his packet as though time was short.

"A reward for what?" The woman eyed his black-gloved hand and the silver tip of his cane.

"Simply for locating them."

"They haven't broken the law, have they? They seem like good children. At first I did not wish to rent to them, but they seemed quite polite. They have been good tenants. Pay their rent on time. Quieter than most. No bother." She blew her nose noisily and scrutinized Hess with renewed suspicion. "So what have they done?"

"They are sought by their families."

"And what are you to them?"

"I am only the man hired to find them and bring them home."

The woman cleared her throat and looked both ways from hall to foyer. "You said something about a reward?"

"Fifty marks to the one who helps locate them."

"Fifty for me, or must I split it with you?"

"Have you keys to their flat?" Hess smiled and looked up the stairs. He had not doubted that he would find them. The surprise lay only in the fact that it had been so easy.

"For seventy-five marks I have keys." She laid her hand on the desk.

"I can knock on each door for nothing," Hess countered.

"They are not home." The hand remained unmoving and unintimidated on the desk.

Hess counted out the bills and then stepped back as she opened a cabinet with numbered keys hanging on the inside of the door. *Apartment 2-C.* She removed the brass keys and passed them to Hess.

"I can see myself up." He nodded his thanks.

She called after him, "It is only fair that I get seventy-five, you know, since you are taking my tenants and I will receive no more rent from them. It is only fair."

————

Hess did not turn on the light in the flat, although the gloom of twilight made it difficult for him to see well. He relocked the door and then stood in the center of the sparsely furnished front room, savoring his victory.

He could make out the shapes of dishes stacked on the shelf above the kitchen sink in the corner. *Clean. Neat.* Nothing seemed out of place. No wonder the landlady had demanded seventy-five marks for betraying such exemplary tenants.

He limped to the open door of a large bedroom. In the last ray of daylight he could see that the double bed was perfectly made up. Two vases of flowers filled the room with fragrance. He shoved the keys into his pocket and went to the window to look out on the narrow street below. From this vantage point he could just make out the corner window of the cabaret. He nodded, as if to congratulate himself on his superb instincts. They would have heard the music. Had they sensed their own peril?

He reached out with his uninjured hand to pluck a daisy from the bouquet on the chest of drawers. Tucking it into his buttonhole, he sat on the edge of the bed and swung his aching leg onto the mattress. Then he removed his pistol and placed it beside him on the pillow.

This would be as good a place to wait for them as any. The muzzle of a gun in the mouth of the first one through the door would hold them all prisoner. A simple matter.

Patting his flask, he considered celebrating with a swallow of schnapps. He thought better of it, and leaned his head back against the headboard as the room grew darker.

———

The Wilson Line steamer *East Sea* eased into the wharf. Though night had closed in around the port of Danzig, Orde could still make out the loading docks and cargo cranes.

Orde ran a practiced military eye over the scene, noting the spread of warehouses along the waterfront. *Journalist's eye,* he corrected himself, but he went on observing strong points and defensible positions just the same.

Danzig was supposed to be a place where war might break out. According to the ravings of Herr Hitler, Danzig must and would belong to the Reich. It was apparent to Orde that warlike preparations were taking place. A convoy of trucks, distinctly German in appearance but bearing Danzig license plates, streamed past the Wilson Line docks toward an isolated and dimly lit warehouse.

They are not transporting tea, thought Orde grimly. He declined the offer of a taxi to his hotel, deciding that he would walk the few blocks instead. From the pocket of his overcoat he retrieved a notebook with the address of the Ibsen children, but he replaced it unopened after realizing that it was too late to go there. He would see them at the docks tomorrow, anyway. Orde's luggage had been shipped ahead to Warsaw, except for the small valise he carried.

The area of Danzig adjacent to the harbor was gloomy and dismal. A trio of drunken sailors paused on wobbly legs, apparently searching their fuddled brains for directions. When the middle of the three men slid down to lie unconscious on the cobblestones, his companions dragged him out of the street, emptied his pockets of a few remaining coins, and left him propped against a warehouse wall.

Up ahead, one bright light in all the grimy dark beckoned to Orde. The polished globe of the lamp spoke of more care and concern than could be seen anywhere else in the quarter. Orde was drawn to the light to see what warranted such pride in the otherwise neglected surroundings.

The neatly lettered sign beside the door read ENGLISH MARINER'S CHURCH. The words were printed in English at the top, but repeated in German and in Polish below that. Orde thought how appropriate that seemed; here was Danzig caught between Germany and Poland with England trying to make sense of it all.

Orde knew that time was running short. If Danzig was a barrel of petrol, then the lighted match was very close indeed. He had heard the reports of how the Nazis were transporting arms and ammunition across the Nogat River from East Prussia by night. The Nazis in Danzig clearly wanted war, but then they had their sights set on a much larger target than just this port.

The rest of the German Danzigers expected to be reunited with the Reich, but without bloodshed, the way Hitler had demanded and gotten the Sudetenland. They wanted to be German, but not at the cost of war and the interruption of their trade with Poland. They were deluding themselves. The war that was most certainly coming would engulf them all.

Some time after dark a bank of storm clouds swept in from the Baltic and erupted over Danzig. Lucy awakened to the soft cry of her baby, tended to his needs first and then set out pots and pans to catch the drips from the leaking roof.

The dissonant clank of water drummed against the pots, and rain sluiced through the gutters. Lucy nursed the baby and then, lulled by the unwritten melody and the coolness of the air, she fell into a deep and untroubled sleep again.

The storm outside raged on, unabated through the long night. After a day of heat and profound exhaustion, Lucy was too weary to worry any longer that Wolf was somewhere in Danzig, perhaps very near. There was only one fundamental issue. She and the baby were both alive, both well. She had no strength to dwell on anything beyond that. Her sleep was dreamless and profound. If her baby had cried, Lucy would have awakened, but he did not cry. The child, too, simply slept on in the illusion of well-being beside the warmth of his mother's body.

The summer storm seemed to sing its lullaby to Lucy. She felt no foreboding at the drum of distant thunder. She never heard the sound of boots against the stairs. She did not stir at the rattle of the extra key that had been bought from the old concierge in the lobby. For these few hours, at least, Lucy was at peace beside her child. Merciful sleep. It shut the unthinkable disaster from her mind even as the lock clicked open and the hinge of the door groaned back.

22   One Moment of Joy

Werner seemed very happy with the large and elegant room at the Sopot casino. There were tabletops to explore and the fringe of a bedspread with which he could do battle. The fixtures in the bathroom were shiny brass, and he could see a kitten reflection in the faucet. There was one big bed for Mark and Jamie to share and a very nice feather cushioned sofa for Alfie. A silver candy dish held perfect round chocolates. Mark poked his finger in the bottom of every one to see what was inside, but Alfie did not mind. He decided not to look at the bottom before he took a bite. He liked surprises as long as they were nice surprises. Butter creams, marshmallow, orange stuff, and cherries.

"This is much better than just going to Sprinter's for lemon ice and sleeping on the beach," Jamie said, finally looking happy.

"Jacob and Lori's room is not nearly so big as this." Mark sat back on the sofa and propped his feet on the coffee table. He punctured another chocolate, peered in, and popped it into his mouth. "You know if *they* were in here, we could not put our feet up or poke the chocolates."

Alfie smiled. Now that they did not have to sleep all crammed into the little room where Lori had slept, he did not mind so much that they were not all together in the same room.

"They... won't have as much fun ... as us," Alfie said confidently, biting into a cherry covered with light chocolate. He offered Werner-kitten a bite, but Werner was not interested. He hopped off the back of the satin sofa and ran to climb the pale yellow draperies.

"It has been a very good day," Jamie said with a contented sigh. He wiped his mouth on his sleeve and watched with admiration as Werner nearly made it to the top of the draperies before sliding down.

"We should fill the ice bucket with sand from the beach," Mark said. "Then Werner will have a toilet."

"Good idea," Alfie said. Then he called to Werner, "Plumbing inside, Werner!"

The cat meowed, much quieter than he had when he had been inside the despised hiding place in the valise. Lori had been right about nobody noticing the noise. Almost nobody had noticed except for the bell captain who sent men everywhere looking for the cat that had slipped into the lobby to hide somewhere. It had been fun to watch them on their knees, poking their heads into corners behind potted palms. They never imagined there was a kitten stashed in the luggage.

"It's a good thing your mother sent us money from England," Mark said. "We could stay here a whole week if we weren't leaving on the ship."

"And there would still be enough for Jacob to get to Warsaw." Jamie tossed a pillow at Werner, who jumped straight up and scampered across the mantel on the fireplace. "If I was him, I'd stay awhile after we leave. Who wants to go to Warsaw when you could stay in the Kurhaus Hotel and eat all the chocolates you want?"

"It wouldn't work," Mark interjected. "He told the man at the front desk that his papers were still in the luggage at the depot. So he didn't have to give our real names. But the clerk will want to see them, all right. He's got to be gone before then."

"Too bad." Alfie mumbled through a full mouth. "Sopot is . . ." He wanted to say that in his entire life he had never been anyplace as wonderful as Sopot and this hotel. This room had more space than three flats like theirs. The lights were bright and clean. The tub was big enough for him to play boats in—except that he had not owned any toy boats since Mama died. It did not matter. Soon he would be on a real boat. A big boat. And now that Jacob and Lori were really married, maybe Jacob could get on a boat to England much sooner.

"Probably it is better that Jacob has two relatives in England," Mark said. "A brother and a wife. I think so. Two of us will be able to make more of a fuss than one."

Jamie raised his head and looked all around the room. "My papa stayed here once, you know. He told us about it."

"My papa too," Mark added, not to be outdone.

"Maybe they stayed in this very room." Jamie smiled at the thought. "Papa will like it that Lori and Jacob had their honeymoon here, I think. Maybe it will make the rest all right. You think so?"

Alfie patted the sofa and Werner jumped up beside him. "They. . . they won't have as much fun . . . as our room." He scratched Werner's head and thought about filling the ice bucket with sand.

Mark and Jamie exchanged *the look*. Alfie wished he knew whatever secret they knew.

Lucy's mother and father stood in the barnyard. The door to the barn was open. It was dark inside, but Lucy could see someone moving from stall to stall. Lucy's father smiled and tapped out the tobacco of his pipe. Then he reached his arms out to take the baby from her.

"What will we call him, Mother?" he asked of his wife.

Lucy's mother pulled the blanket back from the baby's face to study the serious blue eyes of the quiet infant. "He looks like Wolf, don't you think, Papa?" She smiled at Lucy. "Would you like to name him after his father, Lucy dear? He looks so much like Wolf. No mistaking he is the son of Wolfgang von Fritschauer."

In her sleep, those words were pleasing to Lucy. In her dream she could not remember everything that had gone on between

Vienna and this arrival at her childhood home.

Lucy opened her mouth to speak, to agree that her son should be called Wolfgang; but the words would not come. She tried to say the name again and again. The word formed clearly in her mind. She could see the letters, suddenly inscribed in black on the red blanket in which the tiny form of innocence was wrapped: W-O-L-F.

"What is wrong, Lucy dear? You can't speak?" her mother asked her sympathetically. "Shall we call your son Wolf? Shall I say it for you?"

Lucy raised her hand to touch the head of the baby, but suddenly he was pulled away from her. The image of her mother's face faded and that of another woman took her place. The woman standing in front of her was the same one Lucy had seen among Wolf's photographs. Here was the wife of Wolfgang von Fritschauer! Her cold eyes glinted with pride as she took the baby from Lucy's father and cried, "Yes! Just like Wolf!"

At the same instant, Lucy's father stepped back, his face pale. "I have to tend to what is mine!" he shouted angrily as he hurried away into the barn. Lucy tried to follow, but she could not move. She tried to call out for her father to come back, but she could not speak.

Her hands hung heavily at her sides. She could not lift them to fight against the woman who smiled over the baby. As Lucy watched, the shadow from the barn stepped into the light. It was Wolf, tall and handsome in his black uniform. He looked at Lucy and smiled cruelly, as she had seen him do a thousand times before. Suddenly she remembered everything! Scenes from their life together replayed in a flash. She remembered the terror of her escape from him; the threat he had made to take her baby rang out clearly in her mind.

She looked at the blanket where her child lay. It was red, but a darker red than it had been before. The fabric seemed to dissolve and melt until it covered the arms of the woman with blood. The black letters of Wolf's name spun like pinwheels and moved together to form the shape of the Nazi swastika. Lucy tried to shout a warning to the woman; to tell her she must guard the baby; but still she made no sound.

Could they not see the blood that would drown the child? Why did they not take him out of the blanket before it suffocated him?

Lucy found the strength to step forward; she opened her

307

mouth and willed herself to shout the warning. They did not hear her.

"What shall we name the Führer's child?" asked the woman.

"He looks like me," Wolf was pleased. "Just like all the rest. We will call him Wolf." Blood had pooled in the baby's eyes. Lucy could see her son open his little mouth and gasp for breath. She ran toward him, to wrench him from the unseeing woman, but as Lucy reached out, they floated just beyond her straining fingertips.

In the barn Lucy could hear the rattle of milk filling the metal pails. She could hear the cowbells banging against the stanchions where her father milked the cows. If she could reach her father, maybe he would help her! But the barn door, like the couple, swung lazily beyond her reach.

She tried to call out for her father, but he did not hear her. The clank of the milk pails grew louder; the baby coughed and cried and . . .

"I am dreaming."

Lucy opened her eyes as the slow drumming of rainwater in the pots on the floor reminded her of where she was. The rain had stopped. The world was silent except for the few stray drops that had not yet found their way off of the eaves. Lucy gathered her baby to her and stroked his face gently with her fingers. No blood. He was fine, breathing sweetly and evenly. Thank God!

She sighed and lay back down in the blackness with a shudder of relief. It had been so pleasant, at first—her dream; her sleep. And then what had happened?

Closing her eyes she tried to recapture the feeling of peace she had felt before the dream had changed so horribly. *A name. A name for the baby. Not Wolf.*

"What will I call you, little one?" she whispered softly, cradling the tiny fingers in her hand. "What name for my son?" Her own voice was drowsy and pleasant in the stillness of the night.

At that moment a match flared behind her. The room was suddenly illuminated with orange light.

Lucy cried out as she sat up on the bed. Wolf glared at her from the glow of his match. He was smiling—the cruel smile she knew so well. His raincoat was draped over the chair. His boots were still wet.

He stepped forward as though he might toss the match onto the bed; instead, he touched the flame to the wick of the gas lamp.

"His name is Wolf," he said with amusement. "Or have you forgotten whose child he is, Lucy dear?"

Morning had come, terrible and swift, to the Kurhaus Hotel at Sopot.

Lori had not slept at all, even though Jacob had slept and then awakened a dozen times throughout the night to her loving touch.

Only one night together, but it was enough to knit their hearts forever. Lori felt as if she had never been a child, never belonged to anyone but to Jacob.

She reached out and touched his muscled back. There was the scar he had gotten when he fell from his bicycle in fourth grade. She remembered that. He was brave even then; he had not cried even though his shoulder had been torn open. Any other boy in their class would have cried. Lori thought now that she had loved Jacob Kalner even then—and long before that day as well. He had tied her braids together in second grade, and she had been so angry. In first grade, he had told her to take a sniff of a jar with a rotten bird's egg, and she had run home crying. His mother had made him bring her flowers as an apology. He had doffed his hat and bowed and made her smile from behind the screen door. There were other memories—birthday cakes shared in Sunday school; family outings on the Spree when she publicly hated him and secretly loved him. And now all of that had come down to one night, the consummation of everything she had ever longed for. Jacob, her friend. Jacob, her hero. Jacob, her lover. Jacob, her husband.

They were not children any longer. After this one night of discovery and joy they were to be separated. For the first time in their lives, really, they would not be able to talk to each other or ignore each other; to tease or listen; to make wishes. Or to embrace again. *For how long, Lord?*

Lori moved closer to him, pressing herself against him and kissing the back of his neck. She did not want him to wake up. When he awoke he would turn and tell her it really was morning. *Don't wake up. Let me listen to your heart while you sleep.* She laid her cheek against his back and listened to the deep and steady beat of his heart. It was much slower than her own heartbeat. Strong and honest. He had loved her far more than she had loved herself. He had forced her to wait for this perfect night until it was right. How she adored him for that, for demanding only the best for her soul! Today at the docks he would demand that for her safety's sake as well.

Don't urge me to leave you or to turn back from you. Where you go I will go.

How could she let him go? How could she keep her promise not to beg him to let her stay at his side?

———

Hess had propped open the bedroom window to hear the cabaret accordion. One sip of schnapps had led to another until at last he had emptied the flask and dozed fitfully on the bed.

The first gray light of dawn illuminated the room. Hess opened his eyes as the memory of last night returned.

They had never come back to the flat! He sat straight up, sending the flask clattering to the floor. Had they been warned? He threw back the curtain and looked out on the still-sleeping street as though he might see them below. He groped toward the closet door and threw it open. *Empty!* Wooden hangers lay in a pile on the closet floor, one lone sock in the corner.

Hess cursed and then rushed to pull open the drawers of the chest. Each one *empty*! In his rage he threw the vase of flowers against the wall and overturned the night table, shattering the lamp.

Only then did it occur to him that perhaps his quarry had never ever been here! Had he been tricked? Seventy-five marks had yielded him nothing but a night's lodging in a vacant apartment.

Drawing his knife, he held the blade up to the just-breaking daylight. The landlady would spend twice as much as he had paid her in the repair of this flat. Plunging the knife into the mattress, he tugged the knife from the head of the bed to the foot.

Within five minutes, dishes were broken into shards, draperies and upholstery alike were shredded.

———

The thin, reedy voice of the newborn's cry covered the sound of blows as Wolfgang von Fritschauer unleashed the rage he had felt against Lucy for months.

She was too weak to resist when he grabbed her by the hair and slapped her again and again. Blood from her nose splattered across the clean white sheets, dotting the skin of the baby like a fulfillment of her worst nightmare. Wolf kicked the table over. He threw the basin against the wall.

"Beg me!" he hissed through clenched teeth as he threw her back on the bed. "I want to hear you beg me!"

"No, Wolf!" she cried. "Please, no more! The child. Please—" She held the sheet up to her face and tried to stop the bleeding. The sheet was soaked with red. "I *am* begging. . . ." She wept and held a hand up to restrain him as he unbuckled his belt and stepped toward her. Hooking his thumbs in his trouser pockets, he rocked upon his toes and glared down at her.

And the infant wailed on. The child's fair skin grew red with terror and outrage as his quiet world became a hell of confusion.

"You think I have forgotten you, eh?" he sneered. Then in a sarcastic voice he mimicked her. *"Oh please, Wolf! Don't make me go to the Lebensborn yet! We have such fun together still!"* He let his eyes linger on her gown where her milk dampened the fabric. He smiled cruelly, a smile she knew all too well.

She shook her head. "Please. The baby was only born last night. Oh, Wolf! Not even you could—" Her face was a mask of terror.

"That's right," he towered over her. *"Beg me."*

"I can make everything like it used to be," she pleaded. "I was just frightened! I did not want you to take my baby!"

"So all your efforts have come to this, eh?" Again he mocked, *"Oh Wolf, you must keep me pregnant!"* The muscles in his cheek twitched. "Why not start now?"

"Wolf!" she sobbed and pressed herself back against the iron bars of the bed where she was captive. "Don't do this thing!"

He threw his shirt across the room, then grabbed her gown at the neck and tore it from her. He laughed when he looked at her. "So this is what becomes of beauty. . . Not quite what you had before, Lucy. But it's been a long time—I do not mind."

She tried to scream, tried to fight him, but he clamped his hand over her mouth and pushed her beneath him.

Lucy's cries of pain were muffled and lost beneath the frantic wails of the baby born into a world gone terribly wrong.

Cocking back the hammer of his pistol, Hess placed the barrel into the ear of the still-sleeping landlady. She awoke with a start and opened her mouth to scream as Hess clamped his hand down hard to silence her.

"Do not scream, dear Frau," he said quietly.

Her terrified eyes rolled wildly as if she would black out. He smiled down at her patronizingly. "So sorry to awaken you so early in the morning, but you see, you have something I want. Something I need."

From beneath his hand she begged him not to harm her.

"I do not like being made the butt of a joke," Hess explained as though he were telling a waitress his coffee was too cold. "You understand?"

She shook her head. She did not understand at all.

"Your tenants are quite sloppy," he continued in a whining voice. "What a terrible mess they made of the flat before they left. Did you know?"

Again the head moved slowly. No. She did not know.

"If I remove my hand, you promise not to scream?"

She nodded, closing her eyes as if to pray. The hand was lifted slowly from her mouth. The gun remained at her ear.

"Please," she breathed. "Do not kill—"

"Kill you?" Hess jabbed the gun into her neck to make his point. "Only if you scream. Or lie. You will tell me everything, will you not?"

"Yes, only please . . ."

"I ask the questions and you answer. Right?"

"Yes. Anything." Tears streamed down her fat cheeks.

Hess gave her another sharp jab. "Shut up and listen. Your tenants in 2-C did not come back last night. Where are they?"

"I . . . I don't know," she stammered. "I am not their mother."

"Yes. Did you know the closet is empty? And their chest of drawers as well?"

"No! I swear! They were there! I saw them last . . . two days ago. They paid in advance until the end of the month. Still more than a week yet on their rent!"

"They are gone," Hess said. "And they left the flat—your lovely flat—a wreck, I'm afraid." He stepped back as the woman's face clouded with anger. At him and also at the children.

"They did not check out. Gave me no notice. Did not collect their cleaning deposit."

"Good. No doubt you will need it after what they have done." He waved the pistol in her face. "You do not know... have no idea . . . where they have gone?"

She lay very still on her back, staring past the gun toward the ceiling. "They had mentioned England. But I thought I would have noticed. I did not think they would just leave."

"England," Hess whispered. "How were they to travel?"

"How should I know?" the woman barked.

Once again he pressed the gun to her ear. A small cry escaped her lips. "Landladies know everything about their tenants."

"They said . . . by steamship . . . but if they left with their luggage, I would have seen them," she protested meekly. "Please. I have told you all I know."

"Not all." Hess leaned down very close to her face until the gray of his blind eye was all she could see. "Where is my money?" he growled. "My seventy-five marks!"

She pointed to her handbag. "There! In there! Take it and go! Please go! And do not hurt me!"

Hess smiled. His soulless eye mocked her terror as he pressed the steel of the pistol hard and steady against the side of her neck.

A sudden movement of his wrist was all Hess needed to slam the gun barrel into her head. Her eyes rolled back in unconsciousness. He dumped out her handbag and took back the cash he had given her; then he slipped out of the building without being seen.

———

Wolf buttoned his shirt slowly as he spoke to Lucy in a patronizing sing-song voice. He acted as though nothing had happened since she left him in Vienna, as though nothing at all had just happened in this garret room—no violence—no brutality.

"You are not hurt," he said lightly. "On the farm we breed back mares to stallions three days after they give birth." He managed a short laugh. "Probably you will be pregnant again from our little passion here."

313

Lucy did not reply. She lay very still beneath the red-spattered sheet. Her eyes were dull as she stared at the window. The baby nursed frantically. His breath trembled against her breast. Only now as she absently stroked his head was he quiet.

Wolf looked down at his clothes. Flecks of blood covered him. The morning light broke through a layer of clouds and streamed across the wood-plank floor covered with wreckage from Wolf's rage. "You are not going anywhere," he muttered, "until I take you."

"Where?" Her voice was barely audible.

"Back home. To the Reich. You would like to go home, wouldn't you?"

She did not reply.

Wolf's tone was still smooth. "There are questions which you must answer, you see. People who want to know . . ." He waited as if she would respond to his words. "Your friend, Otto Wattenbarger . . ."

"I do not know." And then she remembered it was Otto Wattenbarger who had hidden Peter Wallich's family in Vienna. A Gestapo agent himself, Otto had helped many political prisoners escape or die without talking. Otto had been arrested the night Peter and his mother had fled to Frau Singer's.

"You must remember him, eh? Maybe you were working together? Maybe you were in on the entire resistance plot in Vienna?"

"Oh, Wolf," she said wearily. "*Oh* . . ."

"You would like me to think you are too stupid and cow-like to be involved in such things. But you left Vienna with the family of Michael Wallich. Remember the Wallich case? Of course you do. Because you must be one of them as well. We would have had a confession from Otto, but he chose to launch himself out into eternity. Dead as a post in his cell. *Tragic.* And with so much he might have told us about the operation in Vienna." He put on his raincoat to cover the stains of her blood. "And so, my dear, I am afraid we will have to get our information from you."

"Let me sleep, Wolf. Please." She closed her eyes as tears crept from the corners.

"Yes. You are not going anywhere." She could hear his smile. "I have phone calls to make. But I will be back. And then you will come with me. You and the baby. A baby needs its mother—until someone else can be found to replace the nourishment."

314

Wolf was right. He had made certain she was too weak at this moment to move, too abused to do more than lie here until she could recover. By then, no doubt, he would be back. And then he would take her child. He would arrest her and give her to men who could, and would, match his own brutality. "By the way, I checked. The door can be locked from the outside. And I have both keys now. Just in case."

What was the use? What was left for her now? He was right. It had all been for nothing.

He stood over her bed and leaned close to her. "This morning's tryst may well be your last experience with physical pleasure. I hope it was unforgettable for you, dear Lucy."

With that, he slipped out of the room and locked the door from the outside, just to make certain she would still be here when he returned.

Lucy slept for what seemed like hours, yet when she opened her eyes the shadows on the rooftop were unchanged. It was as though the sun had not moved and no time at all had passed.

The bells of Marienkirche boomed out over the city. Lucy lay still and counted the tolling of the hours. *"Four . . . five . . . six . . . seven . . . eight . . ."* And then silence.

Could this be? Only eight o'clock? Wolf had just left the flat a few minutes before! His footsteps no doubt still echoed against the pavement of Heiliger Geist Strasse!

Lucy sat up slowly as if to test her fragile strength. She felt as though she had been asleep for days, as if the terror Wolf had brought into this room had happened days before.

She frowned, wondering if perhaps it really had been days ago that he had come to her. Perhaps something had happened to him and he had not been able to come back, she thought. Had she slept so long? Locked in some delirium of grief and pain had days instead of minutes passed? Had she cared for her baby without knowing what she was doing?

She touched his forehead. He was sleeping a deep, contented sleep. His diaper was dry. And yet, the blood—*her blood*—on the sheets was bright and fresh! She touched her nose. It was still bleeding slightly from Wolf's blows. Not broken, but tender and bruised, as was her right cheek.

Lucy ran her hands over her arms. The welts from Wolf's belt were bright red, *new*! There were the marks made by his fingers as he had held her down.

She swung her legs around and stood, gripping the iron bed for support. Her legs still trembled and her mind reeled, sending the room and the bright square of the window spinning until she sat down on the edge of the bed again.

She turned her head to the silver crucifix above the bed. "What day is this?" she asked aloud. "How long have I been sleeping?" With that, she stood once again, more slowly this time. The world did not spin. She kept her eyes fixed on the cross as she walked toward it and put her hand out to touch it. "You saw what he did," she moaned and began to weep silently. "Help me. Please . . ."

Taking the crucifix down from the nail, she clutched it to her. Wrapping herself in a sheet, she walked to the door and tried the knob. *Locked! From the outside!* Wolf had not returned. Only minutes had passed since he had left her! How much time did she have before he returned? And how could she get out?

Behind her through the partially open window, she heard the soft cooing of a pigeon. She turned to look as the bird walked along the ridgeline of the adjoining roof. Lucy frowned as she stared hard at it. She had never really looked at the roof before now. Always her eyes had swept up to the blue sky or the starlit night above the buildings.

But this was the only way.

Three brick chimneys protruded from the slate shingles, marking the division of houses. The structures all butted up against one another, providing a narrow tight-wire path along the high peak. Three buildings away was the smaller peak of a dormer window almost identical to the one where she stood now. She could not see inside. The angle obscured that view from her. She did not know if it was someone's apartment, or an office, or simply an empty garret room. *But if she could get to it!* If she could walk that narrow precipice, perhaps it was a way of escape!

She caught a glimpse of her reflection in the dingy glass. Even if she made it across the roof to the window, she could not walk three steps through the street without being noticed. Bruised face and matted hair. Ashen complexion and trembling hands. "Help me," she prayed as she turned to look with pity upon her baby. "Help me take him to safety. And then . . . it does not matter what happens to me. But for the baby! Sweet Christ Jesus! Have mercy on me!"

How long would Wolf's telephone calls take? There was no time to think about that now. Lucy found the washbasin and filled it with cold water. She bathed quickly and washed her hair. Dressing was more difficult. Each thing was done slowly, even though her mind rushed and her spirit shouted that she must *hurry*!

She donned a loose cotton dress. How strange it seemed to wear this dress now! She had bought it for a picnic by the Danube. Wolf had not liked it; he had ordered her never to wear it again. Clean and soft, it felt good against her skin. Somehow wearing it seemed to give her added strength to defy him. She braided her damp hair and then covered her head with a scarf. The finishing touch was a pair of dark glasses that she had worn on the ski slopes last fall. The glasses helped conceal the bruise beneath her eye. She powdered her nose to cover the redness, then added a touch of lipstick to give her deathly pale skin some color.

The bells of Marienkirche tolled the half hour. How long until Wolf ascended the stairs? She must be gone when he opened the door! No time to rest! No time to sit and let her trembling muscles gather new strength!

The basket of baby things was already packed, as was Lucy's own valise. But there was no hope that she could carry more than the basket and the baby across the roof. She stuffed some of her things into the basket. Underwear. One thin dress and a sweater. What was left of her money and the crucifix went on the bottom with her papers and the little green book, *Waiting at Table*.

The rest would remain for Wolf, proof that she had really been here—evidence, along with the blood-stained sheets, that Lucy Strasburg had been within his grasp.

The baby did not awaken when she gathered him up and placed him in the basket. "Let him sleep, dear God," she breathed. "And let him wake in heaven, or in safety somewhere...."

With that, Lucy leaned her weight against the chest of drawers until it scraped a few inches across the floor to partially block the door. It would not hold Wolf up for long, but even seconds might make the difference.

The window jammed halfway open, making it difficult for Lucy to squeeze out onto the ridgeline. Wolf could not pass

317

through the small space. Here again, he might be delayed.

The Baltic breeze blew hard against her, penetrating the fabric of the dress to awaken every nerve in her body. For just a moment she looked off down the steep slate precipice that fell away onto the shadowed street, and she doubted and feared what she was doing. But did she not fear Wolf more? And if she fell, and the baby fell with her, was not that end better than a future controlled by a man like Wolfgang von Fritschauer and his great Reich?

The thought gave her courage as the bells of Marienkirche tolled three quarters of an hour. Lucy could almost hear the tread of Wolf's returning footsteps resounding from the street below. She fixed her mind on the four-inch ridge along the peak of the roof and hooked her arm through the handle of the basket. She let go of the window sash and turned to put one foot in front of the other. *Like a child walking a rail fence,* she told herself. She did not look down. She did not think of the weakness of her legs or the momentary dizziness that threatened to draw her into the abyss. What was behind her was much more terrible than death. Her past *must not* become her future or the future of her baby! The cobblestones of Heiliger Geist Strasse were a gentler bed on which to sleep than the bed Lucy was running from. And so when the pigeons sailed past, she heard their wings and was unafraid. When the echo of traffic below filled her ears, she did not let herself dwell on those things.

Step followed step. She tottered toward the first chimney and then reached out to embrace it. *The first landmark of safety!* She paused there only long enough to catch her breath. Then fear crept up behind her and shouted that she was a fool, that she should go back to the room and find some other way! Lucy brushed the terror back and once again stepped away from the safety of the brick island to balance herself and launch out toward the next.

23   God Bless the Child

Hess limped into the lobby of the Deutscher Hof, only to be greeted by the eager face of Gustav Ahlman. Ahlman seemed as cheerful as Hess was grim.

"Herr Hess—" Ahlman motioned that his superior officer should join him for a short stroll outside.

"This had better be worth my time," Hess growled. "I have had a very difficult night and I am in no mood for—"

Ahlman seemed not to notice Hess's irritability. The news he had was too good to be short-circuited. "I was looking for you. Called the hotel three times last night from a public telephone in the Heiliger Geist District." He slowed his pace to match the halting step of Hess, who merely glared back at his exuberant expression.

"What of it?"

"I followed Major von Fritschauer as usual yesterday. He stopped at several of the derelict boardinghouses in the district."

Hess's eyes widened. Here it was, the evidence he had been expecting. Wolfgang von Fritschauer had been in the same district where the Ibsen children had lived. *So it was Wolf who warned them!* Hess stopped mid-stride. He shook his head angrily. He had been a fool. Why had he himself not followed Wolf? His throbbing leg held part of the answer to that question. "What did he do?" Hess demanded.

"He has found Lucy Strasburg for us, just as you predicted he would." Ahlman's voice grew tight with excitement. "He went up to her apartment and stayed several hours. I watched him from across the street."

"How do you know he was with the woman?"

Ahlman pulled out his dog-eared photograph of Lucy. "I showed this to the concierge of the building. Positive identification. He wanted to know if she was a criminal. Told me there was another fellow up there with her. I told him there was a reward for her capture, and that he must keep an eye out for her until I returned. And then I went to telephone you. Three times, as I said."

Hess paled with the realization that no doubt Wolf had warned Lucy of the danger of remaining in Danzig, just as he had warned the Ibsen children. "And you followed Wolf when he came out?" Hess was not pleased. "Why did you not stay at the boardinghouse to guard against the escape of the woman?"

Ahlman looked puzzled. "You ordered me to follow Major von Fritschauer. And so I did." He shrugged. "He is at his hotel. Two blocks from here. At least he was there a few minutes ago. I came straight here to tell you."

It was true that Hess had instructed the young agent to do nothing but follow and observe. Heinrich Himmler had given him this young, inexperienced agent from the Gestapo roll sheet. And now this was the result! Ahlman had followed the hounds and possibly let the fox go free!

Hess hailed a taxi. "Heiliger Geist District," he commanded; then he turned to the puzzled junior agent. "The name of her hotel?"

"Hanseatic. But what of von Fritschauer? Is he not the one we should apprehend?"

With a gesture, Hess ordered the underling to be silent. His patience had grown thin. The night had been long and unproductive. Hess could only hope that he was not too late.

Lucy dropped to her hands and knees as she neared the dormer. Holding tightly to the basket, she inched forward until the roof of the window was centered beneath her. Like a child descending a playground slide for the first time, she eased herself off the ridge and braced her feet as she scooted down onto the dormer peak to straddle it like a horse. But how to get through the window? She dared not get off the dormer roof. To do so would be to fall.

She crept forward and peered over the eaves and through the soot-caked glass into an attic storage room. The window was hinged to open at the center. Generations of pigeons roosting on the sill had pushed the right window in, leaving just enough of the edge exposed on the left side for Lucy to grasp and pull. "Please, God!" she cried out at the effort.

The hinges tore loose at the top, and with a groan, the window frame crashed forward to hang crazily from one corroded piece of hardware.

320

Lucy gauged how she might swing the basket and her baby safely through the opening and onto the attic floor from this position. With a sense of regret she looked back toward the window of her own apartment. There at the base of it were the sheets she had put out earlier. She wished she had thought to bring them. She might have made them into a rope by which she could lower the baby and herself to safety. But she had neither the strength nor the time to traverse back across the rooftops to retrieve them. Instead, she rummaged through the basket and pulled out her sweater.

Tying one sleeve around the handle of the basket, she lowered her baby out over the empty air; as her heart pounded in her ears, she swung the basket in a gentle arc passing it over the ledge into the attic. Twice it bumped against the broken window frame and then skittered across the glass to dangle above the courtyard four stories below. Lucy prayed. *Not for me. For the baby.* She tried again. The slowly swinging rope of yarn stretched beneath the weight as it swept out over the edge of the roof and then back toward the opening. The wicker passed through the narrow space and over the boards of the floor. At that instant, Lucy released her grip and let the weight of the basket carry it inside, where it thumped loudly to the floor.

The baby wailed as his cradle jarred him awake. At the sound of his cries, Lucy called out and forgot her own fears. In a moment she lowered herself off the dormer roof. Blindly, her foot groped for the solid feel of the windowsill. The broken window frame gave way beneath her weight as she probed the air. The cries of her child drove thoughts of the cobblestones from her mind! Was he injured? Had the basket fallen open and spilled him out on the dusty floor? "Oh, God!" she cried. "Help me!"

As if a hand touched her groping leg and guided it inward, the sole of her foot found the ledge. Bracing herself, she reached down first with one hand and then the other until she crouched half in and half out of the window. Staring into the dim room, she did not step down until she saw the basket, still closed, beneath her on the floor. Then Lucy tumbled forward, her energy all but expended as she tore open the hamper and picked up the child. He was frightened, wet, and hungry, but uninjured by the fall.

Lucy could not walk, not unless she rested here a while. But how long could she rest before Wolf made his way across the route of her escape and found her here?

Unbuttoning her dress, she reasoned that she could not go until the baby was nursed and at peace again. For the time being she decided that maybe God had taken an interest in this child, and so perhaps it would have to be God who kept Wolf at bay and helped her find her strength again. She closed her eyes as the baby nursed. She did not mean to fall asleep at such a time. It simply happened.

"Fourth floor." Ahlman raised his eyes to the steep staircase leading up to Lucy Strasburg's room.

"Go up. Wait there," Hess instructed. "I'll get the key from the concierge."

"What about Major von Fritschauer?"

"We will deal with him later." Hess knocked hard on the door of the concierge as Ahlman took the stairs two at a time.

The old concierge recognized Hess immediately. "Ah, but it was you who were looking for some wayward children yesterday. Why did you not show me the picture of the lady also then? She is right upstairs. She has been there for several months. A decent tenant, her and the boy, both." He turned down the radio and then began to paw through a drawer containing dozens of loose keys. "I gave the duplicate to the other gentleman last night." The old man showed off the small swastika pin that he wore openly on the collar of his frayed shirt. "You see where my loyalties lie," he smiled, revealing toothless gums beneath his drooping mustache. "Anything I can do to help, I told him. He paid me well also."

The boy. Certainly the tenant who lived with Lucy Strasburg was Peter Wallich. And so the entire nest would be cleaned out at once.

"If I had known she was a criminal," the old man babbled, "well, of course I would have notified the police. Soon enough we will have the criminals removed from Danzig, eh?" The man's accent was that of a Prussian. His sentiment was that of nearly every German who lived within the shadow of Poland. "A small key, it is. It was just the attic, you see, and so the key is different and—"

He held up a small, black iron key. "This is it. But I have no more for myself, and so you will have to pay me."

Hess slapped down a handful of loose change and snatched the key from the old man.

"Good luck," chuckled the concierge. "Bring back the key when you are finished. Heil Hitler, eh, brother?"

———

Wolf had showered and changed. He felt pleased with himself as he rounded the corner of Heiliger Geist Strasse. He looked up at the ornate baroque facades of the ancient buildings that housed thousands in this city. He congratulated himself. He had found the proverbial needle in the haystack.

This morning on the telephone to Berlin, he had noticed that the voice of Gestapo Chief Himmler had also sounded pleased at the news of Lucy's capture. Now, perhaps, the disapproval that Lucy had brought upon his head would finally disappear. He had sensed the suspicion of his superiors after the Wallich case went sour. Bringing Lucy back to Berlin to undergo interrogation would certainly dispel the last doubt anyone might have about Wolf's loyalty.

As for the child, a handsome baby boy, Wolf had already called his wife, asking her to meet him in Danzig tonight to pick up what he told her was the "motherless infant of an S.S. officer." No doubt she would see the resemblance the baby had to Wolf, but the woman was smart enough not to ask him too many questions. In these days women knew their place. If they presumed to step out of line, divorce was accomplished by a phone call to the Reich Ministry of Information. Only a phone call.

Wolf could not see the window to Lucy's room, but he imagined that the tiny garret was already hot and steamy from the humidity after the rainstorm. He had no desire to stay up there with her; instead, he would move her to his own hotel where he could watch her in some comfort until she recovered enough to travel back to the Reich.

There was no automobile traffic on Heiliger Geist because the street was too narrow. Even if she got away, she would have to walk three blocks in order for them to get a taxi. Judging from the condition she was in when he left her an hour before, it would probably take her most of the day to regain the strength for such a walk. His abuse had weakened her, but Wolf had no regrets. She had asked for it, and he had given her just what she deserved.

Wolf was humming as he swung into the lobby of the dilapidated hotel. Such cheerfulness was unusual for him. It lasted only until he reached the top of the stairs and saw that the door of Lucy's room was slightly open.

Alexander Hess and another man stood in the middle of the wreckage of the room. Hess's face was purple with rage as he turned his gun on Wolf. "Where is she?" Hess demanded. "You see! You will not get away with your treachery, Lieutenant von Fritschauer! You will tell us where she is, or you will take her place at the interrogations!"

———

It was hot in the attic. Stifling and miserable.

Lucy heard her name drift through the window. Distant shouting. The voice of Wolf. A second voice that she had heard before . . . somewhere.

Get up, she told herself. *A matter of seconds and they will be here!*

Mercifully, the baby slept again. She returned him to the wicker hamper and closed the lid. Staggering to her feet, she swayed in the center of the dark room as she searched the gloom for the way out.

Behind crates and old trunks, Lucy could just make out the outline of a door. She clambered over stacks of old books, sending them clattering to the floor. She prayed the door would be unlocked. Her fingers grasped the hot metal of the knob and . . . turned. The door squealed open. A narrow ladder led down to a landing. Every muscle in Lucy's body shook as she climbed down unsteadily. The air cooled as she descended. She was on the top floor of yet another warren of deteriorating apartments. Voices of tenants penetrated paper-thin walls. The rank odor of cooking grease and fried fish filled the air. Lucy grasped the loose banister and walked down the stairs. She tried to carry herself as though nothing were wrong, as if she belonged in the stinking place.

The doors of flats were all open for ventilation. No one seemed to look up as she walked down the long musty corridors and descended from one floor to the next. She could feel the presence of Wolf just behind her. The image of his face reminded her of the huge deer hounds she had seen as a child, their long legs gobbling up the field as the dogs pursued a doe and her fawn. Slowed by the progress of the baby, the doe had been dragged down and torn to pieces as the fawn screamed like a wounded eagle in the high, piercing voice of terror. And then, it too, had been killed.

Lucy clutched the basket tighter to her as she reached the foyer. The concierge of this building was playing solitaire at a table in the lobby. The woman did not look up as Lucy swept past and rushed toward the light that streamed through the glass in the door.

Once again she froze. *Voices behind her. But were there watchers in the street?*

"Looking for someone?" asked the concierge in a lazy voice.

"My friend is late," Lucy muttered and then she pushed out into the crowd of pedestrians wandering from shop to beer cellar up the sloping street.

Lucy wildly scanned the faces in the crowd. She resisted the urge to run. Like the doe in her memory, she did not want to attract the attention of the hounds. She did not want to be dragged down onto the cobblestones and watch her baby tumble out at the feet of men who would tear his soul to shreds!

She leaned briefly against a streetlamp as a fresh wave of dizziness threatened to knock her to her knees. And then, when the world slowed its lazy spin, she fixed her eyes on the bright scarf of a broad-backed woman and matched her pace.

Three blocks, and there were trams. Three blocks, and she could blend in with the bustle of thousands who traveled to Langer Market. For three blocks, Lucy lowered her head and looked neither to the right nor the left as she tramped behind the stranger whose width protected her from an oncoming view.

Not for me, her heart whispered. *For the child . . .*

Lucy could not let herself think what she must do after these three long blocks. She had come this far. There must be some place to run.

———

Lori was still in bed. She was very sad, Jacob explained, and probably would not come out until it was time to go. But there were important matters to attend to, so Jacob was up early.

Werner-kitten did not like the taste of beer. He would not

drink it. Three of them together could not get more than a thimbleful of the stuff down his throat.

"Not enough to do any good," Jacob said, glaring at the indignant kitten who licked its chest and shook its head as if to spit out the vile-tasting brew.

Jacob went downstairs to the casino and ordered a glass of famous Goldwasser schnapps. Made in Danzig, the liqueur had tiny flecks of gold in it. But its potency, not its precious metal, had made it known throughout the world. Jacob looked plenty old enough to consume the schnapps if he wanted to, but the bartender looked twice at him because it was breakfast time. Only the most hardened drinkers could stand Goldwasser this early in the morning.

Claws out, ears back, Werner started his yowl in a low voice and ended it with a high shriek as Jacob and Alfie held him. Jamie opened his mouth, and Mark dribbled the potent schnapps down his throat.

"I'm sorry, Werner," Alfie said as tears of pity coursed down his broad face. He understood about terrible medicine that hung in his throat and made him want to throw up. But sometimes even kittens had to take medicine. "Don't hate me, Werner," Alfie pleaded as the kitten struggled to free himself.

"Hold his mouth open, will you?" shouted Mark as needle-sharp teeth tried to close around his finger.

"You see," Alfie explained to the kitten, "you have to be asleep and quiet in your box or they won't let you go to England. If you yowl, they will hear you and throw you off the boat." A terrible thought. Alfie thought of how his own papa had drowned in the water. It made him hold Werner a little tighter, but not too tight because the little bones were very small. Alfie did not want to crush Werner, only make him drunk. "Don't hurt him," Alfie said to Jacob. Jacob did not answer. He had a faraway sort of pain in his eyes. Alfie supposed that Jacob was wishing there were a secret box big enough to hold him, too.

"How much do I have to get down him?" Mark's face was flushed red from the effort, and he had the easiest job of anyone. Who would think that one little kitten could fight so hard?

"How much have you gotten down him?" Jacob leaned over and peered into the shot glass.

"Almost all," Mark said with relief.

"Well, three of those will lay a man under the table," Jacob replied with satisfaction. "Werner should be out for a while, I'd say."

But Werner was not out yet. He bit Jamie, who screeched. Then he turned to bite Alfie, who jumped back in hurt surprise. Werner had never behaved in such an angry way before. Jacob got claws down the arm as he turned loose too late to get back.

Then Werner began a wild dash around the room. He dashed across the back of the sofa, sending pillows flying. He swerved up the wall and back down again. He screamed up the curtains, turned, and jumped down to explode across the floor and into the bathroom. All the while he made a low sound like an electric motor whirring.

The boys looked at one another and held their wounds as the sound of Werner's claws across the marble bathroom counter told them he was not finished yet.

That instant a streak of black and white fur flashed across the floor and through their legs and up the wall beside the fireplace. Werner seemed to hang there in midair for an instant and then, claws still out, he slid down to the hearth.

Slowly, Werner turned around three times. He sat down and cocked his head quizzically to one side as he studied the traitors whom he had considered his friends. His wide cat eyes blinked lazily. He licked his paw and tried to clean his whiskers but instead, he fell down, curled up, and went to sleep.

A mighty cheer rose up from Alfie, Mark, and Jamie. Jacob did not cheer. Nothing could make him smile this morning, it seemed. Alfie felt very sorry for Jacob. Alfie knew what it was like to be left behind. He knew what it was like when friends went away and he had to stay.

Alfie wanted to hug Jacob, but he did not. That would not have made Jacob feel better. So Alfie said, "I wish you would be with us when Werner wakes up."

Jacob looked at the thin red claw marks. "Why? You scared to take him out of the box?" Jacob almost smiled. Alfie knew that Jacob did not understand what Alfie meant at all.

"He's going to be one mad cat," Jamie agreed. "We'll open it up and run for cover."

Mark added. "Too bad we can't turn him loose on a Nazi." He meowed and hissed to make his point.

Jacob still was not amused. "We've got an hour," he said.

"Get your bags ready." And then Jacob left to go back and be with Lori again.

Rabbi Aaron Lubetkin was sitting in a chair by the window. Peter noticed how much stronger the great rabbi looked today—not so much the frail old man with one foot in the grave. There was some color on his cheeks. His beard filled out the hollowness of his face, and the hair on his head, though streaked with gray, was quite thick and healthy-looking.

Rabbi Lubetkin was dressed in a loose-fitting cotton caftan, belted at the waist over trousers that were much too big for his thin legs. Peter caught a glimpse of his own skinny reflection in the mirror. So why was he so concerned about the rabbi? Even after months in prison and a near-death joust with rheumatic fever, the rabbi looked healthier than Peter.

A copy of the book *Galilut Erez Yisroel,* by Halevi, was turned facedown on the table next to the water pitcher and a pair of reading glasses. The book was a good sign, Peter thought. Michael Wallich had loaned it to his son just days before the Nazis had arrested him in Vienna. Peter had read the book by flashlight under the covers after that. The book inspired men to long for a home in Israel. Yes, Peter thought, it was good to see that the rabbi was reading it. Such a book would make him listen to what Peter had to say.

The rabbi recited a blessing on Peter as he entered. Peter thanked him, even though he did not believe in such things. It was a matter of being polite, socially correct in a world that, to Peter, seemed centuries out of step with reality.

"I see you are reading the work of Gershon Halevi." Peter started there, with something they had in common.

"You know this book?" Rabbi Lubetkin seemed surprised.

"My father gave it to me before his death," Peter volunteered. "A fantastic book. But very deep." He paused. "Of course, when we fled Vienna it was something precious which I left behind. It would not do for me to carry such a book out under the noses of the Gestapo on the railway."

Rabbi Lubetkin passed the book to Peter. "I have read it through. Here. Take my copy. It is yours, Peter."

To this kindness, Peter responded bitterly, as though he could not see the depth of the rabbi's eyes. "You might as well keep it here. The Nazis will be in Warsaw soon enough, and then I will only have to run from them and leave the book behind to be burned once again."

The rabbi's kind smile did not waver, but the depth of those chocolate-brown eyes reflected pity. He replaced the book on the table and folded his hands placidly on his lap. So much for Halevi's book. "So," said the rabbi, "Rachel tells us that you had an idea about how to find the address where your mother and sister might be staying here in Warsaw."

"I have heard nothing back from my friend in Danzig. I hope she will write me, but—" He shrugged a who-knows shrug.

"And none of the leads I gave you helped?"

"Half of them left Warsaw during the time you were in prison. The other half had no information."

"I am sorry," Rebbe Lubetkin said. It was clear by his expression that he truly was sorry for a lot of unspoken things in Peter's life. "I hope you find your way."

"That is why I am here, Rabbi Lubetkin." Peter scooted forward until he sat on the very edge of his chair. His eyes lingered on the spine of the Halevi book. "I have decided that I will find my way. No matter what else happens, I am going to Palestine!"

"Mazel tov, Peter!" Aaron Lubetkin seemed not only pleased but surprised. "You have gotten your papers then? Some miracle?" Everyone in the entire district knew that Rabbi Lubetkin was trying to procure papers for his children to go to Rabbi Lebowitz in Jerusalem. Every door had been closed to them. Curiosity sparked in the rabbi's face.

"I have come to offer you some help," Peter said with confidence—almost arrogance. "Because you helped me, I return the favor. Yes?"

The rabbi looked at his folded hands. Useless hands, helpless to remove his own children from the danger of Warsaw. "What is your plan, Peter?"

"You know that the British Captain Samuel Orde is coming here soon. He will be teaching the young people of Hashomer Hatsoir."

This was the Zionist youth movement where boys and girls worked together being trained as potential emigrants to Palestine. There was no mention of God in such training. It was a political movement to Aaron Lubetkin's way of thinking. There was much about it that he and others among the Orthodox disapproved of.

"I am happy for you," the rabbi said. "You will spend time on the Hachsharah." He spoke of the farm outside Warsaw that was used for summer training. "Maybe they will feed you and you will put on a little muscle, nu?"

"I am not going to the Hachsharah," Peter corrected. "There will be no time for such things. When the captain comes here, there is a rumor—or maybe it is the truth—but anyway, it is something I have heard whispered by someone who should know."

"And what is this whispered word?"

"The captain is not coming only to work on a newspaper! We all wondered how a man of such renown could resign his commission. Now it is said that he never resigned! He has come here to hand pick a few who will return with him to Palestine! Like Gideon, he will choose only a few." He inhaled deeply and stared straight ahead. "I will be among them."

"Mazel tov," the rabbi said wryly. His bearded cheek twitched as if to suppress a smile. "You have gotten your letter of acceptance to this school of Gideon's soldiers?"

"You are making fun of me, Rabbi Lubetkin. But I have come to tell you what I know."

"What you *think* you know—"

"What I know about the mission of Captain Orde." No arguments would stop Peter. He had thought it all through. "This great military genius, this brave and stalwart Englishman . . . he happens to be a friend of your father-in-law, Rabbi Lebowitz in Jerusalem. True?"

"True."

"And he is coming here to take tea with you, I have heard."

"I have never heard of an Englishman who will refuse tea if offered."

"Well, then . . ." Peter paused. "Now that you know the real reason he is coming to Warsaw, I thought maybe it would be a good thing if you would ask him to help you get Rachel out."

"Rachel? My little bird? Why, yes, the captain has offered to intervene with British authorities. We expect him to bring us good news from London. But, only Rachel?"

"If you cannot get your visas," Peter pushed ahead, "here is the plan. She should join Hashomer Hatsoir today. Come with

330

me to a Zionist Youth meeting. That way when Captain Orde selects his few, no one will deny that Rachel should come with us to Palestine. You see? They will not say the captain is playing favorites, that he has chosen her over another girl or boy because she is the daughter of Rebbe Lubetkin and the granddaughter of Rabbi Lebowitz." He sat back and crossed his arms. "All fair, you see? Then over tea you can tell him she is a member, and that you wish her to go to Palestine."

Rabbi Lubetkin held up his finger to stop the flood of youthful excitement. "How did you think of all this?"

"I was thinking of her last night—" Peter blushed. "I mean . . . she handled herself bravely in the altercation between David and Mordechai. She is brave. And . . . worthy."

"And she has also taken an interest in your well-being." The rabbi did not speak of the fact that something about Peter made his daughter want to turn and run. "We have hoped you would find your way to your mother and sister. But Rachel is not the sort of girl for Hashomer Hatsoir." A soft smile. "She is betrothed to a young man named Reuven who lives in Lodz. The family would not—"

Peter leaped to his feet. "So what does it matter what his family thinks? Can't you see that there is no other way for us to get out of here now?"

"I am still praying for the visas. My children will go to be with their grandfather. In an Orthodox home. Not in the Hashomer to live on a kibbutz. You see, your way does not fit."

"You had better make my way fit, because pretty soon—" He picked up the Halevi book. "People who burn books, Rabbi Lubetkin, will also burn people. I have seen the wall of fire. It is not like the pillar of fire you say your God used against the Egyptians. No, this is a different kind of fire. It burns an impassable wall just at the border of Poland. I do not know what you will do with the rest of your children when it sweeps into Warsaw. But maybe you can help Rachel get out. Ask the captain about it!"

The boy's anger had receded into a hopeless desperation. By his tone, the rabbi knew that Peter Wallich cared for Rachel. *Hopeless.* Perhaps this outburst had been motivated by love, but even love was inappropriate in this instance.

Aaron Lubetkin tried to be gentle in his reply. But he did not let the boy hope for something so impossible. He simply nodded his head and said, "A good idea. We will see. Perhaps the captain will bring our travel documents with him, and then the problem will be solved."

24 Goodbyes Are Never Good

It was very early in the morning in the Red Lion House. Through the ceiling, Charles heard the groaning boards as Murphy got out of bed. Then the new baby cried a bit, and a second groaning of boards filtered down as Elisa got out of bed.

Other than that little bit of activity, the house and the world of London seemed very still this morning. Last night the sirens had wailed on and on, very late. Charles and Louis had finally gone to sleep in spite of the terrible sounds. But now everything was like a drowsy summer morning should be.

The scent of flowers drifted in from the roof garden and mingled with the rich aroma of coffee. Murphy always made coffee for Elisa in the morning. Charles liked the smell of the dark brew much better than that of tea. It was an aroma that reminded Charles of the long-ago days in Hamburg. The images were very distant, like a dream, but coffee brewing in the morning was something Charles remembered from that time when he and Louis had been with their mother and father.

Elisa opened the door a crack and called in, "Big day today, boys. You awake?"

Charles sat up slowly. "Big day?" Then he remembered that the last refugee children's ship was leaving Danzig this afternoon. There was shopping to do, Elisa had told them, and Charles and Louis could both help push baby Katie's pram through the market.

They did not leave for market immediately, however, even though Elisa usually liked to get vegetables before the day warmed them in the farmer's stalls.

This morning Charles and Louis pushed the new pram toward the little church at the opposite end of Red Lion Square. Murphy and Elisa held hands and walked slowly behind, as though they were just a family out for an early morning walk.

There was hardly any traffic. It was still too early for people to be going to work. This walk seemed unusual to Charles, but maybe babies, like vegetables, needed to be out in the early morning before the sun got high and wilted them.

The doors to the inside of the church were locked. But this did not seem to bother Murphy at all. He opened the gate of the churchyard and stepped aside, warning the boys that they must push the carriage carefully over the path between headstones, because it was rutted and they must not tip Katie out.

Then in a quiet voice, he said to Elisa, "The new area is over there." He gestured toward the newest headstones—shining marble without cracks. They did not lean or look as though they might crumble to dust.

"It does not matter when the date of death occurred," Elisa answered him. "Date of birth is what matters. I would think that something between 1919 and 1922 would do for him."

"That much range?"

"He was always such a big strapping child. His mother, Leona Kalner, said he outgrew his one-year clothes at six months."

And so this conversation went on as the happy family of five strolled leisurely through the cemetery of St. John the Evangelist Church.

Charles and Louis resisted the urge to roar along the path with the pram. They maintained a sedate pace as Elisa and Murphy peered down at names and dates of birth. Here was a date that was correct, but the name was a girl's name so it would not work. But Elisa wrote down the information anyway because she said it could be used for the Lubetkin girl in Warsaw.

At last, Murphy gave a happy exclamation. "Here it is! That Sam Orde is an absolute genius!" He explained. "Look! Look here! This is perfect."

Elisa stood at his side and frowned down at the tiny headstone of a baby boy.

WILLIAM HOWARD JOHNSON
BELOVED SON OF
HOWARD AND SUSAN JOHNSON
b. July 20, 1920
d. August 19, 1920

"Yes. It will work," Elisa said in a quiet voice. But her voice was not happy like Murphy's. She was seeing something besides the dates, and it made her sad.

Murphy scribbled down the names and dates. They began to walk back much faster now. Birds chirped above their heads. Elisa picked Katie up from the carriage once they were outside the churchyard and nuzzled her gently. Elisa looked as if she might cry, which seemed very strange indeed.

"What do we do now?" she asked Murphy.

"There is nothing to it." He tucked the paper into his pocket. He was smiling, looking around the square as the red omnibus stopped at the corner, then grumbled on its way. "I'll stop in at the birth registrar . . . No, better to just drop them a line, requesting a certified copy of the birth certificate. The department is down the hall from the death records. *Beautiful.* The right hand has no idea of what the left hand is doing. As far as birth records are concerned, William Howard Johnson is a big healthy nineteen-year-old Englishman. As far as passports are concerned, William Howard Johnson will be a big healthy Englishman about to take his first trip abroad."

"And Rachel Lubetkin?" Elisa looked at the name of the little girl who was about to lend her identity to someone in faraway Poland.

"Better have that birth certificate sent to your parents' address." Murphy frowned thoughtfully. "As a matter of fact, we should set up a number of different post boxes. That way the registrar will not be sending birth certificates to the same address." He grinned back over his shoulder toward the headstones in the sunlight. "A strange sort of resurrection, isn't it?" he muttered. "We'll have to be careful, but I think it can work."

———

Always before, Lori had acted the part of Mother to the Lost Boys. But this morning at the docks, Alfie could see that something had changed about her.

She made certain that each traveler had his identity tag properly tied to the center button of his shirt. Those tags matched the special travel permits and the luggage tags that were also properly attached. Very quietly, she spoke the names of Mark and Jamie and Alfie and gave them strict instructions about which line to stand in and how they absolutely must stay together so they were not separated.

But her attention was not really with the boys, Alfie noticed. Even as she spoke, she was looking mostly at Jacob. Touching his hand, leaning her head against his arm in between sentences. It was plain to see that Lori was not ready to be here. Her skin was very pale. Her blue eyes were bright with loving Jacob, with missing him terribly even before they were apart.

Jacob stood tall and very adult-looking in the suit he was wearing for the second day in a row. His hat was pulled down lower than usual over his forehead, making a shadow over his eyes. But Alfie could see all the same that Jacob was not ready for the parting, either. He looked at the ship. And then he looked so softly at Lori. He looked at the teeming crowds of children. Eight hundred tagged and ready. And then he looked at Lori. Her hair. Her hands. Her cheek. Her neck. His eyes wandered to a mother on the dock who cried and hugged her little girl goodbye. And then he looked back at Lori. He touched her hair without thinking about the fact that they were in the middle of hundreds of people. He breathed in so deeply that Alfie thought Jacob's lungs could not hold any more air. His eyes beneath the hat brim were sadder than any eyes Alfie had ever seen, except for the boys at the hospital. They all had eyes like that. Eyes that looked on and wished while other boys ran and played, eyes that lived in helpless bodies while minds were bright and *smart*.

Alfie saw all of this. It made his heart hurt for Jacob and for Lori. People with sad eyes like theirs hardly ever got well from whatever it was that made them sad, Alfie knew. He remembered what Herr Frankenmuth of Fresh Fish Daily had told him: *"Somebody is always being left behind these days."*

Only Werner-kitten seemed to be at peace in all this noise and confusion. Tucked into his secret compartment in the bottom of the valise, the kitten had not made even one peep since he had fallen asleep. Alfie thought it would have been easier if they had stuffed the Goldwasser down Lori and packed her away to sleep until England. As it was, she was barely holding on to her emotions. Everything was *right there*, on the edge, ready to break her into little pieces.

"John Murphy says you mustn't worry," Lori said above the din. "The fellow you are working for is here in Danzig right now. And do you remember where you are to meet him?"

Jacob nodded and pointed to the office of Hamburg-Amerika shipping just a few feet from where they were all standing.

"Don't worry." Jacob touched her lips with his finger. "I will be lost without you, even though I will not be lost."

The emotion came again, glistening in her eyes. She kissed his finger, nodded, then looked away. Children were already walking up the gangway. She did not want to see that, so she stooped to flip the luggage tags, making certain that they were all as they should be.

The line inched forward for the luggage examination. English officials from the ship stood beside Polish customs men. The checks were not very complete. Sometimes a bag was opened, but mostly the children and their tiny parcels were simply waved through. Not like Germany. Not at all. This is what the Danzig Gang was counting on. Most likely the bag containing Werner would be looked at briefly and passed over the table, and then Alfie would carry it up into the ship.

"Murphy says we will be together again by the fall." Lori's voice grew more desperate as the line moved up again. Jacob held her hand. Their fingers were twined together, like Alfie's hands when he prayed.

"In the meantime this job . . ." The whistle of the ship boomed the warning that there was only half an hour to cram all these children onto the boat! Jacob's words were lost beneath the bellow of the horn.

"You can go to school in London and work part time at the newspaper office," Lori said.

"And we'll get a little place of our own."

"And I will plant a garden. . . ." Every word brought them a step nearer to the luggage table. Beyond that, the gangway and the ship waited.

"It will be fine for us, Lori. Wait and see." He put his hands on her shoulders, his eyes skimming the side of her face.

"This may be something you really enjoy doing. And . . . it will be all right. A lot of people . . . newly married . . . are . . . they have to be apart awhile." Tears welled up. Her chin trembled as she spoke.

Jacob lowered his head and looked her in the eye. "Don't. Or I will cry." He bit his lip. She brushed away the tears.

Lori did not let herself cry because she did not want to do that to Jacob. It was a very brave thing. Yes, Alfie thought, very brave.

Then they reached the luggage intersection. The bags were

hefted onto the table, including Werner's secret hiding place.

"Well, what have we got?" the Polish inspector and the Englishman stood side by side. "Personal items?"

"Personal," Lori said in a very businesslike manner. "Clothing and such things as that."

The English inspector checked the luggage tags against the tags that were tied to their buttons. He took out his red pencil and began to check each bag.

At that moment Werner's bag let out the most mournful, terrible howl. The inspectors both jumped back and put their hands in the air. The yowl began again. Alfie knew they would find Werner now and not let him go, and he felt sick.

"Heavens!" exclaimed the Englishman. "What is in there?"

It was a most terrible calamity. All their bags were put to the side. They were told to stand over by the office, while others in line were checked right through. Werner continued his racket even then.

Jacob patted Alfie on the shoulder. "Sorry, old friend," he said. And Alfie knew that Jacob really was sorry. "We will have to let Werner out of the bag or they won't let you on the ship."

Alfie talked softly to Werner so he would not squirt out and run away when they opened his hiding place. Then Alfie lifted him out carefully. He was still drunk, Jacob said, but just awake enough to yell. So Alfie held Werner for the last time while they waited for the inspectors to come over and have a stern word with them. Alfie remembered how Lori did not cry, and so he did not either.

The line moved on. Two hundred remained. Lori and the boys would be last on board. Lori did not mind, she said. It gave her more time to spend beside Jacob. She drank him in, like Alfie drank the cool lemonade his mama had fixed on a hot day. That was a good way to think about how Lori and Jacob looked at each other. They were lemonade to each other on a hot day.

"You are an idiot!" Wolf glared at Hess and then looked at the gun in his hand with a careless disdain. "I had her here, and now you are letting her get away!" He gestured toward the window through which she had obviously escaped and the roof over which she had climbed.

Hess was unmoved by Wolf's pleas of innocence. "You

warned the Ibsen children to abandon their flat," Hess snarled. "You have now warned Lucy Strasburg to leave this place."

Wolf paced, and the barrel of Hess's gun paced with him. He ran his hands through his hair in the frustration of encountering this moronic obstacle that even now kept him from tracking Lucy down. "She could not have gotten far." Wolf's eyes flashed angrily. "And if you will work with me in this matter, we will bring her in and settle once and for all who helped her escape. I, for one, believe it was *you*, Major Hess. And I shall not hesitate to report that you held me at gunpoint while the object of a massive manhunt slipped away through the streets of Danzig unhindered!"

Hess and Ahlman exchanged glances. "You were here with her last night, Wolfgang." Hess's voice was high and whining with perverse amusement. He wanted nothing more than to see this haughty Prussian aristocrat brought to trial. And Hess himself would deal with Lucy Strasburg—without assistance from Wolfgang von Fritschauer.

Wolf exploded with rage. "Look at the blood, Herr Hess! Does this look like I embraced her as comrade and fellow conspirator?" He gestured at the dried stains on the sheets, the dark splatters on the wall.

With this, the first doubt struck Hess. Yes. There was blood. Had von Fritschauer beaten the woman? If so, why? Seconds ticked by as he considered the implications of such a thing. Wolf would have beaten her only if . . . *if she had somehow betrayed him*.

Hess did not reply. He kept the weapon leveled at Wolf's gut, yet that unspoken doubt shouted to Wolf that perhaps he was getting through. "So. You think I have something to do with the Karl Ibsen case? Or perhaps that I am one of the conspirators with Michael Wallich and Otto Wattenbarger? You believe this insanity, even though it was I who arrested *both men*?"

"Wattenbarger took cyanide in his cell," Hess persisted. "Who provided it to him?"

"Would I arrest him only to kill him before he gave us names?" Wolf mocked everything in the dossier. "Someone else in the department made it easy for Otto—not me. And the woman we are both after betrayed me, just as she betrayed you and the Fatherland. Your own failure in this matter has made you suspicious of someone who might help you!" He whirled around to face Hess and he stared into the clouded eye. He was close enough to snatch the gun from him, but he did not. "You are looking for the Ibsen children? And for Lucy? I will tell you where they will be." Wolf could clearly see that he had gotten through to Hess at last. "Today is the day of the last children's refugee transport to England. Or have you forgotten such a minor point as that?"

"I'll take care of Werner," Jacob said, thumping Alfie on the back. "Don't worry about that, Alfie."

Alfie was not worried. He was only sad. He cradled the kitten in his arms and stroked its head with his big finger. Werner breathed in and let every breath out with a low, unhappy growl. He looked very sick, even though Jacob said it was just the Goldwasser that had done this to him. Werner looked as sick as a cat could look, Alfie thought. He wished the kitten had stayed asleep in his hiding place.

Alfie looked at all the mothers kissing their children goodbye and it made his heart squeeze and his chest ache. He remembered how he had cried when Mama told him the Bible story about the mother of Moses putting her baby in a little boat and sending him away from the sword of the bad king. And now here were all these mothers, all these children. Their voices mixed together in one low groan. So many. So many. And certainly these mothers who were sending their children away felt even worse than Alfie, because they had their babies a lot longer than Alfie had Werner. And Werner was a kitten, not a human baby. Alfie felt terrible. It was hard to imagine how much worse these mothers and fathers felt seeing their babies walk up onto the ship.

Alfie had learned about goodbyes. There was nothing good about them.

Little faces peeked over the rail of the ship. Tearful eyes searched for familiar faces. Handkerchiefs fluttered at the tips of tiny hands. The air echoed with calls of *Mama! Mother! Mama! Mama!* And every woman there answered to that one name, as if no one had any other name but Mama and all the hearts became one huge broken heart. Hands raised up and hands reached down; love and sorrow bridged the gap between the children at the rail and the women on the dock.

But Alfie did not cry, even though he felt like it—for himself and for everyone else that day. He remembered how brave Jacob and Lori were and he did not cry.

Alfie turned to Jacob. "Will you write and tell me how Werner is?"

Jacob was touched by Alfie's question. "Sure. And you write me, too."

"I don't write so good," Alfie frowned.

"I'll help you," Lori said.

"I don't know where to write." Alfie noticed everyone else had addresses to write to.

"We will send our letters to TENS in Warsaw." Lori stroked Alfie's arm as tenderly as Alfie was stroking Werner's little head. "And Jacob will read your letters to Werner."

Well. That was something, anyway. *Letters*. But letters could not hug a kitten or a child.

He could not stand watching it anymore, so he turned and faced the other way. He looked at the giant loading cranes, at the crates and warehouses all along the waterfront. He looked at the dock workers, who were also standing with their arms crossed and watching the scene at the docks.

This was the last boat for children, Alfie knew. There would be no more after today. He thought of all the mothers who would like to put their children on such a ship and cry and wave farewell because they knew it would save their children. He remembered the long lines of mothers and children at the Jewish church in Berlin who had hoped they could get their little ones onto a ship like this. Not all of them made it, he knew. That was a different kind of sad.

And then he saw her.

Alfie recognized the woman right away, the same woman he had seen running through the fish market when he had taken Werner to eat at Herr Frankenmuth's Fresh Fish Daily. She had the same frightened look on her face then as she did now! On that day she had a baby in her stomach. But today, the lady held the baby in her arms.

She was standing in front of three people. One was the nurse from the ship, Alfie knew. The other two were men, both dressed like the other Englishmen who helped organize the children. The faces of the three were hopeless, wearing the kind of expressions that said they were sorry but they *could not* . . .

340

The woman held out the little bundle to the three. She begged them. Her face—such a sad and pretty face—seemed to have caught all the hurt from every heart on the dock that day. She looked over her shoulder. *Was someone still chasing her, like that day in the fish market?* Alfie remembered that she had been on the same train out of Germany. *Maybe she was being chased even on that night.*

Alfie looked where her eyes looked. He could not see anyone walking toward her. He could not find who was chasing her. Yet, like the mama of the baby named Moses, she was holding this brand-new baby out to three people who shook their heads and crossed their arms and would not take the baby no matter how she pleaded.

"Why don't they hold the baby?" Alfie asked out loud.

Lori asked Alfie if he had said something.

Alfie nodded. "Yes. Jacob," he asked politely, "would you hold Werner for a minute?"

Jacob took the kitten.

"Thanks," Alfie said. "I'll be right back."

They let him walk away. The toilets were just around the corner, and so no one thought anything about Alfie leaving just for a minute. He was glad no one followed.

He walked toward the woman and her baby and the three people with their arms crossed. Alfie stopped and watched and listened from the corner of the Hamburg-Amerika Line office.

"He is so small," the woman was crying. "You see? So small and helpless. *Oh, please!* He won't take up much room. And someone will want a baby. You see? Look how sweet, how beautiful . . . I have no place else to go. I am begging."

The nurse looked very sad. But she spoke first. "I have other things to attend to. You will handle this?" And then she left, hurrying back to her own table at the base of the gangway.

The two men looked at each other. Which one should do the talking? The short one shrugged and shook his head. "There is nothing we can do, madam." His German accent was very bad. "You see we are packing to the gills."

"But he is so tiny—"

"No room. One thousand children from the Continent. We have spent weeks choosing which children, documenting their need."

"But you see, this baby. . ." She lowered her voice until Alfie could barely hear her. "Nazis . . . take him . . . take my baby . . . raise him to be . . ."

The men glanced uneasily at each other and backed up a step. They put their hands out as though she were trying to hurt them instead of give them the bundle. Still, she begged. They backed up farther, shaking their heads. It was settled. No. They would not hold her baby, would not take the little one to safety.

Alfie frowned. Did they not know the story of Moses and the bad king and all the little ones who were killed by the soldiers? Could they not see that no mama made up such a thing, that only a very desperate mama wanted to give her baby away?

The men turned and walked away, each in a different direction, leaving the woman in the middle. She closed her eyes and held the baby close to her as she shook her head. Her lips still moved, but now she was not speaking to anyone. *Except maybe to God,* Alfie thought as he walked toward her. Her skin was very pale, like the delicate porcelain statues that Mama had kept on a special shelf so they would not get broken. This woman looked as if she might fall, as if she might break into pieces if she fell.

Alfie put out his hands to catch her. He did not think as he put his hands beneath her arms. She did not look at him as he guided her back through the crowds and the noise and helped her sit on a wooden crate.

Then he took the baby from her arms and sat down beside her. Did she notice? Her eyes were shut. Her hands were open on her lap.

Alfie looked at the baby that the others would not take. The baby, unlike its mother, was awake—wide awake, looking right up into Alfie's face and sucking on a little fist. Alfie's heart felt glad and sad at the same time when he smiled down at this very new human kitten. Such perfect hands. Fingers no bigger than . . . than what? Alfie had never seen such tiny little fingers before. The baby was squinting because the sun was so bright. Alfie held up his arm to shade it.

The woman still did not move. Alfie could see her face was bruised. Someone had hit her. He knew this because his own face had been bruised just the same way when the orderlies at the hospital had hit him. Alfie did not know if he should speak, because she seemed to be resting even though she was sitting up. But time was short. He looked at the baby. He put his finger out, and the tiny hand curled around it.

The ship's whistle blew. Fifteen minutes and everyone would have to be on board.

"You have a very nice baby, lady," Alfie said softly, as if he were waking someone up.

She opened her eyes and tears spilled out over the bruised place on her cheek. She looked at Alfie. Her eyes told him *thank you,* but she did not say anything. Maybe she could not talk anymore. Alfie knew about people who could not talk, because some of his best friends in the hospital could only talk with their eyes. But Alfie could see plainly what their souls were saying to him. Then he did most of the conversation, and they agreed.

"I saw you on the train to Danzig," Alfie said gently. "You were running from the Hitler-men."

She nodded. Only once. Her eyes lingered on the face of her child. *Such love.* Alfie saw it. He knew about that, too, even though people thought he did not.

"We ran away, too. We lived here in Danzig. And now they are letting us go to England."

She bit her lip and swallowed hard. Alfie could see that the woman wanted nothing in the world so much as for her baby to go to England.

"I saw you in the fish market when you were running," Alfie continued. "The Hitler-men are still chasing you?"

The nod said yes. The eyes said that they were very close behind her now, that they would hurt her and take the baby away. Alfie knew all of this in his heart, even though she did not speak it.

"They are not interested in me anymore, even though I am a Dummkopf. I am not in their country no more. So I do not think they will bother me."

At this, the woman looked surprised. Her face told Alfie that she did not think he was a Dummkopf, but a very kind gentleman to help her sit down and to take her baby in his arms until she could find the strength to hold him again.

And then her mouth opened and a voice croaked out, "What . . . is . . . your name?"

"Alfie Halder."

"Thank you, Alfie Halder. For helping." She was talking about helping her just for these few minutes because she knew there was no help beyond that very instant. It was all coming to an end for her, for this perfect little baby in Alfie's arms. There was no room on the ship. No room anywhere. She could not put this baby in his basket like the mother of Moses had done. The basket would not float. There was no one left to lift it from the water. The swords of the soldiers were drawn and the order had been given.

"What is the name of your baby?" he asked.

For just a moment he saw a twinge of something—*embarrassment?* Ah well, he understood. When someone has just had a baby and then had to run away, maybe there was not time to think about names. That was understandable. Names were things that needed lots of thinking.

"He hasn't a name yet," she whispered, and she looked at the baby's hand wrapped around Alfie's finger. "My name is Lucy."

"Lucy is a pretty name. Do you want to hold him again? The ship is leaving soon." He passed the baby back to her, although he hated giving up the feel of that little hand on his finger. His own fingers were so big and clumsy. He began to work on the tag that was tied around his button. Lori had knotted it so he would not lose it because, she explained, this was his ticket to get on the ship and get into England. It had his name on it and the official stamp saying that he was one of the specially chosen ones who got to leave this place and get away.

Alfie explained this to Lucy as he worked on the stubborn knot. Finally he jerked the button of his shirt off and held up the precious tag.

Lucy looked at him as if she did not know what he was up to. He held the tag for her to see clearly. "You see? There is my name. And I can spell it, too. *A-L-F-R-E-D H-A-L-D-E-R.* Except my friends call me Alfie. I am glad you like the name." He smiled big. He felt very glad inside for what he was doing.

The baby had a pretty blue gown on with little buttons down the front—very small buttons. Alfie chose the third button and began to tie the tag onto the baby's gown. What clumsy fingers!

"What are you doing?" Lucy asked in a frightened voice.

"There is not a lot of time to explain," Alfie answered. "Except I am going to stay behind with Jacob and Werner who they won't let go to England."

"But . . . your ticket . . . how—"

"There is no time to argue." Alfie had often heard Jacob say that when someone was wasting time. "We will call your baby

344

Alfie. Lori will carry him on the ship to England like you want, and he will be safe."

Then Alfie remembered a very important thing. *Writing!* Every mother needed letters written to her. "Do you . . . have a place . . . an address? So Lori can write to you for the baby and you will know?"

Lucy was crying now. Crying very quietly, but also quite a lot. She gave the baby back to Alfie and stumbled toward a wicker hamper that she had left out in the middle of the concrete. Sitting down beside Alfie, she began to search through the basket. Her hands were shaking terribly. Tears drummed down on the things in the basket. She pulled out a little green book and opened it; then she took out a slip of paper with writing on it. She copied down the writing in her book and gave the address to Alfie. "Here," she said. "If I make it I will be at this place in Warsaw."

"We are going there, too. We will work in a news office called TENS." He frowned toward the place where he knew everyone would be waiting and worried about him. "Now you should go so Lori won't want to give the baby back."

She gathered up a few little things from the basket. "Take this. Diapers. Canned milk . . . bottles. It is his." And then her face filled with the pain, like the face of every other woman on the dock. Lucy took the baby back and held him for a moment. "Oh, God! Dear God! Help me let him go! Take care of him for me!" She laid her cheek against his forehead, her hand over his heart. One final kiss. Desperation laid the baby back in the arms of big Alfie Halder.

He stood in front of her with the baby in his arms and the basket in his hand. "We will see you in Warsaw," he said. He was certain of this because he had seen her three times already. Three important times. And God did not make such things happen for no reason. He knew that in his deepest heart. "Now," he said in a grown-up voice. "If they are looking for you, go back to my friend in the fish market. Herr Frankenmuth. He said he would help. And he does not like Hitler. He puts fish guts on Hitler's face in the newspaper. He will help you, Lucy. Tell him Alfie and Werner said so."

She nodded, reached up and touched the baby one last time, and then Alfie turned from her and hurried away. Goodbyes were never good, and she had to go away quickly. He was sure of that.

25   The Loving Heart of Jesus

From the high platform of a cargo crane, Orde had a clear view of the entire Danzig wharf. He scanned the faces of the children who had already boarded the ship and then traced back the slowly moving line to the gangplank in search of Lori Ibsen and the boys.

His search was rewarded as he spotted the young people standing together in a worried little knot. They, too, seemed to be looking for someone.

The queue was growing shorter. Perhaps Lori would not board the ship until she had seen Jacob and Orde standing together. He started to climb down from his perch, when he noticed three men on the far end of the crowd. At first glance they were not there to see anyone off.

For a few seconds he traced their rough progress through the crush of people. At the point was a tall, aristocratic-looking man in a summer suit. His face was grim; his eyes never stopped moving. Behind him was a shorter, older man who pushed men and women from his path with a walking stick. The three fingers of his right hand were stiff beneath his gloves. *Gestapo*. Orde knew at once what he was seeing. The third man was young, probably not much older than Jacob Kalner. His brutish, muscular body seemed to enjoy shoving past those who were even remotely near him.

These three headed directly toward the line that shuffled toward the passenger gangway. They were moving toward the office where Jacob Kalner leaned down to gently kiss the lips of Lori Ibsen!

Orde clambered down the stairs and into the mob on the wharf. He had no illusions about whom the Gestapo agents were after.

The mother of baby Moses placed his basket into the water and then turned away, leaving her daughter to follow through the reeds to learn the fate of her son. But Lucy Strasburg could not turn away. She could not leave, as Alfie had warned her!

Lucy *had to know*! She had to see for herself what happened when Alfie presented the baby to his friends and told them what he had done. So Lucy followed along after him. She crouched behind crates, and peered through spaces between the cartons. She spotted a small group of young people who hailed Alfie and pointed to the last of the line moving up the gangway.

Lucy gritted her teeth as the grief of this distant parting tore through her. *There was the girl called Lori! Pretty. Fine-boned and delicate. A very young face. Seventeen, maybe eighteen years old.* Lori leveled her gaze on Alfie and scolded him with a look for being late and making them worry.

Lucy pressed her ear against the space and tried to hear her words, but the sound of a thousand other voices drowned out this one small drama.

Big Alfie was smiling happily as he stretched out his arms to present the baby to Lori. Lori's face registered disbelief, then outrage, then panic. She did not, *would not*, take the child. She shouted something at Alfie; then the ship's whistle exploded! Lori was shaking her head, denying that this could happen; refusing to accept the story that Alfie Halder explained patiently to her as he continued to hold the baby out to her.

Lori turned to a strong-looking young man for help. She clung to his arm, pleading for him to do something. The young man questioned Alfie, gestured as if to ask where the woman was who gave him the baby. Alfie shrugged. His smile did not diminish as he held up the tag on the baby's gown and then looked toward a little black-and-white kitten nestled in the arm of the young man.

Alfie shook his head slowly. *He was not going. He would not get on the ship!* Lori was ashen-faced, helpless. She could not grasp it! She, too, looked around through the mob. Lucy knew the girl was searching for her, that she would, indeed, give the baby back. Lucy fought the urge to run and snatch her baby from Alfie Halder's arms and find some other way. *Some other way!*

Looking from side to side along the wharf, she tried to think what she must do. This had been a terrible mistake! Several officials were gazing at the group of children, wondering what was going on. With a nervous glance, Lucy saw the nurse at her station checking papers. Would the woman recognize the baby that Lucy had begged her to take? Would she call out to the guards that a tiny imposter had stolen the identity of Alfie Halder and was trying to slip illegally into England? Would they come and take the baby away to the Danzig Foundling Home? *"Please! Oh, dear God!"* Lucy prayed. And then, at the far end of the tearful crowd, Lucy glimpsed the sunlight on the head and shoulders of someone who looked like— *It was Wolf!* Lucy did not take her eyes from him as he moved through the press of bodies. He searched faces; he scanned across the tops of heads in search of Lucy, *in search of the child he claimed for the Führer!* Two other men trailed behind him, heading directly toward where the little band of travelers stood together absorbed in pitched debate!

Lucy bit her hand in an effort not to cry out. She felt the blood drain from her face. The world and the sky spun in opposite directions. "Take him!" Lucy cried silently. "Take my baby! Before Wolf comes to you! Get on the ship! Go *now!*"

Alfie held up the baby. He nudged the tiny form against Lori's body. A fragile little arm raised from the bundle. It waved below the girl's face for a moment as if to beg. *Take me!*

Wolf seemed to see the hand. *How could he know?* He called to his companions as the horn bellowed one last warning! They looked at Wolf and then at one another; then the three merged and pushed people out of their path in a frantic rush toward Lori and the tiny infant.

And then, a miracle! Before the swell of the whistle faded, Lori reluctantly took the baby from the arms of still-smiling Alfie. The gentle young man with the mind of a child patted his namesake and then retrieved the baby's basket for Lori.

Two dockhands stood at the base of the gangway to move it from the ship. Big Alfie raised his hands and stumbled forward to stop them. He pointed at Lori. At the baby. At the two other frantic-looking little boys with her. Then Alfie took the kitten from the other young man who pulled Lori to him in a final, careful embrace. A kiss, loving and desperate, passed between the two. All the while, Lucy's child was held by both of them.

The nurse at the table asked to see their tags as Wolf led his companions closer to the edge of the crowd. A wall of grieving mothers, ten deep, kept them back. They struggled and raged in their places while this final embrace took place. Then Lori, holding Lucy's baby, backed up the gangway. She waved and called back to the young man who loved her. She touched the fingertips of her right hand to her lips.

Wolf leaned hard against the human barricade. No one seemed to notice his roughness. He lunged past a man and a woman who simply turned their heads to look around him as they waved up to a little boy at the rail.

Lucy willed Lori to hurry up the gangway! Could she not see the dark and menacing looks on the faces of the three men who struggled to reach her and tear the baby from her?

Halfway up, Lori stopped. She gripped the rail for support as though she might run back down. *"Run!"* Lucy cried as Wolf reached the inner perimeter and at last broke through.

At that moment, the little boys with Lori nudged her along, pulling her with them up to the safety of the ship. The three disappeared with baby Alfie through the arch of a doorway and then emerged an instant later to take their places among the others at the rail.

Wolf moved forward toward the two young men who still gazed up at Lori. Then another man stepped from the crowd. He stood just behind Alfie and faced Wolf and his companions.

Strong, muscular arms crossed over a barrel chest. His sunbrowned face was set, his eyes hard, yet he smiled at Wolf. It was the sort of smile that boys in the schoolyard smile before a fight. Lucy had not seen the stranger before this. She did not know where he came from, but now he stood as a tangible barrier between Wolf and the boys and the gangway where Lori had taken the baby. The newcomer looked British, Lucy thought, his sandy hair and mustache sun-bleached like that of a dock worker. He seemed unafraid of the odds of three to one. Perhaps he welcomed the chance to fight.

Wolf stopped mid-stride, pretending not to see the Englishman who had intervened with a look.

Lori and the others were not aware of the nearness of danger. Crouched behind her crate, Lucy watched the stand-off and wondered who the newcomer was.

Still the stranger grinned, daring Wolf to come near.

Wolf and his men also crossed their arms. They spoke quietly among themselves. *They were too late!*

Lucy could feel the air tremble from the power of their hatred. Their faces were set hard and ruthless against the young people who called out to one another in their grief. Wolf jerked his head, and the trio turned away from the unspoken challenge of the bodyguard at Alfie's back. For the moment it was over.

Lucy looked back to the bundle in Lori's arms. The final bellow of the ship's horn vibrated the air around her. Dock lines were cast away, and the first perceptible movement of the great liner caused the voices and shouts to grow even louder.

"Goodbye, Mama!"

"Don't forget to write!"

"Say your prayers!"

"I will think of you every hour!"

Lori reached her hand out over the slowly widening gulf. Alfie and his friend reached up as though they could touch her fingertips.

The bodyguard stood as a sentinel at their backs.

And in all the tumult the tiny hand of the baby reached up, fluttering for just one beautiful moment as if in poignant farewell to his mother.

No one else seemed to notice. Only Lucy, hiding at the edge of the water to see what fate awaited her child.

————

The massive brick spires of Danzig's Marienkirche receded in the distance, shrinking at last to tiny dark slivers against the late afternoon glare of the sky.

Lori sat beside Jamie on a thick mound of coiled rope and cradled newborn Alfie in her arms. A white crescent of sand framed the bright blue waters of the Bay of Danzig. Behind a thread of breakers, she could still make out the matchbox-size structure of the Kurhaus Casino and Hotel. The pier that had seemed to jut out so far into the bay was now only a dark stub of a pencil protruding from the land. Lori imagined children sitting with their mothers on the benches that looked out to sea. They would point at this black dot of a ship and wonder where it was going.

"We are going to England," Lori muttered in a joyless voice.

Jamie glared at her. "I know that." Her comment made him somehow indignant. Or perhaps he was just upset at the unhappy way events had unfolded today. "Who are you telling? The baby can't understand anything."

Lori could hear in Jamie's voice that her brother was angry at this helpless little one for taking the place of big Alfie. It was not what anyone had expected. Not what they had planned or prayed for.

She looked down into the face of innocence and knew that, given a choice, the mother of this baby would not have given him away. Lori held in her arms the most desperate evidence of love that could be demonstrated on earth. Here was love so strong that a mother had torn her heart out and sent it away, perhaps never to belong to her again.

Jamie scowled. "Alfie *is* a Dummkopf! Imagine, giving away his ticket to stay with a cat!"

Lori wanted to slap his face for uttering such blasphemy; she wanted to shake him and tell him to open his eyes! For months they had been living beside the purest heart, the wisest soul; yet Jamie still could not see what Alfie Halder was! But Lori did not hit Jamie. She did not scold him for thinking the obvious.

"Alfie knows much more than we give him credit for," Lori said as she touched the cheek of the infant. "He sees . . . things you and I do not see."

"Well, giving away a ticket to England is easy enough for any-one to do these days in Danzig," Jamie mocked. "Walk out on any street corner, hold up your ticket and your visa, and then watch out. A thousand people would mob you in thirty sec-onds." His eyes narrowed. He felt somehow betrayed. Jamie loved Alfie, and Alfie had chosen to stay behind. "Why would he do such a thing?" Jamie shook his head from side to side. "After all the trouble everyone went to get us here, and Jacob *wanting* to come, but Alfie gives his ticket to a complete stranger, and—"

Lori put a hand on Jamie's arm to stop the tirade. "Oh, Jamie, don't you see? *Alfie*—Alfie the Dummkopf, Alfie who was judged unworthy by the state to live, Alfie who can never be like other people—Alfie gave this little baby more than a ticket to En-gland." She held up the tag for Jamie to see again. "Alfie gave the baby *his* name. His *life*! All new and bright in the Promised Land to start over!" She frowned at the bigness of what she knew was true. "It was what Jesus would do, Jamie. You see? Our Alfie is closer to heaven's heart than anyone I know!" Jamie grew pale and silent, wanting her to help him understand. "Today Alfie was the answer to some woman's prayer."

"Right!" Jamie scoffed. "*Help me give my baby away!* Some prayer!"

"No," Lori said. "You are wrong." She opened the basket at her feet and took out a delicate satin gown wrapped in paper and labeled with these words:

TO WHOM IT MAY CONCERN: PLEASE PLACE MY BABY IN A HOME WHERE CHRIST IS KNOWN. THIS GOWN IS FOR THE CHRISTENING. I WILL THINK OF HIM DRESSED IN THIS AND HOLD THE THOUGHT IN MY HEART LIKE A MOTHER'S MEMORY. MAY YOU BE BLESSED FOR SEEING TO THIS SMALL REQUEST. I WILL PRAY FOR YOU WHEN I PRAY FOR MY CHILD. THANK YOU. LUCY STRASBURG.

Jamie read and reread the words. He swallowed hard. He looked away and then back at the baby. *So new!* What darkness there was in the world when mothers wrote such notes and shipped their babies over the oceans in little baskets! Jamie resented having to contemplate such heartache. "I wish I was a baby again," he said softly. "When I see Mama I'm going to climb up in her lap and lay my head against her shoulder and . . ." His eyes clouded with emotion. He looked hard at this motherless child. "Can I hold him awhile, Lori?"

She carefully passed the sleeping infant to Jamie, showing him how to support the head and the back as he took the new Alfie into his arms. And then for the first time all day, Jamie smiled. He knew for himself what Lori had been trying to explain, and his resentment melted away. "Alfie's *heart* is a genius, isn't it, Lori?"

She nodded, wishing only that she could have been near enough to have given her ticket away to this child's mother. Lori's own heart had remained behind. With Jacob.

———

At the Danzig train station, Alfie and Jacob took turns making Werner jump for pieces of bologna out of a stale sandwich. Captain Orde stared out at them from the little square windows of the red telephone booth. He was talking long distance to London, Alfie knew, explaining to Lori's mother why a baby named Alfie was coming to England instead of a big Alfie.

Alfie also knew that everyone was blaming the whole thing

on Werner because, as Captain Orde said, "The cat is a loud drunk, is he?"

This made Jacob laugh, and Alfie had laughed, too. Alfie decided that anyone who could make Jacob laugh on a day like today was worth liking. So Alfie liked Captain Orde. He even liked calling him *Captain*, because it made him feel as if he were in the army. A soldier, just like the little tin soldiers in his bag. It was exciting, and Alfie was very glad that he had decided to stay.

When Werner had eaten the last of the sandwich, Alfie looked all over the loading platforms to see if he could find Lucy. Captain Orde had told them about the three men who were coming after them, and Alfie had worried that maybe they had gotten Lucy. He was glad to know that the baby got away with Lori and Jamie and Mark. But he certainly was worried a lot about Lucy. He prayed for bright angels with swords to cover her. He also prayed that she would find Herr Frankenmuth of Fresh Fish Daily because sometimes he seemed like a gnarled-up old angel to Alfie. Herr Frankenmuth would see the bruises on her face and help her. If only she could find him.

The captain stepped out of the telephone booth and waved the phone at Jacob. "Come here, lad." He was smiling at Jacob. "Your *mother-in-law* wants a word with you."

Alfie laughed at the strange, nervous look that came over Jacob's face. Jacob looked very guilty at first; then as he walked up to the captain and took the phone, he straightened up and made a gruff and brave face.

But his voice was like a little boy. "Hello, uh . . . Frau Helen?" He shut the door behind him so that Alfie and the captain could not hear what he said. Captain Orde was enjoying the way Jacob was sweating and squirming in there, Alfie thought. It was fun to see Jacob look as if he had just knocked over a lamp in someone else's house.

Alfie picked up Werner and held him up to the glass pane of the booth so Jacob could see him. "Heh-heh, Jacob—" Alfie pretended that Werner was talking. "You should have thought about what Frau Helen would say before you married Lori! Heh-heh!"

Jacob was not amused. He put his big hand over the pane so Werner-kitten could not talk to him. The captain seemed very pleased by the whole thing. Jacob's face was very red, but when he slid the glass door open Alfie heard him say, "Give her a kiss for me. Tell her . . . I love her." And then as he hung up, his face seemed satisfied and relieved.

He looked straight past Alfie to the captain. "You warned them?"

Captain Orde nodded. "There will be an armed escort at the docks to meet the ship. Murphy says that his family is well protected. He was not surprised by the news, just surprised that they have just now caught up with you." The captain looked very serious. "If you had not been warned to leave your flat, well . . . things would not have turned out this nicely. Danzig is a powder keg." He looked toward some tough-looking young men at the entrance to the station. "And Herr Hitler has already lit the fuse. It is a good thing you contacted London when you did."

Jacob looked at Alfie, who pretended not to notice. "That was Alfie's idea, Captain Orde," he said quietly. "You'll see. Alfie *knows* things. Lori says angels speak to him."

Captain Orde did not make fun of Jacob. He put his hand on Alfie's shoulder and looked him straight in the eyes the way other people seldom did. "And a little child shall lead them," he whispered. Then in a louder voice he said, "Well, what shall we name you? You have given your name away. Who would you like to be?"

A slow smile spread across Alfie's face. This was probably the best thing anyone had ever said to him. "I gave my name to the baby," he repeated. "He will wear it good. He is a smart baby. I can tell."

Jacob joined in. "But now you have to pick a name! The name of a prophet, don't you think so, Captain Orde? Pick someone from a Sunday-school lesson, Alfie! Someone you like a lot."

Alfie frowned in deep thought. This was important stuff, the choosing of a name. He wished that he could have also spoken to Frau Helen on the telephone, because she had been his Sunday-school teacher and maybe she could help him.

"A prophet," Captain Orde said as the train whistle blew. "Exceptional idea. Very good."

It was a simple choice after Alfie ran all the stories through his mind. He did not want to be Jonah, because Alfie had seen the inside of fish bellies at Herr Frankenmuth's Fresh Fish Daily. The smell was most unpleasant. It would not be fun to be burped up by a fish.

He likewise did not want to be Jeremiah because the king's men had put him down a muddy well and left him for a long time. For a moment, Alfie considered Daniel; then he remembered how bad it felt when Werner nicked him with his little claws. A lion's den would be a scary place to spend the night.

There were others who had done good things, but Alfie did not especially like their names.

He smiled and held up Werner-kitten. Werner's mother had thought her baby kitten was dead, hadn't she? She had pushed tiny Werner with her nose and looked at Alfie for help. Then Alfie had worked and worked on Werner until his little kitten ribs had heaved up and down.

In a way it was like the story of Elisha, Alfie thought. Elisha was a good-hearted sort of prophet who did the same thing for a little boy that Alfie had done for the kitten. He had brought the boy back to life and given him back to his happy mother.

Alfie very much liked stories with such happy endings. It made him think of seeing his own mother alive in heaven. It made him imagine hugs and sitting together in the park to feed the ducks on the banks of the Spree River.

"Well?" Jacob asked impatiently. "What do we call you, Alfie? Now that you have given your name away."

"I like Elisha a lot. He was a very nice man. He watched his friend Elijah ride to heaven in a chariot with fiery horses. That is a good story too," he frowned. "And then Elisha did even better things than Elijah."

"Ha!" the captain exclaimed, as if the choice pleased him very much. Then he added, *"And as Elijah and Elisha were walking along and talking together, suddenly a chariot of fire and horses of fire appeared and separated the two of them. And Elijah went up in a whirlwind. Elisha saw this and cried out, My father! My father! The chariots and horsemen of Israel!"*

Jacob seemed surprised at the way this English captain could quote scripture as easily as Pastor Ibsen. But Alfie . . . or Elisha . . . was not at all surprised. "I like this," Alfie cried, thinking of his little tin soldiers on fiery horses that could fly through the air. "I like this a lot!"

Jacob looked doubtful. "An unusual name. This will take some getting used to." He looked mildly unhappy, as if maybe this was not such a good idea after all.

"A perfectly good name," said the captain.

Jacob disagreed. "You couldn't pick something simple. Like Daniel? or Samuel?"

"Samuel is taken," said the captain. "That is my name."

The announcement was made calling for passenger boarding on the Warsaw Express train.

"Elisha." Alfie repeated it slowly. He wanted to make sure.

"Come on, then," said the captain, putting an arm around Alfie's shoulder the way Alfie's papa used to do. "I will tell you the story of how I stood on the very spot where Elijah was taken to heaven in a whirlwind! The exact place where the fiery horses rode between Elijah and Elisha!"

"You were *there*? Did you get to see the horses?" This was better than anything, Alfie thought.

"Only the hoofprints on the rocks," the captain said as Jacob looked at him suspiciously.

Alfie walked toward the great locomotive and imagined smoke rising up from the chariots. He decided that he loved the English captain very much. He was more happy than ever that he gave Lucy's little son his ticket and his name.

"A clever woman, your Fräulein Strasburg." Hess rubbed his sightless eye as he appraised Wolf.

"Clever, ja, Agent Hess. You learned that on the train to Danzig, did you not? But she is not my Fräulein."

"Somehow I have come to believe you in this matter," Hess said in a patronizing tone, like a schoolmaster reluctant to discipline a tardy pupil. "My assistant, Gustav Ahlman—" He swept a hand toward the empty place where Ahlman would soon sit. "He has followed you everywhere in Danzig. To the priests. And to the maternity wards." He smiled as Wolf squirmed beneath his knowledge. "So. You made her pregnant and she ran out on you. She made a fool of you, did she not?"

Wolf inclined his head like a puppy who was watching his master thoughtfully. "She and Peter Wallich also made a fool of you, Agent Hess." He flicked his fingers toward Hess's right hand, where the leather glove covered places where the fingers should have been. He stared hard at the gray film across Hess's eye. "At least she only wounded my dignity. And that, only as an insect might irritate a horse."

"We have one thing in common, von Fritschauer. The woman

has made fools of both of us, ja? Perhaps such commonalities are the stuff great bonds are made from." He smiled at the thought that there could be any bond at all between him and this haughty Prussian aristocrat. "For some time I suspected that you were part of the escape of Peter Wallich and Fräulein Strasburg. The boy described you as a great friend. A brother and ally, really."

Wolf snorted at the thought. "But now you know the truth."

"Yes. Peter Wallich is also a clever boy, is he not?"

"I met him only once," Wolf said slowly, remembering the night he and Lucy had gone to Otto Wattenbarger's flat in Vienna. Lucy had argued with him about whether the Walliches were Jews or, in fact, relatives of Otto Wattenbarger. All along she must have known the truth and bought them time by convincing Wolf to delay his arrest. Clever. Yes. And as for the boy? He had spoken of wanting to be an S.S. officer like Wolf. He had admired the belt buckle of his uniform and the inscription engraved on every S.S. dagger. And all the time the Jew had been laughing up his sleeve at Wolf. Lucy had been laughing as well. The memory brought a fresh rush of anger to Wolf. He clenched his fists and stared out at the traffic rushing below the Deutscher Hof.

"I have no doubt that you will be given opportunity to deal appropriately with these clever people." Hess looked at his watch impatiently. Why was Gustav Ahlman not back? They had a plane to catch to London, after all. They had been on the Danzig wharf to see the Ibsen children off, and they would be there to greet them when they stepped off the ship tomorrow in England.

"She was not at the ship as I supposed," Wolf remarked darkly. "By now she could be anywhere."

Hess raised a finger to correct him. "But if the infant in the arms of Lori Ibsen was in fact the child of Fräulein Strasburg, well . . . there is no bond as strong as motherhood. Unless it is the bond of two fools who do not wish the rest of the world to know what fools they are." He shrugged. "Why did you not simply kill her?"

"I wanted to clear my name, wanted her to confess that I had nothing to do with her plots in Vienna," he blurted out. It was plain that he wished he had killed her. It would have been much simpler.

"I have already sent a wire to that effect to Berlin. In it I have stated that you carried out your duties here in an exemplary way." He grinned again at the surprise on Wolf's face. "So you see, I am not such a bad fellow. We must keep in touch, you and I. If the child is hers, some word will come from her sooner or later. And I know where to find the Ibsen family. As a matter of fact, I read the intelligence report from London on Monday, giving me the name of the man who was with the two boys at the docks."

Wolf leaned forward. "You have his name? But how?"

"He is Samuel Orde, a former army officer—now a journalist scheduled to begin work in Warsaw. This is of little importance to me, since I am going to England. Probably it makes no difference to your case, either." He spread his gloved hand as if to show he was giving Wolf everything. "I tell you this only to let you know that there is nothing which happens in London that does not find its way back to me. And if Fräulein Strasburg should attempt to make contact with the Ibsens in England, I will forward that on to you."

Gustav Ahlman appeared, interrupting Wolf's speech of cold gratitude in which he spoke of the comradeship of the Aryan soul. *It is just as well,* Hess thought. Such speeches bored him terribly.

Ahlman stood breathless in the center of the hotel room. "It is just as you predicted!" He directed his exuberant admiration to Hess alone. "The man and two boys got on the Warsaw Express train."

"Did anyone else approach them?" Hess queried.

"No one. But I was close enough to hear. The man placed a trunk call to London. He closed the door of the booth as I neared and shut out his conversation from me." Ahlman pulled a rumpled letter from his pocket. "I went back to her apartment, as you instructed. I broke open her letter box, and—" He passed the envelope to Hess with a broad smile. He had saved the best for last.

The envelope was addressed in a childish handwriting to Fräulein Lucy Strasburg. There was no return address on the outside, but the postmark was from the main post office in Warsaw.

Hess tore it open carefully, his three missing fingers causing some awkwardness. Wolf stared at him impatiently, then leaned

358

forward with interest as Hess removed a single sheet of note-book paper.

Hess looked at it a moment, squinted in the dim light, then passed it to Wolf. "My vision is poor for reading. You will read it out loud."

A muscle in Wolf's cheek twitched as he read the words:

My dear Friend,

I have managed to arrive in Warsaw. That is the only thing that has gone as I expected. A clumsy oaf on the train spilled coffee on me, soaking my clothes and rendering the address of my destination undecipherable. I have managed to find my way to the Muranow Square Community Soup Kitchen for meals. I may use that address as a temporary mailbox, they tell me. I still have not found my dear mother or Marlene. I pray that you have not discarded the Warsaw address that I wrote out for you if you should decide to come and join me here. How fortunate it is that I left a copy there in Danzig with you. Perhaps I am not altogether lost. Only delayed.

Please send the address to me quickly. Or, if you have finally come to your senses and wish to have a safe haven for your baby, come join me here soon.

I think of you fondly and hope all is well with your baby.

A friend always,
Peter Wallich

Wolf scanned the note again as Hess clapped his hands together in deep satisfaction. He rose. "You have done well for us, Gustav." Then he bowed slightly to Wolf. "Peter Wallich. Delivered into our hands."

Wolf folded the note carefully. It was so easy! "Perhaps Providence has had pity on two fools, Agent Hess."

"There can be no doubt. Eventually Lucy will find her way to Peter Wallich. Or he to her." He gestured toward the still-grinning Gustav Ahlman. "I will need Gustav in London. My legs are not strong enough to run after children. However, there are several agents already in Warsaw who have been looking into various matters concerning fugitives who have fled the Reich. I will send a wire. Reichsführer Himmler has put an entire force at my disposal in this matter." He raised his hand like a priest reciting a blessing. "Peter Wallich has blazed our trail to Lucy, has he not? And every scrap of information that I receive in London will be immediately relayed to you." He indicated that Ahlman should make a note. "Your address?"

"Europejski Hotel. Warsaw."

"A fine establishment." Hess approved of his choice. "And I, in London, take more modest lodgings. In the Bloomsbury District, 107 Gower Street. Mills University Hotel."

Providence may have had pity on two fools, thought Hess as he watched Wolfgang von Fritschauer leave, *but I am no fool.*

He telephoned Berlin immediately and expressed his suspicion about Wolf. He was sending Gustav Ahlman to Warsaw to keep an eye on every movement of the Prussian officer. "He has allowed Lucy Strasburg to escape," Hess told Reichsführer Himmler with certainty. "And he thinks he is free simply to walk away. It is best if we let him do a little work on our behalf before we bring him in."

At that, Hess was ordered to stop in Berlin for a few hours before he continued on to London. A memorandum regarding this case had fired the imagination of the Führer. There were a few details to discuss in regard to timing the demonstration for the greatest effect against the arrogance of England.

Adolf Hitler had spent the day touring Germany's West Wall, the massive concrete structure that was the Reich's answer to the French Maginot Line. He praised the engineers and decorated several for conspicuous contributions to the Thousand-Year Reich. The Führer called the engineers "soldiers who fight with their intellects, but are no less brave because of that."

Hitler was in a jovial mood when he retired to his quarters for the night. The Siegfried Line was an impressive array of fortresses. Much propaganda mileage would be gained by focusing the attention of the democracies on the extreme defensive measures Germany was being forced to take. Goebbels' broadcasts would see to it that the British pacifist movement had plenty of ammunition (Hitler chuckled to himself at the play on words) with which to accuse the British government of pushing for a showdown against poor, abused Germany.

Hitler, Joseph Goebbels, and Gestapo Chief Himmler were meeting to review the slant in the program Goebbels was preparing. "Not only can we show the world to what great lengths we will go defensively," observed Goebbels, "but it will be well received by our own citizens to be reminded how well protected they are, and how invulnerable Germany's border is."

Hitler held up his hand in a familiar gesture that meant *Silence, I've thought of something.* Goebbels raised his eyebrows expectantly, and in a moment Hitler spoke.

"Invulnerable. Yes, that's it. Goebbels, you have reminded me of a dream I had last night."

The propaganda chief knew that Hitler put great stock in dreams and omens. "Something to do with the West Wall, mein Führer?" he asked.

"No," corrected Hitler, "about England. The British are so smugly superior because they feel secure on their tiny island. This quality allows them to meddle so confidently in the affairs of others. In my dream, I saw that smugness shattered as their invulnerability went up in flames! Stone monuments crashed down on the heads of the sanctimonious Britishers. Yes, I'm sure that's it!"

"But it cannot be an attack linked to us," protested Goebbels as he saw where this conversation was leading. "That would undo all our efforts to keep the appeasers in power."

"Not us directly," agreed Hitler, placing his hand on a concrete pillar as if testing its strength. "Himmler—" He beckoned to the bookish head of security. "Isn't it true that the IRA bombing campaign is going well?"

"Quite well, mein Führer. The Irish have successfully detonated over a hundred devices and disrupted transportation and communication."

"You see, Goebbels," said Hitler, "it need not be us who remind the British of the need to put their own house in order."

"Did you have a vision of a specific target?" questioned Himmler, since this operation would clearly fall into his domain.

Hitler closed his eyes and covered them with both hands. He stood that way long enough for Himmler and Goebbels to exchange a glance; then he replied.

"I see a dramatic moment when a revered British institution, a part of their cherished history, crashes to the ground. A bridge perhaps, or a famous building. And—" He held up an instructive finger. "If it should happen to fall on a political opponent of ours—if Mr. Winston Churchill, say, should have the misfortune to be killed—why, we would not shed many tears, would we, Goebbels?"

26 The Last Fortress of a Broken Heart

Herr Frankenmuth had made a bed for Lucy on the canvas tarp that lay in the bow of the twenty-foot fishing boat. She looked up at the myriad of stars passing overhead as the craft chugged against the slow current of the Vistula River. The thrumming of the small gas engine could not drown out the high whir of a million crickets that serenaded their passing from the riverbanks. A soft breeze carried the scent of new-mown hay from the broad green fields of the Polish countryside. Lucy scarcely smelled the heavy aroma of iced fish packed in crates for transport to the Polish markets.

The river cut through the heart of Poland on its lazy journey from Warsaw to Danzig and the Baltic Sea. Its summer mists were cool against Lucy's fevered skin. Several times, Herr Frankenmuth left the helm and came forward to touch her forehead with his rough hand.

"When we reach Warsaw," he promised, "you must see a doctor. I have friends there."

Lucy thanked him quietly. She had little strength left for more than that one word. She stared up at the spray of crystalline stars and considered the miracle of her escape aboard the fish monger's boat.

Twice a week Herr Frankenmuth and his son traveled the river from Danzig to Warsaw. Had Alfie remembered that small detail? she wondered. How had he known that at the mention of Alfie Halder and Werner, the fishseller would look at her bruised face and know somehow that she needed help?

When the refugee ship had gone, Lucy had stumbled into the marketplace and found the stall just as Alfie said she would. She had managed to mutter Alfie's name and then Herr Frankenmuth had gently guided her to a cot behind the stall, where she had collapsed and slept until evening.

He fed her supper as she told him only the barest details of what had happened to her—how she had met Alfie and given up the child. "And somehow I must get to Warsaw," she breathed the request.

And now the request was being granted. It seemed as though some other hand had guided Lucy, first to Alfie Halder and from him to Herr Frankenmuth.

It was a long journey up the Vistula to the Warsaw fish market, but the old man promised her that she would be out of reach of anyone who might harm her. As if to emphasize that assurance, he pulled a loaded shotgun out from between two crates of mackerel. The port of Danzig was crammed full of Nazi agents, he explained with a grin. And if it came to war, he would simply load and shoot into the blackshirted mob like shooting into a bait tank. Such a gun as this could drop an entire swarm of S.S. vermin, he claimed. He patted the stock of the ancient weapon and then patted Lucy on her arm. If a German battleship entered the harbor of Danzig, Herr Frankenmuth explained that he was well armed and ready to withdraw upriver to the fortress of Warsaw.

"The Nazis will never be in Warsaw," he declared. "There are a million and a half Polish soldiers and millions more just like me who will fight them if they try it." He swept his hand along the dark shadows of the riverbank. "In the daylight you can see Polish guns guarding the Vistula. This is our highway, and I tell you, the Nazis will not pass over it." He replaced his aging weapon in its hiding place. "You will be safe in Warsaw behind a wall of Polish gentlemen." Then, as an afterthought, he explained, "This German name of ours comes from a great-grandfather." He thumped his chest. "But we are Poles as sure as anything."

Lucy managed a smile of gratitude in reply. But she could not help wondering if all of Poland was equipped with such ancient guns. Pride and the courage to fight would mean nothing against new German tanks and modern aircraft. Lucy had heard Wolf say it a hundred times. She had listened while he laughed at the ill-equipped cavalry of Poland; while he had scoffed at the thought of Polish biplanes in combat against the new Heinkels being turned off the German assembly line.

She was too weary to think about it now. Perhaps all of Warsaw was safe from the designs of the Führer, perhaps not. All that mattered to Lucy was that her baby was safe. She was traveling to Warsaw so that there would be an address for her, a place where a letter might come to her from England with news about the child.

She raised her head slightly to look as the bright headlight of the express train to Warsaw washed over the berm beside the river.

"Look there," said Herr Frankenmuth proudly. "You can see our Polish guns along the tracks."

The old man was right. An artillery piece that had been new when Herr Frankenmuth was young now resumed its duty as a rusty sentinel between rail line and river. The silhouettes of soldiers waved up at the lighted windows of the passenger cars. Uniforms, helmets, and guns all seemed unchanged from photographs Lucy had seen of the Great War. A picket line of horses stamped and snorted a protest against the noise of the train.

Lucy laid her head down against the rough canvas and closed her eyes. It was not enough—horses and ancient artillery beside a river were nothing compared to what she had seen at every corner in the Reich. Tonight Lucy had no illusions about the security of great nations. Probably Warsaw was not the fortress that Herr Frankenmuth imagined it to be. But for the moment, none of that mattered to her. There was only one thing she cared about for herself now, that a letter would come for her in Warsaw and she would *know* where her baby was. She would hold it to her heart and imagine that the hand which had written it had just touched her child. That was all. That was enough. It was the last fortress for her broken heart.

———

Alfie Halder and Jacob Kalner slept soundly as the express train to Warsaw rattled over the rails. The black-and-white kitten that had disrupted the best-laid plans now curled peacefully on the lap of Samuel Orde.

The lights from the train reflected in the dark waters of the Vistula River. Houses and tiny villages huddled at the river's edge. Lanterns of ships and small boats glowed like fireflies in the night.

How peaceful the night is! Orde thought as he stroked the kitten. And yet, a Polish soldier had been shot and killed today on the frontier between Poland and Germany. Tonight, in answer to that, Warsaw had mobilized all Polish troops, moving their Army into the forward positions facing the Reich. Orde spotted evidence of this troop movement on the unpaved roads of the Polish countryside. He had noted the horse-drawn carts among outdated vehicles in the columns. What he knew about the German divisions on the opposite side of that unfortified border made him shudder inside.

Orde knew that Poland could not afford to remain mobilized for long. Unlike Germany, which directed every resource toward remaining on a war footing, Poland's Army was not equipped for months of standing on guard against aggressions.

What Orde had witnessed in Danzig convinced him that war here was inevitable. Certainly it must come before the first rains of autumn made the primitive highways of Poland impassable.

"September," he whispered, turning his gaze on his peacefully sleeping charges. He would have to find a way out for these boys and the Lubetkin family by then, or it would be too late. The fate of Poland would be their fate.

In the end it was not a coded report from a clandestine agent that caused Adolf Hitler to make up his mind. Nor was it a newspaper account of doings in Parliament that decided Hitler on his action against Winston Churchill.

Dr. Schmidt had been reading to the Führer from *The New York Times*. It was innocuous stuff—FDR's calm reassurances to some Chamber of Commerce about how the European situation would not damage the U.S. economic recovery. Roosevelt agreed with the businessmen's resolution that Americans should maintain strict neutrality, not getting entangled in foreign affairs that were of no concern to the U.S.

Hitler was relaxed and jovial, nodding pleasantly as he made a circuit of the great room at Berchtesgaden with its magnificent views of Alpine scenery. In Dr. Schmidt's view, it was the purest of bad fortune that Hitler's wanderings about the room took him past the hewn oak coffee table at the precise moment when Schmidt turned to page six of the first section.

There, opening directly under the Führer's gaze as if brought to his attention by some sinister force, was the abhorrent face of Winston Churchill. Hitler stopped in his tracks. He stared down at the page and his breath surged audibly through his nostrils.

It was an advertisement for an upcoming issue of *Collier's* magazine. With Churchill prominently displayed as the cover photo, the caption read: "HITLER IS ON THE RUN—THE INSIDE STORY FROM THE MAN WHO HAS BEEN WATCHING HIM SINCE 1933."

"Since 1933!" exclaimed the Führer. "Yes! In my way, hounding me, barking at me! But no longer . . . not one moment longer!"

Hitler practically ran to the telephone that stood on a small mahogany table in the corner of the room. "Himmler!" he demanded of the operator. "No, I'll wait!" His tone suggested that his wait had better not be a long one.

Dr. Schmidt heard the moment when Himmler must have come on the line. "No questions," ordered Hitler. "Commence Operation Edifice at once, exactly as planned."

———

Suddenly bread crumbs were not enough. As the hungry chirping of naked chicks filled the cell, mother and father sparrow embarked on a frenzy of journeys to and from the nest. They always carried morsels of food in their beaks, which they crammed into the wide-open throats of their offspring.

Four baby birds, as near as Karl could figure, maybe five. He could not see them, but he could hear them in their endless demand for nourishment. The bits of Karl's black bread were reserved for the adult sparrows, even though they no longer seemed to notice the meal Karl placed for them on the window ledge.

Caring for their children had driven every thought of self from their tiny minds. This fact made Karl smile to himself. Sparrows were not so unlike humans, after all, were they?

When moments of doubt and worry over the fate of Jamie and Lori came to Karl, he only had to look up at the sparrows laboring over their little ones. If the God who watched sparrows was aware of how the little birds loved their babies, then the God who loved him certainly understood the times when Karl Ibsen grieved for his own children.

And like the sparrows, Karl was prone to neglect nourishing his own soul when he worried so much about the nourishment of his children.

Today, once again, his feathered guests preached a sermon to him. "The Lord pities us as a father pities his children." If such a thing was true, then no doubt the Spirit of the living God hovered over Karl and Jamie and Lori. Like the sparrows, the Lord carried nourishment to them. He spread His wings to cover them and shield them from the danger that even now surrounded them.

Outside the window of his cell these days, the endless drone of aircraft could be heard skimming the tops of the trees, prowling along the border of Poland. Karl knew what this meant. He was certain of what was coming. The sky would not be safe for baby sparrows to learn to fly. The earth would not be safe for human children to walk to school. There was nothing he could do now to change that fact.

———

It was the last refugee children's transport ship. The last miracle. *The last chance!* Some said that it was easier for those who left than for the mothers who were left behind. After all, they reasoned, the children had a whole new world to learn about and exciting things to experience. The mothers, on the other hand, turned their faces from the last glimpse of the ship and returned to face empty rooms, scuffed little shoes left in the closet, a much-loved toy left behind.

And just beyond the horizon, the wall of fire loomed higher and brighter and swept ever nearer. Could those mothers dare to hope that they would ever see their little ones again?

A full twenty-four hours had passed since that last embrace. The ship arrived at Southampton. It was nothing like the arrival of a busload of children at summer camp. No smiles. No cheers. No little hands raised in greeting. Anxious, homesick faces looked down at the beginning of a new life. Anxious, hopeful adult faces looked back up at them from the quay. A small group of musicians played the bright music of Mozart. The music was nice. It was something familiar in this unfamiliar world.

Here and there among the waiting crowd, uncles and aunts, old family friends who had left Germany *in time*, called up to children whom they had not seen in years. Those children were considered the lucky ones by their companions. At least someone *knew* them, yes? This distant connection was better than nothing.

Exuberant joy, the tearful happy reunion of a mother with her two children was a miracle not expected on the docks of Southampton. Such a sight might have broken the little hearts who had no more mama to hold them; no more papa to lift them up and carry them away on top of broad shoulders.

For this reason, Helen Ibsen waited for her children in the privacy of a cluttered shipping office. She sat very still between Anna and Elisa while one thousand immigrant children were sorted between those who had *someone* and those who had *no one*. It was a lengthy process; an hour and a half that seemed as long and as terrible as all the months which had gone before. All the while doubts and fear hovered close and black in the little room.

When at last the door groaned open, Helen's heart hung in her throat. The grim face of a balding clergyman appeared.

"Mrs. Ibsen," he said in a soft voice. A sad and sympathetic voice. "We have a bit of a situation here. Something concerning one of the boys."

Helen, Elisa, and Anna stood together. They grasped each other's hands. As if their blood supply was linked, they grew pale at the same moment.

And then the clergyman stepped aside.

First Jamie ran to the arms of his mother with a shout! Then Mark entered—poor Mark, no mama among the three women. Had he guessed the fate of his mother and father? He looked hopefully at Anna and Elisa. He had been hoping for a surprise; hoping that his mother would be here. Like a gift that was expected, but not received, the absence of Mark's mother caused him to burst into tears. Helen reached out for him; pulled him close. She ran her fingers through his hair and touched the tears on his cheeks just as she did her own son.

And then came Lori, cradling the baby in her arms. Her eyes were red from crying. She looked exhausted from the ordeal of walking among so many little broken hearts.

She hung back, hesitant to run to her mother. Almost shyly she greeted Anna and Elisa. Four men and women wearing official identification tags crowded in behind Lori, interrupting the reunion with nervous coughs and uneasy looks.

"Mama?" Lori asked and then, she, too, fell into her mother's embrace.

It was well known and discussed openly among the older children on the refugee ship that in many cases infants were to be placed in British homes for permanent adoption.

Lori kept this in mind as she faced off with the tribunal of the immigration committee who questioned her about why this tiny baby was given Alfred Halder's identity when the records showed that Alfred Halder was quite a bit older, indeed.

When it was discussed that the infant should be placed immediately into the home of a loving British couple who had been longing for a newborn child, Lori wept with all the sincerity of that long-ago mother who stood before King Solomon to plead for the life of her baby.

She would not let anyone lay a hand on the baby. She claimed that the child was her own; that she and Jacob Kalner had conceived it in New Church, and that she had given birth to it prior to their hasty marriage.

Then, as a final touch, she presented her copy (one of two) of the certificate of legal and holy matrimony. It was dated, signed, and sealed by Pastor Douglass of the English Mariner's Church in Danzig.

A very shocking affair, indeed! The grandchild of the famous Pastor Karl Ibsen had been born out of wedlock! These words were whispered in urgent, barely audible voices by the committee.

However, they believed the story and enjoyed repeating it immensely in the coming days. The baby was allowed to stay with Lori. Papers were adjusted and the accounting showed that there was nothing irregular here as far as the correct number of children who passed through the line. One thousand ordered. One thousand delivered. And that was the end of that.

Even though Helen Ibsen knew the truth behind the story Lori had told, she did not mention it as she rode back to London with her arms around Lori. She cuddled the baby. She praised God for such a beautiful miracle as this!

Then Lori explained everything to Anna and Elisa and her mother. She told them how dear Alfie Halder had given his place to the baby—his life to save this life! She showed them the christening gown and the silver crucifix at the bottom of the basket. She laid the note before these women, *her family*; and they read it and wept for Lucy and circled around Lucy's baby like a herd of mother buffaloes protecting a calf!

Elisa knew as she held little Katie in her arms that the woman who had written such a note had love as strong as iron! Should the baby of Lucy Strasburg be given away and adopted and never be seen by her again?

Elisa, Anna, and Helen agreed with Lori. There was no arguing with the wisdom of Solomon that the mother who loved the child enough to give it up must be the woman who should ultimately raise the child.

Elisa decided that she had milk enough for two. Room enough for two. Clothes which she had not yet returned from baby showers intended for a baby boy. Lori would come and live with the Murphys and help out. And all of them together would begin to pray for Lucy Strasburg, whoever she was and whatever kind of trouble she was in that had driven her to such desperation. God paid wise attention to such prayers, Anna said, as she held the tiny baby boy in her arms.

And then, as if to shout His approval, the Lord himself saved a remarkable surprise for the last.

"She gave this address to Alfie." Lori took the torn page from her pocket. "She said she wants to know that the baby is well. She would like it if we could write."

Lori gave the paper to Elisa, who read the name and gasped and grew very pale. "Where did you. . . ? Where did she. . . ? *This name!* Lori? Can this be right?"

Anna took it from Elisa. She clamped her hand over her mouth and blinked in wonder at the hastily scrawled name and address.

FRÄULEIN LUCY STRASBURG %RUDOLF DORBRANSKY
2334 NISKA STREET APARTMENT 3A
WARSAW, POLAND

Rudy Dorbransky was dead, of course. He had died in Vienna, paid the ultimate penalty for moving Jewish children beyond the reach of the Reich. Elisa knew his family remained in Warsaw after Rudy had been killed. Somehow, seeing his name at this moment was a reminder of all that had gone on before; a verification that perhaps the children who had arrived on this *last ship* to the West *must not be the last!*

The train cars of Elisa's nightmares had been peopled with children guarded by Nazis and all had been headed *east!* *To Warsaw?* The children had dissolved into heaps of bones before her terrified eyes. But now, perhaps that dream had a different meaning than Elisa had imagined.

By carefully picking the identities of children long dead, they might give the children of Elisa's nightmares another chance at life. Alfie had given his own precious papers to this baby. It was the clearest sign to Elisa that they must not abandon hope of turning those eastbound trains back toward life and freedom!

———

The public house known as Lamb's Tavern looked out over the pleasant, tree-studded Red Lion Square. From the corner window overlooking Lamb's Conduit Road, the house of Elisa and John Murphy was in full view.

In this convenient perch, Alexander Hess and Allan Farrell shared a plain English midday meal of blandly flavored roast, mixed vegetables and cheese with a pint of Newcastle Brown Ale for each.

Hess inhaled the yeasty aroma of the dark brown ale. It reminded him of the smell of fresh baked bread. Although he carried the credentials identifying himself as a wine merchant, Hess would not touch the stuff. When quality schnapps was unavailable, there was nothing quite so welcoming as a glass of good beer.

It had been a hectic few days, but now everything seemed to be heading for a satisfactory conclusion. He relaxed, sipped his beer and listened as Allan Farrell filled him in on the progression of events that had occurred inside the Red Lion House.

"They were due home"—Farrel checked his watch—"over an hour ago."

It did not matter. Hess ordered another pint of Newcastle's. All the work and worry had been done in Danzig; now it was simply a matter of watching and waiting for the right moment. He was unconcerned by the late arrival of the Ibsen children. They would come. Helen Ibsen would be there. Anna Lindheim. Theo Lindheim was home on leave for the occasion. John and Elisa Murphy.

A scholarly-looking man holding the hands of two towheaded boys swung around the far corner.

Farrell leaned forward and whispered urgently. "There he is. That is Grogan."

"And the children?" Hess asked, picking at his vegetables.

"German refugee brats. Being adopted by the Murphy family. Grogan uses them as a cover."

"Sensible," Hess remarked. "Who could suspect a man of

371

anything sinister if he has won the hearts of children, eh?" Then he looked again at the harmlessness of the man's physical appearance.

Farrell smiled slightly and looked down at his hands. Who would look at Allan Farrell and imagine that he was any threat at all? And yet, he had turned England on its head. "His looks are deceiving," Farrell said in a matter-of-fact tone.

Hess watched Grogan and the boys stand and chat for a moment in the sunlight. Grogan leaned down and said something to one of the two children. Then he mussed the boy's hair affectionately and followed them up the stairs and into the upper story of the tall old house. At the top of the steps, Grogan turned around and swept the square with his eyes. Satisfied, he disappeared into the house.

"Very good," Hess remarked. "But any man who knows would spot him as an agent. He has *the look*, you know. Like a very dull sentence with an exclamation mark at the end. It labels him like a sign."

"Murphy has a bodyguard, of course. An ex-prize fighter named Freddie Frutschy. You cannot miss him. He is not a young man, but he will be like the Maginot Line. Something to go around. Or over. You will not get through him, however. His wife is as protective as a hen. She squawks, but we shall wring her neck."

Hess smiled his old, patient smile. "When the time is right." Hess patted Farrell's arm. "You new fellows. Everything must be done yesterday." Hess shook his head. "We have opportunity here to change history if we do not rush. Yes? You must not forget which English statesman is the object of our mutual concern, the enemy of your people as well as mine, yes?"

"Churchill." Allan's eyes narrowed in unspoken hatred of the man. "He is responsible for the legislation against us. Thousands of Irish have left England."

"But not Irish Americans." Hess swallowed the last bit of ale. He was feeling very relaxed. "And that is the beauty of it. One of the reasons you have been so tremendously successful. Your work has not gone unnoticed. You may have heard the Führer's speech? We are all struggling against the same thing, are we not? The oppression of our respective races."

Allan's eyes flashed a moment of resentment. "No one has joined me in my struggle until now. I have gone it alone."

372

Hess laughed. "I assure you, your memorandum was personally approved by the Chancellor. You see, it is all a matter of timing. Perfect, impeccable timing. Surely you know about such things. The fuse must be lit at the right moment, you see. Now we are laying the groundwork together." His eyes flitted toward the heavy, old-fashioned black car that pulled to the curb in front of the Red Lion House.

Dressed in the summer uniform of a chauffeur, Freddie Frutschy got out and opened the door of the vehicle. A large man indeed. Formidable in a close situation. But perhaps he could be taken out at a distance. No doubt he carried a weapon and knew how to use it.

Out of the back compartment appeared faces that Hess knew well: Helen Ibsen. Lori Ibsen. James Ibsen. A dark-headed child of no importance. Then Anna Lindheim and Elisa Murphy, who was holding an infant.

Hess frowned as Grogan came out on the landing to greet them. The two blond boys flanked him and shouted their welcome. Grogan looked out over the square again. His eyes brushed over the corner window of Lamb's Tavern without stopping.

With the proper timing, Operation Edifice could be accomplished to the complete and total satisfaction of the Führer. Hess would watch, he would wait and listen, and then at the precise moment the fuse was lit in Poland, London would hear the deafening roar of the explosion in its own streets.

Rachel pretended not to notice the boys of Peter Wallich's little Zionist Youth brigade as they marched by with broomsticks over their shoulders.

Herr Menkes, the baker, came out from behind the counter. He dusted his powdered hands on his powdered apron and watched the *right, left, right, left* progress of the group. They did not march with the stiff-legged arrogance of the Nazis or the pomp of the Poles. This was the purposeful stride of the British soldier. Their arms swung in time, their broomstick rifles poised on their shoulders for action!

They were secretly called the Broomstick Brigade by the younger boys who were jealous and not allowed to drill with them. The oldest of the troop was nineteen. The youngest fourteen. There was a waiting list for those who wanted to join up.

Peter Wallich shouted his commands in English and was rewarded with precision responses from his soldiers.

"Why do you watch them?" Rachel asked irritably. Her purchase was left on the rack as the baker looked on with a big smile.

"They are quite good," said the baker with pride. "Look at the way the feet rise up and come down all together. An unusual accomplishment, for Jews to walk in step, nu?"

"Let the Germans march in step," she said scornfully. "And the Poles. Let them beat each other's brains out, and then maybe we Jews will have peace."

Menkes paid no attention to this clever daughter of the rabbi. "It is good for our boys. Good discipline."

"Why does Peter Wallich shout his orders in English?" she demanded. "No one speaks English in that whole bunch, but he calls out and they lift their sticks this way and that as though they understand."

Menkes watched them all the way to the base of the clock tower. They stood in straight rows while Peter walked up and down and pretended to inspect uniforms. Of course, there were no uniforms. Only ragged shirts tucked more neatly than usual into ragged trousers.

"I have spoken at length with this young mavin, Peter Wallich. He has good reasoning on the subject. He says that when the Germans attack Poland, the English will come in to fight against the Nazis. Now, everyone knows that the Poles do not think much of us Jews." He paused as the next command was given and the group whirled around in one splendid movement. "The Poles will not want us fighting with them, you see, but—" He held up a finger. "Since the Englishman is coming to visit, some say that the British government has sent him to train our boys."

"He is not a soldier anymore. England was unhappy because Captain Orde too much favored the Jews in Palestine. He was sent away because of that."

Menkes scoffed. "Just what they *want* the Germans to think. Just what they want the Mufti to think! England is not so foolish that they would turn out one of their best officers! Captain Orde saved the pipeline in Galilee and trained our fellows there to fight the Arab gangs! Would England punish him for such success?"

Rachel blinked in a puzzled way. It did not make sense. "But that was what my grandfather wrote us from Jerusalem."

"Well, I tell you, Peter Wallich has it figured out! So do some of the other people around here! This is just a *decoy*! The English want him to train our fellows to join them when they rush to the aid of Poland, you see? That is why Peter trains his boys in English. When the British come, the Poles will not know a British *right* from *left*." Menkes had learned the words by watching the daily parade through the square. "But *we* will know. We can fight with them right here in Warsaw."

"I don't think there will be a war," Rachel said. Maybe she did think there would be a war, but she did not want to think about it. "Everything will get worked out. All this is for nothing."

"We can hope." Menkes went back to his work. "It is a nice summer activity for them, anyway," he added paternally. "And if they don't fight here, maybe they can go to Palestine. Captain Orde, they say, plans to return and become the general of the Zionist Army one day."

"Quite an ambition for a Gentile," Rachel remarked dryly. "Especially since the newest British policy says there will not be a Jewish homeland and *nobody* can get into Palestine anymore. Not even us. I don't want to go anyway," she added. "Warsaw does not have buildings blowing up or Arabs slaughtering helpless settlers. Everyone is just all excited about this and that, and none of it means anything. They just want to march in step and beat their drums."

Menkes packaged the sugared rolls apart from the golden brown loaf of challah. "We can hope, nu?" he said, but his voice did not sound hopeful.

Rachel left the bakery feeling particularly irritated at Peter Wallich for parading around Muranow Square. There were Zionist Youth camps out in the countryside for such nonsense. Why did he have to show off right here? Who wanted to listen to the tramping of feet outside the window for hours at a time? *Unpleasant.* And David and Samuel were unhappy because they were not old enough for his little soldier games.

More terrible than all of that was the strange effect it had on Papa! He sat by the window and asked Rachel if perhaps *she* would not like to join the Zionist Youth movement?

"There are plenty of girls . . ." he had said in an off-handed way. It was as if he had lost his mind. *Those* girls were not from religious families, certainly not from the family of Rabbi Aaron Lubetkin!

She was indignant and she let him know by raising her nose slightly and becoming very silent. *Those* girls, she told Mama later, held hands with boys in public and smoked and even passed for Polish. Assimilationists! They were trying to forget who they were. Rachel asked Mama to ask Papa not to bring such a thing up because it was upsetting. She would not fit. She did not want to fit. Her life was here in Muranow Square with Mama and Papa and the boys until she was old enough to marry. She did not like to think of the world turned upside down. She did not like to think about the great Captain Samuel Orde coming into their home. He was an honored friend of Grandfather Lebowitz, perhaps, but he was also partly what inspired all this marching and saluting and looking so grim.

She wished it were last year. Or maybe the year before. Things had been even better the year before those years. Nobody thought about anything but who was getting married and who was being born and who was sick or who had gotten well. Nobody was running away from Warsaw. People weren't coming to Warsaw who had no business being here!

Rachel entered through the kitchen door. She could hear the voice of Father Kopecky in the other room. He was talking very quietly to Papa and Mama, but Rachel could hear every word.

"Not a pleasant thought," Papa said.

"Must be realistic," Mama added. "There is not a mother here who would not wish to send her child if it comes to that."

"The Nazis will be much harder on Jews than on ordinary Poles. I have compiled a list of a few trustworthy people in the church who will be willing. Small babies. Not yet speaking. Girls will be easier for us to manage. You should know that there are still a few good people willing to take them in."

"But the Polish Army?"

The priest did not sound hopeful. "Provided England and France come in on our side in time. But now it looks as though we may also have the Russians allied with the Nazis. If that is the case, men who know say that Germany will cut through Poland like butter, and England and France will wait on the sidelines. There is too much at stake not to have this little plan. Of course it involves only a handful of children. But . . . it is something."

Rachel had heard enough. She turned around and slammed the door loud as though she had just come in. Silence dropped like a curtain. Then Mama called, "Rachel? Is that you?"

She tried to sound cheerful. "Yes." She did not feel cheerful. She felt afraid. Why couldn't life just be ordinary again? Why must they think only of this? Why must they talk about Jewish mothers giving their babies away?

"Are you all right?" Mama heard it in her voice. Rachel was not all right.

"I have a headache," Rachel said. "Too much sun. *Too much* . . ."

27   Preparing the Way

Passport photos for Jacob Kalner and Alfie Halder arrived among a sheaf of photographs showing the Polish Army parading toward their frontiers with Germany. Harvey Terrill opened the envelope to scan through the material, his critical eye evaluating what could be cropped to fit in a number of different places in the paper.

He dumped the discarded photos in a basket and then presented the pictures of Jacob and Alfie to Murphy.

"Passport pictures?" he asked Murphy.

Murphy attempted to brush off the photographs as routine. "Just mug shots of the kids with Orde in Warsaw."

Terrill tossed another handful on the desk. A man, dark and very Jewish-looking. A pretty woman in her late thirties. Two little boys with very close-cut hair and serious eyes. "How about these?" he asked wryly. "Also employees?"

"I dunno. I'll ask him. He didn't send captions?"

"No. Nor immigration applications, either."

Murphy shrugged it off, scooted the mound of pictures to the side and pretended to be distracted by other things. He would warn Orde to send the photographs to Murphy's personal attention. There was no getting around the fact that Terrill had the cynical mind and the nose of a journalist. No use arousing his curiosity.

Twenty minutes later, Terrill was still smiling as if he had a secret. Smiles were rare on Terrill's face, and somehow Murphy liked him better sour.

Word came from the London agent soon after Wolf settled into his hotel in downtown Warsaw. A follow-up note from the Berlin office explained that the name of Lucy's Warsaw host was the father of the notorious Vienna resister, Rudolf Dorbransky.

Could there be any question left of her guilt? Any doubt that Lucy had been closely allied with the ring of anti-Nazis in Austria?

The Führer had been apprised of this, and was most anxious, therefore, that Wolf apprehend Lucy Strasburg and bring her back to Berlin.

At this news, Wolf had frowned. Hess had said it would be simpler just to eliminate her, but orders from the Führer were orders. Every traitor to the Führer and the Reich must be exposed. No doubt she knew much, Himmler wrote. Hitler believed completely that an appropriate interrogation of this woman would lead to an entire ring of disloyal army officers. With the plans in place for Case White against Poland, it seemed imperative that those traitors be rooted out.

At such a command, something stirred uneasily in Wolf. Certainly he was not still suspected? Had his association with Lucy Strasburg put his own life in jeopardy?

That possibility filled him with a fresh sense of anger toward her. He should have killed her in Danzig, and then there would not be this question remaining in anyone's mind.

He pressed the ammunition clip into place in his pistol and held his fingers out before his face to watch them tremble. Wolf was afraid. No doubt they were watching him even more closely now from the heights of Berlin's citadels of power. Nothing could go wrong this time in Warsaw.

"Why should it?" he reasoned aloud, staring down at the Dorbransky address. He had her cornered. It should be a simple matter of scooping her up.

The Bristol Hotel in Warsaw was the gathering place, a home-away-from-home for most of the English-speaking journalists assigned to cover the present chaotic politics of Poland. Not far from the government offices and the Royal Palace, motorcades containing every variety of diplomat streamed by. On the first day after Orde's arrival with the boys, the French foreign minister whisked past the uninterested residents of Warsaw. He met with the Polish foreign minister, Józef Beck, to urge Poland to *try a little harder* in negotiations with the German government.

Two hours after the French vehicle passed, Orde stood on the roof of the Bristol and reported the motorcade "live" to London through Polski Radio.

Murphy sent a telegram of congratulations. He did not guess that the French and Polish officials had already uttered frosty farewells.

On the second afternoon, a representative of the government of the Soviet Union also passed by. Polish policemen on horses lined the avenue in case there were demonstrations of any kind. They need not have bothered. Orde stood at his microphone and reported that spectators simply had not come.

He did not mention the one elderly man walking his dog. The mutt lifted his leg on the rear tire of the Russian limousine parked outside the great baroque government palace. Nor did Orde report that not one Polish policeman attempted to interfere with man or beast on this solemn occasion.

On the third day, there was a demonstration of a different sort. An emissary of the Pope arrived in Warsaw, and the square was packed curb to curb with cheering Poles. Now this was worth reporting! The Pope had sent a spokesman to plead for peace and restraint in this border dispute with Herr Hitler. The bells of the cathedrals rang out welcome.

Orde had to shout into the microphone to be heard above the tumult. Blue-coated policemen linked hands to restrain the crowds. What the French and the Russians and the British could not accomplish in Polish corridors of diplomacy, perhaps the prayers of the Pope could.

What passed between the Vatican spokesman and the Polish foreign minister was not reported. Later, a Mass was held at St. John's. The overflow crowd filled the streets for ten blocks around the cathedral.

The cardinal prayed for peace. The people prayed for peace.

No doubt the Polish foreign minister prayed for peace right along with them.

That night there was a shooting incident at the border. Three Polish soldiers were killed by Germans. The frontier between Poland and Czechoslovakia was closed. The spokesman of the Pope went home, and another million Polish military reservists were ordered to report for duty.

All of this was dutifully discussed and reported by the Western journalists. The rumble of motorized and horse-drawn equipment echoed throughout Warsaw where the bells of St. John's had sounded.

It was decided by those exalted members of the press who had never seen military duty that this war would begin at dawn. *Wars were supposed to begin at dawn, weren't they?* A pool was formed for taking bets on the exact hour of the first shots. Then another pool for choosing the exact date, *and* the time of day! This was an American idea. For one buck a pop, the reporter who guessed the closest would win the entire jackpot.

The hat and the calendar were passed.

Orde looked at the hat full of money and IOU's. He looked at the list of guesses. Then he stood up and excused himself from the proceedings.

"Hey, where'ya goin', Orde?" called a fairly soused journalist from McCormick News in Chicago. "Come on, what's yer guess? When's the Blitzkrieg going to begin?"

Orde checked his watch and waved. "There's a new movie playing at the English theater. I'm treating my crew. So sorry."

"Whatcha say? Dawn? *What time is dawn?* This one gonna start at *dawn,* Orde?"

Orde continued to smile pleasantly, although making a game out of something so deadly and inevitable made him feel angered and sickened.

He had his opinion. He kept it to himself. He hoped he still had time enough to keep a promise to an old rabbi and, if he was lucky, to the Zionist Youth of Warsaw.

Upstairs in the hotel room, as Werner played with his shoelaces, Orde placed a telephone call to the home of Rabbi Aaron Lubetkin. In careful Yiddish he explained that he had been asked by Rabbi Lebowitz of Jerusalem to pay a call when he reached Warsaw. *Would Monday be acceptable?*

The voice was that of a young woman. She replied with polite dignity, but just before the receiver clattered into its cradle, he heard her shouting, *"MAMA! He's here in Warsaw!"*

Warsaw is lousy with Jews, thought Wolf as the taxi rolled to a stop in front of the Niska Street apartment building where Lucy imagined she was safe.

"Wait here," Wolf ordered in clear, unaccented Polish. His dialect was that of an aristocratic Pole. He managed to fit in quite well in *Gentile* Warsaw. But here in the Jewish District heads turned as he walked into the shabby foyer of the building.

He did not give the concierge time to ask his business or call ahead to warn the occupants of apartment 3A. Taking the steps two at a time, he reached the third floor before the antique elevator would have made it up one level.

Wolf fingered the gun in his pocket and fixed a smile on his face as he knocked on the chipped blue paint of the door.

"Who is it?" a woman's voice called through the thin wood panel.

"A friend," Wolf replied. He did not ask himself if the Jewess within would wonder who among their friends spoke with such refined accent. Indeed, her curiosity got the better of her. After a moment of hesitation, the door opened slightly. A chain was in place, intended to keep strangers out. She was not worried as she peered out at him.

"Who are you?" she asked. Her thin, serious face was still unafraid.

"I told you," Wolf lied. "I was a friend of Rudy Dorbransky in Vienna. The *younger* Dorbransky, I mean. Rudy was a great violinist. He spoke often of his family here in Warsaw. I thought I should look you up and—"

"They don't live here anymore," the woman replied quietly, but she did not slam the door on the handsome face of Wolf. She continued to look at him as if she hated to disappoint him.

"Oh yes." Wolf read the address aloud. He checked the number on the door. "This is the address."

"I am sorry." And she was. "But the Dorbransky family left some months ago."

"They are surely still in Warsaw?" Should he believe her? Behind her two small children chattered and played house.

"No. Not Warsaw." She looked skyward as though she could

not remember. One of the children knocked something over with a clatter. She scolded in Yiddish, then turned back to Wolf in an embarrassed manner.

His smile was frozen on his face. He felt she was lying, and yet, he did not yet want to force the issue or the door. "You have a forwarding address?"

She shrugged. "No. Nothing. Some letters have come for them, but we send them back." She was reluctant to end the conversation, and yet . . . was there something behind that gaunt, mousy face?

"Why don't you open the door?" Wolf asked. "Maybe we can think of who might know how I can find my friends. I have come a long way."

The woman blushed. "My husband is not at home. I cannot . . . and I cannot help you in any way. We are from Cracow ourselves, you see. We were just very lucky to find this flat empty. They were just leaving. They sold us the furniture." She gestured at the furniture that Wolf could not see and shrugged. The children shouted and laughed, and at that moment, when she decided she was quite through, Wolf decided he was just beginning.

He braced his foot in the door as she attempted to close it. "Who was with Rudy's family?" He retained a pretense of friendliness even as he forced the door to remain open against the woman's wishes.

"I . . . please . . . don't remember. They were just leaving."

"A red-haired woman was with them, perhaps?" He remembered Peter Wallich's desperate note about his mother. This was the very place where Karin Wallich had fled from Vienna, Wolf sensed. And why not? It was Lucy's last refuge as well.

"Yes! A red-haired woman! A little girl! Also Viennese." She repeated this news with the hope that he would now go away.

Instead, powered by the awareness that Lucy also had this address, he shoved hard against the door, pulling the chain loose with a snap. The woman opened her mouth as if to scream. Wolf waved his weapon in front of her face and shook his head in a warning that she must remain silent.

The place was as thin on charm as the woman trembling before him. One severe square table and four chairs sat in the center of the room. A bookshelf stood against the wall. A few elegant pieces of porcelain sat upon the shelves as a stark reminder of how far these people must have fallen in society. The children played on, oblivious that anything was wrong.

"Where is Lucy?" Wolf asked with a smile, as if this was some sort of elaborate joke. Her joke on him? Or his on her?

Confusion mingled with terror in her eyes. "Lucy?"

Again he waved the gun beneath her nose. "You think I will not use this?"

"Please! Sir! I don't know anyone by that name! We are from Cracow! From Cracow, you see? They sold us the furniture and went away. I don't know where they went! No one named Lucy has come here!"

The fear was genuine. Wolf backed up a step in the tiny space that passed for the main room. He nudged open the bedroom door with the heel of his hand and then looked from the empty bed toward the rack that served as a closet. The bed was made up. From this one fact, he was satisfied that perhaps this living broomstick was telling him the truth.

At that, he pocketed the weapon, looked once more around the shabbiness of the flat and straightened his fingers for a small, unspoken Nazi salute. The woman did not recognize the gesture, Wolf knew, but soon enough it would be common in Warsaw. Perhaps then she would remember the man who entered her flat uninvited and know that the visit had been only a small foretaste of what was about to come upon the Jews of Warsaw.

Wolf could hear her crying as he descended the steps of the flat. He imagined what she would tell her husband when the man got home. Then he hurried to his hotel room to telephone Heinrich Himmler at Gestapo headquarters in Berlin with the news that the London agent had sent inaccurate information. Lucy was not there. But sooner or later, he knew she would contact the people in London who had the child. It was a matter of patience, Wolf told them. Of course, patience was not a virtue he possessed himself. He only asked that it be extended to him in this difficult situation.

Wolf apprised Berlin of his plans. He had Peter Wallich's address. He did not doubt that Lucy would eventually be in contact with the boy, he assured Himmler. When that moment came, Wolf would be on hand to arrest them both and bring them back to the Reich for the trial which the Führer desired so urgently.

The fact that Lucy Strasburg was not where the London agent

said she would be was not Wolf's fault, was it? It certainly did not mean that she was not in Warsaw and within the reach of Nazi justice.

Wolf sensed that the impatience of Himmler was placated by his assurances. He only hoped that the Führer could also be soothed in the meantime.

"Six months' rent in advance," said the Polish landlord as Wolfgang von Fritschauer counted out the bills without argument. "And if you would like to pay for twelve months, of course there will be an additional discount."

"Six months will be sufficient," Wolf replied. The discount did not interest him as much as the location of the apartment.

Kowalski was a typical Polish landlord. Physically fat and soft, the man was nonetheless hard and shrewd in his dealings. He did not care what reason Wolf had for renting an upstairs flat on the corner of Niska Street and Muranow Square. The affairs of the tall, iron-jawed young man did not matter as long as the rent was paid. But Kowalski was *curious*!

Why should a well-groomed, well-educated businessman like *this* wish to rent a flat in the Jewish District of Warsaw? Certainly it was possible that the fellow had some business transactions with the Jews. Such a thing was quite common in Warsaw. After all, Kowalski conducted matters of a financial nature with the Jews on a daily basis. He owned several buildings in the Jewish District that were leased to the Jews. But Kowalski made the Jews come to his office in downtown Warsaw. He did not have an office anywhere near the noisy, medieval world in which they lived.

Well, then, was the business of this gentleman of a personal nature, perhaps? *A Jewish mistress?* At first Kowalski thought this was a logical explanation. Jewish women were known for their beauty. Polish wives were jealous. Polish men often discussed the desirability of the Jewesses. It was well known that certain members of the Polish nobility kept Jewish mistresses. Their fiery temperaments and lack of care for the proprieties of the church, it was said, made them excellent distractions for wealthy Poles. The joke was that a gentleman did not have to worry about his mistress making confession to his personal parish priest if she was Jewish. Such reasoning made sense, did it not?

But why would this fellow set his mistress up in the most religious sector of Jewish Warsaw? The Orthodox Jews had their own standards of moral behavior. They did not like their women running around with Polish men. In such an area, a Jewish mistress would have difficulty walking down the street without being reviled. Shops would be closed to her. Life would be unbearable.

This fellow could not have rented the flat for the keeping of a courtesan.

What was left, then?

Kowalski leaped to the only conclusion. Everyone knew that the Jewish District was a nest of Bolshevik dissension. The Polish government always worried about the Jews making plans with the Russians. Kowalski himself worried about such things. After all, if Poland was taken over by the Communists, he would lose his apartment buildings. The Jews would form collectives and take over everything Kowalski owned. They would not pay him rent anymore. He would be poor—as poor as the people who now rented from him.

"You are a government man, are you not?" Kowalski asked.

Wolf looked up sharply. "I would not tell you if I was."

That reply was as good as a yes. "You are going to be keeping an eye on the Jews?"

A slight smile. "That is not your business, as long as I pay the rent."

Kowalski felt pleased. He had figured it out. "As I told you. A very prominent apartment. You can see the whole of Muranow Square all the way to the Community Center. There are so many Jews coming and going these days. Terrible times. We must be careful of the Jews or they will feed Poland to the Russian bear, eh, my friend?"

Wolf shrugged. He did not reply. But that was as good as a yes, was it not? Kowalski felt honored that his building was somehow in a very small way being used for the defense of Poland against the intrigues of the Jews. Everyone knew the Jews were plotting with the Communists. And now this government fellow was going to be right in Kowalski's own building, protecting the Polish state and Kowalski's property in the bargain.

For a moment, Kowalski considered giving this government

agent a discount. He thought better of it. After all, Kowalski's taxes paid this fellow's salary and also paid the rent on the flat on Muranow Square.

Kowalski gave him the keys with a knowing smile. "Good luck then," he said. "You will enjoy the view very much."

The letter Elisa had sent to the Warsaw address of Lucy Strasburg returned to the London TENS office covered with large, angry-looking Polish words indicating that there was no one there by that name.

It lay open on Murphy's desk with the rest of the mail. The photograph of tiny baby Alfie at his christening poked out sadly from the torn envelope.

Murphy reread the letter Elisa and Lori had written. It was long and newsy, in the warm, friendly tones of someone who had lived among the outgoing people of Austria.

Harvey Terrill was just on his way home after what had been a very newsy night, but without any warmth of friendliness at all. Exhaustion reflected in Terrill's face.

"Thanks, Harvey," Murphy encouraged. Then he held up the letter. "When did this come in?"

"Yesterday," Harvey answered in a flat tone. "I opened it by mistake. Took me a while before I translated it and figured out it was talking about the baby." He frowned as if something just struck him. "I thought that baby was Lori Ibsen's kid."

"Long story," Murphy waved him off. "Go home and get some rest. The Nazis and the Russians are having a pow-wow tonight in Moscow. You'll have to be awake for that one."

Murphy waited until Harvey left the office before he picked up the letter again. He called Elisa and told her that the letter had been returned, and then he slipped it into the outgoing mail packet back to the Warsaw TENS office and Samuel Orde.

David and Samuel had blabbed the day and the time of Captain Samuel Orde's planned visit to the Lubetkin home.

Apparently, this time no one doubted their veracity. At 6:30 A.M., the first of the young men began to gather on the sidewalk outside the Muranow Square house. They chose their places along the curb, dusted off the pavement, and sat down to wait for the arrival of the great *Hayedid*!

After breakfast, Rachel looked out the window. The little knot of young men had grown to a crowd. Black coats mingled with the white, short-sleeved shirts of the nonreligious. The curb-sitters had multiplied to at least two hundred, with more coming from every direction like lines of ants on the march to the ant-hill!

"Mama!" Rachel shouted in alarm. "Hurry! Come look!"

There was no need for Etta to hurry. These men and boys were not going away. They had staked their claims on little parcels of pavement so they could see *him*! Like the Deliverer, he was! The one who had been in the newspapers and had trained the Special Night Squads *and so on and etcetera*, until he was practically a legend. *And so what if he was not a Jew? He probably really was a Jew, only nobody was telling it!*

Etta gasped in astonishment at the ever-spreading mass that began at her front door and moved outward into the square like an ink spill on a tablecloth! Among them near the front steps gleamed the red hair of Peter Wallich.

"Have they come to see the captain?" Etta breathed. "But how did they know he would be here today?"

At that, David and Samuel, dressed for Torah school, peeked their heads around the corner. If ever there were guilty faces, David and Samuel had them. Their eyes were wide with *who—me?* looks, their mouths clamped shut as if they had never opened to spill the news to friends and classmates.

Etta turned and glared at them. She put her hands on her hips and shook her head to let them know that they had better not pretend they had said nothing!

"Well? Nu? You should see what you have done! Next thing you know the Polish Secret Police will accuse us of hosting a riot!" She crooked her finger. *They should come see.*

Guilt made them tiptoe to the window. They gazed solemnly at a thousand below. More were coming. Brooms were being set aside and stoops were left dusty and untended. Now it was no longer just young men who flocked, but *everyone* was coming!

"We didn't tell," Samuel said in his sweetest voice.

Etta replied with a threatening look. *"Samuel!"*

"We just said . . . that is . . . *I* told *Mordechai* that—"

"Mordechai!" Rachel snarled the name. "You were showing off!"

"I told Mordechai that if he did not believe he should come here to our house at eleven o'clock." Samuel finished indignantly. "So?" He gestured toward the thousand and some Mordechais who had all come to *see*.

Etta's face reflected her puzzlement. "You think this many will show up when the Messiah comes?"

"If they do, then the Messiah will not be able to get through them all." Rachel glared at the smirking face of David. "What are you so happy about?"

"Mama?" David addressed his happy question to Etta and ignored his sister entirely. "How will Samuel and I get to Torah school this morning?"

Etta looked from the angelic face of her son to the teeming mob of spectators. "David, it would have been easier if you had told me you had a stomachache."

"You only told Mordechai?" Rachel challenged. "They must have sent out printed invitations to everyone in Warsaw so they would not have to go to school!"

"Not true." Samuel looked at her in a dangerous way. "Only Mordechai I told."

David never said *who* he had mentioned the event to. But everyone out there had heard from someone who had heard from *someone else* that the great and mighty English Zionist soldier, Captain Samuel Orde was coming to tea. Like the Messiah, he was coming. Like Gideon. Who in Jewish Warsaw could doubt such a marvelous tale? The Eternal always answered prayers during perilous times, did He not? Blessed be He! Was there even one Jewish male who was not in the square?

Maybe Mordechai was not there. Everyone knew that Mordechai was a poor loser.

28 The Deliverer Comes

Something was up with the Jews in Muranow Square. In all the days Wolf had been watching from his perch, he had never seen a gathering quite like this.

The clatter of milk bottles announced the arrival of the grocery delivery boy outside Wolf's door. He turned away from the window and fixed a smile on his face before he opened the door to the diffident youth who stood with his arms full of boxes.

A Polish language newspaper was folded and wedged between a small bottle of cream and another of milk. The boy looked red-faced and harried today.

"You are late," Wolf scolded in a friendly fashion. The building was without an elevator. The delivery boy was always later than promised.

"Did you see the mob in the square?" the boy blurted out, setting the boxes on the table and then going to peer out across the crowded square.

Wolf pretended that he had seen the demonstration but that it did not really interest him.

"Did someone die?" he asked, as he took the bottles of milk to the old-fashioned icebox. Always Wolf made the boy wait for his payment until the grocery boxes were empty. Jews talked too much for their own good, Wolf knew. This young fellow was like the others of his race in this way.

"No one died," he answered. It was not like him to leave the explanation incomplete.

"A wedding, perhaps," Wolf said knowingly and then he let the matter drop.

The boy stared distractedly down at the ever-expanding mob. It was plain he wanted to be among his people. He turned as if to leave. The tip seemed of little importance. "I have to go," he said, touching his hand to his cap. His voice betrayed excitement.

"The tip," Wolf replied. "Just a minute. Only a minute." He moved slowly toward the bedroom, where his wallet was. When he emerged, the boy stood rooted at the window. His eyes were wide with anticipation. Wolf stood unspeaking at his shoulder. "Will there be a riot?" Wolf asked.

The boy scoffed. "A holy man is coming," he said quietly. "No riot. You will be safe." He seemed amused by Wolf's question.

Wolf slipped him a few loose coins, then opened the door for him. *These Jews,* he thought with disgust. *A holy man, indeed!* At that, Wolf stretched out in his chair beside the window. He had just raised his field glasses to scan the crowd when the bright flash of the morning sun reflected off the windshield of a car with blinding intensity. The dull throb of a headache clamped across Wolf's skull like a vise.

He lowered his head for a moment and closed his eyes against the pain. It did not diminish. Instead, the dull throb became a roar in his ear. Small lights and shadows flickered at the edges of his vision.

He blinked rapidly and tried to focus his eyes. Lights shifted and danced, distorting his eyesight until he was unable to see even his hand clearly. He held his fingers up before his face. He could see only thumb and index finger. The agony in his skull gripped tighter. Wolf completely forgot the gathering in the square below. He groped toward the bathroom and felt for the aspirin bottle. His hand knocked the water glass to the floor with a crash. He gulped the aspirin without water and then stumbled to his bed and fell across it.

The light through the window seemed to focus down through the darkness that played across his vision. He struggled to sit up and draw the window shade, leaving the room in semi-darkness. With a low moan, he lay back on his pillow and closed his eyes. Today was one day he would leave the Jews to their holy man. It did not matter anyway.

The gruff, unshaven Polish taxi driver grimaced and ran his hand over the stubble of his beard in concern.

"Something is up with the Jews," he said in a displeased voice.

Jacob and Alfie had been invited along so that they might explore the Jewish District while Orde made his call on the family of Rabbi Lubetkin. Both of them leaned forward to stare at the mass of black-coated backs blocking all traffic into Muranow Square.

A Polish traffic policeman was detouring all vehicles down Niska and away from the mob.

"What is it?" Orde muttered to himself.

"Oh, you know these Jews!" the driver scoffed. "Always something. A wedding or a funeral maybe. They always wear black, so who can tell?" He flicked his hand toward the crowd. Head out the window, he shouted profanities at them. Then with a shrug, he said, "Blocking traffic! *Troublemakers!*"

"Pull over," Orde commanded, "at *once!*" As he paid the man he asked pointedly, "Were you among the crowd at St. John's when the envoy of the Pope came?"

"Of course!" The man said.

"Then you blocked traffic as well, my friend."

"The Jews have cost me my full fare!" the Pole exclaimed.

"No! *You* have cost you the full fare! I do not ride with ill-mannered anti-Semites. At least not on purpose."

"No tip?"

"A tip? Yes, here is my tip to you. Keep your mouth shut if you are an ignorant bigot. And cut off your tongue before you ever curse the Jews again. Or have you not heard that *God himself will curse those who curse His chosen*?" Orde's eyes blazed like a fiery preacher during a revival meeting in a small country parish. The Pole had never seen anyone quite so crazy looking. A frightening thing to have hanging over the backseat while a mob of wild Jews blocked escape in the front of the taxi.

"*Just get out!*" he shouted. He made the sign of the cross as the hair on the back of his neck stood on end.

He had already shifted into reverse and was looking for his escape as Orde jumped from the vehicle.

"What did you say to him?" Jacob asked. Jacob did not understand the exchange that took place in Polish.

Orde grinned broadly as the wheels of the taxi squealed against the cobbles. "Discussing the prophet Balaam." Orde marched forward toward the mob, five to six thousand people filling the square.

Alfie was also smiling as he fell in line behind Jacob. With one backward glance, Orde could see that Alfie . . . *Elisha* . . . was looking upward toward the tops of the buildings. His eyes were bright with amusement. He raised his big hand and

391

waved . . . a broad, signaling wave toward the Star of David that graced a synagogue poking up beyond the square. It was the sort of wave that said, "Yes, I see you!" But no one was there!

Orde too felt the hair on the back of his neck prickle. He stopped at the outermost perimeter of the crowd and turned to Alfie. In a quiet, certain voice, he asked, "*They* are here, aren't they?" Did Alfie understand the question?

Alfie nodded happily, swept his hand to the top of the Star; then upward to a line of buildings at the far end of Muranow, on to the peak of the clock tower, and finally to the big house that was their destination. Then, one more startling gesture; Alfie smiled at the empty air just above Orde. At that moment, the murmuring thousands grew strangely silent. A corridor of humans parted as though a hand had opened the way for Orde and Jacob and Alfie to walk through. The path led straight to the house of Rabbi Aaron Lubetkin.

There, on the sidewalk in front of the house, like soldiers waiting for the arrival of their general, a troop of fifty boys, from fourteen to nineteen, snapped to smart attention. Commands from a tall, gaunt red-headed boy were shouted in English.

"*Ten-hut! Huh-bout-TURN!*"

Five rows of ten ragged soldiers each saluted Orde as he approached them and smiled slightly with appreciation. Orde paused, responded in kind, and then prowled the line as if inspecting the readiness of his soldiers. Alfie and Jacob hung back and watched in amazement. The soldiers did not have guns, but they carried broomsticks as though they were rifles. At the barked commands of their red-haired leader, they progressed through a series of maneuvers as Captain Orde stood back and watched them with all the dignity he would have accorded the Highland Light Infantry.

A small pattering of applause rose up from those among the spectators who could see. When it was finished, Orde spoke quietly to the leader of the group.

"Captain Peter Wallich, First Warsaw Hashomer Platoon, reporting for duty!"

"Your English is excellent, Captain Wallich," Orde said. "And your men are well trained." He looked the stiff-backed rows up and down once more. "Where did you learn to drill?"

"Books, General Hayedid."

"Books?"

"Books. Rudyard Kipling, mostly. A lot of different books. And then there are movies. Errol Flynn."

"Ah." Orde nodded once and suppressed a smile. He knew the movie the boy was speaking of. *Charge of the Light Brigade*. That explained a number of peculiarities in the demonstration. But no matter. It was a tiny, unequipped and untrained bunch; yet as Orde looked up toward the metal outline of the Star on the synagogue, he felt the certain presence of other captains and other troops and the approving nod of their Commander here watching today. *God looks at the heart,* Orde thought. *And so must I.*

"Where are our headquarters, Captain Wallich?"

"The basement of the community soup kitchen." A pause. A moment of embarrassment. "There are more of us than this. These are the best."

"A well-disciplined group. Admirable. Well done." Orde did not let his gaze linger on the worn-out shoes or torn coats and trousers cinched with string or cracking leather. "I will have a word with your community leaders, and then we will begin immediately. You may dismiss the men."

At this, the crowd began to disperse. Had they come to meet Orde, or, like Alfie's angels, had they come to see the future army of Israel?

From the corner of his eye, Orde saw the scornful expression on the face of Jacob Kalner. Was it any wonder he was not impressed? He had seen a hundred thousand Hitler Youth dressed and polished, carrying real rifles over their shoulders! He had heard their voices raised in one song, to one Reich and one Führer! What was this pitiful little show compared to what Jacob had seen throughout Germany?

Jacob crossed his arms and watched as the Zionist Youth marched off in time. He looked with revulsion as the sole of one boy's shoe flapped an extra beat. The hands of many spectators reached out to tap the boys proudly on their shoulders as they passed through the square and on toward the synagogue.

"Pitiful," Jacob said.

"Very good," said Alfie, as if he wished he could line up so straight and march in step like that.

"Pathetic," Jacob said again.

Orde did not blame Jacob for his scorn. And yet he could not let it stand. "What is it?"

"Do they think they can make any difference against Nazi guns and tanks and planes?"

Orde smiled and turned to Alfie. "How many soldiers are on our side, Elisha?"

The light of admiration was bright on Alfie's face. He spread his arms wide and looked up into the sky where streaks of thin clouds passed above the earth like the trails of smoking chariots. "Look Jacob!" he cried.

Against his own volition, Jacob looked up. He stared hard at the vapors passing overhead on the wind until it felt as though the earth itself were moving, not the clouds. Were they just clouds?

Orde saw the goose bumps on Jacob's arms.

Alfie waved. *"Auf Wiedersehen."* Then he turned to Jacob. "They will be back. But don't worry. The General is still here." At that, Alfie pulled out the toy tin general he always carried in his pocket. The one he called *General Jesus.* "You want to put him in your pocket?" He tucked the toy soldier into Jacob's shirt pocket.

Orde smiled. "You are the one who told me he sees things."

Jacob nodded. He could not speak.

The door behind them opened. Etta Lubetkin stood framed in the doorway. Had she heard their discussion? She, too, was looking into the sky as the clouds dissipated above Warsaw.

————

Other men of importance were meeting with Rachel's father and the British Captain Orde. Two representatives of the Zionist community had come, as well as Father Kopecky and three other men whose positions Rachel did not know.

While Mama tended to full teacups and little sandwiches on a tray, David and Samuel were banished to play outdoors. Rachel sat beneath the shade of the elm tree in the garden and watched as baby Yacov struggled to pull himself into position to crawl.

Masculine voices drifted through the open window of Papa's study. Although Rachel could not understand all the words, the tone of the conversation was unmistakable. *Frightening.*

Rachel looked up into the green-leafed branches. Bits of blue shone through. Sunlight played against the leaves as they stirred in the slight breeze. Beneath the kitchen window, David

394

and Samuel drilled with stick rifles over their shoulders in imitation of Peter Wallich's marching troops. Rachel missed the summers when play had involved which tree to climb and what book to read or how much blackberry jelly to make. The sounds of summer were the same. The aromas from the kitchen still drifted out. But along with those sweet things came the dark voices of the strangers who had come to Muranow Square all with the same concern.

"The children will be the first to suffer."

"The Nazis in Prague right now are making even children . . ."

The grass was thick and soft beneath the blanket where baby Yacov lay. He lifted himself up on his pudgy arms and smiled a drooling smile at Rachel.

His eyes were bright and proud. Happy. He did not hear the droning voices speaking of threats against his innocence. His trusting confidence that all was right with the world and his patch of Warsaw made Rachel's heart ache.

"Mama says you are ready to crawl," she crooned to him, hiding her misery.

As if in reply, little Yani pulled one knee under his stomach and then the other. Crouched on all fours, he was in position to crawl, but he did not know what to do next. He rocked back and forth. He became very excited as he looked at his hands and then at Rachel.

She wriggled her fingers on the edge of the blanket. "Right here. Crawl over here and I will tickle your fat belly!"

"Evacuation seems to be . . ."

"Evacuation to where?"

"The Catholic Poles may not be better off if . . ."

"Your opinion, Captain Orde?"

"Expect . . . siege against Warsaw . . . hold on until England . . ."

Yacov put out one tentative hand. Now what?

"Yes. That's it! And now the other! Move your other hand."

The baby moved a knee forward instead. It was effective. He was crawling! Another drooling, surprised grin. Rachel praised him loudly as if to shield him from this terrible talk of siege and hunger and bombing in Warsaw—*and the evacuation of babies!*

"The logistics of transporting little ones is . . ."

"Can we speak of logistics? These are the most helpless . . ."

"The smallest could be hidden among the Poles, as I have said before."

"Captain Orde, you have seen the corps of young boys who can be taken out on foot."

"Peter Wallich has been—"

"We are attempting to acquire papers for. . ."

And Little Yani crawled another step. He crept in unsteady excitement toward the sunlight that touched the edge of the blanket. Such an accomplishment would have given Rachel great pleasure some other time. She would have dashed in to summon her mother to witness the baby's little miracle.

Life had been that simple once. "So wonderful, Yani," Rachel praised her baby brother as she picked him up and walked into the house, wiping away tears with the edge of her apron.

————

Father Kopecky and Captain Orde left Papa's study together. *What else? The goyim!* They had made their plans together— made their lists and talked about how Jewish babies must be taken into Catholic homes if the worst really came to Warsaw!

Rachel was angry. She hoped they saw it on her face as they walked past her and Yacov and smiled their polite smiles! She wanted to shout at them, *You'll never have my brother! Nor any one of my family! We would rather die together than be separated!*

Instead, she smiled politely and saw them to the door with other members of the *Kehillot* who had come to talk to Papa about hospitals and the overflow of children at the orphanage.

Papa spotted her as she walked back toward the kitchen.

"Rachel?"

"Just going to help Mama in the kitchen." She felt angry at Papa, too. Was he actually thinking of sending Yacov off somewhere? Or David? Or Samuel? Or—God forbid—Rachel herself?

"Come here, daughter," Papa ordered in a businesslike way.

She sighed and entered the study without looking up at him. "Yes, Papa," she said.

"You were impolite today."

She wanted to shout at him, but she did not. "I was nowhere close enough to anyone to—"

"Enough!" He really was angry. "It is as hot as the fires of Baal's altar today. So the window was open, and you sat beneath it purposely."

"Just under the elm tree, Papa. Because it *is* hot and I was watching Yacov. You should like me to sit in the sun?"

Papa was silent a moment. Drumming fingers on the big desk. "And singing your brother lullabies, were you?" He paused and then began to sing the words that Rachel had indeed been singing beneath the window as the meeting progressed.

Let's be joyous and tell our jokes,
We'll hold a wake when Hitler chokes.

She shrugged. A slight flush of shame crept to her cheeks, but not enough for her to admit. "Peter Wallich sings it with his Zionist Youth friends. They sing that and worse up and down the square all day. One cannot help but hear it."

"Yes. We all heard. The best men in the community. All trying to sort out major problems, and we all heard."

Her eyes flashed anger. She raised them in challenge to her father. "And *I* heard. You are planning to give us away if the Nazis come. Send us away to be Catholics, to live with the Saturday people! Well, I won't go! I won't leave Muranow Square or you and Mama and the boys."

"Enough!" Papa commanded in a tone he had not ever used with Rachel before. "While I was gone you developed an independent mind, I see."

"I won't go to Palestine!" She stamped her foot. "Or watch my brothers being taken away! This is my home and I will fight them and die before—"

Papa rose to his feet. He had never seen such defiance in Rachel before. "For now you will be silent and listen to me. For I will never speak to you on the matter again. Sit." She hesitated. "*Sit!*"

Rachel sat—primly and rigidly, to show her father she was not happy about sitting. He remained standing, as though this were the synagogue and he was in the bema and she was the congregation who *would* listen!

His voice moderated. "We have a saying, Rachel, that he who saves one life has saved the universe. You have heard this. An important thing, you will agree?"

She nodded. Of course. Everyone knew the saying.

"So." Papa stroked the beard that was only partly there now. "Perhaps the time is coming upon us when only one Jewish life will be saved. In the eyes of the Eternal the survival of only one

Jew in all the world would be enough for Him to still perform every promise He made to Abraham. You will agree to this?"

Rachel shrugged and smoothed the folds of her skirt.

Papa continued. "God promised Abraham only *one* son from Sarah! *One son.* One miracle. And through that son a covenant was made. The Eternal promised the nation of Israel. Promised the Messiah. Promised the redemption of all mankind. It only takes *one!* Can you imagine how that fact must distress God's great enemy, Satan? For this reason, since that time the Evil One has sought actively to deceive and destroy every descendant of Abraham's promised son. And that means you, Rachel. And Yacov. And David and Samuel as well!"

Rachel raised her eyes. A congregation of one, her attention had been captured by the great Rabbi Lubetkin. She opened her mouth in a soundless *oh*.

Papa nodded. "Every Jew who survives openly sanctifies the covenant God made with Abraham. Now is the time for the sanctification of life. *Kiddush Hashem*. Once when our enemies demanded our souls, the Jew martyred his body. Today, Rachel, if the enemy demands that you die, it is your obligation to defend yourself and preserve your life so that God's covenant with Israel may be fulfilled at the coming of Messiah."

He waited as this sermon settled on her. She nodded. Meekly.

"Do you understand why our children must live? Who the true enemy of every Jew is, Rachel? Not the goyim. No. It is the *Evil One* who is God's enemy. It is *Satan* we must fight by remaining alive!"

Rachel did not like any of this. She wished she were wise enough to reply. "I know why I must stay alive. But if you were not . . . *alive*, it would be easier to die, Papa. Easier to die with us all together than to live alone like . . . like Peter Wallich!"

"But you are the daughter of Rabbi Aaron Lubetkin. The grand-daughter of Rabbi Shlomo Lebowitz! It is important, *daughter of the seed of Abraham*, that you *live*! Even if it means going to Jerusalem without us."

She jumped to her feet. This was too blatant. It was no longer a discussion on living or dying and the obligations of being a Jew! Papa was talking about sending *her* away! Too much! "I will *live* wherever you and Mama are! I *won't* leave you! Or my brothers! Because . . . because . . . *Papa!* Can't you see my heart would no longer be alive in me without you? I would be sick for you all . . . I would."

It was a terrible thing. She was losing the argument and all she could do about it was run into Papa's arms and hold on tightly while she cried and cried.

After a moment he stroked her hair. He patted her back. "Well, now. It is not all that bad. You would never survive Yeshiva school if you cannot discuss a little thing like *Kiddush Hashem*. True? Of course true. Go on now. Wash your face. Stop this weeping. And no more singing of ditties beneath the window of important meetings."

———

It was dark when Wolf awoke from his deep sleep. His head still ached—as if he had a night of too much schnapps. But the agony of the morning was past.

He sat up carefully, slowly swinging his feet to the floor. He was still slightly nauseous and decided that he had experienced a touch of food poisoning. He raised the shade and peered out over the quiet square. Here and there lights shone in the windows of Jewish houses. The shops were closed tight. There was no sign at all that the Jewish holy man had come and gone—Muranow Square.

With a sigh, Wolf realized he had not eaten all day. He switched on the light and made his way to the kitchen. On the table was the open newspaper. The words emblazoned across the newspaper were the obituary for Poland: *GERMANY DENOUNCES POLISH MOBILIZATION.*

From the perspective of this Polish rag of a newspaper, this was called foolish propaganda. *Germany* had been rearming for years. No doubt London would also be crying foul as well. But for the Führer, Wolf knew, this was a necessary step. Now there would be opportunity to accuse *Poland* of aggression and increase Nazi demands.

Wolf read the accounts and then smiled down at the Jewish District of Warsaw. Soon there would be no holy man to stop what was coming on this place.

The Führer had set his sights on Poland. On Warsaw. On the Jews who took the living space that rightfully belonged to the German race.

Knowing this made his view of Jewish Warsaw seem like a

very old silent motion picture. Wolf saw the movement of people in the square below him, but they seemed like gray apparitions of a people and a culture long dead. They did not know it, but the requiem had already been played for them. *They were no more!* The mind of the German Führer had decreed their end long ago. The headlines of today's news simply confirmed what was written against them.

As the reel spun out before Wolf's eyes, he watched the Jews with the fascination of one who knows the end of the story. Only the characters of this present scene seemed unaware that their destiny was already written.

The outlying English churchyards had been scoured for possible candidates for premature resurrection. Names were selected carefully for date of birth and gender. Lori joined her mother, Anna, and Elisa on these daily picnic excursions where identities were stolen from the dead so that they might save those condemned to die. Captain Orde had the new passport photos of Jacob and Alfie and Rachel Lubetkin. He had also chosen his own candidates for life from among those who had clamored to join his group of young Zionists. The criteria were simple: an Anglo-looking face and a passible grasp of the English language. Among the young men, only 157 fit those standards. At last word, the passport photos of that handful were on the way to London. If the photographs arrived before the powder keg exploded beneath Poland, then perhaps there was hope. But every day, it seemed, Germany and Poland moved more irrevocably toward confrontation.

The certainty of war struck terror in Lori's heart for two main reasons—along with a host of smaller reasons. If there was a war and England did indeed take sides with Poland, she would probably never see her father again. If there was a war before Jacob got his passport and got out of Poland—well, she could not let herself think about it.

She wrote Jacob every day and included little notes to Alfie and Werner as well. Three times a week the mail steamer brought Jacob's return letters to her. She read the newsy bits aloud to Mark and Jamie and her mother, but the other parts she saved for her own heart. She carried his love letters around in her pockets. When the day was too long or too slow or lonely, she would pull out a letter and read it over again until she felt that Jacob was right there with her.

If there was a war, the mail would stop. That realization evoked another kind of dread. She knew what it was like to live on without knowing the fate of the one you love more than your own life. She could see such brave grief in her mother. A hundred times a day Helen Ibsen looked off somewhere, and her eyes reflected the hope and memory of Karl Ibsen.

"Please, God," Lori prayed. For her father and now for her own husband, this little unfinished prayer helped her get through the hot summer days in London. *"Let them come home!"*

Then a miracle happened. Lori waited beside the mailbox and took the letters from the postman. At last, the passport of William Howard Johnson had arrived! Inside, the image of Jacob Kalner grinned out, daring anyone to challenge that he was a true Englishman!

Lori stood with one foot on the bottom step as she smiled back at Jacob. She wanted to shout for joy! She wanted to run into the little church across the way and blow kisses at the cross above the altar. She wanted to kneel on the weed-covered grave of the little boy who had lived only one short month in this life and say, "Thank you! Oh, thank you!"

In the midst of this miracle, Lori did not see the shadow of Doc Grogan at her elbow. She could not say how long he had been peering down at the passport before he finally spoke.

"William Howard Johnson. A good English name."

"Oh!" Lori snapped the new passport cover closed and put it behind her back. "I did not see you."

"I thought not," he said with a wry smile as he stepped around her. "I understood his name was Kalner?" He walked lightly up the stairs.

It was the day for the Thursday excursion with Doc Grogan. Most of the refugee children were settled in new homes. That left only Charles and Louis, Lori, Jamie, and Mark for today's outing.

From the beginning, Doc Grogan called Lori *Missus Kalner!* He peered over her shoulder when she held baby Alfie and said, "He looks just *exactly* like your husband, don't you think so, *Missus Kalner!*"

This usually made Lori blush, which was the purpose of the

comment. He said he liked to see a little color on her wan and pale cheeks.

Wan was not a word Lori knew, so she looked it up in her English-German dictionary. It meant "pale." "So my cheeks are pale and pale?" She teased him. "I will not ever understand how English has so many words for the same thing!"

Then Jamie chimed in, "For instance, the word *Schwein* in Deutsch can be said *pig. Or swine. Or hog. Or pork. Or Nazi.*"

At this, everyone dissolved into laughter. Doc Grogan pointed out how wonderfully pink Missus Kalner's pale and pale cheeks were. And then how good it was to hear that she really could laugh. Mothers needed to laugh a lot, he admonished, so their babies could grow up hearing laughter. Then he made up a wild theory about how babies that don't hear a lot of laughter never quite know how to talk properly.

Lori had long ago decided that she liked Doc Grogan. He was chubby, round-faced and jolly. His skin was also *pale* and *pale,* but covered with a fine frosting of freckles. He was Bavarian in character, she decided, rather than austere and dry like someone from Prussia.

The bottom line was that he reminded her of her favorite history teacher who had left Germany for safer places in the middle of Lori's seventh-grade year. After that, school had been very dull.

On Thursdays Elisa shooed her out the door and told her to have fun. On this particular Thursday Anna and Helen took the babies while Elisa practiced her violin.

"Be sure you laugh a lot," Mark called as Helen and Anna pushed the pram the opposite direction. They did not need to be told. They prattled on about the babies like two grandmothers should do.

Moments later, through the open window they could hear the high, fine soprano voice of Elisa's violin as it played a Mozart rondo.

"There you have it." Doc Grogan walked backward and waved his arms as though he were conducting. "As good as laughter, is it not, Missus Kalner? Ah! How lovely to see you smile for a whole minute at a time! I feared you had forgotten how since you came to jolly old England and jolly good Red Lion Square."

"She is just Misses Jacob," Jamie teased.

Lori silenced him with a look. For these ten minutes she was doing just fine. Smiling. Feeling almost like breathing. Fine. She did not want to be reminded that there were moments when she missed Jacob so badly that she could barely speak, that at night she lay in bed and ached from missing him.

"My mother was married younger than you," said Grogan in a matter-of-fact tone. "Married ten days, and then he was off to the war. Spanish-American War. Teddy Roosevelt and the Rough Riders. He came home and *POP,* there was the first of eleven babies. Just that easy." They lined up to wait for the red bus. "Eleven children and imagine, none of them looked like him! Not like your little Alfie, eh, Missus Kalner."

Jamie and Mark howled at this because they knew the real story about the baby. How big Alfie had shoved him into Lori's arms and said, *Auf Wiedersehen!* Of course they were not permitted to tell the truth of it, or the immigration adoptions people would be standing on the doorstep demanding that the baby be given to some childless couple who ran a bee farm in Sussex or something. Murphy had warned them sternly. They could not even tell Doc Grogan the truth. Dangerous stuff, he said.

But they could laugh at Doc on Thursdays all the same. He took them here and there and made them speak like every educated Englishman should speak. Proper vowels and no making of W's into V's, like old Hildy Frutschy. *"Ve ist goinggg!"*

Today, like every Thursday, they joked and laughed as they waited for the bus. He sometimes withheld their true destination from them until they had already passed it once. This made them pay attention, he said—made them use their imaginations as they wondered which place was worth seeing and which was only mediocre.

The dome of St. Paul's Cathedral loomed ahead of them. Grogan did not bother to hide their destination from them.

"How would you like to see the place where the remembrance ceremony for your father will be held?" he asked Lori and Jamie.

Not even Charles and Louis had ever been inside St. Paul's with Doc. And to see anything in London without him was like not really seeing it.

A chorus of cheers arose. The wind on the top deck of the bus blew through Doc's thin hair. He looked hard at the dome in a very thoughtful way. "It will take us all day. You have your lunches?"

Five bagged lunches by Hildy were held up. She made wonderful bratwurst sandwiches, Hildy did—as long as the onions did not get warm. Then the bags made heads turn.

Grogan held up his own bag. "Good. We will eat at the top in the Golden Gallery. At one o'clock, so we can hear the ringing of Great Bell."

He made it sound so wonderful. For just a moment, Lori looked down at her photograph of Jacob. Could she help it if she missed him, wished beyond anything that he were here?

"We will begin in St. Dunstan's Chapel and then on to the crypt where they keep the old famous people in storage for posterity."

Charles and Louis exchanged puzzled looks. Should they tell him they did not understand this big English word *posterity*?

In predictable Doc-like fashion, he knew they did not know. Possibly that was why he used the word. "Future generations; children just like you, only fifty years from now, who will wander through history. Depending on the teacher, they will see nothing in the crypts but marble, chiseled and cold. Ah!" He held up a sausage finger. "But if their teacher is like me, then they will hear the voice of Lord Nelson shouting to his men! They will hear the tap-dancing step of those who once were and those who have yet to be!"

29   Requiem for Poland

Warsaw was a vast city spread out along the wide banks of the Vistula. It was a tangle of narrow streets and broad, proud avenues that expanded into wooded parks or cobbled squares, or erupted into the towering spires of the Cathedral of St. John and a very tall skyscraper on Napoleon Square.

To this large and beautiful city Lucy Strasburg awakened. She had a view from the room where she was carefully nursed to recovery by Herr Frankenmuth's widowed sister. At night the expanse of Warsaw seemed limitless. Lights spread like a carpet of jewels far into the late evening. Parts of the great city never slept. The heart of Warsaw glowed against the black sky, lighted by the neon marquees of theaters and clubs.

Lucy often lay awake with that view before her. She wondered about the fate of Peter Wallich. Had he found his mother Karin and sister Marlene? Had they then struck out for some safer, more distant place than Warsaw? Would they one day be reunited with baby Willie in America and then perhaps travel on to Jerusalem?

Such thoughts made her happy that she had stumbled on the Wallich family. How fortunate she was in this one instance that something good had managed to come out of the darkness of her life. She felt no pride for her help to the Wallich family; only a sort of humble gratitude that someone so worthless could be used. Beyond that, she only hoped that the Walliches would manage to slip from Warsaw before the next apocalypse descended on them. She held no such hope for herself.

Sensing the presence of Wolf, even here, she had no illusions about her own safety. Lucy longed for only one thing: to know the fate of her baby. She had put her son into the arms of a stranger. Where had the child gone once he arrived in England? Did he have both mother *and* father, as children should have? Was he loved? Had he been christened in the satin gown as she dreamed a hundred times as the days passed?

These small details were the stuff that nourished Lucy's broken heart. She could close her eyes and imagine her baby in a carriage being pushed through a shady park in London. She awoke sometimes to his cry. Her breasts filled again with milk as she reached out in the darkness only to find that he was not there. And in those moments of fierce longing, she did not ask God if she might hold him once again. Such a prayer from one like her was doomed to go unheeded, she believed. No. Lucy did not pray for her own longing. She prayed that he was held when he cried. That he was fed when he was hungry. That he was loved, all the time.

And then she asked that she might know that these small prayers were answered on behalf of her son. She showed the address Peter had given her to Frau Berson. Frau Berson had dug out a well-worn city map and dragged her bony finger along Niska Street to where the Jewish District of Warsaw began. It was the other side of the river, the other side of Warsaw—a different world, Frau Berson warned her.

Lucy had nothing to pay the good woman for her care. Frau Berson gestured toward the cross hanging above her corner table. The woman took no more credit for helping Lucy than Lucy took for helping the Wallich family. Instead, Frau Berson dipped into her coin purse and presented Lucy with tram fare across Warsaw. She made her a lunch and filled a canning jar with apple juice to drink because it was hot today and Lucy might need something cool to drink.

"You intend to stay with these Jewish friends of yours?" Frau Berson asked as though she doubted the wisdom of such mixing of cultures.

"Peter asked me to go with him to Warsaw. I should have done so." That *should have* held all the regret she had ever felt. *If I had gone with Peter, I would still have the baby. If I had gone with Peter, Wolf would not have—*

She shuddered and stopped herself from thoughts that could not change anything at all.

"You might be back." Frau Berson straightened her collar as though Lucy were her daughter going off to school. "You have not seen the way *they* live. It is not like the Jews in Berlin. Or the Jews in Danzig. They are a different people than you or I. A world in which we do not belong."

This warning clanged in Lucy's head like the bell of the tram. The long tram car slid across the face of Warsaw mile after mile as Lucy stared at the city and listened to the unfamiliar language of the Polish passengers. Their tongues cracked against their palates in greeting and in discussion of the terrible reports that were splashed across the front pages of undecipherable newspapers.

The world of the Poles was strange enough to Lucy. Could the Jewish District possibly be more unfamiliar and frightening than this? She saw sandbag barricades and taped windows everywhere, yet downtown Warsaw was bustling with activity. Admiring women scanned shop windows. Lucy supposed that they could understand what the signs said and what the prices meant. The marquees of theaters displayed names that Lucy could not pronounce with letters turned oddly this way and that like the Russian alphabet.

Could it be that the Führer had not been lying when he said

that Poland was near to being Russian in politics and culture? Is that why the German people feared and hated the Poles so desperately?

Lucy did not see people she need fear. She saw women holding the hands of their children as they walked down the streets. She saw ordinary shoppers passing in and out of the revolving doors of department stores. She saw men in uniform sitting in the parks beside pretty girls, an organ grinder with a monkey on a leash, a blind beggar standing beside a lamppost.

Ordinary people, except when they opened their mouths and gibberish flowed out in an incomprehensible torrent. Maybe that was the only difference between ordinary people here and anywhere.

An airplane passed overhead. All heads pivoted upward. Hands shielded against the sun. Anxious eyes wondered and then, a man in the uniform of an ordinary soldier announced, "Polski!"

People smiled and shrugged, sighing with relief. These people were also afraid. And Lucy pitied them because they had not seen anything yet. They had not even imagined what they were about to see. There would be no mistaking it when the German aircraft swooped down on Warsaw. No one would look up. Everyone would be too busy running for cover.

Wolf had told Lucy what the bombing was like in Spain. He said that when Warsaw had its turn, the Luftwaffe would be one hundred times more powerful.

She looked at the slip of paper with the address on it. She held it lightly between her fingers. Lucy knew that when the German bombers came to Warsaw, she would stand unmoving in the street. She would look up into the sky and welcome whatever fell on her.

There were only these little questions to clear up. She wanted to *know* that all was well with the baby. And then it did not matter any longer. She would not cause her own death, but she would not run from it, either. She did not think that welcoming death was a sin.

Wolf had reminded her of how little she was worth. That knowledge made living seem of little importance. And she prayed that perhaps there was some tiny attic room reserved for her in God's mansion.

She patted her pocket where she still carried the little green book with all the details of life as a parlormaid. She would never see the freedom of England or America. She would never hold her baby again, she knew. But she would be content to wait on tables and sweep up crumbs in heaven. This was the mercy Lucy Strasburg asked for.

—————

The rumble of thousands of horses' hooves against the packed soil of the parade ground drowned out all conversation. Orde stood on the platform among dozens of other Western journalists to observe what was supposed to be a display of Polish prowess.

Dutiful to his newly acquired vocation, Orde snapped photographs with the cumbersome news camera, and took copious notes as to the state of readiness of the Polish Legion. To his right, Jacob Kalner watched with the wide-eyed admiration of one who could not conceive that *so many troops* could not stand up against the German divisions. On Orde's left, Alfie, the new Elisha, gazed over the scene with a strange smile on his lips, as if searching for legions of fiery angels. Sadly, he did not see them among the Poles.

At the front of the platform, Edward Smigly-Rydz, inspector general of the Polish Army, stood at attention. He had acquired the nickname of Smigly, meaning "nimble," as a young man fighting the Russian Bolsheviks in 1920. After an hour of conversation with the general, Orde had decided that he was more arrogant and shortsighted than nimble. The strength of the opposing German panzer divisions would require more than nimble cockiness to be defeated.

The endless sea of Polish cavalry spread out before the platform was crowned with old-style French helmets. Their weapons were lances, sabers, and rifles of the vintage of the last war.

Throughout the prancing troop were horses as white and glowing as neon signs in Piccadilly. For any man to ride a white horse into battle was certain suicide. Only a blind enemy could miss such a target. Such animals were meals on legs for the buzzards that now swooped low over Poland.

This display of tens of thousands of horses caused the Polish general to glow with pride. "You can see," he told Orde, "our cavalry is adapted for rapid movements over the Polish plain."

Orde knew that the plain was the flattest country of its size in all of Europe. This level vastness made Poland the least defensible of any nation on the Continent. Feeding horses would be a nightmarish logistical problem on the field. There was only one hope for Polish victory that Orde could see, although he did not express his pessimism aloud. The world must pray for an early rain to clog the dirt roads and turn the fields into mires that would suck down the German might. In such a case, horses might have some advantage against three thousand heavy German tanks. *Otherwise . . .*

The Polish Army had six hundred light six-ton tanks, built on the English Vickers' design. These tin cans had been effective against the rifles of the Arabs in Palestine, Orde recalled. But crude land mines had taken out a number of the tanks easily even when wielded by primitive bands hiding among the rocks. Orde looked at Jacob's face beaming with envy. He would love to be a tank commander in such a force!

Orde shuddered involuntarily. He saw before him images of charred men in charred machines, of dead and bloated horses being scraped from the roads like so much manure from the floor of a barn.

Behind the tanks came horse-drawn light and medium artillery of the same manufacture as the world war.

The Polish general looked on proudly, his cruel face twisted into a perverse smile. Was he remembering, perhaps, how these same units swept across a portion of Czechoslovakia after the Munich Agreement last year? Was he under the illusion that Hitler's forces would simply lie down and roll over? General Smigly-Rydz had played the role of a scavenger when Czechoslovakia had been dismembered. Now, perhaps, the brutality of that action would come back on Poland. The general was more interested in nationhood than democracy. He was anti-Semitic; perhaps he was a man of courage, yet Orde had sensed great darkness in this man's soul.

Herr Hitler had been quite happy to send photographs of his weapons and troops out from the Reich for publication. He gloated in the fact that his army and air force were the most modern in the world. Had this Polish general not seen those photographs? Could he not hear the trembling of earth and sky as German divisions moved into place on three sides of the Polish border?

When war came to this place—and Orde did not doubt that

inevitable occurrence—the Poles would be forced to fight a re-treating action to hold back the Nazis from Prussia in the north, Czechoslovakia in the south, and Germany in the west. If they could cling to their plain until Britain and France arrived, then perhaps the rains would bring General Mud to their rescue.

The Reich surrounded all sides of Poland except one. Soviet Russia towered like a bear at their eastern back door. Here was one small reason to hope. England had sent an emissary to Moscow to attempt to form an alliance, a nonaggression pact which would guarantee that Russia would not tolerate any German aggression against Poland. That alone might cause the German Führer to rethink the million troops posed at Poland's front door. The horses of Poland's cavalry might be nothing to slice through, but did Hitler wish to face three hundred Russian divisions on the other side?

The crack of rifles and the boom of field guns announced that this glorious display of might had come to an end. Men stood at attention as the Polish national anthem was played.

Tears stood in the eyes of general and troops alike. But to Orde as he listened respectfully, the anthem sounded like a requiem that resounded over the spires of Warsaw in the distance.

———

Lucy noted a perceptible change in the dress and language of the tram passengers at the edge of the Jewish District. Frau Berson had been correct in saying that this large, sprawling expanse of Warsaw was like stepping into a different world.

In the showcase windows of the shops, none of the latest Paris fashions were displayed. Hat makers displayed the newest Jewish headgear, which in fact had not changed in style for several hundred years. Marquees were written in Yiddish or in Hebrew, depending on the nature of the shop. The world of floral print dresses and pin-striped suits had vanished. Here were long severe dresses on the women; caftans of black that reached well below the knees of the men.

Lucy saw old men, white-bearded and stoop-shouldered, conversing animatedly with young men who dressed exactly the same. The only difference was the white hair and wrinkled skin.

Like rows of blackbirds on a wire, men crowded onto the tram. Women came along as well, but they sat in the back of the vehicle with their youngsters. Men and women alike stared at

Lucy. *What are you doing here?* their looks asked. The tram moved slowly from stop to stop, and still Lucy did not get off. Two women looked at her curiously and then whispered behind their hands. *Maybe she is lost? Maybe she is blind? Maybe . . . who can say? Very strange, nu?*

Lucy had not imagined how different it could be. The neat rows of Hebrew letters on street signs and shop windows looked like little hands raised up in prayer. Words inscribed in that strange alphabet seemed like tongues of fire painted in a line.

Yet here, too, women stood chattering on street corners while their children ran around their legs or balanced to walk the curb. Delivery boys carried packages to doorsteps. Huge dray horses pulled wagon loads of cheese, vegetables, and ice through the streets.

A paper boy stood on the corner hocking his publications. The headlines, in large type, proclaimed only one word that Lucy recognized: *NAZI!*

Men young and old clustered around whoever had purchased a paper. They waved their arms and argued loudly. They gestured toward the east and then toward the west. Black eyebrows arched upward in concern.

What could these separate people possibly have in common with the world of the Poles that surrounded them?

Then Lucy saw it. The drone of a single airplane passed overhead. All faces peered skyward with ominous expectation. Hands shielded eyes from the glare, and then someone sighed and said, *POLSKI.*

So that was it. Fear was the common bond between Jew and Gentile Pole. But one thing was missing in the way that fear was dealt with. In Catholic Warsaw, everyone carried the obligatory gas masks. But here, as Niska Street grew ever more narrow and ever more crowded, there were no gas masks to be seen.

Mothers pushing baby carriages had no gas masks. Old men and young delivery boys carried no gas masks. Small, serious-faced scholars carried no gas masks.

Could it be that Jews did not believe in such a precaution? If that was the case, Lucy decided, they were foolish. Everyone knew about the mustard gas that had been used in the last war. Every day Frau Berson had talked of blistered skin and blind men and seared lungs. Just thinking of what Hitler might do with the gas made the old woman tremble. She had gone out on the first day the Polish government had issued them to all civilians, and after hours in long lines, she had returned with two. Lucy carried hers in a little cardboard box slung over her shoulder. Everyone in Gentile Warsaw had one. Lucy had seen them everywhere outside the borders of this district.

She frowned and looked at her own case; it must have been an obvious curiosity to the plump old woman sitting across from her.

"Polski?" the blue-eyed Jewess asked quietly. She was questioning Lucy's presence on the train.

"Nein," Lucy answered, surprised by the human voice addressing her.

"I see you are of *German* heritage," the old woman said with a twinge of sarcasm. Her eyes lingered on Lucy's gas-mask container. Other heads swiveled to look at Lucy.

"Ja. Deutsch," Lucy replied quietly.

"And you are wondering about our gas masks?" The woman's voice was heavily accented, but her German words were well chosen.

Again, a hesitant nod from Lucy.

The eyebrows of the woman rose slightly as though she knew some joke but was not sure if she should tell it. Then, she told.

"There are no gas masks for Jews, you see. Jews in Warsaw have no protection from the gas if the Führer should decide to use such a weapon against Poland." A shrug. "You see?"

The tram bell clanged loudly. This was Lucy's stop. She was grateful for the interruption. She inched through the other passengers, and as she stepped onto the sidewalk, she slipped her own gas mask into the large paper lunch sack Frau Berson had sent with her.

She looked unusual enough on this street, she reasoned. She did not want to flaunt that difference. *No protection for the Jews of Warsaw!*

She shuddered and lowered her eyes so she would not have to look into the faces that turned toward her and wondered. She took the scrap of notepaper from her pocket and looked at it again, although she knew the number well. *2334 Niska Street, Apartment 3A.* The name above the address was RUDOLF DORBRANSKY.

Lucy studied the row of mailboxes in the lobby of the gloomy building. Most had names above the numbers. Apartment 3A had an empty place behind the little glass window.

No matter. This was the correct address. The number Lucy had given to Alfie so that they could write her from England! She looked up the steep stairs, half expecting to see Peter Wallich and his sister appear on the landing above her!

Her mouth was dry with excitement. She hoped there had been time enough for a letter to get here about the baby. She dashed up the steps, using the banister to pull herself upward toward the answer she had come all this way to find. *No doubt the letter has come! Peter will know all about the news from England before me! Oh, won't it be good to see him again!*

Lucy was flushed and out of breath as she raised her hand and knocked on the door of Rudolf Dorbransky, Apartment 3A. She could hear the happy squeals of small children through the thin wood door. Had they heard her knock? She raised her hand again and then the door was opened just a crack. A timid slice of pale face peered out at her. Dark, frightened eyes filled with a freshly revived fear at the sight of her.

"Please, bitte—" Lucy leaned against the door to keep the woman from closing it on her face. "I am looking for—" She held out the address and managed to smile hopefully. She looked over the head of the woman, who glanced at the note and then pushed to close the door on Lucy's face.

"Not here!" the woman said in poor German.

"Please!" Lucy leaned harder on the door. "Peter!" she called. "Peter Wallich? Peter, *it is Lucy*! I have come here all the way from Danzig! Peter!"

"Wrong place!" The woman was angry. She pushed hard in an attempt to keep Lucy back.

"Please!" Lucy cried, unbelieving. "You are making a mistake! Ask Peter Wallich who I am! He will know me! *Lucy!* I am *Lucy Strasburg!* A friend of Peter and Karin and Marlene Wallich! I was told to meet them here!"

The woman let out a garbled cry for help. Then a large hairy hand pulled the woman aside and Lucy tumbled forward into the tiny flat.

The faces of two ragged children gaped up at her in terror as a burly man stepped between Lucy and the rest. "You got the wrong place," he growled. He snatched the address from his thin, trembling wife and thrust it back at Lucy.

"But surely Peter Wallich can vouch for me."

He crossed his thick arms. His teeth were clenched between his black beard. His eyes smoldered. "No Peter Wallich here. No Rudolf Dorbransky. They move out. Who knows where to." He flung his hand up and Lucy winced as though he had struck her.

He had struck her, in a way. "But this is the address." Her voice was small and pitiful.

"I'm telling you." He was warning her as well.

Lucy backed up a step. "But did they come here? Peter? Marlene and Karin?"

The woman took pity. "A woman and a little girl?"

"Yes!" Lucy resisted the urge to grab the woman's hands. "Where did they go? Did they leave an address?"

"They left," the man said, "like everyone else. Now this is *our* place. Get out!"

"But were there letters?" Lucy directed this question to the brow-beaten woman who cringed beneath Lucy's pleading eyes.

The man stepped to the side, blocking Lucy's view of his wife. "No letters! We send the letters back! Nobody lives here by these names! Why should we keep letters when these people don't live here? Probably dead!"

He moved his bulk another step forward. He knew that Lucy was not *one of them,* and he hated her! He hated her as much as Wolf hated a Jew! Only he was not so cruel. He did not strike her physically. He simply slammed the door on her hopes and clicked the lock and snapped the chain into place.

"Not here," she muttered as she walked slowly down to the foyer. "How could that be?"

No Rudolf Dorbransky family. No Karin Wallich. No Peter Wallich. No letter from London. No hope.

Where can I go now? Lucy wondered. *What options are left to me?* She felt faint. She sat down on the bottom step and stared at the checkerboard tiles on the floor of the foyer. She cradled her head in her hands and tried to remember everything Alfie Halder had said to her in those last terrible moments of farewell on the Danzig wharf.

"See you in Warsaw . . . newspaper. . . TENS. See you in Warsaw!"

St. Paul's Cathedral was an immense building. Lori guessed that several churches the size of her father's church could have fit in it side by side. Probably another half dozen or so could have stacked up to fill the vast dome of the cupola.

The giant lantern on the top of the dome was easily seen from the Red Lion House, but Lori had not imagined that it could be so big or so high.

"It weighs seven hundred tons," explained Doc Grogan as he craned his neck back to look up into the misty heights of the cupola. "I do not speak of the weight of the dome itself," he warned. "Only the lantern and the cross on the tip top. An amazing feat of engineering."

That was the last thing Doc Grogan said for quite a while. He paid one shilling per head for the privilege of climbing 616 steps of a nearly vertical staircase that twisted upward between the walls of the inner dome and the outer shell. The views might have been awe-inspiring, but in this case, the trek was also breathtaking in a literal sense.

———

Allan Farrell stood staring out over the city of London from the vantage point of the Golden Gallery high atop St. Paul's Cathedral. Down the Thames in the middle distance was the arch of the Tower Bridge. Part of the great fortress called the Tower of London was visible as well.

Allan shook off the urge to take in the sights and forced his attention back to the slope of the roof that spread out its great bell-shaped curve just below where he stood. The lead-covered expanse fell away gently for the first few feet, then swooped abruptly downward. Anything sliding down that surface would shoot out into space with the acceleration of a meteor slamming to earth.

Allan's inspection turned upward toward the towering structure called the lantern that surmounted the dome. He looked up toward the cross on the very top, then over the railing again.

The terrorist circled the base of the lantern, pausing every so often as if gauging something in his mind. When he reached the west side of the gallery, he attempted to see the spot where the Gunpowder Plot conspirators had been executed, but even from that great height it was not visible. The bulk of the west facade of St. Paul's hid the exact location from view. "But I know it's there, just the same," he murmured to himself.

He was rounding the circuit of the Golden Gallery once

more when he ran squarely into a line of children. A swirl of blond and brunette heads bobbed around him. Small necks craned to see everywhere at once, and fingers pointed a hundred different directions.

Allan waited impatiently for the children to move out of the way; then, the adult who was apparently their guide puffed and wheezed slowly out of the stairwell. "Children," he gasped, "stand aside and let this gentleman—"

The man's voice trailed off so abruptly that Allan looked to see what had caused the sudden change of tone. It was Grogan! Then these children must be... Allan ducked his head, then decided that his movement was suspicious, raised it again and found himself staring into Doc's direct gaze.

Grogan looked puzzled, then worried. He seemed about to speak, but Farrell roughly pushed through the knot of children and began a clattering descent of the stairs. Allan resisted the urge to run down the twisting iron corkscrew and forced himself to maintain a careful, deliberate pace.

All the way down the steps and up the aisle of the cathedral to the west entrance Allan thought about how this chance encounter could ruin things. Something would have to be done— and quickly.

No one had ever heard Doc Grogan so silent. He *was* gasping for breath, of course. But he was speechless, unable to utter one coherent syllable until long after they leaned against the stone railing of the parapet and looked over the sloping lead roof of the dome that slid off into the tiny London streets far below.

Lori snapped pictures of the shining ribbon of the Thames, of the boys crowded around the sweat-soaked, red-faced Doc; of the far distant landmarks of the Tower of London and the twisting lanes of the city.

They unpacked their lunches on this perch that seemed almost too high even for the pigeons. The ten-foot hands of the clock struck one, and the tolling of the Great Bell began.

30   The Scent of Death

It seemed as though the tolling of the bell of St. Paul's struck a discordant note in Doc Grogan. He stared out over the stone parapet and then looked up to the golden ball of the great lantern atop the dome.

Suddenly he barked, "That's it." In an angry-sounding voice, he ordered everyone down the stairs. He led the way, clattering down the iron steps almost at a run.

Jamie and Mark teased him about how much easier it was to go down the steps than up. He did not respond to their jokes, but instead glanced up at the inner brick shell of the dome and then back up to where the iron braces linked the interior cone to the lead-covered exterior roof.

Lori caught his sense of uneasiness. She felt a terrible sense of vertigo as she followed him down and down on the frail spiral of stairs. She wanted to shout for him to slow down. What if the little boys should slip? It was six hundred steps to the bottom, and as she peered over the railing, she could imagine falling straight to the stone floor below.

Jamie and Mark, however, enjoyed the rapid pace. They thought Doc Grogan was simply paying them back for the fact that they had left him in the dust on the way up. Lori let them go by. She was angry at Doc for this game. She hung back with Charles and Louis.

"Let them go," she said. "We don't have to hurry."

Grogan, Mark, and Jamie were already two twists of the spiral below them.

Louis and Charles seemed grateful for the fact that she slowed her pace to match their careful descent.

"Going up was easier," said Charles as he clutched the rail. "'Cause we couldn't see down."

It took them ten minutes longer to reach the floor of the cathedral than it had taken Doc and the older boys. When Lori emerged from the exit, Jamie and Mark were sitting on a bench just to the side of the opening. Doc was nowhere to be seen.

They answered Lori's question before she asked.

"Doc said he had something really important to do. He told us we should all go back to Red Lion House and wait for him there."

Jacob paced the length of the small TENS office and back again. He was careful not to knock over the overflowing trash can or the stacks of military books beside Captain Orde's desk.

Werner sat on the windowsill, his head moving back and forth as he watched Jacob. Alfie thought Jacob's face looked as if he had found something he had always wanted. Alfie knew what that something was, too.

"All my life I have wanted to fight those arrogant, goose-stepping Nazis," Jacob said in an excited voice. "And now I can do it! There were plenty of soldiers marching in the legion today who are no older than I am! If war is coming, I want to join the Polish Army!"

The captain pressed his fingers together at the tips. Tap. Tap. Tap. Alfie could tell that Captain Orde did not like anything Jacob was saying. As a matter of fact, Alfie did not like it either. When the Nazi tanks came, they would kill Jacob in no time. Alfie frowned at the thought. He wanted to tell Jacob that, but it was better for the captain to talk about such things.

"You have a wife to think of," Orde said. He was not joking. Lori was a good thing to mention right now, because otherwise Jacob would run out the door and down to the recruiting office to enlist.

Jacob stopped pacing. He ran his fingers through his hair. Had he forgotten Lori was waiting in London? "She would expect me to be brave, expect me to fight the men who killed my parents and are keeping her father in prison!"

Alfie stuck out his lower lip. It was no wonder Jacob was ready to sign up with the Polish Army and go off to the border to wait until the shooting started! Jacob had not been thinking quite right since he found out about his father and mother. He had wanted to fight everyone since the captain had broken the terrible news. Mostly he wanted to take as many Germans with him as he could get hold of.

"Joining the Polish Army will not bring back your mother and father," the captain said above the tap, tap, tap of his fingers. "It will simply make certain that you join them much sooner than you would like to.

"Defeatist!" Jacob spat.

"Realist," the captain replied calmly. "Or have you forgotten the German counterpart to what we witnessed today?" He lowered his head and looked up at the still-pacing Jacob. "Have you forgotten that the Poles are driving pygmy tanks compared to the big ones you saw rolling through the streets of Berlin?"

"I saw them too," Alfie volunteered. "Much bigger. Lots more noisy, too."

Jacob glared at him unpleasantly. "Stay out of this, Elisha!" he cried. "Aren't you supposed to see angels all around? Fiery angels with drawn swords, protecting the righteous?"

Alfie shook his head. "Not today," he said slowly, trying to remember if he had missed something.

Captain Orde interrupted in a very captain-like way.

"If you want to fight the Nazis, I will help you. But not here. Not in Poland." He raised his head and sniffed the air. "What do you smell, Jacob?"

Jacob sniffed. "Polish sausages," he said in a flat tone.

Alfie knew that the captain was catching the scent of a dead dog out on the street. Alfie had just said how bad it smelled.

The captain narrowed his eyes. Tap. Tap. Tap. "That is death, Jacob," he said in a quiet voice. "Call it Polish sausages if you will, but I am telling you that unless there is a miracle, there will not be any place in Warsaw or all of Poland that does not stink like death."

"Then I will die bravely!"

Captain Orde stood and faced off with Jacob. "Better to live bravely. And sensibly!" He picked up a long narrow strip of paper from the teletype machine. Werner jumped down; he thought this would be a good thing to play with. The captain held it up for Jacob to see.

"I cannot read English," Jacob said in a proud and angry voice.

"Then I will translate." Orde began to read. "Today after failures in talks between Moscow and Great Britain to sign a mutual nonaggression pact, Moscow has announced that high German officials are flying to the Kremlin to discuss matters of mutual national interest." He stopped and looked at Jacob's blank face.

"So what?" Jacob snapped. "So Hitler is breaking every

promise and finally climbing into bed with the Communists."

"You really do not know what this means, do you?" Captain Orde said.

Alfie thought that he might know, but he did not say it out loud. Stalin and Hitler hated each other a lot. Did this mean they were now going to be friends?

Captain Orde looked very pale. "The mutual bed on which Hitler and Stalin will lie is Poland." He swept his hand toward the lovely old buildings of Warsaw just outside the window. "Take a last look, Jacob. Then inhale deeply and remember the smell. The child these two monsters conceive is called Death. This will be its playground. Here. Warsaw." He sighed deeply and sat down on the squeaking desk chair. Then he looked at Alfie. "You understand, don't you, Elisha? There are no angels around Warsaw. No chariots of fire. No flaming swords or—" He placed the tape in a jumbled pile on his desk. "I promised Helen Ibsen I would do my best to get you out of here, Jacob. I intend to do that." He looked at Alfie, then back to Jacob. "Join the Zionist Youth organization. They train young men to travel to Palestine. To work there. To fight there if they must. The odds are not perfect, but much better than this. I have contacts. Several hundred young men were brought in illegally to the Mandate. There may still be time—"

"To run away," Jacob said bitterly.

"You have never seen running until you see what is about to happen here in Poland. They will run and they will be massacred. On all sides, I have no doubt. The Nazis will come in from the north, south, and west. The Russians will come in from the east. Both sides have been waiting twenty years to divide up Poland like a beef carcass."

All the fire left Jacob's eyes. He turned away and sat on the edge of a shipping crate that had not yet been unpacked since they arrived. Werner jumped up on his lap and Jacob scratched the kitten behind his ears. This was a good thing, Alfie thought. Jacob had remembered that Captain Orde was an honest man, a soldier who knew things just by looking.

"I want to fight them." Jacob's voice was sad more than angry.

"You will have your chance," Captain Orde said in a soldierly voice. "As a matter of fact, I have the hope that I might train you myself."

Jacob smiled a little. "You're retired."

"Temporary insanity on the part of the British High Command, I assure you." He squared his shoulders. "They will need me back soon enough. After what I saw today, I have no doubt of that." He raised his eyebrows and Alfie could tell that he was relieved. "Until then, you must promise me that you will not join the Polish Army."

A shrug. A nod from Jacob.

Captain Orde tapped his fingers in a happy way. "Good. A good strong lad like you will do well under my command. But you must learn to obey orders first." He looked over at the overflowing garbage can. "You will empty that, please. And then put the books on the shelf."

———

Alfie had been looking for Lucy Strasburg ever since they arrived in Warsaw. He had not been wandering around *looking* for her, but rather he had been expecting to see her around every corner.

Today he swept the step and the broad sidewalk in front of the TENS office. Werner played tag with the broom, crouching and pouncing on the straw and then attacking wildly as Alfie pulled the broom across the pavement.

Busy people hurried past with gas masks hung from straps around their shoulders. Faces were grim. Alfie noticed that the eyes of everyone darted up to look into the sky every time an airplane rumbled over.

There were Polish uniforms everywhere. Long, shining sword scabbards dangled from wide belts and clattered noisily along the sidewalk. The swords made the sound of tin cans banging on the ground. The soldiers seemed not to notice the racket they made as they walked and talked to one another. But Alfie noticed. Along with the engines of automobiles and trams, Warsaw had become a very noisy place, indeed.

Like the Tin Man in the moving picture show that Captain Orde had taken them to last night, Warsaw rattled. Its old, rusty knees knocked together. Its jaw hinge groaned as it stood shaking in front of the Great and Terrible Oz of a Führer. Hitler's voice boomed out in a most terrifying way. Alfie replayed the scene in his mind.

"I AM THE GREAT AND TERRIBLE OZ!" This had been spoken in English with Polish subtitles and translated into German by Captain Orde.

Alfie looked down at Werner, a small version of the cowardly lion. Werner's ears went back when Alfie talked loud like the Wizard.

"You are supposed to try and run away, Werner," explained Alfie. "And then Dorothy and the Scarecrow and the Tin Man grab your tail and pull you back."

Alfie looked at his broom. He forgot his place in the story. The bad witch rode on the broom, didn't she? And then Dorothy threw water on her and she melted.

"Oh well," Alfie said. There would be no happy ending for the Tin Man this time. Captain Orde had said that England was the Cowardly Lion. It seemed to fit. He said that the French were like the Scarecrow—no brains. It made the moving picture show much better because in the end everything worked out. But Alfie thought it could have just as easily gone the other way. The heroes do not always win just because they are nice, Alfie knew. If that was true, then his friends at the hospital would not have been killed. The Hitler-men would not have put Pastor Ibsen in prison and killed Jacob's parents and burned down Jewish houses.

Alfie thought about this very hard as he swept. Countries like France had to be stuffed with more than straw in their heads. And a strong nation like England had to have more than just big muscles. England should have been brave, should have growled loud a lot sooner than it was doing now. *Cowardly Lion*.

One of the Polish Tin Men rattled past. He had a lot of bright medals on his chest. His boots were tall and shiny, and his uniform was just like one of Alfie's tin soldiers. He greeted a pretty lady in front of Cafe de Paris and they went in to eat lunch.

Alfie scratched his head and looked at Werner, who was chewing on the broom head ferociously. Alfie felt bad that he had called Werner the Cowardly Lion. He bent down and scooped the kitten up. He kissed Werner's nose and said, "Oh, I'm sorry, Werner. You are brave to attack something so big and unfeeling as a broom. I didn't mean *you* are a coward. I meant England."

Werner did not seem to mind. He purred when he smelled the tuna on Alfie's breath. It was good to have a friend.

The tram clanged by. There was a black hood over the headlight with a small slit in it. Only a tiny bit of light was allowed from trams and cars at night because everyone expected that the Nazis would soon bomb Warsaw.

Alfie looked up with everyone else as an airplane hummed over. *Just Polish.* Alfie looked down, then over at the people getting off the tram. Then he saw Lucy Strasburg, crossing the street behind the tram. Alfie was not at all surprised. He was just very happy to see her.

She looked much better than the day she gave the baby away. She was very thin, but her cheeks were not white like sheets. Her eyes looked serious, but bright and alive. She was checking a slip of paper with an address and then checking numbers on the fronts of the buildings. There was no sign yet for TENS, so Alfie raised up the broom like a flag on a stick and began to call her in his loudest voice.

"Lucy! Lucy *Strasss-burg*! Hey, Lucy! Lucy! LUCY!"

The effect was tremendous. Everyone looked at Alfie just the same way they looked at the planes. *Worried.*

"It's all right," Alfie said to a woman who walked far around the swinging broom. "The baby's mother—" He pointed the broom toward Lucy, who smiled wide at the very sight of Alfie. She was running now, dodging traffic to get to Alfie.

Alfie decided that he would have to tell her that he had gotten a new name and she would have to call him Elisha like everyone else. But first he wanted to know everything! He wanted to hear the whole story, because he was sure he had seen the bright ones follow her. Had she seen them, too? He squinted hard, but they weren't there. Well, they would be there when Lucy Strasburg needed them. He was sure of that.

She was out of breath and very happy. She took his hands and kissed them. "Oh! It is you! Oh! Alfie Halder! Bless you . . . *bless*! I thought I was lost. So afraid I had heard wrong and that I would not find you!"

"Why? I told you . . . we will be in Warsaw." He twisted his mouth around because he was embarrassed. Nobody had ever been so happy about seeing Alfie before—except maybe Werner when he was locked up a long time in the hotel room and they came home and turned on the light. Then Werner bounced all over the room.

"The address—" She held out a crumpled slip of paper. "The address Peter gave me was . . . the people have gone away, you see. So I . . . have you heard anything from England? Anything about my baby?" Her eyes held part of the sky in them, like the blue part with a heap of clouds moving in. She was worried. She was lonely. Alfie knew all about such eyes. He had seen them many times before.

"Baby Alfie is very well," Alfie said. "See?" He held up Werner as an example of how babies can do well even if they miss their mothers. Even if they have to go somewhere else to be safe.

Lucy bit her lip. "Tell me what you have heard."

"You want a letter?" he beamed. "Captain Orde has the letter. I can't read it . . . but I bet it is a good letter!"

———

Through the window of the TENS office in Warsaw, Orde, Jacob, and Alfie watched as Lucy opened the fat letter from Lori and Elisa. Pictures spilled out onto the park bench where Lucy sat.

She put her hand to her heart and then scrambled to retrieve them as if she feared some cruel wind would see and begin to blow out of the still air.

She held them like playing cards. Choosing one at a time, she gazed at them. Her face reflected joy and sorrow, then joy again. There were tears on her face. At this distance they could not see the tears, but she brushed her cheeks the way mothers do when they are happy about something wonderful.

Lucy went on this way for a long time. She did not open the letter until she tucked the edge of each photograph in a line beside her thigh. Then she read a little and looked down. She read a little more and then looked down once again at the pictures.

It was not as fine as it would have been if they could put that baby back in her arms, but it was a start, anyway, Orde told them in a gruff-sounding voice.

"Should we be looking at her like this?" Jacob asked. "Lori always hates it when I stand off and look at her and worry when she is . . . being . . . emotional."

"We should keep an eye on her," Orde said.

Alfie nodded. He wanted to go sit beside her. "Yes. We should. The man hurt her bad before she ran to the docks." Alfie put his hand to the place on his face where he remembered her terrible bruises.

Orde looked sharply at Alfie and then back at Lucy. Alfie's words made the captain nervous. Alfie could tell. Orde rose up on his toes and clasped his hands behind his back. He looked all around the square.

"I'll recognize him if he shows up," he muttered.

Jacob bumped his big fist into the palm of his hand. "A fellow like that. I almost wish he would try something."

"She shouldn't go away," Alfie warned with a frown.

"We can't stop her if she wants to go, Elisha," Jacob said. "Can we, Captain?" Was there a way to keep her from leaving?

Alfie looked at her, so bright and pretty in the sunlight. It was a terrible thing that somebody wanted to hurt someone so nice and pretty as Lucy. But Alfie was certain she should not go. He was as sure of that as he ever was about things. He bit his lip and felt scared inside. "How do we make her stay here, Captain?" Alfie said. "That man has hurt her bad. They will kill her if she goes. Maybe kill her if she stays. But for sure if she is not with us."

Orde and Jacob looked at each other around Alfie. "No angels around her, Elisha?" Jacob asked. He was not making fun.

Alfie frowned and looked everywhere. "No. No angels. Just us."

The letter from London. The photographs of her baby. It was all so much more than Lucy had hoped for. If she never heard another word, maybe she could manage now that he was safe.

A thousand times Lucy had replayed the escape of her baby from Wolf on the docks of Danzig harbor. Time and again she had seen it in her mind. *Lori carrying the child onto the ship. And then Wolf appearing with Hess and the other man, only to be stopped by the grim smile of the sun-browned stranger who stepped between them and the gangway to block their path.*

Lucy sat across from Sam Orde and repeated the story as it had happened to her. She did not tell everything, of course, but she knew from the way he looked at her that he guessed the details she left out. He had the eyes of a priest, full and kind, yet also wondering how Lucy had come to such a condition.

He did not question her about her relationship with Wolf. It was enough to say that Wolf was S.S. and that he had fathered the child with the intention of taking it from Lucy. At that, Orde merely frowned more deeply, his eyes reflecting both pity and perhaps a fleeting moment of revulsion. *Ah well,* Lucy thought, *this Englishman with the eyes of a holy man was only human, after all.* Should she blame him if his disgust for her was revealed for an unguarded instant?

She sat erect in her chair and looked straight ahead at the wall as she had done as a child in trouble at the convent school. No doubt Mother Superior would have looked at her more harshly than this fellow did!

Lucy deliberately passed over her days and nights of anguish as she had grieved and wondered about the baby. Best to stick to cold facts.

"So you see, Wolfgang von Fritschauer was not in pursuit of the children. He wished only to take the baby away." She bit her lip. "And I am certain he saw the baby in Lori's arms." She turned her eyes on Orde's face. The emotion she saw there surprised her. *Sadness?*

He exhaled loudly as though letting out a pain, deep in his chest. "And the address you gave Alfie?"

"My friends—the people I expected to be there—have moved away. No forwarding address. Apparently the address is months out of date." She could not stand the intensity of his sympathetic gaze, and so she focused her eyes on the wall again.

"I am glad you remembered us. The letter only arrived yesterday. I was hoping you would come. Your baby is beautiful."

Do not be so gentle or I will cry, Lucy thought as she stood to go. "Danke. Thank you," she said in English, which made him smile for the first time.

"You are learning English. Good. Planning to join your child in England?"

Planning was too strong a word for a dream that was only a prayer. Lucy pulled her green book from her handbag and passed it to him, hoping for a sign of approval.

"Ah." He smiled more broadly, but there was a doubt in his eyes. "Studying to be a parlormaid. Good. Yes." A long pause—too long. "But where are you going now?"

Lucy pointed toward the park across the street. She held up her sack lunch. She stepped back and extended her hand for the precious little volume. "I will not keep you from your work."

She swept a hand over the cluttered mess of the office. "I have my lunch, as you see."

"But do you have a place to stay in Warsaw?"

"I will go back to the home of the woman who took care of me. I was unwell, you see." This was one of the details she had not mentioned in her recitation. "Until I can find a place of my own and work."

"Ah." Orde held up his finger. "*Work!* The very thing I was getting at, Fräulein." He looked embarrassed as he stepped around an open crate of books. "Work. You see, I have been in need of . . . here in Warsaw . . . a secretary. You were a secretary in Vienna, you said?"

"Only German." Lucy tried not to look too disappointed. *Work as a secretary until she could get to England! Oh, God! But certainly he needed someone who spoke Polish and English!*

Orde indicated that her parlormaid instruction book was in English. "German is what I need. Partly, at least. You do take shorthand? The office is in need of someone who can take down the various speeches of the German government, then transcribe them. You do type as well?"

Her hopes began to rise. She resisted the urge to clap her hands together in joy. "Yes. I was fastest in the typing pool. I can . . . but my English is very poor," she concluded doubtfully.

"Good enough," Orde said in a businesslike manner. He inhaled and exhaled. A great concern had been lifted from him. "Other office work is required, of course." He frowned down at the jumble of files left by his predecessor, a Pole who was addicted to vodka as the drink of choice for breakfast, lunch, and dinner. Orde opened the dusty file drawer full of empty vodka bottles. "Not mine," Orde said. "But, as you see, more than anything we are in need of organizational skills. Typing. Clerical things." His lower lip protruded with concern. "And if this fellow, von Fritschauer, should come around, I should not like for you to meet him . . ." Orde's gaze lingered on the remaining trace of a bruise on the side of her nose. "If he has followed you here, as he followed you to Danzig . . ."

And so, he said the very thing that Lucy sensed. *The thing she feared!* She looked through the office window to the sidewalk, where Alfie and Jacob stood talking to a Polish gendarme as they waited for Orde and Lucy to complete their interview.

Maybe she should go away, Lucy reasoned—simply melt

away and call Samuel Orde later when he had more news of the baby. She had come only for news, not expecting sympathy or a job. "Wolf has never let anyone stand in the way of what he wants."

"He did not get past me on the Danzig quay," Orde responded. "I was in his way then." He smiled the schoolyard brawl kind of smile she had seen that day. "Frankly, this chap is just the sort I enjoy standing in the way of, Fräulein Strasburg. No need to speak further of it. You will need a room in which to stay. Appropriate clothing for work. TENS will assist in this. An advance of perhaps two weeks' salary? Yes? Good. Then it is all settled. Have your lunch here and then—well, start where you wish."

———

Doc Grogan crouched behind an ivy-covered wall on the corner of the street opposite Mills University Hotel. Twice he had pretended to be tying his shoe for the benefit of a passerby, but fortunately there was very little traffic to wonder about why the man remained in one spot for so long.

At last the only pedestrian Grogan cared about appeared at the top of the steps of the hotel. Allan Farrell looked up and down the quiet street repeatedly before proceeding, as if he were trying to cross Piccadilly without using the subway.

Farrell apparently satisfied himself that no one was observing him, and he strode purposefully down the steps carrying a small leather satchel. Grogan waited until the young man was out of sight around the far corner before leaving his place of concealment and rushing into the hotel.

Grogan mentally reviewed what it was he was seeking, even while another part of his mind was complaining about having still more stairs to climb! He was panting again when he reached Allan's door. He started to try the knob, then decided to knock first instead.

After a moment's delay brought no response, he tried the door and found it locked. After a quick glance up and down the hall, Grogan's hand extracted a small ring of oddly shaped keys from his pocket. He squinted at the lock, then at the keys.

Selecting one, he inserted it in the lock and was rewarded with a satisfying click. The door swung open, and Grogan stepped inside quickly and locked the door behind him.

A glance around the room showed very little that was out of the ordinary. The table had an untidy look, with bits of paper and twine lying about, as if something had been hastily wrapped.

Grogan's inspection of the closet revealed a curiosity: nine small leather cases, twins to the one Farrel had been carrying. They were all empty, but identical in description.

The language professor ran his fingers over the walls and floor of the closet and soon found what he was seeking. The edge of one board protruded past the others just enough for Grogan's fingers to grasp it and pull it free. He reached through the opening into a recessed compartment, and his hand closed around a small glass bottle.

Extracting the bottle very carefully from its hiding place, Grogan gently unscrewed the lid. One whiff of the contents told him all he needed to know. He was even more careful as he replaced it.

He was about to reinstall the board when his fingers brushed something else inside the cubicle. Grogan brought a leather-bound book out into the room with him and carried it to the window to inspect it.

It was a small red volume entitled *BAEDEKER'S LONDON AND ITS ENVIRONS*. The book fell open in Doc's hand to the place marked by a red ribbon. The indicated section was labeled "St. Paul's Cathedral—The Dome."

———

A terrible suspicion forced itself to Doc Grogan's attention. He cursed at the cabbie for driving too slowly and shoved pedestrians out of his way after he jumped from the traffic-jammed taxi.

Grogan's face was distracted, nervous as he appeared in the doorway of Red Lion House. He was sweating ferociously.

"Come on!" he called to the little boys.

"Where?" Charles wondered in a puzzled voice.

"Get out here!" Grogan insisted; then he hefted the twins and hauled them downstairs.

"What?" Lori insisted. "Why are we—?"

"Take the children over there," Grogan demanded. There was no arguing with his tone of voice. He left her on the sidewalk and ran back up into the house with more urgency. She heard him shout now, angrily, for the other boys to get out.

Moments later, puzzled and irritated, Jamie and Mark emerged and at Grogan's urging, hurried into the square to join Lori.

"Wait for me," he said. Then he pointed to the bench at the farthest end of Red Lion Square, "Over there."

"What's wrong?" Lori asked him as a cold knot of fear formed in her stomach. She had felt this way at New Church when the Nazis had come in to search and Jacob had pushed them into the bellows. It was the sense of panic, thinly veiled beneath a calm exterior.

Grogan did not reply. He jogged across the grass of the square as though he did not hear her question. Then, not waiting until the street was clear, he dodged traffic and recrossed the street in front of the house.

He knocked on the door of the downstairs flat where Freddie and Hildy lived.

"They aren't home!" Lori shouted. Did he hear her? "Gone shopping! And to pick up Elisa!"

He turned the knob cautiously, hesitated a moment, then gave the door a shove. It opened. It was not locked. Had extra-careful Hildy ever left the door unlocked before?

"What's he doing?" Jamie asked with alarm.

Grogan reached inside the pocket of his tan linen jacket, and then with a glance over his shoulder toward the children, slipped into the flat.

"What's wrong?" Mark echoed. Charles and Louis, who stood apart holding hands, unexplainably began to cry. They had never seen their beloved Doc act so strangely before!

Suddenly the crash of broken glass sounded from the lower flat. Windows were broken one after another as Doc Grogan threw pieces of furniture out into the street. And then, as if pursued by someone or *something*, he dashed out the door!

In that instant there was a great flash of light behind him! A rolling pillar of fire lifted him off the ground and spun him over and over into the air like a bird.

It seemed to happen in slow motion. Doc Grogan floated above the shrieking cars as the children screamed in horror from the far side of the square. Windows from neighboring houses trembled and shattered inward with the blast. The leaves and limbs of the trees moved as if a giant wind had smashed against them.

Lori covered Charles and Louis with her body as debris swirled in the sky and clattered down with the same slow motion as the rag-doll body of Doc Grogan.

And then everything was very quiet. *So quiet!* Traffic completely still. No birds chirping. No voices calling. Seconds ticked by. The hiss of a car radiator erupted. The crackle of the fire that had flashed and devoured the inside of the downstairs vanished. From far away there came the faint wail of a siren. The boys looked up from where they had fallen. They knew Doc Grogan was dead. The house did not matter. Doc was dead. He had gotten them out, and now he lay in the rubble beside the curb in front of the lovely old Red Lion House.

People began to shout. A woman holding her bloody forehead stumbled from the house next door. A dazed man climbed from his wrecked car and walked carefully over the broken glass to where Doc Grogan lay. He stooped and peered at the body. He leaned closer, then jumped to his feet and shouted, "He is breathing! He is alive!"

31   In the Balance

Hildy Frutschy was hysterical. She sobbed and trembled as the Scotland Yard detectives interviewed her. She blamed herself for everything while big Freddie sat forlornly beside her and wrung his cap in his enormous hands.

Had she left the gas on after brewing her tea? She had worried about that after she was gone. She frequently worried about such horrible things, and now it had come true, hadn't it? Her very worst nightmare had come true, just as she had always worried about it. The children were almost killed. And now poor Doc Grogan lay on the very threshold of death and . . . oh! It was the absolute fault of her own carelessness, wasn't it?

Anna and Helen and Theo comforted the boys in a private sitting room at the hospital. Elisa and Murphy sat with Lori as

Scotland Yard Detective Thompson asked her to replay the incident once again from the beginning.

The ordeal had lasted for hours. Lori's brow furrowed as she repeated the story once more. "He seemed agitated . . . No, I did not smell gas from the house. He ran up the stairs and got the boys out . . . ran back, smashing windows and then—" At last Lori began to weep. She leaned her head against Elisa's shoulder and cried very softly.

If it was an accident, why go through this again? Why put Lori through the horror of reliving it over and over?

Yet another detective opened the door and motioned to Detective Thompson with a crook of his finger. "Grogan died a few minutes ago."

Murphy and Elisa exchanged sorrowing looks. Doc Grogan *dead*! Lori covered her ears and buried her face deeper in Elisa's shoulder. Elisa held her as if she were a little girl.

"Do you want your mother?" Elisa asked gently; then she shot a withering look at Detective Thompson. Why was he pressing so hard? "She needs her mother," Elisa said to Murphy in a voice loud and indignant enough that Thompson could hear her. "And then she needs to sleep!"

Murphy stood and crossed his arms across his chest in a defiant way. He waited until the second agent slipped out, leaving Thompson to glance at his watch apologetically. Yes. It had been going on a long time.

"I suppose you overheard?" He looked at the door. "I am sorry. I was hopeful Grogan would survive this. Shed some light."

"The girl is worn out." Murphy indicated that there was to be no more questioning.

The agent nodded and swept his hands toward the door where the others waited. Then as Elisa and Lori moved out, he put a hand up to stop Murphy. Waiting until the two women were out of earshot he said quietly, "There is someone here you should talk to."

Murphy was convinced that there was nothing more to the headline than *CARELESS HOUSEKEEPER LEAVES GAS STOVE ON—BLOWS UP HOUSE—ONE KILLED*. This continued probing seemed needlessly cruel, and he was angered by it. Murphy sighed and nodded. It was ten minutes more before anyone came.

The door swung back, revealing the bulk of the man Murphy

recognized immediately as Mr. Tedrick, of the British Secret Service. It had been over a year since Tedrick had arranged for Murphy and Elisa to meet together in the cottage of New Forest. This was one man Murphy had hoped never to have to see again.

"Hullo there, Murphy." Tedrick extended his meaty hand. He was too cheerful for a time like this. His smile was too broad, his voice too eager to spill the bad news.

"What are you doing here?" Murphy did not shake his hand. He was finished for the time being, and he wanted to gather up his family and find a nice quiet hotel to sleep in for a while.

Tedrick would not be put off. He sat down heavily in the one comfortable chair and indicated that perhaps Murphy should sit somewhere as well. Murphy continued standing.

"Suit yourself," Tedrick said. "I suppose you've already written the story. Let me guess—something about a careless housekeeper? A gas burner left on? Household accident?"

"Something like that."

"Print whatever you like. Probably that is the best story to circulate in a case like this."

"What case?" Murphy asked in an unmistakably angry tone.

"What was Patrick Grogan to you?"

"Dr. Grogan . . . Doc . . . was a speech therapist. One of our boys—" He ran his hand through his hair. The effort of telling even this small detail seemed too great. Murphy could not believe that Doc was gone. He needed to think about that. Digest it. Try to understand the loss. Instead, Murphy was standing in a little room across from an arrogant government man who manipulated personal lives like a game of chess. "What difference does it make?" Murphy finished and sat down.

"Grogan was more than that." Tedrick looked at his nails and then back to gauge Murphy's response. "He was an agent."

Murphy shook his head. He looked toward the stony face of Detective Thompson. "Yours? Or theirs?"

"Actually," Tedrick said with a half smile, "yours. American."

"Well, well," Murphy said with disgust. "Is that for publication, Tedrick? Remember who you're talking to. My profession." His voice was thick with sarcasm.

"Suit yourself." Tedrick was not threatened. "Your government might not be too happy about it, though."

"Listen," Murphy growled. "It's late. The bottom of my house blew up today, just about taking my kids up with it, killing a man

433

we were all genuinely fond of. I don't much like you, Tedrick. Never have. So if you've got something to say, just get to it, because I'm taking my family someplace quiet in about three minutes."

Tedrick's amused expression did not change. "Well, then. You always were a rather direct chap."

"That's what makes me a newsman and you a professional sneak. So? What's up?"

"Grogan was an American agent, working closely with us on the link between the Nazis and the American Clan de Gael. Recognize the name?"

"The American version of the IRA. Yes." Still angry, he showed little interest in the news, as though nothing surprised him. Maybe nothing did anymore.

Tedrick continued as if he were talking about the weather or a motoring trip to Blackpool. "We have known for some time that information about you . . . your family . . . has been of great interest to the other side. The Nazis. With your wife's former activities and personal associations—"

Murphy narrowed his eyes threateningly. If this clown brought up the fact that Elisa made a mistake once a long time ago with a former Nazi, Murphy decided he would knock him cold. Patience was gone. Tedrick seemed to sense that and backed off a bit.

"Her connection, for instance, with Pastor Karl Ibsen, on the one hand. And on the other, her activities in Vienna. Smuggling children out of the Reich. Children like . . . your boys, for instance. Charles and Louis Kronenberger. Such things are all an active irritant to the sensitive stomach lining of the German Führer, we are certain. For this reason we thought it best if your . . . bodyguard—" He was openly amused at Freddie Frutschy. "Well, Grogan was a healthy backup, as you can see from today's incident."

"Not an accident? Then what?"

"Grogan lost his life. The bomb—"

"Bomb?"

A slow nod replied. The irritating smile remained as if to say, *What else, you idiot?* "Bomb. Yes. We are ninety percent certain. It was a botched attempt on the lives of the Ibsen children. On your children. No doubt your wife and the babies were supposed to be there for the event as well. If Grogan had not broken out the windows, the whole block might have been lifted up and sent elsewhere."

Murphy's stomach lurched. He felt cold and then hot. Beads of sweat formed on his forehead. There was no room left for defiance, no matter what he felt for Tedrick.

"Okay. *Why?*" he pleaded.

Tedrick studied his nails again; then rubbed his hands together thoughtfully. "Have you ever heard the name Paul Golden?"

Murphy played the name over in his mind a few times. "Golden? Paul Golden?" He sighed and scratched his head in confusion. "No," he shrugged.

Now Tedrick looked concerned. "Grogan said the name. Three times before he died. *Paul Golden* and *light wells.*"

"He spoke?"

"Paul Golden. Light wells. Ibsen. Churchill," Tedrick replied. "He was on to something big. Told me last week—"

"Told you?"

"Yes. Grogan was not hostile to me, as you are. We did have a bit in common. Like rooting out the scum from London's gutters before someone innocent slipped and—" He waved his hand. That was all beside the point. No use discussing political ideologies in the face of cold, brutal murder. "So, he told me there was someone in your organization bleeding you dry for information. The leak is from a stationary agent in your house, possibly at the TENS office. From there it is passed to the IRA and then on to the Nazis." He paused, letting the implications sink in.

"You mean someone close to us?"

"I was hoping Paul Golden worked for you," Tedrick said in a distracted way. "Have you noticed things missing? Or maybe out of place?"

"Come to think of it," Murphy shrugged, "I thought it was just me." He frowned as he considered the times he had misplaced things. The postcards warning Elisa that she might still be in danger had vanished completely. There were plenty of other things as well. But Paul Golden? The name meant nothing to Murphy.

"I just had a word with the ladies about it." He held up his hand to stop Murphy's reaction. "No one knows Paul Golden." The smile was gone. "Where would you like to stay? Savoy, perhaps? You will need a round-the-clock bodyguard. I'll get my best man on it right away. Freddie Frutschy and his wife are leaving for Wales tonight. They have a son there. Freddie told me the Missus needs to get away." Tedrick talked rapidly. "This is beyond him anyway," Tedrick said grimly. "I am making arrangements for Mrs. Lindheim and her sister to leave London with the boys before the first public orders for evacuation are announced tomorrow."

"Evacuation?" Tedrick had said the word in such an offhanded way that it sounded as though the event were common knowledge. He left no room for argument. Decisions had been made.

"Yes. School children. They are being evacuated out of the areas most likely to be targeted by the Luftwaffe." He cleared his throat. Evacuation was the final admission by the British government that things had become hopeless. "There is a cottage in Evesham near the Avon. Charles and Louis Kronenberger, Jamie Ibsen, and Mark Kalner will be happy there until you can make arrangements to get them back to the States. I suggested that Elisa leave as well. She refuses to consider it until after the memorial concert at St. Paul's. She says now, more than ever, it must go on. Lori Kalner is adamant that she will stay until Elisa leaves London."

"You've already talked this over with them?" Murphy challenged. His weary brain replayed the news of mass evacuation of English school children. Again and again he rolled the news over until the implications of it made him feel a little lightheaded. And Tedrick had already spoken with Anna and Elisa about it!

Evacuation! Refugees here in England? First in Germany, then in Austria. The Sudetenland had followed. Prague in March. Danzig. And now that Poland was certain to be swallowed, the evacuation order was finally to be given right here in London!

"So it has come to this," Murphy replied in a hoarse voice. "I hoped it wouldn't."

"But it has. And now we will make the best of it."

———

"It is hard to believe that there could be any good news on a day like this." Anna gently put her hand on Murphy's arm.

He looked up at her, barely able to comprehend what she was saying. She pulled two envelopes out of her handbag. The

436

return address was the passport office. The passports of Alfie Halder and Rachel Lubetkin had arrived in the mail today.

Lori carried Jacob's document in her handbag. But 157 birth certificates had gone up in the flames of the Red Lion House. Destroyed with them were the hopes that they might be used to obtain additional passports for the boys in Orde's Zionist Youth brigade.

A number of applications were pending, however. Twenty-nine were currently being processed. But the political situation deteriorated by the hour. Should Murphy take these three passports to Warsaw? Or should they wait until more arrived?

Murphy gazed at the solemn faces inside the slick blue folders. Rachel Lubetkin. Jacob Kalner. Alfie Halder. Their safety seemed to hang in the balance with that decision.

Peter Wallich was taller, it seemed to Lucy, when she first spotted him at the long table in the Community Center soup kitchen. He was definitely thinner and more tattered. She recognized the plaid shirt he wore—the same shirt he had on the day he left her in Danzig.

The center of attention among a group of young people his own age, Peter gestured broadly as he related some story to his audience.

Lucy looked around for some sign of Peter's mother and sister. Where was Karin Wallich amidst the clamor? Where was Marlene, with her dark and sullen face?

No one had yet noticed Orde's entrance into the enormous room, or spoons would have been silent against bowls, and conversations would have fallen away. Orde had deliberately come early. The photographer was scheduled to arrive at seven o'clock to begin the arduous task of taking several hundred passport photos. Orde had not explained that he was sending them back to England a few at a time in hopes that they would come back inside shiny new British folders. Lucy had heard Orde gruffly inform the photographer that what happened to the photos was of no concern as long as he was paid.

"What is it?" Orde leaned in to Lucy as he noticed her gazing with mild wonder in the direction of Peter Wallich.

"Peter," she answered.

"Yes. A member of the Zionist Youth. How do you know him?"

"I know him," Lucy said as the boy happened to look up and see her.

He gaped at her a bare moment before he leaped to his feet and dashed through the narrow aisles between tables to where she stood.

"Lucy!" he shouted, loudly enough that his cries of joy turned heads. "Lucy! It's *you*!"

Suddenly everyone noticed that the woman Peter Wallich was shouting at happened to be in the company of the great and magnificent British Zionist, Samuel Orde. So who was this Lucy, anyway? And how did Peter happen to know her?

All propriety was thrown to the wind. Peter charged up and embraced her, laughing and shouting her name! A small group of his companions made a curious semicircle around him as he and Lucy embraced and looked at each other with delight.

"Last I saw you, you were not so thin!" Peter exclaimed.

"And I could say the same for you," she replied.

"You got my letter?"

"No."

"Where is the baby?"

"In England."

A moment of dark comprehension flashed in his eyes; then he brushed it away. "But you had to get the letter—you found me here. I lost the address where mother and Marlene—"

"They are not there anymore," Lucy said in a rush.

And so the reunion stumbled from one revelation to the next as members of the Zionist Youth lined up to have their pictures taken in the basement.

Peter and Lucy talked for three hours in a quiet corner of the now-deserted dining room of the soup kitchen. When Orde and Jacob and Alfie emerged from the evening's instruction, the red-haired youth leader's countenance had changed from one of joy to somber concern.

The conclusion of their rambling conversation had come to a frightening possibility that Peter shared with Orde.

"So you see, when I lost my address, I wrote to Lucy in Danzig inquiring of her to send the information to me. I gave this place as my return address."

"I never got his letter," Lucy added.

"It is possible that the man who pursued her in Danzig could have intercepted that letter," Peter finished. "He would have this address, you see. He arrested the man who helped my family in Vienna, and I do not doubt that he is still—"

Orde nodded and looked at Lucy with a new concern. "Yes. It is best that you remain with me. He will show up, sooner or later." The prospect seemed to please him. "In the meantime, the photographer is still waiting downstairs. Both of you . . . if you please."

———————

Allan Farrell coupled the wires of a small black device to a bundle of explosives on his kitchen table. Another of the leather satchels stood open on the floor beside him. There was a sharp rap on his door.

Farrell started to sweep all his material off the table and into the case when he heard two more knocks, followed by a pause, and then two more. He continued putting everything out of sight, but in an unhurried manner. Then he went over to the door and admitted Hess.

"Ah, Mr. Farrell," said Hess. "Sorry to interrupt you." He tugged on the glove covering his crippled hand. "Is all proceeding as planned?"

Allan nodded. "Soon everything will be in place."

"What a great pity that the explosion that removed the man Grogan did not eliminate a few more nuisances as well."

Farrell stiffened, expecting a rebuke for his rash act.

Hess noted the worried expression that crossed Allan's face. "Don't be alarmed, Mr. Farrell. You did very well in removing a potentially troublesome opponent, and as for the rest—well, they will not be around to bother us much longer, will they? But I have come to say goodbye. Other important events are going forward that demand my presence elsewhere, so I leave you to the completion of your mission. Do you have all that you require?"

"Everything."

"Good. If you find the need for additional supplies, just leave your request in the usual way. Between our technology and your courage and resourcefulness, I am certain you cannot fail." Hess straightened his necktie. "That's it, then. I'll be listening for the sound of your success. The echo will undoubtedly be heard throughout Europe."

——————

Two days later, Hess stood in the bowels of Gestapo headquarters in Berlin, reviewing Allan Farrell's progress.

"You are certain that Operation Edifice is positioned and will take place as planned?" demanded Himmler.

"Quite sure, Reichsführer," responded Hess. "And there will be no way to link the activity to anyone but the IRA."

"And will all the principal targets be in place?"

Hess nodded a contented agreement. "The Murphys, the Ibsens, and the Lindheims will all be attending to hear Winston Churchill deliver an address on what is sure to be a memorable occasion."

Both men chuckled slightly. "You have done well, Agent Hess. Your reward will be participation in another event of great significance."

"Thank you, Reichsführer," Hess nodded modestly. "And the nature of my new assignment?"

"It is the opening scene of what is called Case White," explained Himmler, waving a handkerchief of that color which he was using to polish his spectacles. "The Führer was very taken with an American radio production called, I believe, *The War of the Worlds*. In it a race of beings from the planet Mars attacks the earth. This is, however, beside the point. The night that the broadcast occurred, a great many Americans believed such a ludicrous invasion was actually taking place! There was widespread panic, and armed citizens fortified their homes against the threat from Mars." Himmler paused and smiled at the puzzled look on the face of Hess.

"You understand that Poland must make a move of aggression against the Reich. The Poles have so far not cooperated, but we will see to it that they attack a radio station in the border town of Gleiwitz. We have arranged that some political prisoners and some traitorous officers are going to be the Poles for this attack. They are even going to be dressed in Polish uniforms."

Agent Hess nodded his understanding. "And my role in this little stage play?" he asked.

"You are to select the participants and see that they are equipped and in position on the morning of September 1."

"And may I ask for your guidance in regard to the selection?" requested Hess.

"I believe that you are acquainted with the prison compound near the Polish border crossing where your unfortunate injuries took place. You should make your selections there."

Hess rose and saluted, then paused. "One additional thought, Reichsführer. May I suggest adding Major von Fritschauer to the list?"

Himmler paused in thought, then agreed. "I will send word that he is needed back here in Berlin. It does not appear that anything useful is to be gained by following him, and most recently he has attempted to hide himself among the Jewish community of Warsaw." Himmler shook his head sadly that a young officer could have fallen so far.

"Shocking," agreed Hess, and he saluted again before leaving.

———

Rachel extended her hand shyly to the beautiful woman who had saved Peter Wallich and was even now, according to Peter, being pursued by Nazi agents.

It was like meeting the heroine of a very exciting story in person. Rachel considered the details of the dramatic escape from Vienna, the chance meeting with Adolf Hitler, the long and terrible ride with the Gestapo agent in the rail car! How much more exciting did a story have to be in order for this Lucy Strasburg to really be a heroine? Peter had recited the harrowing tale a hundred times. And now *here* was the very Lucy!

"Is she Jewish?" asked the old yentas in the soup kitchen.

"She must be."

"Probably raised in an assimilated family. Ignorant of Jewish ways, you can tell."

"So what? That is what helped her save Peter Wallich! I'd like to see how you would handle meeting the German Führer, God forbid! Oy! Makes my head ache to think about it!"

Thus everyone *knew* the secret that Lucy Strasburg was really Jewish, even though it did not show. Just like they knew that Captain Samuel Orde was also really secretly Jewish. Peter had not mentioned the part about the baby, which might have caused the yentas to view her with less kindly eyes. That part of the adventure being left out created room for speculation about what a lovely couple Captain Samuel Orde and Lucy Strasburg would make standing together beneath a chuppa! *Nu?*

All the talk among the women in the soup kitchen made Rachel blush deeply when she finally got to meet Lucy. *A real heroine. Oy! And maybe even a little romance in her future as well.*

For the moment at least, with the spark of her imagination ignited, Rachel thought about something besides the turmoil that had turned her peaceful existence upside down. Only much later in the night, when she lay on her bed and contemplated the past of such a beautiful woman as Lucy, did it occur to her that Lucy was not in Warsaw because she wanted to be. Like all the rest, she was running, running, running away!

———

"I am in love with her," Peter blurted out to Lucy, nodding absently at Rachel Lubetkin as she carried yet another stack of pillowcases down to the basement.

Lucy smiled slightly. "Then I envy you both. First love." She dried the tin bowls as they spoke.

Peter looked miserably at the empty doorway where Rachel had just disappeared. "She hates me. At least I think she does. Just my luck, huh? To fall in love with the prettiest girl in the district, who also happens to be the rabbi's daughter."

"She will come around." Lucy tried to console Peter.

He shook his head in disagreement. "She is already engaged. To a boy named Reuven in Lodz whom she has never met."

"Hmmm," Lucy said with surprise. "They are still doing that sort of thing?"

"And I am not religious. Obviously. But . . . I have spoken with her father."

"Courageous, Peter."

"I told him she should leave Poland with us." He looked at Lucy. "Already Hayedid has sent out ten groups of twelve to go to Yugoslavia. Soon enough they'll be in Palestine, papers or no papers."

"And will your Rachel leave her family?" Lucy thought it might be the family of Rachel Lubetkin that tied her to Poland, not this Reuven fellow in Lodz.

"If her father orders her," Peter said hopefully. "And he might if—" So here came the point.

"Just say it, Peter."

"All right then. If you use your influence and speak with the captain, then he will speak to the rabbi, and—"

"And your Rachel will go with you to live on a kibbutz."

"Yes."

Lucy nodded. "I have no influence with the captain," she said softly. "He is a kind man who has employed me. That is all."

Peter looked at her in disbelief. "Everyone talks about the way he looks at you."

Lucy frowned and looked away. She did not want to hear this. She knew how men looked at her. She hoped the captain was not like other men. "It is your imagination."

Peter took her wet hand in his. "Tell me you will speak with him about Rachel. She is too pretty to stay here." His eyes were desperate. "And you know what I am talking about. If the Nazis come here . . . Well, there is no use saying they don't do whatever they want to women, is there?"

His comment had not been intended to hurt Lucy, but it did. "Yes. No use denying it. And I will speak to him about her. Although I think you could get further with him than I can."

Peter kissed her hand in gratitude and then stumbled clumsily off down the stairs after Rachel.

———

TENS Warsaw acquired the last two-bedroom suite available at the Bristol Hotel. Perhaps they rented the last suite available anywhere in Warsaw. With the enormous influx of Western journalists crowding into the city to follow the shuttling politicians, every hotel was packed, and no one seemed to be checking out.

Alfie knew that this fact was a relief to Captain Orde, because it had settled the issue of where Lucy would be staying.

"Of course you must stay with the TENS staff at the Bristol," he told Lucy in a very businesslike tone. "Elisha and Jacob will move into my room with me. You may have the other room. You *must* have the other room until things in Warsaw settle down a bit."

Alfie knew that the captain did not really believe anything in Warsaw would settle down. As a matter of fact, he had made a tour of the basement of the Bristol Hotel, which had been converted into a bomb shelter. The captain had told Alfie that when the siren blew, he must very quickly put the kitten in his hiding place in the valise and carry it with him down to the basement.

The captain did not say *if* the siren blows, but *when* it blows. The people in charge of the bomb shelter would not let a kitten in if they knew it was a kitten. But if they thought it was just a piece of baggage, they would not make a fuss about it. For this reason, Alfie had kept a few extra cans of sardines in Werner's valise. That way, if they were in the basement shelter a long time, Alfie could feed Werner and maybe Werner would not yowl so loud and upset the other people in the shelter.

All of this had been discussed long before Lucy arrived at the TENS office, and also a long time before Warsaw filled up with so many people. The point was, Jacob explained to Alfie, the captain most likely was very pleased to give up his room to Lucy. He did not seem to want to let her out of his sight.

Jacob was right about that. When Lucy went down to the delicatessen to pick up sandwiches which Captain Orde ordered, the captain paced nervously in the office and stopped at every turn to look out over the street. He muttered, "Shouldn't let her go." Then he rocked back and forth on his toes and looked almost angry.

Jacob nodded at Alfie as if to show how right he was. Alfie shrugged and nodded, then said to the captain, "Why didn't you go with her?"

At this, the face of Captain Orde brightened. "I'll just go see what's keeping her." Then he dashed out the door.

Jacob looked smug. He put his feet up on the desk. "Don Quixote," he remarked with a grin. "And he has met his Dulcinea at last."

Alfie did not understand what Jacob meant and he did not want to ask because Jacob might think he was a Dummkopf. "Yes," Alfie said as though he understood perfectly. This made Jacob look at him with surprise.

Maybe Alfie did not know about Don Quixote, but he could tell easily that the captain was very worried about Lucy Strasburg. Captain Orde would fight for her. He would very much enjoy smashing the face of the man who had hurt Lucy.

"Look at this." Jacob grinned and took his feet off the desk as Orde and Lucy walked together toward the office. Orde was carrying the paper bags with sandwiches. He was talking to her in a pleasant way. A kindly way. Alfie could not tell what they were talking about, but Lucy Strasburg had the same misty smile she had on her face as when she saw the pictures of her baby.

"The protective instinct of the chivalrous British knight." Jacob pretended to read a newspaper, but he was watching all the while. "King Arthur and Guinevere," he said under his breath.

"Yes," Alfie agreed. He did not understand this either, but it made him very happy to see the way their lonely captain worried over Lucy, who was also a very lonely person. Alfie knew about lonely people. He knew all about that even if he did not understand what Jacob was talking about exactly.

The captain did not talk to Lucy in the same gruff manner in which he discussed things with Jacob and Alfie. That evening at the hotel, he told her about the complete safety of the bomb shelter beneath the hotel. He said that the sirens would no doubt blow, but that she must not be frightened by such an event. Even if there were some sort of German aggression against Poland, he told her, she was not to worry. The British Army was pledged to protect and defend, the captain said confidently.

Alfie had heard the captain talk about the way he felt the war would go. Poland would not be able to hold on until England and France came to help. Warsaw might come under siege. If that happened, they would have to get out any way they could.

What Orde told Lucy sounded different from what he had told them. Alfie did not think that the captain was lying to her. Maybe he was just putting the best face on what was really a very, *very* bad future for Poland.

And what did the captain mean when he told Lucy that the British Army was pledged to protect and defend? Alfie figured it out when Werner knocked over Lucy's water glass at supper. Orde had scooped up the kitten and locked him in the bathroom, then had come back to the table with towels.

"In the British Army we call this mopping-up operations."

Lucy's face had gotten very soft as she watched him blot the spill, as if she had never seen a man clean up anything before. It was a very gentle thing to see, Alfie thought. It made him feel good inside. And then he knew that Samuel Orde was her own personal English army to protect and defend.

Maybe later, Alfie decided, he would ask someone about King Arthur and the other fellow, Don Quixote. If they were like the captain and Lucy Strasburg, they must be very good stories.

Alfie hoped they had happy endings.

32 New Orders

Captain Orde was a kind man—perhaps the only really kind man Lucy had ever met. Why then did she fear his look? Why could she not lift her gaze to meet his? Was it because she knew he would see how broken she was inside, and knowing that would give him power over her?

She approached his desk with a neatly typed list of provisions for the Torah school air-raid shelter. He was poring over other lists; names of young men he had slated to slip out of Poland and across the borders of Hungary and Yugoslavia, then on to Palestine. The TENS office of Warsaw was barely a news office. Samuel Orde's primary mission was to rescue as many young Jewish men as could be saved. Lucy found this amazing. Incomprehensible. So very different from Wolf, whose mission it was to kill the same young men.

She waited for him to finish. He looked up, and she gazed at the corner of his desk rather than chance a look into the depth of his eyes.

"Peter Wallich asked me to speak with you," she said almost shyly.

"Peter? My future general of Israel? He can't speak for himself?"

"We are old friends. This is a matter of the heart. A very tender heart, Peter has."

"A heart you know well, I do not doubt." He sat back in his squeaking chair and smiled up at her.

She raised her eyes only briefly and let her gaze take in the smile lines at the edge of his sun-browned face. Even his skin, rough and weathered, was different from Wolf's cool, smooth complexion.

"We were together a long time," she said briskly, wanting to get past that.

"Yes. He has told me about it."

She felt her color rise. *What had Peter told him?* Had he spoken of the way she looked when she carried the baby? The silly songs she had sung as she sat in the chair beside the window and dreamed of holding the little one? Had every vulnerable expression and word been shared with Captain Orde?

"He told me you were someone to be trusted," Orde added. "Utterly and completely."

She let her breath out with relief and tried to organize her thoughts. "He has asked me . . . well, it is foolish that he asked me at all, but it is a matter of his personal . . ." She faltered.

"Yes?" He thumbed the edge of a sheaf of papers impatiently.

"He is in love, you see." She lowered her voice, aware that Alfie was looking at her quite openly. "With the rabbi's daughter. With Rachel Lubetkin."

"Ah, yes." Orde seemed amused. "So is every young male in the Zionist Youth brigade. Rachel is a pretty girl."

"And Peter is concerned about her staying here in Warsaw, you see. There is such danger. Especially for . . . young girls who are pretty." The words came out like a shrouded confession of her own past, her own involvement with a man who had won her over by making her feel desired. All because she was attractive. But of course her life was nothing like Rachel's. "You see?" she asked lamely.

Orde hung on her words for a moment. She could feel him looking at her, wondering if being pretty had made her own life hard in some way. Better to be homely than to live as she had lived. But that was not what they were discussing here.

"Peter is anxious to get her out of Warsaw. Is that it?"

"Out of Poland. Yes. To Palestine."

"I have seen what the Arab gangs do to pretty Jewish girls in Palestine," Orde said under his breath.

She looked up at him with surprise. "What?"

He waved away the thought. It was nothing he wanted to get into now. The issue was Rachel Lubetkin. Lovely. Innocent. A girl any boy could fall in love with. And here she was with a million other girls just like herself. Some more attractive. Some less. But all of them Jewish and all in the path of a Nazi steamroller that crushed all women and children equally to serve its purpose.

Orde inhaled deeply. "Her father has spoken to me already of his concern. And her grandfather in Jerusalem before that. There are people in London working on getting a passport for her. So, you see—" He smiled and shrugged. "Peter Wallich is not the only one who loves her. The question is whether the girl wants to be loved away from her home here in Warsaw. She is

447

not at all happy with the suggestion, I can tell you. And I don't imagine she would return Peter's affection if he tried to get her to leave with the Zionist Youth brigade."

"I'll tell him then. Tell him that other ways are being explored to help her leave. He will be relieved." Lucy backed away, nodded her thanks, and managed to slip back to her desk without ever once having to look the captain full in his face.

Even after she returned to her typing she could feel his thoughtful gaze hot on her back. She did not need to look up to know he was wondering about her. Her shame made her clumsy and slow in her work.

After breakfast, Rabbi Aaron Lubetkin announced that he would get out of bed and go see for himself the work being done on the shelter in the basement of the Community Center.

Etta helped him bathe, then made him rest before he dressed. After he dressed in his finest Shabbat clothes, she made him rest again and eat.

Word had gotten out, no doubt through young David and Samuel again, that their father was coming to see the defense efforts, and so in anticipation, the efforts were doubled.

Far beneath the floor of the soup kitchen, salvaged timbers were hoisted in place to reinforce the walls and ceiling of the basement. Outside the structure and within, pillowcases and flour sacks alike now held earth from every flower pot and garden plot in the district.

Menkes the baker recruited a number of refugees who had in faraway lives been bakers themselves. Mounds of golden-crusted loaves grew like heaps of sandbags to defend against hunger in the quarter should the Nazi threats prove real.

Older men from among the Zionists directed the younger men from the Yeshiva schools. The English Captain Orde moved among them all, indicating which barricade should be strengthened and how best to brace walls and ceilings against shelling. Groups within groups coalesced around him, then scattered in a dozen different directions as others moved in for new orders. *Water to be stored. Canned goods. Flashlights or candles. Blankets and bandages.* These supplies were gathered and then distributed to the shelters of the Community Center, the Torah school, and a dozen smaller buildings around the district.

Into this beehive came the word that Rabbi Lubetkin was coming to inspect the work of his congregation, coming to bless the work that had been done and that which was being done.

Groups of bearded Hasidim came first, as if to prepare the way. Their black caftans flapped like the glossy wings of crows in the sunlight as they moved steadily toward the soup kitchen to form a welcoming committee.

———

Wolf's view of Muranow Square from the window of Kowalski's apartment reminded him of a swarm of insects. Since dawn the square had been attracting Jews by the hundreds. More continued to come, and none ever seemed to leave until the area was filled with milling bodies.

They seemed to be doing nothing more than talking. The Jews created knots of conversation that unraveled and formed anew as different speakers approached and earlier members broke away to join other groups.

What was all the discussion about? Wolf raised his field glasses and tried to discover the topic by examining newspaper headlines over the shoulders of black-coated gesticulating speakers.

At last one front page remained still long enough for him to make it out. In Yiddish phrases the paper announced an obituary for Poland: *GERMANY AND RUSSIA SIGN NONAGGRESSION PACT.*

Wolf was exhilarated by the announcement of the event. The three hundred Russian divisions would be kept on the sidelines! It was still important that the Nazis not fire the first shot, but a Polish response to provocation would undoubtedly happen soon, and then the attack on Poland would begin.

But it also meant that Wolf would have to hurry. He would have to locate Lucy and return her to Germany quickly. He again raised the field glasses to his eyes.

On the far side of the square, directly in front of the Community Center building, a double line of marchers appeared. The twin ranks, providing the only orderliness in the whole chaotic scene, instantly attracted Wolf's attention. One quick glance and Wolf snorted in derision. These were not soldiers at all, but the ragged boys who played at being soldiers.

As Wolf watched, the rows of broomstick warriors marched

and counter-marched as if oblivious to the surging crowd that surrounded them. When they halted, they were facing Wolf. He noted the scarecrow-thin figure, his too-short trousers flapping against his bony shanks, walking up and down the ranks with his back toward the Kowalski building.

Wolf snorted again at the ludicrous figure of the boy playing officer; then his snort turned into a strangled cough. The officer-boy had turned to salute a sandy-haired man who had stepped out from the crowd.

The features of the man seemed to leap through the field glasses directly into Wolf's apartment. It was the Britisher who had interfered on the dock in Danzig! Wolf swung his gaze back to the thin, pinched face of the boy. Peter Wallich! Lucy must be close at hand!

———

As the word of Rabbi Lubetkin's imminent arrival leaped from the parapets and ricocheted from the buildings of Mura-now Square, Peter Wallich laid aside his shovel and called his troop together in front of the community building.

Lucy left her work in the kitchen and joined the throngs out-side in the square who gathered to welcome back their beloved rabbi from his long convalescence.

From her place beside Alfie, she could see Orde talking seri-ously with Peter. The boy had dust in his hair, giving it the ap-pearance of tarnished copper.

Everyone had heard the unveiled threats that the German Führer had hurled at the Jewish population of Poland last night, and then this morning came the terrible news about Russia. Without equivocation, Hitler promised to wipe the Jews from the face of the earth. The Jews of Poland, he claimed, wanted to plunge Germany into war, and he would retaliate if they contin-ued their agitation against the Reich!

Lucy had transcribed the speech for Orde. He had rewritten his daily story and focused on the pillowcase sandbags that formed the pitiful bulwarks of the Warsaw Jewish community. He had compared them to the concrete bunkers in Germany that had been under construction for years.

Lucy watched Peter Wallich and his little band as they per-formed their drills as the ragged honor guard for the rabbi. She could not help but compare them with the hundred thousand

Hitler Youth she had seen at the Nuremberg rally last September. They had marched with burnished shovels over their shoulders. Lines had been straight. Voices had roared.

Behind Lucy, the baker Menkes blustered about the preparedness of the Polish Army and about the readiness of the Jews of Warsaw! "If the Germans come here, we will show them a fist! Fight the rats!"

Just then a small boy darted past and climbed the brick wall beside the Community Center. Poised on the top of the wall like a bird on a wire, he reached deep into his pocket, whipped out a piece of chalk, and with five bold strokes drew a picture on the bricks.

Then he flapped off the wall and disappeared into the crowd, leaving behind him the likeness of Hitler scraped upon the gray bricks! There was no doubt about the identity of the face in the cartoon. The oval shape of the face; one definite stroke curving down over the forehead in the Führer's cowlick; that tiny brush of a mustache! And over the entire face was drawn an insulting, dismissing, enormous *X*!

A small ripple of laughter rose, then the pattering of applause. Lucy smiled with the rest, but her heart grew heavy with a sense of uneasiness for these people and this place.

Involuntarily she looked up and remembered that Wolf had told her about the German Führer's plans for Poland. *The bombs will fall here first.* Hitler had said as much in the broadcast last night. No matter how many times he changed his policies; no matter even that he had now signed a pact with Stalin, the one thing that never changed in Hitler's rhetoric was his hatred of the Jews. He had drawn their caricature in his mind and crossed them out with the vengeance that the little urchin had used when marking on the brick facade of the Community Center.

Attention returned to matters of real importance to the people of Muranow.

"Here comes Rabbi Lubetkin!"

"See how pale he is!"

"He is walking without help! The Eternal be praised!"

———

Wolf hurriedly scanned the ebb and flow of the crowd around the sandy-haired man and Peter Wallich. Lucy must be nearby, she must be! He sensed her presence even before he saw her, then lined up the field glasses on the back of a woman he knew was Lucy, even before she turned.

At last! A feeling of urgency filled Wolf. He would not wait a single minute longer. He would follow her, capture her, and take her back to Germany.

A last quick glance through the field glasses confirmed that Lucy was not leaving. She and the Britisher were watching Peter Wallich drill his pitiful troop. Wolf tossed the glasses down and turned to the door to go.

Halfway down the stairs, someone was coming up. The figure called out to him, "Herr von Fritschauer. Good! I have news."

Gustav Ahlman! What was he doing in Warsaw? "Not now, Ahlman," said Wolf, starting to push past. "I've spotted her at last."

Ahlman moved in front of Wolf, blocking the stairs. "Important news," he repeated. "New orders."

An angry sweep of Wolf's arm caught Gustav off balance, shoving him against the banister. "Get out of my way," Wolf shouted, and he ran down the stairs.

Wolf scarcely heard the echo of Gustav Ahlman's voice calling out, "New orders!" In Wolf's mind there was only one objective, one focus of all his attention: to capture Lucy.

It was indeed time for Wolf to return to Berlin. Great things were happening, events in which he had the duty, the right, to participate. But Wolf knew that he could not go until this duty was accomplished. He could not leave Warsaw having failed to erase the shadow on his reputation.

How could he have been so deceived? A mystery surrounded Lucy Strasburg. The woman he had believed to be an ignorant peasant was standing by the side of a military Britisher. She was obviously connected somehow with the largest community of Jews in all of Europe.

Wolf dodged a knot of black-coated men standing in a circle. Their beards and earlocks bobbed in rhythm as they gestured gnarled fingers toward newspaper headlines. A babble of voices rose from the square and assaulted Wolf's ears; Yiddish, Polish, German, even Slavic tongues for which he had no names. It was as if all the Jews from all of Europe had been poured into Warsaw and stirred together.

Wolf darted to one side of the crowd of men and bumped into two short plump women walking with linked elbows. With heavily laden shopping bags hanging from their arms, they revolved slowly around like a gate swinging on rusty hinges and blocked Wolf's path. Wolf tried to pass by them, only to have them pivot in front of him and bar his way again.

He bounced up on his toes, trying to see over the crowd. Lucy had seemed so near through the field glasses! Up close, the square was both expansively broad and packed with bodies! It was almost as if they were deliberately preventing Wolf from reaching her!

He pushed between the elderly women and a group of schoolgirls. The girls, a flock of twittering birds in dark blue jumpers, braids and freckles, pointed at him and giggled. What could this Saturday person be so anxious to find in Muranow Square?

Wolf hopped up on a low brick wall and scanned the crowd in the direction of the Community Center. He thought he had lost his way completely until he spotted again a file of broomsticks marking time to the marching steps of their bearers. There she was! Lucy's glowing blond hair was unmistakable. She was still where he had seen her last.

Wolf started to jump down from the wall, but found the crowd pressed in around him. He turned, looked down into faces that stared back at him. Jewish faces, every one. He turned again and saw a completely solid ring of people watching him with anticipation.

They think I'm going to speak, he thought with confusion. *They must believe I have a message to deliver.* Indeed, those in the ring nearest Wolf were asking for silence, shushing the others around them.

"Husband!" a voice cried out. "It's him! The man I told you about." Wolf tried to see whom the words came from. He located an arm pointing at him and followed it back to the mousy face of the woman from the Dorbransky apartment.

Wolf was confronted by a powerfully built man whose curly black hair seemed to spill off his head and flow over his brawny arms and out the collar of his shirt. Cracow, the woman had said . . . no doubt her husband was a steel worker!

Wolf attempted to stride past. "What do you mean, breaking into my home? Scaring my family?" demanded the man.

Wolf touched the pistol in his pocket, but saw how awash he was in a sea of angry, questioning eyes and left it undrawn.

"Must be some mistake," he argued. "I don't know you."

"We'll see whose mistake it was," said the man, reaching out for Wolf.

"Von Fritschauer, wait!" called Gustav Ahlman from just behind Wolf.

Ahlman lunged through the ring of people, clutching for Wolf's sleeve. Wolf jerked aside, and Gustav's rush carried him into the face of the steel worker.

"What's this, another one?" shouted the man. He drew back a fist the size of a pipe wrench and crashed it against Ahlman's nose. Gustav's nostrils exploded in spurts of crimson and an audible crunch of cartilage and bone.

Wolf seized on the distraction as an opportunity to shove two onlookers out of the way and plunge on in pursuit of Lucy. He must not lose her now!

Allan Farrell skirted the rim of the Whispering Gallery that overlooked the rotunda of the cathedral floor without even glancing at the paintings or the statues. He had many other things to think about, and his mind had long since ceased to contemplate the art work.

When this operation had first begun, Allan had worried that making so many trips up the hundreds of steps might attract unfortunate attention. But none of the priests or lay attendants paid the slightest attention to one more tourist amid the crowds of sightseers.

In the satchel he carried was another, smaller leather bag. This inner bag was actually one of the packages Allan was making the repeated trips to deposit. Eight packages meant eight deliveries to the Golden Gallery high atop the outside of the dome.

When Allan reached the last of the spiraled iron stairs and emerged into the breezy London afternoon, he congratulated himself on his timing: he was alone on the platform. This simple fact meant that he would not have to wait for an opportunity to make another deposit.

Allan listened at the top of the stairs for the clatter of footsteps that would give away the approach of more sightseers. When he heard nothing but the soft sighing of the wind, he immediately opened the satchel and removed the inner bag with its already attached length of light rope.

A quick check showed that the wires connecting the radio receiver and the explosives were firmly attached. Allan counted stone pillars around to the right from the stairwell. When he reached the fourth one he stopped and lowered the bag over the railing and into the opening in the lead-sheathed curve of the roof.

When the bag had gently come to rest at the bottom of the opening, Allan dropped the end of the cord in after. Out of habit he leaned over the rail to see if any trace of his handiwork could be seen, but nothing was visible. Perhaps if someone had hung by their toes over the parapet and dangled headfirst they could spot the little bag, but not otherwise.

Allan picked up the outer carrying case with a great sense of satisfaction. *Six eggs in the nest*, he thought. *Almost home.*

The linking of Rachel Lubetkin's arm through her own startled Lucy. Cradling her baby brother on her hip, Rachel led Lucy into the packed gathering that had assembled to hear Rabbi Lubetkin speak publicly for the first time since his arrest in November.

The synagogue itself was not large enough to hold the numbers of men and women coming into the auditorium. The enormous hall was filled to standing room only and still the crowds trailed out the double doors and into the square.

Yet room was made for Lucy Strasburg. *A heroine, was she not? One who saved the life of one Jewish boy?* And now she stood beside the rabbi's daughter.

Wolf had escaped from the clutches of the steel worker from Cracow and from the pursuit of Gustav Ahlman, but neither of these successes amounted to anything. Lucy was gone! By the time Wolf had reached the far corner of the square, she had vanished as surely as if the earth had swallowed her up.

The Britisher had also disappeared, and the last definite connection with Lucy, Peter Wallich, was marching out of Muranow Square at the head of his ragged band of play soldiers.

Wolf revolved slowly around in place. In his mind he cursed Ahlman for delaying him, cursed the couple from Cracow for interfering, cursed all the Jews of Muranow Square and his own excruciatingly bad luck.

What to do now? He could only think that if he had once spotted Lucy from the window of his rented apartment, he could do it again. He went back to the Kowalski flat, this time skirting the edge of the square instead of forcing his way through the middle. He was careful to turn up a side street in order to avoid the spot where he had encountered the woman and her husband.

Deep in thought, he ascended the stairs toward his apartment. Perhaps it was time to enlist additional aid from Berlin. If he could reach Himmler, and explain how close he was to success, next time he would have a ring of operatives around the square. That was the answer, no doubt of it. Perhaps Reichsführer Himmler would shed some light on what the new orders involved—in code, of course.

Wolf pushed open the door of his room. It had been stupid of him to rush out and leave it unlocked, but he had been in a hurry: Ahlman's interruption had delayed him, and the result had been failure instead of success. Wolf decided that he would give Ahlman the cursing of his life when next they met; he might even denounce the oaf to Himmler.

Two strides into the living room, Wolf saw the oaf already present to be cursed and denounced. Ahlman was seated in a chair with his back toward the view of Muranow Square and a Luger semiautomatic pistol pointed at Wolf's midsection. His eyes were surrounded by saucer-sized purple rings, and where his nose had been was an ungainly mass of tape and sticking plaster.

"Major von Fritschauer," Ahlman said flatly, "your new orders are that you will accompany me back to Berlin at once."

———

Have you selected a headquarters for the Gleiwitz operation, Agent Hess?"

"Yes, Reichsführer. There is a schoolhouse in a nearby village that is suitable," answered Hess. "My assistant has already made the necessary arrangements."

"Excellent. And have the participants been identified?"

"Yes, Reichsführer, we have selected thirteen, including Wolfgang von Fritschauer. I trust you approve the selection of Karl Ibsen as well?"

"Considering the timing," commented Himmler with a thoughtful look in his eyes, "it is absolutely poetic."

"And the code name that has been assigned?" inquired Hess as he stood to leave.

"I am certain you will appreciate the subtlety," smiled Himmler. "Your code is *Konserven*—Operation Canned Goods."

The entire block of solitary cells groaned aloud as morning came with muggy regularity. Karl opened his eyes to the insistent peeping of the young sparrows. A few moments of just-breaking sunlight slid across the bricks and illuminated the nest where four feathered heads with bright button eyes poked up from the lip of the nest.

On the window ledge, mother and father sparrow looked at their offspring with a kind of dare in their expression. It was nearly the last of August. Karl knew this from the marks on his brick calendar. It was time the young sparrows learn to fly. Already they had hopped up on the edge of the nest and flapped their stubby wings in imitation of their parents. But today was different. For some reason Karl could not understand, this was the day when they would fly.

He did not make a move to sit up even when the clatter of the meal tray sounded outside in the corridor. The steel trap slid back and the bread and porridge were shoved through. The black water that passed as coffee was already cold. The mush was cold as well. It would not matter if Karl ate now or waited awhile. He dared not disturb the small drama being played out above him.

Lady Sparrow leaped from her perch and flew toward the nest. With a flurry, she brushed her children firmly, urging them up. Pushing them toward the edge. Then just as abruptly the big male rushed toward the nest, pushing his mate aside. She resumed her place on the window ledge while he took over. He was much rougher with his children. Today they would fly. He would not accept excuses. If they did not fly, then they would go hungry. They might die. No exceptions. He beat the inside of the nest with his wings. The down lining flew up and floated down to land on Karl's bed. Welcome to the real world.

457

All four young birds beat their wings frantically. The big male shoved them one after another from the nest. And one after another, they flew clumsily to where their mother sat beside the bread crumbs on the ledge.

Karl wanted to cheer! This was the first time he had seen them all at once. But he lay very still as the young birds were lectured and then directed to fly back to their little home. The largest of the young sparrows spread his wings and flapped, raising himself off the ledge a few inches. Then, his father's stern feathers at his back, he leaped up into space and hovered a moment, sank down, and then with his father at his side, he weaved back to the nitch in the bricks.

His three siblings followed after, each with a different degree of skill. All of them made it home and only then were they fed. By this event, Karl marked the end of summer. The end of a sermon that God had been whispering in his ear for months.

When the door to his cell crashed open, revealing the grim faces of the prison warden and four armed S.S. guards, Karl was not surprised.

The sparrows watched silently from their nest.

"Prisoner Ibsen," said the warden, "your stay here with us is at an end, I'm afraid."

Karl managed to stand. His clothes hung in tattered rags from his thin frame.

"He will need a bath. *Mein Gott!* This one stinks! Come on, pig! Out of your filth!"

Karl did not look up at the family of sparrows as he tottered from the cell. He did not want to reveal their hiding place to these men. The butt of a rifle would easily crush the nest and the sparrows. Such men would take pleasure in destroying in a moment the miracle that had come to Karl in his cell. He wanted to look over his shoulder. He wanted to whisper goodbye. And thanks. But he did not.

The rifle urged him hard from this nest. The door slammed shut behind Karl and the family of sparrows was safe.

"Where are you taking me?" Karl asked. His voice was strong and untroubled.

"The Führer has arranged a little party for you at the border," sneered an S.S. guard.

"Silence," ordered the warden, then, "For now, Prisoner Ibsen, a shower. Clean clothes. A meal perhaps?"

Karl did not need further explanation. Was this not the kindness offered a condemned man? Maybe this was the day when Karl Ibsen would finally be nudged from the nest. No longer bound by earth, he hoped that soon, like the young sparrows, he would fly.

From high atop the fifteen-story platform of Warsaw's Prudential building, Orde broadcast the scene of imminent war by shortwave to Belgium and then to London. In the morning sunlight, anti-aircraft batteries were clearly visible. Like the nests of storks, machine guns perched among the red brick chimneys of buildings overlooking the main highways.

A cloud of dust rose up like smoke from a convoy of antiquated military vehicles. Private automobiles, commandeered in the last week by the Polish Army, were blanketed with soldiers on hoods and roofs and trunks and running boards.

From the high perspective, it looked more like an army in retreat than an army moving forward to face the massive German Wehrmacht.

As the military traffic rolled out from Warsaw in creeping black columns, thousands of people struggled against the tide as they oozed into Warsaw from the threatened battlefields of western Poland. On the other side of the city, thousands more were leaving Warsaw on highways headed east.

Every road and rutted lane was crammed with human flotsam drifting from the shipwreck of failed politics. There seemed to be no beginning of the mass, and no end.

Orde spotted the massive traffic jams at the Warsaw aerodrome and at various rail terminals throughout the city. Even as he spoke, he scanned the horizon for the way he would take out of Warsaw in order to lead his little group to safety. His broadcast was an unspoken plea that somehow the passports be sent. He was certain that Murphy was listening in London.

33 The Pain of Not Being Good Enough

Lori knew what the Warsaw broadcast meant before Murphy explained it to her. Stalin and Hitler had signed a mutual non-aggression pact. Hitler had annexed Danzig.

Poland had not yet officially declared war, but it was coming. Why should anyone try to raise her hopes? There was going to be a war, and Jacob was still in Warsaw with Alfie!

In England, a general mobilization had been announced. Soldiers home on leave had been called back to ships and army bases. Tonight London was to be in complete blackout in anticipation of German bombing.

All of this was reality, yet still the precious passports of Alfie and Jacob had not been sent to them in Warsaw! *Why?*

Three passports were laid out on the bed of their Savoy Hotel room—one for Jacob, one for Alfie, one for the Jewish girl named Rachel.

Lori held them in trembling hands. "I will go to Warsaw myself if you are afraid," she challenged Murphy angrily.

"Fear has nothing to do with it." Elisa tried to calm her. "In the first place, it is practically impossible to get a flight to Warsaw."

"Can you honestly think it will be easier when the war begins?" Lori asked. "Or are you hoping this will all go away? *Look!* Three of them—three passports to get them out! And here we are waiting for dozens more that might not come until the whole of Warsaw is up in smoke! And these three will go up in smoke with it when we might have saved them!"

"We were hoping more would come, Lori," Murphy said gently. "There are passports in process. One for Lucy Strasburg, others for kids your age, and younger, trapped in Warsaw. There will not be a second chance to get them out. When I take the passports to them, there may not be another opportunity to go back with the documents that arrive a day or two later in the mail!"

"In a day or two, maybe it will be too late for these. Then

what about Jacob? What about Alfie?" She was pleading. "Go now," she begged. "I know there is no time left!" She pulled back the curtains and looked down at the sandbagged buildings all along the Strand. Shop windows were boarded up. Helmeted members of the Home Guard talked together on the street corner outside the theater. Taxi drivers at the curbs covered their headlamps with black cloth.

"What more proof do you need? The government has announced that every English citizen should come out of Poland," Lori cried distractedly. "Look at these!" She held up the passports. "These make Jacob a British subject! And the same for Alfie. But if England goes to war with Germany, then *they* and their passports are no longer neutral, are they? Then the Nazis can march right in and arrest them for being British, just the same as they arrest someone for being a Jew or a German Christian like my father!"

She ran her hands through her hair and paced back and forth in front of the window. "Tomorrow, Elisa, you are playing a concert to remember my father in a Nazi prison. And Churchill is speaking. The bells will ring, and everyone will remember what could have been done to stop Hitler! Please . . . I don't want to sit there and have to remember that there was a chance to get Jacob out of Poland! I don't want to think about him running through Warsaw streets while *German bombers*—"

Suddenly she grew silent and sank down beside Elisa on the bed. Elisa wrapped her arms around Lori as she finished her tirade with tears of frustration.

Murphy leaned against the mantel of the fireplace and rubbed his hands nervously across his lips. The girl had a point. She had several points. He could not argue with even one of them.

The twelve men in the back of the transport truck from Nameless camp had no idea where they were being taken. The truck's canvas flap was tied shut securely, and the prisoners were told that even to loosen the fabric to get some air in the stifling interior meant severe punishment for all the occupants.

The one positive result of this demand for a cloak of concealment was the opportunity it provided for the men to talk. They shared names, stories, and the crimes against the state that had brought them to this place. The discussion soon turned to speculation about the mysterious exercise. Some claimed that they were going to be exchanged for German spies who had been captured by the Poles. Others said flatly that they were going to be executed. Neither argument made much sense; either release or execution could have been accomplished without all the secrecy.

Soon the atmosphere was so suffocatingly hot that even the will to speculate about their destination or fate required too great an effort. At last all discussion ground to a halt, while the truck continued to grind onward.

In a final effort at conversation, one of the prisoners asked, "Does anyone know what the date is?"

Karl consulted his memory of the scratches on his cell wall. "Near the end of August," he said. "I think it is the thirty-first."

———————

Orde's Zionist Youth brigade was out in force—but, then, so was all of Jewish Warsaw. Orde stood on the brick wall in the center of the square dispatching orders to the various corners with Peter Wallich's troops as messengers.

"Take Jacob and Elisha and three others and deliver this load of lumber," Orde directed Peter. "You and your men stay and aid the residents in boarding up their ground-floor windows."

"At once, Hayedid," agreed Peter, and he gave a snappy salute.

Three men and a woman appeared in the square behind Orde and arranged a group of chairs and music stands. "Is this where you want us?" one called out.

"Quite right," returned Orde. "Please remember to keep it light and cheerful." A few moments later the sounds of a string quartet mingled with the hammering and sawing noises of Muranow Square.

Orde watched a group of men filling pillowcases with earth from the flower beds. A fine layer of dust settled on their black hats and in their beards. It coated their faces with a pallor that reminded Orde of corpses. But the eyes of these men were lively, interested, and pleased to be doing something in defense of their homes.

The Hayedid stepped down off the wall and approached an aged rabbi whose frame was nearly bent in two by the weight of his years even before he started filling sandbags. "Rabbi," said Orde respectfully, "it is not necessary for you to do this labor. There are plenty of younger men."

"So," replied the rabbi, "where is it written that a man becomes too old to work with his hands?"

"Ah, but, Rabbi," countered Orde, "I have other important duties for you. Soil we have in adequate supply and laborers also, but we will soon experience a shortage of pillowcases. Will you please take personal charge of collecting more?"

The string quartet soared into a breezy composition, a waltz-tempo piece that Orde could not name. He went over to the Community Center, where the women of Muranow Square were preparing to feed the workers. From the doorway the delicious smell of freshly baked bread mingled with the aroma of potato soup.

Orde spotted Lucy standing with Rachel Lubetkin, stacking bowls next to the cauldrons of soup. He thought how fine Lucy looked, even dressed in a plain blue skirt and white blouse, with her hair pulled back under a scarf. She felt his approving glance and looked up, then smiled shyly and looked away again.

A voice at Orde's elbow caused him to turn. "Excuse me, Hayedid," said a young man named Avriel. The scholarly-looking youth wore round spectacles and had prematurely thinning hair. "You are wanted at the barricade."

At the main street leading out of Muranow Square, Orde found a Polish army staff car. Its exhaust was churning out a foul cloud of bluish smoke, but at Orde's appearance, the engine was shut off and a pear-shaped man in the uniform of a brigadier general appeared.

"Captain Orde," said the officer, "I am General Wojoski."

"I am not military," corrected Orde. "I am a correspondent with TENS news service, and today I am here helping my friends."

The general waved off Orde's protest. "We know who you are really, Captain Orde, and it is about your help that I have come. We could use your expertise in planning the defenses of Warsaw proper. Not," he added hastily, "that they will be necessary. Strictly as a precautionary measure."

Those nearest the barricade stopped shoveling and hammering to listen to Orde's reply, but it came without any hesitation. "I am sorry, General," he returned, "but as you can see, we have more than enough to keep busy with here. However," added Orde thoughtfully, "I wonder if you could look into something for us? It seems that by an unfortunate oversight there have been no gas masks distributed in this quarter."

The general swelled up slightly as if about to respond to the thinly veiled accusation, then abruptly changed his mind. "I'll see what I can find out," he said gruffly, and returned to his car.

"Bravo, Captain," said Avriel. From the center of the square, the string quartet continued to play.

Only three passports out of dozens. Murphy paced the length of the bedroom and back again. He looked out the French doors to the balcony. Block by block, London was evacuating school children. Lori was right: tomorrow might be too late.

Elisa spread the precious passports out on the bed. One each for Jacob, Alfie, and Rachel Lubetkin.

"Orde will not leave Poland unless they leave with him." Murphy shrugged. "But that includes Lucy Strasburg, obviously. He's a good man." Murphy sat beside her and took her hands in his hands. "I was hoping we could . . . that there would be more passports to smuggle in."

Elisa's face reflected the disappointment. There had just not been enough time. "So close," she managed. "Oh, Murphy." She looked at the three new folders. "But *these*! You'll have to take them to Warsaw. To wait even one more day will mean that they are lost as well. And Sam Orde lost with them."

"It should not be this hard. Just a few more days. I was hoping—"

Elisa opened her violin case, took the blue silk scarf from the Guarnerius, and removed the violin from its velvet nest. With practiced fingers she found the hidden panel and lifted it. Then, as she had done a dozen times before, she placed the precious passports into their hiding place and sealed it securely once again. Then, she replaced Rudy's violin. "There are still jewels behind the tuning peg that may be useful," she said.

Murphy telephoned three airlines. KLM was the only one still with service to Warsaw. "You'll touch down in Vilnyus, Lithuania, tonight," explained the agent. "We Dutch are neutral, so, if it is possible to fly through German and Polish air space—" He laughed nervously. "Well, then, we will get you to Warsaw." There

464

was a long pause. "I assume you are leaving Warsaw again shortly?"

"Yes. The next flight. And I will be traveling with companions."

"I will have to wire ahead, sir. We cannot guarantee any seats on flights leaving Warsaw unless we wire ahead. If you will stop at the ticket counter before you depart, I should have an answer for you."

The agent asked a few mundane questions about the weight of each of the passengers. Murphy guessed at the weight of Rachel from Elisa's weight. For Orde, Jacob, and Alfie, he placed their weight within a pound or two of his own.

The agent gave Murphy a stern warning about the luggage allowance. One case per passenger. Murphy signaled Elisa to stop packing. The violin case was all he would be taking on this trip. He rolled up clean socks and underwear and stuffed them into his pockets. He took his overcoat out of the closet and folded one clean shirt into a minute square, which he likewise stuffed into the deep pocket.

Then he took Elisa's face in his hands. "I hope this is right. There won't be a second chance to get in. Not if the war breaks."

Elisa nodded. She laid her head against Murphy's chest for a moment. Could he feel how frightened she was to have him leave today? She did not speak of fear. She did not ask him to wait until more passports arrived, until this whole terrible thing blew over. She knew, as he did, that there was no more time.

"I'll get Lori," Elisa said softly. Then she opened the door to the adjoining room. Lori sat beside the open window overlooking the city and the hulk of St. Paul's.

"Tonight they are turning off the lights," Lori said bleakly. "They finally believe us, don't they, Elisa?" The voice was so small and sad that Elisa almost forgot that Lori was not the tiny girl she had played dolls with in the backyard of the old Wilhelmstrasse mansion.

"Murphy is going to Warsaw," Elisa answered—a practical answer that shouted all was not yet lost!

Silence. Lori stood up. *"When?"*

"Today."

"Oh, Elisa!" she cried, running to embrace her.

"He is leaving in an hour. Tonight he lands in Warsaw. If God is willing, Murphy will take them the passports and bring your

465

Jacob back with him on the next plane."

"Oh, Elisa!" Lori broke into tears. "I am so afraid. So very afraid! My father is still . . . even if Jacob is free and with me, my mother will be alone. With the war there will be no more hope for Father. No more . . . all of them. So many. Has God forgotten them, Elisa? And all the children? All the birth certificates we collected. Useless." Silence. "It is so dark, isn't it, Elisa?" She was not speaking of the fact that the lights would be blacked out throughout London.

"It is dark. But God can see, even in the darkness." As she said it, Elisa regretted the trite, simplistic sound of the words. But the words were true. God had eyes that could pierce the blackest night and illuminate the darkest heart.

The gentle drumming of rain sounded on the awning over the window ledge. "Yes," Lori said, reaching out to touch the drops. "He is crying, too."

Murphy stood in the doorway behind them. "I'm leaving now. I called down for a taxi. Stay here with Lori and the babies." Then, to Lori, "Don't worry, Missus Kalner. We'll do our best."

———

Gustav Ahlman was standing outside the schoolhouse when the truck arrived from Nameless camp. He stood by with an air of importance as the flap was untied and the parched prisoners tumbled out, blinking in the afternoon sunlight.

"Bring them some water," he ordered. A bucket and a dipper made the rounds of the twelve men. It had to be refilled four times before all were satisfied.

In a stupor induced by the long airless ride, and now water-logged as well, the men stumbled into the schoolroom as indicated by Ahlman. In a heap on the floor was a pile of jackets, trousers and boots. "First, new clothing," announced Ahlman cheerfully, "then supper."

"What are these jackets?" asked one man as he hunted for a size that would fit him.

"They look like army uniforms—Polish, I think," offered another as he searched for a matching pair of boots.

"No talking," said Ahlman. "Anyone who breaks this rule will not be fed."

The men got dressed in silence.

Wolfgang von Fritschauer arrived at the schoolhouse headquarters in a staff car with Agent Hess. "When can you tell me what this mission involves?" he asked.

"I see no reason not to inform you right now," offered Hess. "You are about to meet those who will also be part of this operation, so it is time for you to understand the plan.

"You are aware," he continued, "that the Führer has promised Russia and Italy that we will take no military action against Poland unless the Poles act as aggressors first."

Wolf waved his hand to indicate that he was as aware of international politics as Hess.

"This operation is designed to furnish that instance of aggression." Hess continued. "You will be involved in a mock attack on the radio transmitter located in Gleiwitz. We will seize the station, broadcast a message of contempt for the forces of the Reich, and retire, having given the Führer ample reason to retaliate."

"Simplicity itself," nodded Wolf. "I am grateful for the chance to prove myself again to Reichsführer Himmler. Was it he who suggested my participation?"

"Actually, I asked for you personally," said Hess, "with Herr Himmler's wholehearted agreement."

———

"These men are not soldiers," protested Wolf to Hess after they had entered the schoolhouse. "They are not Gestapo, either. What is going on here, Hess?"

Hess pulled Wolf into an adjoining room. On a schoolteacher's wooden revolving chair lay the uniform of a Polish officer. "Get dressed, and I will explain," said Hess, gesturing toward the clothing. "It is necessary to furnish some bodies as proof of the validity of the attack. All these men were political prisoners. They have been promised a reduction in their sentences for their participation. After we are through here, no one will question what has happened to them."

"Ingenious," complimented Wolf. "But how can we prevent them from escaping before it is time for them to become casualties?"

"That is your first duty to this mission," said Hess. "As you can see, you are dressed the same as they, so they will trust you. They will be told that they are to receive a standard military inoculation. They will not protest the administration of the narcotic because they will see you receive an injection of a harmless saline solution first."

"Now everything is clear to me," agreed Wolf. "You will find that I am eager to cooperate."

———————

It was very late. Warsaw was entirely dark because of the blackout. Jacob was asleep beside Alfie. Werner-kitten was also asleep, curled up in a warm ball on Alfie's pillow. His soft kitten breath fanned Alfie's cheek. The night seemed very peaceful. All the darkness of a big city without lights also seemed peaceful, but Alfie knew that it was not. Not really.

Captain Orde was awake, his chair pulled up beside the window. The curtains were open wide because all the lamps were off. This was so a Nazi airplane would not see the light in their hotel room and drop a bomb on the Bristol.

There was just enough starlight that Alfie could see the serious look on the captain's face. His eyes were lost in the shadow of his frown. He tapped a pencil on the arm of the chair. The tapping was like the sound of a drum. One little drum for the one-man army who had pledged to protect and defend Lucy.

Lucy was in bed in the other room. Alfie did not know if she was asleep or awake like the captain. Alfie smiled quietly. It would be funny if he asked if anyone was awake and everyone answered *yes* at the same time.

Alfie considered asking. He decided against it because he was sure that the British Army was thinking very serious thoughts about the one-woman nation he pledged to protect.

All evening long, Orde had looked at Lucy when she was not looking. Then, when she raised her eyes toward him, the captain would look away quickly. And then it would be Lucy's turn to look at the captain—until he looked up. It had gone on like this, both of them trying not to look at the other when the other was looking.

Once when their eyes had accidentally bumped, Lucy had gotten red and Orde had looked very embarrassed.

Alfie had noticed this, and it reminded him a lot of the way Jacob had looked at Lori and then had tried *not* to look at Lori.

It seemed to be very painful. Alfie wondered why Orde did not just hold Lucy's pretty face in his hands and look and look and look. Like having all the ice cream a person could eat, only free.

Captain Orde sighed loudly. A lonely sigh. Alfie had heard their captain make that sort of sound before. "Why don't you help him, Jesus?" Alfie prayed. He had not meant to say the words aloud, but sometimes thoughts came out on their own.

"Hmmm?" asked Orde. "Did you say something, Elisha?"

"Not to you," Alfie answered truthfully. "Just *about* you."

"What about me?" The captain talked to Alfie as though he really mattered. Alfie liked that.

"Jesus should help . . . you."

Silence. "Yes. I hope He will."

Silence. "Her eyes are sad," Alfie said.

His comment startled the captain. "Her . . . what are you saying?"

How could Alfie tell the captain what he had seen in Lucy Strasburg's eyes? Alfie had not been afraid to look at her. Not at all. He had looked at her face all evening long when the captain was trying not to. In her eyes, Alfie had seen so many friends who had all gone away to the Promised Land . . . dead. All dead on the night that the Hitler-men had burned Berlin. When he looked at Lucy, he could easily remember the way his friend Werner had looked when other children walked by and he could not walk. Alfie remembered Dieter, who could not feed himself. Heinz, who could not move his legs or arms without shaking. And there were others.

They had all worn their hearts in their eyes. The terrible ache was the same. It was not pain that came from being crippled; it was pain that came from not being loved. Not believing that anyone would ever love them because they were not straight and tall or strong or smart. When the Nazi orderlies were cruel to them, they thought somehow it was their fault. Sometimes Alfie had felt that way, too. Yes, sometimes Alfie had the ache of his heart in his eyes, too. Because Alfie was not smart. But then Alfie remembered that he did not have to be smart to be loved. He knew that Jesus loved him and that made the hurt of being *not good enough* go away.

Lucy was broken inside, just like Alfie's friends had been broken on the outside. It kept her from playing, it kept her from

469

speaking, and in a way, it made her helpless even to feed her own soul.

What Lucy needed was somebody to love her, like Alfie had loved his friends at the Sisters of Mercy Hospital before the Hitler-men killed them.

But who would carry Lucy until she was strong enough inside? And how would she get strong unless someone loved her enough to feed her soul? If there was nobody to do that for her, then Lucy with the sad heart would die inside. The darkness would steal her too, just as surely as it had stolen the lives of the boys in the ward.

How could Alfie tell all of this to a man so smart as Captain Samuel Orde? "How can I, Jesus?" he asked out loud again.

Orde turned away from the window as though he wanted to hear Alfie's heart tell him all about Lucy and himself, too.

"What do you see, Elisha?" Orde whispered. "What is it?"

Alfie reached up and touched Werner-kitten on his pillow. The soft rumble of a purr erupted like a laugh, and then Alfie knew how he could say it.

"My kitten was almost . . . *dead*. His mother Joseph did not want him. But I took care of him. Just like Werner . . ." He tried not to confuse Werner the kitten with Werner the boy, even though the stories were a lot alike. "I took care of him because he needed more than the other kittens, or his heart would have died." Alfie smiled as Werner purred louder. "And now . . . you hear him? He loves me a lot, too." Werner got up and moved against Alfie's head. "Lucy is like Werner was. You should take her face and hold it."

At that, the captain laughed a small, nervous laugh. "I . . . don't know her, Elisha. Not at all. How can I?"

"Just look at her eyes. She don't have to tell you anything. Her heart . . . just barely hanging on. Somebody's got to love her back to life."

"What have I got to give her?" Orde asked in a truly puzzled way, the sort of voice that *wanted* to do something right, but did not know how.

"Oh, Captain." Alfie thought maybe he had forgotten. "You know . . . Jesus. He made lame people walk and blind people see. He loved them before they were well . . . loves me, even if I'm . . . not smart. You tell Lucy. You can say it . . . in a smart way. Huh?"

470

Captain Orde sat a long time in the dark. He did not move. He just looked into the dark place where Alfie's voice had come from. And then he got up and came to the side of the bed. He reached out and touched Alfie's forehead. He smoothed Alfie's hair back like Mama used to do. And then he kissed Alfie on the forehead and went back to sit in his chair beside the window.

And now the night was peaceful. Alfie went to sleep.

34   The Ant and the Cricket

"What will happen to us now, Papa?" Rachel sat at the feet of her father in the dark study. The baby was asleep on Etta's lap, and David and Samuel rested on pillows nearest the open window.

Somehow, tonight, on what was possibly the last night of peace, they all wanted to stay together in this room. The walls were filled with Papa's books—wisdom from floor to ceiling. The books were old friends, like relatives, in a way, to the family of Rabbi Aaron Lubetkin. Who could say what would become of those leather-bound friends if the war began tonight and the Nazis came tomorrow?

Papa was silent in his big leather chair. He turned his face toward the sound of crickets chirping in the garden.

Why did he not answer?

"I am afraid, Papa," David said from his pillow.

Then little Samuel began to cry softly.

"Listen!" Papa said with a smile in his voice. "I will tell you a story. Listen now, Samuel. David. Rachel. A story you must remember. It is a story about an arrogant cricket and an ant."

He cleared his throat, still rusty from his months of illness. But his voice was very strong as he began.

"Once there was an ant who was carrying a very large bread crumb home to his family. He was very proud of himself because the crumb was ten times bigger than he was. All of a sudden he heard the loud whining voice of a cricket high above him. 'Tsk-tsk! You are a tiny fellow to be carrying such a load. Let me help you.'"

Here he paused to let them imagine the voice of the cricket.

" 'Thank you,' said the ant in a squeaky voice. 'You are very kind.' At that, the cricket picked up the bread crumb and gulped it down in one enormous bite. A very cruel and unfriendly act, don't you think, David?"

At this David replied indignantly that it was, indeed.

"The ant thought so too, and told the cricket just that! The cricket said, 'Hold your tongue and feelers. I see you are a strong ant! I have work that you must do, or I will eat you, too!' "

By now Rachel noticed that little Samuel was no longer crying. He sat up and glared at the imaginary cricket as Papa continued.

"At that, the cricket stated he wanted to travel, and the ant must drag along the cricket's things, which were wrapped in a birch-leaf case. The bundle was even larger than the bread crumb. The ant obeyed as the cricket hopped a big hop, then lay down to snooze and wait for the ant to drag the case after him. The poor ant got no rest and was very worried about his family."

The evening air seemed cool and pleasant now as Papa spoke about the ant and the cricket. The terrible chirping of the German Führer did not seem so threatening.

"One day the cricket came to a puddle," Papa continued. "The ant said, 'I'll wager a year of my servitude that you cannot jump across that puddle!' The cricket stretched his leapers and hopped across in one hop. 'I did not think you could do it,' cried the ant.

"The cricket mocked him when the ant caught up at last. 'Now you owe me a year of servitude!' "

"This is not such a good story," David said grimly.

"But wait!" Papa said knowingly. "The ant was a smart little fellow. Day after day as he dragged the bundle along he challenged the cricket to jump over this and that. A path. A wall. A stream. And each time the ant doubled the wager. Every time the cricket leaped easily over the obstacle and won the bet."

"Why is this good?" David asked Papa again.

The rabbi waved his hand in the dark. He was getting to the point. " 'You will notice,' said the ant, 'that I am betting double or nothing every time. I am sure there is nothing you cannot do, Herr Cricket!' The day after that, the cricket and the ant came to the sea. 'I will wager you 16,384 years of service that you cannot jump across the sea.'"

David listened with renewed respect for the ant. The crickets in the garden chirped on brashly as Papa finished his tale.

"The cricket stood up. He stretched his leapers. He had a wild look in his eyes and he cried, 'There is nothing I cannot do!' With that, he bent his leapers double. Beads of sweat formed on his forehead. Then he gave a mighty jump into the sea, where he drowned. The ant smiled. He picked up the cricket's belongings and started for home."

Samuel laughed a high, happy laugh. Satisfied, David sat against the wall. Rachel smiled at the bookshelves and wondered if their printed pages were jealous of her papa.

"When you wonder what will happen to us, you must never forget. We are the ants. One day Herr Hitler will leap once too often. Perhaps he will leap into Poland and be surprised, nu?"

"It is a nice night, Papa," Samuel said. "Tell us another story."

Lori was not asleep when the telephone rang. The insistent bell was a jarring interruption to thoughts and prayers. Lori could hear Murphy's cheerful voice on the telephone as she joined Elisa.

"We're refueling. KLM has seats for all of us leaving Warsaw tonight at 11:30," he babbled happily. "I've been trying to reach Orde in Warsaw. No luck. Nothing getting through."

"What should we do?"

"Orde is going to have to meet me at Warsaw airport. The plane turns right around and leaves fifty minutes after I get off. There's no time for me to chase them down in Warsaw." He sounded mildly distracted. "Maybe a direct wire from London TENS to Orde at Warsaw TENS. I talked to Harvey Terrill and told him I was off to Warsaw, but now I can't reach him. Hope the phone isn't out."

"I'll take care of it," she promised. Certainly tickets on a plane leaving what was soon to be a battle zone was a small miracle!

After quick goodbyes, Elisa dialed the number of London TENS. No answer. Where was Harvey Terrill?

"What is it?" Lori sat on the bed beside her.

"Murphy got the tickets out of Warsaw, but Orde has to have

everyone ready to leave at the airport when Murphy gets there." The TENS phone continued to ring. "Murphy can't reach Orde. The telephones in Poland are not taking long distance." She let the telephone clatter into the cradle. "I'll have to go to the office. Send the wire on our equipment."

Lori looked out at the blackout. "Now?"

"It's two blocks." She waved her hand as if to say how safe she would be.

"Take the Secret Service agent then," Lori warned.

Elisa frowned and bit her thumb. How could she take this government man into the TENS office and send a wire to Orde telling that Murphy was bringing passports and then naming the recipients of the prized illegal documents? She half suspected that the agents had been put in place less to protect them than to keep an eye on everything they did. This would ruin everything!

Elisa explained briefly to Lori and then they considered how she could get around them.

"Lori," she instructed. "Open your door. Talk to them about . . . anything. The blackout. Tell them you are frightened. Keep them talking for a few minutes, and I'll slip out my door, down the stairs, and to the office. I'll be back before they even notice I've been gone."

Lori really was frightened. She clasped Elisa's hands. "Are you sure you should go?" Lori had seen what a bomb could do. She knew how really terrible things could get. "Isn't there some other way?"

Elisa rang up the TENS number once again. Still no answer. *Where was Harvey?* Twenty rings and no reply. "I can send the wire," Elisa said lightly.

Lori agreed reluctantly. At that instant, baby Katie wailed a hungry protest.

The two women exchanged glances. This was one thing Lori could not attend to.

"I can go," Lori said with a grin. "I can run faster than you, anyway."

Katie woke baby Alfie. His lusty cry filled the room as Elisa printed out a message for Harvey Terrill to transmit to Warsaw.

"Harvey can't have gone far," Elisa said. "Not on a night like tonight. Wait for him at the office. Tell him I tried to reach him by telephone, and that this message needs to be sent to Orde immediately in Warsaw."

Lori opened the paper. ORDE: MURPHY DUE TO ARRIVE 4:30 P.M. WARSAW AIRFIELD TOMORROW. BE THERE WITH . . ." The names followed as though there were nothing unusual about such a message at all. Would Harvey be curious about the required immigration papers for Alfie and Jacob?

"If he asks, tell him you think it's all straightened out," Elisa answered. "He's just nosey. Don't let him intimidate you." Elisa always got along with Harvey Terrill. Lori preferred to give the sullen man a wide berth.

What else was there to do? The airline would sell the tickets to someone else if Jacob and the rest were not there to claim them! That thought was more terrifying than the blackout!

It was simple for Lori to slip out of her room and down the hall; she trembled at the thought that it might also be simple for someone to enter the Savoy Hotel and make his way up to the suite. Elisa talked to the kind and patronizing agents who assured her that everything was quite under control.

At the far end of the hall, Lori sneaked into the stairwell and disappeared. *Round little Hildy Frutschy at the bottom of the stairs at the Red Lion House had made a far better watchdog than these two fellows,* Lori thought. They droned on about the closeness of air-raid shelters and the vigilance of the anti-aircraft crews who even now watched the skies above England.

Lori did not have any sense of danger from German planes tonight. She remembered too clearly that the explosion which had taken Doc's life did not come from a Nazi bomber.

———

Lori made her way quickly through the blue-lit lobby of the Savoy Hotel. A strange, confused atmosphere pervaded London. Among some small cliques of citizens, the voices were low and serious as the reality of the crisis was discussed. Among others, the laughter and the conversation were especially loud and bright. *Those Londoners are whistling in the dark,* Lori thought, pushing her way through the revolving doors into the still night air.

Thin slits of light from covered headlights were all that was visible of the automobiles that crept up the street. There had already been a number of traffic accidents, Lori had heard.

Passing groups of people along the way, she listened to snatches of conversation. *"Parachutists . . . that's most likely what the Nazis will do. They'll send in parachutists first and saboteurs to blow the bridges, and . . ."*

"They've set up thousands more beds at the hospitals. They're digging an underground passage from the railway to the hospital."

"What good are sandbags gonna do, I ask you, if a bomb falls on your house?"

Word had just come over the BBC that a million and a half children were being evacuated from London.

Lori was relieved that the younger children were already safely tucked into bed in a farmhouse in western England. After everything that had gone before, what would scenes of mass evacuation have done to the emotions of the boys?

Lori tried to read her wristwatch by the starlight. Surely Murphy's plane would have taken off again by now. She looked skyward and prayed for him as she rounded the corner and half jogged down the alley to the side entrance of the TENS building. She prayed for Jacob! She prayed that she would be able to reach Sam Orde in Warsaw, to warn him to be at the airport with Jacob and Alfie in plenty of time!

The glass of the transom window was covered with black paper. Lori could hear muffled voices within. She heaved a sigh of relief! *So Harvey Terrill was there! Probably overwhelmed with business,* she reasoned as she slipped Elisa's key into the lock. *Maybe in a meeting or on the phone?* It would be best to simply send the message to Warsaw and slip out without interrupting him. The harried night editor was seldom pleasant these days. She did not want to get underfoot on a night like tonight.

Conscious that she must not let interior light spill out, she squeezed quickly through the door into the coffee room of the TENS office. Terrill's voice in the adjoining office was tense, almost angry. Lori stood for a moment, not wanting to interrupt what was obviously an important conference.

"He's gone to Warsaw, I tell you. Out of the way."

Lori had a sense of indignation at Terrill's obvious pleasure over Murphy's absence! She stiffened and stood silently in the anteroom as her eyes adjusted to the scene through the door in front of her.

The newly installed blackout curtains were pulled tightly across the windows. A single bank of lights was burning, creating a pool of dim illumination in the center of the room while leaving the corners in shadow.

Underneath the light and bent over the conference table were the figures of Harvey Terrill to one side, and a small, thin man with his back to Lori. Some sort of blueprint was unrolled on the tabletop and weighted in place at the corners with two dictionaries and two telephone books.

The night editor jabbed his finger toward the plans. "You can drop the dome with just eight charges?"

What was he saying? Lori backed up a step deeper into the shadow. *Drop what dome? What was he talking about?* Her heart hung in her throat and a feeling of cold fear welled up in her.

The man across from Harvey answered in a youthful, excited rush. "See now, this is the way it works. Not the whole dome. We don't need the whole dome, you see? The lantern tower is plenty." He sounded pleased, like a little boy showing off some grand scheme. "The lantern tower is eighty-five feet tall. Seven hundred tons."

Lantern tower? The tower of St. Paul's? She tried to silence her breathing, which suddenly seemed unnaturally loud.

Harvey peered at the plans. "You've put the charges in the light wells?"

"Right. You see here." The small man slid his finger in a tight circle. "Wells through the roof to catch the light at the top of the Golden Gallery. The lantern tower rests right there on the top of the inner cone. Nothing but brick supporting seven hundred tons! When we blow that, the lantern will drop through the dome three hundred feet to the pavement of the church! It won't stop there. It will carry the floor of the rotunda and everyone right down with it into the crypt."

There was a heart-stopping silence as Harvey Terrill digested everything that was before him. Lori felt the ground sway beneath her in one terrible moment of realization. This was what Doc Grogan had been trying to tell them!

Paul Golden. Light wells.

Not a name! It was a place! St. Paul's! The Golden Gallery! The light wells at the base of the lantern tower were set with explosives!

The young man paused in blissful contemplation as Harvey Terrill smiled grimly with understanding. "Your mother would be proud of you, boy," he said softly in appreciation. "Blowing up the parish church of the British Empire."

A pleased chuckle sounded. "If we time this right, old Nelson and all the moldering British corpses will have a host of new neighbors joining them. Including Winston Churchill."

"You're sure these little satchels will do the job?"

"The eight 'little satchels,' as you call them, are sitting right on the brick. They'll all go at once when I send the radio signal. I'll be in the bell tower at the front of the west facade with the transmitter. When Churchill climbs the pulpit and begins to speak, you walk out of the building. That will be all the signal I need to press the button. And—"

Enough! Lori stood with her back pressed hard against the counter. She inched her way back toward the door. *Paul . . . Golden . . . light wells . . . Churchill . . . Papa!*

All of this had been planned for the special service at St. Paul's for her father and the other pastors. But *why*? Why had Harvey Terrill done this?

Her hand dripped with perspiration as she groped for the doorknob. The slippery metal resisted her grasp. She whirled like an animal trapped in a corner, and Elisa's message fluttered away. Her elbow caught a coffee cup and sent it crashing to the floor!

A cry of alarm pursued her as she threw the door back. In only an instant she would have been free, but the strong grasp of angry hands slammed against her, pulling her back from those few steps into the alley!

A vise-like ring of arms clamped around her, wrestling her through the open door, then slammed her down hard against the counter and onto the floor.

Lori tried to cry out, but a hand pressed down over her mouth.

Terrill swore angrily. "It's Lori Ibsen!" He grabbed her hair and held her head close to his scowling face. "Little snoop. How much did you hear?" His eyes were blazing even in the dim light.

The other man sat squarely on her. "However much she heard, it's too much, Harvey. She knows too much."

———

Karl Ibsen was the last to receive the injection. By then there were vacant stares on some of the faces of the men who had

478

preceded him, and he knew what was being done. In a few moments several of the others were completely unconscious and passed out on the floor, including the man dressed as a Polish officer who had not come with the prisoners from Nameless camp.

Karl looked knowingly into the eyes of the doctor as he received his shot. "We were told that we might win our freedom today," he said.

The doctor looked away uncomfortably. "I am sorry for the prison that you are in," Karl said.

"*I* am not a prisoner," remarked the doctor in a startled tone.

"There is no answer at that number," said the Savoy Hotel operator impatiently.

"Please," Elisa argued. "Let it ring. I know someone is there."

"I am sorry, Mrs. Murphy. We cannot keep the lines tied up. If you would like to ring the number later—"

Elisa had already telephoned the TENS office six times in the last hour. Why did Harvey not pick up the receiver? Where was Lori?

Elisa paced the room nervously. She stopped to lean against the rail of the crib where Katie and Alfie lay peacefully sleeping at opposite ends. Her head throbbed. She regretted that she had let Lori go alone on a night like this. Murphy had warned her to be careful of going out during the blackout. People would be running down pedestrians like chickens crossing a highway, he said. Headlamps were all but blacked out. Streetlights were out entirely. Pickpockets were no doubt out in droves!

Lori had only two blocks to walk to the office. Where had she gone? Why did she not telephone Elisa at the hotel? Had she been hit by a car? Or thumped over the head by some back-street Artful Dodger taking advantage of the new blackout regulations? Elisa felt as though *she* had been hit on the head. Her temples throbbed. She opened the French doors and stepped out onto the balcony. The noise of traffic emanated up from the dark canyons of the streets stretching out from the Savoy. Far across the city, Elisa could hear the howl of a siren. She could easily spot the black mountain of St. Paul's Cathedral silhouetted against the starlit sky.

It was dark, and so Allan Farrell did not bother to conceal the pistol. His right arm held Lori's shoulders as they walked from Fleet Street to Ludgate Hill, directly toward the dark hulk of St. Paul's. He held the barrel of the weapon in her left side. "I will blow your heart out," he explained softly, "if you make one wrong move. You understand?"

She answered with a nod. She could not speak.

Impatient with her, he jabbed her harder with the pistol. "Don't think I won't do it," he whispered in her ear as they passed the dark forms of a group of people standing on the corner of New Bridge Street and Ludgate.

"It's saboteurs they're worried about, luv. They've put extra men patrolling every bridge across the Thames. . . ."

Lori heard the soft, knowing chuckle of her captor as the nervous conversation of men and women mingled with laughter and jokes. No faces. Just shadows with voices.

The shadow that held her whispered, "No one would even see you fall if I shot. Just the sound of a gun and there you would be with your guts hanging out all over the sidewalk. I would just walk away."

Lori was trembling all over. Her legs felt as though they would not support her. She believed this man. She was certain he would do what he threatened, and so she stumbled on beside him up the gentle slope toward the cathedral.

Framed against the starry sky were the two bell towers flanking the entrance. The dark mound of the dome loomed from the center.

Lori lifted her eyes to the pinnacle of the lantern tower high atop the dome. She tried to make out the cross that crowned the lightless lantern. Always before it had been easily discernible, but not now. The hour of darkness had enveloped even that one fragment of hope and comfort.

She phrased her question carefully. "Where are we going?"

He did not reply. A harsh squeeze to her shoulder warned her that she must not speak. She knew the answer anyway. He was taking her to St. Paul's, which would soon enough be one vast crypt. Lori had no doubt that he intended her to be entombed there as well.

Should she scream and try to break away? Get it over with?

Oh, God! Life was so precious that she clung tenaciously even to these few terrifying minutes! Her thoughts flew to Jacob and to Papa! She prayed for courage, and prayed somehow to survive! She fought the urge to beg this man to let her go. If she spoke, if she begged or wept, he would simply shoot her and be done with it!

Why doesn't he shoot? she wondered as they passed the statue of Queen Anne in front of the cathedral. She looked up at the edifice of St. Paul's. Soon it would be tons of rubble. It would collapse in upon itself by the will of this man, and Lori would vanish with it in a roar of light!

Involuntarily she croaked, *"Why?"*

She winced, expecting the utterance to be answered with a rough jerk or a painful jab of the pistol in her ribs. Instead, he stopped and craned his head upward. A quiet, almost inaudible whisper rasped in her ear. "This war is very old." The voice was strangely detached, inhuman, escaping like steam from his throat. "Like the tide, it rises and recedes, but always it is here. Millions drown. Millions more will die before we are finished." He tightened his grip on her flesh. "You are nothing compared to that. We cannot let you live to fight us. You know too much for us to ignore you. You know enough to stop us." And then, a shove forward and a calm, patronizing voice, "You see?"

At that, he prodded her on through the gate of the churchyard on the south side of the structure. There were workmen everywhere, filling sandbags, stacking them against the outside of the church for protection against bombs. They could not guess that the devastation was already planted within the structure. They did not see that the fire waited within the walls to collapse the great cathedral inward and take them with it into the crypt!

No one looked up as Allan Farrell led his captive through the wide open doors. No one stopped them as they passed, or challenged their purpose there. By the pale glow of candles, some prayed silently at the altar for peace, for salvation, for the tide of darkness to be turned! *But it was too late!* Too late they were shoring up the walls of their church, too late the workers climbed their ladders and built frames to protect the windows!

Eight little satchels had been placed in the light wells. One man would walk out and raise his hand in signal, and all the prayers, all the fortifications, all the work would come crashing down on the heads of the Christians in this place!

The destruction comes from within! Look among you! Lori wanted to shout as they walked easily past a group of parishioners who had come to help.

They walked past the baptismal font and then past Lord Nelson's monument. Along the wall, Lori could see two men carefully removing the painting of Christ holding His lantern and knocking on the door.

Tor Auf! her heart cried. *Open the gate! Open your eyes!*

Allan nudged her toward the door that led to the honeycomb of stairs within the walls. "To the top," he whispered. "Climb."

Twice on the spiral stairs they met men coming down. They talked and laughed over their shoulders. They nodded greetings to Allan and Lori as if to say they were grateful they had come to help. Allan seemed undisturbed by the presence of people on his killing grounds. He was certain of himself. Certain of his purpose.

From the dim glow of a blue lantern, Lori could see the expression on his face. He gloried in the fact that even in these final hours people worked to shore up what he, one man, would soon destroy!

Allan was right. She was nothing compared to this, and yet she was *everything* because she knew enough to stop it! *But how?*

He forced her to the top of the edifice, to the Golden Gallery at the base of the lantern tower. No one else was there. Buckets of sand and water had been carried up by workers as protection against incendiary bombs, but the platform was deserted. The others had descended to bring up more little buckets. Over the edge of the parapet, Lori could see the dark wells in the roof that were meant to catch the sunlight and channel it into the interior of the dome.

Allan twisted her arm and dragged her to the door that led into the forbidden interior of the lantern tower. Deftly, he manipulated the ancient iron lock and pushed the door back on its groaning hinges. Then he forced her up an almost vertical set of steps and into a tiny sealed room in the interior of the tower.

Once there, he gagged her and tied her to a large winch-like machine in the center of the space. She lay in dust that had been undisturbed for years.

"Don't waste your time," he said, touching the gag as a warning that what little noise she might make would go unheard. "You are insulated by seven hundred tons of stone in this tower. No one will hear you."

He stood over her for a moment. The rough corduroy of his trousers brushed her face. "It will not hurt," he said gently, as though talking to a child. "You will not feel anything at all."

Stepping back, he waited a moment more, then descended the steps, closing a massive trapdoor after him.

Lori could not hear the door at the base of the pinnacle as he slipped out. She could not hear anything at all except her own breathing.

"She might have gotten lost," offered the burly Scotland Yard detective, replacing the receiver of the telephone. "No one answering her description has been taken to the area hospitals."

The blackout curtains were drawn tightly in the hotel room. Elisa sat on the edge of a striped chair and stared at the telephone. Something had happened. She was certain of it now. Something had happened to Lori!

The second agent had called only moments before from the TENS office. Harvey Terrill said that he had not seen Lori at the office tonight. He had been out for a few minutes when he found that the telephones were out of order, but other than that short time, he had been right there all evening long.

"I gave her my key to the office," Elisa managed to whisper. "She could have let herself in. Waited for Harvey."

The agent's tone implied a reprimand. "It was nonsense for her to sneak out alone. That is why we are here. Either Tom or I could have accompanied her." He frowned at the bowl of fruit on the table. "Absurd for a young woman to be out alone with the blackout in full effect." He looked at Elisa resentfully. This incident would no doubt reflect on his performance, and it was Elisa Murphy's fault. "What was the nature of her business at such an hour?"

"My husband telephoned. He wanted a message delivered to the news office. The telephones—" She waved a hand helplessly in the air. Tears stung her eyes. *Lori!*

"Probably took a wrong turn," said the agent again doubtfully. "Probably got on the tube and ended up in Kent or some-place."

It was the most hopeful scenario. But why had she not called?

"She is a thoughtful person," Elisa said softly. She bit her lip at the certainty of what she was about to say. "If she could, Lori would call me here. No. Something . . . something has happened to her."

35   Judas Kiss

Tedrick arrived at the Savoy half an hour later with a cadre of agents in tow. Two were sent immediately to the London TENS office, where Harvey Terrill was found hard at work. He had not seen Lori. Except for a small break for a quick meal, Harvey claimed that he had been in the office all night. "The telephone exchange was apparently out of commission," he explained when asked why he had not answered repeated calls.

Elisa's head was throbbing. She ached with exhaustion and worry. Tedrick placed one more call to the little cottage near Evesham where Helen Ibsen and Anna had taken the boys.

If Tedrick had known Lori, he would not have bothered to place the call. Lori had slipped out of the hotel this evening, he explained in an unconcerned-sounding voice. Probably just missing her mother. Probably sick of all the fuss in London. No doubt she would show up on their doorstep soon enough. The train service was drastically curtailed because of all this, and no doubt the impetuous young lady would be arriving later today.

It was nonsense. They all knew it. Still, Tedrick maintained this charade of mild concern until he put down the receiver.

His angry voice penetrated the door to Elisa's room as he took apart the agents for negligence. Tedrick's harsh reprimand pierced her with shame. *How had she been so foolish to let Lori go out alone?* She had never made it to the office. The message had still not been sent to Orde in Warsaw, and Lori had van-ished! Lori had gone out for nothing!

Within hours, Murphy would arrive at the Warsaw aerodrome and Orde would not be there to meet him! The realization of that doubled the sense of futility in Elisa.

Alone in her room with the babies, she paced like a caged lion as Tedrick's rage reached a crescendo in the next room. Elisa looked at the telephone and decided that probably Tedrick had it tapped. *But what else was there to do?*

For the last time, Elisa telephoned the London TENS office. In an uncharacteristically friendly voice, Harvey Terrill answered on the second ring.

"Ah, Elisa! Did the lost sheep come home yet?"

The too-cheerful words were like a knife. "No. Now listen," she said in an urgent whisper. "She was coming to tell you to contact Orde in Warsaw. Tell him to have Jacob and Alfie and Rachel Lubetkin ready to go at the Warsaw airport at eleven o'clock tonight."

"That's it? You could have called."

She almost choked. "I tried . . . please, Harvey! It's urgent! Just send the wire."

"Murphy got the passports for them, does he? You think the immigration officers aren't wise to phoney passports?"

Tedrick's fury slowed to a dull roar. The muffled replies of the recalcitrant agents were punctuated by Tedrick's mocking replies.

"Send the message, Harvey. That is all she was coming to tell you."

"You know kids. She got distracted by something . . . or someone, maybe. Some bloke in a uniform."

Elisa closed her eyes in frustration. Harvey Terrill did not seem to comprehend what was happening here. "Harvey, Jacob Kalner is Lori's husband. She did not wander off like a stray on a side street. *Tell me you'll wire the message to Warsaw!*"

Harvey sounded slightly wounded. "Sure. Right away."

Elisa placed the telephone easily back into the cradle as Tedrick's voice rose one last time. *"You're through! Finished! Done! Back to pounding a beat in Soho!"*

Moments later he emerged, beads of sweat lining his brow. Behind him the two chastised agents stood staring dully at the floor.

"Listen," he said to Elisa, "if there's something you're not telling me about this, the girl's life could depend on it."

485

Elisa sat silently in the chair and looked out over the city toward the blacked-out dome of St. Paul's. What could she tell him? Lori was delivering a simple message to Harvey Terrill at TENS. She never arrived. The content of the message did not matter. It had nothing to do with anything. How could it? She had told the truth about everything but the passports. "Murphy wanted the Warsaw correspondent to meet him at the airport. It is that simple."

Tedrick crossed his massive arms. "The girl was with Grogan the day he was killed. She saw something . . . *someone* . . . who did not want to be seen."

"She would have told us."

"Not if she didn't know what it was."

———

Harvey Terrill hummed to himself as he flipped through his file in search of the emergency telephone number for the Polish Embassy in London.

He dialed and let it ring as he edited the front-page story Orde had wired in from Warsaw. *The Polish government has given up all hopes for a peaceful solution to the annexation of Danzig by the Germans. In Warsaw, small children and old men are filling sandbags. Even in the Jewish District of the city, rabbis and Yeshiva students are digging slit trenches in city squares. The basements of synagogues are being fortified for use as air-raid shelters. Meanwhile, citizens of Warsaw carry on. The cafes are still filled. Theaters are crowded. In the English movie house, the motion picture "Stagecoach" is playing with Polish subtitles to a packed house.*

It was an interesting study in contrasts, Harvey mused. Slit trenches and bomb shelters on one hand; cafes and American movies on the other.

Life went on. Like ants moving in an orderly line beneath the shadow of a raised boot, Poland marched along.

Tonight the embassy took a little longer to answer the telephone, but Harvey's call was eventually put through.

"I have information you may wish to relay to your authorities in Warsaw."

"Your name, please?"

"There is a gentleman arriving tonight at 11:30 in Warsaw on the KLM flight from Vilnyus. He is an American newsman named John Murphy."

"*Murphy?*"

"John *M-U-R-P-H-Y*. Yes. I have learned from a reliable source that Mr. Murphy is carrying forged passports into Poland. I am not certain if they are American or British passports, but they are intended for two members of the staff of Trump European News Service. Something you will want to follow up."

The KLM flight touched down in Warsaw a few minutes after midnight. The atmosphere of the place was thick and humid.

"Mr. Murphy? Mr. John Murphy?" The thin man in the dark blue uniform of a Polish customs officer was polite but firm. Murphy was asked to accompany him to an office for questioning that was clearly not routine.

Murphy felt as if the violin case tucked under his arm had suddenly turned bright orange and sprouted a sign that read "Look here for contraband!" He decided that his best approach was wounded innocence.

"What's the reason for this delay? I'm here on business for Trump European News, and I have only a short time before I need to catch a return flight to London." Waving his passport, he added, "I'm an American, as you can plainly see."

"Yes, Mr. Murphy, we know all about who you are, and there is no problem with *your* passport."

Murphy's blood begin to pound in his ears at the significantly emphasized word. "Well, then," he said with all the brass he could manage, "I'll just be on my way," and he started to stand.

The customs officer gave a brief shake of his head and waved Murphy back to his seat. "A moment more, if you please. Regulations permit us to search for suspected smuggled items. Would you be so kind as to tell me what is in the case you are carrying?"

Murphy did his best to act unconcerned. "This is a violin that belongs to my wife, who is a professional musician. Since I was making this trip to Warsaw, she asked if I would deliver it to a friend here who has asked to borrow it."

"And the name of this friend in Warsaw?"

Stupid, stupid, stupid! Murphy had no ready answer and anything he might make up would sound suspicious. At the obvious delay in replying the officer continued, "Perhaps I should examine the case, then?"

Murphy held on to the case. "Say," he said calmly, "I'm sure we can work this out. Isn't it customary to offer a little gratuity for good service? After all, I am in a terrible hurry, and my internationally known firm would be grateful for any assistance you can provide."

"Bribery, Mr. Murphy?" the man said grimly. "At this point, I really must insist on seeing the instrument." A thin, bony arm snaked out of the uniform sleeve and a hand extended expectantly toward the violin. Reluctantly, Murphy handed it over.

The American was surprised when the officer raised the lid of the case and removed the violin. Setting the case aside, the Polish official studied the violin with great care, even holding it at an angle so that the light from his desk lamp would shine inside.

There was a long, uncomfortable delay. Murphy tried not to look at the case, tried not to rub his sweaty hands together, tried not to think about what he knew of Polish prisons. When the officer at last gave a long sigh, Murphy almost jumped out of his chair. He fought down an insane urge to yell at the man to stop playing and get it over with.

"It is a genuine Guarnerius," the customs officer commented.

"What? Oh, right. Absolutely genuine. So?"

"Mr. Murphy," said the man, folding his hands in an attitude of sincerity and gazing at Murphy with the demeanor of a doctor about to inform a patient of a terminal illness, "smuggling is an extremely serious offense, particularly in these tense times."

Murphy nodded his understanding, but made no comment.

"What would you say," the man continued, "if I told you that this violin is very suspect and must be confiscated?"

For a moment Murphy acted as if he did not understand, and then for another instant, he thought of protesting. How could he give up Elisa's violin? Then he thought of Lori Ibsen. *Kalner,* he corrected himself. He thought of the terror that was certainly coming to Warsaw, and that the next KLM flight was the last one out. All this went through his mind in the space of one deep breath. "All right," he said. "You keep the violin, and I'll keep the case."

———

Cradling the empty violin case, Murphy emerged from the Polish customs office into the airport waiting area.

The room was stifling and crammed with desperate people. The noise of competing voices gave the area the frantic atmosphere of the stock exchange on a hectic day of trading. While some people waited anxiously for a flight to be announced, others argued loudly with clerks of customs officials, or with one another. Some waved wads of money and offered to buy tickets to anywhere, as long as it was away from Poland and nowhere near Germany. Polish money was scorned. French francs and British pounds were considered by the more cool-headed of the ticket holders. American cash was looked on with some interest, and here and there a few precious passages from Warsaw were purchased.

Murphy stood on a bench and scanned the crowd in search of Sam Orde and his little group of travelers. Were they here? Had they already checked in at the KLM counter and picked up their tickets?

He worked his way through the jostling crowd to the long line for KLM Air Service. Precious minutes slid away as Murphy moved forward too slowly.

If Orde had received the message from London TENS, he would be here by now, Murphy knew. He continued to scan the mob expectantly.

Holding tightly to the case that had contained Elisa's violin, he thought how much more valuable the passports were. *But where was Orde? Where were the faces that matched the photos on these priceless documents?* Jacob. Alfie. Rachel. They would not be able to pick up their tickets without the passports.

At the head of the line, a florid-faced man was shouting that there must be more tickets available. The man looked as though he might have a stroke as his color grew redder and redder and his voice shriller and shriller. At last the man seemed to believe the clerk that there were no more tickets to be had, and he deflated like a punctured balloon. From loud and demanding, the man shrank in on himself till he meekly moved aside and went to sit forlornly on a bench next to a woman and two small children.

"Next!" the harried clerk shouted and pointed at Murphy impatiently.

Murphy produced his return ticket. "I expect to be joined by some business associates," he said. "Has anyone been here asking for John Murphy? Trump European News. Four reservations out of Warsaw were confirmed for them in London." He gave the names slowly. She scanned the list with an air of indifference. Could Mr. Murphy not see that there was near panic here? Could she keep track of all the people looking for someone?

"No," the girl replied, "not yet. What's more, your friends should already be here and checked in. Don't you know that this is the last flight out of Warsaw? There are lots of others waiting to use those tickets."

"Can you give me a little more time?" Murphy asked. "I'm sure they are on the way."

The clerk consulted a clock on the wall behind her, "Five more minutes! The plane leaves in fifteen."

The head of TENS walked rapidly out the front doors of the airport and looked frantically for Orde and the boys. On the street corner he waved off some taxis; there was not enough time for him to reach the news service office and return to catch the plane.

Murphy went back inside the airport to a bank of pay phones. Every telephone was dead!

When the American turned away from the phone, he found the ticket clerk waving at him. "Has the rest of your party arrived yet?" she asked. "Your time is up."

"No," he said, "but they are on the way. Any chance of holding the flight?"

The woman looked shocked. "Absolutely not," she replied. "Do you see this case?" she asked, pulling a small bag out from under the counter. "This is my bag, and this is my flight. If your friends aren't here, it's just too bad." She waved to the florid-faced man, who jumped up eagerly. "There are now three seats available," she said.

Murphy ran back outside. Up the sidewalk a block in one direction, then back past the terminal building and a block down the other way. No Orde! Murphy heard the engines of the KLM plane turn over with a roar.

He came to a sudden decision and hurried over to the first cab in the taxi stand. "Do you know the office of Trump European News?" he asked, and he gave the address of TENS, Warsaw. "I want you to take this case to the man in charge there. His name is Samuel Orde. Have you got that? Samuel Orde." He thrust the violin case into the man's hands, along with twice the requested fare. "Take it right now," he directed.

One glance over his shoulder at the departing taxi, then he ran straight out to the tarmac. "Hurry!" called the KLM clerk from the bottom of the boarding stairs.

As the last KLM flight out of Warsaw taxied away from the gate, Murphy's final view was of a large man waving bravely over the fence. He could not hear the man's sobs, but Murphy had no doubt that they echoed the ones coming from the seats beside him and across the aisle.

Pastor Karl was unable to move his legs or his arms, but he was perfectly awake. He watched the burly S.S. guards come into the room where the prisoners had been drugged and sling the men over their shoulders like sacks of potatoes.

When it came his turn, Karl had the odd sensation of being swept up high in the air. It brought back long-forgotten memories of Karl's own childhood, occasions when a toddler named Karl Ibsen had been lifted high by his father and swung through space.

He had no ability to feel the hands that roughly reached around his thin frame, or of the brawny shoulders over which he was tossed. If he closed his eyes, he could imagine that a completely invisible force was carrying him.

Karl opened his eyes in time to see the truck into which they were being loaded. The prisoners were stacked carefully, face up, so they would not suffocate, but otherwise they rested all over each other like sacks of grain in the back of a wagon.

After a short ride in the truck, the human cargo was unloaded again and carried through a shady, wooded area. Karl enjoyed the sweet breeze that played on his eyelids. He liked the sounds of crickets chirping along a stream, and when he was at last dumped without ceremony against a tree trunk, Karl was grateful that he was propped upright and could look around him.

Alfie knew he was dreaming, and yet it was not a dream.

He could smell the scents of the woods. Crickets fiddled and bullfrogs boasted on the banks of the Vistula River. It was very dark everywhere except for fireflies that bobbed drunkenly in the branches of the bushes.

Alfie was walking in a line of men. He lifted his feet high like a soldier marching. He did not stumble when he walked, even though the path was dark. Werner-kitten rode on his shoulder and rumbled in his ear. Ahead of him, Alfie could see the forms of the boys from Sisters of Mercy Hospital. They, too, were being carried. Slung over the shoulders of strong men, they were being taken some place . . . someplace. But where?

His friend Werner looked up at him. Alfie was glad to see his face.

"I thought they killed you," Alfie said to Werner the boy.

"Yes," Werner replied. His eyes looked worried.

"Where are they taking us?" Alfie asked. He hoped that Werner would answer him. Werner was smart. He always knew the answers.

Werner could not point. His hands dangled over the shoulders of the man who carried him. Werner moved his eyes to show Alfie where they were marching to. Alfie looked up to a high hill with a big metal tower on top. There was a square cement building on the hill as well. Alfie thought that the tower looked very much like the radio tower on top of the Polski Radio broadcasting studio where the captain had gone to send his report to London. But it was not the same. There were crickets and bullfrogs. This seemed a very lonely place.

"What is this place?" Alfie asked Werner.

"Look behind you," Werner said.

Alfie looked over his shoulder. The kitten stopped purring. Marching along behind Alfie was a Hitler-man in his uniform. Over his big shoulder was Pastor Ibsen. Pastor Ibsen was also wearing a uniform, but it was like the ones Alfie saw on all the Polish soldiers.

"Are you awake?" Alfie asked Pastor Karl, who had his eyes closed.

Pastor Karl opened his eyes. "Hello, Alfie," said the pastor just like always. "I like your kitten."

Alfie wanted to hug Pastor Karl, but he could not stop marching. "Where are we going?" Alfie asked.

"There." Pastor Karl's eyes pointed to the tower.

"Why is the Hitler-man carrying you?" Alfie asked.

"I cannot walk," Pastor Karl replied.

The bullfrogs bellowed loudly, almost drowning out pastor's voice.

"Why?" Alfie asked, but the sound of bullfrogs became so loud that he was certain the pastor could not hear him.

Then the pastor looked up into the starry sky. There were lights moving above them, bright lights. Suddenly Alfie knew that the sound he was hearing was not bullfrogs, but the rumble of airplane engines.

"You must run!" shouted Pastor Ibsen. "Run and tell them!"

Alfie could not run. His feet kept marching in the line with all the rest. He looked down at his clothes and saw that he was also dressed in the uniform of a Polish soldier. Why was he marching between these Nazi soldiers?

"I can't run!" he cried to Pastor Karl. His heart was pounding. He was sweating because he was afraid. Something terrible was ahead on the path. He knew it, and yet he could not make his legs stop marching forward.

Pastor Karl raised his arm to the tower. "Tell them." Small spouts of flame erupted in the blackness. A popping sound rattled all around the ground where Alfie marched! There was a great explosion beside the tower. The light from it made the metal frame glow like a skeleton against the sky.

Alfie looked at the face of his friend Werner. "RUN, Alfie!" Werner shouted. "It has begun!"

"I can't run!" Alfie cried. His legs marched on toward the fire and the spurting lights that Alfie now knew were guns firing down on them. "Help me!" Alfie cried to Pastor Karl.

"Step aside," replied the pastor in a kind voice. "One step to the side, Elisha. Tell them. Tell your captain."

Alfie stepped one step to the side, and now he was no longer marching with the rest. He backed up as other Hitler-men, carrying men on their shoulders, marched on without seeing him.

"Where do I run to, Pastor Karl?" Alfie shouted after him as fire began to fall from the sky in sheets like a waterfall.

There was no answer. In the glow of the fire, Alfie saw the Nazi soldiers lay their burdens down in the grass of the hillside.

––––––––

Hess brought a staggering Wolfgang von Fritschauer to the grassy knoll on which the transmitter stood. "Now," he observed in a friendly fashion, "now is your opportunity to prove your loyalty to the Führer."

"Yes, I see," slurred Wolf. "Now we can strike at Poland after such pro . . . what's the word?"

"Provocation. Exactly," agreed Hess.

"And my part?" asked Wolf. "Do I lead . . . attack the town, or stay here and broadcast?" he mumbled.

"Neither," said Hess quietly.

"Then do I lead the prisoners so we can be seen retreating?"

"Nothing as involved as that," corrected Hess.

"What am I expected to do, then?"

"Why, Wolf," said Hess in a kind voice, "you are expected to die." He shot Wolf through the neck with a Polish army-issue pistol.

Wolf's body was laid out on the grass. Hess placed the pistol in Wolf's outstretched hand. It would be clear to any observer that the man had been killed while directing a Polish attack on the German radio transmitter.

―――――

Operation Canned Goods continued in the woods between Gleiwitz and the Polish border. Karl Ibsen was wide awake when he was placed against a tree trunk, but he had no strength to escape. To Gustav Ahlman, he remarked, "What will you say to the Judge of the Universe? You know this war is going to bring great destruction and sorrow on Germany. Is that what you want?"

"It will bring your destruction first," Ahlman said, pressing the muzzle of his pistol against Karl's head.

"Oh, God," Karl cried, "receive my spirit!"

Then Ahlman pulled the trigger.

―――――

"Where do I run to, Pastor Karl?" Alfie whispered the question once again as a wide gulf of water separated him from the pastor. Would he find no answer? "Where should we go?"

Silence. No crickets. No bullfrogs. No explosions or thrumming engines. Only silence and a very bright light all around Alfie, as if a silver cocoon had suddenly surrounded him and made him safe. Alfie was not afraid any longer. But still he asked the question.

"Where?"

The voice of Pastor Karl was soft and happy. "The Promised Land."

"A good idea," Alfie replied.

The light began to fade. "More with you . . . than are with them."

"Very good," Alfie said, feeling happy. He reached up and stroked Werner-kitten, who purred in a sleepy way on the pillow.

Alfie knew he was dreaming. Werner was on Alfie's pillow. Jacob was fast asleep in the bed beside him. There were no crickets chirping. No fire or explosions. But something was coming to Warsaw. Alfie was sure of that when he opened his eyes and sat up.

"Are you awake?" Alfie shook Jacob's shoulder.

"Huh?"

"Wake up." Alfie shook Jacob again.

"What?" Jacob sounded angry. He fumbled for the clock and held it close to his face. "Elisha, it's 4:30 in the morning. Go back to sleep."

"No." Alfie said, feeling very sure that he must not go back to sleep. "We have to tell the captain. The planes are coming."

Jacob lay very still with the clock in front of his nose. It ticked loudly. There was another sound. Alfie knew that Jacob was now awake. The sound was the terrible buzzing of engines.

"Planes."

"Coming to Warsaw."

"Now? Luftwaffe?"

"Yes," Alfie said, climbing out of bed and looking for his trousers. "We should tell the captain. And then we should go to the Promised Land."

Hess was inside the radio station and on the air. In excellent Polish he announced that the forces of the Polish Army had liberated Gleiwitz from German oppression. Hess called on Poles working nearby to rise up in revolt.

He ordered machine guns to open up on the concrete building. Moments later, all the windows were shattered and there were convincing pock-marked walls to prove the reality of the attack. The gunners were extremely careful not to damage the antenna or the transmitter.

36 The Promised Land

Orde awoke suddenly. Something terrible had happened. The air was filled with the unending rage of a beehive buzzing full blast. Without realizing what was on his face, he brushed plaster and glass from his cheeks and groped for the lamp that had been on the table beside the couch. It was not there. Plaster was on the table, strewn on the floor of the hotel suite.

There were planes overhead, planes so near that they seemed to be in the room! Double-engine planes. *Luftwaffe!*

He put his feet on the floor and cut his right foot on glass from the broken lamp. Outside, not far from the Bristol, another bomb crashed down. The floor shook. Then another boom! And another, moving closer in a perfect rhythm. The whole building shuddered. Another huge chunk of ceiling crumbled down, filling the room with choking plaster dust.

Orde coughed. He tried to call out to Alfie and Jacob in one room and then to Lucy in the other! Their names caught in his throat. He gasped for breath and wondered why it was so dark. The blackout curtains hung crazily from a broken rod. The glass of the windowpanes was gone. Orde could see fires in the distance, the eruption of flame like a waterspout in the direction of the airport!

Orde remembered the light switch in the bathroom. Maybe it still worked. But he could not walk across the floor because of the litter of glass shards. Orde groped in the darkness for his slippers, miraculously finding them where he had left them by the sofa. They were full of rubble. He shook them out and slipped them on the wrong feet.

"Jacob!" he cried, shuffling toward Lucy's room in confusion. He tripped over an upturned chair. "Lucy!" he shouted.

Behind him he heard the voice of Alfie in a sing-song cadence above the incessant droning of the motors. "We have to go now, Captain! Get dressed, Lucy!"

Alfie emerged from the room, the kitten tucked into his shirt. The little black and white face peered out at the neck just beneath Alfie's chin. A second head.

"We're all right, Captain," Alfie said.

Then, behind Orde, Lucy came to the other door in her nightgown, her hair falling over her face. By the light of yet another explosion, Orde could see that she had a cut above her right eye that was bleeding. She held her hand to it, then looked at the black liquid that was her own blood. "I'm not hurt," she muttered.

"Get dressed," Alfie said. "We have to go. Pastor Ibsen said it's time to go to the Promised Land."

———

There was no traffic in Muranow Square. No taxis. No trams running. Peter Wallich slept on an iron cot in a long line of other iron cots in the dormitory of the Community Center.

He opened his eyes to the sound of distant motors and a thumping, like a paper bag filled with air being popped. He sat up and listened. Other men and boys in the room snored and wheezed on as though nothing were out of place in the sounds of early morning.

Peter got up and pulled his trousers over his nightshirt. He found his shoes and undarned socks and stumbled through the unfriendly iron frames of the cots.

It was hot, even though it was not yet light. The thumping sound grew louder. Not nearer. Just *louder*.

He pushed through the swinging door out into the dining room. It was deserted, dark. He threaded his way through the long wooden tables and benches to the entrance, then out through the doors, where the buzzing sound increased in volume.

Peter searched the vaguely lightening sky. It seemed empty, except for bright morning stars. Daylight was coming, slowly turning the deep purple of the eastern sky to hues of violet. Pastel shades reflected in the taped and boarded windows of houses and shops all around the square. The gold of newly stenciled letters on baker Menkes' shop caught a ray of light. But it was not sunlight!

Far across the rooftops, in the direction of the angry whirring sound of a buzz saw, a flash of light exploded like lightning. *The*

497

airport? Had a plane gone down? Several seconds later the resounding *boom* of that explosion reached Peter's ears.

Several others joined him on the steps. "What is it?" asked a boy of about twelve.

No one wanted to answer what they *thought* it was. What they *feared* it to be!

Peter looked toward the open window of Rabbi Lubetkin. Why was that window open? No tape. No boards. Did the rabbi not believe that *they* could come here?

The distant humming of the bee swarm was suddenly accompanied by a *slap! slap! slap!*

Bombs?

Across the square, Peter could just make out the form of Rabbi Lubetkin as he ran out on his front steps, his wife at his side.

Had they left their windows open so they could clearly hear this terrible moment?

―――――――

Pulling her robe around her shoulders, Rachel followed her father and mother out into the tepid morning air. The scents of the river drifted around her.

Papa walked slowly down the steps and then out into the street so he could see better. He held his hand up like a scout looking for a trail or shading his eyes against the sun. But there was no sun—only distant fire and the sound of airplane engines. So it had begun! He stared to a faraway place on the horizon, where puffs of smoke erupted like little mushrooms.

"The airport," he said. "It is true." He turned. "Downtown Warsaw. There." He pointed to a spiraling purple plume of smoke. "Polski Radio, maybe."

"But will they bomb us, Aaron?" Mama's voice trembled.

"No." He sounded so certain. So *confident*! Why, then, was Rachel still so afraid?

Across the square, Dolek's horse-drawn milk wagon plodded up the street. Ludicrous, because it was so ordinary on such a morning, it turned lazily into Niska to continue its regular route.

Rachel watched it with astonishment, and then she remembered that the old milkman was mostly deaf. Probably his horse was deaf, as well.

"What do we do now, Aaron?" Mama's voice was still shaking.

"No air-raid sirens," Papa said in that same confident tone. "No doubt the Polish Air Force is giving them a beating." He turned away and walked back up the steps. Then he gathered Rachel and Mama into his outstretched arms and urged them inside.

Once in the foyer, Rachel felt almost normal. Nearly unafraid. This was her house. Everything was just the same. No matter if a little something was going on at the airport, nu? Even so, her heart was pumping hard.

Papa looked around him. He looked at the ceiling and at the walls. His gaze was not friendly. "Maybe the Poles have fallen asleep. Maybe the sirens do not work. Make a call, Etta," he instructed. "Get the telephone chain up and busy. Sirens or not, have morning prayers in the air-raid shelter, I think."

A hint of daylight pushed back the darkness, creeping over the broken windowpane, then through the torn black-out curtain. Outside the hotel room, women wept noisily in the corridor, while others shouted. Someone was yelling for everyone to get down to the air-raid shelter. Still there were no sirens wailing over the city.

Lucy bandaged Orde's foot while Alfie stood beside the window and peered out across the rooftops. Jacob sat quietly in the chair beside him. His eyes were closed, his lips moving silently. Orde knew the boy was praying and he was glad for it. His own thoughts were laced with prayers, but his mind was jumping like a bullfrog from puddle to puddle.

The corner of the ceiling was down. Lucy was on her knees, worrying over his foot as though there were nothing else. *Dear God, where to take them? How to get them out? I waited too long.*

Two walls were cracked with diagonal fissures running top to bottom. *How was the outside masonry holding up?* The sound of engines was almost gone. Very far away he heard the sound of feeble anti-aircraft fire. Probably this one raid over downtown Warsaw was nothing more than the Germans leaving a little calling card, a brief memo that the real stuff would soon be arriving. Right now the battle was far to the west. Some impatient Luftwaffe pilot had not been able to resist the urge to wake up Warsaw and then scoot back to business.

Still no sirens. Yet the cry came, *"Get to the shelters!"*

Orde made a sudden decision. He looked at Lucy's face, at the cut over her eye. The sad resignation and worry on her expression. "I'm going to the office," he said. "You all go down to the shelter until—"

Alfie turned. He was not smiling anymore. "Not the shelter, Captain," he said without doubt.

"I'm going to get to the shortwave radio. Try to find out what's happening," Orde replied quietly. "It's a long way to the office, and the shelter here is—"

"We should stay together, Captain," Alfie said. He turned back to the window.

Lucy looked into Orde's face as if to beg him to listen. Alfie had seen something. Orde frowned, considering what it would be like for the four of them to be caught out in the street in the open if the bombers came back.

Lucy put a hand on his arm. She bit her lip, and her eyes held the silent entreaty, *Do not leave without me.*

Jacob looked up as the distant popping sounded in the morning air. "I don't want to go to the shelter," he said. "If a bomb falls on me, I want it to be just a bomb. Not a whole building along with it."

Outvoted, Orde nodded agreement. The voice in the hall was still shouting for everyone to get to the shelter. The weeping women had been led away down the stairs.

"We should hurry," Alfie said. "They will be waiting."

Orde slipped his shoe over his bandaged foot. Then he reached down to help Lucy to her feet. It was a strange time to tell her what he wanted to tell her, and yet, maybe there would not be another time.

Jacob and Alfie looked on as he took her face in his hands. This time, for the first time, she did not turn her eyes away from his. He did not speak for a moment as they stood there in the dust and rubble. Alfie was right. He could clearly see the beauty of her broken heart and he knew. *Orde knew!* He *loved* this woman!

"I will not leave you," he whispered. "The Lord has never stopped loving you. He has let me see you, Lucy. *Come with me.*"

She nodded, still searching his eyes and believing him. She was no longer afraid. No longer ashamed. In that moment she laid her heart in his hands to carry.

The hall outside had grown silent, as had the street below. Orde took her hand in his.

"We should hurry," Orde said.

"Yes." Alfie agreed. He was smiling again, that knowing smile. "A long way to go."

———

Everyone was moving too slowly. David and Samuel got up at their mother's urging, but they were cranky and belligerent from a long night with little sleep.

Rachel dressed more quickly than her brothers. She took over the job of phoning friends and neighbors with the news that Papa thought it would be better if everyone went ahead to their assigned shelters.

Yes. Yes. The battles seemed very far away. Why should anyone waste time or bombs on the Jewish District? But all the same, send the children on. Gather up your belongings. It was only the first day. Just the first day. A good day to practice in case the conflict should develop into something serious. School could start early for the young ones. It could be held just as easily in the basement of Torah school, where there were sandbags and canned food and water—just in case a bomber should get lost.

David and Samuel, wide awake, were excited by the prospect of a real war. After all, they had been practicing marching in the shade of the elm tree. Now they would really see something!

They dressed as though it were a regular school day. Mama gave them their haversacks and asked Rachel to escort them to the corner, to watch them all the way to the school. There were still phone calls for Mama to make. Things to do. No doubt by the evening more refugees would be coming into Muranow Square.

"We'll be along in a bit." Mama kissed the boys lightly. She seemed not at all afraid, and yet her eyes held something in them that cut a cold knife of fear through Rachel's own heart.

For David and Samuel, walking out into the newly breaking day was an adventure. School chums from all over the district emerged onto Muranow on their way to early school in the air-raid shelter. They hailed one another. They pointed to distant sounds of guns whumping. Such small sounds, they were; it was difficult to believe that they were more than sounds, that men

501

were dying, being blown to little pieces every time a gun cleared its throat.

Rachel was glad nothing had come so close to Muranow! Glad and relieved that all the children were going into the shelter. She was not anxious to join them, because she wanted to look, to watch the fly-sized airplanes climbing high and then falling off to drop their deadly little eggs on some unknown target.

Six-thirty in the morning. Hundreds of children surged around her. She waved goodbye to her brothers on the corner. The excitement was like some sort of game. She was smiling. David and Samuel did not turn around to wave. "I'll bet the Polish Air Force is giving them a beating!" David said to his brother.

There was pride in that statement. The Polish Air Force at that moment was *their* air force, protecting the Jewish community.

Rachel turned to go back home. She took three steps and then stopped. Suddenly the air filled with the high, undulating wail of the Warsaw sirens!

What?

All conversation ceased in that instant. Little faces turned upward in confusion. Could this wail be meant for them? For the Jewish Quarter of Warsaw?

Suddenly, as if drawn by the screaming of the sirens, a formation of German planes appeared just at the level of the housetops! How many? Ten? Or maybe fifty? Or a hundred? No! It was only three, but the terrible crooked cross of the swastika was plainly visible on their tail rudders!

Hundreds of screams, the shrill screams of children, rose up, only to be lost in the spinning props of the planes. The roar of engines was deafening!

Rachel stood, rooted with fear on the sidewalk. She could plainly see the features of the pilots. They flew unopposed, no Polish planes pursued them! And they were smiling as they flew overhead.

Then the screams were drowned out by the terrible shriek of the bombs. The children all began to run at once as spouts of pavement erupted behind them and in front of them and beneath them. The bigger ones outran their little brothers and sisters. Rachel screamed and fell to her knees as little Samuel was knocked to the ground. David threw himself over Samuel, kicking back the others who stumbled on in blind terror toward the school. Then little ones struggled to follow the bigger ones, and all of them reached the steps just as the entire building exploded outward, tumbling down on top of the children to betray their belief that someplace was safe for them.

Rachel screamed at the sight of cart-wheeling bodies and tumbling bricks. The dust, the noise, the horror of it made the whole world shake. Sandbags were nothing. Boarded windows simply disintegrated behind the protective covering. Rachel covered her head as a shower of debris rained down and the drone of the engines sped away in search of other targets.

Then came the silence, eerie and dark in its implication. Silence where laughter and excited voices had been a moment before. Silence covering prostrate bodies like the masonry dust. No birds. No more sirens. Rachel heard her own sobs as she peered up through the cloud that covered what had been Muranow Square.

No more children. No more childhood. It vanished forever in that terrible moment.

"God!" she called. Had the bombs also silenced the Almighty? Could three men, three planes, do this? Only *three*?

Rachel pulled herself to her knees. She raised her hands, imploring the silent heavens to help her stand. To walk forward to look for her brothers.

At that moment, she saw them. They walked . . . stumbled . . . out from the gray cloud of fire and destruction. Hats off. Clothes askew. Their knees and hands were bloody, their faces streaked with tears, but they were alive!

Behind her, Rachel heard other voices. Mothers. Fathers. Running toward the scene, calling out the names of their children!

And then the high, terrible wail of the siren began again, calling those who were left to the shelter of the Community Center.

———

Orde and the others were only five blocks from the Bristol Hotel when the Heinkel raiders struck. The bombs dropped in four installments, lifting the hotel from its foundations. When it came down again, the roof collapsed from the center as the walls puffed out in a weird orange glow of fire and rolling black smoke.

Orde shielded Lucy as debris rained down all around them. He raised his eyes to watch the retreating tails of the planes. No one could have survived the bombing in the shelter of the Bristol. The threatening hiss of escaping gas from the mains made Orde jump to his feet.

Alfie and Jacob were already steps ahead of him. Lucy stumbled after, her head turned back in horror to gape at the remains of the Bristol.

As they ran up the deserted street, Orde could see smoke billowing up from the Jewish District near Muranow Square. Three German bombers scooted away unopposed just above the level of the rooftops.

Telephone lines had been installed in Elisa's suite at the Savoy Hotel. The hope was that Lori's abductors would ring with ransom terms.

With Tedrick towering in the background, he raised his hand in signal for Elisa to answer when the telephone rang. At the same moment he picked up the extension.

No sinister voice replied to Elisa's tentative "hello."

It was Winston Churchill, growling over the lines from Chartwell. "They've started, Elisa," he said gruffly. "The Nazis are bombing Warsaw and Cracow right now."

Tedrick replied with an unexpected expletive. "Great heavens, Winston! Are you *certain*?"

"That you, Tedrick? Yes. Certain. Straight from the Polish ambassador a few minutes ago."

Elisa felt faint. She lowered herself onto the sofa. *Bombing Warsaw!* Had Murphy made it out? Had he managed to connect up with Orde and the kids?

Winston asked the question that showed that nothing escaped his attention, even as she framed it in her mind. "Have you had word from Murphy in Warsaw?"

"Not yet," Elisa said in a faltering voice.

"You do not know if he was able to meet Orde?"

"We are praying so."

"Yes," the voice drawled in a kindly way. "And as for the young lady? Your cousin Lori?"

Tedrick replied. "No word. No ransom demands. I fully expected that some demands would be linked to the service at St. Paul's this morning. Perhaps some note, a political statement to be read from the pulpit—possibly by you, Winston."

504

"The world, it seems, is run by blackmail and extortion these days," he replied in a gloomy voice.

"Shall we go ahead with the service, Winston?" Elisa asked painfully.

The answer was definitive. "Yes! By all means in our power! As Hitler explodes his bombs on the churches of Poland, we shall gather to pray before the righteous throne! Can the God of heaven ignore the difference in the way we begin a conflict and the Nazi disregard for heaven? Yes! By all means we shall continue with our plans." He paused. "I suppose that your father will be on alert, unable to come. But your mother? And Helen Ibsen?"

Tedrick replied again. "We will send a car for them. If there is some demand made, some political statement to be read, perhaps Mrs. Ibsen should be on hand." He frowned, deep in thought. "The Nazis have not been able to break her husband. It seems logical that this might be a ploy to extract some statement from her. Especially now with the Polish war."

"Well then—" Churchill sounded satisfied. "Elisa, perhaps you should also consider bringing the boys along. They are young, but not too young to remember the prayers of England on a day such as this. I would like them in the front row as I speak."

It was a kind thought, made from a great heart. Elisa hung up and immediately telephoned Anna and Helen with the request.

————

Allan Farrell paused beside the statue of Queen Anne that stood just below the steps leading to the grand entrance of St. Paul's Cathedral. Allan knew very little about the reign of the real Queen Anne, but he hated her memory just the same. After all, was she not depicted as standing above a prostrate Ireland? In the terrorist's twisted mind, the queen seemed to be smiling spitefully down at the spot where the Gunpowder Plot conspirators had been executed. He vowed to wipe the smile off her face.

He was several hours early for the Remembrance Service, well before the dignitaries and the crowd were due to assemble, but already well into his plan. Allan reached into the leather satchel and extracted a camera that he hung around his neck.

Among the contents of the bag were another camera, a light meter, and the radio transmitter, which Allan believed he could pass off as one more piece of camera gear.

Allan had been prepared to find a cordon of policemen surrounding the church in response to the news that Poland and Germany were finally at war. The fragile and deceptive calm of the day before had been shown for what it really was: the collectively held breath of all of Europe. Now that wishful thinking was shattered.

But there were no policemen surrounding St. Paul's, no special security measures, no troops patrolling the streets. Despite the fact that the early editions of the papers had announced the start of the war and the mobilization of British troops, it was clear that Britain was still not prepared to have the war on its doorstep. Allan was anxious to prove just how wrong the British were.

Once inside the building, Allan wandered up to the spot directly beneath the dome where the two arms of the great edifice crossed. He noted with particular interest the placement of the chairs for VIPs in the very front row, just below the pulpit. He also saw the provision of chairs for the musicians, to one side of the south transept. And his thoughts went to the girl tied up high above his head.

"Excuse me, sir," inquired a wizened little man. "Do you need assistance?"

"I'm a photographer," announced Allan, holding up the camera. "I'm looking for the best spots from which to take pictures of the proceedings. Sort of scouting the ground before the crowds arrive."

"Right you are too, sir. Just you let me know if there's anything you need. We certainly want to have a fine record of the doings here today."

"We certainly do," agreed Allan. "Say, there is one thing. I suppose that the dignitaries will be brought in the grand entrance, won't they?" At the man's agreement, Allan continued. "Then where would be the best place to get a view of their arrivals? I mean, I'm sure the steps in front will be crowded with onlookers."

"I've got just the thing," said the old man. "Leave it to me. What you want is the bell tower, just above the entrance. I'll take you there myself."

The KLM plane refueled in Amsterdam for the return flight to London. Murphy telephoned Elisa with his own list of bad news and was met with a catastrophic roster from her end.

Lori was missing. Elisa had managed to phone Harvey Terrill to send Orde the wire in Warsaw. But Harvey had obviously not gotten through. Now the violin was gone, the passports sent off across war-torn Warsaw in a taxi. Who could tell what was coming in the next few hours?

One bright spot remained. The prayer service at St. Paul's would continue as planned. *If ever the world needs prayer, this is the moment,* Murphy thought as he dashed back to the waiting plane.

————

The horse stood a little way apart from the overturned milk wagon and the crumpled body of Dolek the milkman. Cans were upended, mingling milk with the blood of the old man and others. The liquid ran in a pink stream in the gutters as the family of Rabbi Aaron Lubetkin ran with hundreds to the safety of the large shelter under the Community Center.

Rachel hung back just a moment as the wail of the useless Warsaw sirens kicked in again. She looked back over her shoulder at the devastation of the square. The linden tree where the birds had built their nests was now an uprooted, shattered mass lying across the churned grass.

Beyond its broken branches, Rachel spotted Peter Wallich's red hair glistening in the sunlight as he leaped a barricade with a dozen other boys from the Zionist Youth brigade.

One by one they vanished up Niska Street. They did not look back. Rachel knew they were getting out of Warsaw. *Warsaw,* where they had all come for refuge, was not a safe place to be.

————

It was hot even though the sun was only barely up. Alfie had sweated through his shirt, and Werner was soggy and unhappy against Alfie's belly as they ran the last two blocks to the TENS office.

The entire building was untouched. For blocks around, the city seemed as perfect and unharmed as it had last week, and for years before that. Except for the distant sounds of exploding shells and the smell of the smoke, it was impossible to tell that there was a war on.

Peter Wallich stood impatient in the sun, his red hair was covered with plaster dust. His clothes were a uniform shade of gray. There were a dozen other boys his age with him, also coated with dust. Their appearance indicated that they had been near the explosions in the Jewish District.

Peter stared up anxiously into the sky. One of his companions spotted Orde and the others approaching and tugged his sleeve. Peter looked at them and then, as if all powered by the same thought, they ran in a bunch to surround Orde and Lucy, Jacob and Alfie.

Talking at once, they recited where they had been when the first bombs fell.

Then the questions tumbled out from every mouth. "What is happening?"

"Are the Poles fighting?"

"Should we stay and fight?"

"Should we leave Warsaw?"

These were the young men scheduled to slip out of Poland in two days. The diving of the Heinkels may have moved their schedule up somewhat.

Orde pushed through them, his hands raised in an attempt to silence the chatter. Did they see the plaster dust on his hair, the cut above Lucy's eye?

Orde dug into his pocket for his keys. He patted each pocket. No keys anywhere. No matter. He gave the glass pane in the door a little kick and let the glass tinkle to the ground and then he reached in and opened the door. As the group bunched up behind him in the entrance, he halted, stooped, and picked up something.

Beneath the broken glass lay a violin case. A strange thing, indeed, to find resting on the doormat of a news office. Left by an itinerant musician in panic, perhaps, as he fled the roaring of the bombs?

The address of the TENS office was tucked into the battered handle. Orde shook the case. He smiled and entered the office.

———

By the time Murphy's KLM flight landed in England, both his

508

clothes and his thoughts were rumpled, and he was in need of a shave. His mouth felt as if the soles of Wehrmacht boots had tramped through it.

Just as they are tramping through Poland right now, he reflected. Somewhere over the English Channel the KLM pilot had picked up a BBC broadcast and relayed it to his passengers. Since before dawn, German planes had been bombing Polish towns, and German tanks were advancing on four fronts into Polish territory.

It had all apparently started with some action involving an unknown village named Gleiwitz, but that fact seemed unimportant. The war, long expected and feared, had begun.

Murphy struggled with deciding what to do first. He desperately wanted to go home to Elisa, but knew that he should go to the TENS office and start gathering the threads of the breaking stories.

Glancing at his new watch, Murphy realized that there was not time to do both. If he went directly to TENS, he could change clothes there and meet Elisa at the Remembrance Service. Maybe he could get through to TENS Warsaw. Then he could at least reassure Elisa about Jacob Kalner. But what to do about Lori?

37   Passport to Life

The harsh voice of the German Führer emanated clearly over the radio from the Kroll Opera House in Berlin, where he now met with his rubber-stamp Reichstag.

Everything inside the London TENS office had been put on hold as staffers gathered around the shortwave to listen to the Führer rasp out his reasons for attacking Poland.

Murphy entered and stood for a moment, unnoticed at the back of the tense and angry group.

The voice cried in fury, *"I should like to say this to the world. I alone was in the position to make such proposals. . . . For two whole days I sat with my Government and waited. . . . I can no longer find any willingness on the part of the Polish Government to conduct serious negotiations with us. . . . I have therefore resolved to speak to Poland in the same language that Poland for months past has used toward us."*

Staff members exchanged disgusted looks. "Bombs," said James Samuels dryly. Then he noticed Murphy. "Hi, Boss." Back to the radio.

The applause of the Reichstag slowed. *"This night for the first time Polish regular soldiers fired on our own territory. . . . We have been returning the fire, and from now on bombs will be met with bombs!"* The roar of approval was tremendous.

Murphy imagined Timmons observing this farce from the press gallery as the heroic voice of the German leader rallied his people to his call to die:

"I am from now on just the first soldier of the German Reich. I have once more put on that coat that was most sacred and dear to me. I will not take it off again until victory is secured, or I will not survive the outcome!"

The familiar chant of *Sieg Heil! Sieg Heil!* erupted from the receiver.

"Well, I guess that is that."

"You heard the man. Victory or death."

"Gives us something to aim for." Nervous laughter followed.

"No," Murphy added. "Gives us something to shoot at." More laughter. Faces turned to see him, recognizing him in a surprised sort of way.

"Thought you were in Warsaw, Boss. Harvey said—"

"Did you get Orde out in time? And the kids?"

Murphy shook his head. "No dice."

All faces were glum at the news. The radio was switched off. Reporters moved like sleepwalkers back to their desks. There was plenty to write about, but nothing to talk about. No one felt like gabbing.

Murphy caught his grimy reflection in the glass of his office. A quick glance at the clock told him he had only minutes to get to St. Paul's to hear what Winston Churchill would say in reply to the lies and distortions of Adolf Hitler.

There had been no further word on Lori Kalner, his secretary informed him. Murphy felt sick. Had there ever been a day so tragic in its portent of the future?

"Where's Harvey?" he asked. To his surprise, the night desk

editor, who always seemed to be present when bad news hit, had left for home. "Said he had to change for the service at St. Paul's," a secretary remembered.

Murphy reflected that he had not even known that Terrill cared enough to attend the Remembrance Service. Murphy chided himself for unreasonably wishing that Harvey had stayed at the office to track war stories.

After a quick change and a washroom shave that caused only two small nicks, Murphy went into the conference room. The bulletin boards there were plastered with maps of Poland. Strands of red yarn were already creeping across Polish territory like the spreading tentacles of an octopus.

Murphy picked up the conference-room phone. "Try to get me Orde in Warsaw," he said to the operator. Then he turned back to studying the maps. The floor was littered with reports and dispatches. The head of TENS picked up a handful and flipped through them, comparing village names with map locations.

About halfway down the pile he came to a note in Elisa's handwriting. It requested Harvey to contact Orde about meeting the plane. The phone rang. "I'm sorry, sir," the operator said. "I can't get through to Warsaw. Shall I keep ringing?" Murphy stuffed the note in his pocket.

"No. Send a wire telling Orde to contact us, although I'll bet he's already trying. By the way, I'm leaving now for St. Paul's. I'll be back in a couple of hours."

———

Allan Farrell watched from his perch in the bell tower as the cars began to arrive at St. Paul's Cathedral. Pastors in clerical collars, musicians lugging instrument cases, and politicians in formal dress arrived in anxious little knots.

Soon after these recognizable professions came the common folks. Some looked sad, others frightened. A cabbie brought a group of people, then parked and joined the crowd now thronging into the church. "Need to teach that Hitler bloke a lesson, we does." He spoke so loudly that Allan could hear every word.

The words "teach a lesson" reminded Allan of his mission, and he checked the transmitter for the hundredth time. He fretted briefly about the lack of opportunity to test the device, then

511

relaxed when he reminded himself of the previous successes of German technology.

He turned his attention back to the front steps. When the terrorist spotted three women arriving together and noted the resemblance to Lori Ibsen, he was certain that he was watching the Lindheim-Murphy-Ibsen family.

The discordant sounds of the orchestra tuning up floated out of the church and drifted up to the bell tower. Allan tried to imagine the noises that would come from the centuries-old building as the lantern tower came crashing through the dome and floor. He compared the kettle-drum sound to the thunder of falling masonry and the plaintive strings to the wail of human voices. Excitement gripped him as he anticipated his symphony of terror.

But where was Churchill? Where was the greatest stroke of all?

As if saving the best for last, a car bearing Churchill and Anthony Eden arrived. The two men, grim-faced and deep in discussion, were obviously hurrying between meetings. It was Allan's intention that they would never hurry anywhere again.

————

Three passports lay in the secret compartment of the violin case.

Only three?

Orde's face was pained as he looked at the folders. He had hoped for so many more. He opened each one. As the boys of the Zionist Youth brigade looked on like starving children, he gave Jacob his identity. Then he smiled and handed Alfie his folder.

As he gazed down at the photograph on the third folder, his face was troubled. *Rachel Lubetkin! And not one for Lucy!*

The thin, dirt-streaked arm of Peter Wallich snaked in over the shoulders of the circle. His fingers clamped around the passport and he pulled it back to stare at it.

"She will be saved," he said.

Behind him, as if to emphasize his thought, the radio announced:

ALL CITIZENS OF GREAT BRITAIN ARE URGED TO REPORT TO THEIR EMBASSY AT ONCE. A STATE OF WAR HAS NOT YET BEEN DECLARED BETWEEN GREAT BRITAIN AND GERMANY. . . .

The group exchanged horrified looks. *Where was England?* Polish cavalry in the west was being overrun by German panzer divisions. Even now tons of dynamite were exploding on fourteen Polish cities. Where was England? Were they not coming? Would England and France arrive in time to save Poland?

Peter's hands trembled. He held up the passport. "With this she can get out?"

Jacob looked down at his own folder. His passport to life, a ticket past the German lines. British citizenship! As long as war was still undeclared, he could walk up to any German officer, flash this passport, and be let through the lines all the way to England.

Did Alfie understand? Alfie looked at his own photograph. He was listening to the devastation being reported over the shortwave. His eyes were sad.

"Where is England?" asked Peter.

Alfie patted Orde on his shoulder. "Right here."

"But . . . where is *England*?" asked another boy, his voice filled with a sense of betrayal. "Who will save us?"

Alfie answered again in the uncomfortable silence. "Here is the captain. He will save us."

Peter whirled on Alfie angrily, "Idiot! Don't you hear what I'm asking? England! *An army!* Will they come to fight for us?"

Alfie was unoffended. He still smiled. "We should stay together," he said. "And see the Promised Land."

Orde had turned away to fiddle with the radio in a preoccupied way. The Poles were taking a beating in the west. New formations of Luftwaffe had passed over the city, bombing indiscriminately.

"Elisha," Orde said. "At nightfall you and Jacob will go to the embassy compound. You will be taken out. You will be safe there. Lucy and the rest of us will—"

"No!" Alfie said. "We stay together! Me and you and him and him and Lucy and—"

"Dummkopf!" Peter shouted.

"Shut up!" Jacob stepped between Peter and Alfie, and for a moment it seemed as though another sort of battle would explode right here. Orde pushed both boys aside as the shortwave continued to blare the bad news of the German Blitzkrieg rolling over Polish defenses.

Sweating and panting in the small space, Jacob and Peter

stared at each other around Orde.

"That's enough!" Orde menaced. "Or I will beat both of you! Now is not the time or the place!"

Alfie was still smiling. He gave Werner-kitten to Lucy. He shrugged and shuffled his feet self-consciously. He had not meant to make anyone angry, but he knew how they would get out and he also knew that they *must* stay together. "Today is Friday," Alfie said. Angry, resentful eyes looked at him, but he pressed on. "I know how we can get out of Warsaw on Friday."

Peter snapped Rachel's passport folder down. "I am going back to the Jewish District," he said, as though Alfie were only rambling. "I'm going to find Rachel and get her to the British Embassy." He backed up a step.

Alfie continued to talk. "On Friday all the Catholics in Warsaw eat fish. Herr Frankenmuth told me—"

"The Germans are bombing that quarter worse than anywhere else, Peter," Orde warned. "You might make it in, but—"

Alfie pressed on. "Werner is very hungry. He has not had any breakfast. None at all."

The kitten yowled at the mention of his name.

Peter looked down at the picture of Rachel. "I know a way, if I can get this to her. Britain is not yet at war. That's bad for Poland, but good for whoever has one of these." He held it up. He was going. Orde could not stop him. Peter looked at Lucy, whose eyes reflected her love for him. Her admiration.

Alfie said loudly, *"Peter!"*

"I'm sorry," Peter said softly to Alfie as the buzz of bomber engines grew louder again.

"Don't miss the boat!" Alfie stepped forward and pumped his hand. "We are going to Herr Frankenmuth at the fish market, you see? He sells fish to the Catholics in Warsaw every Friday, and he will take us on his boat! The fish market! Hurry!"

The planes had returned again over the Jewish District of Warsaw. This time they were serious. Why, after all, bomb a military target when there were so many Jews down below to exterminate?

Rachel finally understood the meaning of the meetings, the discussions of how to protect the Jewish children of Warsaw— where to take them, how to get them out of here if the worst

514

should come. Well, the worst had arrived. It *had* come! And this was only the first morning of the war!

Rachel held baby Yacov, his eyes wide and troubled by the rhythmic thumping noise and the trembling of the earth. Women in the shelter wept for their lost children. Men prayed.

At last Rachel understood why Mama had talked of sending her children away. Rachel would gladly give up Yacov, give up David and Samuel forever, if only they could escape this terror!

Papa stood, his face lost in the shadow of the strange light of carbide lamps.

All eyes turned to the great Rabbi of Muranow. They looked to him for hope, for comfort. He raised his hands and gradually the weeping died away, except for one woman who huddled by the door and called the name of two children who had fallen on the steps of the Torah school. Her quiet sobs accompanied his prayers like the counter-melody of a sad symphony.

"For the sake of heaven, Jews, don't despair! The salvation from God appears in an instant!"

And then he began to sing this summons to believe, this cry for salvation found in a Yiddish melody as old as the hope for the coming Messiah:

> O look down from heaven and behold,
> Look down from the skies and see!
> For we have become as a derision,
> A derision among the nations. . . .

Hundreds in the packed shelter joined in. Papa closed his eyes as he sang. The song was heard in heaven, Rachel knew, but how would God answer it? Would He save them all in one miraculous sweep of His hand? Or, as Papa had explained to her, would He save only one? For God's plan, even one Jew would be enough to keep His covenant! Because of this He cared for every Jew as though each was the only one! Rachel felt the presence of the Eternal One among them. He came to them in the calling of their hearts. One to one, the Lord of heaven was very near.

> Therefore we plead with you ever:
> Now help us Guardian of Israel,
> Take notice of our tears. . . .

The bereaved mother wept on. Only one woman crying, and

yet she cried for everyone, every Jewish mother who had ever lost a child. Rachel knew this as she sang.

> Now take notice of our tears,
> For still do we cry aloud, "Hear O Israel."
> Show all the peoples that you are our God,
> We have indeed none other, just you alone,
> Whose name is ONE.

Papa prayed again, and even the weeping mother, the one woman, raised her head and was comforted.

The orchestra assembled to remember the plight of the imprisoned pastors soared into their contribution. It was the *Elijah* by Mendelssohn.

Fret not thyself because of evildoers . . . the words of Psalm 37 reminded the listeners, *For they shall soon be cut down like the grass.*

In the front row of the congregation, three women joined hands and hearts. They prayed for the missing Lori, for absent Jacob, for Theo who was even now flying patrol missions with trainee pilots along the English coastline, for thousands of children represented by those sitting bravely beside them.

The Lord knoweth the days of the upright: and their inheritance shall be for ever.

They prayed for the Poles, for the free nations to resist Nazi aggression, for the Jewish people trapped in the middle.

The wicked watcheth the righteous, and seeketh to slay him.

They prayed for the righteous men of honor and courage who stood up to evil when they could easily have saved themselves instead. For Karl Isben: pastor, husband, father. They prayed for courage for themselves to be as strong.

The salvation of the righteous is of the Lord: he is their strength in time of trouble.

The melodic strains floated up and up into the shining bright dome where the soft glow was like looking into heaven. Lifted by the prayers of hundreds of anxious hearts, the sounds and thoughts reached past the galleries of stone to the ears of the frightened girl imprisoned overhead.

"Oh, Papa," she whispered. "Mama, Jacob. I'm here."

Charles remembered that the last time they had been with Doc Grogan on their Thursday excursion, they had been right here—St. Paul's Cathedral, in this very place. It was a peaceful place. A happy memory, as long as he did not think past the time they spent here in St. Paul's.

Today rows and rows of chairs filled the space just beneath the dome. There had been no chairs here on the day they had climbed high up into the Whispering Gallery and then on to the Golden Gallery. The polished marble floor had been empty that day. Louis had leaned far over the rail and considered spitting, but Jamie had reminded him that this was a church, a holy place. Although it would have been fun to watch his spit fall so far, it would not have been a nice thing to do.

So here they were, all in a row far below the place from where they had looked down. Mr. Winston Churchill had asked for them to be here today, and Charles was glad for that. Although it had hardly been any time at all since he had been with Elisa, he had missed her terribly and wished she was with them all in the little cottage. Elisa had stayed in London to practice for today's performance. Lori had stayed to help with the babies. *Now where was Lori?*

Little Katie and baby Alfie were parked in their carriage next to Elisa at the end of the aisle. Charles could see them sleeping. He could make out the box that contained the little tent which served as a covering for little ones in case of a chemical gas attack by the Nazis.

Charles supposed that now everyone throughout England would carry their gas masks all the time. He looked over his shoulder at the worried faces of the grown-ups. All of them, indeed, had their gas masks with them.

Charles, Louis, Jamie, and Mark seemed to be the only children in the whole vast gathering. Already half the children in London had been evacuated because everyone knew what was coming. And here it was. A war, just like Mr. Churchill said would come if someone did not stop Herr Hitler. Charles was very glad that Mr. Churchill was going to speak today. It would be a terrible thing if everyone in England was quiet on a day when Germany was dropping tons of bombs on Poland.

That thought made him remember the long talks Murphy and Doc Grogan had about that very thing. Charles looked far up into the misty heights of the dome, where shafts of light beamed through from the light wells in the Golden Gallery. Louis also looked up. Then Mark and Jamie leaned their heads back and stared at the golden glow so many hundreds of feet above them.

The music swirled—very pretty music. Charles touched Elisa's arm. "Look," he whispered. "It looks like heaven."

She nodded. Her face was sad and worried. She looked over her shoulder at the entrance in hopes that Murphy would come soon. Harvey Terrill stood to one side, beside the stairs that led up through the interior of the dome.

Charles smiled and thought how tired Doc had been when they climbed all the way up, how long it had taken him to tell them all the stuff he knew about St. Paul's because he could hardly breathe.

He leaned his head back on his chair again. "We were up there with Doc." He pointed up and up. "Golden Gallery."

Elisa looked at him strangely, as if she were thinking about Doc again. She craned her neck back with the boys as the pretty music drifted on the light beams.

Then she leaned down and put her lips against Charles's ear. "Doc climbed up there?" She also remembered that it had been his last day.

Charles nodded. Her head went back again. "No windows," she whispered to herself.

"Light wells." Charles was pleased that he remembered what Doc had showed them. He pointed up toward the highest gallery just beneath the lantern tower. He would tell her more if she wanted to know. But after the service. It was almost time for Elisa to play. She was using her Steiner fiddle today. It was out across her lap. She had practiced here with it a dozen times, and—

Elisa's face grew very white. She was looking up into the dome. Even though the time for her to play was very near, she was searching the light beams of the dome as though she could see something there. *Something*. Maybe Charles would take her up there after the service. Maybe they could all climb up inside together and sit on the stone benches and remember good times with Doc. Maybe Jamie and Lori and Aunt Helen would also want to remember good times with Pastor Ibsen. A picnic on the Golden Gallery would be as good a memorial as this, Charles reasoned. He would tell them his plan after this was all over and everyone else went home.

Looking up and listening to the music, Charles could almost

imagine that there were angels playing on the beams from the light wells. He did not even have to close his eyes to imagine such a thing.

It was perfect, except that Theo was gone in a plane. Lori was not here. And where was Murphy? Well, it was almost perfect. Just about everyone was here today.

Jacob Kalner tucked his passport into his pocket and then said firmly, "I am sticking with you, Elisha." He had a peculiar smile on his face as the other boys looked at him with amusement.

Who among them would not have jumped at the chance to flash that precious document in the face of a British Embassy official and simply slip in behind the high metal gates to be taken out of Poland in safety? But here was this *meshugge* actually choosing to go with them into the Warsaw fish market as if nothing at all might fall on his head and kill him! *Oy!* They could understand the confusion of this big oaf called Elisha—after all, he was not all there. He acted as though something had already hit him on the head and knocked a few brains loose, nu? But Jacob Kalner had always seemed a sensible fellow. Why, then, did he refuse to go to the British Embassy? And why did Captain Orde, who also could go to the embassy, insist that everyone was leaving together or no one was leaving?

It was an amazing thing to see. The one called Elisha marched on one side of Lucy Strasburg and the captain on the other. The kitten poked his head out of the neck of Elisha's shirt in front. Lucy, who knew just exactly where Herr Frankenmuth should be, was giving directions. *Turn here. Then go left here. His boat was moored halfway down the quay.*

All the while as they tramped down the streets, the German Heinkels buzzed persistently above. Their shadows brushed the cobblestones behind and in front of where they ran. Why then, did they not run faster?

"Herr Frankenmuth will be there," Alfie assured them. "He is waiting for us to come."

A haze of smoke from burning buildings drifted across the sky above Peter. He could hear the sounds of pitched battle not

519

far away. The engines of the airplanes seemed always the same, neither far nor near, only sometimes louder and softer. He knew when they climbed because the pitch changed, and he knew when they came down against their targets because the roar turned into an angry scream, followed by dull explosions. Peter did not look up as he ran through the deserted streets of the Jewish District. He did not stop to look at the lifeless faces of the children who had died there this morning.

He ran on toward the cavernous doorway on Kozhla Street, the winding little lane where the animal market was. He passed beneath the archway and there, in the smoke, he saw something enormous moving toward him! It moved quietly and took shape. Yes! It was the great horse of Dolek the milkman! Its reins hung down from the bridle. It took a step and stepped on the end of a rein and stopped. Its enormous hoof held the leather fast against the cobblestones, and so the horse did not move when Peter walked to him. The horse's liquid brown eyes were watering—probably from the smoke, and yet, for a moment it looked to Peter as though the beast were weeping silently.

He crooned to the animal and stroked his thick neck. He took the leather rein, lifted the foot, and then led the horse to a heap of rubble. Peter climbed the rubble nervously and then slid his leg across the broad, sweating back. Grabbing a handful of mane, Peter turned the animal back toward the square and nudged him forward.

The hollow *clop, clop, clop* of iron horse shoes against the pavement beat a rhythm in time with the explosions of Nazi bombs on the train stations and warehouses on the outskirts of town.

Every newspaper in London had a special edition already on the streets. War news was already being shouted from the news kiosks that lined Fleet Street.

Cars and taxis pulled to curbs or hailed the newsboys who ran through slowly moving traffic selling their papers. Murphy took one look at the traffic jam and headed up the street toward St. Paul's on foot.

His brain was dull from lack of sleep and the unending on-slaught of events over the last twenty-four hours. He looked at the clock tower of the cathedral. Still a few minutes before Elisa was scheduled to play. How he regretted the loss of her violin—the beautiful Guarnerius, given over to a crooked customs inspector who seemed to know very well the quality of the instrument.

Murphy's head ached. He brushed past pedestrians on the packed sidewalks and began the ascent up Ludgate Hill to St. Paul's. He was angry at himself for his failure. No Orde. No Jacob or Alfie or Rachel Lubetkin. And the violin, gone, for nothing.

He bit his lip and paused mid-stride for one instant. How had the Polish customs' inspector known to challenge Murphy about *passports*? "Not *your* passport," the man had said.

Murphy turned the incident over in his thoughts once again. It seemed that the inspector had come looking specifically for Murphy.

Elisa had told Murphy that she had managed to sneak a call to Harvey Terrill. That she had asked him to send the cable to TENS Warsaw.

Murphy reached into his pocket and pulled out the note he had found in the office just a few minutes before. Elisa's handwriting: a note to Harvey.

Murphy stopped walking. He frowned down at the message. He looked up at St. Paul's. People pushed past him, but he did not notice.

He knew without a doubt that he held the note that Elisa had sent Lori to deliver to Harvey last night at the TENS office! *The message—and Lori—had reached TENS!*

He began jogging rapidly up Ludgate Hill toward the cathedral. Why had Harvey lied? Why would he lie about seeing Lori? And how had Polish customs gotten the tip to detain Murphy?

Harvey Terrill!

———

Allan Farrell watched a flock of pigeons swirl in a figure-eight pattern around the clock tower and the bell tower of St. Paul's. He was growing impatient for the time to push the button.

He toyed with the idea of pushing the button without waiting for the signal. After all, everyone was inside already, weren't they? Did it matter whether Churchill died while speaking or while sitting in the audience? How much longer was the orchestra going to play, anyway?

Igniting the charges right now, however, would kill his accomplice as well. He wondered how much trouble he would get into for that. Of course, he could always explain that it was a mistake. He doubted that anyone really liked Harvey Terrill enough to care very much anyway.

The transmitter lay on top of the satchel. A flick of one switch turned it on, then a long push on the button, and . . . Allan's eyes again sought the top of the dome. Would the tower drop straight into the inside like a candle being pushed down into a cake? Or would part of the fabric of the dome collapse, too? Allan was eager to find out.

38   Live and Be Well

Outside the packed shelter, the steady *whump! whump! whump!* of falling bombs penetrated the thick walls of sandbags.

Rachel huddled close to her mother. She was frightened but not terrified as many others seemed to be. Everywhere the sounds of sobbing could be heard—mothers who had lost children, sisters who had lost brothers.

Rachel looked at the dust-covered forms of David and Samuel. There was blood on the knees of David's torn knickers. Samuel had a trickle of dried blood on his right cheek. How had they survived? It was a miracle when so many had perished this morning!

But how long would this go on? Would the Germans run out of bombs soon? Would they be shot out of the skies by the Polish Air Force—or by the English?

"Where is England?" someone muttered. "They will surely come and stop this!"

As if in reply, a desperate pounding sounded against the barricaded door of the shelter.

"You think that is England, already?" A ripple of nervous laughter filled the room.

"Maybe Hitler got lost and wants in." More laughter.

It was an odd thing to have someone knocking on the door with destruction raining down outside. And then everyone realized at once that it was not odd—someone had found his or her way to the shelter!

"Let them in!" cried a dozen voices in unison.

First the question was shouted, "Who is it?"

"Peter Wallich" came the muffled reply. "Please! Let me in! Is Rabbi Lubetkin inside? I have an urgent message!"

Heads swiveled to look at the rabbi. "Let the boy in," he urged.

Rachel shuddered at the thought of the door swinging back. She did not want the terrible noise of the explosions to fill the shelter. She snuggled closer to her mother and leaned her face against Etta's arm.

"*Please!* No, Papa!" Rachel begged. In the small storage room of the shelter, she wrapped her arms around her father's waist and clung to him.

Mama held the British passport in her hands as though it contained her every hope.

"Rachel," Mama said gently. "God has heard my prayers and answered." She put a hand on Rachel's shoulders, and the girl turned and buried her face against her mother.

"Mama! I don't want to leave you! Don't make me go with Peter! Oh, Mama! Let me stay with you!"

Aaron Lubetkin swallowed hard and stepped back. He could not bear to look at the misery of his only daughter. It would be easier for her to stay right here with them. Much easier for Rachel. Maybe even easier for him to allow her to stay.

"You must *choose life,* Rachel," he managed to say. His voice did not carry the authority of the spiritual leader of his community. Instead, there was only the grief of a father who must now bid his daughter farewell, possibly for the last time.

Peter Wallich waited outside the metal door. He had warned them that they did not have long. He had risked his life to come for Rachel. He would be risking his life to take her to the gates of the British Embassy to safety. And then he still had a journey to make.

How much longer did they dare take in this parting? Mama held Rachel close and stroked her hair. She kissed her daughter on the head as she perched on the crate and begged with an embrace that they not be parted.

523

Then Etta reached behind her and grasped Rachel's clasped hands. Finger by finger she pried them loose; all the while she whispered Rachel's name gently, as if she were trying to wake her from a nightmare. "Rachel? Rachel? Sweet Rachel? It is time. It is time to go now. We will meet again. Please. Rachel? You must go now. *You must*."

Rachel sat back in a daze on the crate. So it was true. It was harder to choose life. Much harder.

"May I say goodbye to David and Samuel? To the baby?"

Papa opened the door slightly. David entered, carrying the baby. Samuel followed. Samuel was also crying, although he did not know why. The door clicked shut. Only one moment more . . .

Rachel embraced little Samuel first. She took his face in her hands.

"What's the matter, sister?"

"I have to leave," Rachel managed to say bravely.

"Will you come back?" His eyes were puzzled, frightened that she would leave the shelter and never come back. The streets were littered with friends who were not coming back.

Rachel looked to her mother for help.

Etta stepped forward and pulled Samuel into her embrace. "Rachel is going to be with Grandfather Lebowitz. To live at his house. She is going to the Promised Land."

"And you will come later," Rachel said. But the tears did not stop flowing; she did not truly believe in this dark hour that anyone would ever be in Jerusalem with Grandfather!

David stepped up and hugged her in a manly way as Papa held the baby. "The Eternal go with you," he said gruffly.

"And give you . . . peace . . ." Rachel broke. Only for a moment. Then she caught herself and took Yacov from Papa. The baby, not understanding anything, only felt Rachel's sorrow. He nuzzled her damp cheek with a sloppy kiss.

Then Mama took him from her and opened the door. Peter stood before her. She gave the passport to Peter, as if the passport were Rachel herself. Rachel's life.

Shalom. . . .

Rachel did not look at the faces of the people in the shelter who watched her leave. She followed Peter out into the smoke-shrouded sunlight. The sun was a red ball in the sky glaring down on Muranow Square.

The big horse of Dolek the milkman was tied to a broken branch on the great fallen tree in the square. Peter held her hand as if she were a small child. He led her through the rubble and helped her stand on the horizontal trunk of the tree and then boosted her onto the back of the animal. He jumped on behind her as the constant boom of bombs and artillery fire pushed against the hot air around the broken city of Warsaw.

———————

Harvey Terrill leaned nervously against the wall of the south aisle of the cathedral. Directly behind him were the circular stone stairs, the first part of the ascent to the dome. Harvey had chosen to stand in that spot so he could see if anyone went up to the galleries. Now he was not at all sure why he did it.

What was he going to do, anyway? Tackle someone to prevent him from climbing the steps? Argue with the person?

Harvey could not take his eyes from the hazy hollow globe of the dome over his head. It seemed so vast and so high and so permanent. It was hard to imagine that in minutes, both peace and permanence would be shattered right here in the heart of London.

The enormity of it made Harvey nervous. He thought of how much stone and lead-covered timber was over his head, and he wondered how impatient his partner with the trigger was getting. He wished this service would speed up. Didn't Churchill have more important things waiting? How long before the man would speak?

Elisa Murphy was shifting in her chair. That meant she was getting ready to play, and Harvey knew she was on the program right before Churchill.

Then Harvey noticed—she, too, was looking upward at the blue shimmer of the dome! Terrill's head snapped back. Was there something up there that gave the plot away? Had she gotten some clue to what was about to happen?

Harvey looked anxiously to see if any of the others were stirring. Had Churchill been warned? No; there he sat next to David Lloyd George and Anthony Eden and others of similar politics. Harvey forced himself to calm down, to think about what a blow would be struck here today. All of the anti-Hitler, anti-appeasement crowd were gathered in this one place.

Still, he wished it would hurry up and get over with. Even if this event was going to be bigger news than the Führer's speech, Terrill wished it would happen soon!

Besides, the two adopted brats of the Murphys' were staring up at the dome as if they knew something. How much longer?

Elisa trembled as she looked down at the reddish hues of the old Steiner violin. What had been Doc Grogan's last words? *Paul.* She raised her eyes to scan the majestic creation of Sir Christopher Wren. St. Paul's Cathedral. Could Grogan have meant. . . ?

Golden. She craned her neck to search up into the heights of the Golden Gallery, where Doc Grogan had spent his last hours with the children. *Paul Golden? A man?* Or St. Paul's? *Golden* . . . Golden Gallery! *Light wells!*

She listened as the last strains of Karl Ibsen's favorite symphony built to a crescendo. *Ibsen!* She looked to where Winston Churchill studied his notes in preparation for his coming speech! *Churchill!*

She let her eyes linger on the violin. Not the Guarnerius. Why had Murphy been intercepted by Polish customs and asked about passports? Illegal passports?

One more look to her far right told her she was not wrong. Harvey Terrill was staring up into the dome of the cathedral as though something was terribly wrong above his head. He glanced at his watch, shifted his weight from one foot to the other as if he wanted to run from this place.

Harvey. St. Paul's. Golden Gallery. Light Wells. Ibsen and Churchill.

Elisa leaned forward and looked around the sides of the sanctuary in search of Mr. Tedrick. Where was he, now that she needed him? Where was Tedrick? Whom should she tell, if not Tedrick? And what, exactly, should she tell? Could she be wrong? Had her imagination simply swirled away into the heights of absurdity?

"What is it, Elisa?" Anna whispered with concern. "Are you all right?"

Elisa nodded, and sat back. She continued to search the gathering for the enormous bulk of Tedrick.

Once again she followed the gaze of Harvey Terrill skyward. Was someone on the gallery, planning to shoot Churchill?

There was no more time to delay. Elisa stood and passed the

violin to her mother. She did not know what she intended to do. She hoped that Tedrick would see her, that he would watch her walking toward Harvey Terrill. That he would see how pale she was, and *know*.

Harvey nodded, with nervous pleasantness, strained at every muscle in his face and eyes. He glanced at his watch. Looking down at the floor and ignoring her approach, he began to walk slowly, *too calmly* back toward the grand entrance.

He then saw Elisa start toward him. This was not right. He did not know what she knew, or guessed, or had figured out, but she was coming toward him instead of going up to play her violin. Something was wrong!

The only thing Terrill could think of doing was to give the signal early. Now, in fact!

He started for the west entrance along the south aisle, walking deliberately at first, then faster and faster as panic took hold. What if she signaled someone? What if she called to him to stop, shouted out for the crowd to run out of the church?

Behind him, he heard Churchill being introduced. Speaker and showman that he was, Churchill was covering for any awkwardness at the change in program, going on smoothly, moving into his talk. "In this solemn hour it is a consolation to recall our repeated efforts for peace. Outside, the storms of war may blow and the lands may be lashed with the fury of its gales, but in our hearts this morning there is peace."

Not for long would there be peace! Just the time it took for Harvey to run out the door and down the steps to the statue of Queen Anne. Then there would be no peace in this place—in this whole nation—except the peace of the grave!

"Close your eyes!" Peter shouted to Rachel as the horse picked its way through the rubble of a residential area.

She saw a child's broken doll. A hat beneath a brick. A photo in a broken frame. The scattered pages of a book. And, aware that this was the death of something . . . someone . . . she closed her eyes and pressed back against Peter's bony chest.

She held on to the mane tightly as the horse picked up its feet in a more steady rhythm once again.

"All right," Peter instructed. "We are past it. Open your eyes."

She did so, and saw a miracle. They trotted down an ordinary street, lined on either side with regular apartment buildings. The windows were taped, but not broken. There were even a few red geraniums in window boxes. A few cars remained parked along the straight, unbroken street that stretched out before them. *The cars must not run,* Rachel thought, *or they would be with the Polish Army right now being blown to pieces!*

She and Peter seemed to be the only living souls on all that long expanse of city street. It was the street that led to the British Embassy, Peter explained. He would make sure she was taken care of, and then he would meet up with Captain Orde on the wharf of the Vistula. From there, he said, they would escape upriver.

This is all like a story in a storybook, Rachel thought. Some other day she might like to sit and read such an exciting fairy tale. But this was a *real* story—her own story—and so for now she wanted somehow to step out of the pages of this living hell and find a quiet place to sleep, to lay her head on Mama's lap and pretend it was not happening!

"Only three blocks," Peter said, nudging the old horse to a faster trot.

Rachel did not reply. She felt no joy, no sense of relief at being so near to safety. She simply clung tighter to the horse's mane. She raised her head only slightly as the deafening drone of Hienkel's engine approached behind them. The horse did not quicken his step until the black shadow swooped down over them.

Peter cried out with alarm as the plane banked low over the housetops and rolled to circle back over them for an easy kill!

The orchestra had stopped. Some part of the program was now complete. Allan did not know exactly what the order of the service was, but he knew they were one step closer to Churchill's speech.

He picked up the transmitter and set it on the balustrade on the side facing the dome. Just as quickly he took it down again. What if he should accidentally knock it off with his excited, agitated movements? Perhaps the impact with the ground would send the signal to the explosives; perhaps not. Allan did not want to take any chances—not now, not when he was so close.

He would go down in history! His name, *his* name, would

ring down through time as the one who dealt oppression one of the greatest blows ever struck. Children would ask their grandparents where they were the day St. Paul's was blasted!

Allan's hymn of self-praise was interrupted by the sight of someone running toward the cathedral. The man sprinted up the hill, dodging around other people on the sidewalk and darting in front of a bus when one side of the street became too crowded. People don't run like that without a purpose. If this were simply a late arrival who did not want to miss Churchill's speech, he would not be running this desperately, this doggedly.

Allan pivoted sharply and grabbed the transmitter. He flicked the power switch on and was rewarded with an answering gleam from a small bulb lighting a dial that masked the device's real purpose. Should he press the button now? Should he wait for Harvey's signal?

There was a clatter on the steps of the cathedral. Even before Harvey Terrill had appeared beside the statue, Allan knew who it was. He braced himself for the blast. Strange how he had never thought about how loud the explosion would be. He wondered if he should have brought some earplugs. Well, it was too late to worry about it now. With deliberately applied firmness, Allan pressed the transmitter button.

———

Peter kicked the clumsy horse hard and pulled the one rein to the left. Urging the animal up three stone steps, he leaped from its back and grabbed Rachel to dash back into the archway of a small church. Peter slapped the big horse hard on the neck. There was no room to shelter it here. Its broad rump was sticking out as if to point to a target for the German airplane!

"Get!" Peter roared at the horse. He flapped his arms as Rachel crouched down beside the door and covered her head. "Run! Stupid horse! Run!"

The horse spun on its heels and trotted off down the road. The rein dragged along beside it. The booming roar of the double-engine plane filled every corner of the street. The burst of machine-gun fire popped a staccato dance as bullets sparked against the cobblestones at the heels of the animal.

Rachel screamed as the roar echoed and the plane climbed up above the city again. But the pilot had other things to do, apparently. He did not come back. The horse trotted a ways and then stepped on his rein again.

Peter grabbed Rachel by her blouse and pulled her down the steps. He ran to the horse, took the leather strap of the rein, but did not bother to climb back on the animal.

There, in front of the British Embassy, stood a small knot of desperate people clinging to the gates as a man in an English army uniform checked documents.

Peter stopped across the street, removed Rachel's blue folder from his pocket and gave it to her.

"There," he said. "Go and be well."

She did not thank him, because she did not feel thankful. She nodded, fingering the folder. "Goodbye, then," she said softly.

"I can't miss the boat." Peter had already led the horse to stand beside a banister. He climbed the banister and leaped onto the back of his mount. "Now get going!" he shouted at her angrily. *"Live!"*

Rachel nodded and turned toward the frantic people at the embassy gate. Peter did not wait to watch her enter. There was not enough time. She stopped in the middle of the street and watched him as he retreated back down the empty street.

The big, slow horse did not vary his gait even though Peter kicked and flapped his arms wildly. *"Get! Get going!"* She could hear him shouting at the deaf animal. "Stupid horse! Hurry! Hurry!" The sun glinted briefly on his hair. He was like a clown— the high comedy of panic. Rachel smiled at his appearance in spite of herself. He looked as if he were trying to fly. Trying to make the aged horse of Dolek the milkman lift off and soar to safety above the dying city of Warsaw.

"Live," Rachel repeated the admonition to Peter. "Live and be well. Find your Promised Land, Peter Wallich."

One Jew! Would that one Jew who lived be someone like Peter? *Ah, the Eternal must have a sense of humor if it is Peter alone among us who lives,* she thought.

Peter turned up a distant street on his way to the river and the fish market. Only then did Rachel pivot and walk slowly toward the desperate people who begged at the gates of Great Britain.

She stood apart and looked at her own likeness on the page of the passport—black hair, serious blue eyes, unsmiling lips.

Rachel scanned the crowd. Maybe three hundred were there. Surely someone among them—some girl or young woman. . . .

Face after face, she studied those who pressed in and shouted for refuge. And then she saw her—a woman of perhaps twenty. She wore a white broad-brimmed hat that shielded her face. Her clothes were modern, stylish. She was shouting loudly, waving a Czech passport in the air. Her face was desperate. Czech passports meant nothing any longer, not since the Nazis had taken over in March.

Rachel smiled and remembered what Papa had told her: *"He who saves a life, saves the universe."*

Yes. This woman might pass for her sister, even without the hat. Ah, but *with the hat,* she could pass for the girl in this precious British passport that Rachel held.

Rachel walked quickly to her, and she pulled her to one side. "This is yours." Rachel extended the passport to her.

"No," said the woman. *She is very pretty,* Rachel thought.

"Yes. It is yours. I saw you drop it. Now go in. Live and be well." Rachel shoved it into her hands, then turned and ran back down the street, back through the broken city of Warsaw. She ran and ran. She would not look back until she reached the smashed square of Muranow.

The sense of urgency that drove Murphy up Ludgate Hill was greater than the war, greater than the death of Doc Grogan, greater than the missing Lori. Elisa was at St. Paul's and Harvey Terrill was at St. Paul's! That seemingly innocuous information filled him with a nameless dread he could not explain.

He zigzagged across Fleet Street to miss a stretch of sidewalk blocked by a man unloading stacks of newspapers. Newspapers! *GERMAN ARMY ATTACKS POLAND,* the headlines screamed. *CITIES BOMBED, PORT BLOCKADED!*

Almost there. The bulk of St. Paul's dominated his path. From under the shadow of the west facade, the great dome itself was hardly visible. Only the lantern tower surmounted by the ball and cross could be seen from this low angle. Closer at hand, the bell and clock towers seemed to lean over the statue of Queen Anne.

From the doors at the top of the steps, Harvey Terrill burst into view and ran down toward the statue. He spotted Murphy at the same instant and skidded to a halt. A hideous caricature of a smile played over his features; the grin of a corpse. "Murphy," he said, and ran out of words.

"Harvey," Murphy demanded, "Lori was at TENS last night, wasn't she? What's going on here, Harvey? Who tipped off the Polish customs? Who's Paul Golden?"

"Not *who*, Murphy, *what*!" Elisa burst out with this exclamation as she dashed down the steps behind Terrill. "St. *Paul's. Golden* Gallery. *Light Wells*. It's *there*, Murphy!" she shouted, pointing up at the lantern. "Whatever it was Grogan died trying to tell us, it's up there!"

Murphy grabbed Terrill's forearm and spun him around with his hand twisted up beneath his shoulder blades. "Let me go!" Terrill cried. "It's too late now. Too late!"

"Too late for what?" Murphy demanded. "What is it, Harvey? Where's Lori?"

———

Nothing happened! Allan pressed his finger against the button again and again! He switched the power switch off and pushed the trigger button again. Still no result—no satisfying roar, no crashing bricks.

He flicked the power switch back and forth. Maybe it was jammed! With each blink of the tiny light he pressed the firing button over and over. No screams of panic, no rush of smoke, no place in history!

Allan began to tear the back off the transmitter. Maybe a loose wire? There was still time . . . if only . . . He tore off one fingernail, then another. No tools! Why hadn't he brought tools?

With bloody fingers, he raised the device over his head and smashed it down on the stones. No explosion agreed with his anger. Allan stamped on the radio with his heel, but the only destruction he caused was to the device itself.

Wait! Perhaps there was another way. He dug into the satchel, tossing out film, light meter, camera strap. Under the false bottom was a pistol.

There was still a chance. No alarm had yet been given. No sirens, no rush of people for exits. To be a living hero would have been nice, but to become famous as a freedom fighter— even martyrdom was not too high a price.

"What's too late?" demanded Murphy again.

Terrill grew strangely silent. He looked intently at the bell tower, then the clock tower, as if he was confused. He stretched up on his toes to look at the lantern, standing as a sentinel against the peaceful sky. "I can't understand it," he mumbled.

"Come on then," said a grim-faced Murphy, dragging Terrill up the steps. "We'll figure it out together."

Once inside the south aisle, Churchill's voice was heard ringing into the thrust of his speech: "This is not a question of fighting for Poland. We must fight to save the whole world from the pestilence of Nazi tyranny. We must accept the challenge laid before us all by those who have so ably and courageously carried the torch of freedom. 'Lift it high,' their examples say. 'Let no tyrant extinguish it.'"

Tedrick met Murphy at the rear of the nave. "What's all this?" he asked in a dark whisper. Terrill was almost limp in Murphy's grasp, but he continued to shoot fearful and shuddering looks up at the dome.

"Harvey knows something about what Grogan was trying to tell us. It has to do with the dome and the Golden Gallery... maybe Lori, too."

"And it's about today," broke in Elisa. "He said *Ibsen* and *Churchill* too."

A young man came out of the doorway that connected with the clock tower. He started to cross the nave directly toward Tedrick, then spotted the small group standing in the shadows and pivoted to walk rapidly down the north aisle.

When he reached a point opposite the stairway to the galleries, he increased his pace to jog toward the opening. Terrill seemed to come out of his stupor at the sight. "Take me back outside," he pleaded. "I don't feel well, that's all—I need air."

Elisa was the first to see the connection. "That man," she said, pointing. "He's going up into the dome!"

———

Alarmed by the disturbance at the rear of the service, a policeman moved to block Murphy's path to the stairs. No time to explain! With a move that would have done credit to a Penn

State running back, Murphy faked the policeman out of position and dashed up the steps.

The left-hand spiral of the shallow steps cork-screwed upward. Above him Murphy could hear the clattering feet of his unknown quarry. Churchill's voice continued to follow him upward: "Our war is not for material gain. It is a war for the rights of the individual, championed by individuals of the highest, most resolute character. Shall we do less than they?"

The painted, glossy black treads curled up and up around a central support pillar marred by centuries-old graffiti. *T.S. 1776* was carved into the stone. *G.C. 1815.*

The footsteps tapping over his head now retreated in volume. Finally, out onto a landing, Murphy found himself at the base of the dome, where the huge half-globe rested on arches above the rotunda. Churchill's voice, echoing up from a hundred feet below, threatened to drown out the sounds of the other man's passage. "We must not underrate the gravity of our task . . ."

There he was! On the far side of the Whispering Gallery, beneath the watchful gaze of a painted St. Paul, the small, delicate-looking man disappeared into another doorway. He threw a look over his shoulder and caught a glimpse of Murphy's pursuit, then increased the tempo of his flight.

The audience reacted to the clattering footsteps overhead with annoyance rather than alarm. Churchill was saying, "We must expect dangers and disappointments . . ." Murphy ran past a scene of St. Paul's shipwreck, around the gallery, and through the exit door. The stone steps grew steep, the passage narrow. He ran ten steps upward to a wider tread for a landing; every few landings a crude wooden bench. But there was no time to rest. Murphy panted with the exertion, and his leg muscles burned.

———

One hundred eighteen steps upward from the Whispering Gallery, Allan Farrell burst into the outside air. He rushed around the circular walkway with its enclosing stone parapet. He no longer concealed his pistol, but carried it in his hand as he ran.

His plan was simple: he would ascend to the Golden Gallery, climb over the rail to where he could see a satchel of explosives concealed in a light well, and detonate the bomb by shooting the blasting cap.

In the instant of his martyrdom, twenty pounds of explosives would erupt three hundred feet above the floor of the church. Maybe the other charges would go off from the concussion, or perhaps just the sudden loss of support on one side of the tower would make it collapse anyway.

Regardless of how great the destruction, debris would shower down inside the cathedral. People would be killed; terror would reign. Allan felt a kind of exaltation at the prospect.

As he circled the gallery, he reflected that with the pistol in his hand he could have run directly at Churchill and fired. Allan was shocked at the thought. He was no common murderer, no assassin! Where was the drama, where was the glory in shooting a man with a pistol?

The Stone Gallery opened in front of Murphy's last step with an expanse of gleaming white railing set against a brilliant blue sky. Which way to turn now? Still another hundred feet to the Golden Gallery, where something waited.

Murphy vaulted up on a block of stone just as the man he was chasing reached another flight of marble steps leading back inside the dome. A small hand holding a large revolver swung upward, waved in Murphy's direction. A shot boomed and the bullet smashed into the stone balustrade with a crack of flying masonry as Murphy threw himself to the side.

Cautiously peering over the marble block, Murphy saw that the man had gone inside, into the space between the outer dome and the brick cone that supported it.

Clanging footsteps rang overhead, telling Murphy that his quarry was still racing up. The stairs here were made of iron, and rattled with every jarring step. A clockwise spiral of metal curved up another twenty feet.

When Murphy looked up, he could see the retreating form of the other man two spirals above him. Allan chose that moment to look down and spotted Murphy crossing a walkway. The gun boomed in the narrow, walled space and the echoes reverberated throughout the dome.

The bullet flashed against the iron frame of the stairs, showering sparks from the ricochet. Another shot followed, making Murphy lunge to get directly beneath Allan, hoping to spoil his aim.

The terrorist returned to fleeing upward. At the last curve of the staircase below the Golden Gallery, he caught his toe on a protruding iron bolt. Allan fell, sprawling across the platform, the pistol jarred from his hand by the impact.

The revolver spun across the grill and teetered on the edge. Allan jumped for it. The swollen and clumsy fingers he had torn on the transmitter case brushed it, knocking if off the stairs.

With an angry cry, Allan watched it tumble to the next level down and bounce on the steps. When the pistol hit, it loosed another shot, this time directly into the bricks of the interior cone. A flattened lead slug zigzagged between the walls before dropping, spent, into the darkness below.

Both men, gasping for breath, stared stupidly at the revolver lying on the platform between them. Their eyes met, locked, challenged. They sprang for the steps. Allan hopped down awkwardly, the ankle that was twisted in his fall buckling beneath his weight. Murphy pounded upward, his legs on fire and his breath ragged in his chest.

Allan reached the landing first and bent to retrieve the pistol. Murphy, from behind, crashed into him, smashing him against the rail. They grappled for the gun. Murphy's greater strength twisted the revolver in Allan's grasp.

Allan's fingers, slipping from the grip, sought and found the trigger. He tried to squeeze off a shot into Murphy's face. Murphy's hands locked around the barrel and pushed it aside just as another round exploded. Powder flashed, burning Murphy's eyes. He threw up his hands.

Allan had the gun; he leveled it at Murphy's head. Murphy's eyes, streaming tears, watched the trigger finger tighten, the hammer start back. Then Farrell stopped.

Only one shot left! Allan needed it to detonate the explosives! He shoved hard against the dazed Murphy, trying to throw him over the railing. Murphy clutched desperately at the iron bar, hanging on. Allan hit him on the side of the head with the pistol, a weak, ineffectual blow.

Others had reached the spiral stairs and were coming up. Allan spun away from Murphy and clambered back toward the Golden Gallery. Outside at last, he hoisted himself up to the rail, preparing to jump down into the light well. At the moment of springing he was hit from behind; Murphy, grabbing for his ankles.

Allan leaped away, kicking back hard—too hard. He missed

the opening; he had overshot the light well. He hung suspended from its lip, clumsily supporting his weight with his one free hand and two fingers of the hand still grasping the gun.

Murphy, staggering, appeared above the rail. "Give it up," he said. "It's over." Above him, he heard a muffled cry.

Allan gritted his teeth and tried to drag himself up and over the rim of the light well. If he could reach the edge and drop inside . . . But his strength failed. His feet could find no hold on the slick lead surface. He could hang there, but he could climb no higher.

Murphy watched, horrified, as Allan tried to aim the pistol over the rim and fire into the satchel. But his injured hand could not steady the revolver.

Allan Farrell had one chance left: if he hung from his elbows, he could use both hands to aim. One shot! One chance! "Don't!" Murphy shouted.

The blast recoiled the gun backward, jerked Allan's elbows loose, and sent him sliding down the dome. His face scraped against the curve of the dome he had sought to destroy. Slower at first, then faster, as the angle of the slope increased.

His body parted company with the dome and hurtled into space. He had an instant of thought, a momentary gleam of comprehension, just before his body struck the rail of the Stone Gallery. He knew he had failed; his last shot had missed.

The German Luftwaffe had smashed dozens of vessels, large and small, tied to the docks along the Vistula River.

The small fishing boat of Herr Frankenmuth was moored beneath a wooden roof beside a garbage scow. Hardly a worthy target for a crack Nazi pilot.

In this unlikely place, Lucy found the fish merchant working desperately on the petulant engine of his boat. Wrenches and screwdrivers were spread everywhere. The old man was covered with grease from head to foot. His son looked very worn out from the ordeal, although it was plain to see that perhaps the broken engine had saved them from disaster. The waters were littered with half-submerged boats that had attempted to flee the gun sights of the German planes.

Herr Frankenmuth barely looked up when a fighter buzzed overhead. This engine was his enemy now!

He wiped his rough hands on a rag that seemed less soiled than his clothes, then he looked up at the sound of approaching feet and chattering voices.

"Hans," he called to his son, "it is Werner the kitten!"

The son poked his head up from the belly of the boat.

Alfie was smiling and waving. He held Werner high over his head in greeting. "Hello, Herr Frankenmuth! Me and Werner have brought some friends."

"Huh?" said the son and the old man in unison. Near and far, the booming of guns accompanied the reunion. Father and son exchanged amazed looks. Should they be surprised?

"No fish today." Herr Frankenmuth stepped out onto the dock and into the center of a circle of sweating, grimy boys. "We have not been able to fish." He waved a hand into the air as a plane passed low over the shed. Its shadow flickered through the cracks between the slats of the roof. "And so far the Luftwaffe has not got our little fish in the barrel either."

Except for Herr Frankenmuth, the docks were empty. A fire was raging at the far end of the wharf.

Orde stepped forward, wiped sweat from his brow, and extended his hand. "Can I help?"

"Engine trouble," said Herr Frankenmuth. "We cannot find what is wrong. Tried all day." He nodded at Lucy. There was no time or inclination to talk. He turned to his son, who sat beside the starter. "All right, Hans, give it a try."

The younger man flipped the starter switch. There was a long pause. Nothing. He flipped it once again, and the motor sputtered and then rumbled to life. The old man's eyes widened. He looked at Alfie and then at Lucy. He reached up and scratched the ears of the kitten. "Well, well," he said, "I should have known you were on the way." Then, to Alfie, "Where are we going?"

"The Promised Land," Alfie answered.

"Ah, I should have known."

Behind them came the hollow clopping of a horse's hooves against the pavement, then a rhythmic *thunk, thunk, thunk,* as the horse came onto the wood of the dock.

It was Peter Wallich, looking very pained and tired but very relieved to see his companions.

The blue smoke of the motor rose up in the little shed. It was getting dark.

"The Germans should be heading back soon," Orde said.

"They have had a successful first day. They'll be here with more in the morning."

Herr Frankenmuth frowned slightly and looked out toward the wreckage on the river. "Do you think it is safe to travel by night?"

Alfie put the kitten on his shoulder. "Look, Werner." He pointed to the far side of the riverbank, where wooden piers had been smashed and burned. "Do you see them, Werner?" He took the paw of the kitten and raised it up in a little kitten wave. Then he waved his big hand and called, "Hello! Yes! I see you!"

The boys beside the boat looked at one another strangely. There was no one over on the other bank. No one at all.

"Who is he talking to?" asked one under his breath.

"Who is over there, Elisha?" asked Peter as he came up to the group.

Alfie smiled. He knew that Werner saw them. After all, they had been following them all day. They had walked before and behind. They had hovered above and sheltered them with their shining wings when the German planes had swept over. How could the other boys not see them?

"Oh," said Alfie. "There are lots more with us than with the Nazis. We don't have to be afraid. They are going with us to the Promised Land, see?" He waved again—a close wave, just above the heads of Samuel Orde and Lucy Strasburg.

Epilogue

The sharp prow of the fishing trawler rose and fell in cadence with the rhythmic beat of the diesel engine. The Mediterranean was mercifully calm tonight. Even so, nearly half of the passengers on board the *Ave Maria* were seasick. The air below deck was rank with the sour odor of vomit and diesel fumes.

Sam Orde and Lucy made their way to the bow of the trawler. The cold wind and stinging salt spray against their faces were a welcome relief. Lucy shuddered from the chill. Orde put his arm around her and gripped the slick rail for support. His keen eyes scanned the midnight darkness for some sign of the British and German ships that prowled these waters.

The refugees on board the *Ave Maria* had been fortunate in their journey. Twice they had spotted the plumes of great naval ships on the far horizons of the sea, but the little trawler had slipped away undetected. Now, only hours away from the end of a long and desperate flight, Orde prayed that the tiny vessel might run the final blockade of British gunboats patrolling the coast. It seemed strange to contemplate that they must escape both Nazi and British ships to win their freedom. Either navy would gladly blow a shipload of Jewish refugees out of the water with never a pause to ask questions.

Sensing the apprehension of her new husband, Lucy leaned her head against Orde's chest. "We are so close now, Sam," she said, "and not one of us lost in all the weeks since we left Warsaw. We are almost home."

"Hmmm," he replied, sweeping his eyes over the star-dusted skies to where the darkness marked the rim of the world. "The coast is thick with patrols. It was true before the war. It is doubly true now."

"Spoken like a military man." She brushed his cheek with her fingertips and tucked herself closer against him. "The Lord

540

would not bring us so far only to let us die within sight of our goal."

Her faith made him smile. He kissed her forehead and then turned his eyes back to the horizon. He believed that her words were true, and yet, this was the hour for vigilance. Alfie, Jacob, Peter, and the others had become the sons of his heart, his own dear family. He would not relax until they all stood together on safe and solid ground, until Lucy held her baby in her arms again.

As if drawn by the drama of these final hours, Alfie stumbled to find Lucy and Orde at the bow. Jacob and Peter followed on his heels, silent with apprehension. They, too, felt the peril of these last few miles.

Alfie cleared his throat and stroked the head of Werner, who was tucked into the boy's shirt. "Werner don't like the ocean," said Alfie. "I told him about crossing the Red Sea and God opening up the water so we could get through, but he still isn't happy."

"Everyone is sick," Jacob said.

"Except us," Peter added. Then, "How much longer, Captain?"

Orde raised a hand to a point where the constellation Orion rose over the black horizon. "Keep your eyes there, boys. You'll see it soon enough. A light. No bigger than a star from this distance, but shining from the darkness. That will mark the place we land."

Heads pivoted to stare hard at the lowest star in Orion's belt. Were they as close as that?

"Any sign of gunboats? Patrols?" Jacob asked. He was a soldier at heart, just like the captain. He believed in the angels that Alfie spoke of, yet still he watched.

"Nothing yet," Orde replied quietly.

Alfie was smiling broadly. The starlight illuminated his broad face with joy. Or perhaps it was his joy that lit the night. "There it is." Alfie pointed as a single beam of light winked on and off. "Look, Captain! Lucy! Look, Werner! Just like they said . . ."

"I didn't see it," chided Peter.

"Me either," added Jacob.

Neither Orde nor Lucy had seen Alfie's light.

"Oh yes!" Alfie insisted. "Look!" he cried, pointing toward where the shoreline certainly lay. "Me and Werner can see it!

541

They are there! Right there where they are supposed to be! Can't you see?"

Still nothing but the stars and the darkness. The group exchanged looks. And then, right where Alfie pointed, a bright light for just an instant did indeed gleam.

"There it is! Look!" They shouted and clung to one another at the miracle of their beacon.

Alfie pulled little Werner from the protected covering and held him high over his head. "Look, Werner! Just like you always said it would be! Werner! It's the Promised Land!"

Authors' Note

The events following the Nazi invasion of Poland in September 1939 pursued a chaotic course, but one foreseen by Winston Churchill. England and France continued to vacillate about going to the aid of embattled Poland. Prime Minister Chamberlain sent threatening diplomatic communiques to the Führer, who was at the front lines in Poland within days of the invasion. No British or French troops, however, were deployed to Poland.

By the time the Allies committed to war, Poland had already been partitioned between Germany and Russia. Stalin used the opportunity provided by his pact with Adolf Hitler to swallow up the Baltic States of Estonia, Latvia, and Lithuania as well. The conflict and turmoil in present-day Europe are deeply rooted in that terrible era.

Where was the United States in all this? Why was the nation with such power to tip the scales on the side of justice simply a spectator from across a wide ocean? And what were the results of American neutrality?

In the research and creation of The Zion Chronicles and The Zion Covenant Series, these were questions we asked ourselves again and again, questions that we feel are worthy of further exploration.

The story of America is the story of our parents and grandparents . . . and yours as well. Eventually, the war raging in Europe would touch us even here. The sons of men who had fought in the Great War now would be called on to fight again in a much more terrible conflict. Ordinary beginnings on farms and in cities led to great bravery and memorable deeds. Boys who might have been considered average by everyone but their loved ones went on to turn the tide of victory against the Nazi darkness that engulfed the world. Wives, mothers, sweethearts remained behind to work in the factories and run the machinery while maintaining the homes that are the heart of a nation.

The gates of history swing on small hinges. The course of all the world can indeed be changed by the life of one man; by the prayers and faith of one woman.

It is the story of these folks that should be told next—ordinary men and women who lived through hard times and kept their faith intact until that moment when their lives became inexorably linked with those whom we have come to know in The Zion Covenant and The Zion Chronicles Series.

The Shiloh Legacy Series begins right here at home with the people we know best of all. . . .

Brock and Bodie Thoene
September 1, 1991
In My Father's House